*The Peculiar Miracles of Antoinette Martin*

# The
# Peculiar
# Miracles
## of
# Antoinette
# Martin

A NOVEL

# Stephanie Knipper

ALGONQUIN BOOKS OF
CHAPEL HILL
2016

Published by
ALGONQUIN BOOKS OF CHAPEL HILL
Post Office Box 2225
Chapel Hill, North Carolina 27515-2225

a division of
WORKMAN PUBLISHING
225 Varick Street
New York, New York 10014

This is a work of fiction. While, as in all fiction, the literary
perceptions and insights are based on experience, all names, characters,
places, and incidents either are products of the author's imagination
or are used fictitiously.

LIBRARY OF CONGRESS CATALOGING-IN-PUBLICATION DATA
Names: Knipper, Stephanie, author.
Title: The peculiar miracles of Antoinette Martin /
a novel by Stephanie Knipper.
Description: First edition. | Chapel Hill, North Carolina :
Algonquin Books of Chapel Hill, 2016. | "Published simultaneously
in Canada by Thomas Allen & Son Limited."
Identifiers: LCCN 2016006236 | ISBN 9781616204181
Subjects: LCSH: Autistic children—Fiction. | Gifted children—
Fiction. | Healers—Fiction. | Sisters—Fiction.
Classification: LCC PS3611.N5744 P43 2016 | DDC 813/.6—dc23
LC record available at http://lccn.loc.gov/2016006236

10 9 8 7 6 5 4 3 2 1
First Edition

——+——

For my daughter, Grace.

People always say you're lucky to have us as parents, but I know the truth. We're the lucky ones, because we have you.

Hug. Tap, tap, tap.

I love you too.

*The Peculiar Miracles of Antoinette Martin*

# ROSE'S JOURNAL
## *April 2013*

——+——

MY DAUGHTER, ANTOINETTE, whispers in her sleep. Real words. Tonight when I hear her voice, I rush upstairs, but I'm too late. She is quiet. And the sounds could have been anything. The wind. An owl. Crickets.

She lies on her side. Her right hand stretches toward the doorway, toward me, as if even in sleep I'm the sun she rotates around.

I reach for her too. But I don't enter her room.

When she sleeps, I can pretend I don't notice her eyes, a finger's breadth too far apart. Her arms are relaxed, not held tight against her shoulders as they are much of the day. Her white-blonde hair, still newborn fine, fans out behind her like a dandelion puff, or as if she were running and the wind caught it.

The window is open, and a breeze flutters the sheer white curtains. It's the first week of April, but already the air is so warm the tulips are sprouting. Kentucky is like that. Unpredictable. Tonight is dark, but here in the country, street lights don't obscure the stars.

I close my eyes and summon a dream. In it, Antoinette sprints through the farm, fingers brushing the daffodils and tulips. Her legs are strong, pounding the dirt like any other ten-year-old girl. But this image ignores the child she is. In a more accurate vision I see her walking toward me, marionette-like, arms cocked, hands curled toward her chest, knees bending and popping with each step.

I move into the past, pulling up memories of us sleeping curled into each other as if still sharing the same body. Swaying in time to field sparrow songs. Dancing under a shower of lavender petals in the drying barn.

She shifts, turning toward the window. Outside I envision the fields bursting with white tulip buds. It's too early for them, but stranger things have happened.

My sister, Lily, used to be fascinated by the Victorian language of flowers, memorizing the meanings for each plant we grew on the farm. It was a game to us. She scattered bouquets around the house, and I tried to guess her message. Daffodils represented new beginnings. Coneflowers were for strength and health.

And white tulips were for forgiveness and remembrance.

My heart stutters, and a familiar pressure builds in my chest. I breathe deeply, counting each beat. When my body calms, I look at my daughter.

A strand of hair sticks to her cheek. I walk into the room to free it, but she turns away from me and curls into a ball. I stop, unwilling to wake her, letting her linger a bit longer in dreams, safe in a place where I can't hurt her.

That will come soon enough.

# Chapter One

Antoinette Martin stood in the kitchen, staring at the alarm above the back door. The red light was not on, which meant it wouldn't scream and wake her mother if she opened the door. She could walk in the garden.

Pops of joy burst through her body. She bounced on her toes, bare feet slapping against the old oak floor. The smooth wood felt like creek water in July. A happy thought. She bounced again.

When her body calmed, she reached for the doorknob, then hesitated. She and her mother lived on a commercial flower farm in Redbud, Kentucky. Though most of their fifty acres were cleared and given over to flower fields, thick woods rimmed the back edge of their property. Antoinette was not supposed to go outside alone. It was easy to get hurt on a farm.

She mashed her nose against the cool glass of the kitchen door window. Outside, she didn't need music or art to block the white noise that engulfed her. The groan of the refrigerator; the swish, swish of the washer; the hum of the air conditioner. Outside, the land sang, and that was better than the Mozart and Handel compositions their neighbor Seth Hastings played on his violin.

At night, Antoinette would sit on the back porch of their farmhouse listening while Seth played the violin, or she would page through her mother's art books. She could name Bochmann's *Lark Ascending* from the first trill of the violin. She could close her eyes and re-create the crooked grin of Leonardo da Vinci's *Mona Lisa* or the slope of the hill in Wyeth's *Christina's World*, brushstroke by brushstroke in her mind.

Unusual for a ten-year-old, but then very little was usual for Antoinette.

The sunlight shining through the door was sharp. Tears filled her eyes, and she screwed them shut. She felt tied up inside, as if her muscles were too tight. The sun still glowed red behind her eyelids, but the hurt was gone and that helped her decide. She needed music to calm down.

With her mind emptied of everything else, she forced her arm outward until her fingertips brushed the flaked paint on the door. It felt sharp against her skin, and she almost recoiled. But when would the alarm be off again?

Summoning control, she flapped with one hand and pushed the door with the other.

The door opened with a sigh, and the light fell harder on her face. With her eyes closed she leaned into the sun, wishing it could draw her outside. Controlling her body was sometimes difficult, but that morning she moved like a ballerina, swiveling her hips and sliding through the door like a ribbon of silk.

On the porch she threw her arms open, ready to fly to the sun. Then she listened. The land sang to those who stood still long enough to hear it.

People had songs too, but Antoinette needed to touch them to hear their music. Sometimes she grabbed her mother's hand,

and the low, sweet sound of a pan flute filled her body. When that happened, Antoinette felt like she could do anything. Even speak.

Today the outside world sounded mournful, like the oboe's part in *Peter and the Wolf*. Antoinette wiggled. She almost opened her eyes, but she thought better of it; if she did, she would be lost. Her brain would lock on to the blades of grass, and she would start counting. One, two, three . . . four hundred, four hundred one, four hundred two. The counting would trap her for hours.

She kept her eyes closed as she climbed down from the porch. A breeze snaked around her ankles, making her nightgown dance. She laughed a high-pitched giggle that bubbled up from her throat. If she raised her arms, she might be light enough to fly. She lifted her hands, then brought them down hard enough to clap her thighs.

The flagstone path would lead her to the flower fields, but today she wanted more than the feel of stone beneath her feet. She left the path and pushed her toes into the soil. The ground buzzed, a tingle of electricity that vibrated up her legs, calming her muscles so that on the way to the garden she didn't bounce or flap, so that her legs didn't fly out from under her.

She walked until her feet bumped against a ridge of soil that marked the start of the daffodil field. From her bedroom window she could see the bright yellow heads nodding in the sunlight, but out here she could *feel* them.

She squatted and pushed her hands into the loamy soil. It slid from her fingers, coating her nails and the creases of her small hands. She inhaled, filling her lungs with the scents of the garden: soil, compost, and new green grass.

With her hands in the dirt, the music was louder. A chorus of woodwinds flooded her body: clarinets, flutes, and bassoons. But the tempo was too slow and some of the notes were off. Sharp in one place, flat in another. Her heart pounded in her ears, and her arms tensed. She needed to flap, but she forced herself to stay still while a picture formed in her mind, a picture of a bulb bound by clay soil, and a plant weakened by root bores.

Antoinette hummed, increasing the tempo and correcting the notes. When everything was right, she stopped. Her body was calm now, but she slumped to the ground, exhausted. Bits of mulch pricked her cheek, but she didn't move. She breathed deep, listening to the robins calling from the nearby woods.

"Antoinette?"

At first she didn't hear her name; she was lost in the sensations around her. Then a rough hand fell against her neck. The touch sent a jolt through her body, and she fell back, her eyes wide with fear.

"Sorry. Sorry," a man said as he snatched his hand away.

She tried to sit up, but her muscles weren't working yet.

"Antoinette." The man was calm. "Antoinette. What's wrong? It's Seth. Look at me. Are you okay?"

He touched her cheek and turned her head toward him. When she leaned into his calloused hand, her heart stopped racing and she relaxed. Seth was as much a constant in her life as her mother. Like her, he understood that speaking wasn't the only way to communicate.

He crouched in front of her, the tips of his long dark hair tickling her cheek. "Can you tell me what's wrong?" he asked.

Her arm felt heavy, but she pointed over his shoulder, back home where the blue clapboard farmhouse rose beyond the sea of daffodils.

"Home?" he asked. "You want to go home?"

She pointed and opened her mouth. *Home*. That's what she wanted to say. The word would be whisper light if she could get it out.

Seth slid his arms under her body. She picked a daffodil before he lifted her. The commercial fields weren't for home flower picking, but the yellow daffodil would make her mother happy.

Seth cradled her as he walked back to the house, and she melted into him. He smelled like green grass and tobacco. Through his thin T-shirt, she felt the steady thump of his heart, which was its own form of music.

THE KITCHEN DOOR popped open with a thud. Antoinette raised her head from Seth's arms and saw that the room was empty. Her mother was probably still asleep.

"Rose?" Seth called. There was no answer. The air inside the house was heavy and quiet. He started down the long hallway that led to the bedrooms.

Through an open door, Antoinette saw her mother, sitting in one of the two blue chairs by the window overlooking the back field, her journal open on her lap. She turned when Seth knocked on the doorframe.

Focusing on faces was difficult for Antoinette; they changed every second, tiny muscles shifting with each smile or frown. One person could wear hundreds of faces. But Antoinette forced herself to study her mother's face. Her lips were rimmed with blue, and deep circles sat under her eyes. Her short blonde hair stuck out in all directions and shadows highlighted her gaunt face.

"I found her outside in the daffodil field," Seth said.

Her mother closed the journal and stood. "She's been wanting to go outside, but I've been so tired." She leaned over Antoinette who was still snug in Seth's arms. "You always were persistent."

Antoinette held out the daffodil.

Her mother smiled when she took it. "Daffodils symbolize new beginnings," she said to Seth. "From Lily's flower book. I can't believe I remember."

Antoinette felt Seth flinch. "Hard to forget." His rough voice was tinged with something that sounded like regret. "She carried that book everywhere."

Antoinette was sandwiched between the two of them. *Content*. The word floated up from somewhere inside her. Her entire body felt warm. She stretched toward her mother, wanting to hear her song.

Her mother drew back. "You need to sleep," she said, her lips forming a sad smile.

"She was lying among the daffodils," Seth said. "Last night, I noticed some of them had browned around the edges. I planned to harvest them today, but then this morning they were fresh when I got there. Antoinette was half asleep in the middle of them. She didn't hear me until I was right next to her." He spoke slowly and his voice was heavy with meaning, but Antoinette was too tired to figure out what he was trying to say.

He sat in one of the chairs and shifted Antoinette so that his arm was behind the crook in her neck.

"She's so tiny," her mother said as she sat across from Seth. "It still surprises me how heavy she gets after a while."

Seth laughed. Antoinette liked the sound. She closed her eyes and let the noise wash over her. She was too tired to flap her hands, but she twitched her fingers against Seth's arm. *Happy*.

She usually was happy around Seth. He could be abrupt with others, but he was always kind to Antoinette and her mother.

Once, some boys at the farmers' market had giggled at Antoinette as she stretched up on her toes and walked in circles under the Eden Farms tent. When Seth heard them, he stopped unloading flats of impatiens, walked over to Antoinette, and put a hand on her shoulder. In his presence, the tension left her body, allowing her to stop walking and stand still.

Seth didn't say a word. He just glared at the boys until they started fidgeting. Then one by one, they apologized.

"They're kids," he said after they scattered. "They don't know what they're doing, but it hurts anyway."

He had been right. It did hurt. Every time someone stared at Antoinette a little too long or crossed the street to avoid her, a small, bruised feeling bloomed in her chest.

Knowing that Seth, along with her mother, understood how she felt eased the hurt a little.

Thinking of her mother, Antoinette cracked her eyes open, and watched the slow rise and fall of her mother's chest. Despite her fatigue, she struggled toward her mother. If she could hold her mother's hand, everything would be all right. She imagined her mother's song—the notes of a pan flute, smooth and round as river rocks.

"Not now, Antoinette," her mother said.

Antoinette didn't stop trying. As she struggled to sit up, she stared at her mother's tapered fingers. At the green-and-purple bruise on the back of her mother's hand. It was from the IV she had in the emergency room last week.

Seth wrapped her tight in his arms and leaned back. Now she was even farther from her mother. "Your mom needs some rest."

Antoinette shook her head hard, making her hair lash against her cheek. *Mommy!* If she could say the word, she was sure her mother would respond.

"She can't do this much longer," her mother said, her voice cracking. "And I . . . well, it's not like I'm going to get better."

Seth sighed. After several long seconds he said, "It's time to call Lily. You can't keep avoiding her, Rose."

Antoinette strained against his arms, but he was too strong. The exhaustion that stole through her body trapped her, making her eyes shut as if tiny weights were attached to her eyelashes. She was tired. So tired.

"I don't know," her mother said. She sounded small and scared. "It's been six years. Antoinette was too much for Lily as a four-year-old. It's not like things have improved. And the way I left things with Lily . . . what if she won't come?"

Antoinette fought to open her eyes but couldn't. Her body grew heavier and heavier.

She heard Seth: "The three of us aren't kids anymore, Rose. Lily's your sister. The girl I know will come if you ask."

Antoinette couldn't fight it any longer. She sank into Seth's arms as sleep overtook her.

# Chapter Two

〜

L ily Martin lived a cautious life. She looked to numbers. Math was consistent: two plus two equaled four. Always. There was no way to make it something else. Rearrange the numbers, write the problem horizontally or vertically, and the answer was always the same. Four. Equations had solutions, and their predictability made her feel calm, settled.

Except today.

She had spent most of the day reformatting death tables for the life insurance company she worked for. They weren't really called death tables. *Life expectancy table* was the correct term, but what else did you call a collection of data that predicted when someone would die?

Lily headed the actuary department, and it was her responsibility to know when someone was likely to die. A healthy, male, nonsmoker could expect to live 76.2 years, whereas a smoker's life expectancy was reduced by 13.2 years. A thirty-two-year-old woman with congestive heart failure—well, she was uninsurable.

The death tables fed the rating engine that supplied price quotes for insurance policies. Over the weekend, the rates for smokers and nonsmokers had been switched until someone in the

IT department realized that a worm had slipped through their firewall and flipped the data.

Lily came in to work that Monday and spent the morning fielding calls from the CEO and the head of IT. At noon, after death had been restored to its rightful position in the insurance world, she grabbed her laptop and left, planning to finish working from home.

Upon arriving there, she opened the door to her study and set her computer on the desk. Sunlight filtered through the two large windows. While she waited for the laptop to boot up, she opened the windows. A yellow finch sang in the redbud tree outside. From her childhood study of the Victorian language of flowers, she knew redbuds symbolized new life, perfect for a tree that bloomed in spring.

She stared out the window, and for just a moment she was not in her house on the south side of the Ohio River; she was back at Eden Farms, in Redbud, Kentucky, where she grew up. April was her favorite time there. The land was waking, and the air tasted like hope.

Covington, where Lily now lived, was in northern Kentucky, on the banks of the Ohio River. The land there was steep hills and deep valleys, not mountainous like Appalachia in eastern Kentucky but different enough from the town where she grew up that she often felt she had moved across country instead of only two hours north.

Redbud was in central Kentucky, just south of Lexington. The land there was draped in Kentucky bluegrass and rolled like soft ocean waves, much of it decorated with white-plank fences that surrounded the area's sedate Thoroughbred farms. Nestled among them, Eden Farms was a burst of color. In summer, the fields behind their farmhouse were a crazy quilt of purple, pink, yellow, white, and red. For Lily, it was a wonderland, and she and her sister, Rose, used to pretend they were fairies, the fields their kingdom.

Outside her house a car honked, and Lily came back to the present. She pressed her fingers hard against the windowsill. Nothing good came of dwelling on lost things. She bit her lip as she turned from the window. Covington was nowhere near New York or Chicago in size, but it was a far cry from the country, where everyone lived acres apart. In Covington, if she stood in her side yard and stretched out her arms, she could touch her house with one hand and her neighbor's with the other.

She lived in the city's historic district, and her house was two hundred years old. The floors sloped in places and the yard was postage stamp size, but she had transformed the ramshackle place into a warm, inviting home. Here in the study, the walls were the color of sun-warmed soil, and three Kentucky landscapes hung above her desk. Her sister had painted them at age fifteen. The colors were too bright and the proportions were off, but Lily liked their slight awkwardness. It reminded her of Rose at that age, lanky but beautiful, child and adult at the same time.

A purple potted orchid and a small framed picture decorated Lily's desk. In the photograph, Rose and Lily stood with their arms wrapped around each other, holding on as if they'd never let go. Their cheeks were pressed together and their hair—Rose's light blonde and Lily's deep brown—twirled over their shoulders. Seth Hastings had snapped the picture right before Rose left for college.

At the thought of Seth, Lily clenched her jaw and quickly looked away. Losing him shouldn't hurt after all these years, but it did.

*Focus on work*, she thought. She sat in front of her laptop, and her stomach grumbled.

"If you'd let me take you to lunch like a normal person, you wouldn't make such awful noises." The voice startled her, sending her heart to her throat.

Her neighbor, Will Grayson, leaned against the doorframe. He slumped into the wall as if he couldn't hold himself up, reminding Lily of how he had looked when he'd been taking morphine. Almost a year had passed since his last chemo treatment, but from his appearance today she guessed he still had some pills left.

Automatically, her mind went to the death tables. A thirty-four-year-old male in remission from lung cancer had a five-year life expectancy of 13.4 percent.

Thankfully, Will stood solidly among that 13.4 percent.

Several months ago, she had accompanied him to his oncologist's office for a follow-up visit. The doctor smiled at them. "I don't get to say this often enough," he said. "Your CT scan is clear. We got it all."

Lily thought she might slide to the floor in relief, but Will was nonplussed. He nodded once and stood. "Cancer's got nothing on me," he said. That's what she liked about him—he made his total self-interest charming.

Now she looked up at him and smiled. "I thought you were finished with that stuff," she said, referring to the powerful pain pills he had taken when he was ill.

His dark hair shot up in surprising directions and smile lines feathered out around his blue eyes. He was an emergency room doctor at St. Elizabeth Hospital. She knew that before his illness he'd had the habit of spending an hour each day in front of the mirror, even on his days off. She'd once asked why he dressed like a member of the Young Republicans club.

Postcancer Will still wore khakis and button-down shirts, but on his days off he didn't tuck in his shirttails, and he no longer smoothed every hair into place. Sometimes Lily caught him taking deep breaths as if testing his lung capacity. When he finished, he'd close his eyes and smile, seemingly content in a way she'd never seen before.

He tugged his shirt cuffs over his still-thin wrists. "I'm not working, and it's too good to waste. Want some?" He fished the prescription bottle from his pocket and tossed it to her.

She tried to catch it but missed. The bottle smacked into her nose. "No," she said, leaning over to pick it up.

He shrugged as he took the bottle. "Suit yourself, but you're missing out. How about lunch? I'm starving."

She shook her head. "I have to work."

"Aw, come on. What's a guy got to do to impress you?"

They went through this routine at least once a week. Will wasn't specifically interested in *her*; he was interested in anything female. Since she fell into that category, he occasionally slipped into Romeo mode with her until she reminded him that she wasn't interested. Which was true. Most of the time, anyway. Sometimes her heart sped when his dark hair flopped into his eyes. Then she forced herself to count the girls she had seen leaving his house that month. Six in March.

"When are you going back to work?" she asked.

A month ago, Will had taken a leave of absence. "To focus on the things in life that really matter," he had said.

Now he crossed the room and spun her chair around till she faced him. Then he leaned down, putting his hands on the armrests. He was so close she felt his breath against her lips. "As soon as you agree to go out with me," he said.

She saw flecks of lilac in his blue eyes and felt her cheeks flush. "Did you get the coffee grounds I left on your stoop?" she asked.

"Thanks. Worked wonders for the azaleas." He pointed at her computer, which now sported the blue screen of death, warning her that a data loss was in process. "I think you've got a problem."

"Shit!" She turned away and jabbed the power-down button then waited for the screen to black out. "What do you want, Will? The key's for emergencies, not your daily drop in." He flinched slightly, and she immediately wished she could take back her words.

"Ah, cut to the quick. You're cruel, Lily Martin. Did anyone ever tell you that?"

She glanced at the picture on her desk then looked away, hoping he didn't notice. She had more photos, but this was the only one she displayed. Under her bed, she had eight boxes of snapshots. On nights when missing Rose made her head ache, Lily stared at the pictures until she fell asleep, surrounded by pieces of the life she used to lead.

She also had baby pictures of her niece, Antoinette. Sometimes Lily tried to imagine what the little girl might look like now, but she never could. As a baby, Antoinette had been different. Trying to picture her as a ten-year-old was impossible.

Will caught her glance at the picture. He snatched it up.

"Give it to me, Will." She held her hand out, but he jumped back.

"You were cute then, but I like you better now," he said. "Even that little wrinkle you get in your forehead when you're mad."

"I don't have a wrinkle." She raised a hand to her forehead and pressed.

"Yes, you do. Right here." He removed her hand and smoothed his fingers over her skin. "There. All gone now."

His fingers were soft, and she relaxed under his touch. He put the picture back on the desk. "Your sister doesn't have anything on you."

That was a lie. Rose was the beautiful one.

"Don't get me wrong," he said. "She's pretty in an obvious way. But who'd want a blonde, blue-eyed Barbie doll when they could have a girl with green eyes and skin like porcelain? Don't sell yourself short."

Lily looked up at Will. His eyes were the blue of the cornflowers that grew wild in the fields back home. No wonder he never had trouble finding women.

"Not funny, Will. Why are you here?" She didn't like being teased.

He grinned, flashing his perfect teeth. "It's an emergency. I'm out of coffee."

"There's a Starbucks down the street," she said as she turned around and shut her laptop.

"But then I wouldn't get to spend the day with you." He rested his chin on her shoulder. "Well? Do you have any?"

"It's in the kitchen, where it usually is."

He kissed her cheek then walked into the kitchen, looking for the coffee she kept on the counter next to the coffeemaker.

Will made her heart flutter and her palms sweat. She had often imagined his lips pressed against hers. Part of her wanted to leap head first into a relationship with him. But Lily never jumped into a pool without first testing the water. That part of her—the cautious side—told her to wait. Will was her best friend, and she didn't want to risk losing him.

She dropped her head to the desk and slowed her breaths, counting each one. The counting had started when she was a child. It grounded her when she was anxious: ceiling tiles, picture frames, flower petals. She counted them all.

When she was younger, and hadn't yet learned to count under her breath, kids at school christened her "the Count." Every day on the way into school, Lily counted the dirty white tiles between the entrance and the library. Her classmates would strike mock Dracula poses, pretend cloaks across their faces, and they'd yell out random numbers.

The teasing continued until one day when Lily was in fifth grade. After school ended for the day, some students encircled her while she waited for the bus. They shouted numbers at her, laughing when tears accumulated in her eyes, until her friend, and neighbor, Seth Hastings, shoved through the crowd. Seth grabbed the ringleader, threw him to the ground, and punched the boy in the gut. Then Seth hooked his arm through Lily's and walked her to the bus. When the stress of the situation made Lily start counting, Seth added his voice to hers. After that, Seth walked her to the bus every day, and no one called her "the Count" again.

Lily had since learned to count silently, but she hadn't been able to stop the habit. She had reached the number seven when Will called from the kitchen. "I can't find the coffee."

She closed her eyes and murmured, "Eight,"—she never stopped on an odd number—before answering. "It's on the counter."

"Lils! It's not out here."

His words were long and rounded, but if she didn't know him, she wouldn't realize he was high. She wondered if he ever went into work at the hospital that way. She pictured him in a white lab coat, sneaking into a supply closet and shaking a few pills into his hand. Maybe thinking you were invincible was a trait all doctors shared. Or maybe it was just Will.

"It's not here!" he said again.

She pushed back from her desk. Today wasn't a good day for work anyway. Every year, as spring beat back the winter gray, a sense of depression stole over her. Redbuds bloomed and daffodils poked their heads from beds that lined the streets. It was beautiful but felt somehow artificial, and it made her miss the farm.

Rounding the corner to the kitchen, she nearly ran into an open cabinet. All twelve doors were open. "I can't find it," he said.

She crossed the room, closing doors as she went, and picked up the bag next to the coffeemaker.

"Thanks." He measured out even scoops. "You want some?"

She nodded and grabbed tomatoes and cheese from the refrigerator. Since she couldn't work, now was as good a time as any for lunch.

As she put the meal together, she glanced out the window. Off of the kitchen was a small wooden deck with rickety stairs leading to a brick patio that filled what passed for her backyard. It was surrounded by a high stone wall. In late spring and early summer, white clematis and New Dawn roses scrambled up the wrought iron lattices covering the wall. It was beautiful and practical at the same time, providing a small barrier between herself and her neighbors. On one side was Will and, on the other, an artist who made kinetic sculptures out of Campbell's soup cans. While she loved her old brick house, living so close to other people was difficult for her, even after six years.

Everything was crowded here. The sidewalks were cracked and not quite wide enough. When passing someone, she had to twist sideways to avoid touching them. Birds fought to be heard over the constant rumble of cars and buses. Plants jumbled together, vying for the little pockets of soil that served as yards around the houses.

Lily carried the plates outside to the bistro table on the deck. Will brought their coffee. He placed her cup next to her plate, but he didn't sit. He paced, sipping his coffee and shading his eyes. There was a slight breeze, but the sun warmed the last of the winter air. Aside from the squeak of a rotating sculpture in the artist's yard and the street traffic, the day was quiet.

"How can you stand it out here? It's so bright," he said as he shoved a piece of cheese into his mouth.

She shrugged and held her face to the wind, feeling the coolness on her cheeks, drawing memories of her younger self to mind.

"That's right, you were a farm girl." Will laughed. "I wish I had seen that. Bet you were cute with your brown hair in braids and pig slop on your feet."

"It was a flower farm. There weren't any pigs." She closed

her eyes and concentrated on the red glow of the sun behind her eyelids.

"I can see you now. Barefoot in the dirt. A chicken in each hand."

With her eyes still closed, she said, "I told you, it was a flower farm. No chickens. No pigs." Her mind, though, was on the numbers of Eden Farms: the percentage she once owned (half), the percentage she now owned after signing her share over to Rose when their parents died (zero), the number of years that had passed since she had been home (over six), and the number of years since she'd last spoken to her sister (also over six).

Being apart from home, and from Rose, was like missing a limb, but going back would be like trying to sew an arm back on.

"Why won't you tell me about it? And when was the last time you went back?" Will asked, pushing her deeper into memories. "It's home. You know, that place where if you show up, they have to take you in?"

*No*, Lily thought. *They don't. And most likely, they wouldn't.*

Will was still talking. "It's half yours isn't it? Just because your sister's crazy doesn't mean you have to stay away."

"She's not crazy. She's mad at me." It wasn't half hers anymore either. Lily pushed her plate back and stood. She and Rose once had been sisters in every sense of the word, when they were young and naive enough to believe that something like blood could tie you together forever. What they didn't know then was that it could just as easily push you apart.

"Which in my book makes her crazy. How could anyone be mad at you? Come on. It's not far. Let's hop in the car and surprise her."

There was a pile of terra-cotta pots and concrete urns under the deck Lily had been meaning to go through. Most were cracked or broken in some way, but she hoped some could be salvaged. As Will prattled on about the farm, she stood and walked down the stairs to the patio.

After a moment, Will followed. The deck boards creaked under his feet. "You know I don't mean anything." He ducked under the deck. "I bet you were cute then. Barefoot in the dirt."

She reached into the jumble of pots and picked up a blue ceramic container. A thin crack slashed across its surface. She turned the pot over: the crack went all the way through. She put it aside. The next pot she removed from the pile had a thin coat of green mold on the outside but no cracks. Definitely salvageable. Inside the house, the phone rang, but she made no move to answer it.

Will took the pot from her and set it aside. He captured her hands and said, "I'm sorry. I promise I'll be good this time. Now come on back up and sit with me." In the sunlight she could see how dilated his pupils were. They squeezed out most of the blue in his eyes.

"Come on, Lils. It's a beautiful day. We'll sit on the deck, and I won't mention your crazy sister at all." Lily struggled not to smile, but he saw it anyway. "That's the Lily I know." This time when he tugged her hand, she let him lead her back up the stairs.

He guided her to the far edge of the deck and leaned against the rail. "See," he said, "I can be good."

"There's a first for everything," Lily said with a smile.

Will bumped his shoulder against hers. The gesture was friendly and intimate at the same time. "I just want you to be happy."

Lily looked out across her small backyard. The roses had

started to leaf out, but it would be a month or more before they bloomed. "I am happy," she said.

"I know you better than that. I see it every spring—you miss home."

He was right, but Lily didn't acknowledge it. Instead, she said, "Why does it matter so much to you?"

He twined his fingers through hers. "You should know the answer to that. You matter to me. What's important to you is important to me."

Her hand grew hot under his.

"Plus," he said, "I've got a thing for farm girls. You in a pair of cutoffs with your hair in braids." He grinned. "I'd die a happy man."

Lily's heart quickened. She was leaning into him when the phone rang again. Startled, she disentangled her hand from his and ran inside to answer the phone. She needed to get away before she did something she'd regret.

"Hello?" she said, out of breath.

Silence. Then, in a voice so soft it didn't sound real, "Lily?"

At first she thought she was imagining things.

"Hello, Lily? Are you there?" Rose's voice was the same, but beneath her soft Kentucky accent was an undercurrent of fatigue.

The surprise of hearing her sister's voice was so great, Lily's knees wobbled. Her response came out like a question. "I'm here?"

AFTER THE CONVERSATION ended, Lily remained seated on the cold tile floor, holding the phone, until a robotic operator voice said that if she would like to make a call, she should hang up and dial again.

Will was still on the deck when she went outside, but he seemed far away somehow. She felt odd, like she stood in a bubble. Everything was distorted.

"You okay?" he asked, surprising her with his concern. "What is it?" He closed the space between them and put his hands on her shoulders.

She closed her eyes, wishing she could hide from what she had to say. "That was Rose, my sister?" Again, it came out like a question. "She has congestive heart failure. She developed peripartum cardiomyopathy when she was pregnant. Most women recover from it. She didn't. I had assumed she'd be okay. She's not."

Rose had already outlived the statistics Lily knew.

Will brushed his hand across her cheek. "A transplant—"

Lily shook her head. "She has pulmonary hypertension. She doesn't qualify."

Blinking hard against the tears that stung her eyes, Lily said, "My sister is dying." The words suddenly made it real, and she began to cry. Will reached out to hug her; this time, she didn't pull away. She buried her face in his shoulder, her tears darkening his rough shirt. She could still hear Rose's voice: "I need you to come home."

## ROSE'S JOURNAL
### March 2003

———+———

FEAR HAS A taste.

I'm sitting at our scarred kitchen table, tulip and daffodil bulbs lined up in front of me. I should be working on my senior portfolio. It's spring break, and I graduate in seven weeks. Instead, I'm writing in my journal and gulping lemonade, trying to wash the taste of copper pennies from my mouth.

My baby is due in late May.

My. Baby. I picture myself sailing across the stage at graduation, my black gown billowing like a circus tent around my belly.

Yesterday, when we arrived home, Lily dropped our bags by the kitchen door, then ran outside and clambered down the porch steps.

"Not going to give your mom a hug?" our mom asked. She stood in the kitchen waiting for us. It was March, but already her skin was dark from working in the fields. Her nails were bright red. Years of pushing seeds into the ground and ripping out weeds left them permanently stained. She always wore nail polish.

Lily glanced over her shoulder. The wind lifted her long brown hair. She looked like something that sprang from the ground. "In a minute. I've got to check something in the greenhouse first."

She returned holding a bouquet of herbs. One plant had airy, fernlike leaves, the other, small scalloped leaves. "Fennel and coriander," she said as she presented them to me. "Strength and hidden worth." She smiled as if I were someone worth looking up to, instead of a pregnant college girl abandoned by her baby's father.

Now I pick up a daffodil bulb and run my fingers over its smooth white flesh. The kitchen is the best place to work. In early morning, light fills the room. I can pretend I'm in an art studio on campus, my stomach still flat, my plans to travel to Italy after graduation intact. In those moments, I'm not returning home to work on the farm to support my daughter—I am an artist.

Briefly, my stomach muscles contract, and I can't breathe. "False contractions. They're called Braxton Hicks," my obstetrician had said at my last visit. He claimed they didn't hurt. He was wrong.

When my muscles unclench, the taste of copper pennies returns. I take a drink of lemonade, but it doesn't help.

I try to focus on the daffodil bulb I'm supposed to be sketching for my portfolio. Earlier, I slipped one of Dad's garden knives through the bulb's brown papery outer layer. I undressed it, removing the paper scales. Then I cut it in half, exposing the flower bud.

Most people don't realize that a tiny plant lies inside of the bulb, already germinating. I plan to create a series of drawings that capture flowers in various stages of germination.

The flower bud is folded over on itself. I set down the bulb and hold my arm out with my thumb up. I squint, aligning the tip of my thumb with the top of the first leaf. I measure the stem against the base of my thumb. The plant is a green so pale it's almost white.

I start drawing. I make my strokes thin and sparse. I concentrate on my arm moving in great swoops over the paper, on the feel of the bumpy cloth canvas under my charcoal.

I'm not afraid when I draw.

The charcoal makes a soft *phft, phft* across the page. I study the bulb and trace the bend of the stem, the pleat in the first leaf. As I work, I try to be the person Lily thinks I am, full of strength and hidden worth. I sit straighter, ignoring the slight pressure in my chest that developed when I hit the six-month mark and never left.

Lost in thought, I jump when Mom puts her hands on my shoulders. She's silent for a moment. Then she bends down and kisses the top of my head. The end of her long blonde braid tickles my cheek. "You're still an artist. Coming home doesn't change that."

When I don't answer, she turns to the kitchen counter. "Do you like the crib?" she asks. Her back is to me as she pours a cup of coffee, but I catch the slight stiffening of her shoulders that says my answer matters. She was disappointed when I told her I was pregnant, but after the shock wore off she and Dad began a campaign to get me to move home after graduation.

"It's beautiful," I say because it's true. My father, Wade, made the white crib that now sits at the foot of my twin bed. I see his hand in the precise curve of the spindles and the solid feel of the wood.

The thought comes before I can stop it. *If Lily made furniture, it would look like this. Solid. Beautiful. Something that will last.*

"I'm glad," Mom says. She looks younger when she smiles, and I wish she would do it more often.

Another pain grabs me. I groan and hunch forward. "Braxton Hicks," I say between clenched teeth. I clutch the stick of willow charcoal so hard it snaps in two.

I hear Mom's coffee cup clatter into the sink. "That's not Braxton Hicks," she says. "We need to go to the hospital."

MY ARMS ARE heavy, and I can't open my eyes.

"Rose?" My mother's voice. "Can you hear me?"

I try to turn toward her voice, but I can't move. I can only flutter my eyes. Wherever I am, everything is dim. I don't know whether the light is off or if I slept all day and it's night now.

"Is she awake?" My father's voice. He sounds tired.

"Almost," Mom says. "Rose? Can you hear me?"

*Yes*, I want to say, *I can hear you.* Something is blocking my throat. I try to lift my hand to my face, but my arm is weighed down by sleep.

"Rose?" Mom says. She sounds far away.

I can't speak, and I am so, so tired.

I try to move again, but I'm trapped. I struggle, shaking my head. The pillow crinkles.

"Rose?" Mom touches my cheek.

When she does, I force my eyes open and try to take a deep breath, but something is clogging my throat. *I can't breathe!* I panic and slap my face. A plastic tube fills my mouth.

"Don't," Mom says. She grabs my hands. "Stop. You're in the ICU on a ventilator." Fear is etched across her face and deep lines furrow her brow. Her nail polish is chipped and hair pokes out of her messy braid.

"You gave us a scare," Dad says. Dark circles ring his eyes.

My brain is fuzzy. Ventilator? ICU?

Mom sinks into a chair next to me and drops her head to my bed rail. "You're okay," she says. The words come out in a rush.

I'm not okay. I'm empty. I drop my hand to my stomach.

It's flat.

*Baby?* I mouth around the tube.

Mom doesn't notice.

*Where is she?* The familiar taste of copper pennies fills my mouth. I wrench myself upright, and yank at the tube. *Where is my baby!*

"Stop," Mom says. She stands over me, cradling my hands in hers. "Wade, help me."

Dad grabs my arms and pulls them down. "Be still, Rose, calm down." His green eyes are rimmed with red.

*Baby,* I mouth again. *Baby!*

Mom, at last, understands. "Your baby's fine," she says, but I don't believe her. Her eyes are so wide the white swallows the blue, and her lips are thin with the effort of smiling. She doesn't let go of my hands.

I can't breathe. Something is crushing my chest.

"She's fine," Mom repeats. "Lily's with her. She hasn't left her side."

"She's little," Dad says. "No bigger than my hand. But she's fine." He holds out his hand, palm up, and smiles.

*What?* I mouth. My mind is white fog. I remember sitting at the kitchen table, drawing. Pain ripping through my abdomen. Then . . . nothing.

*What?* I mouth again. This time, Mom understands I mean: *What happened?*

She looks at the ceiling. "When we got to the ER, your blood pressure spiked. They had to deliver the baby. You had a heart attack on the table." Her voice wavers.

I shake my head. She's wrong. I'm twenty-two. Heart attacks happen to old people.

Dad takes over. "It's called peripartum cardiomyopathy. The pregnancy caused your heart to enlarge, and the muscle was badly damaged."

If Mom weren't holding my hands, I'd clap them over my ears. I am a child again. *La, la, la. I'm not listening.*

Her last words are small, and I almost miss them. "You're still here," she says as if to convince herself. "I didn't lose you." Then she drops her head to my chest and closes her eyes.

THE NEXT DAY, a doctor I've never met removes the vent tube. His long fingers curve around it, then he yanks like he's starting a push mower, and just like that, I'm breathing on my own again.

When he leaves, I press my hand against my heart. It beats like it always has, but now I know I'm broken.

When a nurse brings my breakfast tray, I turn away. I keep my eyes closed when she checks my vitals. I keep them closed when a nurse's assistant comes in to sponge me off. The girl lifts my arms and runs a damp cloth over them, chattering the entire time.

"You're a lucky one," she says. "Still young enough to get better. Most of the people in here are old. They don't have much time left."

I realize I've never thought about time before. My life used to stretch before me to a vanishing point on the horizon, the end always out of sight. Now it contracts until it's a small dot. How much time do I have left?

A week? A month?

The aid moves to my legs, running the cloth against my skin in soft circles. I count my heart beats. Nothing seems different, but I can't trust my body anymore.

When she's finished, Mom and Lily come in. Mom sways on her feet, and Lily's skin is pale.

I turn away from them.

"Get up," Mom says. She's pushing a wheelchair. "We're taking you to see your daughter."

I don't move. What kind of mother can I be if my heart might give out at any moment?

Lily sits on the side of my bed, and I roll toward her. "She's two pounds fourteen ounces," she says. "All even numbers, so it's good. She looks like you."

My heart flutters. My daughter is three days old, and I haven't seen her yet. "Really?"

Tiny strands of brown hair have escaped Lily's ponytail. Dirt fills the creases of her fingers and smudges her left cheek. She works in the garden when she's upset.

"Really." She squeezes my hand.

Mom guides the wheelchair toward the bed and helps me into it. When she bends down to ease my feet onto the footrest, I notice streaks of gray running through her hair. I smooth them down. Suddenly I don't want to see time passing.

"She's a fighter, Rose. Like you." Mom looks at me as if I've accomplished something great, instead of merely surviving.

They wheel me out of ICU and to the neonatal intensive care

unit. Mom pushes me to a double sink next to the doors. Several plastic scrub brushes are stacked in a cabinet over the sink.

Lily grabs three of the brushes and hands them out. "Make sure you get under your fingernails," she says as she shows me how to squirt soap onto the sponge and lather every inch of my hands.

She's fast, scrubbing her hands with the brush, then scraping under her nails with a tiny plastic file. She counts as she works, and I mouth the numbers with her. We stop at thirty-two.

Lily blots her hands with a paper towel, and then dries mine for me. When we finish, Mom wheels me down an aisle lined with cube pods, each of which houses a baby in a plastic bubble. It looks like something from a science-fiction movie. Quilts in bright colors—orange, pink, and purple—cover the bubbles.

"There are so many." I whisper, afraid of disturbing the babies. I had expected crying, but other than the beeping monitors, the room is silent. Nurses bend over babies. Some of them sing. Some stroke tiny feet or hands. Others adjust IVs and oxygen sensors.

Lily turns down an almost-empty row and stops next to a bubble draped in an orange quilt. A round nurse dressed in SpongeBob scrubs pushes buttons on a monitor. She looks up when we enter. "Is this Mom?" she asks.

Mom. Hearing that startles me. I need to grow into the word.

"We've been waiting for you." The nurse adjusts something on the monitor and writes the displayed numbers on her palm. Then she folds the orange quilt down, opens a curved plastic door on the bubble, and I see my daughter for the first time.

She is tiny, so small she looks more like a doll than a baby. She is asleep, lying on her stomach. Her hands are balled into fists. A purple plaid hat covers her head, but a fine mist of hair pokes out from under it. Blonde, like mine. I touch the tips of my hair and smile.

Other than the hat, a diaper, and booties on her feet she is naked. "Can I touch her?" I ask the nurse.

"Just slide your hand into the isolet. She's having a little trouble regulating her body temperature today. It's been low, so she needs to stay in there, but she'll know you're here."

I run my fingers along her back. At my touch, she sighs and moves her head to nuzzle my hand. I melt.

"We took her off oxygen this morning. She's been fine."

I nod as if the words mean something, but I'm only half listening. I'm too busy studying the eggshell pearl of my daughter's fingernails, and her toes, which look like tiny peas.

"She knows you," Lily says.

"How can you tell?"

"She hasn't reacted this way to anyone else. She normally doesn't move much, even when someone touches her. I've never seen her lean into anyone. Have you, Mom?"

"Never," Mom says softly. I hear pride in her voice.

My baby's eyelids flicker. I lean forward, hoping for a glimpse. "Has she opened her eyes yet?"

The three women glance at each other. "Once," Mom says.

I take in their glances. "What is it? What's wrong?" A list of problems flash through my mind. Blind. Missing eyes. Cataracts.

"Nothing. Her eyes are unusual. That's all."

"Can she see?" I ask the nurse.

She nods. "We think so. Some preemies have vision problems because of the oxygen, but we don't think that's the case with her."

Lily says exactly the right thing. "Her eyes are just an unusual color. They're not dark blue. They're pale blue, like cornflowers."

"Like yours, Rose, when you were a baby," Mom says.

I run my fingers over my daughter's back. Her spine is a string of pearls. "Does that mean anything?"

The nurse shakes her head. "No, it's just unusual."

Mom leans over me. "What are you going to name her?"

"Antoinette," I say. I picked the name two weeks ago after flipping through a baby name book Lily gave me. "It means praiseworthy."

At my voice, Antoinette opens her cornflower blue eyes and turns toward me. My heart stops again, but this time it's from love.

## Chapter Three

L
ily sat on the edge of her bed, a well-worn book in her lap. Its white cover had grayed over the years, and the rose on the front was more peach than pink.

Tomorrow she would drive to Redbud and see Rose for the first time in years. She had already called her boss to request a leave of absence. She knew she should be packing now. Her barely used black suitcase sat open on her bed, a pile of T-shirts and jeans beside it, but she was spellbound by the old book. She flipped through the pages until she found what she wanted. As she looked down at the artist's rendering of honeysuckle, her mind drifted to the last time she had been home.

Two years ago, on the first Friday in June, Lily had called in sick to work. She shoved T-shirts and jeans into a suitcase. Then she sat in her car and counted to fifty before heading south to Redbud.

It was Rose's thirtieth birthday.

When they were children, thirty had seemed mythical, like a land they'd never visit. Like China, real but out of reach. They used to sit in the rafters of the drying barn, legs dangling over the beams, eating lavender shortbread cookies while conjuring their futures.

"Paris," Rose said once. Her daydreams played out anywhere but Kentucky. "I'll paint the Eiffel Tower and the Louvre. By thirty, I'll be exactly where I want to be."

*I want to be here*, Lily thought, though she didn't say it out loud. Her dreams seemed small next to her sister's.

"Promise me, you'll be there when I turn thirty," Rose said as she stretched out across the wide wooden beam. "Wherever we are in the world, we'll spend our thirtieth birthdays together. First mine, then yours."

They hooked their pinkie fingers and swore to be together. Rose might have meant they'd be together on their birthdays, but Lily had meant forever.

Yet here it was. Rose's thirtieth birthday. They were apart and neither of them had the life they imagined.

Lily had arrived in Redbud early that Friday morning. She checked into her hotel room, but instead of leaving the room and driving to Eden Farms she stood at the door, twisting the knob first left, then right, counting each turn. She was stuck. It was late afternoon before she could stop.

When she finally left the hotel, she drove north, to Richmond. She ate at a diner that looked like a 1950s museum. Her legs sweated against the red vinyl booth. She drank her sweet tea and picked at her country fried steak. Then she walked around town, ducking into antiques shops and candy stores until it was too dark to do anything except drive back to the hotel.

The following day, she drove even farther north, stopping in Lexington at the Kentucky Horse Park. She bought a ticket and watched the Parade of Breeds. She looked at the statue of

Secretariat and measured her steps' length against Man o' War's impressive twenty-eight-foot stride.

Finally, on the morning she was heading home to Covington, she gathered her courage and drove to Eden Farms. She pulled off on the side of the road and stared at the blue clapboard farmhouse where she grew up. The house stood well back from the road, the drying barn several yards to its left. Oak and birch trees arched over the drive that split in front of the house. One path led to the house and the other to the drying barn.

Their land was wedge shaped, with the widest portion of their fifty acres in the back. Most of it was cleared, but a thick stand of woods made up their back border. The commercial fields were behind the house, and on the right side were two ornamental gardens—the house garden and the night garden.

The Hastings family property bordered theirs on the left, but Lily forced herself to ignore it. After Seth completed his sophomore year in college, he decided to enter seminary. When he did so, he made it clear that there wasn't room in his life for both Lily and God. Besides, the last she had heard, he didn't live there anymore. He was probably off somewhere, saving the world.

Lily turned her attention back to her home. She wanted to climb the back porch and knock on the door, but her knees locked. She stayed where she was, on the side of the road.

As a child, she had been captivated by the Victorian language of flowers. Her interest had started on a trip to the library, where she found a heavy book with a thick white cover. Each page had an artist's rendering of a flower with the meaning the Victorians assigned to it written in script below.

She flipped through the book until she found lily. There were seven entries. White lilies meant purity. Lilies of the valley meant return of happiness. Water lilies meant eloquence. Her name could mean something different every day of the week.

She spent hours memorizing the meanings for each flower. When it was time to return the book, she hid it under her bed and told her mother she lost it. Twenty years later, she still knew that white daisies meant innocence and ivy meant friendship.

Honeysuckle meant the bond of love.

She looked down at the honeysuckle growing along the fence line and broke off three long strands of the vine. She braided them together and twined the garland through the white fence.

Then she drove home without looking back.

It was hard to believe two years had passed since that day. As Lily sat among her folded jeans and T-shirts, she prayed that the courage she had lacked on Rose's thirtieth birthday would sprout up inside of her like that honeysuckle, spreading until it was impossible to ignore.

SHE SNAPPED THE book shut when Will knocked on her open bedroom door. He cocked an eyebrow and held up a bottle of wine. "Merlot. An excellent packing wine. Cherry undertones with a hint of wood smoke." He poured two glasses, then sat in the plush chair next to the window. "Your bedroom is surprisingly drab, Lils."

Lily accepted the glass he held out to her. He was wrong. Her mother had made the blue-and-white star-pattern quilt covering the bed. The oil painting hanging on the opposite wall was from Rose—a yellow lily resting on a porcelain plate. "Bright. Like you," Rose had said when she presented it to Lily. A pewter mug filled with dried rosemary—for remembrance—sat on her dresser. Sheet music, rolled into a tight scroll and tied with a black ribbon, leaned against her mirror. And a tiny purple baby cap hung from the knob of her top dresser drawer.

Her room wasn't drab, wasn't boring. It held the most important parts of her life. Will just didn't know where to look.

"Talk to me, Lils," he said. "You're troubled. I can see it on your face."

The afternoon sunlight slanted across the floor. The tiny room was stuffy. She set her book on the bed and her wineglass on the nightstand, then crossed the room and opened the window.

The ever-present sounds of traffic and birdsong drifted in with the breeze. She pressed her forehead against the screen and watched cars drive past. "I'm fine," she said. Every three seconds, a sculpture in the artist's yard squeaked.

"Yeah, and I'm a monk." When she didn't respond, he grabbed the book from her bed. "What has you so fascinated?"

"It's a book on the Victorian language of flowers," she said as she counted the cars parked on the street. Ten.

"What?" He leafed through the pages.

"The Victorians. They assigned a meaning for every flower. They'd send each other bouquets with hidden messages." Her fingers twitched, and she laced them together. Rose was the only person Lily allowed to look through the book without her. "Sometimes I think of people as a flower. Rose was—"

"Let me guess—a rose?" Laugh lines framed his mouth.

Lily shook her head. "Oak-leaf geranium. It means lasting friendship."

He flipped through the pages until he found the flower. "Pretty," he said. "What about me? What flower am I?"

Her face heated, and she bit her lip. "Give me the book."

He drew back until he was just beyond her reach. "Come on, Lils. Play along. You need to relax a little. This day has been hard enough." He stopped flipping pages. "Here I am. A red rose. Passionate love." He grinned, and her heart turned over.

"Put the book in my suitcase when you're finished," she said. She had to focus on Rose, not the way her skin tingled when Will looked at her.

"I'm teasing. Let me help. I know this isn't easy for you." He tossed the book on top of the stacked T-shirts, then walked over to her.

Her back was to him, and he put his hand on her shoulder.

"I have to pack," she said, without turning around.

He squeezed her shoulder slightly. "Sometimes it's like there's a wall around you. You need to let people in. Talk to me."

She shook her head. Her heart was still bruised from the last time she let someone in. Besides, if she started talking, she would crack right down the middle. The only way she'd be able to help Rose was to stay strong. That meant she had to focus on the business at hand. Packing. "I have to get home. Rose needs me."

Will sighed. "If you change your mind, you know where to find me." As he walked back to his chair, he stopped. "What's this?"

She looked over her shoulder. He nodded at an old shoebox sticking out from under her bed.

"Nothing." She reached for the box, but he was faster.

"Friends shouldn't keep secrets." He let the lid slide to the floor. "Pictures." He ran his fingers across their tops. "Hundreds of them."

"Four hundred twenty-two," she murmured. She reached

for the wineglass on her night stand and took a drink, focusing on the burn in the back of her throat. There were seven similar boxes under her bed.

Will flipped through photos until one caught his eye. He held it up. Three young women stood in shirt dresses, their arms looped around each other as they smiled at the camera. He pointed to the blonde in the center. "Is this Rose?"

Lily shook her head. "My mother, Portia. Rose is just like her." Rose and Portia not only looked alike, they each saw the world the same way—a patchwork of colors and shapes.

As in everything else, Rose and Lily were opposites when it came to their parents. Rose was their mother's daughter, but Lily took after their father, Wade. Rose and Portia knew purple irises rising from a semicircle of yellow pansies would look beautiful next to the gray drying barn. But Lily and Wade knew the exact amounts of nitrogen and phosphorous to feed the plants. Gardening was a synthesis of art and science.

The science came easily to Lily. She and Wade plotted the commercial fields. They worked compost into the soil, transforming it from thick clay into light loam. Before planting, they measured the ground's pH, making sure it was a perfect neutral 6.5 (unless they were planting azaleas or hydrangeas, in which case they added coffee grounds and pine needles to lower the pH to a more acidic 5). They mapped out a field rotation schedule to build up fertility and mitigate pests. They debated the merits of buckwheat or clover as cover crops.

The art of gardening was another story. Lily and Wade ruled the commercial fields, but Portia and Rose designed the display gardens. They filled the house garden with crimson William

Shakespeare roses, English lavender, and yellow coreopsis. They trained wisteria over the gazebo, and then encircled it with pink hydrangeas. It shouldn't have matched, yet it did.

But Lily's favorite was the night garden planted against the stacked stone wall on the side of the property. Everything there was white. Astilbe and sweet alyssum. Foxglove and columbine. The flowers glowed as the sun set. Standing in the garden when fireflies came out made Lily believe in magic.

That's why Eden Farms was successful. Everyone played their part.

"I see Rose in your mother," Will said, yanking her back to the present, "but I also see you. Here, in the sharp line of her jaw. She looks stubborn as hell."

He handed Lily the picture, and though she didn't say so, her heart warmed at the thought that something of her mother lived on in her.

She studied the women standing next to her mother. It had been years, but she recognized them immediately. The plump woman on her mother's left was Cora Jenkins, who owned the Italian restaurant in town. Teelia Todd, whose family owned an alpaca farm, stood to Portia's right. The three women had been inseparable when Lily was younger. After her parents' car accident, they had promised to watch over the girls and the farm. But Lily hadn't talked to either woman since her parents' funeral six years ago.

"Mom *was* stubborn," she said. "She had to have the last word in every argument." It was strange for Lily to realize she was now older than her mother had been when that picture was taken. Gently, she placed it back in the box.

Will selected another photo and held it out to her. A young man with brown hair curling around his ears leaned against the hood of an old Ford pickup. He was smiling, but his eyes were dark, and his shoulders were tense. "Who's this?" Will asked.

"Seth Hastings. Just a neighbor." She glanced at the rolled sheet music on her dresser as she took the picture from Will.

Another photo had been stuck to its back. It fluttered to the floor, but Lily ignored it as she slid Seth's picture inside the box.

"Should I be jealous?" Will asked as he retrieved the picture that had fallen to the floor.

*Of what? A ghost?* Lily thought.

Will turned the other photo right side up and cradled it in his hands. He drew a sharp breath.

At the sound, Lily glanced at the picture. It was summer, and a little girl sat on the porch. The girl's head lolled back, and she gazed up and to the right, fixated on something over the photographer's shoulder.

"My niece, Antoinette," Lily said, before Will could ask. She went back to her suitcase, hoping to put an end to the questions.

Being around Antoinette made the need to count worse. *Much* worse. She counted her T-shirts and jeans, making sure she had six of each. Fancy clothes would be wasted at Eden Farms. She tucked the Victorian flower-language book under a yellow and white shirt.

Shoes. She needed shoes. She fished around in the back of her closet until she found an old pair of garden clogs.

"You never talk about her," Will said.

Shame rose up in Lily, but she was going home. It was time to face her mistakes. She dropped the shoes on top of her suitcase and sank onto the bed. "I stopped going home after Rose realized Antoinette had problems." The words came out in a rush, and her ears burned.

Will frowned. "Why?" he asked. "I thought you loved it there."

She took the picture and clasped it in her hands. "I do. I did." If she closed her eyes, she could see the farm glittering with starlight. Her mother's face, lined, but still youthful. Rose as a child, long-legged and graceful, running through the stream that rimmed their property, the tips of her blonde hair dripping wet.

Then Antoinette's face flared in her mind, and Lily began to count. She reached thirty-two before she forced herself to stop.

She looked down at the photo of her niece. The girl's eyes were too far apart, and her head looked too heavy for her neck. "Our parents died in a car accident. The day of their funeral, Rose asked me to move home and help with Antoinette and the farm."

Lily's chest tightened. She could still see Rose's face, a mix of fear and sorrow, as she had begged Lily to stay. But being around Antoinette . . . Lily sighed. "I couldn't do it. And when I realized I was wrong, it was too late. Rose was so angry."

Will looked down at his wineglass. It was almost empty. He poured some more and cocked his eyebrow as he held out the bottle to Lily. She shook her head.

"Surely she would have forgiven you—"

"I called to apologize, but Rose wouldn't answer the phone," she said. "For the first month, I called every day. I left message after message." She shook her head. "Nothing. Rose was angry. I can't blame her. Antoinette is her daughter and I . . ." The words stuck in her throat.

The first time Lily held Antoinette, it had been in the neonatal intensive care unit, and her niece was only two hours old. At a little under three pounds, Antoinette was barely longer than Lily's hand. When Lily came home on visits, she used to carry Antoinette through the fields, naming the flowers and telling her their meanings.

Life continued that way until Lily returned home when Antoinette was two. That day, Lily and Rose sat side by side on a bench next to the library playground. The sun was a ball in the sky. Everything was gold. Antoinette turned in circles on a small patch of grass and waved her fingers in front of her eyes. It wasn't a random gesture. Not like she was moving for the fun of it. Her movements were methodical. Like she was counting each flick of her fingers.

*Oh, God. She's like me*, Lily thought, stunned at the realization. "Something's wrong," she said when she found her voice.

"What?" Rose followed Lily's gaze. "Nothing's wrong with her. She's just playing."

Lily shook her head. She stared at Antoinette, counting each twitch of her fingers.

"She's fine," Rose said, biting off each word.

"No," Lily said, unable to tear her gaze away from Antoinette. "She's not."

The little girl's head lolled to the left. She moved her hands back and forth. One, two. One, two. She didn't stop, even when Rose scooped her up.

"Nothing's wrong with her," Rose said as she walked back to their car.

Lily looked up at the sky and counted the clouds. She didn't know anything about being a parent, but she knew about being different.

That night, when their mother asked Lily to stay, she said she had to work the next day. Then she drove home, counting the entire time.

Now she looked at Will. His blue eyes were intense. "What if I'm not strong enough to handle Antoinette?" Her fear was that she would take one look at her niece and become paralyzed, would start counting and never stop. She would disappoint Rose all over again.

She reached for her glass and drained it.

Will took her glass and set it on the windowsill.

"Do you know why half of medical school is spent in residency?" he asked.

Lily looked out the window. It was getting late. Clouds drifted in front of the sun and the room grew dark.

"You can read every anatomy and physiology book on the planet, but until you're standing next to a patient who's having a stroke or bleeding out, you don't know how you'll react. You're thrown into it, and you figure it out as you go along."

Will leaned forward until their foreheads touched. "You'll do the same."

# Chapter Four

S omething wild was in the air. Antoinette felt it as soon
as she clambered out of the van. The temperature had
dropped and wind rushed through the trees. Her mother
always said April weather could turn on a dime. An hour ago, the
sky had been a crisp blue. Now it was so dark it almost looked
like nighttime.

Seth had parked right in front of the Bakery Barn. Years ago,
Eli and MaryBeth Cantwell had turned the run-down barn in the
middle of Main Street into a bakery. A small roof jutted over the
entrance, and baskets filled with yellow pansies and blue violas
hung from the white beams. Several metal tables sat on the concrete patio in front of the bakery. They were all empty.

The air smelled like lightning, and the scent made the tiny
hairs on Antoinette's arms stand. When the rain came, the land's
song would change. Right now, Antoinette heard the low moan
of a cello, an eerie sound.

Antoinette flapped her hands. *Change, change.* She wanted
to stand outside in the rain, listening to the land's music. She
imagined water streaming down her back, flattening her hair
against her head, her whole body bright with sound.

"I still say you need to tell Lily *everything*," Seth said as he led Antoinette and her mother to a table near the bakery entrance. He had been saying the same thing since they left the farm.

Antoinette's muscles felt short and her joints stiff. In spite of that, when her mother pulled out a chair for her, she didn't sit. She leaned against the table, hands curled tight against her shoulders and her head cocked to the side, listening. The music would change soon.

"The rain should hold off," her mother said as she sat down. The walk from the van to the outdoor table had been short, but she was out of breath. "At least until we get back to the farm."

"You need to tell her," Seth said again.

This was one of the few times Antoinette had heard her mother and Seth argue. It bothered her, and she pulled her hands even tighter against her shoulders.

"You don't need to protect Lily anymore," her mother said. "Besides, she was anxious around Antoinette before. Knowing *everything* will scare her away. I can't risk her leaving."

Antoinette didn't like it when people talked about her. It made her feel bound up inside, like she was tangled in rubber bands.

She tried to focus on the music, but over the cello she heard the distant buzz of traffic. She also heard a bird calling from one of the Bradford pear trees lining the square and the rush of wind in the tree leaves. But most of all, she heard her mother's voice. It was light as a bell with Seth's lower voice her counterpoint.

Her mother spoke easily. Words fell from her mouth like water flowing downstream. Seth was deliberate in his speech. Antoinette wondered whether he spent hours in silence, storing his words, savoring their taste before doling them out one by one.

"You don't know that," he said. He sat with his elbows braced on his knees, like he was waiting for something.

"Why do you care?" Antoinette's mother asked. She leaned forward and stared at him as if studying his face. "You haven't talked to Lily in years."

Seth pushed his chair back from the table and stood. "It's not about Lily," he said. "It's about what's best for Antoinette. She deserves someone who knows the whole story. And Lily's stronger than you think. Have faith in her."

"Faith was always your purview," her mother said, "not mine."

Antoinette watched as Seth walked to the corner of the patio and pulled a pack of cigarettes from his pocket. He leaned against the wrought iron railing as he shook out a cigarette, lit it, and inhaled deeply. His closed his eyes as he blew out a stream of smoke.

Her mother stared at him through narrowed eyes. "You still have feelings for her," she said.

Seth didn't answer. He took another pull on the cigarette.

Her mother pressed on. "When you talk about her, your voice softens, and you get these little lines about your eyes, as if you're smiling." She pointed at his eyes. "You're doing it now."

Seth turned away and stared out across the street. "We were talking about Antoinette. Not Lily."

"You might want to figure out how you feel about Lily before she gets home," Antoinette's mother said.

He hunched his shoulders and stubbed out the cigarette. "Thanks for the advice."

Antoinette cocked her head. He didn't sound thankful. She rose up on her toes and rocked her head from side to side, trying to loosen the tension in her body. She felt thunder in the sky.

"She has a right to know how you feel," her mother said.

Seth laughed, but it wasn't a happy sound. "She has a right to know *everything* about Antoinette."

"Touché," her mother said as she leaned back in her chair.

"There y'all are." A tall woman with hollow cheeks approached their table. Her gray hair was clipped short, and her eyelids drooped slightly. MaryBeth Cantwell. Her left hand was behind her back. "With the weather, I was afraid you wouldn't make it. They said on the radio that a storm's rolling in." Her right hand shook slightly as she shielded her eyes and looked across the parking lot. There the sky faded from gray to black.

"We can use the rain," Seth said. "The ground's starting to crack, and it's only April." He seemed grateful for MaryBeth's presence. He tossed the spent cigarette on the ground, then walked back to the table, pausing to kiss the older woman's cheek before sitting down.

"I appreciate you coming out to test my new cupcakes before the show, but I don't want y'all to get stuck here because of me." A constant tremor shook her right hand, and her head lolled to the right. She leaned down and whispered in Antoinette's ear. "Don't tell your Mama—or Seth"—she winked at them—"but I've got something special just for you."

MaryBeth pulled her left arm from behind her back. She held a small silver platter. On it sat a white cupcake swirled with pale lemon frosting. The little cake was crowned with a candied purple pansy. "I made it special for you. I'm selling them at your mama's garden show next weekend, so you tell me if it's good." She placed the plate on the table.

Antoinette had overheard her mother talking to Seth and knew MaryBeth was sick. She looked at MaryBeth's trembling hand and thought the woman must understand what it felt like to be unable to control your body. She wondered what MaryBeth's song would sound like. Would it be slow and sweet like her mother's? Or ragged around the edges, like Seth's?

The wind picked up, lifting tendrils of Antoinette's hair. She bounced once and looked sideways at the cupcake. It was lace and sugar, like the snow that covered the farm each winter.

Eli Cantwell walked out of the bakery. He looked like skin stretched across a skeleton, and when he smiled his lips disappeared. He carried two porcelain saucers. Each one held a cupcake. One cake had pale green icing dusted with coconut shavings. The other had lavender icing topped with thinly sliced strawberries.

"We didn't forget about you two," he said as he set the saucer with the green cupcake in front of Antoinette's mother. "Tell us what you think. We want to be ready for the garden show."

"You'll be ready before we are," her mother said. "Two weeks doesn't seem like nearly enough time." She peeled the wrapper from her cupcake and took a bite. "It's delicious."

Antoinette loved their yearly garden show. Her mother invited artists from all over Redbud to set up exhibits in the garden. Then she opened the farm to the public. All day people milled through the fields, gazing at the flowers and art. The air was always filled with music that day.

Thinking about it made her happy. She flapped her hands.

MaryBeth took the other plate from Eli. She held it in her bad hand, and it shook slightly. "Would you mind helping us haul some tables out to the barn before the show?" she asked Seth. "Eli and I aren't as young as we used to be."

"We've got plenty of extra tables at the farm," Antoinette's mother said.

"We'll set them up for you," Seth said.

That was one of the things Antoinette loved about Seth; he was always willing to help.

"I don't want you to go to any trouble," MaryBeth said. She set the plate in front of Seth, and as she did, her hand twitched. The cupcake ended up in Seth's lap, and the saucer shattered on the concrete.

"I'm sorry." MaryBeth pressed her good hand against her mouth. "I . . . I'll clean it up."

"Don't worry about it," Seth said. He grabbed some napkins from the dispenser on the table and wiped the icing from his pants. "That's one good thing about working on a farm. A little mess doesn't bother you." He smiled at her, but she hurried back to the bakery without noticing.

Antoinette's hands stopped flapping, and she managed to take a bite of her cupcake. She would make MaryBeth feel better by eating every last bit. Her first bite was all icing. Smooth and lemony.

Eli watched his wife leave. "She's having a bad spell. She likes doing things herself, but I don't think she can keep it up much longer." His voice wavered, and he looked older than he was.

"She seems worse than she was last month," Antoinette's mother said gently.

Eli nodded. "Her strain of ALS is particularly aggressive. I don't know what I'll do when she's . . ." He stopped and spread his hands. "God will provide. He always has. Excuse me, I'd better go check on her."

Antoinette wasn't sure about God providing. He never answered her prayers. She stared at the purple candied pansy. It looked like it was covered in glass.

"You can eat it," her mother said.

Antoinette knew that. Cora Jenkins often stopped by their house to collect edible flowers. She tested her recipes on Antoinette and her mother before serving them in her restaurant. She made flower-themed food for the garden show. Last year, she made a spinach salad tossed with tiger lilies and dried cranberries. It had been the perfect mix of bitter and sweet.

Antoinette felt the temperature drop again. She flapped her hands in excitement, then calmed enough to take a big bite of her cupcake.

Seth took another napkin from the dispenser. Most of the icing was gone now, but he kept working. He kept his head down, avoiding her mother's gaze. "Do you really think Lily will come home?"

Antoinette tapped her fingers on the table. *Why is Lily coming?* She wanted to ask, but no one paid attention to her.

"She'll come." Her mother's voice was low, but she sounded confident. "She would have come home years ago if I hadn't been so stubborn."

Seth tossed the napkin on the table, then put his elbows on his knees and laced his fingers together. "She's going to find out about Antoinette sooner or later."

"Let's hope it's later," her mother said. Then she did what

she always did when she didn't want to talk about something, she changed the subject: "Why didn't you let Lily know when you came home?"

Seth sighed and shoved a hand through his hair. "I tried. When Mom told me that Lily had moved to Covington, I found her address online and drove to her house. I parked on the street and sat in my truck, trying to get up the nerve to knock on her door." He lifted one shoulder in a small shrug. "I didn't exactly end things on a good note, and I wasn't sure she'd be happy to see me."

He shook his head. "God, I was stupid. I should have known seminary wasn't right for me. I was always more Peter than Paul."

Antoinette's mother gave a small laugh. "I always thought Peter was easier to take. At least he seemed human."

"Yeah, well that was my problem. Too human." Seth frowned. "School was about following a set of rules. I learned which people were too damaged to love and that being a good Christian meant staying away from them.

"No one was *real*. No one ever sat down and said, 'You know what, there's this place in me that's broken. I'm not sure whether God exists and, if he does, whether he gives a shit about me. I felt like I was wearing a mask the entire time I was there."

"Did you tell Lily any of this?" Antoinette's mother asked. A chilly wind was blowing and the sky darkened. Her mother shivered. "The storm will be here soon."

"Wait here," Seth said. He jogged back to the truck and returned with a sweatshirt that he wrapped around her shoulders.

"I wanted to tell her," he said as he sat down. "That's why I drove to her house that day. But just as I found my nerve to get out of the truck, Lily came outside. A man was with her. A good-looking guy, I guess. Dark hair. Neatly dressed even though it was a Saturday."

Seth reached into his pocket for his cigarettes. He pulled one out but didn't light it. Instead, he tapped one end against the table, then turned it over and tapped the other end. He repeated the action several times. "The man had his arm across Lily's shoulder, and she was laughing at something he said. They seemed . . . close."

"Did you talk to her?" Bundled in Seth's sweatshirt, Antoinette's mother looked small, but the blue tinge had left her lips.

Seth shook his head. "She had obviously moved on. I didn't want to interfere. I had hurt her enough already, so I left before she noticed me."

Antoinette's mother reached across the table and placed her hand over his, stopping his nervous fidgeting with the cigarette. "Will you be okay with her here?"

Seth pressed his lips into a thin smile. "I'll be fine," he said. "I always am."

The first drops of rain fell as MaryBeth and Eli returned. MaryBeth carried a white bakery box tied with a red ribbon, and Eli carried a broom.

"I'm so sorry," MaryBeth said to Seth. "I can't always control my arm anymore."

Antoinette knew how that felt. She took another bite of her cupcake, hoping it would cheer MaryBeth. *It's good*, she tried to say, but no one noticed. She tapped MaryBeth's leg and smiled. Her teeth were coated with icing.

No one paid attention to her. She stomped her feet. Still, no one listened.

Eli swept the shards of glass into a dust pan. "What's life without a little adventure?" he said with a smile, although his eyes looked sad.

Antoinette took another bite of her cupcake. Lemon and vanilla combined together. Two of her favorite flavors. She wanted to tell MaryBeth that she understood being different.

Antoinette tapped MaryBeth's hand. She wanted to hear the older woman's song.

"Don't," her mother said, concern in her voice.

"She's okay," MaryBeth said. "I see you finished your cupcake. Did you like it?"

Antoinette flapped her hands. *Good*, she thought. *It was good.*

"I'll take that as a yes," Eli said with a laugh, but MaryBeth's shoulders sagged. She seemed sad.

The sky started spitting rain. "We'd better go," her mother said, but Antoinette wanted MaryBeth to smile.

Seth stood and held his hand out to Antoinette's mother. "You look tired," he said. "Lean on me. I'll help you to the car."

"MaryBeth, the cupcakes are wonderful," Antoinette's mother said. "You'll sell out of them at the show." She hugged the older woman.

With her mother distracted, Antoinette caught MaryBeth's hand. Bells filled her mind. Antoinette closed her eyes and followed the threads of the song. In most places, it was light as a hummingbird's wings, but in one spot the notes were round and flat.

Antoinette hummed along with MaryBeth's song. She had just reached the part where the notes felt off, when her mother noticed. "Antoinette, stop." She grabbed Antoinette's shoulder and pulled. Through her thin cotton shirt, Antoinette felt her mother's cold fingers, but she didn't let go of MaryBeth's hand. She pictured the way the woman's song should go and hummed, correcting the notes that were off.

"Seth?" her mother said. There was an edge of panic in her voice. "She's going to seize."

Antoinette's hands tingled, and her neck twitched. She squeezed MaryBeth's hand hard.

The woman groaned. "You're hurting me, Antoinette."

"What's going on?" Eli asked.

"Antoinette, let go!" Her mother was loud, but Antoinette didn't stop.

"It hurts," MaryBeth said.

At the same time, Seth grabbed Antoinette under her arms and pulled her away. The connection broke, and the song faded.

The rain fell harder, but no one moved. Antoinette slumped against Seth, fighting to keep her eyes open. MaryBeth twisted her neck from side to side.

*Are you happy?* Antoinette thought. She tried to focus on MaryBeth's face, but it looked fractured, as if her eyes had traded places with her mouth. Antoinette had to look away.

"What happened?" Eli asked.

"I don't know," MaryBeth whispered. Her voice was different, stronger.

Fireworks exploded behind Antoinette's eyes, and her arms started to shake. *Not yet*, she thought, but she couldn't stop. Her eyes rolled up, and color filled her brain.

"She's having a seizure," her mother said. "We need to get her to the van."

Seth turned, but Eli grabbed his arm, stopping him.

"What just happened?" Eli said. "Look at MaryBeth. She's not shaking. Antoinette *did* something!"

The colors came faster now, brilliant blues and reds like lightning that colored the sky at night.

Just before darkness overtook Antoinette, she heard her mother's voice, soft with compassion: "Eli, you're looking in the wrong place if you're looking for a miracle. She's just a little girl."

———+———

I AM A mother.

A mom.

Mommy.

I chant the word as I ease Antoinette from her car seat. If I say it enough, maybe I'll believe it. Maybe I won't shake when I hold her.

It's early. The sun is just now climbing over the hills, and the chill of the night still hangs in the air. Antoinette is six weeks old and barely weighs five pounds, yet I've never held anything heavier in my life.

Until now, she has spent every minute of her life in the NICU. Mom and Dad offered to accompany me to the hospital to bring her home, but in the past month and a half I've grown small with fear. How can I be a mother if I'm afraid to be alone with my daughter? I went to the hospital alone to prove to myself that I could.

A shock of blonde hair pokes from beneath Antoinette's purple plaid cap. Her eyes are closed, and she snuggles into my arms as if there's no place she'd rather be.

But my heart could stop beating any minute. How can she trust me when I don't trust myself?

My knees are jelly as I carry her up the back porch steps. I move carefully, monitoring my heartbeat. I go to brush my hair away from my shoulders, forgetting I cut it off four weeks ago. I am not the same person I was before I went into the hospital. I needed my appearance to reflect that. Several heartbeats pass before I can open the door.

A bundle of cinquefoil sits in the center of the kitchen table. The shrubby plant spills out of the old glass someone used as a vase. The flowers are paler than they should be, more butter yellow than lemon. I'm not sure whether something's wrong with the plant or with me.

Before I became ill, colors were vibrant. I saw pink and blue and yellow housed in a white rose petal. After all, white is a compilation of every color.

Things are faded now. I only see white. Or butter yellow in this case.

"They mean 'beloved daughter,'" Lily says.

I startle. I was so intent on carrying Antoinette without dropping her that I didn't see Lily beside the table.

My heart shudders. I take several deep breaths, calming only when Antoinette wraps her hand around my little finger. "What are you doing here?" I ask Lily.

"Can I hold her?" When Lily takes Antoinette, it feels like a huge weight has been lifted from me instead of a tiny baby.

She removes Antoinette's cap and tosses it on top of her bag, then presses her nose against Antoinette's scalp.

"Why aren't you at school?" I ask. There is a week left in the semester. Lily missed several classes while I was in the hospital, so I know she has to be behind.

"Couldn't miss my niece's homecoming. Besides, I took my exams early."

Of course she did. Jealousy swallows me. I should be graduating next Saturday. Instead, I dropped out in the middle of my last semester.

"Do you think she remembers me?" Lily rocks gently as she talks. Antoinette looks comfortable with her.

"I'm sure she does," I say, though I don't know. The nurses at the NICU know my daughter better than I do.

Lily starts singing. Not a real song. She strings numbers together to the tune of the alphabet song.

"You're home for the summer?" I ask. In spite of the envy I feel as I watch how easily she interacts with my daughter, Lily is my touchstone. I am strong when she is here.

She curls around Antoinette. Her long dark hair swings forward, screening her face. "I'm taking summer courses this year. I'll be home for the garden show, but then I'm going back to school." There's a slight tremor to her voice, and when she looks up, her eyes are red.

I am about to ask her what's wrong, when Mom and Dad rush into the kitchen. Lily hands me Antoinette and slips away.

"I thought I heard you," Mom says. "Did you have any problems? Are you okay?" She holds me by the shoulders, examining me as if I might have a heart attack right here in the kitchen. She's aged in the past two months. Frown lines stretch across her brow.

I want to reach for Lily, but the worry in Mom's eyes holds me here. "I'm fine," I say, though my heart tumbles through my chest, and I see black spots before my eyes.

"You're sure?" Dad hides his concern better than Mom, but I see anxiety in the way he holds his hands perfectly still.

I look around them, trying to see Lily, but she has disappeared.

I force a smile and turn back to my parents. "Positive." I am lying.

LATER THAT NIGHT, I sit on the edge of my bed, peering into Antoinette's crib. Is she breathing? I place my hand under her nose. I don't feel anything. Panic stings my throat. Then I feel a warm puff against my hand, and I relax.

Lily sleeps in the twin bed closest to the door. I have always slept under the window. Her soft snores fill the room. The familiar sound helps me breathe easier.

Our room is still a large square box. The walls are still painted faded rose; the floor is still scarred where Lily and I carved our initials into the soft wood beneath our beds. But Antoinette's crib changes everything.

I tiptoe across the room and sit on the side of Lily's bed. I never got to ask her what was bothering her earlier in the day. After Mom and Dad came in, she slipped out to the garden and stayed there until after dinner.

"Lily?" I nudge her shoulder.

She groans. "What's wrong?" she asks, without opening her eyes.

"Can I get in?" I crawl beneath her covers before she answers. As a child, Lily would slip into my bed at night when she didn't want to go to school the next day.

Funny how our roles have reversed.

She makes room for me, and I roll onto my side so that I can see her face. Lily is tall and dark. The exact opposite of me.

"Why were you upset earlier?" I ask. Her eyes are still puffy, and I know it's not from sleep.

She is fully awake now. "It's nothing," she says. "Is Antoinette sleeping?"

I don't want to talk about Antoinette. I want to pretend we're teenagers again, sharing secrets. "I know you. You don't cry easily."

"I cried a lot when you were in the hospital," she says. She rolls over on her back. Her lips move, and I know she's counting.

I cried then too, but I don't say so. I used to be the one who comforted her. Now that I need her comfort, I don't know how to act.

"Seth broke up with me," she finally says. "That's why I'm taking summer courses. I can't be on the farm, knowing he's next door."

Whatever I was expecting, it wasn't that. Seth and Lily have been together for so long that I think of them as one person. *SethandLily.* "Why?" She must have misunderstood him.

"He's decided to go to seminary. Apparently, I'm a distraction." She puts a hand over her eyes.

That doesn't sound like Seth. I'm about to say so, when a soft bleat comes from Antoinette's crib. I don't want to leave Lily, but she shoos me away. "Go check on her."

I hesitate. "I'm fine," Lily says. "Go get her."

This time I listen. I lean over Antoinette's crib. Her eyes are open. I freeze, hoping she'll go back to sleep. When she doesn't I say the first thing that pops into my mind. "I'm your mom," I whisper. "Do you remember me?"

"Of course she remembers you," Lily says. She flings back her sheet and sits on the side of her bed. She sleeps in one of Seth's old white T-shirts. It's only May, but her legs are already brown.

Antoinette kicks her feet and waves her hands in front of her face.

"Have you called him?" I ask as I pick up Antoinette. Her hand wraps around my finger. She has a tight grip for a little girl. As usual, her touch calms me.

"He won't answer my calls." Lily traces the lines between the wood planks with her toe.

I carry Antoinette to the rocker in the corner of the room and sit down. "I could talk to him."

Lily shakes her head. "You have enough on your plate."

Antoinette closes her pale blue eyes and nuzzles against me, causing a few drops of milk to leak from my breast.

Quickly, I lift my shirt. I haven't been able to breast-feed her yet. My first job as a mother was to carry her for nine months. My second is to feed her. Antoinette is only six weeks old, and already I've failed at everything a good mother should do.

"Your body experienced too much trauma," the nurse said at my last checkup. "If your milk hasn't come in yet, it's not going to."

I whisper a prayer. *Please, let me get this one thing right.*

Antoinette latches on and begins to suck, but within seconds she curls her fists into tight balls and screams. I want to cry. I squeeze my eyes shut and push my toes against the cold wood floor to get the rocker going. The motion soothes Antoinette, and she settles into a hiccupy sob. "Is there a flower for disappointment?"

I hadn't meant to ask the question, so I'm surprised when Lily answers: "Yellow carnations."

"But they look so happy."

Lily stands and stretches. "Appearances can be deceiving."

Antoinette opens her mouth wide, but no sound comes out. She's hungry. I need to go downstairs and warm up a bottle. I push myself up, but when I stand the room swirls.

I fall back into the rocker. Antoinette wails. "Lily," I say over Antoinette's cries. "Can you go downstairs and warm up a bottle?"

She is out the door and down the hall before I stop speaking. How am I going to get through the summer without her?

Antoinette still screams. I start rocking again, but this time, the motion doesn't soothe her.

"Hush. Hush." I place my lips next to her ear and whisper, but she doesn't stop.

"Let me take her." Mom leans against the doorway, eyes red from lack of sleep.

I shake my head. *I can do this. I can take care of my daughter.*

"Rose," Mom says in a voice so soft I almost miss it, "let me take her."

"But I'm her mother." I don't want to let go. I want to get one thing right.

"Part of being a good mother is learning when to ask for help." Mom smiles to soften her words. "Not your best quality."

She leads me to my bed and eases me onto it. She cradles Antoinette in one arm and me in the other. As Antoinette settles into her grandmother's arms, blessedly silent, I realize I will never be the kind of mother I want to be.

# Chapter Five

L ily left Covington before sunrise. After 111 minutes on the road, she reached the outskirts of Redbud, Kentucky. The town was named for the trees that grow wild over the hills, making the air in early spring smell sharp and sweet.

It had rained last night, and the grass was still wet. The road was narrower than Lily remembered, and as she rounded a bend her tires slipped onto the gravel shoulder. An unwanted thought pushed through her mind: traffic fatalities were the leading cause of death for people ages eight to thirty-four.

She eased off of the gas pedal and positioned her hands at nine and three o'clock on the steering wheel. Her knuckles were white, but she didn't loosen her grip. She hunched her shoulders to loosen the knots between them.

Around her, white-plank fences stood in front of houses tucked into the hills. Puffy white-flowered Bradford pear trees dotted the landscape. The trees were invasive, able to grow anywhere, including the thick Kentucky soil. They spread like the honeysuckle in the woods behind Eden Farms, but Lily liked them. There was something to admire about a species that planted itself anywhere, even if it wasn't wanted.

The road widened slightly as it turned into Main Street and ran past Cora's Italian Restaurant, past the Bakery Barn, and Teelia Todd's shop, Knitwits. Lily passed the library with its Georgian columns making it look as if it belonged in a grander town. The farmers' market sat across from the library, taking up an entire block.

Redbud was known for Eden Farms' flowers, and in two hours the market would be full of daffodils and hyacinths, the air thick with their scent. Moms in baseball caps would meander through the aisles, towing toddlers behind them.

On impulse, Lily turned into the lot and parked in front of the Eden Farms' booth. It still anchored the market the way it had when she was young.

Teelia Todd's booth stood across from theirs. She sold hand-spun alpaca yarn. Her husband had died when Lily was in kindergarten, leaving Teelia to raise their son, Deacon, alone. On cool days, Teelia would bring one of her alpacas, Frank, to the market with her. She'd loop his lead line around a beam where he'd nuzzle everyone who passed.

Lily smiled at the memory as she walked to the Eden Farms' booth. She ran her fingers over the rough wood planks. The years fell away, and she was sixteen again, sitting on a metal stool, surrounded by cut sunflowers and hydrangeas, fanning herself with a folded price list.

Rose was supposed to help, but she usually snuck off before the day got too hot. "I'm out of here as soon as I finish school," she'd say. "Who wants to spend their life pulling weeds and spreading manure?"

Lily tried to explain the peace she felt sitting in the booth, answering questions about which flowers tolerated the heavy

Kentucky soil, or why a blast with the garden hose was the safest way to get rid of Japanese beetles, but Rose never understood.

Flowers were predictable, like numbers. Black spots on rose leaves indicated a fungus. Prune the damaged leaves, apply a fungicide, and the plant should survive. Brown hosta leaves meant the plant needed more shade or water. Move it to a shady spot or increase the waterings and it would be fine. Plants spoke a language she understood. To those who paid attention, they revealed whether they needed more phosphorous or nitrogen, less water, or a good soaking with the hose.

A large pickup truck rumbled past. In only minutes, the lot had started to fill with the farmers and artists who had booths at the market. Looking out across the market, she pictured it full. Handmade soaps. Chocolate-dipped strawberries. Hand-harvested honeycomb. Teelia's booth stuffed with yarn.

Lily wanted to settle onto the metal stool behind the Eden Farms cash register, but Rose was waiting at home, and although Lily's heart hammered nervously against her ribs she longed to see her sister.

A white truck, its bed filled with yellow snapdragons and pansies in rainbow colors, slid into the parking space next to hers. Lily dipped her head, letting her dark hair fall like a screen across her face.

"You're early. The market doesn't open for another two hours," a man said.

Even with her back turned, she knew that voice. Her heart raced and her cheeks flushed. She looked up as Seth Hastings stepped out of the truck, his unruly brown hair already streaked with summer gold.

Seth wasn't handsome. His cheekbones were too sharp, and

his forehead too broad. His dark eyes were framed by thick brows, and he was almost too tall. As a child it had made him look awkward. But now, as Lily studied him, she saw that he had grown into his body.

She flashed to an image of him at seventeen, lanky in a teenage boy way, supporting his weight on his arms as he rose above her. Despite the crisp breeze, her whole body flushed. She had no idea he was in town.

"Lily?" He frowned, looking surprised to see her.

Years ago, talking to Seth had been as natural as breathing. Now, seeing him made her mute, and she started counting. She was on six when he leaned in and hugged her. His arms were stiff, and the hug seemed more out of obligation than anything else, but without thinking she gripped him tightly. His hair still smelled like strawberries and summer.

"Sorry," he said. He pulled away and ran his hands through his hair. "I didn't mean to—"

She wanted to look away but couldn't. His hair was longer now. It brushed his shoulders, curling up around the edges. The look softened him, lessening the air of seriousness he had as a boy.

"It's like time stopped," he whispered, "and you're still seventeen."

His comment caught her off guard, and she laughed. "You know how to flatter someone, don't you?" She was thirty years old. Her hair might still be long and brown, her eyes might still be moss green, but when she looked in the mirror, there were tiny lines around her mouth and a melancholy look in her eyes that hadn't been there when she was younger.

Seth tilted his head. "No," he said. "You're the same. But

why are you at the market instead of the house?" He seemed to have recovered from the initial surprise of seeing her, and he took a step back, putting some distance between them.

That's when Lily noticed the Eden Farms' logo—a nodding lily—on his truck door. The same thing was on his green T-shirt. "You're wearing an Eden Farms' shirt," she said, shock coloring her voice.

"Rose didn't tell you?"

She shook her head. "I didn't even know you were in town." She had been so startled at seeing him again that until now she hadn't wondered why he was here. "Shouldn't you be heading up a church or off saving the world?"

"Yeah. That didn't work out so well." He shrugged and pulled his hand through his hair again. She recognized the gesture. He was nervous. "Round peg in a square hole and all. They didn't take my questioning the tenets of the faith as well as you did. I should have been sure of God's existence before entering seminary instead of hoping seminary would prove his existence to me." One corner of his mouth quirked up.

"Did it?" Lily asked.

He shook his head. "I didn't figure that out until after I came home and bought into Eden Farms. Spending time with Antoinette helped me realize that he exists, even when I can't feel his presence.

"It's funny, I used to think my messed-up life was proof that God didn't exist. But when I finally found him, it was because of a little girl whose life was more broken than mine had ever been." He shrugged and smiled.

A familiar anxiety prickled along Lily's spine as he spoke of

Antoinette. "She sounds special," she said, resisting the urge to count.

"She is," he said. "Between Antoinette and working on the farm, I feel . . . settled. Like I'm where I'm supposed to be."

Lily had signed over her share of Eden Farms to Rose years ago and no longer had a say in what happened there. So why did it feel like a betrayal to know someone outside of the family owned part of it?

An even worse feeling arose. Why hadn't Seth called her when he left seminary? Going to school had been his reason for ending their relationship. Why didn't he try to resume it once he was no longer in school?

She drew the inevitable conclusion: his feelings for her were not as strong as her feelings for him. At the thought, her knees wobbled.

*Stop it*, she told herself. *Focus on Rose. Coming home is complicated enough without dwelling on the past.*

The pansies in the truck bed caught her eye. Getting her hands dirty always helped her calm down. "Need some help?" She pointed at the flowers.

Seth raised his eyebrows as if he had expected her to say something else. "Sure," he said. "We can set these out, and then I'll ride back to the farm with you." He paused as if he had misspoke. "That is, if you want me to."

Lily took a deep breath and counted to eight. *You can handle running into an old boyfriend*, she told herself. Seth was just someone she used to know. Nothing more. Besides, seeing Rose again would be easier if she wasn't alone.

At her nod, he dropped the tailgate and took a pair of gloves from his back pocket. She shook her head when he offered them to her. "You know what to do?" he asked.

"I haven't been gone that long." She grabbed a flat of yellow pansies. Dirt spilled over the edge, coating her hands. She slid the flat onto a metal rack behind the counter and wiped her hands on her jeans, leaving behind a smear of mud.

Seth worked fast. There was a rhythm to the way he walked over the curb and grabbed flats from the truck, as if he moved to music Lily didn't hear. They didn't speak as they worked, but then, they never had. Between the three of them, Rose was the one who always had something to say. Without her, a soft silence stood between them.

When they shoved the last of the pansies into place, Seth tugged his gloves off and stuffed them in his back pocket. "I'll drive you back to the farm if you'd like," he said.

His tone was formal, and despite her resolve to ignore their past, she felt something small and bruiselike form in the center of her chest. She looked down at her hands so he wouldn't see the hurt in her eyes. Dirt from unloading the pansies was trapped under her nails. She focused on it as she climbed into his truck. They could return for her car later.

Seth took a deep breath, then blew it out. "I should have handled things between us differently," he said as if reading her mind. He started the truck and drove out of the market. "I didn't want to hurt—"

Lily held up her hand, cutting him off. "Tell me about Antoinette," she said as she rubbed her hands together. Dirt was everywhere. Under her nails. In the creases of her palms. "Is it bad?"

For a long moment he didn't respond. They drove a mile before he said, "It's not bad. She's different. She can't speak. She communicates by touching or pointing to what she wants. But she's smart. Rose taught her about art. I play for her. Mozart and Handel mostly."

"You still play?" Seth's father had taught him how to play the violin. It was one of the few things they shared. Lily remembered summers in the flower fields, sitting at Seth's feet as he played. Even scales were beautiful in his hands.

Seth nodded. "Antoinette connects with music and art. She spends hours staring at Rose's art books. If you ask her to find a certain painting, she'll page through the books and locate it in seconds."

The image he described didn't match the child Lily remembered. Antoinette had been almost four years old when Lily last saw her. It was during the funeral for their parents. Antoinette flapped her hands in front of her face the entire time. Then she bounced up to the rosewood coffins and banged her hands against them until Rose pulled her away.

"Did the doctors ever diagnose her?" Lily asked.

"No. At first, they thought it was autism, but that never fit. She's affectionate. Sometimes when Rose holds her, Antoinette sinks into her as if Rose is her whole world." He glanced at Lily. "It's like she's locked in her body and can't get out."

"And Rose?" Lily knew the statistics. Rose should have died already.

He tightened his grip on the steering wheel. "It's bad."

Lily's stomach twisted. She stared at the land rushing by.

Too soon, they left town and passed Seth's place. His family owned the twenty acres bordering Eden Farms. A white-plank fence marked the property line.

Before she could blink, they were at the white sign with black scroll lettering: EDEN FARMS, FLOWERS. The shoulder dipped slightly. Honeysuckle and scrub brush grew along the side of the road, but several feet of land was cleared on either side of the farm entrance.

Seth turned in, and Lily noticed a locked black iron gate in front of the driveway. "What's that about?" she asked as Seth pressed a button on the remote clipped to his visor, and the gate swung open.

"Antoinette wanders off. When she was six, I found her walking down the main road. After that, Rose installed the gate." Seth punched a button and it closed behind them. The oak and birch trees arching over the drive had budded. Soon they would leaf out, shading the way to the house.

Lily watched Seth. Small lines creased his forehead. The angles of his face had sharpened over the years. But at that moment, she saw the ten-year-old boy who had saved her from bullies all those years ago at school. Despite the way things ended between them, Seth had always looked out for her. Now it sounded like he was doing the same for Rose.

"I'm glad you were here for Rose," she said. "And Antoinette."

He bobbed his head once, an almost imperceptible nod.

The forsythias lining the drive were still in bloom, making Lily feel like Dorothy following the yellow brick road. In minutes, she would see Rose. Every muscle in her body tightened, and she started to shake. *What am I getting myself into? Will Rose still be angry? Can we ever be close again?*

Asphalt changed to gravel as the drive split, one half leading to the farmhouse and the other to the drying barn. At the intersection, a profusion of yellow daffodils bloomed. In a week or so, pink tulips would also sway in the wind.

Seth parked and shut off the engine. "I'm sorry I hurt you," he said, without looking at her. Then he climbed out of the truck and shut the door before she could respond.

Lily sat in the truck, hand pressed over her heart as if holding it in. Driving up, she felt the way she did each time she came home. Her body recalled every dip, every bump.

Seth rapped on the window. "Coming in?" he asked.

Unable to stall any longer, she stepped out of the cab. Like it or not, she was home.

# Chapter Six

~~~~~~

Early morning sunlight fell in pale streaks across the wood floor. Antoinette lay sprawled in the middle of a sunbeam, her arms stretched over her head, her legs bent at the knees. If she were a cat, she'd arch her back, then curl into a ball and let the heat sink through her skin.

The kitchen smelled like vanilla and cinnamon, which was a Saturday smell. But today was Tuesday, and the kitchen should smell like coffee and toast. Also, Antoinette should be sitting at the table with flash cards spread out in front of her.

She was homeschooled, but she didn't study math and English. Each day, Jenna, her therapist, arrived at their house carrying a black bag filled with bits of chocolate, animal crackers, and pretzels.

Weekdays, Antoinette and Jenna would sit at the table. Jenna would take two laminated flash cards and hold them up. On the cards were words like *home* and *chair* and *Mommy*. Antoinette understood the words when they were spoken, but the letters swam when she looked at the cards.

"Show me 'Mommy'!" Jenna would say in her bright voice. Staring at the cards hurt Antoinette's head, so she never looked at them. Some days when Jenna said, "Show me 'Mommy'!" Antoinette would point to her mother who often sat at the table with them, going over the farm's financial records.

"No, silly," Jenna would say as if Antoinette were two years old. "On the card. Show me which card says 'Mommy.' I'll give you an animal cracker if you get it right."

Antoinette was not a baby, and she was not a dog. She didn't want an animal cracker.

They'd continue this way until Antoinette either randomly tapped a card and by chance landed on the correct choice or, more often, started screaming.

That was usually when her mother would intervene and suggest that they were finished for the day.

But not today. Today they were up early, and her mother had already told her that Jenna wasn't coming.

Plus, they had company. Cora Jenkins sat at the large oak table, across from Antoinette's mother, their heads bowed toward each other, their voices rising and falling.

Antoinette didn't like the morning therapy sessions with Jenna, but disruptions in her schedule made her feel like there were ants crawling over her. She twisted on the ground, trying to calm the itchy feeling. Everything had felt off since last night's storm. Even her seizure had been worse than normal, and her body still didn't work right.

"Lily's the only family Antoinette will have when I'm gone," her mother was saying.

*I don't need any family except you.* Antoinette shoved her feet against the floor and tried to push herself out of the room, but her knees were locked. She couldn't move.

"Lily hasn't acted like family," Cora said. She stood up and walked to the counter. "I can't just sit here waiting. I need to do something. Your mother always brewed a pitcher of hibiscus tea for company."

"Lily's not company," Antoinette's mother said.

Antoinette squirmed. Her skin still itched. She wanted to leave the room. If she tapped on her mother's leg, she would understand. She would pick Antoinette up and carry her away.

Cora shrugged as she opened the blue canisters on the counter. "She hasn't been home in years. That makes her company." She measured out a cup of dried hibiscus petals and one-half cup of fresh lavender. She emptied the petals into a large saucepan, filled it with water, and then added one-third cup of sugar. She found a glass pitcher in the cabinet beside the sink and set it next to the stove. "I'll make enough to last several days," she said.

"Family isn't company," Antoinette's mother said, but she didn't tell Cora to stop brewing the tea.

Antoinette closed her eyes and focused. Everything would be better once she left the room. Her feet were bare and the floor was slick. *Move.* She willed the muscles in her legs to contract.

Nothing.

She groaned in frustration.

At the sound, her mother said, "I know. This isn't a normal Tuesday. Cora, turn on my iPod. It's docked in the speakers next to the stove."

Cora hit a button and Vivaldi's "Spring" rolled out of the speakers. Still, the familiar music didn't help Antoinette.

If Seth were here, he would play for her. His music was alive. He would slide the bow across his violin, and she would move.

"Better?" her mother asked.

Antoinette groaned. The violins soared, but they didn't mask the whir of the refrigerator or the sound of water dripping from the faucet. They didn't mask the sadness in her mother's voice.

"What should I do?" Her mother had turned back to Cora. "Pretend I don't have a sister?"

Cora took two white mugs from the cabinets by the stove. While she waited for the water to heat, she put a spoon of raw brown sugar in each mug. "You could ask Seth," Cora said. "Or me, for God's sake. Either of us would help with Antoinette. She probably doesn't even remember Lily."

That wasn't true. Antoinette remembered a woman with dark hair and moss-green eyes. A woman who looked like something that bloomed at night.

Cora put the lid back on the canister. "Have you ever thought about expanding into flower-based products? You could sell teas, handmade soaps, lotions."

The whole room smelled sweet. Antoinette squeezed her eyes shut and clenched her jaw until a hard ache formed behind her teeth. It helped her focus. She bit down harder, catching a piece of cheek between her teeth. This time her hands flopped against the floor, but her arms didn't budge.

"Seth and I have thought about it," Antoinette's mother said, "but we decided not to make any major shifts right now. Maybe once Lily's here—"

Cora sighed. "Who says she'll stay, even if she does show up? And Antoinette doesn't know her." The water finished boiling. Cora turned off the burner and fit a metal strainer over the pitcher.

"Seth called from the market," her mother said as Cora poured the tea through the strainer. "He ran into Lily there and is driving her home. Besides, it's my fault Antoinette doesn't know her aunt. I should have called Lily before things got this bad. Antoinette needs her family."

*I don't need anyone except you.* Antoinette tried to scoot closer to her mother, but her feet wouldn't budge.

"Seems like she's done just fine without Lily for all these years," Cora said. She dumped the spent hibiscus and lavender into a bowl by the sink. "I'm experimenting. How do you feel about candied hibiscus flowers?"

*That's right. I'm fine.* Sometimes when Cora spoke, Antoinette leaned against the older woman's leg. When she did, Cora's voice vibrated through her body, and Antoinette pretended the woman's words were her own.

She loved the way Cora's hair, black laced with silver, hung straight to the middle of her back. Once, Antoinette had tangled her fingers in a hunk of that hair. It was thick and coarse, and Antoinette had not wanted to let go. Thinking about it now made her hands flick open and snap shut.

Flick. Snap. She giggled at the movement.

"Antoinette might have been fine without Lily," her mother said, "but I haven't been. I was just too stubborn to admit it."

In the stillness, the house creaked. Water dripped from the faucet. The refrigerator whirred. Vivaldi's violins hummed.

"And candied hibiscus flowers sound too pretty to eat," her mother added.

Again, Antoinette thought about Cora's rough black hair tangled around her fingers. This time, she was able to lift her head and let it thunk to the floor. For a moment, everything was beautifully quiet. She could move. Quickly, before the noise returned, she pushed her feet against the floor, scooting along on her back until she was under the table.

Cora handed Antoinette's mother a mug of tea and sat down. Antoinette's mother shifted in her seat and tucked her feet under her chair. When she did, her pajama leg moved, exposing a band of skin above her slippers.

Antoinette wanted to hear her mother's song. The last time she had touched her mother, the tempo had been too slow, and every once in a while a sharp note grated against her ears.

Recently, her mother stepped away each time Antoinette reached for her. Antoinette missed the feel of her mother's hand against her cheek. She missed curling into her mother as they sat side by side on the couch, the heat from her mother's body pulsing through Antoinette like a bright orange sun. If she could wrap her fingers around her mother's ankle, everything would be better. But anxiety forced her knees to her stomach and her arms to her chest. If she were normal, she would sit up and take her mother's hand. Instead, she lifted her head and dropped it to the floor.

Thump.

Again. Thump.

The tension in her body broke when the back of her skull hit the hardwood, and she let out a happy shriek. Her mother sighed, but she didn't press her hand against Antoinette's forehead and say, "Stop." So Antoinette hit her head again.

"I worry about you," Cora said between Antoinette's head thumps.

The words made Antoinette's hands twist into tight balls. She worried about her mother too.

Her mother sipped her tea. "This is good. It tastes just like Mom's."

"Who do you think gave me the recipe?" Cora said. "And don't think I'll give up just because you ignored my remark."

"I know you worry." Her mother sighed. "But you don't need to. On my thirtieth birthday, I found honeysuckle twined through the fence. Lily had been here. As girls, we had promised each other to be there when we turned thirty. I forgot, but Lily remembered. She might have caused our rift, but I kept it alive. I don't have time to be angry any more. And I suspect Lily knows that."

"I don't know, Rose, you might be asking too much. Lily might come home, but will she stay? You asked her once before and she ran off."

"I know. But I have to try. I want Antoinette to know her family, and Lily's the only family I have left."

Antoinette drew her legs up and pushed against the floor. She was all the way under the table now. Outside, a car door slammed.

Both women started. "She's here." Her mother stood.

Antoinette shoved her body until she was at her mother's feet. She concentrated and flung out her arm.

# Chapter Seven

A deep porch encircled the blue farmhouse. White rockers flanked the door, and baskets overflowing with yellow pansies hung from the eaves. It was inviting, but Lily and Seth walked around back—only strangers used the front door.

The back porch had a crisp new coat of white paint, and purple clematis scrambled up the posts. The swing where Lily and Rose used to sit and watch as storms rolled in was still there. Lily gave it a small push as she passed.

"Is it how you remembered?" Seth asked. The steps creaked under his feet.

Lily went to the clematis. The flowers were so full and heavy she was surprised the plant didn't topple over under its own weight. Last night's rain drops were scattered across the vine, each one a miniature crystal. "Yes and no," she said. Coming home was like rereading a beloved childhood book as an adult. The same, yet different.

She cupped a blossom that was as big as her hand. It was a double bloom, the petals like layers of tissue paper. "It's too early for this to flower. Did you have a warm spell?"

Seth wasn't listening. He was looking over her shoulder, through the screen door. Lily dropped the flower and followed his gaze. Inside, she saw Rose and Cora Jenkins. The skin under Rose's eyes was the color of old pewter, and she stood hunched over, as if her body were caving in on itself.

"Oh no you don't," Seth murmured as he ran into the kitchen.

Lily followed him but once inside folded herself into a corner of the room. An iPod on the counter played Vivaldi's "Spring."

Rose's gaze skimmed past Seth and lingered on Lily. They locked eyes, and Rose smiled.

Lily took a step toward her sister and only then noticed the little girl lying at Rose's feet. Her white-blonde hair fanned out behind her, and her legs were akimbo. She stretched one hand toward Rose as if trying to grab her mother's ankle.

"There she is," Seth said as he reached for the girl.

"Antoinette?" Lily whispered. The young girl was fragile-looking, like a glass figurine. Her skin was so pale it was almost translucent, and her eyes seemed too big for her face.

Startled, Rose looked down, then quickly stepped away as Seth scooped up Antoinette and tossed her into the air. Lily drew in a sharp breath, worried the girl would shatter. Without thinking, she reached for her niece, ready to catch her should she fall.

"You came," Rose said, her voice wavering for an instant as she wrapped her arms around Lily.

Lily was a head taller than her sister, and Rose's arms were thin as willow branches. Lily felt like she was hugging a child instead of her older sister. "Of course I came," she said. Her throat burned, and she clutched Rose as if afraid she might disappear.

"It's good to have you home," Cora said when Rose pulled

back. She pressed her lips into a tight line and nodded. "Rose has been on her own for too long."

"She hasn't been on her own," Seth said, his voice sharp. Antoinette struggled in his arms, still trying to reach Rose. "I've been here."

Antoinette groaned. She smacked Seth's back with one hand and reached for Rose with the other.

"Calm down," Rose said, stepping out of Antoinette's reach.

"It's not the same as family." Cora tucked her long dark hair behind her ears and directed a pointed look at Lily.

"Cora—" Rose started.

"No," Lily said. She stared at the hardwood floor, more scuffed now than it had been the last time she had been home. "She's right, I should have—"

"Not your business, Cora," Seth said. Antoinette squirmed and he tightened his arms around her.

Cora arched her brow, but she stopped talking.

Antoinette threw her head back and screamed. She put both hands on Seth's chest and pushed.

"What's wrong?" Lily asked.

"Is it a seizure?" Cora asked. "Should I call the paramedics?"

*Yes*, Lily thought, *paramedics are a good idea*. Epilepsy was associated with an increased mortality rate.

Seth paced, trying to calm the girl, but she continued to scream. He just held her tighter and kept walking.

"No," Rose said with the voice of someone who had been through this scene a million times before. "She's not having a seizure. She's mad. Calm down, Antoinette. You can't get down until you stop screaming."

But Antoinette didn't stop. Lily was amazed that such a loud noise could come from such a little child. The urge to count crept over Lily, and she pressed her fingernails into her palms to keep it at bay.

"Take her to the family room, Seth," Rose said. "Maybe she'll stop if she can't see me."

Antoinette's face was pinched and red, and the tears rolling down her cheeks made her hair stick to her face. Seth seemed unfazed by her behavior. He carried her to the adjacent family room and walked in circles, holding her close.

Lily counted the kitchen's wood floor planks, pressing her lips together so she wouldn't say the numbers out loud. She was on ten when Rose said, "Antoinette gets frustrated."

On the iPod, a new symphony had begun. *Vivaldi's "Summer,"* Lily thought.

"It's hard for her," Rose said, "not being able to speak."

Lily mouthed, *Sixteen,* then closed her eyes and breathed deeply.

"Still counting?" Rose asked.

Lily blushed, but she nodded.

Antoinette whimpered, and Rose peeked into the family room. The little girl slumped against Seth's shoulder. A thin line of drool ran from her mouth down his back.

Rose went to him and touched his shoulder. "Thank you," she whispered. "You can set her down now."

Gently, Seth lowered Antoinette to the floor. Her knees folded under her like an accordion, and she plopped down, spent from her temper tantrum.

Rose sank down next to her daughter.

Seth stepped back to give them room. He crossed to stand next to Lily. "You okay?" he asked in a low voice.

"I don't know." Lily watched her sister. Rose's skin had a blue tint, but her eyes were bright. "Does she do that a lot? Antoinette, I mean."

"Does it matter?" Cora asked. "You're family."

Lily repressed a sigh. "No, it doesn't matter."

"Only when she's upset," Seth said. "And with Rose's health, she has a lot to be upset about."

Rose ran her hands through Antoinette's thin hair. The little girl let out a sob. "Shh, it's okay," Rose said. As she spoke, Antoinette's eyes closed and her breathing slowed.

Lily felt like she was intruding. She stepped back and bumped into the wall. Seth touched her back, steadying her.

"You're good with her," Lily said to him.

"She's just a little girl," Seth said. "No different from anyone else."

Lily frowned but didn't say anything.

Cora turned off the music. The sudden silence filled the room. "Is she okay?" She walked over to Rose and peered at Antoinette.

Rose dropped her chin to her chest, and her shoulders slumped. "She's fine. She'll sleep for a while."

"Want me to carry her to her room?" Seth asked.

"No," Rose said. "Let's pile some pillows on the floor. She can sleep here."

Seth went upstairs to get some pillows and Cora followed.

When they left, Lily felt like a spotlight had been turned on her. "I'll just—" She gestured to the kitchen and walked to the back door. She turned the doorknob; it squeaked the way it had when she was a child.

"Don't go," Rose said. She rocked back on her heels and

closed her eyes. "I need you. I've needed you for a long time. I was just too stubborn to admit it."

Lily glanced at Antoinette and took a deep breath. Her hands shook as she walked toward her sister. This was why she came home. "Don't worry. I'm not going anywhere."

ASIDE FROM ANTOINETTE curled on a nest of pillows at one end of the family room, Lily and Rose were alone. Cora left once Antoinette was settled, and Seth was upstairs getting a quilt. Lily stood with her arms wrapped around her middle, hoping she didn't look as awkward as she felt.

The room had changed. If she had thought about it logically, she would have realized that with their parents gone, Rose would change the house to suit her needs, but home was the one place Lily's heart ruled, not her head. Over the years, whenever she thought of home, the house was frozen in time, remaining the way it had been in her youth.

The family room used to have beige walls and a desk over-flowing with receipts and flower catalogs. Now the walls were moss green, and the desk was gone. Coffee-table art books were stacked on the floor. The biggest difference, though, were the black-and-white photos of Antoinette hanging above the plush couch.

The pictures were fascinating. In one, Antoinette knelt, her nose brushing the petals of a coneflower. In another she stood with her head thrown back, a wide smile splitting her face. In most of them she looked like a normal little girl.

"Did you take these?" Lily asked.

Rose sat on the couch, her elbows on her knees. She nodded.

"It's not easy getting a good picture of her. She's almost never still."

"I can tell it's your work," Lily said. "The contrast between light and dark reminds me of the plant studies you did for your college portfolio."

For the first time that morning, Rose brightened. "I haven't thought about that in years." She craned her neck and looked up at the photos. "College seems like a lifetime ago."

"Like we were different people then," Lily said, shifting nervously, afraid of saying the wrong thing.

When they were children, Rose had seemed to her like a giant. Though just over five feet tall, she filled a room when she entered it.

"We *were* different then," Rose said. "Younger, at least. Naive—"

"Scared," Lily said at the same time, their voices overlapping.

Seth returned and covered Antoinette with a blue quilt. "She calmed quickly this time," he said, placing a hand on the girl's shoulder.

Lily looked again at the photos hanging over the couch. There were seven. The odd number and their asymmetrical arrangement made her uncomfortable. She pushed her hair back from her face and plucked at her shirt. "Cora said Antoinette has seizures?" she asked to distract herself.

"Yes. And they're getting worse."

"Seizures can shorten life expectancy." Lily had not meant to say that. She pressed her lips together wishing she could recall the words. "I'm sorry," she whispered. "Of course you would know that."

"I know exactly how dangerous seizures are for Antoinette," Rose said as she sank deeper into the couch.

"Hello?" A man's voice called out as the back door opened. "Is anybody home? It's Eli."

Seth gave Antoinette's shoulder one last pat and stood. "I'll see what he wants."

Lily turned her attention to Antoinette. She was amazed that this was the same little girl who had fit in her hand when she was born. "Why did she get so upset?" Lily asked.

Rose let her head fall back against the couch. "It's complicated."

Muffled voices drifted in from the kitchen. Lily spread her hands. "What about this has been simple?"

At that, Rose smiled. "I'm glad you're home," she said.

As if Lily could have stayed in Covington, waiting for the call that told her Rose had died. "We're sisters," she said, and that explained everything.

Seth returned with Eli Cantwell. Lily remembered visiting Eli as a child. Each time their mom took Rose and Lily into town, they'd run to the Bakery Barn while their mom chatted with Teelia Todd in Knitwits. MaryBeth was always waiting for them with yellow smiley-face cookies.

Now Eli held out a bakery box tied with a yellow ribbon. "I heard you were home," he said to Lily. "Welcome back."

Lily smiled her thanks and took the box. She glanced at Eli's thin body thinking he looked like a stork, with spindly arms and legs, and a beak nose.

"Go on, open it." Eli waved his hand. "MaryBeth thought you'd like them."

Lily opened the box and peered inside at the stack of iced

cookies. They weren't yellow this time. They were pastel shades of blue and purple and pink, but each one had a smiley face. Lily grinned. "I can't believe she remembered. Tell her thanks."

Eli nodded toward Antoinette. "She still tired from last night?" he asked. "I've never seen anything like that before in my life."

"No. She's just napping," Rose said quickly. "She got upset this morning with all the commotion—Lily coming home and all. Wore herself out. She'll be fine with a little sleep."

Eli didn't seem to hear her. "Never seen anything like it," he said again.

Seth moved to stand between Eli and Antoinette. "You can get used to anything if you're around it enough. Spend some time here and a seizure won't seem like anything."

Eli nodded and his face softened. He stepped around Seth and knelt down next to Antoinette. "She sure is a blessing. MaryBeth can't stop talking about her since y'all stopped by last night. She's having a real good spell right now." He brushed a stray piece of hair from Antoinette's face.

Lily noticed that Rose looked troubled as she clenched her jaw and twisted her fingers together while watching Eli.

"You have any trouble getting home?" he asked. "I haven't seen it rain like that in ages."

"We were fine," Seth said as he put his hand on Eli's back. "I'll walk you out. I'm headed back to the market."

Eli took one last look at Antoinette and stood. "You ought to get an alarm system," he said. "Anyone could walk right in. With the way things are today . . ."

"We're okay," Rose said as she nodded toward the kitchen.

Lily followed her gaze and saw a light above the door. "Antoinette wanders off sometimes. I usually keep it on. Today's just been real busy. I didn't reset it after Seth and Lily arrived."

Lily didn't let herself watch Seth leave. She looked out the window at the hoop houses behind the commercial fields. Six. When she had last been home, there were only two. Hoop houses functioned like a greenhouse, extending the growing season, but since a hoop house was only a white plastic tarp stretched over flexible piping, they were a lot less expensive.

"Seth missed you," Rose said.

Each sister had always known what the other was thinking. Lily smiled at the realization that not everything had faded between them, but she shook her head. If Seth had missed her, he would have called. Besides, she was here to help Rose. Not to revive an old romance.

Upon hearing Rose's voice, Antoinette stirred in her sleep. She opened her mouth and a soft "Mmmmaaa" fell out.

"What do you think she dreams about?" Lily asked.

"The same things we do," Rose said. "Why would her dreams be different from anyone else's?"

"I used to dream about being you," Lily said shyly. "Everything seemed easy for you. You were the one everyone liked. You had all the friends. You were the pretty one."

"Everyone wants to be someone else sometimes," Rose said, her voice sounding young and wistful. Then her tone transformed into that of a woman who knew the weight of sorrow: "I dream about staying right here. Having more time with my daughter."

The anguish in Rose's voice finally pulled Lily across the room. She sat next to her sister, so close that their knees touched.

"Are you scared?" Lily asked as she reached for her sister's hand. It was so warm and real it seemed impossible that one day soon Rose's heart would stop.

Rose twined her fingers through Lily's and squeezed as if their linked fingers were enough to keep her in this world. "Ter-rified," she said as the distance that had existed between them collapsed and they became sisters again.

## ROSE'S JOURNAL
### September 2005

———+———

THE OAK-LEAF HYDRANGEAS surrounding the library play-ground are still blooming even though it's late September. Lily has taken a few days off work and is visiting. She and I sit on a park bench across from the swings, while Antoinette twirls on a small patch of grass. The blades under her feet are green, but everywhere else, they're brown. The summer has been hot and dry.

Antoinette stands on her toes and stretches her arms toward the sky. Other than the crook in her elbows and the way her head lolls back, she looks like any other child.

Except she looks younger. Antoinette is two and a half but looks half that age.

My heart clenches as I compare her to the other children on the playground. They hang on the swings and climb up the slide. All of them—even the babies—seem bigger than Antoinette.

Most of them speak.

A switch flipped when I became a mother. One day I didn't worry about anything; the next, everything became a concern, a possible source of danger.

Most of all, I worry about leaving her. Who will take care of her when I'm gone?

"Does she always do that?" Lily asks, staring at Antoinette as she turns in circles.

I look at Antoinette and notice a clump of out-of-season daisies blooming at her feet. How did I miss them before? It's a strange but beautiful picture.

"She likes to spin," I say. I keep my voice casual, as if Antoinette's constant movement doesn't bother me. But it does. As a mother, I find that everything bothers me.

I sleepwalked through Antoinette's first year. Suddenly, I was a single mother and a college dropout diagnosed with severe heart disease. The changes were overwhelming and I emotionally checked out. I wasn't a *bad* mother, but I wasn't the mother I wanted to be.

I hope I'm making up for that now.

Across the playground, a little boy laughs as he climbs the steps to the slide. He moves so easily I have to look away. Antoinette wears her body awkwardly, always on the verge of falling.

"How long will you be home?" I ask before anxiety claims me. Mom told me not to compare Antoinette to other children. Someday I'll listen.

Lily's visits have grown less frequent. After graduating early, she accepted a job as an actuary for a life insurance company in Cincinnati and bought a home on the Kentucky side of the Ohio River. When I asked why she moved, she said she needed a change of scenery. She didn't mention the breakup with Seth at all.

"Just the weekend," she says.

"Have you talked to S—"

She cuts me off. "I don't want to talk about it."

We both like to ignore our problems.

The sound of laughter sweeps over us. I look across the playground to see a group of preschoolers scrambling up the slide.

"Do you want to play with the other kids?" I ask Antoinette. She doesn't stop spinning, and I wonder if I should make her quit. No one else is turning in circles. I want to ask Lily what she thinks, but she's watching Antoinette and counting.

"Rose," Lily says, without looking at me. Her voice is so soft I almost miss it. "I think something's wrong." She nods toward Antoinette.

I follow her gaze. Antoinette has stopped spinning. Her head hangs to one side, and she flicks her fingers in front of her eyes. Her arms are bent at the elbows. She looks like a marionette.

Lily is giving voice to my own concerns, but I can't listen. If I do, my fears will become so big that they'll swallow me. My chest burns as I stand. "I need to get Antoinette home. Nothing's wrong with her." If I say it enough, maybe I'll believe it.

Eli and MaryBeth Cantwell come out of the library when we're almost at the car. MaryBeth sees us and waves. She is solid, like Mom.

"How's my favorite girl?" MaryBeth asks as she kneels in front of Antoinette. A strand of Antoinette's hair hangs in her face, and MaryBeth gently tucks it behind her ear. I try to focus on the joy in Antoinette's face instead of the pressure building in my chest.

"She's getting big." When MaryBeth looks up, I see longing in her face. I hurt for her. If anyone should have had children, it's MaryBeth.

"You think so?" I ask. "She seems small to me."

"You see her every day," Eli says. "Trust me, she's growing like a weed." He stands behind his wife and puts a hand on her shoulder. I don't think I've ever seen them apart.

Eli pulls a bunch of wrapped hand-pulled taffy from his

pocket. "We're trying something new at the bakery. Let us know what you think. You too, Lily. Are you home to stay this time?"

"Not yet," Lily says as she accepts the taffy. She is easy around the Cantwells. We've known them since we were little and they were newly married. "But if I can't find a decent bakery in Cincinnati, I might have to move back."

"Sooner rather than later," MaryBeth says. She sits on the sidewalk and pats her lap. Antoinette plops down and flaps her hands.

My heart squeezes the air from my lungs. The flapping is another strange thing Antoinette does.

MaryBeth laughs and waves her hands. "Are we birds?" she asks.

And just like that, my heart is lighter. Make-believe. How had I missed it? The pressure in my chest eases, and I fill my lungs with air. I forget Lily's concerns. I forget my own. I watch my daughter without fear, and for the first time I think we might be okay.

LATER THAT NIGHT, when the sky seems low enough to touch, I sit on the porch swing with Mom. Antoinette sits at my feet, waving her hands in front of her eyes.

The peace I felt earlier vanishes, and an image flashes through my mind: Lily in second grade, sitting on the edge of the school playground, counting blades of grass while everyone else whirled around her.

"Are Dad and Lily still out there?" I ask Mom. I know the answer. The hills around the farm are draped in red and gold; they'll be digging up dahlias until the sky is black.

After we got home, Lily disappeared into the fields. I haven't seen her since. She's different. Distant. Losing Seth changed her. She never trusted easily, but now it's like she's built a wall around herself.

Antoinette stops waving her hands in front of her face. She stares out over the fields as if counting the blades of grass. "Pretty, isn't it?" I say.

As usual, she doesn't answer.

"Antoinette." I tap her shoulder, but she ignores me and starts rocking. The uneasy feeling I had at the playground comes back.

"Mom," I say, trying to sound casual. "When did I start talking?" The books I've read say Antoinette should be talking by now.

My mother looks up at the porch roof. The white paint is flaking. She sighs. "One more thing to do." She closes her eyes, then says, "You were an early talker. You said your first word at nine months and never stopped."

I can't breathe. Antoinette is thirty months old.

"Lily was a different story," Mom says. "When she was four, her pediatrician thought something was wrong because she wasn't talking yet. *Mental retardation*, he said. He sounded like he was talking about a dog, not my daughter."

Lily is the smartest person I know. Different, but brilliant. Hearing the doctor's words makes me angry. Lily might have a few quirks, but nothing is wrong with her. That's the thing about being sisters. We fight, but love always wins in the end.

"I never went back there," Mom says. "Lily started talking in complete sentences a few months later." She pats my knee and smiles. "Antoinette will talk when she wants to. And if she doesn't . . . well, we'll love her anyway."

I try to nod, but I'm drowning. The air is too thick. I gasp, trying to force my lungs open. Then I feel a small hand around my ankle. My daughter, who doesn't even babble, starts humming. I'm so shocked, I forget my panic.

Her voice is clear as a glass bell. I am lost in her sound, and the pressure in my chest eases. I stare at her until her voice trails off.

Then her hand loosens. Her eyes gently close.

And I realize how much love feels like falling.

# Chapter Eight

〜

The sisters sat folded together on the couch for so long that Rose fell asleep with her head against Lily's shoulder. Lily leaned down, pressed her nose to Rose's thin blonde hair, and breathed in her scent. It was the same after all these years: peaches and warm soil.

Once, when they were girls, Lily had told Rose this was how she smelled. Rose put her nose to her arm and sniffed. "I don't smell like dirt," she said. Then she stomped out of the room before Lily could explain that the scent of freshly tilled soil made her feel safe.

Family legend had it that Rose was born perfect. She didn't look wrinkly like other babies. Her skin was smooth, and her eyes morning-glory blue, as if she knew from the beginning she was special and wanted the world to know it too.

Lily never saw Rose in that perfect baby stage, but their mother told the story of Rose's birth so often that Lily could recite it by the time she was four.

"What about my story?" Lily had asked once, sitting at the kitchen table while her mother pounded out biscuit dough.

"What story?" her mother said.

"You know," Lily said, impatiently kicking her feet against the rungs of the chair. "The story of when I was born." This was where she would find out why she was different. Why she felt like the world spun wild around her, and she needed to hold on tight.

Her mother shrugged. "Not much to tell. You were an easy baby. Three little pushes and you slid right out. No fuss at all."

That wasn't what Lily wanted to know. "But what did I *look* like?" She pictured herself as a baby. Maybe her fists were clenched so tight her mother had to pry them open.

"Look like?" her mother said, only half listening as she pounded the dough, sending puffs of flour into the air.

"You know," Lily said. "Rose had pale blue eyes like she just came from heaven. What about me?" She held her breath.

Her mother went to the sink and rinsed her hands. "I'm busy, Lily. You've seen your baby pictures. You know what you looked like. Go on outside and play." She dried her hands against her frayed apron and went back to work.

Lily had seen her baby pictures, and unlike Rose, she *did* have wrinkly skin and black baby eyes. There was nothing in those pictures that explained her fear that gravity was not enough to keep her from floating away.

Rose shifted in her sleep, drawing Lily back to the present. Her sister had welcomed her home, but Lily felt like the bond between them was tenuous, as if they were held together by spider's silk.

She slid out from under Rose and went into the kitchen. Here everything was the same—yet different. The white cabinets. The blue tile backsplash. The bleached oak floor. That was the kitchen Lily remembered from childhood, but small things were off. The canisters where her mother stored lavender and flour weren't to the right of the sink anymore. Now they were on the opposite end of the counter—all the way down by the refrigerator. The speckled ceramic container that sat beside the stove holding spatulas and wooden spoons was gone. The braided rag rug that lay in front of the sink was also missing. These small changes made Lily feel off balance, and she was overwhelmed by homesickness. She was a guest in her own home.

When they were younger, their mother made lavender bread each spring. The delicate bread was Rose's favorite. Before it finished cooling on the wire rack next to the oven, Rose would cut two large slices, one for her and one for Lily.

Each year, Rose said the same thing as she bit into the bread. "It tastes like love."

That's what they needed now, Lily thought. Something to remind them what they meant to each other. Something that hadn't changed over the years. She went to the jars in which her mother had stored dried lavender. She opened the lid, praying Rose had continued the tradition.

She had. The sweet scent of lavender wafted out. The flowers were fresh, which was strange because it was early in the season, but Lily didn't question her luck. She grabbed two white bowls and shook petals into one. Then she searched the refrigerator for a lemon and some milk.

Next she combined flour and sugar in the second bowl, then set it aside as she poured milk into a small saucepan and sprinkled the lavender petals over it. When the milk warmed, the lavender seeped through it, turning the mixture a soft purple. As Lily worked, she thought back to the last time she sat in this kitchen. It had been the morning she and Rose buried their parents.

THE DAY OF the funeral, snow covered the ground. Lily stood at the graveside, trying not to stare at the two gaping holes, but looking elsewhere was worse. Rose bent forward like a tree snapped by the weight of ice. Antoinette shrieked at the falling snowflakes. Behind them stood a row of mourners.

Snow caught everywhere, on Lily's hair, her eyelashes, her cheeks. It was obscenely beautiful, like standing inside of a snow globe. A minister she didn't know stood at the head of the graves reading from the Bible.

Their parents had died in a car accident on their way to a flower growers' convention in Missouri. Each time Lily closed her eyes, she pictured the accident. Her parents rounding a bend as they merged onto the expressway. Snow everywhere. Their wipers steady against the windshield but not fast enough to keep the snow from piling up.

A black Chevy Suburban sped up behind them. Horn blaring. Lights flashing. Crossing the yellow line to pass them.

Lily pictured her father hunched behind the wheel, murmuring, "Idiot." The other driver was going too fast and started to spin.

Her father cut the steering wheel hard. Maybe he thought they would make it. But they turned sideways and slid into the SUV.

Her mother screamed. The windshield shattered, showering the interior of the car with tiny glass pebbles. A sharp crack as her father's head snapped forward, hitting the steering wheel. The car rolled twice, and when it came to rest it was upside down, and her parents were dangling from their seatbelts like rag dolls. This was how Lily saw it in her mind, and she replayed it over and over.

Movement to Lily's left caught her eye, and she shook her head to clear the image of her parents' accident. She saw Antoinette flapping her hands and bouncing on her toes. Lily rearranged her face into a calm expression, hoping it masked the dread tiptoeing through her body.

Her last visit home had been in October. She and Rose had sat at the kitchen table while Antoinette stood in the corner, banging her head against the wall.

Rose bowed her head. "You were right. Something's wrong."

Lily stared at the little girl, and the urge to count grew until it burst out of her mouth. She counted each thump of Antoinette's head. Out loud.

It continued until Rose carried Antoinette from the room, and Lily was finally able to stop.

After that, Lily stopped coming home. She had spent her adult life locking her idiosyncrasies inside and was afraid that if she spent more time with Antoinette she would start living her quirks out loud. Someday she might start counting and not be able to stop.

Everything threatened to unravel when Lily was around her niece, not because Antoinette was different—though she was— but because Lily felt she and Antoinette were so much alike it frightened her.

She remembered the conversation she and Rose had the morning of their parents' funeral.

Rose had been shaking so hard her coffee cup rattled. She was thin, as if her skin were pulled too tight. "Please," she begged. "Come home. I can't run the farm and care for Antoinette by myself. I need your help."

Lily opened her mouth to say yes. Sisters helped each other.

She knew that. But when she looked at Antoinette, who sat under the table flapping her hands in front of her eyes, "I can't" came out instead.

LILY WAS TAKING the lavender bread from the oven and placing it on a cooling rack next to the sink when Rose padded into the kitchen. The room was stuffy from the afternoon sunlight streaming in through the windows, but Rose rubbed her arms as if she was cold. "How long did I sleep?" she asked. Against her pale skin, her blue eyes stood out even more.

"Just long enough." Lily gestured toward the loaf. The sloped brown crust split open along the top to reveal a light purple middle. Perfect. She ran a knife along the edges to loosen the bread from the pan.

"You should've woken me. I would have helped." Rose leaned over the bread, inhaling its aroma. "Reminds me of Mom. It's almost as if she's right here."

"I thought we could have a picnic. Like we used to." Lily flipped the pan upside down and twisted it to free the bread. For a moment they weren't women who hadn't spoken for years but girls holding a shared past.

"Except this time," Rose said, "I won't have to steal the bread from Mom." When she smiled, the fatigue faded from her face.

Lily sliced the bread and packed it in a basket as Rose woke Antoinette. In minutes the three of them walked outside and into the house garden.

Their property was separated into six areas. Thirty acres were reserved for the commercial flower fields that produced most of their income. A small greenhouse and a drying barn sat a short walk from the farmhouse. The house itself was surrounded by an acre of private gardens. There was a kitchen garden that abutted the back porch, the night garden that occupied the west side of their property, and a walled house garden. The back of their land was wooded and a small creek ran through it. Seth's property bordered theirs on the east, sharing a traditional white Kentucky board fence.

The house garden comprised several square flower beds, edged by clipped boxwoods. The beds were empty now, but in a few weeks lilacs and lilies, roses and lavender, would spring to life. A wisteria-draped gazebo stood in the middle of the garden. Large purple blossoms dripped from the latticework. Lily knew the vine shouldn't be blooming yet, but somehow it was.

She stopped just inside the stone pillars that marked the entrance.

"What's wrong?" Rose asked. Antoinette stuttered to a stop beside her.

"I forgot how beautiful everything is," Lily said.

Rose looked at her daughter. "Yes, I suppose it is."

"I missed being here." Lily looked down at Antoinette, and her stomach tightened. "She's grown a lot."

Antoinette bared her teeth and growled, and Lily stepped back. Then the girl stretched up on her toes, flapped her hands, and walked away. Her steps were slow and careful as she made her way around the garden.

"You'll love her once you get to know her," Rose said.

"I already do," Lily said. It wasn't a lie. She remembered holding Antoinette when she was only hours old. The little girl had curled into Lily as if she was someone safe.

Love had never been the problem.

Lily spread one of their mother's quilts over a patch of fresh grass in the middle of the garden and they sat down. Kentucky springs were volatile. Evenings could be cold enough for winter coats. Afternoons could be so hot the flowers wilted. Some years, snow piled up on the ground until May.

This April was hot. The heat made Lily's shirt stick to her back. She plucked at it and fanned her face with her hand. "Is everything this difficult for her?" she asked.

"A year ago things weren't so bad. Lately, though . . ." Rose called to Antoinette, but the little girl ignored her. "She's stubborn."

"Like every other Martin," Lily said. Now that they were together, she didn't know what to say. She tried to sit still, but anxiety made her fidget. A purple thread was loose on the quilt. She wound it around her finger.

Rose gave a small laugh. "I guess so." Then her voice softened. "Her seizures are getting worse. And she's so frustrated . . ."

Lily watched Antoinette. Sometimes the girl squatted and pushed her hands into the dirt. Then, just as quickly, she'd remove her hands and continue on her course.

"How much does she understand?" Lily asked. She counted as she watched Antoinette walk. Each time the girl put her foot down, Lily mouthed a number.

"All of it. She might not look or act like other kids, but she understands everything."

"She knows what's happening to you?" Lily kept picking at the loose thread. Her mother had made the quilt for her before she left for college. Purple lilies and pink roses twined around the edges. "So you'll feel at home wherever you are," her mother had said. Yet here she was, home but not *home*. For the first time in her life, she felt awkward around Rose.

"She does," Rose said. "I wish she didn't."

Lily gathered her courage and asked the question she had wanted to ask since she first arrived. "How much time do you have?" The words sounded cruel, and immediately she wished she could take them back, but she needed to know.

Rose stared at Antoinette. The little girl was at the gazebo. She placed her foot on the bottom step then removed it. She repeated the motion four times. It looked like she wanted to climb the stairs but didn't know how. "Not nearly long enough," Rose said. "Six months. Probably less."

Lily felt like she was falling. She ran the numbers. Six months. One hundred eighty-two days. *Probably less.*

Why hadn't she come home sooner? She and Rose had lost so much time.

"My heart is weakening. It can't pump enough blood through my body. My lungs are filling up with fluid." Rose's tone was so matter of fact that it sounded like she was rattling off a grocery list, not describing the way her heart was shutting down. "The worst part is needing someone to care for Antoinette. She comes with extra . . . complications."

Lily pulled the thread tighter around her finger. "Has it been hard?" How silly. Of course it had been hard. One look at Antoinette and anyone could see that.

Antoinette heaved herself onto the gazebo's bottom step. She clamped her fist around the wood railing and hopped up and down.

"When she was younger," Rose said, "Antoinette climbed

those stairs twenty times a day. She'd get to the top, then turn around and start down again. Over and over. It was exhausting. I tried to make her quit, but she screamed each time I picked her up.

"Then one day, she just stopped. We came out here, but instead of climbing the stairs she locked her knees and refused to move.

"I felt overwhelmed. I wanted to talk to you about everything. About nothing. Some days I just wanted to hear your voice." Rose spread her fingers wide and put her hand down in the grass, moving it back and forth.

"I tried to call you so many times," Rose said. "I'd have the phone in my hand, ready to punch in your number, but I was afraid. I hung up every time."

"Why?" Lily asked. "You didn't do anything wrong—"

"I did. I was a single mom with a bad heart and a special-needs kid. After Mom and Dad died . . ." She leaned back. Her short hair fell in messy spikes around her face. "Being mad at you was easier than dealing with everything else. Plus, I needed help, and I was afraid to ask you again. Now I don't have a choice.

"Seth is here, and Antoinette loves him. He's been a father to her, but he's not *you*." Rose's eyes looked tired, as if decades had passed instead of only six years. "I don't have time to worry about the choices I've made in the past. I miss you. You're the only family Antoinette has left. Will you help me this time?"

Lily didn't say anything. She was afraid she would open her mouth and the wrong words would fall out again. Instead, she reached into the basket and held up a piece of lavender bread. She handed it to Rose, hoping that one act spoke for her.

Rose took a bite and looked up. "Funny," she said. "It still tastes like love."

## ROSE'S JOURNAL
*December 2006*

—✛—

THE WAITING ROOM at Cincinnati Children's Hospital's Department of Developmental and Behavioral Pediatrics is too small. Children are everywhere. Some shove beads through a wire maze bolted to the floor in the center of the room. Others bounce on their toes, hands curled against their shoulders, as if afraid to touch anything. One boy stands in the corner, banging his head against the wall while a woman—his mother?—tries to hold him still.

I can't watch.

Antoinette sits on the chair next to me, bouncing. Her small green coat is folded over the armrest. She is three and a half. Her feet don't reach the floor. To bounce, she pushes against the armrests, lifting herself out of the seat. Then she lets go. Gravity does the rest.

It took three months to get this appointment. Now that it's here, I want to be somewhere else, anywhere else.

This morning, Dad held Antoinette as he paced the kitchen. She arched her back and groaned. In the past three years, he has grown soft around the middle and most of his hair is gone. He puffed as he tried to calm Antoinette. "What do you want, sweetie?" he asked. He is big enough to wrap his arms around her twice, but Antoinette is difficult to contain.

"She wants to get down," I said. After scheduling this appointment, I started making lists. The first time Antoinette walked. The first time she crawled. Her first bites of solid food. There had to be something that would prove she was normal. The lists were in my purse somewhere, but I needed to find them.

"We can cancel our trip," Mom said. They were attending a commercial flower growers' conference in Missouri. It was the first weekend in December and a light snow had fallen.

Antoinette rocked back and forth in Dad's arms like a metronome. I found the crumpled pages on the bottom of my purse and flattened them on the kitchen table. "We'll be fine, Mom."

Antoinette shrieked.

"Just put her down, Dad," I said as I dumped everything back into my purse.

As soon as Antoinette's feet touched the ground, she toddled over to me, her gaze locked on something over my shoulder. When she reached the table, she buried her face against my knees and wrapped her arms around my legs. Then she sighed with contentment as if I were her whole world.

Now, in the waiting room, she sighs the same way and stops bouncing. She leans into me, and despite the pressure building in my chest, I smile. She's happy. That has to count for something.

Finally, the waiting room door opens, and a nurse in pink scrubs says, "Antoinette Martin?"

I pick up Antoinette's green coat, take her hand, and follow the nurse out of the waiting room. As I walk, I remember the last thing Mom said before they left. "You're still her mother. Nothing can change that."

But that's exactly what I'm afraid of. What if I can't mother a broken child?

SOMEONE PAINTED BLUE and yellow fish on the walls of the exam room. White bubbles float from their mouths to the ceiling. All of a sudden, I'm Lily. I count the fish. Five. Then I count the bubbles. Seventeen.

Not good. My chest tightens, and I slip a nitroglycerin pill under my tongue.

"Is she always so tactile?" Dr. Ketters asks. She is at least sixty. The gold buttons on her purple dress gap about the middle, and two inches of white slip show beneath her dress.

Antoinette sits on the exam table, scratching her fingers across its surface. *Phft. Phft.* She laughs at the sound her fingers make. Her green coat is next to her. It's so tiny.

Dr. Ketters stands in front of Antoinette, studying her. She hasn't listened to Antoinette's chest or looked in her eyes or ears.

"She touches everything," I say. That must be normal. Kids grab things. "I have lists." I give the crumpled sheets to the doctor. "When she walked. What she eats. Textures she likes . . ."

Dr. Ketters glances at my papers, then puts them aside. "Does she make eye contact?" Like a magician, she pulls a pink feather from her lab coat pocket and waves it in front of Antoinette.

Antoinette ignores it. She looks up and to the left. "She stares at paintings for hours," I say. I stopped painting after Antoinette was born, but I still have my art books. Antoinette and I flip through them at night. "And music. She loves music." The nitro pill has dissolved, but my heart still hurts.

Dr. Ketters jots some notes in Antoinette's file. She has been in the room for less than five minutes. When she looks up and smiles softly, I know something is wrong.

"Antoinette displays a lot of autistic behaviors," she says.

"She's not classically autistic. She's affectionate." Right now, Antoinette is leaning into me, lacing her fingers through mine.

"You don't see that a lot in autism," she says, "even though it's a spectrum disorder, and people can be anywhere from high functioning with Asperger syndrome to severely impaired." With the words *severely impaired*, her eyes slide to Antoinette.

I nod as if we are talking about the weather, but I don't want to hear anything else. I set Antoinette on the ground, ignoring her upraised hands. I gather her green coat and hold it out to her. "Thank you for your time. Come on, Antoinette. Put your coat on."

Antoinette flaps her hands and pushes the coat away.

Dr. Ketters continues as if I haven't said anything. "I can't give an exact diagnosis. She doesn't fit neatly into any one category. But I can tell you that she will most likely require lifelong care."

*Please stop talking.* The pressure in my chest grows until I think it might explode. I shake the coat at Antoinette. "Antoinette. Let's go."

"Is her father in the picture?" The sympathy in the doctor's voice is painful.

Finally, I drop Antoinette's coat and shake my head. I'm dizzy with grief. "It's just me."

"Institutions are nicer now. Caring for her by yourself is going to be hard."

I lose my breath and I feel something crushing my chest. Then I feel a small hand in mine. When I look down, Antoinette's eyes are closed and she's humming.

She hasn't hummed since last September, and I realize how

much I missed the sound of her voice. The pressure in my chest eases. Her touch has always made me feel better. When I pick her up, she closes her eyes and rests her head on my shoulder.

Dr. Ketters is still talking when I walk out of the exam room, but I'm not listening. As we leave, I think of the second list I made. The one I didn't show the doctor. On it, I listed the way Antoinette's fingers clasp mine when we walk in the garden. The way my heart beats easier when she is next to me. The way she taps my back, and I know it means *I love you.*

LILY'S HOUSE HAS a view of the Ohio River. I see a slice of the river through the window above the kitchen sink. It is late afternoon, and the day has turned gray.

Antoinette slept briefly in the car on the drive from the hospital to Lily's house. Twenty minutes. When she woke, I picked her up and whispered in her ear. "Do it again." Then I hummed, trying to re-create the noise she made at the doctor's office. She didn't make a sound.

Now in Lily's house, she sits on the floor, tracing her fingers along the grout lines in the tile. Lily and I lean against the kitchen counter. I am too agitated to sit.

"The doctor said something's wrong?" Lily asks. She taps her fingers against her leg.

I nod, because I can't say the words out loud.

Something is wrong.

With my daughter.

"I'm sorry," she whispers. I see my pain reflected in her eyes.

"Will she get better?" Lily starts counting. Her lips barely move, but I know what she's doing. If I thought counting would help, I'd do it too.

"No," I say. "She won't get better." The words crush me. I drop my head to my hand. "Could I get a drink?" Though it's cold outside, Lily's house is warm.

Antoinette is sitting in front of the sink, and Lily avoids walking near her. Irritation flashes through me. Antoinette isn't contagious.

I had hoped that stopping by Lily's house on the way home from the doctor's office would help me feel better. Instead, I feel worse. Lily is more reticent than usual.

A holly wreath hangs from a brass hook on the door leading from Lily's kitchen to her deck. I picture her walking alone through a parking lot filled with cut Christmas trees, selecting the wreath.

Lily takes a glass from the cabinet next to the sink and drops some ice into it. She fills it with tap water, watching Antoinette the entire time. Then she hands me the glass.

I set it on the kitchen counter. "I miss you."

"Is there a treatment?" Lily asks. She looks at Antoinette, who has closed her eyes and is rocking side to side.

I don't want to talk about it. "Mom and Dad are at a conference in Missouri. Come home with me. Just for the weekend." I don't want to be alone. I don't want to think about Dr. Ketters's words. How can I provide a lifetime of care when I don't have a lifetime left?

Antoinette kicks her heels against the floor.

Lily appears mesmerized. "I can't," she says. "Not this weekend."

"It's getting late," I say. "I need to get back to the farm." I drink the water, and as I take my glass to the sink it slips from my hand and shatters on the tile floor.

I kneel to pick up the glass shards and slice open my index finger. Bright red blood drips from my hand, staining the floor.

"Are you okay?" Lily grabs a napkin from the table and presses it against my finger. In a minute, it's soaked through with blood. She folds it until she finds a clean section and dabs at the cut. "I think you need stitches."

"I'm fine." I don't need her help. I take the napkin and press it against the cut.

"I'll wrap it for you." She runs to the bathroom and returns with a Band-Aid. "It's deep," she says as she holds my hand under water. She dries it and applies the bandage.

As she does, I feel a hand against my leg. Antoinette taps my leg and raises her hands. "It's okay," I say as I pick her up. "Mommy's fine."

Antoinette rests her head in the crook of my neck and pats my cheek. Then, for the second time today, she hums, and I forget the pain in my finger.

"How about next weekend?" Lily is saying. "I'll come home then."

I nod absentmindedly and walk toward the front door. I'm fixated on the sound coming from my daughter's lips.

"I miss you too," Lily says, but she sounds unsure of herself. She hugs me and holds on tight.

A tall man with dark hair is standing on Lily's doorstep when she opens the door. "Didn't know you had company, Lils," he says.

He is handsome in a too-perfect kind of way. Not at all the type of guy I picture Lily with. "We're just leaving," I say as I carry Antoinette to the car.

The man nods his head and waves his hand in a flourish as if tipping a cap. "Will Grayson, at your service."

I nod, but I'm not paying attention. I'm fascinated by the sound of my daughter's voice.

LATER, I PUT Antoinette to bed. She slept the entire trip home, and she was still asleep when we pulled up to the farm. I don't blame her. It's been a busy day.

It's only after settling her into bed that I remember my finger. I go into the bathroom and sit on the edge of the tub. It doesn't hurt, but I want to clean it again.

I undo the bandage, expecting to see a long gash on my finger, but my skin is intact. There isn't a single mark anywhere.

# Chapter Nine

A ntoinette kicked off her shoes and curled her toes into the grass. The air at the farmers' market was thick with humidity, and the canvas tent shading their booth only served to trap the heat.

She turned in slow circles, listening for the land's song. Today she thought it sounded like redemption—a French horn low and soft—but she wasn't sure. Everything was muffled.

Since her seizure at the Bakery Barn, her muscles had been tight, and the world often went silent. Yesterday she had shoved her hands wrist deep into the ground. That far down the soil was cool. She squeezed the earth between her fingers and listened, but she hadn't heard a thing.

Today she could hear the music, but she had to work to do so. If she didn't concentrate, the sound slipped away completely.

Three customers browsed their booth. Two women walked through the main aisle, and a man wearing a Go Green! T-shirt knelt among eight-inch pots of English lavender. Racks of pansies and violas lined the sides of the booth, at the center of which two white work tables formed an *L*. Antoinette's mother worked at one, and Lily at the other.

Gallon pots of azaleas and rhododendrons sat below the table where Antoinette's mother put together an arrangement of white tulips and daffodils. She used an old steel watering can as the container and selected flowers from buckets of sugar water. The green buds had just cracked open. "Never use flowers in bloom," her mother had said once. "They don't last as long."

Lily sat on a metal stool behind the cash register at the second table. Cut yellow pansies lay scattered across its surface. She twirled one between her fingers. "I can't remember the last time we worked the market together," she said.

Antoinette glared at Lily. *Shut up.*

"Not my best moments," her mother said with an awkward laugh. They seemed uncomfortable around each other—Lily fidgeting and Antoinette's mother's voice too bright.

"I can't believe you never told Mom I used to leave you here alone," her mother said.

Antoinette would have left Lily too. She'd leave right now if she could. It was Wednesday. She should be at home with her therapist. She'd rather spend the morning pointing at flash cards than at the market with Lily.

That morning, her mother had looked at Antoinette and said, "How about we spend the day together? It'll be a girl's day. Just you and me and Lily. You two will love each other." Her mother's smile was too wide, and at Lily's name the excitement that fizzed through Antoinette's body died.

*Not Lily.* She tried to shake her head, but her neck muscles wobbled, and her chin fell to her chest. Lily had only arrived yesterday, but Antoinette already knew she was *not* going to love her. She already had a mother. She didn't need another one.

Plus, Lily's name was wrong. The lilies in the house garden

were yellow and orange and pink, but there was nothing bright about her aunt. Her hair was brown like tilled soil, and her eyes were a deep mossy green. She was more oleander than lily. Antoinette imagined the flower blooming in Lily's footsteps. *Beware*, it would say as she walked past.

If Antoinette could bite Lily, she would. She opened her mouth and snapped it shut.

Lily flinched. "I'm making things worse," she said. "Maybe I should go home."

Antoinette flapped her hands. *Yes! Go home!*

"Give her some time," her mother said. "She doesn't know you yet."

*I don't want to know her.* Antoinette growled at Lily.

Lily dropped the pansy she had been holding. It fluttered to the ground, and when she walked away from the cash register she stepped on it. "Are these from the greenhouse?" She stopped in front of the lavender. "I didn't see them when I walked through yesterday." She knelt and lightly touched each plant. Her lips moved, and it looked like she was counting. She whispered, "Twelve."

The strangeness of it made Antoinette pause.

Her mother trimmed a dogwood stem and inserted it into her arrangement. The red branch was stark against the white flowers.

Lily shook her head. "They shouldn't be blooming now. Everything's out of sync." She pressed her hands into the grass as if the earth was spinning too fast.

"Lily Martin!" Teelia Todd, who sold hand-spun yarn in the booth across from theirs, walked toward them. Teelia was wiry, and her skin as brown as a walnut. Her gray hair swirled around her head in a mass of curls. She carried a milk crate filled with yarn. Frank, one of her alpacas, trailed along behind her.

Antoinette liked Frank. His white fleece was soft, and sometimes he pressed his nose against her shoulder. She shook her hands and wiggled her fingers. She wanted to touch him.

"You found your way back to us," Teelia said as she set the crate on a table in her booth. Frank was out of Antoinette's reach right now, but she stretched toward him anyway.

"I knew you weren't a city girl." Teelia tied Frank's lead line to her booth and hurried over to them

Frank hummed. Antoinette loved the sound. She pressed her lips together and sang along with him.

"Is that Frank?" Lily asked as she stood up. "I can't believe he's still around."

Teelia nodded and hugged Lily. "I'll be gone long before he is. We all missed you."

*No. Not everyone.* Antoinette stopped humming and again tried to shake her head.

"Now that you're home," Teelia said as she released Lily, "maybe Seth won't seem so lost."

"Oh, Seth and I aren't . . ."

"I don't think Seth is lost," Antoinette's mother said. She inserted a white daffodil into the watering can and tucked moss around its stem. "A little too serious, maybe. But not lost."

Antoinette stretched up on her toes and walked to her mother's side. She opened her fingers and placed her palm against the old steel can. The metal was so cold it made her teeth hurt. It felt like Christmas and icicles and knee-deep snow.

"Maybe 'lost' isn't the right word," Teelia said. She paused. "'Agitated.' That boy is agitated. He looks like he's searching for something."

Standing this close, Antoinette saw her mother's pulse beating below her jawline. It wasn't a steady thump-thump. It was more a thump-pause-pause-thump.

Antoinette reached for her. She wanted to hear her mother's song, but her mother walked across the booth to Lily.

Antoinette balled her hands and stamped her feet. Lily needed to *go away*.

"You know Seth," her mother said. "He's probably pondering the meaning of life. Besides, it's spring. Opening the farm is a lot of work. If he's more bothered than usual, that's why."

Her mother was wrong. The last two nights, Antoinette had looked out of her bedroom window. She expected to see deer at the edge of the woods. Instead, she'd seen Seth coming in from the drying barn, carrying his violin. He only played in the barn when he was upset.

"I've known that boy since he was six years old, running around covered in bruises from his father," Teelia said. She pointed at Lily. "The only time he had any peace was when he was with you. He hasn't been himself since y'all broke up."

Lily pressed her thumb against her index finger and then moved it to her middle finger, her ring finger, her pinky. With each touch, she whispered a number. "That wasn't my doing," she finally said.

"The garden show's in less than two weeks," Antoinette's mother said to Teelia. "Are you ready?"

"Almost," Teelia said. "I want to do a spinning demonstration this year. Do you think Seth could come over and pick up the enclosure for Frank and a few crates of yarn? I'm getting too old to haul everything around myself."

"I'm sure he won't mind," Antoinette's mother said.

"Maybe Lily could come with him and help out." Teelia

winked at Lily, and at the same time Frank resumed humming. Antoinette swayed along with him.

"I don't know if that's a good idea," Lily said. "Things aren't the same as they used to be. We're not"—she waved her hand from side to side—"together. Besides, I only got home yesterday, and he seems fine without me."

"Haven't you learned yet?" Teelia asked. "Just because a man *seems* fine doesn't mean he *is* fine. Trust me, even if he doesn't know it yet, that boy needs you."

Frank's humming had grown steadily louder. He wagged his head back and forth. It looked like fun. Antoinette dropped her chin to her chest to imitate him. When she did, she lost her balance and pitched forward.

Right into her aunt.

Lily grabbed Antoinette's shoulders. "You okay?" she asked.

Antoinette bared her teeth and growled. *Don't touch me!* Her arms twitched and flew up over her head.

Lily let go and backed away. "What did I do?"

Antoinette's mother sighed. "Nothing. She just doesn't know you yet."

That wasn't it. Antoinette could have known Lily her entire life, and she still wouldn't like her. She growled. The few customers in the booth stared.

"I'd better get back," Teelia said. She took Lily's hands. "Your parents would be proud of you for helping out." Then she headed back to her booth.

The man in the Go Green! T-shirt came up to the cash register and set three pots of lavender on the counter in front of Lily. "I've never seen lavender bloom this early," he said.

"Neither have I," Lily said. She brushed the gray foliage.

"Would you like to pick out another one? I plant mine in groups of four."

"I've only got enough room for three." He held out a bill.

Lily didn't take the money. Again, she touched the plants, counting as she did. Her behavior was strange. Antoinette cocked her head to the side and watched.

Lily said, "Three." Then she recounted, as if she would come up with a different number this time. "You could plant two in the garden and two in containers in your kitchen. I do that. Then when I make lavender bread or lavender cookies, it's easy to snip off some flowers."

"No, I don't—"

"Here." Lily selected another plant. "We're running a special. Buy three, get one free."

"I don't want four." The man sounded irritated.

"Lily," Antoinette's mother said, "he doesn't want it."

Lily put the four plants on a cardboard box lid and shoved it toward him. "Take it."

"You're one weird lady," the man said as he walked away.

Antoinette giggled. She flapped her hands and turned in a circle. *Weird Lily. Weird Lily. Weird, weird, weird.* For once, she wasn't the only strange one.

"Tell me something I don't know." Lily swept the remaining yellow pansies from the table. They fluttered down, creating spots of gold in the grass.

Antoinette's mother stepped back to look at her flower arrangement. She plucked out a flower that was too tall and trimmed its stem before reinserting it. "Do you remember the garden show before you left for college?"

Lily's cheeks turned bright red. "Of course I do."

Antoinette's mother laughed. "I thought Mom was going to have a heart attack when she found you and Seth kissing in the drying barn."

Lily shook her head. "That was a long time ago."

Her mother sat down on the stool and brushed her hair back from her forehead. Her cheeks had a pink glow, but dark circles sat under her eyes. "You should talk to him. I know he missed you. He carries a picture of you in his wallet."

*Go away, Lily*, Antoinette thought. She slapped the table.

Her mother glanced at her, then dunked a measuring cup in the bucket of water she kept under the table and drizzled it over her flower arrangement.

"Is he okay?" Lily finally asked.

"You know better than to listen to Teelia," Antoinette's mother said. "She exaggerates. If he's troubled, it's the stress of the show. It's in a week and a half. Plus, he's been taking on more responsibility around the farm as I've been slowing down."

When Lily spoke, her voice was soft and tentative. "Maybe you should cancel the show this year. Not just for Seth, but for everyone involved."

Antoinette's mother shook her head and went back to work on her flower arrangement. "I want to keep everything the same for as long as possible."

That was exactly what Antoinette wanted. Which meant Lily needed to go home. She snapped her teeth shut. She might not be able to say *I don't like Lily*, but there were ways to communicate without language. Her mother would know that when she chomped down on nothing but air, it meant *I don't like Lily*.

Sure enough, her mother glared at Antoinette. "Stop it, Antoinette. That's not funny."

Antoinette stopped biting the air, but her mother was wrong. It *was* funny. She shrieked. *Bite. Bite. Bite*, she thought as she circled past shelves packed with flowers.

A woman trailing a toddler placed two potted azaleas on the counter. "They like acidic soil," Lily said as she rang up the plants. "Work coffee grounds around their base when you plant them."

That was true. Antoinette remembered pressing her fingers into the ground near the azaleas flanking the drying barn. The sharp taste of lemons always filled her mouth.

Antoinette stretched up on her toes and walked to the edge of their tent. Frank saw her and hummed. No one was watching. She could slip away, pet Frank, and be back before her mother noticed she was gone.

Antoinette felt light with anticipation. For once her body moved easily. Her knees didn't pop, and her arms didn't fly skyward.

She was halfway to Teelia's when her mother looked up. "That's too far, Antoinette."

From somewhere behind her, Antoinette heard her mother's voice. "Lily," she said. "Could you go bring her back?"

Lily's voice was soft. "How do I do that? Will she listen to me?"

"Just pick her up and bring her back here."

Antoinette hurried. Lily was *not* picking her up. Antoinette would pet Frank, and then she would walk back to the booth by herself. She didn't need Lily. She didn't need anyone except her mother.

She imagined running from Lily, and she moved so fast the wind tugged her hair back from her face. Two more steps and she'd bury her face in Frank's neck. She stretched for him.

Just before her fingertips touched his soft nose, Lily snatched her away.

Antoinette arched her back and screamed. *Don't touch me! You're not my mother!*

Lily tightened her arms around Antoinette's waist and started counting. "One. Two. Three. Four." Her voice shook.

Antoinette flailed her arms and kicked her feet. She screamed until her throat burned. She flung her head back and raked her nails down Lily's arms. Blood beaded up from the cuts she made, but Lily didn't let go.

Antoinette kept screaming. *I hate you!* She imagined yelling the words so loud all of Redbud would hear.

They were back at the booth, but Lily didn't set her down. Antoinette kicked her feet, aiming for Lily's shins, but this time her body didn't cooperate. She didn't hit anything.

"Antoinette, stop! You're hurting Lily." Her mother put her hands on Antoinette's face, trying to hold her head still.

Lily kept counting. "Ten. Eleven. Twelve." Her arms trembled, but she didn't let go.

*Leave us alone!* Antoinette screamed until she was empty. Until her mother felt so far away that Antoinette couldn't reach her, even when she stretched out her arms as far as they would go.

# Chapter Ten

❧

Any confidence Lily had in her ability to be Antoinette's guardian evaporated as she carried the girl out of the farmers' market. Her arms bled from multiple crescent-shaped gouges. Her muscles shook from the effort it had taken to hold on to the girl while she flailed. And now her hands were numb. She wiggled her fingers to get the blood circulating, but it didn't help.

When she realized she was counting, she shook her head and forced herself to stop. Instead, she focused on the spruce pines edging the parking lot. Three trees stood in front of their van. On all three, the needles along the lower branches were brown, most likely caused by a fungus. If the branches weren't cut all the way back to the trunk, the fungus would spread and the trees would die. Even with immediate pruning, it might be too late.

"I don't know what got into her," Rose said as she walked beside Lily.

Antoinette sagged in Lily's arms, heavy as a bag of wet potting soil. Her behavior wasn't mysterious to Lily. The girl didn't like her.

"Let me take her," Rose said. Her cheeks were pale, and though she tried to hide it her breathing was labored.

Lily wanted to hand Antoinette over, climb in the van, and speed back to the farm. Instead, she hoisted the girl up to get a better grip, and said, "We're fine."

Antoinette let her arms flop back and her head nod forward. *Someone so small should not be this hard to carry*, Lily thought.

They were at the van when a white truck turned into the lot. The sound of Beethoven's Symphony no. 7 poured through the windows. Seth. Rose had called him to take over the booth after Antoinette's meltdown.

Seeing Seth made Lily's skin feel like it was on fire. She thought she had stuffed her feelings for him so far down that they had died, but the moment she saw him at the farmers' market, everything came roaring back.

If Teelia was right and he was troubled . . . Lily tried to suppress her concern but couldn't. From the day Seth's mother showed up at their back door, holding his violin, Lily and Seth had been inseparable. She could no more turn off her feelings for him than she could turn off her need to count.

Lily had been eight years old the day Seth's mother unexpectedly showed up at their house. She was sitting at the kitchen table with her mother, stringing green beans, when they heard a knock on the door.

"Who could that be?" her mother said. She dropped the beans she had been holding into the bowl and went to the door.

Lily shrugged and kept stringing beans. She loved snapping the tops then zipping the string free.

Snap. Zip. Snap. Zip. It sounded like summer.

"Margaret," her mother said. "What a surprise."

Lily looked up. The only Margaret she knew was Seth's mother, but that couldn't be right. She never went outside. Lily got up from the table and went to the door. To her surprise, Seth's mother stood on their porch.

Lily stared at her. Margaret was nothing like Lily's mother—she was darker and a head taller. Though she shared Seth's dark eyes and angular face, she seemed insubstantial, as if the wind might blow her away. Once, Lily saw her standing on the front porch of the Hastings' family farmhouse. When Margaret noticed Lily, she jumped like a startled jackrabbit and hurried back inside.

Now Margaret stood in their kitchen, holding Seth's violin case. "I can't stay," she said, glancing over her shoulder. "Would you mind if Seth stored this in your drying barn? His father taught him to play several years ago, but now . . . well, his dad wasn't feeling so good the other night. A little woozy, I guess. Anyway, he accidentally stepped on Seth's first violin."

She smiled and gave a small laugh, but her lips were so tight they were colorless. "I . . . I didn't want Seth to stop playing so I bought him this one myself." She held out the violin she carried. "Sometimes his dad gets a little . . . clumsy. I'd hate for Seth to lose this one too."

Lily's mother didn't blink. "I've read that plants respond to music," she said. She wiped her hands on the blue-and-white dishcloth hanging on the stove handle. "Maybe he could play for them? It would be better than just storing it. And he'd be helping us out. The harvest was low this year, music might boost production."

That was a lie. The harvest had been so big they had to hire high school students to help out.

A look of gratitude flashed across Margaret's face. "If it's no bother—"

"No trouble at all." Lily's mother took the violin. She paused a moment before adding, "Of course, he'd need to be over here more. He wouldn't be home as much."

Lily didn't know how it was possible to look pained and relieved at the same time, but Seth's mother did. Her shoulders relaxed and color returned to her lips, but her eyes filled with tears as she whispered, "Thank you."

After that, Seth came to the farm every day. He played warm-up scales in the drying barn, then went out into the fields and played.

Three weeks later Lily noticed Seth had a bruise. He was running scales in the drying barn while she sat on a straw bale, looking through her Victorian flower book. She stopped at a drawing of rose acacia with soft pink flowers. It meant friendship, but so did ivy. "Acacia or ivy?" she asked Seth without looking up. "Both mean friendship."

Seth didn't stop playing. He was used to her calling out plant names. "I don't know what acacia looks like," he said as he climbed the scale.

She got up and brought the book over to him. "Here's a picture."

He flicked his eyes over to the book. "Pretty," he said. "Use that one." He played down the scale now. When he raised his arm to move the bow, his sleeve fell back. A green-and-yellow bruise encircled the top of his arm.

"What'd you do? Walk into a wall?" she asked. She put the book down and pushed his sleeve up. "It looks like a handprint." She touched his skin, trying to fit her fingers into the four long bruises that wrapped around the top of his arm.

"It's nothing," he said, pulling away.

Lily was only eight, but she knew a hand-shaped bruise wasn't *nothing*. "Was it one of the boys at school?" They teased her for counting; maybe they bothered Seth too. But even as she asked, she realized the handprint was twice as big as her hand.

"Oh, your da—" she started as understanding clicked into place. Her mother's lie about the harvest. The fear in Margaret's eyes.

Seth snapped open his violin case. He put the instrument away without wiping it down. "Don't feel sorry for me," he said. His eyes were hard, and he held himself tall and rigid. He glared at her, as if daring her to let the tears stinging her eyes fall.

Lily didn't say anything. She grabbed his hand and led him to the straw bale where she had been sitting. When he sat down next to her, she opened her book to the page for ivy.

Acacia was pretty, but ivy was permanent. The dark green leaves weren't flashy, but ivy grabbed on to walls and fences and wouldn't let go. Even if you cut it back, shoots popped up in unexpected places. It took years to root out ivy. "This one," she said, pointing to the picture. "This is friendship. It lasts."

LILY WAS STILL thinking about Seth when they got back to the farm from the market. People hadn't been as willing to report abuse back then, especially in Kentucky, where folks tended to mind their own business.

Lily knew the instability in Seth's childhood had created his need to understand *why* life was hard. They spent hours sitting in the rafters of the drying barn, pondering God's existence. And if he did exist, why did he let bad things happen?

They never found the answer to that question.

Would things have been different for Seth if someone had reported his father? Maybe, but "different" might not be better. Most likely, Seth would have been carted off to a foster home and who knows what would have happened there.

And despite the pain his father caused, Seth still loved him. Lily thought that was why Seth had never stopped playing the violin. It was one good thing they shared.

"Earth to Lily," Rose said when they parked. She waved her hand in front of Lily's face. "You've been lost in thought the entire drive home."

"It's nothing," Lily said. "Just remembering the way things used to be." She glanced over her shoulder at Antoinette in the back seat. "Want me to carry her in for you?" She didn't actually want to touch Antoinette, but she wanted to talk about Seth even less. She used to tell Rose everything, but she had only been home a short while, and the bridge between them still felt tentative.

"Could you? She's so big it's hard for me to carry her." Rose smiled apologetically. "I lose my breath easily nowadays."

As Rose made her way to the back porch, Lily opened the van's back door and reached for Antoinette. The little girl shrank away from her touch, but she didn't resist when Lily picked her up. Lily carried her stiffly. "Don't scratch me this time. Okay?" she said. The porch steps creaked as she climbed them.

Lily eased Antoinette onto the swing next to Rose. Antoinette leaned into her mother much like a sunflower turning toward the sun.

"Sit with us," Rose said. She patted the seat next to her.

Lily shook her head. The urge to count had been pounding through her since they left the market. She needed to get inside before it exploded, forcing her to number the wooden slats of the porch floor or the pebbles in the gravel drive. She said the first thing that popped into her mind. "I need to make a phone call."

After the words left Lily's lips, she realized they were true. She wanted to talk to Will. She had dreamed about him last night, something vague and troubling she couldn't quite remember. When she woke, the room seemed full of his voice.

Rose looked hurt. Lily could tell she was trying hard to mend things between them, and just like always Lily was running away. She paused before slipping inside. "Tonight," she said. "I promise. We'll sit on the porch and tell stories, just like we used to when we were kids."

Rose looked up. Her face was earnest, and her blue eyes were clear. "Antoinette will love you. You're too much alike for her not to."

Lily pictured sitting on the swing with her niece. Antoinette would smack her hands against the armrests while Lily counted the stars. Both of them trapped. "That's what I'm afraid of," she said as she stepped inside.

She went upstairs and walked down the hall toward the guest room. Once there, Lily sat on the corner of the bed, took out her cell phone, and called Will.

He answered on the first ring, as if he had been waiting for her call.

"Will." She closed her eyes as she said his name.

"Bored out there already?" he asked. "How is it in Sticksville?"

She sighed into the phone. "Everything feels . . . off." She thought about the strange things that had happened since returning home. Seth's presence. Flowers blooming at odd times. Antoinette. She was in a category all by herself. Lily ran her hand over the scratches on her arm.

"Why? Did you lose a tractor-pulling contest? Maybe I should come down and cheer you up. Adding a little Will to your life makes everything better."

She laughed in spite of everything. "Yeah. That's all I need."

"If it's that bad, come home. We miss you here. Your plants are droopy. I didn't have anyone to talk to last night. And get this, our neighbor even asked where you were. I didn't know Soup Can Artist could talk."

The allure of her house was strong. After this morning with Antoinette, Lily wanted to jump in her car and drive there right away. Covington was two hours north. She could be there before dinner.

But the thought of disappointing Rose again made her stomach tighten. She traced her toe along the grooves in the hardwood floor. "Rose wants me to be Antoinette's guardian," she said. "I don't think I can do it." Shame made her whisper the words.

Will tapped his fingers against the phone. When he spoke again, his voice was steady and calm. Far from the animated Will she knew. "Lils, I've treated kids with special needs in the ER, and what you've got to remember is that they're still just *kids*. People get all tied up believing that they're different. That they don't want the same things we do. But that's not true. They want friends. A family. They want to be loved. To be accepted. Just like everyone else."

Lily pressed her fingers against the bridge of her nose. A dull throbbing rose behind her eyes. "Tell me I can do it," she said. "Tell me I'm strong enough."

"Lils, you cleaned my incisions after surgery. You sat with me during chemo. You saw me almost completely bald. If you can do that, you can handle one small girl, even if that girl is a little different. Trust me. When have I ever been wrong?"

She laughed softly. "Do you want me to list each time?"

Will didn't play along. "I mean when it counts. Have I ever been wrong when it comes to something like this? Something that matters?"

She paused, thinking back over the years. "No," she admitted. "You haven't."

## ROSE'S JOURNAL
### *June 2007*

—+—

I'M THINKING ABOUT Lily when the phone rings. Antoinette giggles at the shrill sound and kicks her heels against the wood floor. She sits at my feet as I clean up from dinner.

I don't answer the phone.

There are two dishes in the sink—mine and Antoinette's. I dunk my hands into the lukewarm water and brush the bread crumbs away. Mom would be appalled. "A growing girl needs more than a grilled cheese sandwich for dinner," she'd say.

I shy away from the thought. Thinking about Mom and Dad makes me feel bruised inside. If I had accepted Mom's offer to come with me when I took Antoinette to the specialist in Cincinnati, they'd be alive today.

I've examined my journal entries from that weekend. If I had known that was the last time I would see my parents, I would have recorded everything: the shirt Mom was wearing; her shade of lipstick; the number of hairs on Dad's head. As it is, I know that Dr. Ketters wore a purple dress with gold buttons when she told me to institutionalize my daughter, but I don't know what my mother looked like when she got in the car and drove away.

The phone rings again.

Though the window above the sink is open, the house is too quiet. I need the night to seep in. I pull the drain in the sink and watch the suds swirl away. Then I rinse the plates and dry them with a dish towel. The plates are white. The towel is white. I miss color.

The answering machine clicks on after the third ring. I hear Lily's voice. "Rose. Pick up the phone. I'm sorry. Talk to me." She is crying, and so am I, but I can't move.

I miss my sister, but Antoinette deserves to be surrounded by people who love her, not by people who are afraid of her. I failed when I was pregnant by not carrying her long enough. I won't fail now. No one will hurt her. Even Lily.

The sweet scent of honeysuckle drifts through the window. Suddenly I'm a child again, sitting with Lily under honeysuckle vines blooming at the edge of the creek. Their branches were so heavy with flowers they arched downward. As we watched, a doe crept out of the brush and lifted her nose to the wind.

I held my breath.

"Do you think I could touch her?" Lily whispered.

"Hush," I said. "You'll scare her off." I was the big sister who didn't have patience for the dark-haired little girl always tagging along behind me. I was the one who was embarrassed when her sister stared at the sky and counted the stars.

Lily was mesmerized by the deer. "I'm going to touch her," she whispered. She crawled out from under the bush.

When Lily moved, the doe lifted her head and sniffed the wind. She tilted her head to the side and stared right at us.

"Don't!" I grabbed Lily's arm, trying to keep her with me, but she was too far ahead.

The doe froze, and Lily stopped. Her lips moved as she counted. She waited for so long I thought she'd give up and come back to me.

Then the doe slowly dropped her head to the creek. My heart raced as Lily crawled closer. I wanted to follow her, but fear held me back. When Lily was an arm's length away, the deer lifted her head and bounded through the brush.

Lily didn't touch the doe that day, but between the two of us, she was the one who wasn't afraid to try.

She's still trying, I think as I listen to her voice on the answering machine. If I was anything like her, I'd pick up the phone and beg her to come home.

Instead, I wait until she's finished talking and then click Save. Later tonight, I'll replay this message along with the dozens of others she's left since December.

Just then, a knock at the door startles me. I peer through the window. "Seth!" Surprise makes me throw open the door. It's been years since I've seen him.

"Lily's not here," I say, without thinking. "She doesn't live here anymore."

"I know. I mean, that's what Teelia told me. I just got back into town. I guess you heard about my mom?"

News travels fast around Redbud. His mother died of a heart attack a few days ago. His father had died a year earlier, so Seth was alone now. I nod, and he looks down at the ground.

"I'm here taking care of things and thought I'd stop by." He is shy. As if we didn't spend every summer of our childhood together.

It crosses my mind that I shouldn't be talking to him after the way he treated Lily. I might be mad at her, but she's still my sister. Then he says, "I'm sorry about your parents," and I crumble.

He holds me while I cry into his shirt. "I loved them too," he says, and I shake harder.

When I finally stop crying, he looks over my shoulder as if Lily will appear and make a liar out of me. I almost wish she would. Antoinette leans into my leg. "My daughter, Antoinette," I say.

"God, she looks like you."

I swell with pride.

He kneels and speaks to Antoinette. "I knew your mom when she was a little thing, just like you."

Antoinette flaps her hands and shrieks.

"She likes you," I say. "She usually doesn't react this well to strangers."

He straightens and stuffs his hands into his jeans pockets. "It's been years, but I hope I'm not a stranger."

"Of course not." I stand back and open the door wider. I ignore a twinge of guilt that makes me feel I'm betraying Lily by speaking to him.

When he walks in, he stops in the middle of the kitchen and turns in a slow circle. "It's the same," he says. Which is funny, because to me, everything has changed.

AN HOUR LATER, we walk through the night garden. The air is cool, and the flowers are budding. So are dandelions and chokeweed.

Mom and I spent weeks planning the night garden. I still have our plans in my old sketch pads. White lilies line the path and moonflowers scale the wrought-iron arch at the entrance to the garden. At night, the arch fades and the moonflowers look like they're floating. Lily used to say it was magic.

I haven't been here since Mom died, and it shows. Weeds are everywhere. I can't look at the ground without that bruised feeling rising up in me, so I look up. The sky is a combination of blue-and-gray swirls, like Van Gogh's *Starry Night*.

Antoinette walks ahead of us, on her tiptoes like a ballerina. Before the doctor told me that toe-walking was a sign of developmental delays, I thought it was cute. Now it's a reminder of everything that's different about her.

Halfway across the garden, she stops and kneels under a maple tree. Snowdrops bloom in a semicircle around her. Odd. I don't remember planting the flowers. It's too late in the season for them. They bloom in early March.

A page from Lily's flower language book pops into my mind. Snowdrops represent hope. The passing of sorrow.

The maple trees have dropped their helicopter seeds, and Seth sweeps them from a stone bench in the center of the garden.

I'm about to sit when I see that something has captured Antoinette's attention. A sparrow lies on its side under the tree. Its wing is outstretched, its head twisted to the side. Its eyes are open. Antoinette reaches for it.

"Don't touch!" I say as I hurry over. "It's dirty."

It's silly, but I cry when I see the bird. Antoinette kneels and softly strokes its head. She runs her fingers across its wing, and all the while she hums. She is careful, as if aware that death is a solemn thing. I don't have the heart to pull her away.

When she stops humming, her head twitches slightly, and the left side of her mouth curves upward. She suddenly looks sleepy and closes her eyes and lists to the side.

"Come on, let's go," I say.

When I bend down to pick her up, the bird hops to its feet.

I gasp and fall back. "Seth!" I point to the bird as it spreads its wings and jumps into the sky.

"Did you see that?" I ask. "The bird. It was dead." I am giddy. Death has surrounded me for so long that this small life is absurdly precious. I start laughing and can't stop.

Antoinette flaps her hands, and I pick her up. She is heavy with sleep.

"Did you see the bird?" I ask Seth as I hurry back to the bench. I shouldn't be carrying Antoinette. Though she is small, she's heavy for me. I'm winded by the time I sit next to Seth, Antoinette on my lap.

"It was probably stunned," he says, "like when they smack into a window but then later fly off."

I look at the snowdrops. I think of the way my heart eases at Antoinette's touch. The cut on my finger at Lily's house, how it healed. Coincidence can't explain everything. I want to tell Seth, but he's right. I've seen birds hit our kitchen window, fall to the ground, and lie there for several minutes before flying off like nothing happened.

"Mom's funeral is tomorrow," Seth says, breaking into my thoughts. "I'd like it if you were there. She didn't have a lot of friends. And with my father gone—"

"Of course," I say, forgetting the bird. "I'll be there."

Antoinette sinks into me. "How long will you be in town?" I ask. I have other questions: Where have you been? Why didn't you come back before? And most of all: have you talked to Lily? But I don't ask them.

Seth picks a piece of long grass and splits it down the middle. Then he ties the thin pieces into a knot. He does the same thing with several other long pieces until he has a grass necklace. "Here, Antoinette." He slips it over her head. She shrieks and flaps her hands.

"That means she's happy," I explain.

"I have to close up the house," he says. "Get everything sorted out. Should take a month or so."

"What about work? Don't you have a church or something?"

He presses his lips together and looks down at his fingers. "Didn't exactly work out."

I don't press for details; he doesn't seem to be in the mood to share, and I'm not surprised. Seth always had a philosophical bent, but he wasn't a conformist. I never could picture him among men who spent more time making sure women stayed out of the clergy than feeding the hungry.

"If you need a hand while I'm around . . ." He gestures toward the night garden.

"Thanks," I say, "but I don't know how much longer I'll be here." The words hurt as they come out. A few years ago I would have given anything to leave the farm. Now it's the only place I want to be. "I can't run it by myself." The season's only beginning and already I'm behind. Several rows of daffodils died because I didn't harvest them in time.

"You're thinking of selling?"

"I don't have much choice. I've got a kid. I'm sick."

Seth looked at me in surprise.

"I developed a heart problem when Antoinette was born. I can't handle the farm by myself." I gesture to the weeds growing at our feet. Pride keeps me from mentioning Lily's phone calls.

"What about Lily?" he asks, as if he's reading my mind.

"We had a falling out. She sold me her share of the farm."

He doesn't ask what happened, and I don't offer details. We both have sore spots when it comes to Lily.

I hate the thought of giving up the farm. Antoinette loves

it here, but I lose my breath walking from my bedroom to the kitchen. I can't manage a fifty-acre farm alone.

"What if I stick around a little longer?" he asks. "Help you get things under control."

"I can't ask you to do that," I say, but in my heart I'm screaming for help.

"You're not asking," he says. "I'm offering. Growing up, this place was more of a home to me than my own house. Let me help."

It's late, and I'm sitting in the middle of a weed patch. But I look at the snowdrops. I think of the bird flying. And for the first time in a long time, I feel almost weightless with relief.

# Chapter Eleven

❦

The next afternoon Antoinette followed Seth to the drying barn. The flagstone path radiated heat. She stepped from the stones to the Elfin thyme ground cover. Her feet brushed the tiny leaves, releasing the strong scent into the air. The plants held her footprints for a second, and then sprang back as if she hadn't been there at all.

Her mother was at the house, sitting next to Lily on the porch swing. They sat on opposite ends of the swing, not close to each other like sisters should. Antoinette growled, but the drying barn was too far away for them to hear. A hard knot sat between her shoulders. She rolled her head from side to side, but it didn't help.

Other than the thick trees lining the creek bank, this was the only spot of deep shade on the farm. Birch and oak trees, their branches interlaced and their roots tangled, encircled the barn. Hostas, ferns, and pink bleeding hearts poked through the soil. A semicircle of dead pansies stood to one side of the barn. Antoinette stretched up on her toes and walked toward them.

"Oh no you don't," Seth said as he pulled her away from

the flowers and guided her into the drying barn. "You stick with me."

It was at least ten degrees cooler in the barn. Sawdust covered the floor and drying lavender hung from the rafters. Steel buckets hung from metal hooks along one wall and wheelbarrows were stacked up against another. Seth upended one of the wheelbarrows and placed several steel buckets into it.

Antoinette tapped the wheelbarrow and raised her hands.

"You want a ride?" Seth asked.

Antoinette flapped her hands. *Yes!*

He laughed and picked her up. "You're getting big." He gave her a tight squeeze then settled her into the wheelbarrow.

"Hold this for me." Seth pressed his iPod into her hands. It was hooked to a wireless docking station. "Are you up for a music lesson?"

Antoinette flapped her hands. She didn't need paper to communicate with Seth. She held the iPod while he scrolled through the songs on his playlist. "John Hiatt on the way to the fields? Classical while we work?"

She bobbed her head. Seth loved music almost as much as he loved the farm. He taught her the names of the instruments and how to tell if a piece was written in four-four time or three-four time.

He pressed Play on his iPod, and Hiatt's "Thirty Years of Tears" started. Then Seth grabbed the wheelbarrow's handles and pushed Antoinette out of the barn. "Hiatt has a great southern folk sound," he said. "This song is in three-four time. Like a waltz."

She rode with her back to Seth so she could look out over the land. The tree leaves were the new green that only came in spring. From the woods, a whip-poor-will called and a mockingbird sang. She tapped her finger against the side of the wheelbarrow, the sound blending with the birdsong and the music until Antoinette felt like she was singing along.

Seth added his voice to the mix. He harmonized easily with Hiatt, the birds, and the wind. He was part of the land.

The song ended when they reached the daffodil field. Seth lifted Antoinette from the wheelbarrow and directed her to a wooden bench at the head of the row. He set the iPod beside her, then squatted in front of her and grinned. "I'm quizzing you today. I think I can trip you up."

He started a playlist then grabbed a steel pail. "The first song's a freebie. You'll get it no problem."

This was the way she learned best. Studying things she loved with people who understood that not speaking was *not* the same as not comprehending.

Over the iPod, a piano started playing. Antoinette raised her chin and flapped her hands. "Für Elise." Beethoven.

Seth laughed. He was at the spigot that stood at the head of the row. "I told you you'd know this one. It's too easy." He hung the pail from a hook and turned on the spigot. To keep the flowers fresh, they had to be placed in water as soon as they were cut.

"We'll do tulips and daffodils today. Maybe the last of the hyacinths if we have time. Your mom asked me to keep back some of the flowers for her to make bouquets for the market. You're in charge of those, okay?" He turned off the water and set the bucket by her feet. The next song started while Seth filled a second bucket. A violin held a single note for several beats, then an organ joined in, giving depth to the piece.

Seth took the pail and bent down among the daffodils. The

muscles in his shoulders were tight with effort as he dug out weeds and clipped buds for market. Soon a thin sheen of sweat covered his arms.

The music still played. The violins were soaring now. Antoinette imagined them as birds looking down over the trees.

Seth straightened and swiped the back of his hand across his forehead. Sweat and dirt streaked his arms, and his brown hair curled around his shoulders. "Mozart?" he asked.

Antoinette sat still. Mozart's music was lighter.

"Beethoven?"

She almost popped out of her seat but caught herself just in time. No. Beethoven's violin concerto started with oboes. This was Bach. "Air on the G String."

He dropped his pruning shears into the bucket of daffodils at his feet. "I can't fool you, can I? You know it's Bach, don't you?"

Antoinette flapped her hands and shrieked. *Bach*. If she could say his name, it would come out like a growl.

Before Seth came to the farm, she used to study men in the grocery store, wondering whether one of them was her father. Her mother was beautiful, and she could speak. No one would want to leave her. But a child who couldn't speak? Couldn't control her body? That was a reason to leave. She imagined her birth father taking one look at her and running for the hills. She hoped someday her mother would tell her about him. But she didn't know how to ask.

Seth grabbed the smooth green stem of a budding daffodil, cut it at an angle, and dropped the flower in the bucket. He made his way down the row, leaving the tight buds that weren't quite ready. Plantings at the farm were staggered to extend the bloom time.

A new song started. This one was easy. "The Grand Theme" from Tchaikovsky's *Swan Lake*. Before Seth could throw out a name, Antoinette stood, raised her arms above her head, and spun on her toes. She moved so fast her knees almost folded.

"You're right," he said as he watched her dance. "*Swan Lake*. Tchaikovsky."

Antoinette stopped spinning and grinned. Now that Seth was here, she didn't search for her father in grocery stores anymore.

The bucket at his feet was full. He picked it up and hoisted it into the wheelbarrow. "Did I ever tell you that my dad was a musician?" he asked as he grabbed another empty pail. "He's the one who taught me."

He hadn't told her. She shook her head from side to side. Seth didn't often talk about his childhood.

"When he was in a good mood, he used to quiz me on the composers." One corner of his mouth quirked up.

Antoinette tried to imitate him, but she grimaced instead.

"Don't worry," he said. "You're better than I ever was. I couldn't tell Bach from Beethoven until I was fourteen." He tousled her hair as he walked down the row.

He walked back to the row where he had been working and knelt. "My dad was first chair violin for the Cincinnati Symphony Orchestra," he said without looking up. He cut three daffodils and put them in the pail. "My mom also played, but she wasn't as good. She was a high school music teacher. My parents met when my mom brought a group of students to the symphony."

The pail at his feet was getting full, but he added a few more daffodils. "It's funny. My dad taught me the violin, but when I play I think of my mother. When my dad wasn't home, she'd put on CDs of Bach and Beethoven. I was little then. I'd stand on her feet, and she'd waltz me around the house." He smiled at the memory.

Antoinette looked out beyond the daffodil bed, across the rows of raised soil. Several rows down, bright green tulip leaves unfurled like flags. She understood how Seth felt. Antoinette saw her mother in every inch of the farm.

"She would have loved you. My mother, I mean." Seth stopped working and looked up at her. "I know it's been hard on you . . . your mother being ill and all. It's never easy to lose a parent. No matter how old you are. But you should know, your mom's trying to look out for you. Lily's her sister. You should try to get to know her. Your mother loves her. You will too if you give her a chance."

Antoinette started rocking. Other than Seth, no one talked to her about her mother's illness. Most of the time, she loved that he talked to her about things others wouldn't, but right now she didn't want to hear what he was saying.

"I used to wonder why bad things like this happened," he said, "especially to good people like you and your mom. I spent a lot of time trying to find the answer to that question, and I still don't have it.

"But I do know that Lily's here to help your mom." He paused for a moment before adding, "And you. I think you should let her."

Some small part of Antoinette wanted to clamp her hands over her ears. She knew her mother was sick. Very sick. It made her feel small and helpless in a way that nothing else did. But she did not want—no, she did not *need*—Lily's help. Antoinette could take care of her mother alone.

Seth nodded toward the house, and Antoinette turned to see what he was looking at. The back porch was just visible from the daffodil field. Antoinette saw the porch swing where her mother and Lily sat, a wide space between them. From this far away, they looked like dolls.

Seth cut another daffodil and added it to the pail. "A long time ago—before you were born—Lily was my best friend. I felt comfortable around her. I could be myself. You know?"

He looked at Antoinette as if to see whether she understood. But she had never had a friend like that, other than her mother of course, and she didn't count. She wondered how it felt to have someone who saw through to the inside of you and loved you anyway.

"It's rare to find someone who knows all your secrets and still accepts you. My dad could be . . . difficult," Seth said. "On the nights that were especially hard, I'd sneak over here and toss pebbles at your aunt Lily's window until she woke. She'd sneak me inside, and I'd lie down on the floor between your mom's bed and Lily's.

"Your mom would fall right back to sleep, but Lily would stay up with me, talking until I could close my eyes."

He sat back on his heels and laughed. "Your grandma found me there once. I was twelve. I thought she was going to skin me alive, but she just leaned against the doorframe and said, 'For God's sake, Lily, don't make the boy sleep on the floor. Put him in the guest room.' Then she went downstairs and made me a plate of scrambled eggs."

The pail at Seth's feet was now full. He stood and picked it up, sloshing a bit of water over the edge. As he placed it in the wheelbarrow, he said, "You need to give Lily a chance."

Antoinette shook her head hard. Seth could like Lily if he wanted to, but she didn't even want to try.

## Chapter Twelve

❧

The sun was setting behind the hills as Lily followed Rose and Antoinette to the drying barn. The temperature had dropped, and the wind picked up. It felt like a storm was coming. She kept some distance between herself and Antoinette. *I can't do this*, she thought every time she looked at her niece. But how could she abandon Rose again?

She kept going back to her conversation with Will. He believed she could handle Antoinette, but Lily wasn't convinced. She started counting her steps.

A series of flagstone paths wound through the farm, but the one leading from the house to the drying barn was more worn than most. The barn was only a few yards away, directly across from the house. Bright pink azaleas flanked its entrance, with a stand of birch and oak trees to the right.

It hadn't always been a drying barn—at least not an herb-drying barn. Years ago, when Lily and Rose were still young, their father had converted it from an old tobacco barn. He ran electricity to power a commercial freezer and installed lights and a phone line.

The rafters, from which farmers before them had hung

tobacco, were perfect for drying lavender, basil, and other herbs. The plants were bound into bundles, then hung from the beams. Securing them had been one of Lily's jobs, and once that was done, she'd stretch out across one of the rough beams, surrounded by the warmth of the barn and the smell of the drying flowers. There she pictured a future in which she and Rose and Seth ran the farm together.

Back then, she never would have imagined spending her adult life away from this place.

"You're falling behind," Rose said, looking over her shoulder.

"Same as always, isn't it?"

Rose held the barn door open for Antoinette, then flicked on the light.

Lily shivered as the wind picked up. She hurried into the barn, accidentally bumping into Antoinette. The little girl growled.

Lily stepped back, then walked a wide circle around the girl. She didn't know how to handle a normal child, much less a child like Antoinette. "I don't know how to be a mother," she said, her voice a whisper. Parenting wasn't math. There wasn't a child-raising formula. No $x + y$ = perfect parent.

At the word *mother*, Antoinette bared her teeth.

"And you think I did?" Rose zipped up her faded green jacket. The barn kept the wind off them, but Rose was cold all the time now. Her face was whiter than usual, and her lips were rimmed with blue. "When Antoinette was born, I cried every night until she was six months old. Mothering isn't something you're born knowing. You figure it out as you go along."

"She doesn't like me," Lily said as she watched her niece shuffle through the cedar shavings on the barn floor.

Seth had left a steel bucket full of daffodils and tulips on a table at the far end of the barn. Rose went to one of the shelves and took down a handful of water tubes. They would fill each of the tubes with water and preservative and then insert one stem into each tube.

Wind whistled through the cracks in the barn's slats. The sound was eerie, and Lily counted the seconds until it stopped.

Thirty-three. An odd number. Not good.

"Fill these for me," Rose said as she handed Lily the tubes. "And Antoinette will love you. You just need to give her time."

"How can you say that?" It wasn't a rhetorical question. Lily really wanted to know. "Weren't you at the farmers' market? She hates me." Lily went to the sink in the corner.

"It's not that bad. Give her time." Rose selected a daffodil and trimmed its stem.

"It's a little early to be doing this, isn't it?" Lily asked. "We've got, what, ten hours until the market tomorrow? The tubes will only keep the flowers fresh for six hours. Besides, the wind is really picking up out there."

Normally, Lily loved storms. She and Rose used to sit on the porch swing and watch the clouds roll in. They'd count the seconds after lightning flashes: "One Mississippi. Two Mississippi," squealing in delight as the time between seeing the lightning and hearing the thunder lessened. But tonight Lily felt off balance. She wanted to be inside the house, preferably in bed with a mug of hot chocolate.

"I know," Rose said. She trimmed another daffodil before plopping it back in the pail. "I won't insert the flowers into the tubes until right before the market tomorrow. I like getting everything ready the night before. It makes things easier in the morning. Put the tubes here." She indicated a plastic container on the table. "And we'll be finished before the worst of the storm."

Lily sensed Antoinette watching her as she placed the filled tubes in the box. She tried to ignore her niece, but even with her back turned, she felt the little girl's stare. "Mom didn't do it this way."

Rose shrugged. "Mom didn't have Antoinette to deal with. Mornings aren't always easy with her."

Lily glanced at Antoinette, who growled and started walking in circles.

"Change always came easy for you," Lily said to Rose as she turned from Antoinette.

Rose flinched. "Easy? You think this has been easy for me?"

"Easier than it is for me, I mean."

Rose frowned. Two sharp lines appeared between her eyes. "I'm dying. I'm leaving my daughter. You think that's easy?" Her voice went up a notch.

Lily shook her head. "I don't mean it like that. Things come easier for you. People like you." At school, Rose had always been surrounded by friends. Lily was lucky if she made it through lunch without someone "accidentally" spilling milk in her lap.

"People like you too, Lily. You just don't let anyone get close to you. So what if you have a few odd habits? We all do. Most people are just better at hiding them—" Rose stopped talking. "Where's Antoinette?"

"By the door," Lily said as she turned around. The door was open. "She was right there."

"Antoinette?" Rose hurried outside with Lily close behind her.

Rose stopped abruptly. Antoinette was kicking her feet through a semicircle of dead pansies. "You can't run off like that," Rose said.

Antoinette kept swishing her feet through the flowers. When she saw Lily, she growled.

The anxiety Lily had felt since coming home threatened to explode. She started to count.

Now that they had found Antoinette, Rose resumed her conversation with Lily. "You said earlier that you used to dream about being me. Well, I'd give anything to switch places with you. You're the one who will be here when Antoinette finishes school. You'll see what she looks like at twenty. At thirty. That's something I can only imagine."

Rose glanced at Lily's lips, which moved as she counted, and grabbed her shoulder. "Are you listening to me?"

At the same time, Antoinette started humming.

Lily stopped counting. "What's she doing?" she asked.

Antoinette was now kneeling in the middle of the dead flowers. She had closed her eyes and was running her fingers over the browning petals as she hummed.

"Shit!" Rose said. "Pick her up. Pull her away from the flowers."

"Why? They're dead. She can't hurt anything." The wind lifted Antoinette's hair, swirling the strands around her head.

Rose's face, already pale, went paler still. "Help me, Lily. I can't lift her."

The desperation on Rose's face spurred Lily into action. In four steps, she was at Antoinette's side. The girl kept humming as she pushed her hands deeper into the soil.

"Your mom wants you to come with me," she said. As she

reached for Antoinette, she prayed the girl wouldn't scratch her again.

Just before they touched, Antoinette stopped humming.

"Pick her up!" Rose yelled over the rising wind.

At the same time, Antoinette looked Lily right in the eye and smiled.

Lily's skin prickled.

"We're too late," Rose whispered.

Antoinette slumped forward, and the dead pansies blushed back to life.

"Oh my God!" Lily stumbled back. "It's not possible." She forgot about the mounting storm, knelt, and cautiously touched a flower petal. It was fragile and unbelievably soft.

Then Rose was there. "Don't let her seize this time," she murmured as she turned Antoinette onto her side.

A statistic flashed through Lily's mind: a major cause of death in epilepsy was asphyxiation due to the inhalation of vomit. She shook off her wonder at the flowers and helped Rose hold Antoinette on her side.

"Is she seizing?" Lily asked. She had never seen a seizure before, but she thought there should be shaking involved. Antoinette was still.

"No," Rose said. "She's sleeping."

Then Rose's earlier words flashed through Lily's mind: "Don't let her seize *this time*."

"You knew." Lily gestured to the now-brilliant yellow pansies. "She's done this before." Everything she had seen since coming home flashed through her mind: the clematis over the porch, the wisteria draping the gazebo, the lavender at the farmers' market— all flowers blooming out of season.

Rose kissed her daughter. "Yes. I knew." The anger in her voice had evaporated. "Flowers. People. She fixes them all. Antoinette's the reason I'm still here. I would have died long ago if not for her."

Lily stared at her niece, numb with wonder. One thought went through her mind. If Antoinette could do this, she could heal Rose.

She could *heal* Rose.

"The healings are temporary," Rose said, dashing Lily's hope before it could fully form. "She seizes with more complicated healings, like my heart condition. And the seizures are getting worse each time. She'll die if she keeps doing this."

Tentatively, Lily stroked Antoinette's hair, unable to believe what she had just witnessed. Lightning flashed, and automatically she started counting. "One Mississippi. Two Mississippi. Three Mis—" A crack of thunder stopped her.

Rose touched Lily's shoulder. "The storm's getting closer. We need to get her back to the house. She'll sleep for a while now."

The wind had begun to roar and rain had started to fall, but Lily couldn't move.

"Come on, Lily," Rose said. "I need your help. I can't carry her anymore."

Slowly, Lily lifted her niece and followed Rose back to the house. As she did, she counted each step away from the spot where Antoinette had performed a miracle.

ROSE'S JOURNAL
*June 2008*

———+———

I MISS MY sister.

More than a year has passed since I spoke to Lily. Every time I pass the phone, I chant, *Ring!* But Lily doesn't call.

I've started talking to her in my mind. I tell her about the flowers we're growing. I tell her that Seth keeps an old picture of her in his back pocket. I tell her that Antoinette loves flowers the way she does.

Then I remember the way she shrank from Antoinette during Mom and Dad's funeral, and I feel a rush of anger. I love Lily, but I live for Antoinette.

Right now, Antoinette toddles toward the Bakery Barn. I count her steps as if, like Lily, I need numbers to make the moment last. A small garden filled with purple petunias, pink zinnias, and yellow daylilies frames the bakery entrance. The zinnias and daylilies are bright, but the petunias have wilted. The sun is directly overhead. It burns my shoulders and the top of my head.

As Seth and I walk to a metal table, I shield Antoinette's view. If she notices the flowers, she'll have a meltdown. When she sees a flower bowed under the summer heat, she stomps her feet and flaps her hands. She seems to have an emotional connection with nature. She only calms after I water the plant.

The patio is empty. Seth selects a table next to the door. His skin is tanned a deep brown, and his hair is streaked with gold. When we were kids, he walked as if he carried a heavy burden, and he rarely smiled. Now he sings while he works, and sometimes Antoinette hums along with him. It seems he has found his place in life.

"Can you watch Antoinette?" I ask him. "I need to talk to MaryBeth." I want to head off Antoinette's meltdown if she notices the plants.

"Sure. But when you come back, I want to hear what the doctor said." Since returning home, Seth has driven me to the cardiologist every three months.

I nod, then pop into the bakery. A young girl with spiky hair and a nose ring mans the counter.

"Is MaryBeth around?" I ask.

The girl rubs her nose ring, a small diamond stud. "I think she's in the back." She points to a room separated from the front of the store by a thick brown curtain.

I walk around the counter and sweep back the curtain. "Eli? MaryBeth?"

The room is well lit. MaryBeth leans over an antique desk that's covered with receipts. Half-moon glasses perch on her nose. Her short hair is messy. She looks like she's been working since the dark morning hours. Judging by the rows of cookies and cupcakes in the bakery case, she probably has.

"Rose!" Her arms are thin but strong, and her tight hug reminds me of Mom. I don't want to let go. "Is my favorite girl with you?" she asks.

"She's outside with Seth. That's why I'm here. Your petunias are a little droopy. Antoinette can't stand seeing flowers in distress. If you've got a watering can, I'll take care of them."

MaryBeth drops her glasses on the desk. "Well, we can't have her getting upset, can we? I've got a can under the sink."

I don't mean for MaryBeth to stop what she's doing, but she waves away my offer of help. "Go sit with Seth and your daughter. I'll be out in a minute." She steps back and looks at me. "And get something to eat. You look hungry."

I've lost weight, but I didn't think it showed. Between working the fields and caring for Antoinette, I'm so tired I often go to bed without eating. Seth's help makes it easier, but he's not the one who wakes when Antoinette has a nightmare. He's not the one who lies in bed staring at the ceiling, wondering who will care for her after I'm gone. I stop at the counter and order three cupcakes from the girl with the nose ring.

Antoinette is sleeping on the ground beside the garden when I come outside. Her hands are covered with dirt.

"Did she scream herself out?" I set a cupcake in front of Seth. It's his favorite, chocolate cake with vanilla icing.

"No," he says as he peels back the paper wrapper. "She saw the flowers, stuck her hands in the ground, and started humming. After she finished, she leaned over and closed her eyes. I think the heat got to her. No one's here, so I let her sleep."

I set the other cupcakes on the table and kneel beside Antoinette. Her eyelids flutter when I stroke her shoulder. "Wake up, sleepyhead. You can't just lie down on the sidewalk and take a nap."

She smiles, and I feel full of light. Antoinette isn't an easy child, but she's *my* child. My past, present, and future are in each breath she takes.

I don't notice the petunias until I help her sit. When I do, I blink twice. "Did I miss something? They were droopy and brown before, right?" The flowers beside the door are a purple so bright it almost hurts my eyes.

Before Seth answers, MaryBeth arrives with a watering can and walks to the flowers. "I thought you said they were brown. I'm no gardener, but they look okay to me."

I shake my head and guide Antoinette to the table. She grabs a cupcake and squishes her hand in the icing. "I must be seeing things. I could've sworn they had wilted."

June isn't Kentucky's hottest month—that would be August when the air burns your lungs—but sweat popped out along my arms as soon as I walked outside. I chalk up my confusion to the heat.

Antoinette shrieks—her happy sound. White icing coats her hands and her mouth. I laugh. "You like that?"

Antoinette flaps her hands. Then she takes another bite of her cupcake. Most of it makes it to her mouth. When she grins, chocolate crumbs coat her teeth.

"There's plenty more where that came from," MaryBeth says. "Eli will be sorry he missed you. He went home after the morning rush. A bakery's not the best place to be during the summer. All that heat.

"Speaking of which, I'll bring out a pitcher of sweet tea," MaryBeth says. "Y'all can't sit out here without something to drink."

As soon as she leaves, Seth says, "What did the cardiologist say?"

I hear him, but I can't get my mind off the flowers. "Did you see the petunias when we arrived? Were they wilted?"

I don't know what I want him to say. If he says no, I'm seeing things. If he says yes, well, I don't know what that means.

"The cardiologist?" he insists. "What did he say?"

I take some napkins from the dispenser on the table and wipe Antoinette's hands and mouth. She finished her cupcake, but more of it is on her face than in her stomach.

"He did an echocardiogram. My ejection fraction was thirty-five percent." Somehow I keep the fear from my voice.

An echocardiogram measures the amount of blood the heart pumps out. Anything over fifty percent is good. Thirty-five percent is low. It means I'm at significant risk for a heart attack.

Thinking about it makes my chest constrict. I take deep breaths and tell myself I should be happy. It's been a little over five years since my heart gave out during Antoinette's birth. My time should already be up.

"I'm sorry." Seth squeezes my hand, and I wonder whether I look as sad as he does. He would have made a good minister, I think. I say so, but he shrugs me off.

"Too many sacrifices," he says.

I wonder if he means Lily.

I pick at the cupcake in front of me. MaryBeth makes them fresh every day, so I know it's good, but I can't eat. I clench my teeth so hard my jaw hurts. I can't talk about my health. If I do, I'll start crying and never stop.

I look at the flowers again. In the year that Seth's been at the farm, we've rarely talked about the things that happen around Antoinette. Flowers blooming out of season. The fact that I'm still here.

Voicing my thoughts seems silly, but I plunge ahead. "You saw them too." I nod to the petunias. "They were wilted before."

Seth folds his cupcake wrapper into a small square. He turns it over and presses the sharp corner into his thumb. "We're both tired from working in the fields today. Or maybe it was a shadow."

It's the closest he's come to admitting that he's seen the peculiar things that happen around Antoinette. I think about the snowdrops in the night garden. The cut that disappeared from my finger. The bird that hopped into the sky after Antoinette's touch.

"It wasn't a shadow," I say, "and I'm not *that* tired." Then I blurt out what I've been thinking for the past several months: "What if Antoinette's causing these things to happen?" I know I'm grasping at straws, but if Antoinette made those things happen, then maybe she can fix me.

MaryBeth returns holding a tray with a pitcher of sweet tea and three glasses. She sets the glasses in front of us and pours the tea.

Seth and I fall silent. I'm embarrassed by my outburst.

"I'd stay to chat," MaryBeth says, "but without Eli, I'm the only one keeping an eye on things." She hugs Antoinette before she leaves.

When Seth speaks, his voice is filled with pity, and that hurts more than his words. "She's just a little girl, Rose. She's not causing anything."

"I'd think you of all people would believe," I say in a stubborn last-ditch attempt to persuade him.

"That's not fair," he says. "There's a difference between faith in God and believing that Antoinette can do miracles."

Why? I want to ask. But I don't say anything, and we finish our cupcakes in silence.

• • •

THE BACK OF my legs stick to the wood bench running along the gazebo, which Seth painted purple and yellow last week. The colors are happy, but they don't help my mood. A bucketful of strawberries sits at my feet. Antoinette is in the middle of the gazebo, stretched up on her toes, twirling.

Seth sits beside me. He hasn't said much since we left the Bakery Barn. I can't blame him. I don't know what to say either.

My chest hurts.

I pluck a strawberry from the bucket, pop off its stem, and bite into it. Fresh strawberries are my favorite part of June. I study Antoinette as she dances, trying to see past her awkward movements. Seth's right—she's just a little girl.

"Earlier, at the Bakery Barn . . . I mean, it's obvious Antoinette isn't making these things happen," I say.

Ever since Dr. Ketters told me to institutionalize Antoinette, I've been looking for some great good to balance out all of the heartache. I used to imagine Antoinette listening to one of Mozart's symphonies and then picking out the melody on the piano at Seth's house. I'd dream of her taking my old paints and producing a perfect replica of the striped fields behind the house.

"I just want to believe something good will happen."

"It already has," he says. He nods toward Antoinette, who is waving her fingers before her eyes, giggling.

He picks up a strawberry and turns it over before dropping it back into the pail. He and Lily used to spend hours picking strawberries. I haven't seen him eat one since coming home.

"Do you miss her?" I ask. I don't want to embarrass him, so I look at my feet. My ankles are swollen, one of the perks of a damaged heart. I make a note to take a water pill when we go inside. Then I steeple my fingers and press them into my chest, trying to dispel the pressure that started building earlier at the Bakery Barn.

"Every day," Seth says softly.

It's getting hard to breathe. "You should call Lily," I say. I haven't talked to her in years, but I'm still her big sister. The need to watch out for her never left me.

"Maybe someday." Seth straightens and stretches his arms over his head.

"I don't understand."

He stares out over the hills. His hair falls over his eyes. "Sometimes the best thing you can do for someone is to stay away from them. She has a new life. I don't want to disrupt it."

It's dusk; the fireflies are out. We should be in the night garden. This past spring, Seth helped me fix it up. The weeds are gone and the trellis is heavy with moonflowers and climbing hydrangeas.

Antoinette stops dancing. I hold out a strawberry. "Want it?"

My chest squeezes again. I should go inside and lie down, but Antoinette is happy, and I love seeing her that way. I want to prolong this moment.

She bites into the berry and red juice trickles down her chin.

I laugh. "Between the cupcake and the strawberries, we'll have to hose you off before we go inside."

When I lean forward to wipe her mouth, my chest tightens. It feels as if someone is crushing my heart. I close my eyes and breathe deeply, focusing on expanding my rib cage and filling every inch of my body with air.

Seth touches my shoulder. "Are you all right?"

I force my eyes open, but I keep taking slow, deep breaths.

The pressure builds, and I shake my head. My nitro pills are at the house.

Antoinette comes closer. My focus narrows to the strawberry she holds. I stare so hard I can count the seeds running up its side.

I breathe. In. Out. In. Out.

"What can I do?" Seth asks, an edge of panic in his voice. "Your lips are blue. Should I call the paramedics?"

I try to say *Call 911*, but my mouth isn't working.

Antoinette drops the strawberry. It rolls toward the stairs, leaving a trail of red juice.

I need to go to the house. I try to stand, then stumble to the ground.

Seth yells my name, but I block out everything except my daughter. I fight to keep my eyes open, wanting her face to be my last sight.

She crouches beside me, and her long blonde hair touches the back of my hand. Her face is too serious for a five-year-old. My vision starts to fade. I open my eyes wider.

Antoinette caresses my cheek. I remember how strong her grip was as a baby. How could I have ever wished her to be more than she is? I want to tell her that she's perfect, but the pain has crawled into my jaw. Suddenly we're both mute.

Then Antoinette hums, and I feel like I'm being turned inside out. The pressure in my chest builds to a single concentrated point, and then it explodes outward. I arch my back and scream.

Antoinette hums faster.

I burn with pain.

Just when I think I will burst, everything stops. I lie still for a moment, afraid to move. Then I feel Antoinette's hand against my cheek.

I open my eyes. She's smiling at me.

"What happened?" Seth is beside me. He tilts my face to his. "The color is back in your face. Your lips aren't blue."

But I don't speak. I'm focused on my daughter.

I put my hand over hers. "Did you do this?"

Antoinette gives me one more brilliant smile before her eyes roll back, and she collapses. Her arms shake, and her heels thud against the gazebo floor.

"Oh God," I say. "What's happening?"

Seth doesn't hesitate. "We need to get her to the hospital." He scoops her up and runs to the truck. I hurry after him, my heart beating as easily and smoothly as it did when I used to run through the fields with Lily.

"I DID THIS to her," I say. I lean over Antoinette's bed in the emergency room. Seth and I stand on either side of her, keeping watch. She had a grand mal seizure. The medicine that stopped it made her fall asleep.

"You didn't do this," he says. "The doctor said seizures are common in children with Antoinette's disabilities."

Antoinette's seizure lasted thirty minutes. Far too long, the ER doctor said. The longer a seizure lasts, the greater the possibility for brain damage.

An IV snakes out of the back of her hand. The nurse had to bandage Antoinette's arm with surgical wrap to keep her from yanking it out.

"The flowers. The bird. And now me. Antoinette's disability didn't cause her seizure, healing me did."

Seth says, "You couldn't have known," and I know he believes now. Antoinette saved me.

When we arrived, Seth told the doctors I had been having chest pain. They did an EKG, an echocardiogram, and drew blood to check for cardiac enzymes. Everything was normal. The echocardiogram—my second today—showed my ejection fraction at sixty percent.

Better than normal.

But at what price? I brush Antoinette's hair from her forehead. I don't know how, but I'm convinced she healed me and that the effort caused her seizure. Which means that I can't ever let her do this again. A broken body I can bear, but a broken heart, well, even Antoinette can't fix that.

# Chapter Thirteen

L ily couldn't sleep. She lay in bed, staring at the ceiling. Every time she closed her eyes, she saw Rose explaining how Antoinette's healing ability worked.

"She can control it," Rose had said. They were sitting on the porch swing with Antoinette between them. As Rose spoke, the tight lines around her mouth disappeared, as if talking about it removed a weight she had been carrying. "She doesn't help everyone, only people she *wants* to heal. And she can't heal herself. She touches the person, and then she hums. I don't know how she actually changes things."

"How does it feel?" Lily asked.

"It's like being turned inside out," Rose said. "Like your bones and muscles are stretching, and your skin can't contain them anymore. You want to burst apart and come together at the same time."

"Does it hurt?" Lily asked.

"Sometimes," she said.

Only three people knew about Antoinette's ability. Rose, Seth, and now Lily. Eli Cantwell suspected. Before they went inside, Rose made Lily promise not to tell anyone what Antoinette could do. "It's the only way to keep her safe," Rose said. "Healing everyone who needs help will kill her."

Despite her promise, Lily wanted to call Will, but how could she explain what had happened tonight? He wouldn't believe on faith alone.

Sleep was impossible. She kicked back the quilt and stood, putting on the jeans she'd worn earlier. She needed to see Seth. He had known about this from the beginning. What had he said in the truck her first day home? Antoinette was different.

What she'd learned earlier went way beyond different.

Before all of this, she had been afraid to be Antoinette's guardian. Now she was terrified.

She tiptoed out of the house and into the night, pausing to slip on the garden clogs she had left by the back door. She trembled as she hopped the white-plank fence between Eden Farms and Seth's property.

His farm bordered theirs. He owned twenty acres, but his house was only a short distance from the fence line. The moon was bright, but she didn't need its light to find her way. It was *his* home. Her feet knew the way.

The scent of honeysuckle drifted on the night breeze, and cornflowers bloomed around her feet. It was too early for them, and she wondered whether Antoinette had been here recently.

A page from her flower book came to her. Cornflowers meant "hope in love." Ridiculous. She didn't love Seth. At least, not anymore. She crushed a blue flower beneath her heel. "I don't love him," she said out loud. She was wading through flowers when his house came into view.

Before Seth's family bought the house, the front porch had sagged in on itself. The white paint was dirty and peeling. Seth's father restored the farmhouse. He shored up the porch, extending it until it wrapped around the first story. He sanded off the chipped white paint and repainted with a soft butter yellow. He removed the overgrown yew bushes that obscured the front of the house and planted pale pink Sharifa Asma roses in their place. He did everything except make the house a home. Given Seth's dark memories of childhood there, Lily was surprised he hadn't sold it long ago.

It was late, but the lights were on. She squared her shoulders as she climbed the porch stairs and knocked on the door. A full minute passed before Seth appeared to open it.

"Lily," he said, his eyes wide with surprise. "Is Rose okay?" He walked onto the porch and shut the door behind him. He wore a pair of faded jeans and nothing else. His stomach was taut. She could count each of his muscles. His brown hair was messy. It curled around his face, tousled by sleep.

"She's fine. Everything's fine. I need to talk to you." Lily couldn't stop moving. She tapped her fingers against her thigh as she paced back and forth on the porch.

"At midnight? Couldn't it wait till morning?" He leaned against the porch railing and yawned.

"No. It can't." She pointed at him. "Why didn't you tell me what Antoinette could do?" Her voice was loud.

"Would you have believed me?" he asked, infuriatingly calm.

"You should have told me." She poked him in the chest. "You said Antoinette was different. This is *way* beyond different."

He caught her hand before she could jab him again. "Does it matter?"

"I don't know," she said after a long pause. "Maybe." This close, she felt the heat from his skin. She could map the tiny lines at the corner of his eyes and around his mouth—could see all the ways his face had changed over the years.

He didn't let go of her hand.

"For what it's worth, I told Rose you needed to know, but even if she had listened to me you wouldn't have believed. I was with Antoinette every day for over a year. Strange things happened around her all the time, but I never thought she was *causing* them until I saw her heal Rose."

He made sense, but Lily was angry. For once, she didn't want logic. She wrenched her hand free.

"She's a little girl who's losing her mother," Seth said, still unruffled. "The rest of it doesn't matter."

His calm manner made her angry. Her face flushed as she turned away from him. "Of course it matters. I didn't know what I was doing before. Now . . ." She waved her hand in the air, searching for the right words, but they didn't exist. "I'm in over my head."

"No you're not. You can do this." He took her by the shoulders and turned her to face him.

A sense of betrayal washed over her, and she fought to hold back tears. "You should have told me," she said. "I thought I was your friend."

"You are," he said, and she thought she saw pain in his eyes.

"No. I meant something to you once. For that, if for no other reason, you should have told me." Frustration and fear overcame her. She turned and reached for the porch railing as tears spilled down her cheeks. "Coming here was a mistake." She hurried down the steps, unsure whether she meant coming to Seth's house or coming home.

Finally agitated, Seth reached for her, but he was too late. "Lily, wait!" he yelled. But she ran home without looking back.

LILY WAS ELEVEN years old when she realized she loved Seth. Before that, she hadn't understood why she smiled when she said his name. Or why her heart fluttered when his hand brushed hers.

They were walking through the fields one morning at the end of a long, hot summer. His right eye was purple and swollen. As usual, he pretended nothing was wrong, and she tried to make it easier for him. "He's drinking again?" Lily asked.

They trailed behind Rose, cutting through tall grass on their way to the creek. The sun was low, but soon it would be overhead, pulling pearls of sweat from their skin. Lily counted her footsteps from the house (forty-six) and plucked a piece of grass gone to seed. She stuck it between her teeth and chewed. It tasted both bitter and sweet.

"You could stay with us," she said, not the first time she made the suggestion. "Mom wouldn't care. We've got an extra bedroom."

Seth didn't say anything, but he never did. He was stuck. The best he could do was spend as much time as possible at their house, slipping home after dinner when his father passed out in the study. Most days he managed, but sometimes he made too much noise as he tiptoed into the house. Those were the nights he snuck out after midnight and ran across the field that separated their houses. Once there, he stood outside, throwing pebbles at the girls' bedroom window until either Lily or Rose woke and helped him inside.

As they walked, Lily held out her hand. He took it, and his hand swallowed hers. When had he grown so much bigger?

"What's holding y'all up?" Rose yelled, over her shoulder. She had draped her shorts over the low-hanging limbs of a river birch so they wouldn't get wet. Her legs were deep brown, and her hair was so long it reached the middle of her back. She looked more like a woman than a child, her body pushing into curves and softening in places where Lily was still narrow and flat.

Seth glanced at Rose, then dropped his eyes to the ground, but not before Lily saw a red flush creep up his neck. For the first time she was embarrassed for him to see her body.

"Come on!" Rose yelled again as she splashed through the creek.

Seth shoved his hands into his pockets and kicked at a rock on the trail. "You go ahead," he said, without looking at Lily.

Rose clambered up onto the flat rock that stood in the middle of the creek. Her white T-shirt was transparent. Earlier that summer, their mother had taken Rose to town and came back with two white cotton training bras. Jealousy twisted Lily's stomach when she saw the outline of Rose's bra through her wet shirt. She counted backward from one hundred, but it didn't help.

Seth kept his back to Rose. He shifted his weight from foot to foot. Every few seconds his gaze slid over to Rose.

Lily wished he would look at her like that, but she knew stripping down to her skivvies wouldn't accomplish anything. For one thing, she was wearing little-girl underwear with SAT-URDAY emblazoned across the back. For another, Rose outshone her in every way.

"Come! On!" Rose yelled again, sitting up on the rock, water glistening on her body.

"I don't want to," Lily said.

"Baby!" Rose called.

Lily clenched her teeth to keep from yelling. Instead, she turned to Seth. "Want to go pick some strawberries?"

He shook his head and mumbled something about forgetting to check the latch on the gate. Then he ran off toward his house, leaving Lily on the creek bank.

She wanted to dash after him, but her feet wouldn't move. A feeling of hate surged through her body. She splashed into the water without taking her shoes off. When she reached the center of the creek where Rose reclined on the rock, her long blonde hair splayed over her shoulders, Lily grabbed a fistful of hair and yanked as hard as she could.

"Ow!" Rose screamed as she toppled off the rock and into the water. "Why'd you do that?"

Lily jabbed a finger at Rose. "His dad hit him again." To her shame, she began to cry. She turned her back on Rose and sniffed hard while she clambered up onto the rock. She hitched up her knee and yanked her shoes off. Her mother was going to kill her for ruining another pair.

Rose stood in the middle of the creek, water rushing around her ankles. "I didn't know," she said.

"If you ever paid attention to anyone else, you would have noticed. It's not like it's invisible."

"Oh," Rose said as she stared at Lily. The anger disappeared from her face. "It's like that."

"Like what?" Lily asked, still mad. She tugged her socks off and wrung the water from them. If she laid them out on the rock, they might dry before she went home, at least enough that her mother wouldn't notice.

Rose shook her head. "Nothing," she said, but she cocked

her head to the side and looked at Lily as if witnessing something she had never seen before.

"Why are you staring at me?" Lily glared at her.

Rose hopped back up on the rock. Her feet dangled in the water. "You like him," she said.

"Of course I do. We're friends." It was true, but as she spoke, she suddenly realized it was more than that. It had happened so gradually, she wasn't aware of it until now. Seth made her feel lit from within, as if by a thousand fireflies.

# Chapter Fourteen

L ily woke with sheets wrapped around her legs. The sun wasn't up, but she kicked back the covers and stood. An image from last night of Seth standing on his porch, yelling after her, flashed through her mind. She shoved it aside, ran her fingers through her snarled hair, and dressed in jeans and a green T-shirt.

Then she reached for her cell phone. She didn't care that it was six in the morning. After three rings, it went to voice mail.

"Will," she said after the beep. "It's me. I need to talk to you. Soon." She clicked off, then walked out of her room and down the hall.

Last night, she had to count backward from one thousand before she could fall asleep. Even then, she woke with knots in her shoulders. Farmwork might loosen her muscles; in the garden, she didn't need to count. Death statistics didn't roll through her mind. She was looser there, her mind not filled with numbers and calculations. With luck, she could harvest some tulips and figure out how to tell Rose that Seth would be a better guardian for Antoinette.

It had taken her most of the night to arrive at that decision, but once she had, it made sense. Seth had known Antoinette longer. He cared about her. Most of all, it didn't bother him that she was some kind of miracle worker.

The window at the end of the hall was open and a warbler's song drifted in. Lily started down the stairs, counting each one. There were nine, which she should have remembered. The odd number made her skin itch.

Eleven paces to the kitchen. Not good.

"You're up early." Rose sat at the large oak table, holding a cup of coffee. Early-morning sunlight streamed through the back door, painting her hair as white as her skin.

Lily stopped at the entrance. She couldn't talk to Rose yet. Not before she worked out everything she wanted to say. "I'll be back," she said, hurrying to the stairs.

"Are you okay?" Rose asked.

No. She wasn't okay. She pushed her heels back until they hit the bottom stair. She moved carefully, imagining herself as a teenager. She was on thirteen when she reached the kitchen.

She shook her head and turned around. Rose watched but didn't say anything.

This time Lily pretended she was a Chinese empress with bound feet, taking dainty, careful steps. It worked. She entered the kitchen on twenty-two, a safe number finally, and sank into the chair across from Rose. The room smelled like fresh coffee and cinnamon.

"Counting?" Rose asked. "Stay there. I'll get you a cup of coffee."

Lily let her. If she got up, she'd start counting again. "I didn't think you'd be awake," she said to fill the space between them.

Rose took a blue mug from the cabinet next to the stove.

"Still load it up with milk and sugar?" When Lily nodded, Rose put two heaping teaspoons of sugar and a large splash of milk into the cup. "Sleeping's hard for me. My lungs fill with fluid. I start coughing as soon as my head hits the pillow."

"I'm sorry. I didn't know."

Rose sat down. "It's been going on awhile. I'm used to it." She handed Lily her coffee.

Lily put the mug to her lips. The confused thoughts from last night came tumbling back. Agreeing to be Antoinette's guardian when she was just a kid with special needs had been hard enough, but adding this weird *ability* to the mix made Lily want to sit on the porch and count each blade of grass.

"About yesterday—we need to talk," Rose said.

No. They didn't. Lily's foot twitched. She took a large sip of coffee.

Rose ran a hand through her hair. "I didn't want to keep secrets from you. Seth told me not to."

He was right, Lily thought.

"It's just that I was afraid you'd leave once you found out about her," Rose said.

The remark hit dangerously close to home. She took another sip of coffee. "I noticed that the white tulips are budding. I thought I'd harvest some of them this morning before it gets too hot."

"You can't just pretend it didn't happen," Rose said, an undercurrent of vulnerability in her voice.

Lily had to look away. She stared out the window, noting that low-hanging fog sat over the fields. "The fog should keep everything cool." Cutting flowers was best done in the morning when it wouldn't stress the plant. She knew the routine by heart. Cut the buds right before they bloomed. Strip the leaves and put the stems in a clean bucket of water so the flowers didn't wilt.

They would store some in the commercial freezer in the barn for close to a month. They had a small greenhouse where they forced bulbs and other off-season flowers to bloom in order to supply the antiques shops and restaurants that formed the town center, but most of their flowers came from the fields or hoop houses.

"Lily," Rose said. "We need to talk about this."

Lily tapped her fingers against her thigh. "Do you still keep a spare pair of pruning shears in there?" She indicated the drawer next to the pantry where her mother used to store twine, bits of ribbon, and anything else that might be useful on a quick trip to the garden.

"Don't ignore me," Rose said. "This is important."

Rose reached out, but Lily stood and took her mug to the sink. It was still half full, but she dumped out the remaining coffee. Then she opened the drawer. It had been a mess when she was a child and it was still a mess now. "At least this hasn't changed," she said under her breath as she fished through metal plant labels, florist's wire, and mismatched garden gloves.

"What's that supposed to mean?" Rose walked over to stand beside Lily.

"Nothing. Things are different. That's all." Lily found a pair of garden shears and grabbed the first two garden gloves she saw. One was pink and the other green. They were both for the left hand. Exasperated, she tossed them onto the counter.

Rose reached around Lily's shoulder, grabbed a right-handed pink glove from the drawer, and handed it to her. "It's a house. Not a museum. If you wanted it to stay the same, you shouldn't have left."

"I didn't mean it that way," Lily said as she put the glove on.

"Then what did you mean?" Rose's cheeks were flushed. This was the healthiest she had looked since Lily arrived.

"Everything's different. It would've been nice if some things had stayed the same. That's all."

"From where I sit, nothing's changed," Rose said. "You're still running away."

"Give me a break, Rose." Anxiety made her short. "You can't spring something like this on me and expect everything to be fine. You should have told me *everything* about Antoinette when you asked me to come home."

"How could I have told you?" Rose's voice went up a notch in both pitch and volume. "You wouldn't have believed me until you saw it for yourself. Seth didn't even believe until he saw Antoinette heal me."

She was right, but Lily couldn't admit that. "You should have told me."

"And you shouldn't have left in the first place," Rose snapped.

Lily stepped back as if slapped. "I called you every day. You never answered. You didn't want me here."

"You're right. I didn't want you here; I *needed* you here. I was sick, and I had a special-needs kid. You think you were scared? You have no idea what fear feels like." Rose was yelling now. "Antoinette's special ability shouldn't change anything, but if you're leaving you might as well go now."

Lily wanted to say she wasn't running away, but wasn't that exactly what she had been planning all morning?

There was a sharp knock at the door. It was probably Seth—someone else Lily was angry with—but she yanked the door open, grateful for the diversion. "What?" she snapped, then stepped back in surprise.

Will stood on the porch, his dark hair meticulously combed and his blue oxford shirt wrinkle-free despite the two-hour drive to Redbud.

"Lily Martin," he said as he opened his arms. "Just the girl I'm looking for."

"What are you doing here?" she asked. In her shock, she was abrupt.

"Do I need a reason beyond missing you?" he asked. He grinned, but something in his eyes said it was more than that.

"To drive two hours south without telling me you were coming? Yes, you need a better reason than that."

"Who is it?" Rose asked. She came up behind Lily and opened the door wider.

"Will Grayson." He pushed past Lily and held out his hand. "Lily's friend. You must be Rose."

After a hesitation, Rose took his hand. "I'm sorry. I don't remember Lily mentioning you."

Will shrugged. "Keeping me all to yourself, hmm Lils?" He smiled at Rose. Then he leaned down as if confiding a secret. "Can't blame her. Women have trouble staying away from me."

Rose gave a shocked laugh. "I can see why."

Lily took his arm. "Why don't I show you around the farm?"

"Wait." Rose pulled Lily into the family room. As soon as

they were out of earshot, Rose said, "You can't tell him about Antoinette. The fewer people who know about her ability, the safer she is." She squeezed Lily's arm.

"You're hurting me," Lily said as she disentangled herself. She was angry, but a small voice in the back of her head said Rose was right. She closed her eyes and counted to ten. "Fine."

Rose didn't look convinced.

"I won't tell him," Lily said. "Besides, what am I going to say? 'Meet my niece, the miracle worker?'" She looked over her shoulder. Will stood in the middle of the kitchen, his hands still in his pockets, whistling. "I'm just showing him the garden."

A pained look flashed across Rose's face. "I would have told you. Eventually. I just wanted you to get to know Antoinette first."

There was a loud thump from upstairs. Rose glanced at the ceiling. "Antoinette's awake. I'd better get her." Before leaving, she said, "I know I'm asking a lot. But I need you. *We* need you. Please don't go."

She didn't wait for Lily to answer. Which was just as good, because Lily had no idea what to say.

Will was still standing in the middle of the kitchen. When he saw her, he smiled. "Surprised you, didn't I?"

"You could say that."

"Rose doesn't look scary," he said, continuing the conversation they had started several days ago on her deck. "No horns—not that I can see anyway. No cloven hooves. Just your average run-of-the-mill sister."

"You never answered me," she said as she held the back door open for him. "Why are you here?"

Will followed her onto the porch. "Simple. You sounded scared on the phone. I'm here to help you feel better." He leaned in to her. "Whatever it takes."

She shoved him.

"Hmm, into the rough stuff." He raised his eyebrows and rubbed his shoulder. "That's all right. I meant what I said. Whatever. It. Takes. I'm your man."

"Seriously, why are you here?"

"You want serious. Okay. I can do that." He stopped smiling. "When you called me and said you couldn't take care of Antoinette, I was afraid you'd leave. I've known you long enough to know that if you did you'd regret it for the rest of your life.

"It might seem easier to walk away, but one day you'd wake up and realize that abandoning your niece was the biggest mistake you'd ever made. I left Covington at five this morning and drove here to make sure that doesn't happen."

Was her fear that obvious? She stared at him, not sure whether she should be grateful, or angry, for his interference.

Will jogged down the porch steps. At the bottom, he said, "Well, aren't you going to show me around the farm?"

Lily counted to ten before joining him.

"So where are the pigs?" he asked.

"It's not a pig farm." She stopped at Will's sharp intake of breath. Without looking up, she knew what had captured his attention. The oak and birch trees had blocked his view of the land from the porch, but as they walked Eden Farms spread out in front of them.

Lilacs bloomed around the farmhouse. Daffodils nodded from beds framing the house. Beyond that, the commercial flower fields stretched. They were striped red, pink, and purple as flowers sprouted from the soil. Pink clematis, blooming a month early, grew over the drying barn.

"You grew up here?" Will rocked back on his heels. "Don't get me wrong, I'm city through and through, but how could you leave this?"

"No pigs," she said, and she smiled for the first time that day.

# Chapter Fifteen

❧

A strange man leaned against the kitchen sink. Antoinette tried studying his face, but when she did it fractured into pieces like the Picasso painting she'd seen, *Weeping Woman*. Focusing on faces was always difficult, but today was worse than normal. She cocked her head to the right and squinted at a spot on the wall above the man's left shoulder.

He was tall and had dark hair like Seth, but that was the only way they were alike. This man was thin and lanky. Seth was covered with a hard layer of muscle. Unlike Seth's warm brown hair, this man's hair was so dark it was almost black. But the biggest difference was the way they spoke.

Seth was quiet, his movements controlled. Sometimes Antoinette thought she heard him thinking before he acted. This man's gestures were big. His voice loud. He held a blue coffee mug and waved his hands as he talked.

"The air smells sweeter here," he was saying. He pointed at Lily with his cup. Antoinette waited for coffee to splash over the edge. "Why didn't you tell me? Trying to keep this place all to yourself? I want to see all of Redbud's finest establishments. The grand tour."

Lily laughed. "I'll give you a tour, but there's nothing grand about it." She sat at the table across from Antoinette's mother. The air between them felt tense; neither woman looked at the other one.

Antoinette stomped her feet. New people kept arriving at the house. First Lily and now this man. She tucked her hands in tight against her shoulders and paced in a tight circle. The house was too loud. The refrigerator hummed. The faucet dripped. The coffeemaker hissed.

"How long are you staying?" her mother asked the man. She seemed anxious. That morning, when she told Antoinette about the new man, she had said, "You can't touch him. Do you understand?" She wouldn't let Antoinette go downstairs until she bobbed her head yes.

"As long as you'll have me," he said. He crossed his legs at the ankles. His shoes were shiny and black, with no mud on them at all.

Her mother glanced at Lily and frowned slightly as if she didn't like his answer.

"Will's a doctor," Lily said. "He could help if Antoinette—"

"Lily told me she has seizures," he said. "Is there a trigger? If you isolate the trigger and remove it, the seizures might stop."

"That's what I'm trying to do," her mother said, but her voice was so soft Antoinette didn't think he heard.

He crouched in front of Antoinette. "I met you once before. You were a little thing. Only three?" He looked to Lily as if for confirmation. When she nodded, he continued. "Your mom rushed you home before we could be properly introduced. My name is Will." He inclined his head toward her in an odd little bow.

Antoinette was captivated. She stole a glance at his eyes. They were a paler blue than the sky at dawn. What would his song sound like? Bright and fast, she decided, like creek water bubbling downstream. She reached for his cheek, but Lily pulled her back.

Antoinette growled. Lily ruined everything. *Go home!*

Lily sighed. "She's never going to like me."

*True.* Antoinette stomped her foot. *Don't like Lily.*

Will walked over to Lily and kissed the top of her head. "Don't forget what I said. She's just like everyone else."

That wasn't true. Antoinette knew she was different and she didn't like it.

The kitchen door opened and Seth came in, not looking at anyone. He went straight to the coffeepot and poured a cup of coffee. With his back still to them, he said, "It's going to be hot today. I thought I'd get started early. Lily, I could use your help. And I'd like to talk to you about last night." His voice turned up at the end, as if he was asking a question instead of making a statement.

Antoinette stretched up on her toes and walked over to him. *Pick me up!* She tapped his back.

"Okay, okay. I'll pick you up." Seth set his mug down and finally turned to face the room. When he did, his body stiffened.

Antoinette turned to see what he was looking at. Will had his hands on Lily's shoulders, his mouth bent low to her ear.

*Pick me up!* Antoinette bounced on her toes. For the first time, Seth ignored her.

Lily shifted sideways, away from Will, but he moved with her, his fingers twitching slightly against her shoulders.

"This is Lily's neighbor, Will," Antoinette's mother said. Her voice seemed loud in the silence. "Will, this is Seth. He owns part of the farm. We all grew up together."

Antoinette patted Seth's hand. He always picked her up when he came over. *Up! Up, up, up.*

"Ah," Will said, "so you're Seth."

"You have company." Seth's words were precise and clipped. "Lily, forget I asked. I'm sure you'd like to spend time with your friend." Then he walked out the door, leaving Antoinette standing alone in the center of the kitchen.

WILL'S CAR WAS a black so shiny Antoinette could see her reflection in the door. She crawled into the back beside her mother. After Seth left, they had spent the day driving through Redbud. They stopped at the farmers' market and the library. Now they were headed for Teelia's to go over preparations for the garden show.

Will drove fast. Each time he rounded a curve, Antoinette listed sideways into her mother. Once, she tried to catch her mother's hand, but she pulled away.

"Time moves slower here," Will said. "I don't even need my watch. I stopped wearing it somewhere past Lexington. Tucked it into my suitcase." He held up his left wrist. A white band of skin showed where his watch used to be.

Maybe he drove fast to catch the time he lost, Antoinette thought.

"Lily tells me you're an artist," Will said to Antoinette's mother.

"I used to be," her mother said. "I gave it up after Antoinette was born and I took over the farm."

"Do you miss it?" he asked. "I've seen the paintings around

Lily's house. The Kentucky landscapes. The yellow lily on blue china. You're good."

"I miss it sometimes, but I have other compensations now." She smiled at Antoinette before turning to Lily. "You kept those old paintings?"

"They reminded me of home," Lily said. "And you."

"It's the only art she has in her house," Will said. "Aside from your paintings, the place is barren."

Antoinette's mother released some of the tension in her body. She leaned forward and tentatively squeezed Lily's shoulder.

Will rounded another bend. This time, Lily touched his leg. "Slow down."

Antoinette didn't want him to stop. She liked the sense of flying along the road, of being thrown suddenly against her mother.

"Turn here." Lily pointed to the string of refurbished houses that made up the Main Street shops. Art's Floral, Knitwits, and several small antiques and craft stores. The Bakery Barn was next to Teelia's. Antoinette bounced with excitement. If she saw MaryBeth again, she would fix her for good this time.

"Park here." Lily indicated an open spot in front of Teelia's shop. "Every grand tour of Redbud includes a stop at the local yarn store."

Will pulled the car in and cut the engine. He squinted as he looked out the front window. "It's just like Mayberry, R.F.D. I didn't think places like this still existed."

"It has its share of issues," Lily said as they left the car.

For once, Antoinette agreed with her aunt. She thought of the old ladies who stared at her in the grocery store, and the kids who teased her at the library playground.

"We won't stay long," her mother said. "I just need to know

when Teelia wants us to come out to her place to load up her stuff for the show."

Knitwits occupied the first floor of a redbrick house with a large white porch. Bradford pear trees lined the property, their branches heavy with puffy white flowers. Antoinette could detect a whisper of music, but she didn't try hard to capture it. Her mother had stopped her from healing MaryBeth, and Antoinette wanted to finish what she started.

MaryBeth's name went through her mind like a song. She started on a high note, then slid down, flapping her hands with each syllable: *MaryBeth. MaryBeth.*

"We're not going to the Bakery Barn today," her mother said as she steered Antoinette toward Knitwits.

This was a dilemma. Antoinette wanted to see MaryBeth, but she liked Teelia. Once, at the farmers' market, Teelia had handed Antoinette Frank's lead line. The alpaca had hummed softly, then nuzzled her cheek with his soft nose.

Thinking of Frank helped Antoinette decide. She would follow her mother into Knitwits. She could visit MaryBeth when they left.

Teelia bustled out from behind the counter. Bead bracelets and bamboo knitting needles hung from a metal counter display. "Who might this be?" She nodded at Will.

"Will Grayson. At your service." He executed a little bow.

Teelia bobbed her head. "A gentleman. We don't get much of that around here."

"Will's my neighbor," Lily said. "He's down here visiting for a few days."

"Days. Weeks. Months," Will said. "Who knows, maybe

longer. This place is growing on me." He looked at Lily as he spoke.

"I thought we'd drop by and finalize plans for the show," Antoinette's mother said.

"I have my yarn ready," Teelia said. "I just need Seth to transport some things to the farm."

While her mother and Teelia discussed details about the show, Antoinette wandered off. The shop was filled with cubbyholes holding yarn in every color imaginable. A group of women sat at a table in mismatched chairs, knitting and chatting. Their voices formed a soft hum.

"The shop hasn't changed since I was little."

Antoinette was surprised to look up and see Lily standing behind her. Anxiety rolled off of her aunt in waves.

"Teelia tried to teach me to knit once," Lily said, "but I kept dropping my stitches. Your mom was good. I think I still have a scarf she made when she was just about your age."

Antoinette didn't like standing so close to Lily, but she didn't walk away. She liked hearing stories about her mother.

"We used to come here after school when the growing season ended. Our mother would sit with Teelia while Rose and I picked through the yarn. In the time it took me to cast on a row of stitches, your mom would be halfway finished with a scarf or a hat."

To Antoinette's consternation, her anger toward her aunt softened. That couldn't happen, not if she wanted everything to go back to normal. She stomped to the corner of the room, as far away from Lily as she could get.

She would *not* like her aunt. She sat in the corner and twisted her hands in front of her face, letting the voices from the women sitting at the table wash over her. She didn't budge even when she realized they were talking about her.

"Is she okay?" a woman wearing an orange flowered shirt said.

"Does she need help?" another said.

Antoinette growled.

Then Lily was there. She stood in front of Antoinette, shielding her from the women. She counted to ten and then said, "Rose, it's time to go."

"I'll be right—" Her mother stopped abruptly as the shop door snapped shut.

"I thought I saw you come in here," Eli said. The scent of cinnamon floated through the air as he hurried over to them.

Antoinette flapped her hands. Eli would take her to MaryBeth. She pushed herself up and walked toward him, but her mother, with Will following, blocked her path.

"Can't stay to talk today," her mother said to Eli. Her voice was artificially bright. "We have to get Antoinette back to the farm. She's not herself right now."

That wasn't true. Antoinette was fine.

"Take Antoinette to the car," she whispered to Lily. Her mother was usually gentle, but this time she shoved Antoinette into Lily's arms.

*No, no, no.* Antoinette screamed and reached for Eli. She needed to see MaryBeth.

"It's not my place," Will started, "but maybe—"

"You're right," her mother said. "It's not your place."

"Will, why don't you help me?" Lily said. She grabbed Antoinette under the arms.

Antoinette bucked and kicked. Lily started counting, but she held on tight. *No, no, no!* Antoinette wanted MaryBeth. *Let go of me!*

"We don't mind if she's a little under the weather," Eli said. "The last time y'all were in town, MaryBeth felt so much better after seeing Antoinette. She had a couple of real good days, but now she's in a bad way again. Seeing Antoinette would help."

He peered at Antoinette, and she reached for him. "Why don't you let me take her? MaryBeth's having trouble breathing. The doctors say she'll need a ventilator soon. A visit from this little girl sure would cheer her up."

Antoinette went still. She knew that healings never lasted, but this one had faded too fast. Something was wrong.

Lily took advantage of Antoinette's momentary calm to head for the door.

"Next time," her mother said. She followed Lily but stopped just in front of the door, letting Lily carry Antoinette outside while keeping Eli inside the shop. "I'm so sorry about MaryBeth," her mother said.

And Antoinette realized it was the only true thing her mother had said since Eli entered the shop.

# Chapter Sixteen

❧

The garden show was in a little over a week. Music would be in the drying barn. Art would be in the house garden. Those two venues would be prepared later in the week. Tonight Lily and Will set up tables in the night garden for the food vendors. Rose directed them while Antoinette walked in circles.

As Lily worked, she thought of Eli. He was going to be a problem. Yesterday, at Knitwits, he had stared at Antoinette as if she were a science experiment. She might not be cut out to be Antoinette's guardian, but she didn't want harm to come to her.

She was surrounded by puzzles she couldn't solve. How to patch things up with Rose? How to get out of being Antoinette's guardian? How to keep Eli away from Antoinette? This was why she liked math—in math, there was always a set solution.

"How about here?" Will asked as he and Lily tugged a table away from the stone wall. He tapped the table twice. He should look out of place in his khakis and polo shirt, but he didn't.

"Back a little," Rose said. "Closer to the wall." She rested on a bench beside the fountain, her portable oxygen tank at her side. That afternoon, she had lost her breath walking from the kitchen to her room. She started carrying the tank after that.

They tugged the table into place and looked to Rose for approval. When she nodded, they moved on to the next table.

To Lily, the night garden felt magical. In addition to the bountiful flowers, concrete benches were scattered throughout the garden, and water trickled from a fountain. Plumes of astilbe swayed in front of the fountain. The plant had airy white flowers that sprouted above the dark green glossy foliage. Astilbe meant . . . Lily couldn't remember. How could she have forgotten?

Will grabbed one end of the table. "Ready?"

"Wait a minute," Lily said. "I have to get the Victorian flower book. I'll be right back."

By the time she returned, Will had maneuvered the table into place. Still holding the book, Lily moved to help him.

"Go sit down," Will said. He plucked the book from her hands and tossed it onto the nearest bench, one right next to Antoinette.

"I'll help," Lily said.

"And lose this chance to impress you with my manly prowess?" Will said. "No way."

"You're incorrigible. You know that?" Lily asked, but she sat down.

"God, I hope so. Where's the fun otherwise?"

Lily ignored him. She had known what quality astilbe represented years ago when she and her father planted the flowers. She could picture him tamping down dirt around the astilbe, see him scattering mulch over the ground. The flowers were still there; everything else, though, was gone.

"What are you doing?" Rose asked.

They hadn't had a chance to talk much since Will's arrival, and Lily hated the tension that had grown between them. Even more, she hated knowing that she would make everything worse when she told Rose she couldn't be Antoinette's guardian. "I can't remember what astilbe means," she said.

Antoinette started walking in tight circles around the bench where Lily sat, so she turned away. If she didn't see Antoinette, maybe she wouldn't start counting.

"Do you think Seth will join us?" Lily tried to sound casual, as if she was just making conversation, but she really did wonder. He hadn't been around much since Will showed up.

Rose glanced surreptitiously toward Will. "I don't think so."

Last night, after they had returned from town, Seth had turned to Will. "You're staying here, I suppose?" His words were careful, his face expressionless.

"If the ladies will have me," Will said with a half smile. "I'll earn my keep. Free physicals for all." His grin was infectious. Rose and Lily had laughed, but Seth left without saying a word.

A soft breeze ruffled the pages of the flower book. At the sound, Antoinette stopped pacing and moved closer. She seemed intrigued. The book was open to a picture of daisies, and she tapped it three times.

"She wants to know what they mean," Rose said.

"Innocence," Lily said, picking up the book but not looking at it.

Antoinette leaned forward and lost her balance. Lily automatically grabbed her before she hit the ground. "You okay?"

Antoinette growled and smacked Lily's hands.

"Are you sure you weren't a baby wrangler in a prior life?" Will asked as he pulled a table in place.

"No more than you were a priest," Lily said.

Antoinette resumed walking in tight circles. When she noticed Lily watching, she growled.

"A priest isn't out of the question." Will raised his eyebrows. "A dark confessional booth has possibilities."

"That's over the top, even for you."

Will grinned. "When will you learn, Lils? I'm a man of extremes."

Lily turned another page. There it was. "Astilbe. *I'll be waiting*," she read. "Can't believe I forgot it."

LILY DIDN'T RETURN to the house with everyone else but sat alone in the darkening garden, listening to the sounds around her. Most people thought it was quiet in the country, but they were wrong. Horses called to each other over their stalls. Cicadas buzzed in the trees. Creek water gurgled over rocks.

And now a violin sang in the distance.

Now was as good a time as any to talk to Seth about being Antoinette's guardian. She stood and followed the stone path to the drying barn. Pieces of a melody floated through the early-evening air, and she pictured Seth, eyes closed, violin under his chin, swaying as he skimmed the bow across the strings.

When she reached the barn, a faint beam of light shone beneath the door. Quietly, she eased it open.

He stood at the far end of the barn, his back to her, a single light shining down on him. Even if Lily had wanted to look elsewhere she couldn't. She had missed hearing him play, missed watching him transform into someone carefree.

Their first kiss had happened here in the drying barn, and she flashed back to that day. It was autumn, and they were both sixteen. Sunlight filtered through cracks in the old wood slats, and the air was crisp with the scent of wood smoke. Seth took off his jacket and spread it over a straw bale.

"I thought we were going hiking," Lily said as he pulled her down next to him.

He picked up a twig and scratched lines on the dirt floor. "I've been thinking," he said.

"About what?" She leaned against his shoulder.

"Do you think God has a reason for all of this?"

She was used to his odd questions. Last week they had been sitting on the rock that rose out of the middle of the creek when he said, "What if this is all a dream?"

"If it is," Lily had said, thinking of her need to number everything, "it's not a very good one."

Now she frowned at him. "All of what?"

"This." He waved the stick in the air, indicating her, the barn, everything. "I've been thinking that maybe my dad is . . . you know, the way he is, for a reason. Maybe something good will come from it." He drew three parallel lines in the dirt.

Lily thought for a moment. If God had a purpose, she didn't see it. "I don't know," she said, choosing her words carefully. "I think things are just the way they are—whether for bad or for good, there's no reason—and you learn to live with it."

Seth frowned and Lily could almost see him considering her words. He had always been serious, sometimes too much so. He tossed the stick aside and ran his foot across the dirt, smearing the lines.

"The whole town knows about my dad," he finally said. "That's what most people see when they look at me. At least the bad parts, anyway. No one talks about the person he is when he isn't drinking."

"That's not true—"

He laughed. "Really? Haven't you lived in Redbud long enough? When's the last time you heard anyone talk about his skill with the violin?" He rested his elbows on his knees and clasped his hands together. He had grown taller in the past year, and his hair was longer. When he leaned forward, it brushed the skin beneath his eyes.

Lily didn't want to admit that he was right. Cora and Teelia whispered about Seth in church, saying he was too serious for someone his age and that it was his father's fault. The kids at school snickered when he walked down the hall. It wasn't as bad as their treatment of her, but it was close.

"You're the only one who sees *me*. Not my messed-up family. Just me. Do you know what a gift that is? To be able to be myself around someone?"

The air was electric. She felt hot and cold at the same time. If she leaned forward just a bit, their lips would touch. "Being with you is easy," she said. It was true. She never needed to count when she was with him.

He wrapped his arm around her hip and pulled her close. He leaned his forehead against hers. "We fit together."

Lily closed her eyes when he tangled his hands in her hair. He smelled like autumn leaves and fresh tobacco. When he kissed her, it felt like coming home, and Lily realized that love grew in familiar places.

Now, as she watched him play, she thought of how much she missed the freedom to be completely herself with someone. She was close to Will, would even say she loved him, but she kept part of herself from him in a way she never had with Seth.

"I know you're there," Seth said as he finished the piece he'd been playing.

She walked deeper into the barn. It was fully dark outside now, and the cicadas sang. "I didn't mean to interrupt," she said. "I was on the way back to the house when I heard you playing. Haydn. Right?"

"You remembered." He took a well-worn chamois cloth from the case and wiped down the violin.

"Why didn't you join us in the night garden?" she asked.

"I didn't want to interfere with things between you and Will." He kept his back to her, but his shoulders tightened at Will's name.

Lily wanted to say there wasn't anything going on between her and Will, but of course that wasn't quite true. She watched as he put the violin in the case, then snapped it shut.

"I've been thinking," Seth said. He was standing so close that she felt the heat from his body. "About what you said the other night. You were right. I should have told you about Antoinette— her special abilities."

This was her chance. Seth loved Antoinette. He'd be a perfect guardian for her. "About Antoinette. I need to ask—"

But he wasn't paying attention. He kept talking. "You have to know that you did mean something to me. You still do."

Lily was too surprised to respond. All thoughts of asking him to be Antoinette's guardian left her.

"I won't interfere with your life," Seth said as he picked up his violin, "because I don't want to hurt you again. But I need you to know that breaking up with you is the biggest mistake I ever made. I *do* care about you, and if I thought that you would've believed what Antoinette can do, I'd have told you, no matter what Rose said." Then he turned and walked out of the barn, leaving Lily staring at the door as it shut behind him.

## ROSE'S JOURNAL
*August 2009*

————+————

I HOIST ANTOINETTE over the fence between our house and Seth's. Since she healed me, everything is easier. I don't run out of breath, and it's been a year since I've had any chest pain. But I can't escape the guilt of knowing that my health comes at a price.

Over the past year, Seth and I have watched Antoinette carefully. We still don't know *exactly* how she works her miracles, but we do know that for the healing to work she must be touching the person or plant or animal.

I miss holding her hand, and I let my fingers linger against her shoulder for a moment before I slide the painting I'm carrying between the fence rails. I'm her mother; she's my child. I want to hold her, to pull her against me—but I can't. The cost is too great.

Once through the fence, I help her up the steps to Seth's house. My hands shake as I knock on the door. I'm not good at thank-yous.

As soon as he opens the door, I thrust out the painting. "For you," I say. It's a rendering of the creek that runs through the back of our properties, the spot where a large flat rock sits in the middle of the water. I haven't painted since leaving school and doing so felt good, but I'm unsure of myself in a way I never was when I was younger.

"Take it." I stumble over my words. "Without you, I would have had to sell the farm."

"The rock," he says as he accepts the painting. His smile is bittersweet. "I spent a lot of time there."

"We all did."

"It's still there." He looks sheepish. "I checked. The first night I was back."

This is a side of Seth I don't often see: shy, soft.

He stands back to let us in. His house is old, like ours. The wood floors are scratched in places, and the French doors leading into the living room sag slightly in the middle. The gray stone fireplace is flanked by a set of bookcases filled with books and photographs.

"Did you build these?" I ask. The wood is solid. I imagine them standing long after the house has fallen down around them.

Seth nods. "I made them for my mother. She loved this room."

It's strange hearing him talk about his parents. I know he spoke to Lily about them, but he rarely did so with me.

Antoinette plops down on the soft beige couch. Her legs stick out from her cutoffs like twin toothpicks. She bounces on the couch, shrieking as she does. I touch her shoulder to calm her, but it doesn't help.

"She's happy," he says. "Let her bounce."

I love the way Seth takes Antoinette in stride.

He holds the painting over the fireplace. "I think it should go here."

"It looks nice," I say. I feel a flush of pride.

"I need a hammer," Seth says. "Be right back."

When he leaves, I examine the bookcase. The wood is

beautiful. Oak stained a rich mahogany color. The streaks of red set off the wood grain. On the middle shelf, beside a stack of books about music therapy, is a picture of Seth and his mother. She has her arm looped around his waist.

When he returns, carrying a step ladder and tools, I nod at the photo. "Your mom was really pretty, especially when she smiled."

He pops open the ladder and climbs up. "Hand me the painting." I hand it to him and he says, "That was the problem. My dad liked to own things. Pretty things. She was just one more possession."

He nods at the painting. "Is it centered?"

I step back and look. "A little high."

He lowers it slightly. "Better?"

I nod and glance at Antoinette, who seems happy twisting her head from side to side and flicking her fingers.

Seth presses a nail into the wall to mark the spot where he'll hang the painting. "He wasn't all bad, my dad," he says. It seems important to him that I know this. "After all, he's the one who taught me to play the violin."

I pick up the photo of his mother. I wonder how she felt about Seth's father. "You don't need to explain," I say. I set the photo back on the shelf, causing some books to slide down. When they do, another picture falls out.

It's of Lily. She's sitting on the creek bank, her arms around her knees. Though the photo is black and white, the sun flashes in her dark hair.

I miss Lily as much as I miss holding Antoinette's hand.

Seth taps a nail into the wall and motions for me to hand him the painting. He hangs it and then sits down on the top ladder step. "I think we're programmed to love our families no matter how screwed up they are."

I look down at the picture of Lily and nod.

Seth follows my gaze. "Have you talked to her?"

I shake my head.

"She'd come home if you asked." He takes the picture from me, holding it gently, as if it's something precious.

Unlike me, Lily forgives easily. But I'm afraid. What if by ignoring her, I pushed her away? "She won't," I say. "Not after the way I treated her."

"Of course she will. She's your sister."

But I shake my head. "I can't call her." I'd rather live with the fantasy that one day Lily and I will reconcile than contact her and discover that I have succeeded in pushing her away forever.

# Chapter Seventeen

Antoinette concentrated on following her mother. The market was busy on Saturdays and getting lost would be easy. The people clumped around the booths could shift, engulf her mother, and then poof—it would be like she never existed at all.

The largest crowd surrounded the Eden Farms' booth; they had the biggest and brightest flowers at the market. People milled about under the green awning, examining black-eyed Susans and purple coneflowers that shouldn't bloom for another two months.

"There are too many people here," her mother said, frowning. She walked carefully, shielding Antoinette from the crowd. A knot of old ladies stood outside of their booth. "Excuse me," her mother said as she and Antoinette eased by them.

Antoinette took two big steps to stay close to her. Normally, she loved crowds—so many people to touch, so many songs to hear. Today was different.

Today it seemed like death sat on her mother's shoulder. She struggled to catch her breath, and she walked even more slowly than normal. As Antoinette followed her, a marigold pushed from the soil, and unaware, her mother stepped on it, flattening its orange petals and filling the air with a sharp scent. Antoinette stopped, mesmerized by the crumpled flower. She tried to move, but her feet tangled, and she pitched forward.

Right before she hit the ground, her mother caught her. "Are you okay?" she asked. She was breathing hard. The short walk from their van to the booth had worn her out.

*Yes.* The word was small and simple. Three letters. *Y-E-S.* Antoinette opened her mouth. A high-pitched squeal came out.

Her mother quickly squeezed Antoinette's hand. "Come on," she said. "You don't want to be late for delivery day."

Faintly, she heard her mother's song through their linked hands, but Antoinette needed all of her concentration to keep up. Healing would have to wait.

One of the old women gathered around the booth turned to Antoinette's mother. "Bless your heart," she said. "Stuck with that retarded girl. As if you don't have enough to deal with."

*Retarded.* The word was a slap across Antoinette's face. It was supposed to mean "slow." It really meant "worthless." *Worth. Less.* Antoinette groaned and curled forward.

"Come on, Antoinette." Her mother tugged her hand.

Antoinette couldn't straighten. The sun bit through her thin cotton T-shirt.

"Poor thing," the old woman said.

"Get out of my booth," her mother said, the words clipped and sharp.

With a sniff the woman shuffled off, and the pressure on Antoinette's shoulders eased.

"Crazy old woman," her mother said. She knelt in front of Antoinette and tapped her first two fingers against her nose. "Look at me."

Antoinette fixed her gaze on a gauzy cloud over her mother's left shoulder.

Long ago, her mother had brought home a prism. "Look, Antoinette," she had said before shining a flashlight through the glass triangle. "All these colors were hidden in the white light. The prism broke it open."

Antoinette's brain was like that prism. In her mind, faces shattered. It was confusing and disorienting, like looking at a puzzle with the pieces scattered over a table.

"Please, Antoinette. I need to know you're listening." Her mother tapped her nose again. The pain in her mother's voice was worse than looking at her dissembled face. Antoinette flicked her gaze from the cloud to her mother, then back again.

It was enough.

"Don't listen to that woman," her mother said. "Everyone's life is hard in some way. Yours just happens to be easier to see than most. Do you understand?"

Slowly, Antoinette looked into her mother's eyes, holding her gaze until her own eyes burned.

"Thank you," her mother said, and Antoinette could feel relief in her voice.

Her mother straightened and looked around the booth. "Where's Seth?" She guided Antoinette toward the back of the tent where they looked across the grassy square separating the market from the parking lot. Seth was at the van, unloading planters of early tulips and late daffodils. When he saw them, he jogged across the grass.

"Ready to go, Antoinette?" he asked as he tousled her hair.

She stretched up on her toes. Saturday was the day she helped Seth deliver flowers to stores and restaurants around town. She loved delivery day.

"Is Lily here yet?" her mother asked.

"I didn't know she was coming." He glanced over his shoulder, an odd look on his face. Antoinette recognized it at once: longing. She imagined she looked like that when she watched kids at the playground—she wanted to be like them.

"She and Will are meeting me here. I want Lily to handle the deliveries today," her mother said. "She and Antoinette need to get to know each other."

Antoinette stepped away from her mother. *No*, she thought. A low moan filled her throat. Seth did delivery day, not Lily. Everything was changing. Her knees buckled, and she dropped to the ground, screaming as she fell.

The concrete stung, but Antoinette didn't care. She screamed until her throat was raw.

"What's wrong?" Lily's voice cut through the noise of the crowd.

"You're late," her mother said.

*No! No! No!* Antoinette kicked the concrete. She did not want to go with Lily.

"Sorry," Lily said. "We lost track of time."

A crowd gathered around them. Someone said, "Would you look at that."

"What a shame," someone else said. The words whooshed through Antoinette's ears, and she screamed again.

"It's my fault," Will said. "I asked Lily to walk through the woods with me."

"All right," Seth said to the people who had gathered to watch. "Show's over."

No one left.

Then Antoinette heard Will. "At least back up," he said.

"It's delivery day," her mother said.

Antoinette stopped screaming and focused on her mother's voice.

"Doesn't Seth—" Lily started.

"I thought you could do it today." Her mother grabbed Antoinette's wrists and tugged. "With Antoinette."

*No,* Antoinette wanted to say. *I don't want things to change.*

"You mean the two of us? Alone?"

"That's exactly what I mean," her mother said.

"I'll get her," Seth said. Antoinette let herself go limp, but that didn't stop him from picking her up.

"Will, come with me," Lily said.

"You don't need me, Lils," Will said.

Antoinette banged her head against Seth's arm. *Not Lily. Not Lily. Not Lily.*

"She doesn't like me," Lily said.

Antoinette stiffened until her spine curved like a backward C. It didn't make a difference; Seth tightened his grip until she couldn't twist free.

"This is why I called you home, Lily," her mother said. "Did you think it would be easy?"

"Well, I didn't think it would be like this," Lily said quietly.

Will pulled her aside, but they were close enough for Antoinette to hear what he said. "When I was in the hospital, you told me stories about growing up here. Just from your voice I could tell how much you missed this place, how much you missed Rose, Antoinette. Don't let fear drive you away. You'll be fine, Lils."

They would *not* be fine. Antoinette kicked her feet, but Seth buckled her into the van's passenger's seat anyway.

Will held the driver's door for Lily. "You can do this."

"I can do this," Lily repeated, but she didn't sound sure of herself.

"We'll meet you at Cora's when you're finished," her mother said.

Antoinette shook her head. *No, no, no!*

Lily slid in behind the wheel. Antoinette sat at the very edge of her seat, as far from Lily as possible. Lily did likewise, leaning against the driver's-side door as she started the van.

As they pulled away, Antoinette forced herself to look directly into her mother's eyes. She didn't break eye contact until they turned out of the market and her mother disappeared.

ANTOINETTE STUCK HER hand out of the van window, letting the wind whistle through the spaces between her fingers.

"I can run into Art's Floral if you want to wait in the van," Lily said as she drove around back to the service entrance. Her voice was so soft Antoinette barely heard her.

Lily's hair swung down her back in a loose ponytail. Antoinette imagined grabbing a handful of it and yanking as hard as she could.

When they stopped, Antoinette bounced on the seat, making the springs squeak. She knocked her hand against the door. *Out.* She looped the word through her brain, attempting to push it past her lips, but the only sound that came out was a low groan.

Lily hopped out and opened the van's back door. Antoinette smacked her hands against the door. She *always* went into Art's. *Out. Out. Out.* She stamped her feet against the floor and flapped her hands.

"Okay, okay," Lily said. She opened the door and stood back. "Do you need help?"

Antoinette pressed her elbows against her sides and wiggled her fingers. *Out. Out. OUT!* She focused all of her energy into pushing the word past her lips. "Ouuu!"

Lily wiped her hands on her jeans. "Rose and Will are both crazy," she mumbled as she reached for Antoinette and unbuckled the seat belt. "I don't know what I'm doing."

Antoinette fell forward. Lily caught her and eased her to the ground. "You okay?" she asked. Without waiting for an answer, she headed toward the back of the van. "Five," she said. "Can't stop on five." She returned to Antoinette's side.

When she noticed Antoinette staring, Lily blushed. "I don't like odd numbers." She pressed herself against the passenger's door and started walking again. Her steps were smaller this time, and she counted out loud, ending on nine.

After three tries, she made it to the back of the van in six paces. "Thank God," she said. She grabbed two buckets of cosmos and set them down. Then she reached for a couple of pails of hoop-house zinnias.

"You want to carry some?" Lily asked.

Antoinette hopped up and down.

Lily held out a small metal pail, and Antoinette curled her fingers around its handle. She worked hard to smooth her gait so water didn't slosh from the pail as she walked. This time, she wasn't the only one with a problem. Lily had to retrace her path twice before she landed on an even number, and they finally walked through the service entrance.

Antoinette loved the back room of Art's Floral. A row of glass-front refrigerators filled with roses, irises, and lilies lined one wall. Spools of ribbon in every color imaginable hung above a worktable. Shelves of glass vases bounced light around the room. Most of the flowers were cut and dying, so there wasn't much music in the room, but as long as Antoinette kept her hands tight against her body the emptiness didn't overwhelm her.

The shop's owner was a thin woman named Ileen. She had dishwater-brown hair and never looked at Antoinette. Ileen was in the back room waiting for them. She flipped her hair over her shoulder and frowned when she saw Lily. "I'm surprised to see you, Lily. Where's Seth? He normally handles deliveries."

"He's taking a break. It's just us today," Lily said as she handed her an invoice.

Ileen accepted the paper, making sure not to touch Lily. "I'll get the check. Don't let her touch anything." She nodded toward Antoinette as she left.

"Don't worry," Lily whispered to Antoinette when they were alone. "She was a bitch in high school too, but don't tell your mother I said that. They used to be friends. Not anymore, I guess."

Lily fiddled with the flowers in one of the buckets. Her lips moved as she ran her fingers over the petals of a zinnia, and Antoinette heard her counting.

"Twenty-six petals," she said with a glance at Antoinette. "That's a good number. Even. I don't have to do anything to fix it. Sometimes if it's an odd number, I have to pinch off a petal to make it even."

Antoinette understood the need to bring order to things. Without thinking, she moved closer to Lily.

"It's like an itch that gets bigger unless I scratch it." Lily ran her fingers over the orange flower petals. "But this one's good."

A potted pothos plant sat on a shelf across the room, its leaves curly and brown around the edges. Antoinette bounced over to the plant. It was potted so there was no point in sticking her fingers into the soil. She couldn't pull water to the roots from anywhere else.

She flapped her hands to get Lily's attention, but her aunt was busy pinching the petals off of a fuchsia cosmos.

Antoinette stretched up on her toes and walked over to the sink. She smacked her palm against the stainless-steel basin. It made a ringing sound, but Lily didn't look up.

A green plastic watering can sat on the floor next to the sink. Antoinette tried to nudge it with her foot, but her muscles contracted, and she kicked the can, sending it across the room.

Lily jumped. "What in the world?"

Antoinette bounced and flapped her hands, bringing them down against the sink. Then she pointed at the dying plant.

Lily followed her direction. "Oh," she said, grasping Antoinette's intent. "You'd think a florist would know better." She picked up the watering can, filled it at the sink, and then watered the plant. "I never could stand to see them dying."

Antoinette wanted to say she couldn't either, but the words wouldn't come. Instead, she stood next to her aunt and flapped her hands, hoping it looked like *Thank you*.

# Chapter Eighteen

～

Cora's Italian Restaurant was their last delivery stop. Lily parked the van and walked to the passenger's side, but this time when she leaned in, Antoinette didn't recoil. Instead, she climbed out and laid her cheek against Lily's hand. Her long blonde hair fell forward, covering her face.

Something inside Lily softened, and the need to count faded. "I missed you," she whispered. When Antoinette didn't move, she continued, "I have pictures of you when you were a baby. I stared at them every night before I went to sleep, wondering what you looked like now."

Antoinette cocked her head to the left. Slowly, she curved her arm around Lily's waist and tapped her back.

"The real you is better than anything I imagined." Lily brushed her hand through Antoinette's hair. It was as thin and fine as it had been when she was a baby. A seedling of hope sprouted in Lily's heart. Maybe she could be Antoinette's guardian after all. Maybe this time, she wouldn't disappoint Rose.

The restaurant door opened, and Seth walked out. "I thought you might need some help," he said. He turned to Antoinette. "Bet you were a big help today."

She stretched up on her toes, flapped her hands, and shrieked. Lily now knew that was her happy noise.

"Did she carry flowers into Art's?" he asked. "I forgot to tell you that's our routine." Lily couldn't help but notice that he was awkward with her, more like a stranger than someone with whom he shared a past.

"Antoinette told me," Lily said. "It's amazing how much she can communicate without words."

Seth walked to the back of the van. "If I've learned anything about Antoinette, it's not to underestimate her."

Antoinette walked in circles on her toes. "Don't think I've forgotten about you, kiddo," Seth said. "Brush up on your Brahms. I'll stump you yet."

For a moment, he was the boy Lily remembered. She forgot herself and touched his arm. "Thank you for being here when I wasn't."

He flinched and pulled away. "I'll unload the flowers," he said as he grabbed two buckets of hydrangea puffs. "Rose is inside waiting for you."

At the mention of her mother's name, Antoinette started across the parking lot to the restaurant entrance. She moved slowly. Several times her knees folded, and she almost fell, but each time she caught herself before hitting the ground.

"I didn't mean anything beyond 'thank you,'" Lily said, confused by his reaction. "I'll leave you alone if that's what you'd like." She hurried to catch up with Antoinette.

They were at the restaurant entrance when Seth called out, "You look comfortable with each other. Like you belong together."

Lily paused at the door. Her fear had vanished in the hours

she and Antoinette had spent together that afternoon. "You're right," she said. "We do." She put her hand on her niece's shoulder and helped her inside.

Cora's Italian Restaurant had changed. The black-and-white floor tile was the same, and the scents of garlic and oregano still hung in the air, but everything else was different.

Years ago, Cora's had looked like a thousand other small town restaurants: cheap, plastic, nothing breakable, and everything easy to hose down.

Now the walls were painted eggplant purple. The metal tables had been replaced with tall red booths sporting cushions covered in a hodgepodge of patterns: zebra stripes, cheetah prints, and splashy old florals. The drop ceiling had been removed, exposing stainless-steel air ducts. Thousands of white Christmas lights were laced through boxwood topiaries that dotted the restaurant.

Rose and Will were waiting for them. "You're both in one piece," Rose said. She seemed tired and had her portable oxygen tank with her, but she looked pleased with herself.

"Antoinette was a big help," Lily said. "We're getting to know each other."

Antoinette gave Rose the same half hug she had given Lily in the parking lot. Then she stuck her hands into a boxwood that had been shaped into a cat.

"What'd I tell you, Lils?" Will said. "Just like everyone else, right?"

"Don't get cocky. Just because you were right once—"

Will pressed a hand to his chest. "Once? You wound me."

"What do you think of the place?" Cora asked, appearing from behind the bar next to the hostess station. She had bundled her long dark hair into a knot. It was more gray than black now, but her face was smooth, as if time were afraid to touch her. "Rose redid the place a few years ago. Said she needed the extra money. I have no idea how she managed for so long without any family around."

Cora was a busybody, and while she never meant for her words to sting, they did.

"She's here now," Will said, nodding at Lily. He didn't touch her, but his presence steadied her.

"I managed just fine," Rose said as she tried to keep Antoinette's hands out of the boxwood.

Cora turned to Antoinette. "I've got something special for you. You want to come to the kitchen with me?"

Antoinette crossed over to Cora and took her hand.

Before they left, Cora narrowed her eyes at Lily. "Your mom and dad would be proud of you for coming home. Don't disappoint them." Without another word, she guided Antoinette through green double doors that led to the kitchen.

Lily was mute for several long seconds. When she found her voice, she said, "Will Antoinette be okay?" She was surprised by how protective she felt of her niece.

Rose threaded her way through the maze of booths and oak tables with ladder back chairs. "Cora's good with her. Besides, she's probably got chocolate back there. Antoinette will do anything for chocolate."

Waitresses dressed in black and white circled through the room, polishing empty tables and folding napkins. The clink of silverware and plates echoed through the room.

"Eccentric place," Will said, taking in the decor.

Rose picked a booth against the far wall and slid in.

Lily sat across from Rose with Will next to her. He leaned down and whispered to her. "It's like a date."

Lily elbowed him. He was so thin, she connected with his ribs more forcefully than she meant to, and he winced.

"You did a good job," Lily said to Rose. "I would have never thought to put all of this together." Separately, the purple, red, and green seemed too strong to ever stand together. Instead, it reminded Lily of the wildflowers in the field behind the farm—beautiful in an unexpected way.

The door to the back room opened and a waitress came in, arms loaded with boxes of flowers. Lily had wondered at Rose's choices when she had picked them: blue irises, green and white hydrangea puffs from the greenhouse, and bright purple hyacinths. As she looked around the dining room, the flowers made sense.

For the first time since arriving home, Lily felt at peace. She leaned into Will, grateful he was there.

There was a bang and a clatter of metal from the kitchen. Rose winced. "Antoinette."

They all turned toward the kitchen, just in time to see Antoinette wobble through the doors. Cora followed, a bright red splat across her white apron.

"Oh Cora," Rose said. "I'm sorry."

Cora held up her hand. "It wasn't her fault. The staff knows better than to leave a pan of Bolognese sauce on the counter where she can grab it."

Antoinette swiveled her face toward Rose and raised her hands.

Lily added another word to her growing lexicon of Antoinette-speak. Raised hands equals *up!*

Rose lifted Antoinette across her lap. The little girl wiggled against the cushions, rocking the booth with her motion.

"Seth finished unloading the flowers," Cora said. "Now he's helping me with a load of fresh tomatoes." She wiped her hands on her apron. "I'm going to check on him, and then I've got something special for you. Antoinette's already tried it, haven't you?" Cora tried to catch Antoinette's eyes, but Antoinette looked away. "Maybe next time," she said, walking away.

Rose shifted. "Switch seats with me for a minute? I've got to use the restroom."

As Lily took Rose's place, Antoinette whimpered. She stretched across Lily toward Rose. If Antoinette was a flower, Lily thought, she would be lavender heather: loneliness.

Lily ran her fingers through Antoinette's hair. "She'll be back. I promise." When she looked up, Will was staring at her.

"You're different here," he said. "Looser. More relaxed." This was Will the doctor speaking. Thoughtful, observant—with anyone else she would have felt uncomfortable.

Antoinette slapped her hands against the wall. Lily touched her shoulder to steady her. There were only a few families in the dining room. No one seemed to notice Antoinette's agitation.

"Some people just fit places. You fit here." His smile was bittersweet. "I wish I had known you when you were growing up."

Lily laughed. "No, you don't. I was the strange kid everyone avoided."

"I wouldn't have avoided you."

Lily knew he probably believed that, but everyone had avoided her when she was younger, everyone except Rose and Seth.

Rose returned before Lily could respond. She was grateful for the interruption; her feelings for Will were complicated.

"Diuretics," Rose said with a shrug. "I can't stay out of the bathroom for long." The bathroom was only a short walk away, but Rose was winded from the effort.

Antoinette shrieked.

"See, I told you she'd be back," Lily said as she slid out of the booth and tried to stand up. When she did, her feet tangled with Rose's and she fell. As she went down, she flung out her left hand.

She felt it snap when she landed.

Pain shot through her hand and up her arm. She curled her body into a ball, her hand cradled in her lap. The last two fingers on her left hand were bent backward.

"Lily!" Will knelt beside her.

"Are you okay?" Rose crouched on Lily's other side. "Your hand. I think it's broken."

Rose and Will hovered over Lily, shielding her from the view of others in the room, for which she was grateful. She felt light-headed. She sat up and put her head between her knees. There was a soft scuffle to her right. Then she felt a little hand on her shoulder.

"I'm okay," she said through the haze of pain. She looked at her hand. Her last two fingers were fixed at a ninety-degree angle against the back of her hand.

"I'm going to be sick," she whispered.

The little hand she felt on her shoulder inched down her arm to her hand. At the touch, electricity sparked through Lily's skin. She cried out and arched her back.

Antoinette was next to her, eyes closed, humming an odd little song.

"Antoinette, no!" Rose yelled, but it was too late.

The spark of pain fanned into a blaze.

Lily groaned as her bones repositioned themselves under her skin.

"Holy shit!" Will said.

Lily's hand burned until she couldn't stand it anymore.

Then, just as suddenly, the pain stopped. She opened her eyes, and when she looked down she gasped.

Her hand was perfectly whole.

"Lils, your hand." Will's blue eyes were wide.

Lily curled her fingers into a fist. "It doesn't hurt."

He grabbed her hand and turned it over. "It was broken. I saw it." He traced the bones from the tips of her fingers to the base of her hand.

"No," Rose said. She caught Lily's eye and slowly shook her head. *Don't tell*, she mouthed.

"It couldn't have been broken." Rose leaned forward, shielding her daughter. "I don't think anyone else saw," she whispered to Lily.

Antoinette moaned. Then her eyes rolled back, and she began to shake.

"She's seizing," Will said, taking charge. "Get her on her side."

A statistic popped into Lily's mind: two percent of people with epilepsy died suddenly from seizures. Quickly, she rolled Antoinette over.

Will grabbed a penlight from his shirt pocket, lifted Antoinette's eyelids, and shined the light in her eyes. "Does she seize like this often?"

"Yes," Lily said, without thinking. "She seizes after . . ." She stopped as she looked down at her hand.

Will followed her gaze. "I saw it. She touched your hand and the bones moved." His voice shook. "The bones *moved*! What the hell is going on?"

"Don't be silly," Lily said. "You're seeing things." She faked a laugh.

"Antoinette!" Seth suddenly appeared from the kitchen. "What happened?"

"I . . . I fell, on my hand. It's okay now." Lily held up her hand and flexed her fingers, horrified that healing her hand had caused Antoinette's seizure.

For the first time since realizing what Antoinette could do, she understood Rose. Lily would rather suffer a broken hand than watch, helpless, while Antoinette seized.

"The seizure's winding down," Will said. He tucked the penlight back in his pocket and sat back.

"We've got it from here," Seth said. He tried to take Will's place next to Lily, but Will wouldn't move.

Cora appeared, her face a mask of worry. "Do you want me to call 911?"

Rose shook her head and clenched her jaw. She glanced at Will. "She'll be fine. She just needs some rest."

As Antoinette stilled, quiet conversation resumed around them. Waiters moved through the charged atmosphere setting bread and wine on tables.

Lily looked up. Eli and MaryBeth Cantwell stood in the middle of the dining room, staring at them. A hostess had been leading them to a table. Eli's eyes were wide in stunned amazement.

Rose pulled Antoinette onto her lap. "She can't keep doing this."

"Eli's here," Lily whispered. She stepped behind Rose, hoping to block his view of Antoinette. "We need to leave."

"I'll carry her to the van," Seth said.

Rose pulled Antoinette closer to her chest. "I can't let go," she whispered. She wrapped her arms around Antoinette and tried to stand, but her knees buckled.

Lily caught her elbow. "Let me help." She slid her arms under her sister's, and together they carried Antoinette outside.

# Chapter Nineteen

❦

It didn't work. Antoinette knew.

She lay with her head in her mother's lap as Seth drove home. She was drowsy but not asleep. Soon she wouldn't be able to fight the fatigue, but she wasn't there yet.

She had hummed along with Lily's song, changing the notes that were wrong, but the seizure came before she could lock everything in place. Lily's bones wiggled like teeth ready to fall out. Healings never lasted, but this one would end sooner than most.

Antoinette twitched, her hand opening and closing on its own. Her mother smoothed her hair back from her face. The van bumped down the road, and Antoinette's eyes became heavier. The thought came again as she fell asleep.

It didn't work.

# Chapter Twenty

✺

Lily stared out the window as she and Will drove back to Eden Farms. Cherry blossoms decorated the trees along the road, but she didn't notice. She also didn't count. Furthermore, she didn't care that failure to wear a seat belt accounted for 51 percent of deaths in auto accidents, and Will was not wearing his.

Instead, she examined her hand, turning it over, looking for a clue that would explain how Antoinette fixed things. But there was nothing. Just her hand, perfectly whole. Her fingers bending. Her skin unbruised.

And yet, something wasn't right. She felt a small catch in her last two fingers. She curled her hand into a fist. As she straightened it, something shifted. Her bones felt loose. There was a sharp pinprick at the base of her little finger.

She dropped her hand and looked out the front window at the rear of Seth's truck, Rose and Antoinette riding with him. Will hummed distractedly and tapped the steering wheel. Lily stole a glance at him. He looked at home driving the Eden Farms' van. His black hair was slicked back making his face seem thinner and his cheekbones sharper.

Had he been this skinny back in Covington? she wondered.

"You keep doing that," he said, glancing at her hand and the way she was flexing her fingers. "How does it feel?"

He reached for her hand, but Lily pulled away. Everything felt fragile. "It's fine." She stretched her fingers as far apart as they could go. There it was again. A small needle prick. This time, she felt it in both fingers.

An image of Antoinette's head hitting the floor flared in her mind. It was one thing to be in pain yourself; it was quite another to cause someone else pain.

"I know what I saw," Will said. "I don't care what you say, your fingers were bent completely back. Then Antoinette touched you, and your bones moved. They *moved*, Lils."

She straightened her fingers again. "Do you hear yourself? What you're suggesting is impossible."

"The universe contains wonders," he said. "You can't be a doctor and not know that."

They were almost at the farm, but he pulled over on the shoulder of the road. "Talk to me," he said. "I was there. I saw what she did. I need to understand."

"I need to get home and help Rose." Lily's stomach twisted.

"Seth will help her. I'm not moving the van until you tell me what's going on."

Lily covered her left hand with her right. "She's a little girl. Nothing's going on."

Will stared at her intently, as if willing her to speak. When she didn't, he closed his eyes and dropped his head back against the seat. "I'd like to believe there's something beyond this," he said. "That the death of the body isn't the death of the soul."

"When did you become a philosopher?" Lily tried to laugh,

but the sound stuck in her throat. She wanted to believe her parents existed somewhere, believe that after Rose died she and her sister would find each other again.

He coughed slightly, then opened his eyes. "I've been rethinking my life. Time to grow up, I guess. Does Antoinette often seize like that?"

Lily pressed her lips together and nodded. She knew Will. He hadn't given up trying to find out about Antoinette's ability; he had just switched to a different puzzle.

"There has to be a way to stop the seizures," he said as he pulled the van back onto the road and drove to the house.

"How?" Lily asked.

"I don't know yet," he admitted.

In the driveway now, they watched as Seth lifted Antoinette from the backseat of his truck. Her skin seemed almost translucent. Then Rose climbed out of the truck. She walked slowly, as if each step was a struggle. Seth caught her arm, and she leaned into him.

"I'll figure it out," Will said as he got out and jogged toward them.

Lily counted to ten before following.

"Lily told me what Antoinette can do," Will was saying as Seth helped Rose up the porch steps. "It's amazing."

Seth glared at him. He had his hands full, Antoinette in one arm and Rose on the other. "I don't know what you're talking about."

Lily ran up the porch steps, only a few paces behind Will. "I didn't—" she said.

"Of course you didn't," Seth said.

Despite herself, Lily felt a warm rush at his words. Seth had always believed the best of her.

Rose stopped on the top step and grabbed Will's arm. "You can't tell anyone. I mean it." She shook him a little.

Will pulled free and raised his right hand. "The Hippocratic oath: first do no harm. I promise. I don't want any harm to come to Antoinette."

"I didn't say anything," Lily said. She needed Rose to believe her.

Rose sighed and closed her eyes. "It doesn't matter. He saw the whole thing." She studied Will for a moment before seeming to come to a decision. "Healing triggers seizures, and the seizures are getting worse. If word gets out about what she can do, I won't be able to keep her safe."

"What about Eli?" Lily asked. "I tried to block his view of what was happening, but I think he saw Antoinette fix my hand." There was no use hiding anything from Will now.

Rose looked worn as she opened the kitchen door. "Then we have to keep him and MaryBeth away from Antoinette."

When Rose went inside, Lily turned to Seth. "You saw Eli. Do you think he'll leave Antoinette alone?"

The little girl let out a contented sigh. She looked so small nestled in Seth's arms. He frowned, his eyes dark. "No," he said, as he followed Rose into the house. "I don't."


LILY AND WILL walked to the drying barn. "What she can do is amazing," he said. "Why didn't you tell me about her?"

"Would you have believed me?" Lily said, noting with irony that both Seth and Rose had asked her the same question.

Will ran his hand over hers. He pressed along her fingers, feeling each joint, then gently bending her wrist back and forth. "Is the size of the seizure related to anything? The difficulty of the healing, maybe?"

"Rose said the seizures aren't as bad when Antoinette does something like bring wilted flowers back to life." She flinched when Will bent her little finger. "Another thing: the healings don't last."

He frowned. "I can see that. She does this with flowers too?"

Lily pointed to a semicircle of dead pansies to the left of the barn entrance. "A few days ago, they were as brown as they are now. Then Antoinette touched them, hummed, and they turned bright yellow. That was the first time I saw her fix anything."

"Something must be taxing her system." Will frowned. "This isn't safe for her. The risk of brain damage grows as her seizures increase. You'll have to monitor her, Lils. She can't keep this up. Meanwhile, we need to get you to the ER. You need an x-ray of that hand."

Lily promised to go tomorrow. Then she knelt and started pulling out the dead pansies. Rose didn't need a tangible reminder that Antoinette was getting worse. It wasn't long before she had a pile of uprooted flowers by her feet. When she finished, she sat down and leaned against the barn.

"Do you ever feel like you have absolutely no idea what you're doing?" she asked. In less than a week, everything she believed about the world had changed. A black ant crawled up the side of the barn, making its way along the splintered wood. She traced its progress, wondering whether it knew where it was going.

Will crossed his arms. The late-afternoon sunlight slanted

across his face, but it didn't warm his skin. He looked tired. "Truthfully, no," he said. "But I have heard that others sometimes feel that way. For me the question isn't whether I know what I'm doing, but whether I'm making the best decision I can at the time. Nothing's perfect, Lils. No matter how much we want it to be." He smiled sadly.

He bent down to pick a yellow viola that sprouted through a crack in the stone path, and he handed the flower to Lily. "I always wonder how something so fragile can survive in such a rough place. But you see it all the time don't you?"

Lily twirled the flower between her fingers. Violas meant faithfulness. A few others bloomed in the cracks between the stones. "They're stronger than they appear," she said as she gathered a handful of blossoms. She needed all the strength she could get.

The ant had reached the top of the barn. It turned around and started down as if it realized it was going the wrong way.

The breeze picked up, ruffling Will's hair. He didn't bother to smooth it back. He looked at Lily as if she was the only thing he saw. "Like you," he said. "And Antoinette. If we can figure out what triggers the seizures, we can stop them. There's a solution for everything. We just have to find it."

# Chapter Twenty-One

L ily woke to the staccato beat of rain on the slate roof. She pulled the quilt over her ears, but it didn't shut out the sound. *Get up*, the rain whispered.

"I don't want to," she said aloud. The light in her room was the pale gray that said the sun wasn't up yet. *Thirty minutes*, she thought. That's when the sun would be completely up. The rain sounded like it was lessening and probably would stop by then.

Across the hall, Antoinette shrieked. "Aey! Aey! Aey!" Then a loud thump, like a hand slapping against the wall.

Last night, Lily stole into Antoinette's room while she slept. The girl was sprawled on her back, and she looked younger, more like a child of five or six instead of ten.

An overstuffed blue chair sat across from Antoinette's bed. Lily was worried about Eli. What would he do if he knew beyond a doubt that Antoinette could heal?

Lily sank into the blue chair. "I'm here," she said. "I'll make sure you're safe." It was a promise she meant to keep.

She had stayed beside Antoinette's bed for most of the night, only sneaking back to her room when her eyes grew too heavy to keep open.

Antoinette shrieked again, and this time, Lily whispered along with her. "Aey! Aey! Aey!" She closed her eyes, shutting out everything except the sound of her voice blending with Antoinette's.

"Lily? Are you awake?" Rose opened the door. Light from the hall fell over her thin shoulders. "Can you help me get Antoinette ready this morning? I don't think I'm up to doing it alone today."

"Let me get dressed." Lily grabbed a clean pair of jean shorts from the dresser and slid them on without changing the T-shirt she'd slept in. She rubbed her eyes and detangled her hair by running her fingers through it.

"How's your hand?" Rose asked.

Lily held it up. A deep purple bruise had blossomed at the base of her fingers. It hadn't been there last night. "Will's taking me to the doctor today."

"I like him," Rose said with a sly smile. "He's nice. And he likes you."

"Will isn't nice," Lily said. He was arrogant and abrasive, she thought, charming if he tried, but not nice. "And he doesn't like me that way. We're friends. That's all." She tied her hair back.

"Maybe you're too close to see it, but he looks at you like you're the only person in the room."

"Will looks at anything female that way. Trust me."

Rose giggled, sounding startlingly healthy for someone who looked like she belonged in the hospital. "Might be worth it, even if only for a night."

Lily laughed along with her. It wasn't as if she hadn't thought about it. Sometimes Will looked at her as if he were hungry, and when he did her knees grew weak. Those were the times she made herself remember the nights after her parents' funeral. When she couldn't sleep, Will sat up with her, watching old movies. He was the one person who had never left her. They had become true friends. Sex would change that.

"I love Will," she said, "but not like that."

"Not like Seth, you mean," Rose said, suddenly serious.

Lily wished she could refute the words, but she could never hide anything from Rose. No matter how hard she had tried to push Seth out of her heart, she hadn't been able to. "No," she said softly, "not like Seth."

"You should tell him," Rose said. "He hasn't really dated since you two broke up. I think he still cares about you."

Lily's heart leapt at Rose's words, but it was dangerous to think that way. After he broke up with her, Lily would not leave her dorm room for hours. She counted lightbulbs, carpet threads, and wall cracks. A year had passed before she could leave the dorm without twisting the doorknob first left, then right, sixteen times.

She couldn't go through that again, and now she had Antoinette to think about. She wasn't going to let Rose down a second time.

"I can't," she said. "Not right now. Not with you and Antoinette . . . If things didn't work out with Seth a second time—" She broke off and started counting under her breath. She felt Rose watching but couldn't stop mouthing numbers.

"I want you to be happy," Rose said.

Her words made Lily stop counting. "I am happy," she said in surprise. "I'm home. I'm with you and Antoinette when I thought I'd never see you again. That's enough for me."

Rose hugged her gently. "But you could have so much more," she said softly.

With the door to her bedroom open, Antoinette's shrieks were louder. Lily pulled away and slipped on an old pair of flip-flops. "I don't need more," she said. And not wanting to discuss Seth further, she changed the subject. "I'm worried about Eli and what he saw."

"Maybe he didn't see anything," Rose said.

"He was looking right at me." Lily could still see Eli's eyes, wide and hopeful.

"He'll go away if we ignore him," Rose said. On the bureau was a teacup filled with the violas Lily had picked yesterday.

"For faithfulness, right?" Rose asked as she ran a finger around the rim of the cup.

Lily nodded. "Isn't that what sisters should be?" She looked at Rose, seeing two of her: the woman she was now, faded and diminished by her illness, and the girl she had been, beautiful and full of life. Lily closed her eyes, committing her sister's face to memory. "Faithful," she said. "In everything."

"We'll keep telling Eli he's imagining things," Rose said. "After a while, he'll believe us."

Lily didn't agree and said so.

"This has happened before," Rose said. "Once, Cora was here at the farm. It was September, and we were walking down the driveway. You know the tiger lilies by the front gate?"

Lily nodded. Every year in late summer, a profusion of the orange flowers framed the entrance to Eden Farms.

"Cora wanted to add the petals to a field green salad she was making. I told her she could pick as many as she wanted.

Antoinette followed us. On the way down the drive, every forsythia was green.

"When Cora finished cutting the lilies, we turned around as Antoinette touched a bush, and it burst into bloom. Every other plant along the drive was already blooming. Yellow flowers were everywhere.

"Cora saw everything. Just like Eli, she thought it was a miracle. I told her she was imagining things. That the bushes had been blooming on our way down the drive. When that didn't work, I faked a heart episode."

"You didn't," Lily said.

Rose grinned. "You play the cards you're dealt. Cora forgot all about the forsythia bushes after that. It'll be the same with Eli."

Across the hall, Antoinette shrieked again. "Come on," Rose said. "Let's go get our little miracle worker."

"Wait." Lily grabbed Rose's hand. She didn't want to leave anything unsaid between them. "I need you to know I won't let you down. I'm not running away. I was scared before, but I'm not now. It's hard being different, and I thought that being around Antoinette would make my . . . my quirks more pronounced."

"But don't you see?" Rose asked. "That's why you're perfect for her. You know what it's like to be on the outside looking in. You know that 'different' doesn't mean broken. Antoinette needs someone who will tell her that."

She squeezed Lily's hand, then walked across the hall to Antoinette's room. When she opened the door, Antoinette shifted, and her eyes opened.

"Good morning, sleepyhead," Rose said. Antoinette reached for her, but Rose stepped aside. "Lily's helping us today."

Rose glanced over her shoulder at Lily. "I know I'm asking a lot, and I wanted to thank you. Having you home makes me feel young again."

Lily had been so long without a sister that she had forgotten the pleasure of being with someone who held your history in her heart. "Tell me what to do," she said. She was nervous, but she knew she could do this.

"Stand over here and let her see you," Rose said.

Lily crossed the room, but her stride was too big. One more step and she'd be at Rose's side, ending on five. She quickly halved her stride and stopped on six. "I heard you singing this morning," she said to Antoinette. "It was pretty."

Antoinette ignored Lily and stretched toward Rose.

"Sit on the bed and let her get used to you," Rose said.

Lily sat tentatively on the far edge of the bed.

"Tell her it's time to get up," Rose said.

"Okay. Hi Antoinette. I'm going to help you get ready this morning."

Antoinette bounced on the bed, and Lily's stomach dropped with the motion. "Let's try this again," Lily said, with a glance at Rose. "Are you ready to get up? We could go down and get some breakfast. What do you like to eat? I don't normally eat breakfast, but I will this morning."

Antoinette hummed.

"Did I do something wrong?" Lily asked.

"She's singing. It means she's happy. You're doing great. Keep going."

"Can you get up?" Lily stood. Antoinette flopped down and rolled to face the wall.

"You have to say it like you expect her to do it," Rose said.

With confidence that was ninety percent fake, Lily said, "Come on Antoinette, it's time to get up." She stood back and waited.

"Get up," she said again, feeling Rose's eyes on her back. Without warning, and much to her surprise, Antoinette sat up and scooted to the edge of the bed. Lily grinned. "Does she need help?"

Rose shook her head. "She knows what to do. You just need to keep her on track or she'll wander off."

Slowly, Lily moved toward the door. "Come on, let's get breakfast." When Antoinette took first one step and then another, Lily felt her world shift, and she wondered how she could have ever thought of abandoning her niece.

# Chapter Twenty-Two

✎

After eating breakfast with Lily, Antoinette stumbled down the back porch stairs, her body hurting everywhere. The happiness she had felt upon waking was gone, replaced by a constant low-level anxiety.

She wagged her head from side to side to loosen her neck muscles. When she stopped, she noticed a sparrow lying on the ground. The bird was on its side, its gray chest quivering. Antoinette hadn't known it was possible for something to breathe so fast.

She crouched down so that she was inches from the bird, so close she could ruffle its feathers with her fingers. The sparrow tried to turn its head toward her but couldn't. Its wing, the one it was lying on, was bent backward. Antoinette mirrored its position, twisting her right arm behind her back and turning her head the other direction.

It hurt.

"Antoinette," Lily called from the porch. "We have to go. Seth's waiting for you in the drying barn. Don't you want to help him get it ready for the show?"

Of course she did. But the bird distracted her. It kicked its legs, but it didn't go anywhere.

Antoinette leaned closer. The bird breathed faster.

Since healing Lily's fingers, Antoinette's arms rarely stayed at her side. She couldn't walk from the porch to the house garden without stopping to rest, and she was tired all the time.

Lily's feet made soft swishing sounds as she walked through the grass. "Come on, Antoinette. Let's go. I have to drop you off with Seth before Will takes me to the doctor."

Over and over Antoinette saw herself reaching for Lily's hand. The tiny bones rearranging themselves. The skin stretching. The muscles lengthening. Everything was almost locked in place. Then the seizure came.

Lily's hand looked normal, but things weren't always what they seemed. The bones weren't properly fused, and it wouldn't be long before they slid out of place again. Lily's hand would be just as broken as it was before.

The bird opened its beak; a tiny squeak escaped. Antoinette leaned forward until she was right over it. Slowly, she dropped her hand to its chest.

*I'm not going to hurt you*, she thought. The bird's heart skittered beneath her fingers. Antoinette closed her eyes, listening.

At first, she didn't hear anything, and her heart raced. The bird opened and closed its beak, but nothing came out.

Antoinette concentrated until a faint song emerged. It was the sound of a piccolo, high and fast, the notes bright.

She followed the melody until she found the spot where the notes were off-key, deep, pain-filled things. The wing was broken. She absorbed the wrong notes and hummed, welcoming the pain into her body, knitting the bird's bones back together.

It took longer than usual, but gradually the song corrected itself. When everything was right, the bird shuddered. It twisted upright, hopped once, and leapt into the sky.

Then Lily was there. "No!" She grabbed Antoinette, but she was too late.

Antoinette tracked the bird, even as she started to shake. She fell sideways but kept the sparrow in sight as it flew higher and higher.

Then, just before the seizure claimed her, the bird stuttered in midair. Its wing folded backward, and it tumbled to the ground.

SEVERAL HOURS LATER, Antoinette sat by her mother's knees, listening to Dvorak's *New World Symphony* on headphones Lily bought for her. Her mother was at the kitchen table, going over her notes for the garden show. "Thirty-two vendors," she said under her breath. "That's up from last year."

Antoinette couldn't forget the bird. After seizing, she slept for a while and woke to the image of the sparrow falling from the sky. She shivered at the thought and pressed her cheek against her mother's knee. The day was hot for April, but she felt cold. She looked around the room, expecting to see icicles edging the table, but everything was normal.

Gold light shimmered through the window on the kitchen door. She wanted to be outside where the sun would warm her.

She stretched her arm up. It was heavy. Dvorak's symphony rolled through her headphones, helping her focus. When her arm was high enough, she let it fall against her mother's elbow. Tap. Tap. Then she pointed. *Outside.*

"Not now. I have to finish," her mother said, without looking up.

Sometimes Antoinette spoke in her dreams. Often she woke sure a word had made it past her lips, but she was always a second too late. The room was silent every time.

If she could speak, her mother wouldn't ignore her. Antoinette would say, "Outside," and they would go. She opened her mouth and tried to push the word out, but not even a whisper escaped.

She scooted across the floor on her rear. At the door, she stood and pressed her nose against the glass. Through the window, she saw Lily and Seth digging weeds in the kitchen garden. Lily worked a triangle of basil. Her back was to Seth so she didn't see him reach for her, as if wanting to stroke her skin.

Will was also outside. He sat on the porch swing, staring at Lily, but she didn't notice him either.

Lily had spent the morning in the emergency room, and she returned home with her hand bandaged. Looking at it made Antoinette's stomach feel hollow, so she shifted her gaze to the plants.

Dill, basil, and oregano grew in wedges bordered by lavender and salvia. Later, marigolds would poke from the soil in a neat circle around the bed. Cora was the only one who used the herbs now that Antoinette's mother no longer cooked. Their names ran through Antoinette's head like a song. *Dill, basil, oregano. Dill, basil, oregano.* She flapped her hands and hummed.

Over the headphones, a flutist began a solo. Antoinette swayed in time to the music. The notes were smooth and round, each one perfect, the sound of loneliness.

Sometimes Antoinette didn't mind being different. When she stood outside and felt the sun on her face—not only its heat, but its essence—when that slipped under her skin, she felt special.

But she didn't feel anything now, so what was she? A weird kid who couldn't control her body. She couldn't completely heal her mother or Lily. She couldn't hear the flowers sing. And now she couldn't even save the life of a sparrow.

She looked back at her mother, curled over her notebook, entering numbers in her neat, even handwriting. She made one last notation, then stood and removed Antoinette's headphones. "Will you come outside with me?" she asked.

Moving was difficult. Antoinette's legs popped most of the time, and when she tried to sit still her arms flew over her head. With her mother's help, she made it outside, but her legs telescoped as soon as her feet touched the porch. She fell, banging her knees on the wood floor.

Will helped her up. "You're going to have a bruise," he said as he brushed off her knees.

She could already feel the bruise forming as she walked to the edge of the porch.

Will stood beside her. "She's fascinating," he said.

The swing sighed as her mother sat down. "Do you mean Antoinette or Lily?"

What a silly question, Antoinette thought. Didn't her mother see the way Will looked at Lily?

"Antoinette, of course," Will said.

"If you say so," her mother said. "But I don't think Antoinette's the reason you drove all the way down here."

Will looked out over the fields. "The reason I came doesn't matter anymore." He looked like he wanted to say more but broke off, coughing.

Antoinette flapped her hands and walked to the edge of the porch. The mountain ash had bloomed. Its branches were a cotton-candy canopy of blooms. Anemones grew around its base, their foliage like thousands of little fingers.

She eased down the stairs and walked to the tree. She sat down and listened to the bees as they darted in and out of the tiny white blossoms.

*Sit*, she thought. *Stay still.*

For a moment, her body was quiet. Then a twitch started at the tips of her toes. She tried to pin her arms down, but the twitch burst out of her body, and her hands flapped over her head.

Disappointment filled her.

Everything was changing.

She looked at the anemones. One plant had leaves that were yellow, but the veins were neon green. That was not normal. The leaves should be a nice even green.

Antoinette wiggled her toes deep into the ground and listened, straining to hear. The flowers were silent.

She pushed her hands wrist-deep into the dirt and closed her eyes.

Nothing.

*No, no, no!* She whipped her head back and forth and slumped over, her face on the ground. Mulch scratched her cheeks and her forehead. She still couldn't hear the plants, couldn't *feel* them. The despair that had been building in her since she had failed to heal Lily's hand finally erupted, and she screamed.

Then Will was there. He slid his hands under Antoinette's arms and picked her up. "I'm taking you to your mother."

Antoinette stiffened until she was board flat, but Will was strong. He carried her to the swing and settled her into her mother's arms. Then he stared into her eyes. "Her pupils aren't fixed," he said. "It isn't a seizure."

Antoinette could have told him that. A seizure didn't fill her with emptiness. A seizure would mean there was still hope, a chance she could heal her mother.

# Chapter Twenty-Three

❧

Y ou worked at the market *every* day?" Will asked Lily on
the way to the commercial fields, Antoinette with them.
"No running around the farm? No chasing boys? You
know there are laws against child labor." He carried a pitchfork,
leaning on it as he walked.

Farming was a never-ending battle against decay, even in
winter, when everything was dormant. There were fences that
needed mending, barns that needed painting, or glass panes in
the greenhouse that needed to be replaced.

The garden show was on Sunday. Broadleaf weeds dotted the
house garden. Overnight, wild onions had sprouted among the
daffodils, and dandelions dotted the night garden. Lily added
weeding to her long list of chores.

But first she would turn the compost heaps at the end of the
peony rows. Instead of one big pile, her father had built several small white containers and placed them among the rows of
flowers, where microbes would transform shredded paper, coffee
grounds, and kitchen scraps into the gardener's version of black
gold.

"It's wasn't as boring as it sounds," she said. "It was peaceful. Fun." She didn't add that Seth often joined her in her work.

Antoinette moved down the path in front of them. Since healing Lily, walking had been harder for her. Her knees frequently folded as if about to drop her in the dirt; yet today she stayed upright. Lily walked with her good hand out, ready to catch her if she fell.

"You have a peculiar idea of fun—" Will broke off and started coughing. Lily thumped him on the back, surprised she could feel his spine beneath her hands.

"That's enough. You can stop hitting me now." His face was pale and his chest heaved.

"Are you okay?" Lily asked. "*Really* okay, I mean." Remission didn't mean his lung cancer was cured, only that there was no evidence of the disease at the moment.

He grinned and gestured to the sky. "It's all this fresh air. My lungs aren't used to it."

She didn't believe him and was about to say so, when a sharp pain shot through her left hand. Yesterday she found out that it was indeed broken. An x-ray showed a fracture at the base of her fingers. The doctor wrapped her hand in an ACE bandage and told her to set up an appointment with an orthopedist in a few days.

Will noticed her massaging her hand. "It hurts?"

She nodded.

"Are you taking your pain meds?"

"They make me groggy. There's too much work to be done." She took the pitchfork from him and opened one of the compost bins. A rich earthy smell wafted out.

"Let me do that," Will said, reclaiming the pitchfork and jabbing it into the bin.

"Not like that," Lily said. She showed him how to dig down to the bottom of the bin and turn the compost over. "Rose and Seth will be here soon." Rose wanted to have a picnic. They didn't have time for it, but Lily couldn't say no to her.

"Your boyfriend doesn't like me, Lils," Will said as he worked. Over the past few days, he had relaxed. He no longer wore pressed khakis and starched shirts. Though his jeans were too expensive for farmwork, he almost looked like he belonged.

"He's not my boyfriend."

Will shrugged. "Could've fooled me. I've seen the way he looks at you. Not that I blame him."

Antoinette stomped her feet and flapped her hands. She turned in a slow circle. Her legs trembled, and her fingers flicked back and forth. The movements seemed random, like she couldn't control her body.

A stone formed in the pit of Lily's stomach as she watched her niece. "Antoinette's getting worse, isn't she?"

Will wouldn't look at her. That alone told her she was right.

She turned his face to hers. He hadn't shaved, his skin was rough. "You're my friend. I need to know."

"Friend?" He leaned into her hand.

"Why would you think you weren't?"

He turned his face a fraction of an inch. His lips grazed her palm.

Lily went still. She felt her face flush, and for once she couldn't find anything to count. "Will, I don't—"

"Are we interrupting?" Rose asked as she and Seth crested

the hill to the commercial fields. Seth carried a picnic basket with one hand and helped Rose walk with the other.

Antoinette shrieked when she saw her mother. She stumbled across the grass and held her hands up. It was eighty degrees out, but Rose wore a long-sleeved yellow cardigan.

Seth set the basket down and swung Antoinette into his arms. "Your mom's tired. You'll have to make do with me, kiddo." His voice was light, but he frowned at Lily's hand on Will's face.

Lily pulled away from Will. "We were just turning the compost piles." Without thinking, she grabbed the pitchfork in her left hand, then flinched when she squeezed her fingers shut.

Rose took the pitchfork. "The healing faded fast."

Lily turned to Will. "You didn't answer me. Is something wrong with An—"

"Antoinette and I are going for a walk," Seth interjected. He directed a sharp look at Lily.

She flushed, knowing he was right. This wasn't something Antoinette needed to hear.

"Come on, kiddo. Let's go find some fun." Seth tossed Antoinette into the air. She flung her head back and giggled, her face bright with joy.

"I don't know," Will said when Seth and Antoinette were out of earshot. He was calm, and Lily wondered if this was the way he delivered bad news to his patients. "This is all new for me. It's not like there's a medical category for child miracle workers."

"But if you had to guess?" Lily asked. "What does the doctor in you think?"

Will stared at the sky for so long she thought he wasn't going to answer. When he did, she saw resignation in his eyes. "How long do the healings normally last?" he asked.

"They used to last months," Rose said quietly. "But lately they've been fading faster and faster." She gestured toward Lily's hand. "This is the shortest I've seen."

Lily was still thinking. Antoinette's seizure after healing the bird hadn't been as large as it had been after healing her hand. Was the seizure larger because of the complexity involved? Maybe the difficulty overwhelmed Antoinette's small body until she seized.

Or maybe that wasn't it at all. Nature abhorred a vacuum. Maybe Antoinette pulled the illness or the pain from the injury into her own body. After all, it had to go somewhere. It couldn't just disappear.

She watched Seth and Antoinette. He held her under her arms as he spun with her—they were a picture of happiness. When they stopped, Seth pretended to stumble, but even as he fell he cradled Antoinette. Their laughter carried over the farm.

"Keep in mind this is just a guess," Will said. He looked like he wanted to be somewhere else. "I'm way out of my league here, but the worsening seizures, the diminished effect of the healings—it all says something is going wrong. How quickly things might get worse, though, I can't predict."

As he spoke, Seth returned with Antoinette on his shoulders. He swung her down but didn't set her on the ground. Instead, he held her in his arms.

"You don't know how strong she is," he said to Will. There was pain and anger in his voice. "You don't know a damn thing about her."

"Lily asked for my opinion," Will said, "and I gave it. I'm

not saying I'm right, but when the body is fatigued or under stress, it doesn't operate as well as it should. High blood pressure, the ability to fight off common colds, certain types of cancer . . ."

"He's right," Lily said. "Something's wrong." She unwrapped her ACE bandage to reveal the deep purple bruise at the base of her fingers.

"Damn," Seth said softly. He set Antoinette down and turned to Lily. "Can I look at that?"

When he took her hand, electricity skittered over her skin.

"Does it hurt?" he asked.

"Not as much as it did at Cora's when I fell, but more than it did last night or even earlier this morning."

He ran his thumb across her palm. "I want to *do* something. Anything. But I can't." He spoke softly, so that only she heard. "Things like this shouldn't happen to kids."

"No," she said. "They shouldn't."

THE KITCHEN LIGHT was on, illuminating the hallway with a soft yellow glow. "Will?" Lily said. "Are you still up?" It was past midnight.

The kitchen was empty. She was about to switch off the light and go to bed when she looked out the back door. In the starlight, she saw Will sitting on the porch swing. He tilted his head back, and every once in a while he'd raise a finger and drag it along the sky as if tracing the constellations. His dark hair blended into the night sky.

A bottle of beer sat on the small table next to him. He took a drink, then shoved his feet against the porch floor, making the swing rock.

Lily bit her lip as she studied his profile. He looked older than he had a week ago and weary.

A light flickered in the fields, drawing her attention away from Will. A thin beam shone beneath the drying barn door. She knew Seth must be out there preparing for the garden show. She should be helping him, but she didn't think he wanted company. Like the rest of them, he was upset at the downturn in Antoinette's health. She knew him well enough to know that at times like this, he wanted to be alone.

She opened the door to the porch and stepped out.

"I was wondering when you'd stop watching me and come out here." Will said. "How's Rose? I figured you'd call me if you needed help."

The past two nights, Lily had sat beside Rose as she fell asleep. They talked about their childhood, Antoinette, or nothing at all. "She's finally asleep."

"You're doing good, Lils." He held up the beer bottle. "Want a drink?"

When she shook her head, he lifted one shoulder. "Suit yourself. You know I'll do what I can to help, don't you?"

"I know." She sat down beside him and rested her head on his shoulder. "Rose is getting worse. It's taking longer for her to fall asleep, and when she does, she wakes a couple of times every night. I don't know what else to do for her."

Will took another swallow. "Do you remember when I was in the middle of chemo? I hated sitting in that open room, tethered to an IV, staring at the other cancer patients. We were all hooked to the same drug cocktail, but most of them had twenty or thirty years on me. Every time I looked at them I wondered whether I'd live to see forty or fifty.

"Then you started coming with me, and I had someone else to focus on. One time you counted the number of chairs in the room while the nurse was flushing my port. 'Twenty-two,' you said. 'That's a nice even number.' Then you counted the ceiling tiles, the nurses behind the desk, the number of patients in the room.

"I don't think you realized you were doing it. When you finished, you looked at me and said, 'Everything's even, so we're good.' You seemed so sure of yourself. So grounded. I held on to your belief that everything would get better when I couldn't believe for myself." Will squeezed her good hand. "That's what you can do for Rose. When she loses hope, hold on to it for her."

"But things aren't going to get better for Rose." Lily stared into the dark. Crickets sang and somewhere an owl hooted. The light in the drying barn flicked off. She squinted, trying to make out Seth as he left, but the night was too dark and she couldn't see anything.

"The point isn't whether she gets better," Will said "The point is whether she goes through this alone or has someone with her who loves her, someone who tells her everything will be all right after she's gone. Love her enough to believe *that* for her. And if you can't believe it, fake it, because most of the time, things work out all right."

Lily looked at him. "How did you get to be so smart?"

He took another drink. "Perception, Lils. It's my gift and my curse. For example, I know you still have feelings for your farm boy."

"Seth?"

"The very one." Will saluted her with the bottle.

She straightened. Her cheeks flushed, and she was grateful for the dark. "I don't—"

"No sense trying to hide it. But he's not right for you." He grew serious. "Where was he these past six years? Where was he when your parents died? He could have found you, but he didn't. That has to mean something."

Will was silhouetted in the light from the kitchen. He drew a finger across her cheek. "I wouldn't have left you," he said.

He was right. He had never left her. And now, he was here again, right when she needed him. She was a tangle of emotion. Though the night was warm, she shivered. "Don't." She took his hand, willing him to stop talking.

"Having cancer taught me one thing," he said. "I want my life to count for something. For me, that means spending it with you. We're good together, Lils. You just have to let it happen."

Everything he said made sense. But still she couldn't forget Seth. "I wish it was that easy," she said.

Will took another swallow of beer. "It is. Life doesn't stand still. You have to move with it. Look at me. A few days ago I was at home in Covington. Today I'm here with you. Easy as wishing."

Even in the dark she could see his smile. It filled his face. "How long can you stay?" she asked.

He lowered the bottle and looked at her. "As long as you need me," he said, as if it was the simplest thing in the world.

# Chapter Twenty-Four

❧

The land was silent. Antoinette cocked her head to the left and listened. Cicadas buzzed. Crickets sang. Wind rustled the leaves on the birch trees. But the music was gone. For the first time, she did not want to be outside.

Her mother walked beside her. Lily and Will walked ahead of them. "It's a lot of work for a garden show, Lils," Will said.

Antoinette didn't hear Lily's reply.

If Seth were here, he would play for her, play until she forgot that she had become deaf to the land. But she hadn't seen him since yesterday when he twirled around with her in the flower field.

Her mother bent down. "Do you remember when you were a little girl?" she asked. "I'd catch fireflies in mason jars for you. Remember the time the whole barn was lit up with their glow? We must have had thirty jars."

Antoinette remembered. The barn had glimmered with their light. Her mother wove a crown of daisies for her. "You're my fairy princess," she had said, and Antoinette believed her—that night anything felt possible.

"You're still my princess," her mother said.

At the split in the drive where one path led to the house and the other to the drying barn, someone called Antoinette's name.

At first, she thought it was the crickets, but then it happened again. She stopped and looked up.

Eli Cantwell stood behind the iron gate at the end of their driveway. "Antoinette!" he yelled again.

Antoinette felt her mother stiffen. "Ignore it," she said. "He'll leave if we keep walking." Her mother motioned for her to move forward, but Antoinette planted her feet.

"Who is it?" Will asked, bringing a hand up to shade his eyes.

"It's Eli," Lily said. She put her good hand on Antoinette's back. "Come on, you need to keep walking."

Antoinette didn't budge.

"I know you're there," Eli yelled. "Please, Rose. MaryBeth's worse. Let her help us!"

"Wait here," her mother said. She walked down the drive to Eli.

The wind carried bits of their conversation to Antoinette.

"She's just a little girl," her mother said.

"I know what I saw!" Eli sounded angry.

"You're confused," her mother said. "You need to leave us alone."

"Please," Eli's voice cracked. "MaryBeth's all I've got."

Her mother wrapped her hand around Eli's. "If Antoinette could help you, don't you think I'd let her?"

"Please." Eli stared at Antoinette as if she were a savior or a saint.

But Antoinette had never been either of those. She looked

at Lily's injured hand. She remembered the sparrow falling from the sky.

This time when Lily gently pushed her forward, Antoinette turned from Eli and kept walking.

ANTOINETTE SHUFFLED THROUGH the cedar shavings and dried flower petals on the barn floor. Twice a year Seth spread shavings throughout the barn—their scent kept flies away. As she walked, she kicked up puffs of sawdust that drifted through the air like dandelion seeds.

At the other end of the barn, a plywood stage had been set up. On Sunday, Seth would stand there, playing bluegrass for the crowd. Bluegrass was happy music, and Antoinette wished he was playing it now. She needed something happy.

They had been in the barn for an hour, and though Eli was gone, she still heard him screaming her name. She balled her hand into a fist and smacked her forehead.

"Shouldn't you make her stop that?" Will asked as he lifted a folding table from the stack against the wall.

Lily looked up from where she stood at the other end of the barn. A can of white paint sat at her feet. She was almost finished painting the walls.

"She'll quit if it hurts," Antoinette's mother said. She sat on a straw bale, too tired to help. Her skin was paler than usual, and every few minutes she took a deep breath. When she did, she steepled her fingers over her heart and pushed.

Antoinette mirrored her movement, pressing her fingers into her heart as if she could tease the grief out. But when she dropped her hand, she hurt just as much as she had before.

Will ran a wet rag over the table, and sawdust slid to the

barn floor. "Won't most of the artists bring their own tables?" he asked. "Seems to me that you shouldn't be doing all of this work for them."

"Each year a few people forget something. Besides, we need tables for our flower arrangements and lavender bread." Her mother closed her eyes and leaned back against the wall. After talking with Eli at the gate, she had grown quiet. She seemed to be withdrawing inside herself.

Antoinette tucked her elbows tight against her side. She felt sluggish, the way she did after a seizure. Except she hadn't had a seizure today. She hit her head again.

"Why don't you go home, Rose," Lily said as she dipped her paintbrush into the can. "We've got this."

"I'm fine," her mother said.

Lily looked at Antoinette. "*You'd* listen to me, wouldn't you?" Her gaze was heavy, but Antoinette didn't mind. As her mother grew weaker, Lily seemed to grow stronger.

Antoinette stretched up on her toes and walked to the far end of the barn. She paced under the herbs hanging from the rafters. Basil, rosemary, oregano. And lavender. They always had lavender.

Her mother used to pick a basketful of the flowers. Then she'd spend the rest of the day baking lavender bread and lavender butter cookies.

The scent would spread through the house. On those nights, Antoinette would dream she was so full of words they popped from her mouth like soap bubbles. She'd wake with her lips buzzing, sure that if she had opened her eyes a second earlier, the room would have been ringing with words like home, love, safe.

And Mommy. Most of all, Mommy.

"What's the story behind this garden show?" Will asked. He popped the metal legs of a table open and righted it.

"It's a family tradition," her mother said.

Antoinette focused on her mother's face. It hurt to do so, but she didn't look away. She studied the sharp line of her mother's jaw, the curve of her cheek, the color of her skin—pale white, like the Honor roses Antoinette had pushed into bloom a week ago.

"Our parents' first year of farming was rough," she said. "Thirty years ago, there wasn't a big market for commercial flower farms. They lost most of their crop and thought they might have to sell the farm."

"Toss me that rag," Will said to Lily.

She threw it to him, her aim true. "They were tough," Lily said, picking up the story. "Mom decided to have a garden show. What did she say, Rose? She wanted to—"

"Spit in the eye of defeat." Antoinette's mother laughed. "Mom was stubborn."

Will wiped dust from his fingers. "Sounds like it runs in the family."

Lily threw another cloth at him. It hit him in the chest with a loud thwack.

Antoinette only vaguely remembered her grandparents—a woman with soft arms and a man with a big laugh.

"Cora and Teelia invited the entire town," Lily said. "To everyone's surprise, the show was a success. Mom and Dad made enough money to hold on for one more season. Since then, we've had the show every year."

That's what Antoinette needed to do—figure out how to help her mother hold on a little longer. She flapped her hands and cocked her head to the left. "Aauugh," she said as she walked over to her mother and tapped her side.

Her mother gently pushed her away. "No touching."

Antoinette didn't stop.

"Antoinette, I said *no*."

Bits of dried lavender fell from the rafters, dusting Antoinette's shoulders. She stomped and a puff of sawdust caught in her nose. Then she smacked her head. Hard. She had to save her mother.

Lily gently tugged Antoinette's hand away from her head. "Don't do that. You'll hurt yourself."

*I don't care.* Antoinette wrenched free and bared her teeth.

Her mother sighed. "Leave her alone. She'll stop when it hurts."

*I hurt now.* She didn't mean her head; her heart hurt more than her head ever could.

Lily whispered in Antoinette's ear. "It'll help your mom. She worries about you." She squeezed Antoinette's hand, then went back to painting the wall.

Antoinette wanted to curl up against her mother's side. They would hold hands. Antoinette would hear her mother's song again. Then she would fix everything.

She screamed and stamped her feet. Her mother was dying and she couldn't stop it.

"I wish you could tell me what's wrong," her mother said.

*Me too*, Antoinette thought. Someday the words would come; she would start talking and never stop. She paced in a tight circle. The rhythm of one foot falling after another was soothing. A minute passed where the only sound in the barn was the scuff of her feet through the sawdust.

Lily broke the silence. "Try counting."

Antoinette didn't realize Lily was speaking to her.

"Antoinette," Lily said again.

This time she stopped. She cocked her head to the right and curled her hands to her shoulders. Her heart beat faster, and her eyelids flickered.

"Try counting," Lily said as she walked toward Antoinette.

"What are you doing?" her mother asked.

"She needs help." Lily stopped just out of Antoinette's reach. "One. Two."

Antoinette's arms uncurled and dropped to her sides.

"Three. Four."

Her jaw unclenched, and her eyelids stilled.

"Five. Six."

Antoinette sighed, and her heart slid back into its normal rhythm.

"It's best to stop on an even number," Lily said. "At least it is for me. That way everything fits together."

Antoinette made herself look Lily directly in the eye. It hurt, but she didn't turn away.

"Counting will help you make sense of things," she said.

Peace settled deep in Antoinette's middle as she realized she wasn't alone. Lily understood.

## ROSE'S JOURNAL
### *April 2013*

———+———

I DON'T REMEMBER the sound of my mother's voice, or the way it felt when she held me in her arms. Since she died, pieces of her have faded away. Sometimes it seems like she was never here at all.

Memory is like that. And one day soon it will be my turn. Pieces of me will start to fade away. Five months have passed since Dr. Teyler told me I was dying. But now that Lily is home, I'm not afraid anymore.

Tonight I sit in the van, watching as she cuts armloads of white Honor roses and Casa Blanca lilies from the night garden. We are going to visit our parents' graves. Her arms overflow as she walks toward the van. I whisper a prayer of thanks for Antoinette's ability to pull life from unexpected places.

I whisper another prayer for Will. He's watching Antoinette for me, and I hurt for him. I see the way he looks at Lily.

But I also see the way Lily looks at Seth. They still fit together.

The drive to the cemetery is short. When we arrive, Lily helps me from the van, then hands me a bundle of flowers. "We probably should have waited until tomorrow," she says as we start toward our parents' grave.

"We're here now." I need to be a family again. Mom, Dad,

Lily, and me. I put my nose in the flowers and inhale. The night is warm as we start up the hill. Lily walks backward, as if not being able to see what lies in front of her makes it easier to face.

"What's it like?" she asks. "Dying, I mean."

I watch my feet. The path is smooth, but lately I fall easily. "You always did get right to the heart of things, didn't you?"

"I did it again, didn't I?" Lily says. The ground changes from flat to a slight upward slope.

"Subtlety was never your strong point."

Lily laughs, and I am young again. "I'll answer your question, but I need you to promise me something." I wait until she agrees before continuing. "Keep Antoinette safe and tell her how much I love her." I shift the flowers to my left hand. "I've got to stop for a minute to catch my breath."

My lungs strain and white dots float before my eyes. I sit on a stone bench next to a grave, shut my eyes, and explain what's happening. Then I say, "Tell me it's snowing." It's a bad joke, but Lily laughs anyway.

"It's a miracle," she says. "A snowstorm in April."

Stranger things have happened.

I catch my breath and open my eyes. Lily has stripped the petals from several roses. She scatters them over my head. "I told you. It's snowing."

She takes my bundle of flowers and adds them to hers. "Maybe we should go home," she says.

"No," I say, "It'll pass." I should have brought my oxygen tank. I take a nitro pill from my pocket and slip it under my tongue. "Do you remember that hollow feeling when Mom and Dad died? The impossibility of it?" Some mornings I still wake expecting to find Mom cutting flower stems at the kitchen sink. When I remember she's dead, I experience that feeling of loss all over again.

"You don't have to talk about it," Lily whispers. "I shouldn't have asked."

"It's okay. Telling someone makes it less lonely." I loop my arm through hers, careful of her broken hand. "Help me walk."

She shifts the flowers to her other arm so she can take my weight.

"Dying feels like that," I say. "Except you're losing everyone you've ever loved at once. There's this panic. You try to hold on because you feel yourself slipping away, but you can't control your body. The weird thing is, you don't think about dying yourself. You think about the people you're leaving behind. It feels like they're the ones dying. Not you."

Mist twirls around us. It's normal here, but tonight it feels like the dead rising up to greet me.

"After panic, resignation sets in. There's nothing you can do to stop it. No one beats death. Not even Antoinette." I wave my hand in air, dispelling the mist. "It's not bad. Make sure you tell Antoinette. Tell her it's not bad."

This day has been coming since the first time I held Antoinette. So much of mothering is about fear. Fear that your child will be hurt. That she will get lost. That no one will ever love her with the same all-consuming intensity that I do.

But most of all, I fear the day I will have to say good-bye to her, because no matter when that day comes, it will be too soon.

We buried our parents side by side, under a shared headstone.

Lily stops shy of the gray stone carved with their names. Then she kneels and I see her lips moving. She's counting, her version of prayer. She rests the flowers beneath the stone, and when she turns to me, I see my past in her eyes. "I promise. Antoinette will *never* forget you," she says.

# Chapter Twenty-Five

❧

Lily had worked harder in the past week than she had in the past six years. Her muscles were knotted in places she couldn't reach, and no matter how much she coughed she still felt sawdust in the back of her throat.

She needed a drink of water. It was early—not even six in the morning—when she padded into the kitchen and flipped on the light.

A low groan filled the room.

"What in the world?" She turned in a slow circle. The room was empty.

There it was again. A moan, like a tree creaking in the wind.

She knelt and peered under the table. Antoinette sat under the farthest end, her knees folded to her chest.

"I thought I heard someone in here," Lily said. She held out her hand. "Why don't you come out here with me? I'll make you something to eat."

Antoinette dropped her head to her knees and started rocking. She had been agitated at the drying barn last night. Apparently, she still was.

"Your mom's asleep, but I don't think she'd mind if we woke her. I know she wouldn't want you to sit out here alone."

Yellow butterflies dotted Antoinette's pajamas. The print was light and happy; the exact opposite of Antoinette's demeanor.

"What about Will? We could wake him up."

Antoinette groaned. If grief had a sound, this was it.

"Well, you can't sit under there alone." Lily crawled under the table and sat next to her niece. Their hips touched, and Antoinette leaned into her.

Lily rested her cheek against the top of Antoinette's head. "I know it's hard watching your mom get sicker. When my parents died, I felt . . . lost. Everything just stopped. Like the world forgot how to spin. I always felt like I moved to a different tune than everyone else, and that feeling got worse after they died. I was so lonely."

She wrapped her arm around the little girl and pulled her close. "I won't let it be like that for you. You'll never be alone. I'll be right here with you."

The planks in the wood floor were old. With time and temperature changes they had shifted slightly, creating tiny cracks between the boards. Lily ran her fingers along the spaces, counting each one.

"Count with me?" She took Antoinette's hand and placed it on the floor. She guided it along a split in the floor by their feet. "One."

Where that crack joined another, Lily shifted Antoinette's fingers. They followed the new line. "Two."

When Lily reached twelve, Antoinette stopped groaning.

On twenty-two, she stopped rocking.

On thirty, she crawled out from under the table and pointed to the back door.

THE DAFFODILS WERE starting to brown, only the tips of the leaves so far, but they'd need to harvest the remaining flowers soon. Tomorrow, or the next day, Lily thought.

She and Antoinette sat in the grass at the head of a row. Antoinette was still in her pj's, and Lily still wore the T-shirt and shorts she slept in. Yellow and white flowers stretched into the distance. If they stored half of them in the commercial freezer, they'd be selling daffodils into May.

Antoinette grabbed a browning flower, but Lily pulled her back. "Leave it alone," she said.

Antoinette struggled for a moment, then sighed and rested her head in the crook of Lily's arm.

"I don't like it when they turn brown either," Lily said. "It's messy, but it's part of the process. They'll come back next year."

Lily sensed someone standing behind them, and she turned.

"You're out early," Seth said.

Lily was unsettled by his sudden appearance but tried not to let it show. They would be working together. To make that possible, she'd have to ignore the heat in her cheeks and the twinge in her heart she felt every time she saw Seth.

"Trouble sleeping." She raised her eyebrows and nodded toward Antoinette who shrieked and flapped her hands when she noticed Seth. "This is the first time she's smiled all morning."

"Well, we go back a ways, don't we?" He sat on Antoinette's other side. She shrieked again and pointed to the daffodils.

Lily and Seth went back even further, but she didn't say so. She kept the conversation safe: "I hate watching them die." She indicated the daffodils. Some people braided the leaves or cut them back before they browned. It was cleaner, but those same people were always surprised when their plants didn't flower the following season. As the leaves browned, they absorbed nutrients the plant needed for the next year.

Seth stretched out his legs and crossed them at the ankle. "After the leaves brown, we'll divide the bulbs. We should more than triple the crop next year." He looked past Lily to Antoinette. "She's happy with you."

He had always known what to say to make her feel better. Lily stroked Antoinette's shoulder. "I hope so."

"I'm going to Teelia's this morning to pick up her stuff for the show. Why don't you two tag along?"

His invitation surprised her, but she tried not to let it show. Antoinette flapped her hands and kicked her feet. She made a happy shriek.

"I guess that's a yes," Lily said, her relief at seeing Antoinette happy outweighing her discomfort at being with Seth. "Let me change and leave a note for Rose."

TEELIA WAS WAITING when they parked in front of her old barn. As they got out of the truck, she ran over, carrying a faded red toolbox. "I'd stay and help, but one of the fences in the back field is down."

Several alpacas stood at the fence by the barn. A brown one nudged Teelia's elbow. "You already ate," she said, pushing it away.

Alpacas hummed. It was a strange upturned sound, as if they were asking a question. *Hmm? Hmm?* Several of them clamored for Teelia's attention.

"Hush up," she said before turning to Seth. "The wheel's just inside the barn, and the yarn's in the blue milk crates. I also need the metal portable pen for Frank."

Seth disappeared into the barn while Lily helped Antoinette from the truck. The little girl tumbled down and headed over to a circle of dead grass by the front paddock. There she sat and pressed her fingers to the ground.

"He smiles more when he's with you," Teelia said, nodding in the direction Seth had gone. She stood at Lily's shoulder, and they both watched Antoinette."You're good for him. And unless I'm wrong, he's good for you. You're lighter around him."

"I thought you had to go fix a fence," Lily said. She was trying to suppress her feelings for Seth. The last thing she needed was Teelia stirring them up.

"What's a fence compared to true love?" She grinned.

"Teelia, you're hopeless," Lily said, glancing over her shoulder to make sure Seth hadn't overheard. Then she dropped the truck's tailgate and hopped up.

"I know what I see," Teelia said. "He's changed since you came home. He's smiled more in the past week than he has all year."

"I'm here for Rose," she said, pitching her voice low. "And Antoinette. I have to focus on them, not on reviving my love life."

At the sound of her name, Antoinette cocked her head. She looked like she was listening for something.

"Who says you can't do both?"

"*I* do," Lily said. She had never been good at dividing her focus. With her good hand, she opened the long silver toolbox attached to the truck bed and fished out several bungee cords which they'd use to tie down the metal pen.

The alpacas stretched toward Antoinette. One with a particularly long neck leaned down and nibbled her hair. Antoinette hunched her shoulders and giggled.

"Shoo!" Teelia waved her hands, and the alpacas drew back. "Seth needs someone who knows his burdens. I warrant he doesn't talk much to anyone."

"Not my business," Lily said, though she figured Teelia was right. She looped one of the bungee cords through an eye hook in the pickup bed. It was hard doing things one-handed. The cord slipped out of the hook several times before she was able to secure it.

"Maybe it should be," Teelia said. She smiled as she turned and started to walk away. "I'll be out to the farm later to set up. Think about what I said."

Lily watched Teelia until she became a small blue smudge on the horizon. It wasn't as if Lily hadn't thought about resuming her relationship with Seth. Of course she had. But there were other people to think about too, like Rose and Antoinette . . . and Will.

"This thing is awkward." Seth startled her, and Lily dropped her head, hoping her thoughts didn't show on her face.

He heaved the collapsed pen into the truck, then grabbed the bottom of his T-shirt and used it to wipe the sweat from his forehead, revealing his taut brown stomach. Lily quickly looked away.

She threaded the cord through the metal pen, then secured it back to the eye hook so it wouldn't fall out on their drive back to the farm. Using her good hand, she tugged on the cord until she was sure it wouldn't tumble out.

"You and Will seem close," Seth said as he sat down on the tail gate. He lifted one shoulder and let it drop as if he didn't care. But that was the thing about growing up together: even after being apart for so long, Lily knew what each twitch of his eyes or shrug of his shoulders meant. He feigned indifference when he was afraid of getting hurt, something he had done when they were kids.

"We're friends," she said, then hopped down from the truck and walked to the fence. Antoinette flapped her hands as Lily passed, thin strands of hair floating around her head like a halo. Four alpacas nosed at Antoinette over the white-plank fence.

Lily rested her elbows on the top rail and watched the animals. They had giraffelike necks and stocky bodies covered in thick fleece. A brown alpaca stretched its neck across the fence and nuzzled her hand.

"That's an awfully *good* friend to drive all the way down here to help you out." Seth plucked a piece of grass and moved to stand beside her. He twisted the grass tight around his finger.

"He is," she said, all the while thinking, *But he's not you.*

She shoved the thought aside. It didn't matter that she felt like she was falling when she stood next to Seth. Or that a deep ache opened up inside of her when she pictured him lying next to another woman. She was here for Rose and Antoinette. Nothing else.

Seth stretched his arm out toward a little white alpaca. It head-butted his hand, then closed its eyes as he scratched behind its ears. "You wouldn't expect something so strange-looking to be so gentle."

Lily felt him watching her, and her blood roared in her ears.

"Seminary was a mistake," he finally said. "I knew that within weeks of arriving."

"What was the first clue?" Lily asked, eager to keep their conversation *away* from their past relationship.

He sighed and uncurled the piece of grass from his finger. "It wasn't just one thing. It was several little things . . ." He pressed his lips together and looked up at the sky as if searching for the right words. Finally, he shook his head. "I was there for the wrong reasons. I didn't want to study the laws in Leviticus or learn how to lead a congregation or counsel newlyweds. I wanted to know why life is so messed up. Why good people get hurt."

Lily didn't have an answer. She suspected no one did.

In the middle of the herd, a baby alpaca rested its long neck over its mother's back. Mother and baby were both white, making it impossible to tell where one stopped and the other began.

Antoinette rocked back and forth on the ground beside Lily. She made an odd buzzing sound and poked at the dead grass. Then she waved her hands in front of her eyes and screamed, "Aey! Aey! Aey!"

Automatically, Lily said, "End on four, remember? Do things in even numbers." Antoinette gave four loud shrieks and calmed a bit. She pounded the ground again, but this time she looked forlorn, not angry.

"Did you find the answers you were looking for?" she finally asked.

"No," Seth said, "but I've learned to live without knowing. 'He makes his sun rise on the evil and the good, and sends rain on the just and unjust.' I could've just read the Gospel of Matthew and saved myself a lot of heartache." He laughed, a sharp, brittle sound.

"It wouldn't have been enough for you." Lily knew him well enough to know that. There had been a restlessness about Seth when he was younger. A need to understand the *whys* of life that mirrored her need for order and control.

He rested his hand on the fence next to hers. "I used to worry about my dad—that I'd turn out just like him. I think that's what started everything. I wanted to know *why* he was so short-tempered. I needed there to be a reason, because if there wasn't one, it meant he didn't love me—or Mom—enough to stop hitting us. It also meant I wouldn't know how *not* to be like him."

He shrugged. "Now I know it's random. Sometimes bad things just happen. Sometimes people make bad choices, but that fact doesn't negate the great good in the world."

He smiled, and his arm brushed hers. Lily couldn't tell where he stopped and she began. "A wise woman I know once told me that. I should have listened to her all those years ago."

"You're nothing like your father," she said.

He smiled, but it was a small, sad thing. "I wish I had realized that before I let you go. Maybe if I had, you'd be leaning on me instead of Will." He cupped her cheek and tilted her face toward his. "I tried to forget you."

Lily wanted to close her eyes and lose herself in the kiss she felt coming. She wanted to run her fingers across his back until the electricity tingling along her skin exploded, but she remembered losing him the first time. The urge to count had overwhelmed her. She couldn't step outside without first counting one hundred twenty-two heartbeats. She couldn't bear to get stuck like that again, and now she had Antoinette to think about too. She couldn't let Rose down a second time.

"I can't," she said. It hurt as she placed her hand on his chest and pushed. "Not unless I know it's real. Not unless I know you won't leave again." She turned away and walked to the truck without looking back.

## ROSE'S JOURNAL
### *April 2013*

———+———

TIME IS SLIPPING away from me. This morning I woke to a note from Lily saying that she and Antoinette were at Teelia's with Seth. Lily and Antoinette have made their peace with each other. It's what I wanted, so I'm surprised that when I think of them together, I feel hollow inside.

"You okay?" Will asks. He pushes a wheelbarrow loaded with steel pails, pruners, and gardening gloves.

I have stopped in the middle of the path leading to the fields. I shake myself and start walking again. "Sorry. My mind was elsewhere for a moment."

His smile is too kind. "You should try music. An iPod? Put the little buds in your ears and the world fades away. At least for a little while."

I appreciate his thought, but that's the problem. I don't want the world to fade away.

Will looks uncomfortable with the wheelbarrow. The land dips, and the wheelbarrow lists left. The steel pails clang together.

"There's an art to it," I say. "You have to distribute the weight evenly in your hands. It'll tip if it's unbalanced."

"Now you tell me," he says as he wipes his hands on his pants. "I thought working the ER was hard. It's nothing compared to farming."

I hear birds call from the woods, and I'm glad of their voices. Without Antoinette, everything is too quiet.

"Can I ask you something," I say, "as a doctor?"

"You can ask," he says. "I might not have an answer."

"Is this my fault? Did I make Antoinette this way?" My words come out in a rush. "If my heart had been stronger. If she hadn't been born so early . . ."

Will sets the wheelbarrow down and takes me by the shoulders. "It wasn't your fault. Millions of babies are premature. Some have trouble. Some don't. You couldn't have done anything to prevent this. You have a beautiful daughter, and a sister who loves you. I'd say you're one of the lucky ones."

"I don't feel lucky."

"You're surrounded by people who love you. There's not much more you can ask from life."

"More time would be nice." I laugh and wipe the corner of my eyes. My cheeks are wet. When did I start crying?

"No matter how much time you have, it won't be enough," he says.

I feel a catch in my chest, and I know he's right. "The tulips are at the edge of this field."

Will follows my lead, sensing that I need to change the subject. "Tell me again what we're doing," he says as we resume walking.

"You know Lily's obsession with the language of flowers?"

"It's kind of hard to miss."

I laugh. He's good at helping me forget.

"Lily used to leave bouquets around the house for me," I explain. "Ivy for friendship. Sweet basil for good wishes. I had to guess what she was saying. I want to do the same for her."

He bumps my shoulder. "She thought about you all the time. She had boxes under her bed filled with pictures of the two of you as girls. One box held baby pictures of Antoinette."

"How do you know what she kept under her bed?"

"I have my ways." He grins.

I laugh. It's been a long time since anyone has made me feel this good. Will has only been here a week, but I feel like I've known him much longer. "I bet you do."

We stop at the edge of the tulip row. The green buds have split open to reveal a flash of white petals. Will rubs his hands together. "Now I know how Lily got so tough. Farmwork isn't easy."

"She's softer than you think," I say as I take a pail from the wheelbarrow. I hook it over the spigot at the end of the row and turn on the water.

"I know. I sat with her when she cried because she missed home. After your parents died, she didn't sleep for a month. And when she finally did, it was only because I slipped Ambien into her hot chocolate."

Regret sits heavy on me. "She did that? Cried that much, I mean?" The pail is full. I try to pick it up, but the weight jerks my hands to the ground.

He takes it from me. "Where do you want it?"

"Just there, at the top of the row."

He sets the pail down among the tulips. "She missed your parents—and you—a lot."

"I shouldn't have been so stubborn," I say as I kneel in the dirt.

"Maybe you should tell her that." Will hands me a pair of pruners.

"That's what I'm trying to do." I run my hand down a tulip stalk and clip it near the base. I put it in the pail and cut another. "I was mad. Not just at her. At everything. Mom and Dad dying. Me being sick. Antoinette."

I sit back on my heels. "Not asking her to come home sooner is my biggest regret."

Will shoves his hands in his pockets and looks out over the fields. "You can't hold on to the past," he says. "Life continues whether you want it to or not."

A car door slams in the distance. I look up to see Lily helping Antoinette from the truck. Seth walks to the back of the truck and drops the tailgate.

"Speaking of regret," I say, "does she know how you feel?" I nod toward Lily.

"What?" He sounds surprised and embarrassed at the same time.

"I'm dying, not blind," I say. "If she doesn't know, you should tell her." I cut another tulip. The bucket is half full. Some flowers stand straight up and some drape over the sides. I'm already breathing hard from just this small amount of effort. I had planned to give Lily the flowers today, but I'm too tired. I'll have to store the tulips in the commercial freezer and fashion the bouquet tomorrow.

"I'm not the one she wants."

"Sometimes we don't know what we want until we're about to lose it," I say. "I used to feel trapped on the farm. Now I can't bear the thought of leaving."

As I did earlier, he changes the subject. "So why white tulips? What do they mean?"

I look down at the bucket. "Forgiveness. Something I should have given Lily a long time ago." I don't mention the other meaning. *Until we meet again.* This is also my way of saying good-bye.

Will takes the pruners from me. "Let me help." He kneels among the tulips, cutting flowers until the pail overflows.

# Chapter Twenty-Six

❧

T hursday afternoon, the kitchen in Cora's restaurant smelled like garlic, oregano, sweet basil, and thyme. Cooks clanged metal spoons against copper-bottomed pots and speed-chopped onions and tomatoes. Antoinette used to love the room, but not today.

Today she wanted to go home.

She had tried screaming, but Cora ignored her. Now she stood in the middle of the kitchen and spun like a top. The room blurred into a whirl of color and scent. When she stopped, her knees bobbled and the walls shimmied.

"Slow down," Cora said, without looking up from a pot of marinara sauce. "You're going to hurt yourself."

Antoinette didn't care if she hurt herself. She didn't want to be here. She wanted to go home and lie down next to her mother. She'd curl into a ball and push herself into her mother's side. They'd sit together all day, Antoinette memorizing her mother's heartbeat until it was so much a part of her, she'd never forget it.

She needed to find Lily—she would understand. Antoinette looked around the kitchen, but aside from Cora there was no one else she knew.

Lily had already delivered the fresh lavender Cora needed to make bread and cookies for the garden show on Sunday. That meant Lily was probably in the dining room setting out extra flower arrangements. And wherever Lily was, Will was sure to be close by. He wasn't as good at deciphering her desires, but he usually figured things out. Between the two of them, they would realize that she needed to go home.

Antoinette tugged Cora toward the door that led into the dining room.

"Wait a minute, I need to check this." Cora left her pot and turned to a plump man searching for something in the walk-in freezer. Cora stared at food the way Antoinette stared at flowers. She would be a while.

Antoinette didn't want to wait. When Cora's back was turned, she headed for the dining room. The restaurant wasn't open yet, and the room was empty.

Antoinette started toward the hostess stand. Maybe Lily was out front in the parking lot.

She had her hand on the door when Cora ran into the room. She pulled Antoinette back. "Don't you ever do that again! You scared me, running off like that!"

Antoinette yanked free. She scanned the room but didn't see any sign of Lily or Will. *I want to go home!*

"Let's go back to the kitchen. I should have chocolate cake in there for you."

Antoinette didn't want chocolate cake. When Cora reached for her hand, she growled.

Cora held her hands up. "We don't have to hold hands, but you need to come with me. I promised your aunt I'd look out for you. I can't have you wandering off."

Antoinette stomped her feet. *No, no, no.* She was not going back to the kitchen. She would find Lily; then they would go home, and she would sit with her mother for the rest of the day.

She whipped her head back and forth, then she screamed as loudly as she could.

"What's going on?" Lily ran into the dining room with Will. "We heard her screaming from the back room."

Cora blew out a breath. "I don't know. She wandered out here and wouldn't go back to the kitchen with me."

Even though Lily was here now, Antoinette couldn't stop screaming.

Lily knelt in front of her. "What's wrong?"

*Home*, Antoinette thought. *I need to go home.* She balled her hands into fists and hit her head. *Home, home, home!*

"Antoinette." Will touched her arm. "You need to stop."

No. She *needed* to go home. She shook her head and stomped her feet. Then she pointed to the door.

"Home?" Lily asked. "You want to go home?"

Antoinette flapped her hands. *Yes, yes, yes!* She knew Lily would understand.

"Will and I haven't finished the arrangements yet," Lily said. "It'll just be a little longer."

Antoinette wanted to leave *now*. Not in a few minutes. She slumped to the floor. She needed to be with her mother.

"Count with me," Lily said. She grasped Antoinette's hand, her skin warm and soft. "One. Two. Three. Four."

Antoinette had heard Lily's song before, so she should be able to hear it now. She closed her eyes and concentrated for several long seconds.

When she didn't hear anything, her last bit of hope drained

away. Without hearing the music, she would never be able to heal her mother. She started to cry.

"Why don't y'all take her home," Cora said. "I'll set up the flowers. I'll keep that chocolate cake for you, Antoinette." Cora blew her a kiss as she hurried back to the kitchen.

Antoinette was ten years old. She knew she was too big to be lying on a restaurant floor, crying, but she couldn't stop.

"I'll carry her," Will said. "You can't do it with your bad hand."

Lily kept holding Antoinette's hand. "We'll go home and see your mom. You'll feel better then."

Antoinette melted into Will when he picked her up. She wrapped her free arm around his neck and rested her head on his shoulder. She hiccuped sobs.

"Hey now," Will said. "It can't be that bad."

But it was. Her mother would never get better. Lily still held one of her hands. Anxiety made the fingers on Antoinette's other hand open and close. Without meaning to, she pinched Will's neck.

He flinched and took her hand, pulling it away.

At his touch, power jolted Antoinette. Two songs—Will's and Lily's—raced through her body. It was as if she had been wearing earplugs until now. She arched her back and tightened her fingers around both of their hands.

She could hear *everything*.

Most of Lily's song was steady and precise, but in one spot the notes were flat and the tempo a count behind.

Antoinette knew she could fix this.

She was sure of it.

She hummed, correcting the flat notes and increasing the

tempo. As she did, a current sparked up one arm and down the other. She was a vacuum, sucking up the wrong notes in Lily's song and sending everything bad into Will.

She didn't mean to, but when they touched her, everything sparked to life, and she couldn't stop.

Lily groaned and tried to twist free, but Antoinette held on tight. In seconds, Lily's song was fixed. Only then did Antoinette let go. Lily's bones were solidly in place, and this time, they wouldn't shift and pop free. Antoinette shrieked with joy.

Will dropped to his knees. "What happened?" He put Antoinette down, staring at her as if he had never seen her before.

At the same time, Lily unwrapped her ace bandage and wiggled her fingers. The bruise was gone. "It doesn't hurt."

The room was turning gray and Antoinette's eyes rolled back.

"She's seizing," Will said. He sounded tired.

"Help me get her on her side," Lily said.

Their voices merged until Antoinette could no longer make out the words, but she didn't care.

Lily's hand was fixed. Antoinette didn't know what had been different this time, but it didn't matter. She giggled as the room went black.

If she could do this, if she could mend Lily's broken hand, she could save her mother.

# Chapter Twenty-Seven

L ily burst through the kitchen door, waving her hand in the air. "It worked," she shouted, but no one was there. She ran down the hall and shoved Rose's bedroom door open. "Rose, something was different this time."

Rose wasn't there either. Her bed was made, the white quilt tucked in around the edges. Lily deflated as she looked around. She wanted to tell Rose what had happened at Cora's. Something had changed, but she didn't know what. She curled her fingers into a fist. Not even a twinge. The bruises and swelling were gone.

She went back out onto the porch where Will sat on the swing with Antoinette. "She's not inside."

A light rain had started to fall when they got back to the farm, but that didn't stop artists from trickling in to get ready for the garden show. Several people wandered about the garden, setting up white tents and unloading tables and chairs.

Antoinette slept in the crook of Will's arm. "You're a natural," Lily whispered.

He looked exhausted. On the way back from Cora's, he had slumped against the van door with his eyes closed.

"Are you okay?" she asked.

Will smoothed Antoinette's hair from her forehead. She shifted in her sleep but didn't open her eyes. "No worse than before."

He was lying. Lily could see it in the way he avoided her eyes. The porch boards creaked as she knelt by his knees. "Tell me the truth, Will. What's wrong?"

The rain fell in a soft patter against the porch roof. The show was on Sunday, and she hoped it would be dry by then.

Will raised his eyes to hers. Flecks of purple mixed in with the deep blue. "Nothing's wrong," he said.

"I know you well enough to know that you're lying."

"Would I do that to you?" He caught her hand and examined it, pressing his fingers along the bones that had been broken. "Does it hurt?"

She wiggled her fingers. "Not at all. Last time, it started hurting as soon as Antoinette let go."

Antoinette sighed. It sounded like a word. "Mmmmaaa."

A tickle of guilt began somewhere below Lily's stomach, and intensified when she looked at Antoinette. The seizure had been smaller this time. That had to mean something. "Is she okay?"

Will kissed Lily's forehead. "She's fine. I'm fine. Go find Rose."

Lily hesitated. She looked from Antoinette to Will and back again.

"Go," he said, shooing her away. "Before the rain gets worse. We're fine."

She took one last look at them, then ran down the porch and into the rain.

LILY FOUND ROSE and Seth as they left the drying barn. Seth carried a basket of white tulips in one arm and steadied Rose with the other.

"Lily," Rose said. She stopped under the barn eave. Seth stood in front of her, shielding her from the rain, which was falling harder now. "I didn't think you'd be home so soon."

Lily's hair was wet and it stuck to her face. The air smelled like ozone. "You won't believe what Antoinette did." The words tumbled out as she recounted what had happened at Cora's. When she finished, she held up her hand. "The seizure was smaller than before. Less than a minute. Something's different this time. I don't have any pain. And Antoinette's okay. Will's with her now. He promised she's okay."

The rain was now a downpour, and Lily raised her voice to be heard. "My hand is fixed, Rose. Completely. If she can do this for me, there has to be a way she can heal you." In her eagerness, the words tumbled out.

Seth set the basket down. "Can I see?" he asked. She held out her hand. "It doesn't hurt?" He ran his fingers over hers.

Lily shook her head. By now they were both soaked, but neither of them noticed.

"She's right," Seth said. There was a trace of excitement in his voice. He held her hand a moment longer. "There's not a mark here."

"What if we're missing something?" Lily asked. "What if there's a solution?"

Rose's eyes were sad as she shook her head. "It's never been about whether she can heal me. It's about the price she pays. It's too high." Rose took Lily's hand and laced her fingers through hers.

"But the seizure was small." Lily squeezed her sister's hand; it felt cold. "What if you both can live? What if it's not a choice between you or her?" She started to tremble.

Seth placed his hand on the small of Rose's back and pressed. "Maybe she's right," he said. "If there's a chance, and we give up—"

"I'm not giving up," Rose said. "I'm making a choice."

Rain now fell in sheets from the barn eaves. It splashed over their feet, turning the ground to mud. "But I can't lose you," Lily said. "Not again." Rivulets of water ran down her nose, but she didn't wipe them away. She knew Rose was right, but it hurt to admit it.

Gently, Rose released Lily's hand. Despite their best efforts to shield her from the rain, she was soaking wet. "Sometimes the best love means letting go." She pointed at the basket of flowers on the ground. "Seth, give them to her."

He took the bunch of tulips and handed them to Lily.

"Forgiveness," Rose said. "That's what white tulips mean—right?"

Lily couldn't stop shaking. White tulips were also a symbol of heaven and remembrance, but she didn't say that.

"I need you to forgive me," Rose said. She raised her voice to be heard over the rain. "For staying mad so long. For taking things out on you that weren't your fault. I can't leave things unsaid between us."

"I abandoned you. If anyone needs forgiveness, it's me." Lily dropped the flowers and gripped Rose's hands.

"We're sisters. There's nothing to forgive."

The rain kept falling. It mixed with Lily's tears as she said what she should have said the morning of their parents' funeral. Unlike then, the words came easily now: "I promise I'll keep Antoinette safe."

## ROSE'S JOURNAL
### *April 2013*

---

I USED TO believe life was easy. You walked in the direction of your dreams, and abracadabra, they appeared in front of you. You only needed to scoop them up and tuck them in your pocket or press them, like a flower, between the pages of an old book.

Now I know the best parts of my life have been the moments I didn't dream. Like Antoinette.

Life is not a straight line. It's a spiderweb that twists and tangles. We crawl along our strands until we touch the people who are meant to be in our lives. The strands can knot, as mine did with Lily's, but they don't break, and the unexpected paths are often the best ones.

The life I planned bears little resemblance to the life I have lived, but I don't mind. Not even a little.

Still, I dream.

In a corner of my heart, the one I don't allow myself to examine too often, I hope for a happy ending. Who doesn't?

Some mornings, when the light is pink and the air is sweet with lavender, I wake believing this is it. This is the morning the room won't spin when I sit up. I'll fill my lungs with air, and hold my breath until I feel like I'll explode. When I let the air out, I won't cough, I won't pass out, my heart won't throw itself against my ribs. I'll run to Antoinette's room, legs steady, heart strong.

Then the best part: she'll be sitting on the edge of her bed, waiting for me. She'll look into my eyes, and I'll find myself reflected there. She'll smile, and it will be more beautiful than any sunset I've ever seen.

"Mommy," she'll say in a bright silver voice.

This is my fairy tale. No prince. No castles or spinning wheels to turn straw into gold. Only my daughter and me, both of us whole, both of us here together.

That's my idea of happily ever after, and it's enough for me.

# Chapter Twenty-Eight

❧

Saturday night, Lily stood on a stepladder threading strings of white lights through the wisteria that grew over the gazebo. She stretched her fingers wide, waiting to feel the bones catch. Nothing.

Rose sat on the gazebo stairs, directing a flashlight beam toward the area where Lily worked. Antoinette was inside napping.

"Still good?" Will asked as he handed her another bunch of coiled lights. He had a faraway look in his eyes, as if preoccupied by a complex math equation.

"Perfect," she said as she wound the lights through the garland of hydrangeas and roses she had made earlier and twined around the gazebo posts. Wreaths of apple blossoms and lilies draped over the rails. The crabapple trees in the house garden had burst into bloom that morning. The night was magic.

She imagined what the garden would look like tomorrow. People would mill about, stopping by Cora's booth, or buying skeins of Teelia's yarn. Seth would stand on the stage they had set up in the drying barn, playing his violin, switching smoothly between Vivaldi and bluegrass.

White tents sprouted throughout the garden, and despite the

rain, the setup was successful. The only issue had been with Teelia's set up and even that was minor.

That morning, Lily had closed the kitchen door and set the alarm before setting out to work. Only seconds later Teelia burst through the door, tripping the alarm.

"My tent ripped," she yelled over the blaring noise. "I need to patch it. A garbage bag or something. The wool can't get wet if it rains."

Teelia ran through the kitchen, opening and closing cabinets, until Lily located the garbage bags for her. Lily wanted to remind her that rain wasn't predicted for Sunday, but given Teelia's agitated state she decided she probably wouldn't pay attention anyway.

After that, the alarm had stayed off.

It was evening now, and most of the vendors were gone. Earlier in the day, the farm had been swarming with artists setting up tables for tomorrow's show, but the majority had finished quickly. A few quilters remained, and Eli Cantwell had just arrived, but other than that the farm was empty.

Until now, Lily had never realized how many artists lived in Redbud. Among others, there was a woman selling handmade soaps and lotions, a silversmith who shaped wire into wrist cuffs, and a man with mounted butterflies in glass frames. Then there were the quilters—five women would have tables with quilts for sale at the show.

Lily grew up sleeping under thick covers her mother made, but her mother's work was utilitarian, more for keeping the cold out than for displaying. But as Lily looked at the women unfolding appliquéd and embroidered quilts, she imagined her mother here.

"Mom would have loved the show this year," Rose said as she aimed a flashlight beam at the tables.

"Shine it over here." Lily gestured to the left where Seth had taped an extension cord up the side of the gazebo.

Rose shifted the flashlight beam, and Lily plugged in the lights. Then she sat back, squinted, and examined her work. It looked beautiful and romantic, like the stars had left heaven and taken up residence under the gazebo.

"Uh-oh," Will said. He nodded at the stone path that led out of the house garden.

Eli Cantwell walked toward them. His face was skeletal, and the lights reflected off his pale skin.

"Want me to handle him?" Will asked.

"No, I'll take care of this." Rose's voice was light, but she pressed a hand to her chest.

Will held out his hand to help her stand and walk down the gazebo steps.

"It's a good thing the rain stopped," Rose said when Eli was a few feet away. Her words sounded forced. "Do you have everything you need to set up?"

"MaryBeth is worse," Eli said. He stopped a hand's length from Rose. He was close enough for Lily to see his knuckles whiten as he clenched his hands into fists.

"I'm sorry to hear that," Rose said, grief in her voice. "Is she here?" She looked past Eli's shoulder, as if hoping MaryBeth was behind him.

It was strange seeing Eli without MaryBeth, Lily thought. They were always together.

Eli shook his head. What little hair he had stuck out in wild tufts. "She's shaking so bad she can't hold a cup of water. Spills it all over herself."

"I'm sorry," Rose said. "I know how hard this must be for you."

"No, you don't," Eli said. He poked a finger at her. "If you did, you'd help us."

"That's enough," Will said, but Eli didn't stop.

"You look awfully healthy for someone with a heart condition," he said. "You're still here—what? Ten years later?"

Lily started counting. She had never felt nervous around Eli before, but he was different now. Angry. Scared.

Rose held out her hand. "You don't understand—"

Eli shoved her hand aside. "I know what your girl can do. It's not right to keep her all to yourself."

Lily stopped counting and scrambled down the ladder. No one touched her sister like that.

"I think you should go," Will said. He stepped in front of Rose.

"You *know* us." Eli stared at Rose, his eyes pleading. "Mary-Beth loves your little girl. How can you let her die?" On the word *die* his voice cracked.

"You don't understand," Rose repeated quietly.

"I understand perfectly. You're letting my wife die!"

Lily took Will's place in front of Rose. "Eli, stop," she said. "You know we love MaryBeth. If we could help her, we would."

"I know what I saw." He nodded at Lily's hand. "It was broken. I saw it. Then Antoinette touched you and it was fine."

Rose was shaking. "I'm sorry," she whispered.

Eli took a step toward Rose.

"You need to stop this," Will said, iron in his voice.

Eli didn't listen. He stepped around Will and reached for Rose. "Help us. *Please*."

"Leave." This time, Will put his hand on Eli's chest and pushed until the older man backed away, then turned, and disappeared into the night.

Lily touched Rose's shoulder. "Are you okay?" she asked.

Rose's eyes glistened. "ALS is complicated. Healing MaryBeth could kill Antoinette. I can't let her do that."

"Of course not," Lily said, although she couldn't help but wish that it were otherwise.

Rose rubbed her eyes. "I need to check on Antoinette. I'll also ask Seth to make sure Eli's gone."

"I'll come with you," Lily said.

Rose shook her head and pressed her lips into a tight smile. Lily thought it was meant to be reassuring, but Rose's eyes were bright with tears. "I need some time alone," she said, and walked away.

Lily watched Rose until she faded from sight. "Do you think she'll be okay?" she asked Will.

"She's keeping her daughter safe. She'll be fine."

Lily wasn't sure. "What about Eli? If he won't leave—"

"Have you seen Seth? The guy's got arms like tree trunks. Eli might be upset, but he's no fool."

"I hope you're right," Lily said. She squinted into the darkness, straining to see whether Eli was still there.

Will sat down on the gazebo steps and patted the spot next to him. "The stars aren't this bright in the city. In thirty-five years I don't think I noticed them. Thirty-five years, and I never looked up. How sad is that?"

"You're looking now," Lily said, grateful for Will's attempt to distract her. He was right. Eli was upset, but he wasn't a real threat.

"Too little, too late, Lils." He flipped his hair out of his eyes. "Did you know that when a star goes supernova and explodes, a new star is born? The force of the explosion shoves clouds of hydrogen and helium molecules together. Gravity makes the clouds collapse and rotate. Once the heat and pressure reach a certain point, a new star is created from the old one.

"It's a transfer of energy from one place to another—ashes to ashes, and dust to dust, just on a much larger stage. One star dies. Another is born. Energy can't be created or destroyed, but it can be transformed."

He grew thoughtful. "What if it's something like that?"

"What?" Lily frowned, not following him.

"Antoinette's ability . . ." He shook his head as if to clear it. "I had the thread of a thought, but I lost it."

Lily sat down and leaned her head against his shoulder. "I'm glad you're here," she said.

"I am too." He stared at her for several long moments, and for the first time since she had known him he looked nervous. "Does he tell you you're beautiful?" he finally asked.

"Who?" Her answer was reflexive, but immediately she understood.

"Seth. Does he know how soft your skin is?" He traced his finger across her cheek.

Despite the tingle of electricity skipping across her skin, she caught his hand. "Don't." She saw expectation in his eyes, and her heart ached knowing she was about to hurt him. "I love Seth. I always have. And I love you too—just not in the same way."

Giving voice to her feelings unlocked something inside of her, and she finally realized how foolish she had been to push Seth away. All because she was afraid of getting hurt. It was the same thing she did the first time Rose had asked for her help with Antoinette.

No more. Fear had already occupied too much of her life.

Will tucked a loose strand of hair behind her ear, then ran his fingers down her neck to the hollow of her throat. His movements were small and tentative.

She froze, unsure whether to lean into him or turn away. "I'm not like the girls you bring back to your house."

He leaned forward until their foreheads were almost touching. "I know. Why do you think I've wanted to do this from the first time I saw you?"

"Will, don't." She put her hands on his chest. "It won't be real. It's not fair to you."

"Let me decide what's fair to me. Just once, Lils. Give me one moment when everything is perfect."

The wind began to blow, picking up a swirl of apple blossom petals and dusting them across his shoulders. Lily lightly brushed them off, leaving her hand on his shoulder. "It won't be true," she repeated. "I'm sorry. I love Seth."

"Ah Lils, haven't you learned? There's more than one version of truth. Let me have my version. Besides, I've been told I'm a pretty good kisser."

She believed him, but that wasn't why she let him press his lips to hers. It was because she remembered his fingers on her cheek, catching her tears after Rose called that first time. She remembered the nights he held her as she cried when her parents died. And she remembered sitting with him through his chemo treatments, when his fear was so heavy she could almost touch it.

She could give him this. She let him hold her close. He slid one hand around her hip and ran the other up her back. He was right. He *was* good at this.

The kiss was long and slow and held all the words they would never say to each other.

THE MOON HUNG in the sky when Lily left Will sitting at the gazebo. It rose above the treetops, speaking of second chances and hope. But it also spoke of regret.

Will had kissed her. It was beautiful and bittersweet, nothing at all like Seth's kisses, which were aggressive and passionate. When she pulled away from Will, she had pressed her hand against his lips and whispered, "I'm sorry."

She loved Will. Through the years of silence from Rose, he had been her only friend. But when she pictured herself sitting on the porch swing at eighty, it was Seth who sat beside her, not Will.

Lily had loved Seth from the beginning, when they were still children. He tied her life together—the good parts and the bad—and that, she realized, was worth risking everything for.

With Will's kiss still on her lips, she started down the flagstone path. A thin beam of light shone beneath the drying barn door. Seth must be in there, raking the cedar shavings and hanging fresh lavender from the rafters for the show tomorrow.

"Seth?" she called as she opened the door. No one answered. She walked deeper into the barn.

Everything was in place: the stage was set up; flowers hung

from the rafters; white cloths covered the tables. But the barn was empty.

Lily sighed. Seth probably forgot to turn out the light. She flipped the switch, plunging the barn into darkness. Once outside again, she decided to go to the creek. She was too restless to go back to the house.

Trees overtook the fields, but moonlight flickered through their canopy, lighting her way. Still, it was dark, and she was cautious, stretching her feet in front of her, searching for the stone path to the creek.

Reaching the water, she rolled her jeans to her knees, then waded in. The creek was stinging cold, and she gasped. The water was lower here than farther down the stream, but with the recent rains even here the creek was deep.

She waded out to the flat rock that jutted from the middle of the creek. When they were kids, Seth, Lily, and Rose would lie on the rock, their heads touching as they watched the sky, calling out shapes they found in the clouds above them.

Tonight the moon draped everything in blue-white light. Lily lay back and put her arm over her eyes. She was almost asleep when a splash to her left startled her. "Who's there?" she asked as she lurched upright.

"Lily?"

Instead of slowing, her heart sped at the sound of Seth's voice. "What are you doing here?" she asked.

"Same as you, I suppose." He crossed the creek and stood at the base of the rock. "Mind if I come up?"

"Suit yourself," she said, scooting over to make room for him.

He pulled himself up in one fluid motion. Moonlight outlined his profile, painting him black and silver.

"I saw the light in the barn," she said. "I stopped in, but you weren't there." She pressed her knees into her chest and wrapped her arms around them. If she touched him now, she knew she would never let go.

"I must have forgotten to turn it out." In the dim light she could trace the planes of his face, the small wrinkles around his mouth, at the corners of his eyes, and across his forehead.

"Rose told me what happened with Eli," he said, placing his elbows on his knees. "I was walking the farm to make sure he's gone when I saw you walk past."

"Is he?"

"He's gone. I checked everywhere."

Lily relaxed. The night was warm, more fit for August than April. She plunged her hand into the cold water, opening and closing her fingers, concentrating on the feel of the water.

Seth ran his hand through his hair, making it wave around his face. "I didn't expect it to be so difficult to see you again."

Lily raised her eyebrows. Whatever she had been expecting him to say, it wasn't that. She curled her hand in the water. The shock of the cold kept her in the present, preventing her mind from slipping back to the summer nights they had spent here. "It hasn't been easy for me either."

"I thought I could forget the past," he said, "but I was wrong. I've missed you. I don't want to interfere with your life. If you and Will are—"

"We're not," she said, the words coming out faster than she meant for them to. She took a breath, deliberately slowing her thoughts. "Do you remember when we used to come here and watch the clouds? You and Rose found shapes, but I couldn't see anything other than the two of you. I wanted to stay like that forever. How did everything end up so differently than I planned?" It was the question she had been asking herself since coming home. She didn't expect him to answer, and was surprised when he did.

"I don't know," he said. "For a long time, I never thought I'd be back here. Now I can't imagine being anywhere else. I believe there are places that get to you. They slip under your skin and won't let you go. Redbud's like that for me."

Lily shook the water from her fingers. Tiny droplets sprayed over her face, cooling her skin where they touched. "What about people?" she asked.

He shifted until their fingers touched. When he looked down at her, she shivered. "Some," he said. "I think it's like that for some people."

"What about for us?" The question was easier to ask in the dark, when the rustle of the trees and the buzz of cicadas covered her words as soon as they were out.

"When I left for seminary," Seth said, "I thought I could forget everything—it wasn't easy for me here. Dad made sure of that.

"But there, no one knew my family. People didn't stare when I walked across campus. No one whispered behind my back. No one pitied me. I felt like I could leave my past in Redbud and just be me, not the boy whose drunk father beat him. For the first time in my life, I was just Seth Hastings.

"It wasn't until I came back for Mom's funeral that I realized leaving didn't free me. Instead, it gave the past that much more power over me. I could never be myself because I was always hiding part of my life.

"I've tried," he said, "but I can't stay away from you. You're the only person I can be myself with. I don't have to hide from you." He moved closer.

"I bought into Eden Farms because I wanted to come home, but I stayed because I saw you everywhere. In the fields, I saw us running through the sunflowers down to the creek. In the barn, while hanging flowers to dry from the rafters, I would see you standing in a halo of sunlight. Sometimes it was so real I thought I could touch you. I'd sit on this rock at night and feel you beneath me."

Seth pressed his forehead against hers. "The best parts of my life have been with you. You see all of me and you love me anyway. Or at least you did."

She watched his lips as he spoke, wondering whether they would feel the same after all these years. She brushed his hair back. The thick strands slid through her fingers. Then she ran her hands over the broad planes of his back and down his arms.

"I still do," she said. "I never stopped."

It felt as if they had been slowly bending toward each other since that first day at the farmers' market. Instead of beating faster, her heart slowed as if trying to stretch this moment into an eternity.

His breath was hot when he lowered his mouth to hers. His lips were as soft as she remembered. He wrapped his arms around her, laid her back on the rock, and covered her body with his.

# Chapter Twenty-Nine

～⌒～

Antoinette was talking in her sleep. She woke from a dream where she rode the wind to the edge of the creek and knelt in the mud. As in real life, ferns grew along the bank, but in her dream the fronds were made of words instead of leaves. She searched until she found a word that calmed her body and made her feel whole. She plucked it and placed it on her tongue. The word tasted like blueberries, sweet and tart at the same time. "Mommy," she said as it slid down her throat.

Dream-talking wasn't unusual. Everything happened in dreams, even the impossible, but this time was different. This time, her lips hummed when she woke as if the actual word had just left her mouth. A breeze blew through the open window, billowing the sheers and sending goose bumps along her arms.

She tried again. "Mmmm," she said. She closed her eyes, trying to remember the ease with which she spoke while dreaming, but it was too late. The word was gone.

It was the evening before the garden show, but the farm was quiet now. Earlier that day, Antoinette had been so tired she fell asleep with her head against her mother's knee. Vaguely, she remembered Lily carrying her to her room.

Outside her window, crickets chirped and an owl hooted. Everything had a voice except her. Even the wind whistled as it swept through the window. She balled her hand into a fist and hit the wall. If she could speak, she could make her mother listen.

"Let me help you," she would say, and for once her mother would be the silent one. Antoinette would hold her mother's hand and sing until everything was fixed. Until her heart was so strong it would never stop beating.

Antoinette's arms were stiff, but she shoved her covers back and concentrated on untangling her legs from the quilt. Some dreams came true. She had fixed Lily's hand after thinking she would never heal again. Why couldn't this dream come true too?

The wood floor was cool under her feet. Her knees wobbled as she stood, but she was calm, still under the thrall of her dream. She didn't twitch or flap as she walked downstairs into the kitchen, and she wondered, *Is this how other people feel?*

In her dream, the words grew on ferns by the creek bank, so that's where she'd go. She would sit there, eating leaves, singing under the moon until her throat was raw. Then she'd run home, wake her mother, and fix everything. Words had power.

Dark shadows sat in the kitchen corners, but Antoinette didn't care. It was easier to see without all the colors getting in the way. As she crossed the kitchen to the back door, her skin prickled in anticipation. What would it feel like to open her mouth and say anything she wanted? She flapped her hands and reached for the doorknob. Everything would change tonight.

She stopped when her fingertips brushed the flaked paint on the door. She had forgotten the red light. If she opened the door, it would squeal. Her mother would wake, and everything would be ruined.

Before looking up, she squeezed her eyes shut. *Please*, she prayed. *Let the light be off.* She flapped her hands twice for good measure, then opened her eyes one at a time. She let her head fall back and looked up.

The light was off.

She blinked hard and looked again. Nothing. The space above the door was beautifully blank. Her heart quickened, and she shrieked twice before she could stop herself. Her voice filled the empty room and echoed through the house, louder than the alarm ever was.

She didn't wait to find out if anyone heard her. She shoved her arm straight out and pushed the door open. It smacked into the wall with a loud crack. She stumbled through, her bones loose under her skin, her knees wobbling.

Antoinette was at the top of the porch steps when she heard a voice from inside the house. "Antoinette? Is that you?"

Her mother.

In a rush, Antoinette tumbled down the porch steps, cutting her leg in the fall. Blood dripped down her shin, but she didn't stop.

The sky was dark and the land silent. No music rolled through her mind, but that didn't matter. Everything would be better soon. Heat shimmered up from the ground. She easily made it to the stone path that led to the woods.

She was at the edge of the field when the kitchen door slammed, and her mother yelled, "Antoinette? Are you out there?"

*Hurry, hurry, hurry.* Antoinette walked as fast as she could. *This must be how birds feel*, she thought. She spread her arms wide to catch the wind.

"I can see you Antoinette!" her mother yelled. "Come back here!"

The woods marking the end of the fields had filled out. The trees' branches twined together to form a thick screen.

Antoinette shoved through. She lost her footing but locked her knees and didn't fall, even when twigs pierced the soles of her feet.

It was cooler and darker under the branches. Instead of following the well-worn path to the creek, she turned off onto a narrow deer trail. It would be easier to hide that way. She wasn't going home until she found the ferns from her dream.

A branch from a birch tree flicked back against her cheek. She felt blood welling along the cut, and she put her hand to her face, willing the edges of her skin back together, but she had never been able to heal herself, and this time was no different.

"Antoinette!" Her mother's voice floated behind her, to her right, so she went left, moving deeper into the woods, toward the sound of creek water.

In the distance her mother called again, closer this time. Antoinette imagined her mother's distress, and she almost turned back, but then she remembered the way her body had felt after speaking. She had to know whether it was possible.

By the time she emerged from the tree cover and onto the creek bank, her face was covered with tiny scratches. Blood trickled from her cheek to the corner of her mouth. It was warm and salty when she touched her tongue to it.

The creek was swollen with rain. Water rose halfway up the

muddy hill. Exposed tree roots hung over the thin lip of dirt separating the woods from the water. She was farther downstream than usual, far from the flat rock that jutted from the center of the creek. She wasn't familiar with this part of the woods, but that didn't matter. Ferns grew all along the water's edge; she could find them anywhere.

Though the moon was out, its light was blocked by the trees, and she could barely see. She found moss and twisted tree roots, but no ferns. She shifted to her left, brushing her fingers along the ground, searching. She was concentrating so hard, she missed the footfalls behind her.

"I thought I heard someone," a man said, startling her. "God must be smiling on me. I went for a walk in the woods to sort some things out and here you are."

Antoinette turned. Eli stood behind her. For a moment, she was happy to see him, but almost immediately she sensed that something was wrong. He stood too close to her, and he whispered as if he didn't want anyone to overhear him.

"I need you to do me a favor," he said. "Then I'll bring you back to your mama. A little girl like you shouldn't be out in the woods by herself."

Normally, Antoinette would be happy to help Eli, but he was different tonight. She tried to scoot backward to put some distance between them but she was at the edge of the creek bank.

"Antoinette!" her mother yelled, her voice closer. She must have followed the flagstone path to the creek, coming out downstream, across from the flat rock.

"Antoinette!" It was Will's voice this time. "Your mom needs you to come home." Her mother must have asked for his help.

Antoinette opened her mouth, but no sound came out. Her dream seemed foolish now. She should have known nothing could fix her.

There was nowhere to go except down the hill. It took all of her concentration to put one foot in front of the other without sliding down to the creek.

"Come on now," Eli said. "I'm not going to hurt you. I want to take you back to your mama. But first MaryBeth needs your help. You love MaryBeth, don't you? You want to help her."

His words made her stop inching toward the creek. She *did* love MaryBeth.

"Be a good girl," Eli said, holding his hand out to her. "That's right. Take my hand. The Lord works in mysterious ways. He must have known I needed your help and sent me out here to find you." Eli turned toward the woods, and this time, Antoinette allowed him to pull her along with him.

"We'll go see MaryBeth, and you'll fix her," Eli said. "Then I'll bring you back to your mom. You'll be home before she misses you."

"Antoinette!" her mother called again. "Where are you? Please make a noise, a sound. *Anything.*"

The panic in her mother's voice made Antoinette stop. She loved MaryBeth, but she loved her mother more.

"Come on," Eli said, tightening his hold on her hand. Though they were skin to skin, Antoinette couldn't hear his song. "We've got to keep going. Hurry."

But Antoinette didn't want to go with Eli anymore. She wanted her mother. *Mommy!* she thought over and over again, and she managed a small shriek.

"Hush," he said, and he gripped her tighter, his fingers pressing into her flesh until she felt the bone bruise. "I'm just taking you to MaryBeth. You like MaryBeth, don't you?"

She did, but Eli was scaring her. She wanted her mother. She shook her head hard. *No!* she thought. *I want my mommy!*

Eli pulled her into the woods, pushing aside tree branches. He was too strong. She struggled, but she couldn't break free. "I know what you can do. Your mama won't admit it, but I saw it. You healed MaryBeth, but she's sick again. I need you to fix her for good this time."

Eli was moving so fast she couldn't keep up with him. Her feet tangled, and she stumbled. She went down hard, scraping her knees on exposed tree roots. She cried out in pain.

"Antoinette?" her mother yelled. "Is that you? Are you okay?"

"I think she's over here," Will said, sounding much closer now.

"We're coming," her mother yelled. "Just stay there!"

Eli pulled her up. "Please," he said, his eyes wet with tears. "I can't lose MaryBeth. She's all I have. Help us."

There was a rustling in the trees on the creek bank. Antoinette strained toward the sound, her mother's face filling her mind.

"Come on." Eli tugged, but she couldn't get to her feet.

Then someone crashed through the trees and grabbed her free hand. At the touch, electricity shot through her, and two songs roared to life in her ears. The first was sad and dissonant, the notes in a minor key. The second was familiar.

Will's.

"Let go of her!" Will said, pulling her hand.

But Eli held on to her hand. "I need her help. Just for a little bit. Please. Let her come with me. I'll bring her right back."

Black spots dotted Antoinette's vision, and her hands were scalding where Will and Eli touched her. She couldn't think with both songs in her head. The discordant music competed for her attention, commanding that she do something.

She concentrated on the spot where Eli's hand gripped her. As when she had touched Lily's hand at Cora's, his song became louder.

Then she turned her focus to Will's hand, and his song flared to life. In one spot, the notes were off. Surprised, Antoinette realized that Will was sick. Very sick. In fact, he was almost as sick as her mother. Almost as a reflex, she grabbed Will's wrong notes—not all of them, there were too many—and pushed them into Eli.

At the same time, Seth crashed through the woods, Lily following right behind. "Get off her, Eli," Seth said. He grabbed Antoinette, pulling her free from both Eli and Will. Her connection to both men broke and the songs faded.

Then her mother was there. She touched Antoinette's face, her arms, her hands. "Are you okay? Did he hurt you?"

Antoinette tried to answer, but the world blinked black and white. Her mother's face disappeared and reappeared in quick flashes.

"Why couldn't you leave her alone?" her mother cried.

Antoinette's vision was fading and she was starting to shake, but she could still make out her mother's voice.

"She's not strong enough to do this. If she keeps seizing like this, she'll die. You could have killed her!"

"I didn't know . . . I would never." Eli sounded shocked. "I just thought . . . MaryBeth is dying—"

"And now Antoinette might be," her mother said. "Put her down, Seth. Roll her onto her side."

Antoinette felt the earth beneath her and hands on her side, rolling her over. She was shaking, but she was still conscious.

"Eli," Lily said softly. "You know we love MaryBeth. If we could help her, we would. But Antoinette can't keep doing this. The seizures are getting worse. Soon one of them might kill her."

"I didn't know," Eli said, his voice tight. "I swear, I didn't know. I would never hurt Antoinette."

Will knelt beside her, examining her. All of a sudden, he frowned; then his eyes widened in surprise as if something had just clicked into place.

"You're a conduit," he said, only loud enough for her to hear. "The sickness doesn't disappear, you just move it from one person to another. Matter can't be destroyed, only transformed. That's what you're doing. Transforming the illness by moving it."

Antoinette's last sight, before the world went black, was of Lily, appearing over Will's shoulder. He turned to face her. "I figured it out," he said.

# Chapter Thirty

~⁓~

On Sunday evening, white lights winked among the hydrangea vines growing up the sides of the gazebo. To
Lily, the garden felt alive. Anticipation buzzed through
the crowd gathered for the show. Every once in a while a person looked up, as if expecting the plants to grow legs and walk
among them.

Who knew? Lily thought. Given what had been happening
there lately, maybe they would.

Strangers and locals milled about the garden, stopping every
few feet to stare at one of Rose's paintings or run their fingers
through Teelia's hand-dyed alpaca yarn. Lily's favorite booth was
the glass blower's.

Earlier that evening, she stood in the shadows with her head
on Seth's chest, watching as a man twirled liquid fire at the end
of a long metal stick. Somehow the orange blaze at the end of
the pole transformed into a glass bowl with bright green streaks
running up the sides.

Seth bought it for her. "So you'll remember this night."

As if she could forget.

He was in the drying barn now, playing for a full crowd.

Tonight he eschewed the classics and chose old-time fiddling, some traditional tunes, but mostly bluegrass. She looked toward the barn and felt her face glow.

"He'll be beside you soon enough," Will said. He sat on the bench that ran the length of the gazebo.

Antoinette stretched up on her tippy-toes. She didn't wear shoes, and her skin was so pale her feet gleamed in the reflected light. Lily looked from Antoinette to Will.

Deliberately changing the subject, she gestured toward the people crowding the garden. "I didn't realize it would be as nice as this," she said. "No wonder Rose insisted on having the show." Right now, Rose was back at the house, resting and recovering from the effort involved with hosting the party.

Will watched Antoinette tiptoe around the gazebo. "Your sister's smart. I'd make a lot of the same decisions she has."

High praise from Will.

Lily cut a piece of lavender bread from the loaf on the stairs next to her and popped it in her mouth. It was sweet and a little lemony. Rose was right; it tasted like love.

She held out a piece to Will, but he shook his head.

Lavender was an herb like basil or oregano, but most people didn't think to cook with it. She turned to Antoinette. "Want some?"

Antoinette flapped her hands and took the bread. That morning, as she walked through the farm, marigolds had bloomed in her footsteps.

Marigolds meant grief.

Except for a light bruise circling Antoinette's wrist, she seemed untouched by her encounter the night before with Eli, but Lily wasn't. Eli's horror upon realizing the price Antoinette paid for healing was matched by his grief when he realized that nothing could help MaryBeth.

Antoinette closed her eyes while she chewed the lavender bread, as if shutting off her other senses helped her enjoy it more.

"It's good, isn't it?" Lily said. Antoinette flapped her hands.

Lily thought back to her conversation with Will last night, when he tried to explain how Antoinette's ability worked. "No wonder the seizures were getting worse," she said. "One little girl can't hold all of that sickness."

Will nodded, picking up on her thought. "It was overloading her system." He paused for a moment, thoughtful. "When she's the only one touching a sick person, she absorbs the illness. But when she's touching *two* people, she pulls the sickness out of one person and deposits it in the other. It's still a strain on her, though. That's why she seizes."

"I should have known you'd figure it out," Lily said, smiling up at him.

He didn't return her smile, though. Instead, he reached for her hand. "I'm better for you than he is. I mean really, choosing a farm boy over a doctor? How does that happen?" He twisted his mouth into a tight grin.

"I don't want to hurt you." She put both her hands around his.

"Can't help the way you feel, Lils, and neither can I. But maybe you could kiss me and make it better?" A string of lights over him winked out, covering them both in sudden shadows.

She kissed him on the cheek. Then she rested her forehead against his. "I'm sorry."

Will brushed his fingers down her face, then dropped his hand to his side. "You're not coming home, are you?"

She shook her head and swallowed. She hadn't wanted to tell him until later. "This is home. It always has been; I just didn't realize it until now. I've already called work and told them I'm not coming back."

"What will I tell our neighbor, Soup Can Artist? He'll be distraught."

She looked into his eyes, and for a moment she was lost. "Tell him I'll miss him every single day." She laid her head on his chest. His heartbeat was strong and reassuring.

The sky seemed darker than it had a few minutes ago, and she wondered whether a storm was coming. The air felt electric.

Antoinette came up behind her. She tapped Lily's shoulder and then pointed to the house. "Mmmm," she said. "Mmmm." She jabbed the air again and again.

"You want to go home?" Lily asked. "You miss your mom?"

Antoinette stumbled down from the gazebo steps. She pointed to the house again.

"Okay," Lily said. "Let's go see your mom." Will followed them.

The night air grew thick. The crowd sounded louder. Antoinette threaded her fingers through Lily's hand. In a moment the house came into view.

Rose sat on the porch swing, but something was off. She was too still. "Oh God," Lily said, "something's wrong."

Will was already halfway up the steps. Lily swung Antoinette up into her arms and ran after him. *Please*, she prayed. *Please. Please. Please.*

They were too late. Rose was unconscious. Her cheeks were pale and her lips blue. Lily set Antoinette down and knelt beside her sister. "Rose? Rose?" Lily shook her hand. This wasn't real. It couldn't be.

Will pressed his fingers against Rose's neck, searching for a pulse. "It's there, but barely."

Antoinette stretched past Lily and took her mother's hand. "No, Antoinette." Lily tried to pull her away, but Antoinette wouldn't let go. When they touched, Lily felt a strange buzzing beneath her skin. "I can't let you do that. I promised to keep you safe."

Antoinette growled and bit Lily on the wrist.

Lily tightened her grip, and the buzzing grew louder. "No, Antoinette. I promised her. I won't let you do this."

"Let her try." Will pulled Lily away from Antoinette.

Lily struggled. "No! I can't let her do this. I promised Rose I'd keep her safe." She didn't realize she was crying until she looked up and couldn't see Will through her tears.

"And you will," he said. He kissed the top of her head. "Don't forget I love you, Lils." He took Antoinette's free hand. Instead of pulling her away from Rose, he leaned down and said, "Send it to me."

"No!" Lily yelled as she realized what he was doing. She dug her fingers into his shoulders, but he shook her loose.

"Death always wins in the end, Lils," he said. "Somebody's got to lose." He locked eyes with Antoinette. "Send it to me. All of it."

## Chapter Thirty-One
### ONE YEAR LATER

❦

**W**ind skittered over Antoinette's skin, but she didn't twitch or flap. She kept her arms at her sides, even when the breeze lifted the hem of her white dress, and it fluttered around her knees. Around her, the land sang of new beginnings and old friends.

She closed her eyes so that she could hear every note. Today it sounded like the violins in Pachelbel's Canon in D. She swayed and raised her hands to the sun, letting the song flow through her and back to the land.

When she opened her eyes, the green hills were brighter, and the wild roses growing along the white-plank fence encircling the cemetery were sunset pink. Normally, the roses wouldn't flower for another month, but last year, after the funeral, Antoinette had pushed her hands into the dirt and they sprang to life. They hadn't stopped blooming since. Even bowed under a blanket of December snow, the pink petals shone like the spots on a butterfly's wing.

"Come on, Antoinette. Your mom's waiting." Lily caught

her hand and led her up the hill. It wasn't steep, but Antoinette slipped on a patch of dew-soaked clover.

"I've got you," Lily said, catching Antoinette by the elbow and steadying her. "I won't let you fall. Lean into me as you walk."

Antoinette was safe with Lily. She nodded, bobbing her head once up and once down. She still wasn't used to the new ease with which she moved. It wasn't perfect, and if she sat too long, her legs popped and her arms flew up over her head, but when she wanted to stand she thought, *Stand*, and she stood. Easy as that.

She bounced once, not because she had to but because bouncing made her happy.

"Maybe I should have brought roses," Lily said. "They have a longer bloom time."

Seth looked at the snowdrops Lily carried, and then across the cemetery to the Martin family plot. Behind the new gravestone black-eyed Susans, red double pinks, and lavender bloomed, all of them out of season. "I think they'll be fine," he said. "Will you?"

Lily blinked as if struggling not to cry.

Antoinette still couldn't look at faces for long periods of time, but she could hold eye contact for three whole seconds before needing to avert her eyes.

"It's been a year. I didn't expect it to still hurt this much," Lily said. Cherry blossoms floating on the wind caught on her hair.

Seth brushed the flowers from her hair. "I know." He wrapped his arms around Lily's waist and kissed her as sunlight glittered over the grass. They kissed a lot. It filled the air with warmth and made Antoinette feel as if love was something she could touch.

She wished she could tell Lily that death no longer felt hollow. Since that day a year ago, when she had held her mother's hand, death had not felt empty. Instead, it felt like waiting for something special, and its taste was unexpected, almost like chocolate, rich and slightly bitter.

A white cherry blossom landed on her shoulder, and Antoinette reached for it. Her arm moved slowly and surely, like someone else's arm.

It was strange thinking *move*, and then having her body respond. She overcompensated, starting too soon, still thinking she needed extra time to reach for a glass of milk or walk down the driveway. That morning she had followed Lily down to the creek. They went everywhere together now. The trip only took five minutes. Antoinette didn't stumble, and Lily didn't stop to count.

They were both almost normal.

Antoinette, though, kept waiting to change back into the girl who couldn't walk a straight line, the girl who bumped into walls or stumbled down the porch steps. Everyone was broken—she knew that. She didn't believe her change was forever; someday she would go back to that girl. But for now, she was free.

In the twelve months since Lily had taken over Eden Farms, everything had been quiet. The land sang with joy, and Antoinette didn't seize when she fixed things. Healings still took energy from her, and she grew sleepy, but for now at least, she didn't seize.

Lily walked forward, holding Antoinette's hand. The wind picked up, and petals danced around Antoinette's feet.

"You look like a snow princess," Lily said.

A snow princess—Antoinette liked the sound of that. She flapped her hands because she was happy, not because she had to.

"Come on. Let's go see your mom." Lily led Antoinette over a small hill, toward the back corner of the cemetery where Antoinette's grandparents were buried. Antoinette didn't remember them, but she could feel them here.

MaryBeth was also buried in this cemetery. After her death eight months ago, Eli sold the bakery and moved away. Antoinette hadn't seen him since.

A new marker stood next to her grandparents' graves. It was gray granite, the name carved in black: WILLIAM GRAYSON. There was one word under the dates that bracketed his life: FRIEND.

Grass didn't grow over his grave. Instead, there were forget-me-nots and blue violas. Lily looked at the flowers covering Will's grave. "Don't worry," she said as she ran her hand over the marker, "we won't forget."

Antoinette's mother knelt in front of the stone. Seeing them approach, she stood up and brushed the dirt from her knees. "You're a little late," she said.

Antoinette grabbed her mother's hand. Her skin was soft and warm. Sometimes her mother pressed her cheek against Antoinette's just because she could. Those were the times Antoinette put her palms flat against her mother's face and hummed. Not because she needed to fix anything but just for the joy of it.

"Do you need help?" Lily asked.

Her mother shook her head and bent to pick up the shovel she had dropped when she stood to greet them. "The lilies were easy." On either side of Will's marker, she had planted six lilies-of-the-valley. "It's the only way I know to say thank you."

The sisters hugged. Lily's dark hair mixed with Rose's blonde hair, and despite their coloring they looked more alike than different.

Seth took the snowdrops from Lily. "Do you also want these on either side of the marker?"

"No," Lily said. She placed the plants in the middle of the marker so that the white flowers stood below FRIEND.

Rose handed him the shovel, and he dug a hole. Lily gently settled the plants into the ground. Antoinette knelt in the dirt and pushed her hands into the soil until she heard the plants sing. The song was perfect, each note in the right place. She hummed along, and when she stopped the buds opened. They would bloom all year.

Her eyelids fluttered. She grew tired suddenly and closed her eyes for a minute. When the fatigue passed, she rocked back on her heels. *Thank you*, she thought.

She couldn't push the words past her lips, but it didn't matter. She looked at the snowdrops, bright white, blooming out of season. There were many ways to communicate; words were only one of them.

"Beautiful, Antoinette," her mother said, lifting her easily. Her mother's cheeks blushed pink, and her skin was firm and smooth.

Antoinette rested her ear against her mother's chest. Her mother's heart beat a steady thump-thump, and to her the sound was more beautiful than any music she knew. The doctors said the heart disease would come back but not for a long time. And when it did, Antoinette wouldn't have to deal with it alone. Lily would be there.

*Thank you*, she thought again.

Lily touched Will's marker and whispered, "You were wrong, Will. Death doesn't always win. Sometimes love does." Then she stood and wiped the dirt from her hands.

"Let's go home," Seth said. He took Lily's hand and walked toward the truck.

Antoinette closed her eyes and settled her head against her mother's shoulder, humming as they started down the hill toward home.

# ACKNOWLEDGMENTS

———+———

THIS BOOK WOULD not have been possible without help from several people.

First of all, my agent, Dan Lazar. When I started researching agents, you were at the top of the list—my dream agent if you will. I couldn't believe my luck when you offered to represent me. After working with you, I realize I'm even luckier. Your guidance and advice has made this a better book and me a better writer.

My editor, Chuck Adams. Your kindness and generous insight helped bring Antoinette to life. It's wonderful working with someone who "gets" what you're trying to do and who pushes you to be even better.

My copy editor, Jude Grant. You work fast and have a great eye. Thanks for catching my embarrassing mistakes!

The entire Algonquin team—you all are the best. Most publishing people are passionate about the books they sell, but I think you all got an extra dose of book love!

To my critique partners, Amber Whitley, Ann Keller, and Doug Clifton, thank you for your patience and comments on early drafts. I'm lucky to count you as friends. (Doug, you can finally find out how the book ends!)

To everyone at Northern Kentucky University Master of Arts

in English program, but especially Andy Miller, Stephen Leigh, Donelle Dreese, and Kelly Moffett. You are the heart of NKU's creative writing program. Your love and dedication to the craft of writing and to NKU's students shows in everything you do.

To the family and friends who put up with me during this long, crazy process: yes, the book really does exist!

To my husband, Steve, and my children Sarah, Zach, Grace, Caleb, Jonathan, and Gabrielle, thank you for understanding my crazy need to put words on paper and for the never-ending supply of coffee, dark chocolate, and hugs. You all are the best part of my life. None of this means anything without you.

Finally, to Marjorie Braman, thank you for taking a chance on me. I wish you were here to share this with us.

# America's Sporting Heritage:

## 1850-1950

# America's Sporting Heritage: 1850-1950

JOHN RICKARDS BETTS
*Formerly of Boston College*

ADDISON-WESLEY PUBLISHING COMPANY

Reading, Massachusetts
Menlo Park, California • London • Don Mills, Ontario

Addison-Wesley Series in Social Significance of Sports

John W. Loy
Consulting Editor

ISBN 0-201-00557-3
ABCDEFGHIJ-MA-787654

# Editor's Foreword

*America's Sporting Heritage: 1850-1950* represents a lifelong professional study, for it is largely an outgrowth of John Rickards Betts' distinguished dissertation written in 1951 on "Organized Sport in Industrial America." Regrettably, John Betts remained a "marginal man" in academia for most of his career. There was little demand for a book on the history of American sport at the time he completed his doctorate, and in ensuing years he found few fellow historians who deemed the study of sport a worthwhile endeavor. It was only in the last years of Betts' life that his several historical studies of sport attracted the attention of colleagues in his own field and that of many historically oriented scholars in physical education.

Stimulated by the much belated recognition of professional peers and encouraged by family and friends, John Betts set forth in the spring of 1968 to write a definitive history of sport in the United States. He had gotten well into his work when he suffered a tragic loss—his wife succumbed to cancer in February, 1971. Thereafter Professor Betts returned sporadically to his research and writing, but his heart was elsewhere, and the final draft of *America's Sporting Heritage* was yet to be written when the author died on August 9, 1971.

Fortunately for the legacy of sport history, the availability of both an early and a late draft of Professor Betts' manuscript permitted the publication of this book. Richard K. Betts kindly permitted the publication of his father's work and performed yeoman service in reading proofs of the book. Dr. Guy M. Lewis offered unfailing assistance at every stage by personally introducing this editor to the author, as well as by providing a thoughtful review of an early draft.

With the assistance of Richard Betts and Guy Lewis the editor was able to successfully reconstruct the author's work. However, he was

unable to locate a page of references for Chapter Nine and had no adequate means for correcting possible inaccuracies in historical dates resulting from typographical errors in the original manuscript. The editor
wishes further to note that consideration of the early and late drafts of
the manuscript indicates that Professor Betts had planned some revision
of his work and had intended to extend his historical analysis through the
third quarter of the twentieth century. These plans, of course, could not
be fulfilled. Nevertheless, this book stands as a singular contribution to
the history of sport, reflecting a unique blend of breadth of perspective
and depth of insight afforded by no other historical account of American
sport.

In substance the book is a social and cultural history of sport in the
United States from 1850 to 1950. The contents fall naturally into two
parts. Part One, "The Rise of Class Sport," consists of eight chapters
which discuss the early years of American sport and describe the development of organized sport between 1860 and 1920. Three themes underlie
this examination of the rise of modern sport: social stratification, technology, and urbanization. Social class lines clearly characterized primary
patterns of sport involvement during the late nineteenth century. Moreover, America's technological revolution transformed sporting activities
from rural pastimes to urban forms of entertainment.

Part Two, "The Prelude to Mass Sport," consists of five chapters
which treat the initial democratization of sport on a large scale for participants and spectators alike from 1920 to 1950. The Golden Age of Sport
in the 1920's is depicted in detail and can be seen as the precursor of the
"new" Golden Age of Sport of the late 1960's. The effects of the Great
Depression and World War II upon sport participation are also dealt with
at some length. Finally, and most significantly, the second part of this
book provides a valuable analysis of the interrelationships between sport
and several institutional sectors of society, including art, business, education, and religion.

The publication of *America's Sporting Heritage: 1850-1950* is a
fitting tribute to the scholarly career of the late John Rickards Betts
(1917-1971). One hopes that his meaningful interpretation of the rise
of modern sport will stimulate other scholars to pursue historical studies
of the social significance of sport in American society.

*Amherst, Massachusetts*                                        John W. Loy
*January 1974*

# Preface

Sport as we know it today is not only the product of its English and American environment but owes much to games and sporting diversions as old as civilization. Ball playing has gone on since "time immemorial," and anthropologists have described mock combats in the religious ceremonials of tribal societies. Chinese, Lydians, and Egyptians had their ball games, as did the Toltecs of Mexico who built courts and played at *tlachtili.* E. Norman Gardiner claims, "The name Ball players (σφαιρετσ) was used to designate young Spartans in the first year of manhood," and Homer had recorded in the *Iliad* the chariot races ("a woman skilled in fair handiwork for the winner to lead home"), boxing, wrestling, running, and archery contests of the heroic age. Bowling and billiards are also games of ancient origin, and some believe Persia to be the home of polo. Sophocles, Alexander the Great, and Dionysius were fond of ball games, and Pindar celebrated sport. Among the Greeks the athletic ideal won out in the fifth century, and city states provided their own sports grounds (gymnasia) and wrestling schools (palaestae). Local games like the Panathea at Athens were held. After the Persian wars athletics were popular especially at the Olympic Games and, later, in the eastern Hellenistic schools under Roman occupation. Of the Greeks we know that they played a team game called *episkyros,* anticipating Rugby football.

Romans were devotees of *Trigon* and the primitive forms of handball and racquets. Augustus sponsored an athletic carnival, and the grammarian Julius Pollux was reputed to be an authority on ball play. By the second century A.D. the Irish, whose mythology claims athletic games of centuries before, were playing at a type of hockey. Sodonius Apollinaris, Bishop of Clermont and wealthy Roman landlord, recorded in his letters the ball and the dice proclivities of the well-to-do citizens of Gaul, medieval nobility maintained their preserves for hunting, and the townsmen of Italy enjoyed a game called *Calzio.* We need only recall the outdoor sports painted by

Peter Breughel, the legends of Robin Hood, and the diversions of Shake-speare's England. Sailing contests, hawking, and *jai-a-lai* (from the Basque country) are of hoary origin. English sport, eclipsed during the Puritan ascendency, revived with the restoration of the Stuarts, and by the middle of the eighteenth century Englishmen were already in the midst of a sporting movement which was to sweep over Europe and America in the next century.

Like drama, dancing, and music, sport is a diversion from the normal functions of life. It has grown into an institution of such proportions that it can no longer be ignored. It is an element to be reckoned with not only as a personal matter but as a factor in our national life. As this study strives to demonstrate, sport is one of the major interests of urban and industrial society in the twentieth century. Although subject to all the vices and perversions which attach themselves to any institution in a highly commercialized civilization, it can, however, be an important factor in the development of national character.

Man has a natural inclination to play and an innate desire to compete, yet he also tends to be gregarious and to enjoy living, at least in part, in a collective, cooperative society. Sport gives an outlet to all these impulses and emotions, compensating for their absence in daily life and offering an escape from the unpleasant realities of everyday life. American sport was to be sporadic, simple, and spontaneous in its early stages, attaining only a precarious place in American society in the early nineteenth century.

Sportsmen of the nineteenth century sought to perpetuate the rural diversions and woodland sports of the pioneers, but the impact of the Industrial Revolution and urban movement of the middle years led to the competitive games and commercialized promotions of the later part of the century. In the twentieth century all the major powers of the world, including those in the Far East, have witnessed a great development of both spectator and participant sports, and the interest has in large part been cultivated and influenced by Americans. It is the purpose of this study to describe the ways in which sports in America have been influenced by historical development and how sports in turn have penetrated our language, literature, arts, educational philosophy, city planning, and other facets of American civilization. As a study in social history, the emphasis will be placed on such themes as the technological revolution, the rise of the middle class, the relationship to democratic aspirations and to the immigrant, and the competitive spirit in a free enterprise society. It is hoped that new light is shed on various aspects of American thought, character, culture, and institutions.

*Newton, Massachusetts*                                                               J. R. B.
*July 1971*

# Acknowledgments

State and local histories, biographies, institutional histories, recollections, government publications, catalogues, record books, almanacs, private and municipal surveys, census reports, rule books, annual reports, and other kinds of materials have been used extensively and are mentioned in the references.

The newspaper collections of the New York Public Library, the Library of Congress, Columbia University, The State Historical Society of Wisconsin, Tulane University, the New Orleans Public Library, and Harvard University have been most useful to this study.

Among the magazines of greatest value are the *American Farmer, American Turf Register, Spirit of the Times, New York Clipper, National Police Gazette, Harper's Weekly, Saturday Evening Post, Collier's,* and the other leading popular sporting, professional, and historical journals cited in the references.

# John Rickards Betts

On August 9, 1971, following a brief illness, John Rickards Betts died at the age of 54, and the academic world mourned the loss of the leading historian of the cultural and sociological impact of sport in the United States. He was born on July 1, 1917, in Bloomsbury, New Jersey but grew up in Pennsylvania. Betts was graduated from Princeton University in 1938 and received his master's and doctoral degrees from Columbia University. Professor Betts began his professional career at South Dakota State College in 1946. Two years later he joined the faculty at Tulane University and served that institution until moving to Boston College in 1954.

Most visible of the several ways that John Betts contributed to sport history were the numerous scholarly works produced during his career. Prior to the appearance of Betts' first study in the history of American sport, only a few historians had given any attention to the subject, and of those who had only one wrote more than a single work. With Betts sport history was much more than a passing interest and his dissertation, *Organized Sport in Industrial America,* completed in 1951, marked the beginning of an involvement that continued throughout his professional career. No author has approached him in effectiveness in the presentation of material; in terms of scope only John A. Krout's *Annals of American Sport* could be considered the equal of Betts' dissertation.

The years following completion of the doctorate were productive ones for John Betts. Much to his credit and to the profit of those interested in sport history, he devoted much of his talent and time to research and writing on various topics in sport, physical education and health . . .

Reprinted by permission from *JOHPER*, March 1972. Guy M. Lewis is in the School of Physical Education, University of Massachusetts, Amherst.

There can be no question regarding the interest of John Betts in the study of sport, but the unusual thing about his involvement is that he was not motivated by those things that have turned the attention of physical educators to the subject.  He was not a participant in organized athletics while in high school or college, although as a youth he did enjoy sand-lot baseball and throughout his life was enthusiastic about tennis.  He did not expect recognition from professional historians for his accomplishments in the area of sport history.  He devoted attention to sport for the simple but all-important reason that the subject excited his intellectual curiosity.

It was during his years as a graduate student that he first became interested in the study of sport.  But, while he knew what he wanted to pursue as a research topic, there was a practical matter to consider.  Sport was not regarded as a subject worthy of the attention of history scholars and the dissertation was extremely important to the career of the professional historian.  After giving the problem much thought, Betts turned to his advisor, John A. Krout, for counsel and from him received the advice that would guide his professional career.  Never, Krout warned him, attempt to confine intellectual curiosity within limits established by the values of others.

Encouraged and challenged by these words, John Betts devoted his career to making the study of sport a respectable endeavor.  He began it with a 757-page dissertation on the impact of industrial advances on sport and at the time of his death he was well along in the preparation of a manuscript for a book entitled *Our Sporting Heritage:  A Social and Cultural History.*

The extent to which Betts' campaign was successful is difficult if not impossible to ascertain, but there are numerous evidences of marked changes that began during the course of his career.  Articles by historians and physical educators have appeared in national, regional, and state historical journals far more frequently during the most recent decade.  In 1970 the distinguished scholar, Eugen Weber, presented a paper at the convention of the American Historical Association. Weber's extended treatment of the subject, "Gymnastics and Sports in *Fin-de-Siecle* France: Opium of the Classes?" later appeared in the *American Historical Review.* An entire session of the American Historical Association's annual convention in December 1971 was devoted to papers on sport.  While these developments do not support the conclusion that a complete revolution in attitude has taken place, they do suggest the emergence of an involvement in the serious study of sport history that heretofore has been absent.

Betts was encouraged by the greater interest in sport shown by professional historians, but he viewed the development as only part of the answer to the problem of how to raise the level of scholarship. He was convinced that professional historians could make substantial contributions, but their work would be limited by a lack of a total understanding of sport. For this reason he welcomed the opportunity to become involved with scholars in the area of physical education.

As a beginning, John Loy and Gerald Kenyon included one of his articles in their book of readings, *Sport, Culture, and Society* (1964), and in 1969 through the efforts of Guy M. Lewis and Bruce L. Bennett, Betts was invited to present a paper at the first meeting of the new History of Physical Education Section of the AAHPER at the annual convention in Boston. In March 1971 he appeared as a speaker at the Big Ten Symposium on the History of Physical Education and Sport at Ohio State University. It was during these periods of relationship with members of our profession that Betts did what he could to encourage physical educators to involve themselves more in the study of sport history. He also received great personal satisfaction from these contacts.

Important as sport was to Betts, it was but one of his many historical interests. Topics in social, cultural, and intellectual history received most of his attention, and he published numerous pieces of research in these areas. He also prepared a book-length manuscript with the title, "A Universal Yankee Abroad: P.T. Barnum in Europe." He was the recipient of a Fulbright Lectureship and a Ford Faculty Fellowship.

The career of John Betts might be viewed from several perspectives and in each case the assessment would result in the conclusion that it was a distinguished one. As a sport historian he had no peer. His contributions to the literature were truly outstanding works, and these studies have been most effective in demonstrating that sport history is a subject worthy of the attention of scholars.

**Guy M. Lewis**

# Contents

# PART ONE

# THE RISE OF CLASS SPORT

## 1850-1920

# Chapter 1

# Early Years of American Sport

" 'And a pretty good price at that,' said the drover to himself, on pocketing the cash, 'for an animal that only cost me 'eighty', and who is so foolish and flighty that she will never be able to make a square trot in her life.' " Mr. Jonathan A. Vielee had a good eye for horse flesh, but he little realized how great a bargain he had made. Proceeding immediately to New York, he sold her for $350 to a horseman who soon changed the "crazy, half-racking and half-trotting little bay mare" into a true stepper with "a clean, even, long, low, locomotive-trotting stroke."[1] From that moment in 1850 Flora Temple engaged upon a trotting career which carried her throughout the Union, made her a household name, and greatly enhanced public interest in harness racing. A new era in American sport was at hand.

In the United States of the 1850's sport was well on the way to becoming a national institution. Great champions of the turf from Post Boy, Boston Blue, and American Eclipse to Lady Suffolk, Flora Temple, and Lexington were already part of the folklore of American sportsmen. Pugilism, in ill repute, had made its boisterous entry into the life of the city. Athletically inclined young men in many communities were joining cricket clubs and baseball teams, while college boys were beginning to organize their campus games. Hunting and fishing, both as work and play, had been the favorite diversions of Americans since the colonial era. Skating, sledding, rowing, yachting, and dozens of children's games were gaining widespread popularity by mid-century. And by the 1850's sport was attracting the attention of more than a few journalists, publishers, gunsmiths, sporting goods dealers, print makers, song writers, artists, professional promoters, and, of course, gamblers. But this is a thumbnail sketch as the nation drifted toward war, and we must turn back two centuries to the diversions and sports of the colonists.

For two hundred years gentlemen of leisure had enjoyed the pleasures of the field; horse lovers had encouraged the breeding of thoroughbreds and boys in every village had developed their own unique games of ball. It is the story of these pioneer years of sport that will help us better understand the enthusiasm of the public of the Civil War era, an enthusiasm upon which the growth of interest in the modern period was so dependent.

Life in the early American colonies was less depressing and monotonous than traditional accounts would have us believe. Only a year after the landing of the *Mayflower* Governor William Bradford dealt brusquely with the boys and young men he found "in ye streete at play, openly; some pitching ye barr, & some at stoole-ball, and shuch like sports." Refusing them the right to play while others worked, he directed: "If they made ye keeping of it mater of devotion, let them kepe their houses, but ther should be no gameing or revelling in ye streets."[2] Within a few years inns and taverns provided ample opportunity to the pleasure-seeking traveler fond of drinking, singing, dancing, or gambling at cards. Football as played in England was a pastime of Boston youths until proscribed by the town meeting in 1658. Training days were often devoted to athletic exercise. Even more than in the English colonies, the Dutch of New Amsterdam celebrated holidays with boat racing, shooting, sleigh riding, skating, nine pins, and a primitive kind of golf.

As Carl Bridenbaugh has shown, sports were enjoyed (and legislated against) in the leading towns of the colonies for a century prior to the American Revolution. Gaming houses sometimes featured billiard tables and fencing schools appeared in various communities, while foot races, athletic games, and turf contests were popular at some colonial fairs. Philadelphia Quakers might rail at "needless vain sports and pastimes," but Charlestonians revelled in cockfighting and "many of the old English sports and games."[3] Yet, as the magistrates were primarily concerned with the establishment of permanent colonies and the Christian Commonwealth, the first century was one of general hardship and little leisure. King James I in his *Book of Sports* proclamation had blamed the Puritans for their austerity and their hostility to sporting diversions. John Allen Krout has suggested, "The English villagers and townspeople who followed in the wake of the *Sarah Constant* and the *Mayflower* brought to the New World the sports and pastimes with which they had been familiar in the Old." But it was also true that the Separatist and Puritan migrations brought their prejudices against English forms of recreation with them: "Dancing, running, jumping and kindred sports of the village green were associated in their minds with profanation of the Sabbath. . . . Had the leaders at Plymouth, Salem and Boston been in Parliament in 1613 they would have voted with the majority that all copies of the *Book of Sports* be seized and burned."[4] Fighting Indians, clearing new lands, and building towns allowed little time for most colonists to devote to merrymaking. Only after two centuries of settlement in the New World was sport to emerge as an important institution in American life.

## Horse Racing and the Origins of Organized Sport

The turf provided the first organized sport in the New World and it was in the South, in Virginia and South Carolina, that it received its earliest encouragement during the middle decades of the seventeenth century. Court records of York County, Virginia, described in 1674 the aristocratic nature of the early American turf:

James Bullocke, a Taylor, having made a race for his mare to runn with a horse belonging to Mr. Mathew Slader for twoe thousand pounds of tobacco and caske, it being contrary to Law for a Labourer to make a race, being a sport only for the Gentlemen, is fined for the same one hundred pounds of tabacco and caske.

Whereas Mr. Mathew Slader, & James Bullocke by condition under the hand and seale of the said Slader that his horse should runn out of the way that Bullocke's mare might winn, w*ch* is an apparent cheate, is ord*rd* to be putt in the stocks & there sitt the space of one houre.[5]

Although New York was introduced to racing by Governor Richard Niccols in 1665, it was in Virginia that the turf made the greatest headway in the late 1600's; numerous race tracks were established, particularly in Westmoreland and Henrico counties. Disputes over racing were settled in county courts; in 1696 a complaint was sent to the House of Burgesses against Saturday races since they often led to Sunday morning contests and the "profanation" of the Sabbath. In the early eighteenth century the neighboring colony of Maryland became greatly addicted to the turf and to pacify a group of Quakers who petitioned against the holding of races in the vicinity of their Meeting House, the General Assembly in 1747 passed "An Act to prevent certain Evils and Inconveniencies attending the sale of strong Liquors, and running of Horse-Races, near the yearly Meetings of the People called Quakers, and to prevent the tumultuous Concourse of Negroes and other Slaves during the said Meetings." Upon the complaint of these Quakers the law was explicit: the Quakers "have for some Years last past been greatly incommoded and endangered in passing and repassing to and from their said Meeting House in Talbot County, by Multitudes of rude and disorderly People that gather together to run Horse Races on the Road between the said Meeting House . . . and a Place near thereto, called New-Market."[6] Racing of any kind was prohibited at New-Market on Quaker meeting days, as well as within five miles of the Meeting House, offenders being subject to a £5 fine. This Quaker attitude toward racing had not changed appreciably since 1716 when an annual meeting of the Society of Friends warned against racing, wagering, and "vain sports, for our time passeth swiftly away and our pleasure and delight ought to be in the law of the Lord."

The fever spread to other colonies. Rhode Island and New Jersey, awakened to the allurements of racing, apparently passed restrictive legislation against the turf during the 1740's. In South Carolina the York Course was built six miles outside Charleston in 1735. After the South Carolina Jockey Club was formed in 1758 and the Blake Track was established two years later on the edge of the city, racing won an ever greater following. Charleston, the center of fashion, soon became the racing capital of the South. Even in New England, where there were no formal tracks, racing was held at Lynn, Medford, and Quincy, Massachusetts.

Nowhere was racing interest so widespread, however, as in Virginia. Hugh Jones observed in the 1720's: "The common Planters leading easy Lives don't much admire Labour, or any manly Exercise, except Horse-Racing, nor Diversion except Cock-Fighting, in which some greatly delight," many of them riding "to Church, to the Court-House, or to a Horse-Race, where they generally appoint to meet upon Business; and are more certain of finding those that they want to speak or deal with, than at their Home." Governor William Gooch's intervention on behalf of the tobacco planters apparently contributed to the period of prosperity after 1730, and organization of the Annapolis Jockey Club as well as systematic breeding of horses in the 1740's gave a lift to turf enthusiasts. English thoroughbreds were imported in larger numbers between 1730 and 1770 (except in the period of the French and Indian wars), but after 1770 only three recorded thoroughbreds arrived as tension increased between Britain and the colonies. Breeding just prior to the Revolution began to shift from the Rappahannock to the James river valley. Subscription meets had been held in the Rappahannock Valley in the 1740's —a pioneer effort toward true organization—while the *Virginia Gazette* mentioned races around a mile track held at the Williamsburg fair as early as 1739.[7]

Young aristocrats attending William and Mary College in 1752 were given the firm admonition:

> Ordered *yt* no scholar belonging to any school in the College, of *wt* Age, Rank, or Quality, soever, do keep any race Horse, at y*e* College, in y*e* Town—or anywhere in the neighborhood—yt they be not any way concerned in making races, or in backing, or abetting, those made by others.[8]

Prohibiting billiards and other gambling games as well as cock fighting, college authorities ordered any horses to be sent off and not brought back, "this under Pain of y*e* severest Animadversion and punishment." Of the Old Dominion John Smyth wrote in his *Tour in the United States of America* (1784) that "there are races established annually almost at every town and considerable place in Virginia," with heavy betting the common practice. George Washington, a devotee of fox hunting, recorded in his *Diary* how he attended the races occasionally both before and after the Revolutionary War. Annapolis, Alexandria, and Williamsburg races lured him to those communities.

Although sponsored by the gentry, people from every class attended as spectators. The effect of an overly enthusiastic racing addiction on the fortunes of some planters was illustrated in the decline of William Byrd III's estate from losses at the races and the card table. Neither financial distress nor death could quell the sporting interest, however. Philip Vickers Fithian, a young tutor in Virginia just prior to the Revolutionary War, attended a race and observed, much to his disgust, that "quite one third of the People were in mourning. . . . Many who wore black & Scarfs I notice swore most desperately!"

## The American Revolution

Turf enthusiasm was forced into the background as events moved rapidly in 1773 and 1774. The Boston Tea Party incurred the wrath of even the most friendly members of Parliament. A series of Intolerable Acts aimed mainly at Boston aroused the colonists to call a Continental Congress in 1774. Article 8, according to the *Journals of the Continental Congress,* "will, in our several stations, encourage frugality, economy, and industry, and promote agriculture, arts and the manufactures of this country, especially that of wool; and will discontenance and discourage every species of extravagance and dissipation, especially all horse-racing, and all kinds of gaming, cock-fighting, exhibitions of shews, plays, and other expensive diversions and entertainments." Many people, even on the verge of war, felt that this was more than human nature could endure. That all were not content is seen in a case arising in New Rochelle, New York, over a horse race held on the Rye "flats" in the following year. The judge was compelled to try the case himself since all the inhabitants refused the oath required to act as jurymen, they being aware of the Congressional proscription.

The British and American armies fought most of the war in New York, New Jersey and the southern states, once Boston was evacuated by the British. Organized racing in the Rappahannock Valley and around Charleston came to a halt. Loyalist planters and owners of estates suffered heavily, and many of their stables were confiscated, dispersed, or destroyed. It is claimed that Lighthorse Harry Lee's cavalry rode many of these steeds. One turf historian has maintained, "This breaking up of the estates of the Colonial magnates meant also the breaking up of their studs and racing stables which already had been decimated by the war. It operated with special severity in Maryland, Virginia, and the Carolinas, the strongholds of the thoroughbred."[9] The flight of Loyalist planters apparently disrupted the breeding of blooded horses. A leading Loyalist turfman, James De Lancey of New York, who had acquired what was one of the largest and finest stables of running horses in the country, sold his racing interests and went to England. When British troops campaigned in South Carolina the owners hid their horses in the swamps and tried to get them out of the invader's reach.

## Revival and Spread of Turf Enthusiasm

The American Revolution had impeded the growth of the turf to a marked degree, and the years immediately following were not conducive to sport. The "critical period" and the depression of 1786 gave way, however, to prosperity and growing optimism, especially with the ratification of the Constitution, the establishment of a new federal government, and the election of George Washington as the first president. By the 1790's another era of the turf was opening. When Messenger was imported in 1788 and founded a new and dominant blood line in America, and when the South Carolina Jockey Club switched its races from the old Newmarket track to the new Washington Course in the same year, the turf entered upon an era of revival. From the formation of the Virginia Jockey Club in 1788 Richmond became a turf center, races being sponsored at Tree Hill, Broad Rock, and Fairfield. Norfolk's race week and opera performances were held simultaneously, with evening balls to give color and gaiety to the social season.

In *Modern Chivalry,* one of our first American novels, Hugh Henry Brackenridge described with a high sense of humor the rustic race meetings of the 1790's. Brackenridge pictured his leading characters, Captain John Farrago and Teague Oregon, falling in with some jockeys at a local race, where the rudiments of organization were evident in the weighing of riders and the racing by heats. The author remarked, "It is needless to describe a race; everybody knows the circumstances of it." Hoping to persuade the jockeys that they should conduct their meetings on the high level of the ancient Olympic Games, the Captain made the mistake of believing that "jockeys and men of the turf could be composed by reason and good sense; whereas there are no people who are by education of a less philosophic turn of mind."

New York had already passed a state law in 1788 prohibiting "travelling, working, shooting, fishing, sporting, playing, horse racing, hunting, and frequenting tippling houses on the Sabbath"—each a violation for offenders over fourteen years of age. Despite this law New York racing returned in force after the Revolution. Although meetings at Jamaica were for only three days in November, Moreau de St. Mery noted, "All New York attends, and the ferries do a rushing business." To the disgust of upright citizens, racing crowds were often composed of the wrong kind of people: "Among the spectators are many of the habitués of the houses of ill repute which debauchery has multiplied in New York."[10] By 1795 a "Society for Aiding and Assisting the Magistrates in the suppression of Vice and Immorality on the Lord's Day" was formed in New York. Inspectors of the state prison in 1802 reported to the legislature that three fourths of the convicts were from the city of New York, where taverns and grog shops, horse racing, animal baiting, and duelling were common. By that date the *Morning Chronicle* was regularly recounting horse and boat races in the vicinity of the city.

While Virginia regained its turf supremacy by 1800, the breeding of horses was already a leading agricultural pursuit of Kentuckians. Within a few years of the state's admission to the Union a French traveler noted, "The horses of this country came originally from Virginia . . . and most of them were brought here by the emigrants who came from Virginia to settle in this state. The number of horses, which is already very considerable, augments daily. Almost all the inhabitants employ great care in breeding, and improving the breeds." Among these horses were many a thoroughbred stallion.

Colonel William Whitley laid out the first circular track west of the Alleghenies by 1788—the Sportsman's Hill track near Louisville.[11] Walter Street in Lexington was the scene of boisterous racing as early as 1787, course racing first appeared around 1790, and by 1797 there was a jockey club. Meetings were held at Georgetown, Bardstown, Danville, and Shelbyville between 1796 and 1798. And it was only natural that migrants from Virginia and the Carolinas carried the racing fever with them to Kentucky, Tennessee, and points west.[12]

Recreation remained a minor factor in the lives of Appalachian settlers building homesteads in the wilderness, but as small communities were established in the wake of the advancing frontier numerous manifestations of sporting excitement appeared in the West. Between the Appalachians and the Mississippi enthusiasm for horse racing mounted with the passing decades. The Pittsburgh area had racing in the first years of the century. Even in the midst of the War of 1812 General Andrew Jackson kept close tabs on his racing horses. Following that conflict a considerable degree of ill will apparently was directed at racing; importations of thoroughbreds had been cut off with the Non-Intercourse Act of 1806 and the Embargo of 1807-1809, and it was only after two decades that the turf was able to make any real progress.

Public racing was legalized in Queens County, New York, in 1821; the New York Trotting Club organized in 1825; the Hunting Park Association opened in Philadelphia in 1828; while thoroughbred racing gradually acquired a following in southern cities like New Orleans, Nashville, Louisville, and Memphis. The opening of the National Course at Washington, D.C. in 1802 and of the Union Course on Long Island in 1821 gave encouragement to the turf in these two areas. Racing at the national capital flourished after Jefferson's inauguration: "Many scores of American legislators . . . went on foot from the Capitol, above four English miles" to attend the race where they found not only "grog" but "sharks" and "sharpers." In 1816 William R. Johnson's Vanity defeated Tuckahoe and won $30,000 for the noted turfman. President John Quincy Adams was not always so busy that he could not take his morning dip in the Potomac, talk about the races with Colonel Richard Tayloe, and feel grateful for the absence of visitors to his office on a racing day. The fever continued to spread and the need of regulation became imperative; the South Carolina Jockey Club published a racing code in 1824 in order to further standardize the rules of the turf.[13]

American Eclipse bested Sir Henry in a famous race at Union Course, Long Island in 1823 and this inaugurated a series of North-South races which continued for about three decades. Hezekiah Niles reported: "For several days before the race, the stages and steamboats arriving at New York were burthened with anxious passengers—many of whom, no doubt, had travelled 500 miles to witness the important contest of speed! It was estimated that not less than 20,000 strangers were in the city of New York —all the hotels, inns, taverns and boarding houses were jammed with people from the bottom to the top, and, on the day of the race, the city was as deserted!" With a glance of disapproval, the writer complained that "the 'sporting world,' from the extreme North to the extreme South of the United States, was engaged in this affair! Few have gained much by it —but many have lost what should have went to the payment of their just debts . . . Never did a case happen before, perhaps, in which *state* pride was so much at stake. It might be excited, we think, by more laudable objects.—The money expended or lost, and time wasted . . . is not far short in its value of half the cost of cutting the Erie Canal."[14]

It was during Jackson's presidency that the first symptoms of a genuinely popular interest in the turf appeared. In 1829 Skinner began publishing his *American Turf Register and Sporting Magazine,* and in 1831 William T. Porter established the most popular sporting journal of the ante-bellum period—*The Spirit of the Times.* Importation of foreign-bred horses had fallen off between the early 1800's and 1830, but the commerce in horses revived thereafter. Dr. Elisha Warfield pioneered in Kentucky racing; his friend Henry Clay was a devotee of the race course and imported horses from abroad. Wade Hampton II was an enthusiast of the turf, and among the breeding and racing titans were Andrew Jackson, John Randolph, and William R. Johnson, more popularly known as the "Napoleon of the Turf."

Meetings increased from 56 in 1830 to 130 in 1839; although there were less than 40 tracks in 1830, ten years later there were nearly twice the number.[15] In 1836 more than $500,000 was involved in sales and transfer of blooded stock—if we are to believe an ante-bellum analyst of the race course.[16] Throughout the thirties there were constant reports of corruption, trickery, and cruelty to the horses. One of the early appeals for reform was made in 1832: "Something must be done to *systematize* the meetings on the various courses. At present there is *no concert* amongst them, meetings are fixed at random, and thus it has, and will often happen, as might be expected, that for the largest purses, there will be the fewest horses, the poorest competition, and the least sport."[17]

In 1830 the Maryland Jockey Club published its rules; racing was reported at St. Louis in 1835; trotting was inaugurated in the South at Mobile in 1837; and by 1839 William T. Porter was proposing an "American Jockey Club" for the settlement of bets, adjustment of weights, regulation of heats, and establishment of general rules of entry. Although John Quincy Adams occasionally was lured to the track, it was during the Jacksonian era that it was most constantly patronized by the president. "The racing on the National Course near the city made it difficult to maintain a quorum in Congress, and the statesmen mounted their horses to ride to the track to cheer their favorites and to bet their money. Even the president entered his horses and lost heavily on his wagers."[18]

The 1830's witnessed a decided rise in public interest in the turf, particularly in the south where the cavalier tradition was still so strong. It was in the following decade, however, that thoroughbred racing apparently reached its peak of popularity. There was considerable excitement over the more spectacular contests, while almost 600 horses were named for the 1842 season which was to be run on 69 recognized race courses.[19] Grey Eagle and Wagner engaged in a memorable contest in 1840; Boston ran against Fashion in 1842; and Fashion met Peytona in 1845—all three of these historic races occurring during the heyday of the thoroughbred turf. North-South rivalries were keen, and the Fashion-Peytona match race attracted well over 50,000 spectators to the Union Course of Long Island. So keen was the popular interest that the New York *Herald* sent eight competent reporters to cover the event, and "extras" were published after each heat.[20] *Niles' National Register* editorialized: "A Horse Race. The sporting and gambling world have just had a glorious harvest. A match between the two crack horses of the north and south, Fashion and Peytona, and in which all the ambition of the sections seems to have been enlisted, 'came off' at the course near N. York on Tuesday last. . . . Besides the purse of $20,000, not much short of one million of dollars are supposed to have been at issue, and won by the south, Peytona beating Fashion the two heats." Such contests encouraged racing in the West, and as early as 1844 the sporting community of Chicago had its jockey club.

A number of prominent southerners were leading turfmen of the 1840's: Thomas Kirkman of Alabama, Thomas J. Wells of Louisiana, Wade Hampton of South Carolina, Isaac Franklin of Tennessee, William R. Johnson and James Williamson of Virginia, Adam L. Bingaman and William J. Minor of Mississippi, and George and Duncan Kenner as well as James L. Bradley of Kentucky. Richard Ten Broeck controlled the Bingaman Course, held an interest in the Metairie Course, and managed a track in Mobile; while Lucius J. Polk, E.H. Boardman, and James Jackson, owner of Glencoe, were leading breeders. The practice of leasing tracks to promoters was popular, thus giving added security to breeders who looked forward to the racing season of a year or two in the future.[21]

Prosperity for some owners was offset by the misfortunes of others, however, and in 1841 Colonel Yelberton N. Oliver sold his Eclipse Course in New Orleans. Competition from the Metairie and Louisiana courses was partially responsible for this move, but the *Spirit of the Times,* which recorded 153 meetings on 106 tracks in 1839, knew of only 38 meetings on 27 courses in 1849. Hard times following the Panic of 1837 hit many tracks. Organized in 1836, the Memphis Jockey Club ceased racing between 1841 and 1847, while it was said of Colonel Oliver, who controlled tracks at Washington, Cincinnati, Louisville, Lexington, Nashville, and New Orleans: "He commenced the Eclipse Course when the country had reached an apparent pitch of prosperity unequalled. . . . But a revulsion took place, which affected Race Courses and other Turf interests, no less than all other species of property."[22] Many areas of the South received the full impact of the Panic several years later; Isham Puckett, promoter of the races in 1842 at Fairfield and Broad Rock, Virginia, advertised: "Owing to the hard times I have concluded to have but one week's racing."[23] As John Hervey has remarked, the Panic had a "shattering effect upon racing . . . relying for its main support upon men of wealth and property."

Adversity alone could not destroy the love of the turf. By 1847 Colonel Oliver was back on the scene in the Crescent City with the new Bingaman Course across the river in Algiers. With stables from Mississippi, Alabama, Kentucky, and even Virginia in competition on the Metairie Course, one observer noted, "The advance in the price of cotton has given an immense impetus to the Turf in the SouthWest, which is most sensibly felt in New Orleans." [24] When a celebrated race between two great champions was held in 1855, the excitement reached fever pitch: "The town is all agog in relation to the great race today between Lexington and Lecomte. The parishes of the state and the adjoining states have poured in their thousands to witness. The hotels and the boardinghouses are all full, full to overflowing; and we know not where they will all find room, unless they contrive to sleep two or three in a bed, and spoon-fashion at that." [25]

Intersectional meetings, however, were almost at an end. With the storm clouds of the slavery controversy growing ever darker after the Compromise of 1850 and the strife in Bleeding Kansas, North-South match races lost their appeal. Forewarning of this might have been seen in the abandonment of racing in 1846 on the national course in Washington, D.C. In the *Spirit of the Times* for November 1, 1851 the lack of interest in Virginia racing was noted: "The truth is, the sports of the Turf are, and have been for many years, on the decline in the 'Old Dominion'. . . . The fall and spring races came off, it is true, over the race tracks near the city; but they fail to excite the smallest degree of interest now, save in the very small circle yet devoted to sports of the Turf." With less confidence in analyzing the causes of this trend than the historian is likely to assume, the journal questioned, "Who can satisfactorily account for this wonderful change?" Even the famous Lexington-Lecomte rivalry failed to arouse the nation's interest as some of the contests had done in earlier years. [26] At the latter races in New Orleans prominent statesmen and public figures from throughout the South put in their appearance, but the northern press gave only scanty attention to this contest between the most illustrious thoroughbreds of the day.

As trotting steadily gained the ascendancy on northern tracks and numerous athletic pastimes began to attract the attention of sportsmen, horse racing no longer held unchallenged title as "King of Sports." Minstrel shows, museums, circuses, and fairs were diverting the public mind. Racing fans of the fifties were already pining for "the good old days," comparing "the palmy seasons of the olden time and the present degenerate days" and lamenting "the declining spirit for the enjoyments of the turf." The Nashville *Daily News* in 1860 complained: "By some means scarcely accountable, turf sports have been pining away, in the middle district of Tennessee, for several years or upwards." Political agitation and religious revivals, along with lavish expenditures on "splendid family residences and business houses," were blamed for this decline to the point where "many of our people have forgotten that there is any such place as the Nashville Race Course." [27]

## Aristocrats, Rabble, and Immigrants

Organized sports grew in the decades prior to the Civil War through stimuli from three major social groups: the American social aristocracy, the metropolitan "rabble," and the immigrant. Successful planters, whose greatest hobbies were breeding and racing, were highly influential in encouraging public interest. First families of Virginia, Maryland, and the Carolinas indulged in fox hunting, while rising New York businessmen occasionally turned to yachting or the trotting course for recreation. Among those sports first engaged in by the social aristocracy were cricket, yachting, baseball, fox hunting, horse racing, trotting, and (in the form of social clubs) hunting and fishing. Work on the plantation was normally a laborious cultivation of tobacco, rice, cotton or other crops, but it was seasonal and permitted recreation in dull periods. The frequent employment of black jockeys to ride the planters' horses on the race course, the pitting of slave against slave in the ring, the prevalence of Negroes as trainers of high-blooded cocks, and the competition of field hands in boat races on southern streams testify to sporting interests on the plantation and also stand as milestones in the black's introduction to American sport.

Planters enjoyed their mounting prosperity as the cotton kingdom grew. Inasmuch as their wives and daughters loved the social whirl and fashionable life of the city, they often spent the slack season in New Orleans, Mobile, or Charleston. South Carolina planters found the life of the city an absorbing but costly venture:

> During the period of the year . . . which they spend in town, they live like princes, in a round of gaiety, hospitality, and indulgence in every pleasure; but this brilliant interval absorbs not only all, but more than they save by living the rest of the year on their plantations, destitute almost of common comforts. . . . [The Carolinians'] amusements are not always of the most elegant kind, and consist less in the theatre and other places of public entertainment, than in horseracing with high bets, and hard drinking till the guest is laid under the table. They follow likewise with ardour all country sports, and are excellent marksmen.[28]

Northern gentlemen who turned to the development of trotting horses and those who formed rowing, baseball, yachting, hunting, fishing, and cricket clubs, were similarly pioneers in the movement towards organization. Members of the social aristocracy deserve much credit for early sporting enthusiasm.

Ante-bellum sporting journals continuously referred to the "rabble" and "rowdies" in sport. Often of a carefree nature, frequently unemployed, the typical "city loafer" and the "town tough" were the first to capitalize on the growth of sport. Early accounts like those of Captain Basil Hall, William Johnson, and Hiram Woodruff recorded frequent riots, while condescending reporters often remarked on the "rabble" at the track. Gambling on prize fights and horse races naturally lured an "undesirable" element to most contests. Often men went armed to a prize fight held in some secluded spot, while a well conducted race was a subject for congratulation by the press. Promoters of sporting contests soon recognized the need for a more genteel atmosphere in order to win the sympathies of the gentry and the growing middle class.

Appeals to the good will of American women were made early in the annals of organized sport: ladies' sections of the grandstand were constructed, plantation belles were persuaded to go fox hunting, and women were encouraged to turn to archery and to attend the track. In 1831 a reporter of the races at Salisbury, North Carolina stressed the "order and decorum" of the crowd and gave a nod of respect to the large number of ladies in carriages "who graced the field, and gave additional relish to the sport." At the celebrated meeting of Grey Eagle and Wagner in 1840 eight hundred ladies attended, and at a race at Natchodoches, Louisiana, four years later the "dark-eyed Creole" was seen "exchanging kindly greetings and joyous smiles with the blue-eyed, fair browed daughters of the far North and West."[29] Although many of the older Protestant families in New Orleans took little part in the amusements and sports of the city, the *Times Picayune* stated that the crowd at the opening of the Bingaman Course in 1847 "was honored with the presence of a large number of ladies, radiating beauty and flushed by the excitement of the sport."[30]

Consciously or not, sporting enthusiasts were engaged in a constant quest for society's approval. John Stuart Skinner referred to the support of exercise and the turf given by Franklin, Washington, Jefferson, Lafayette, Marshall, Randolph, Calhoun and other notables. As secretary of state and as president John Quincy Adams attended the Washington races, and Mrs. Adams was also known to grace the track. "Mr. Adams, we know never misses an opportunity of attending the Races, or the Theatre; and we apprehend no man living holds in greater detestation all the *vices,* which may sometimes be incidental to the *abuse* of these rational amusements." Resolutions were passed against Sunday racing in New Orleans in 1844, hoping to remove "a very serious objection to the Sports of the Turf . . . as urged from the pulpit." One of Grey Eagle's races attracted several distinguished senators and most of Kentucky's congressmen, as well as "the elite of the beauty and fashion of the State."[31]

Just how respectable the turf was considered in ante-bellum years presents an interesting problem in social history. The evangelical sects looked upon racing with strong disfavor and even worldly politicians pursued their sports with circumspection. In 1832 Jackson made ready to fight for reelection against Henry Clay and the United States Bank, he worried over the effect of racing upon his reputation. Opposed to his son's training of horses on any "track in my plantation," Jackson feared having "my farm made a training stable of, the very way to injure me." Whereas he had intended to race Polly Baker and Sir William at Baltimore, he apparently dreaded the prejudice in the Nashville area. The president confided "how loth I was to have any horse trained on my farm. It was that which might have been construed that I was encouraging racing." John Spencer Bassett has noted that as Old Hickory's "position became established as a member of the highest class he dropped cock-fighting," and in 1839 Francis Blair referred to "the sound judgment by which you kept yourself always apart from the class with which achievements on the turf is apt to identify one." Even George Wilkes stated in 1852 that the English turf was "a national amusement of high character, and being patronized by the Queen, is popular with all classes," whereas "with us it is resigned almost entirely to gay men of the world, gayer women, and gamblers."

If racing was not yet universally approved, however, it was approaching respectability. In 1860 the Nashville *Daily News* reported the progress being made, promising "the discipline on the ground will be such as to secure order and decency." Later it claimed that the beautiful belles "threw a refining influence over all on the course who had any susceptibility of refinement, and gave assurance that it will soon be as fashionable to visit the race course as the operas."[32]

William T. Porter boasted that, through his *Spirit of the Times,* "We claim to have elevated the character of the pursuits of the Turf to a pitch they had never before reached in public estimation on this side of the Atlantic." Ante-bellum newspapers—at least those which reported turf meetings—constantly reiterated the appeal to women. The reporter of races at Mobile in 1851 flatteringly stated, "Another strong evidence of their influence was, that during this week not a squabble, dispute, or angry word, took place upon the course. Then hurrah for the whole race of women!"[33] The race course, then, was a scene of gaiety and excitement and it presented one of the best opportunities for intermingling of the sexes; if we are to believe contemporary accounts it readily developed into a carnival of finery and fashion. Yet one must question how much this publicity on feminine attendance accomplished. When the sky was fore-boding and the weather inclement, women seem to have shown little sporting enthusiasm.

The quest for sporting respectability was found, above all things, in the prize ring. Frank Queen of the *New York Clipper* attacked "the un-founded and unreasonable objections entertained by certain classes against pugilists and sparring exhibitions. . . . There is no class of men who are more prompt and willing to assist others than the pugilistic profession, and none who are more grossly misrepresented."[34] An estimated throng of 25,000 to 35,000 spectators swarmed to the Beacon Course opposite New York City in 1844 to watch "Gildersleeve," "Jackson," and three English runners in a match race for $1000. When the overflow crowd swept over the track and infield an annoyed writer in the *American Turf Register* could not refrain from criticizing these "specimens of the tag-rag and bob-tail denizens of New York." Even private enterprises took the same approach. In 1847 the Gothic Hall Bowling Saloon in New York advertised through the *Spirit of the Times* "the largest and most magnifi-cent establishment of the kind in the city, (or world), . . . visited only by the most respectable company . . . also, a Billiard-room, the most quiet and respectable in the city." Most pool and billiard halls, frequented by less reputable characters, had no need to follow this precedent to main-tain a clientele, but the quest for respectability was to be found in virtually every form of sport.

The immigrant and the alien visitor to American shores also contri-buted to the rise of organized sport. By the 1840's the prize ring had gained a considerable following in metropolitan areas although fights had been held since the turn of the century. With the flow of Irish immigration as a result of the potato famine in the late forties, the ring became an important part of the sporting scene. There was some ignorance of earlier sentiment in the claim that: "The American people before this date had descended from a class of Englishmen who had little taste for the ring, and about the only slugging-matches to be seen in the United States were those among the negroes in the cotton plantations." But, after the Irish began arriving, one did hear of the Big Four, "James (Yankee) Sullivan, Tom Hyer, John Morrissey, and John Heanan, who were but the most promi-nent champions of the prewar era."[35]

Other immigrants also brought their games with them. Cricket was played widely by those English immigrants who came to the United States after the start of the British athletic movement in the 1830's. One cricket enthusiast claimed that in 1850 there were nearly a thousand clubs be-tween the Atlantic and the Pacific. Germans brought an enthusiasm for lawn bowling and for gymnastics. The great Turnfests of the 1850's attracted German athletes from all over the United States. Even the Scotch pioneered in introducing track and field sports to the New World with their annual Caledonian games.

International athletic rivalry was almost undreamed of in ante-bellum days but an English cricket team did visit the North just prior to the war. Sportsmen toured the United States to engage in pigeon shooting contests and numerous pugilists arrived from Britain and from Ireland, while native fighters went abroad to win fame and fortune. The dependence of horse breeders on imported thoroughbred stock continued throughout the era and Richard Ten Broeck began racing his horses abroad. French billiards experts put on exhibitions and oarsmen from British ships often raced Americans in harbors along the Atlantic Coast. There was not yet enough popular interest to encourage regular international contests, but the seeds were being planted. When the *America* triumphed at Cowes in 1851 Anglo-American sporting relations received a stimulus which grew steadily in post-Civil War decades.

## English Sport Captivates America

As far back as the early colonial period homeland sports were played in all the colonies, and the debt of early American sport to the English can hardly be exaggerated. As Jennie Holliman so ably pointed out in her study, *American Sports (1785-1835),* "Practically every phase of sporting life in America was tinged with English influence." Horse racing was usually conducted "in accordance with the rules and regulations of New Market;" sporting equipment was imported from Britain; English books and journals were the only source of sporting literature; British soldiers and sailors stationed in America helped stimulate interest in cock fighting, boxing, and other sports of the homeland; and in the visits of sons of the gentry seeking an education or making a tour much information was handed on to friends at home.[36]

Horse racing and the pugilism of the late eighteenth century laid the foundations of popular interest in Britain; cricket was played widely by 1820; rowing contests were already a popular diversion in the 1830's; association football caught on in the "public schools" of the 1840's and 1850's; and in 1850 track and field athletics were first conducted on an organized basis.[37] The enthusiasm of the nobility soon penetrated the masses living in highly congested urban communities. The annual Derby became a great institution in the early nineteenth century, and with the extension of the English railway system tremendous throngs attended the great races.

A typical racing holiday is described in the following report: *"The*

*Ascot Heath Races* have been the aristocratic attraction of the present week. The Queen, Prince Albert, the Court, the distinguished guests of Her Majesty, the leading nobility, and foreigners from every nation—have enjoyed the Ascot week on the Heath. . . . Tens of thousands of persons were gratified, and after the races they all departed, in carriage, coach, cart, van, or on foot, for Windsor, where monstrous trains were rapidly filled and started for the Metropolis."[38] So far advanced was England in the athletic movement that Americans of the pre-Civil War era often read more of English sport than they did of their own. Books and sporting journals, like *Bell's Life in London,* were loaded with information on English racing, prize fighting, and cricket. The *North American Review* of 1842 regretted the English monopoly on sports literature; in a review of English publications on angling, hunting, and rural sports the magazine noted, "With this super-fecundity of British sportsmen in book making, we are not aware of the existence of a single American work in the same department. . . . Sporting is, with us, for the most, not an art but a trade, and needs no teacher but personal experience."[39] The English preceded us by several decades in the organization of sport, and they maintained this early advantage throughout most of the century. The influence of the English was a major factor in the rise of organized sport in the United States.

# Chapter 2

# Rural and Urban Influences Before the Civil War

# Chapter 2

# Rural and Urban Influences Before the Civil War

> A strong body makes the mind strong. . . . Games played with the
> ball, and others of that nature . . . stamp no character on the mind.
> —Thomas Jefferson to Peter Carr, August 19, 1785

For more than half a century we have been aware of the tremendous
influence of the West on American social history. Since Frederick Jackson
Turner's epoch-making analysis in 1893 the one great challenge to the
frontier thesis has been the emphasis on European traditions and institutions as modified by American conditions in the emerging urban-industrial
society of the late nineteenth and twentieth centuries. Even so, the works
of Charles Beard and Arthur M. Schlesinger, Sr., which paved the way to
new understanding of the complex of American civilization, have not
diminished the enthusiasm of Americans for the drama of the westward
march of empire.

## The Westward Movement

On the frontier in the early nineteenth century sport was almost always
informal and spontaneous. Jefferson, like most of his contemporaries, had
favored walking, riding, and field sports as a means of maintaining physical
vigor. As early settlers spilled over the mountains into Ohio, Kentucky,
and Tennessee and then throughout the Mississippi Valley, they carried
their simple diversions with them. Pioneers in Arkansas engaged in shooting matches (usually for a quarter of a beef), as well as in wrestling, foot
races, horseshoe pitching, and one or another type of physical contest.
Rail-splitting or log-cutting contests were popular at picnics and socials.
Arkansas folks rode as many as thirty miles to watch and to bet on Indian
games of ball. Despite the opposition of temperance societies and the isolation of Fort Smith, turfmen apparently brought horses from St. Louis
and as far away as Kentucky. Memphis in the 1820's "was a frontier town
with frontier habits and ways" where the turf was the favorite pleasure and
pastime with Indians as well as whites, attracting gamblers "who at this
time literally swarmed in all the river towns."[1] Horse racing developed
into something of a popular pastime in Texas during the era of the Republic, and race courses followed the advancing frontier. Houston, Velasco,
and Galveston became racing centers on the Gulf Coast, while tracks were
laid out in many an interior town.[2]

Racing was reputed to be "almost a positive mania" in the Texas
Republic, and meetings were usually terminated with the festive spirit of
a ball. The gambling fever raged and brawls broke out among the motley
crowds. When Ferdinand Roemer traveled through Texas in 1846 he noted
with reference to the edge of the frontier "the love for this national sport

asserted itself in these places, far removed from civilization."[3] Rev. Z.N. Morrell, on a visit to Springfield "on the edge of settlement," swam several rivers only to discover that a race track had preceded him.

Texas sport was, naturally, of informal frontier variety. As William R. Hogan has shown, many diversions lay "in the border zone between sport and the actual labor of searching for food. Fishing and hunting of varied kinds, including cooperative bear and buffalo hunts and wolf chases, naturally had more of an aspect of sport to visitors than to many permanent settlers, except on a few coastal plantations."[4] Few famous horses got as far west as the Republic where many of these tracks were of temporary and localized interest, and truly organized racing was common only in the coastal area and in a few rising inland cities. A letter to the *Spirit of the Times* in 1850 lamented, "To the shame of San Antonio, it must be confessed that not a number of your . . . paper is received here." But the spirit of organization gradually penetrated Texas as it had other frontier areas, horses were occasionally imported from the East or Europe, and, through exploitation by the gambling element, racing established a foothold in the land of Stephen Austin and Sam Houston.

When the Great Plains marked the limit of westward settlement from the East, another frontier was already working eastward from the Pacific Ocean toward the Rockies. In California, after the fall of Mexico and during the era of the Gold Rush, sport made its appearance almost as soon as the "49'ers" began their prospecting. Pugilists rushed to the Pacific Coast and a number of contests were held in the flush gold prospecting period. John Morrissey, the noted pugilist from New York, engaged in several big fights in 1852.

San Francisco became the center of social life for miners throughout that area and they bet heavily on all kinds of contests. Although San Francisco women expressed their indignation, two rings were built within the city limits in 1850 for the holding of bull fights. Cock fighting, bear baiting, and even boating regattas were popular. What was probably the first regular race track was opened in 1850, and many prospectors looking for a good time attended the Pioneer Race Course in 1851. They were reported as "laying out their dust at all sorts of odds—a large crowd just down from the mines with large bags full." Nor was the fun confined to the Barbary Coast, for camps and towns of the interior pitted horses against one another to settle local rivalries, and also held amateur and professional foot races. Enthusiasts formed a Jockey Club in 1850 in Sacramento City, where a fight and game of ball always attracted a large crowd. When a grizzly bear and bull were let loose in a ring at San José, the California legislature adjourned to see the fight![5] The air of excitement and the enthusiasm for such entertainment naturally faded with the passing of the gold-rush fever, but mining camps of the West were to remain centers of sporting activity even in post-Civil War years. Life on the fringe of settlement had become a significant factor in the spread of sporting interest by midcentury.

## Steamboats on Western Waters

With the surge of westward migration and the mounting importance of the Mississippi Valley after 1800, the river itself contributed to the growth of sport throughout the West. Louisville, St. Louis, Memphis, Natchez, and New Orleans developed into centers of business and social activity. Southern planters brought their horses to metropolitan tracks and sportsmen held foot races, cock fights, and boxing "exhibitions" in secluded areas outside city limits. By 1830 a large fleet of steamboats had replaced many of the earlier flatboats, and rival owners had already begun to compete for river traffic by decorating their floating palaces or by setting new speed records up and down the valley.

During the 1830's steamboat racing attained widespread popularity, although captains were normally cautious not to endanger their crafts. Many side-wheelers caught fire from overheated boilers, however, and a series of catastrophes in 1836 and 1837, costing numerous lives, aroused a meeting at Natchez to issue a popular demand for the prevention of these reckless river rivalries. Racing continued despite public hostility, and passengers were usually as deeply thrilled as they were frightened by such an adventure. The upper Mississippi was less subject to this racing fever, but the fame of a fast boat encouraged captains to accept a challenge. The usual incentive to arrive first at the next wharf in order to capture the trade spurred even pilots on the upper river and churning side-wheelers like the *Grey Eagle* under Captain Daniel Harris won great reputations. When Queen Victoria sent a message to President James Buchanan on the laying of an Atlantic cable the *Grey Eagle* raced the *Itasca* to St. Paul, then a city without telegraph, to announce the news.

The fame of such contests spread far beyond the Mississippi Valley and in the 1850's promoters introduced racing on the Hudson and lesser rivers, on the Great Lakes, and in California. It is claimed that "the organization of the California Steam Navigation Company apparently had a slightly sedative effect on racing. . . . But the little independents still yapped at the heels of the wicked monopoly, and so racing and lax maintenance continued." After a "brush" between the *Pearl* and the *Enterprise* in 1855, the *Daily Alta California* attacked racing even at the risk of losing its steamboat advertising.[6]

Romantic narrators of the West may have done much to magnify the frequency and the importance of steamboat racing, and Mark Twain with his *Life on the Mississippi* was at least one of the culprits. One writer maintained: "Racing, as racing, was an expensive if not a risky business. Unless the boats were owned by their commanders, and thus absolutely under their control, there was little chance that permission would be obtained for racing on such a magnificent and spectacular scale as that usually depicted in fiction."[7] Spontaneous as it may have been, times were carefully recorded, agreements were made as to the conduct of the race, crowds gathered to watch famous boats pass down the river, and results were reported to sporting journals and the regular press. In that limbo between early spontaneous frontier diversions and more formalized contests of an urban society, steamboats were the first product of the Industrial Revolution to affect the rise of sport. Racing helped brighten the lives of those who traveled the river or lived along its banks, and was destined to rank high in the folklore of the Mississippi Valley.

River boats belching steam were also instrumental in more utilitarian ways to the rise of sport. They served as carriers of racing or prize fight news up and down the Valley and as transport for the planters' stables. In the thirties they carried thoroughbreds to such turf centers as Vicksburg, Natchez, and New Orleans. When the renowned trotting mare Lady Suffolk embarked from St. Louis for the East on the packet *Pennsylvania,* "thousands gathered on the wharf" while house tops were crowded with people paying tribute to the great champion. In 1856 Lexington and Lecomte attracted thousands of visitors to New Orleans and numerous stables were brought in for the meeting. "The fast 'uns are gathering for the coming sport at the Metairie Course. . . . We have already mentioned the arrival of Messrs. Lecomte & Co.'s stable, and now we have the pleasure of announcing that the steamboat Natchez has arrived this morning, bringing Col. Bingaman's and Cap. Minor's stables in good order and well conditioned."[8]

Caution must be taken not to exaggerate the role of the frontier in the rise of organized sport. With the exception of steamboat racing, most sports which flourished throughout both the West and the South were of English origin. In many ways it was only with the passing of the frontier westward and with the rise of prosperous communities that organized recreation took hold: "While it is possible from fragmentary records to overestimate the amount of time which gentlemen of leisure devoted to out-of-door sports, there can be little doubt that as the frontier was pushed westward recreation assumed a larger significance."[9] One might theorize that sport flourished best in the city and on the frontier, the settled rural areas and isolated farms in every region of the United States being the greatest resistant force in the trend toward organization. In both the frontier town and the eastern city there was constant activity and social change; in both there was a decline in religious restraint and in Puritan orthodoxy. Certainly, the frontier, hard and discouraging as it always proved to be, was seldom preoccupied with sport. But in the boisterous pioneer years on the fringes of settlement men responded to the competitive spirit and enriched their lives with the increasing popularity of sporting diversions.

## Agrarian Attitudes Toward Sport

Rural Americans emerged slowly from their intellectual and social insularity, and their reaction to what little sport they saw was most conservative. Small farmers, whose fields were overrun by gayly dressed ladies and gentlemen on a fox hunt, became increasingly aroused. Their posting of lands seems to have had little effect on the planter and his friends. The feelings of irate farmers was expressed by one critic of the hunt: "The manly sports of the field, cherished as they have been by our fathers for generations past, will, we are sure, never be abandoned by our people. They afford healthy exercise and cultivate social feelings. There is, however, a limit to all things. When one's farm is invaded time after time, ransacked, and the game shot down without mercy, without stint, for private use and market sale, it is time to fix a limit to the sport." Hunting and fishing enthusiasts were already facing the problem of nearby preserves. In 1853 John Krider could complain: "While the passion for field sports is largely on the increase with us, agriculturists are improving their lands on the great water courses, and market shooters striving to be in advance of the sportsman on all the choice grounds; so that the chances are, that unless you go farther and spend more time on your excursions, you will hardly get your share of snipe shooting." [10]

Each receding frontier left behind isolated homesteads and rural villages whose people had little time for merrymaking. While some of the early forms of recreation on the frontier survived in the more settled communities of the South and the Trans-Appalachian West, the advance of civilization prevented many from taking root. Almost from the beginning, as we shall see, horse racing and cockfighting became a passion which westerners were reluctant to suppress. But the gander pullings and the beef shoots, the gouging contests and the bear baitings which took place in frontier communities were hardly the proper recreation for respectable Christian settlements in the agrarian West. With the coming of the circuit rider and the country church, soon to be followed by the arrival of the

schoolmaster and the one-room school house, the more genteel games of
the East diffused to the new Canaan. What sporting diversions there were
retained a rustic flavor, but the cruel and wild sports of the frontier were
seldom seen in the new land of settled farms, thriving villages, and busy
towns. In the 1820's and 1830's hunting and fishing remained highly
individualized, simple sports for rural youths, and it was only in larger
urban areas of the South and West like Richmond, Charleston, Savannah,
Cincinnati and New Orleans that devotees of cricket, the hunt, fishing,
fowling, or boating organized clubs.

Religious prejudices against sport remained strong among the rural
folk of the South and the West. When Reverend Francis Asbury of the
Methodist Church visited Charleston in 1795 he lamented in his *Journal*
the "unparalleled wickedness of the people" and confessed, "I have been
lately more subject to melancholy than for many years past, and how can
I help it: the white and worldly people are intolerably ignorant of God;
playing, dancing, swearing, racing; these are their common practices and
pursuits." Baptists as well as Methodists were strong opponents of the
sporting fraternity. With the coming of the "Conservative Reaction" the
sobriety and the purity of Christian people was constantly defended by
the clergy against the temptations of frivolous recreation and of the
gambling fever. Rural recreation was often keyed to church socials, Bible
societies, and camp meetings; or to lyceum lectures, school festivities,
and, occasionally, traveling carnival shows. The pleasures of the athletic
field and the sports of the social aristocracy came into vogue only after
the establishment of settled communities like St. Louis, Lexington, Nashville, and Memphis. It was far more than coincidence that the rise of sport
as an institution in American life began to increase rapidly in the 1820's
and 1830's, when the growth of towns and cities began to outstrip the
increase in the agrarian population. The sporting clique of the established
town or city supported, for the most part, the prize fights, bear baitings,
and cock mains of prewar decades. Well might the enthusiastic sportsman
and judicious editor of the *American Farmer* recognize these prejudices of
Christian farmers and take "special care always to keep clear of and to
reprobate gaming, cockfighting and milling."

Abuse of the Sabbath by sportsmen aroused the local clergy. James
Hall recorded how even the hunter often rested on that day for reasons
of piety or for fear that he might ruin his chances for the rest of the week.
Religious and moral opposition to gamblers as "sporting men" cast a cloud
over the race track and the cock fighting arena for many westerners. Puritan prejudices flowed into the West and lingered long in the mind of the
sturdy farmer, who even questioned the morality and propriety of "speed
trials" at agricultural fairs. Although many of the crude forms of frontier

sport lingered on in rural western areas, it was in or near rising urban centers that sportsmen formed clubs and established officially recognized tracks. It was only with the rise of western cities that the sports of the East began to win the farmer's favor.

Despite these urban influences, rustic lads in all sections enjoyed their traditional games. Rural sports, with their simplicity and spontaneity, were deeply rooted in the hearts of settlers who had swept over the Appalachians and into the Mississippi Valley. Even in New England and the seaboard southern states marbles, skating, sledding, battledore, quoit pitching, town ball, swimming, hunting, fishing, and impromptu horse races were popular in many a rustic village. Country stores or wayside taverns served as fields of battle for horseshoe experts and farmboy jockeys. Saturday afternoon race meetings were arranged in rural areas of the South. In North Carolina the Hillsborough *Recorder* noted a Mocksville race in 1825 and went on to complain that "as is too frequent the case at similar Saturday meetings at country stores, too much wiskey had been drank." Life in the larger cities was already considered too confining in the 1820's; excursions to the country to enjoy rural sports were encouraged; and the *American Farmer* championed the trek from the city to the countryside by warning, "The sedentary and oppressive occupations of a city life . . . require to be counteracted by refreshing amusements that are only to be found in the country." Quoit games were played at county court meetings or log rollings and were sponsored by proprietors of inns and taverns. And the village blacksmith's forge brought farmers together to discuss their nags and to acquire "plates for plating race horses . . . in the best English style."[11]

## Urban and Rural Sport of the Ante-bellum Era

It was the concentration of settlers in villages soon to become towns which in turn would rapidly develop into thriving cities that made it possible to spread the gospel of outdoor sports and organized games. Towns and cities were natural centers for organizing sporting diversions in colonial and ante-bellum years. Horse racing centered in New York, Charleston, Nashville, Louisville, and New Orleans, while, as Jennie Holliman has claimed, "There was hardly a town of any note in the South that did not have its jockey club." Baseball first appeared on an organized basis during the 1840's and 1850's in such communities as New York, Boston, Chicago, St. Louis, Cincinnati, New Orleans and San Francisco; the main agricultural fairs were held in the larger cities or state capitals; boating regattas, foot races, billiard matches, and other contests were usually held before city audiences. Even the trotter, favorite of the farmer, raced most frequently on tracks of private promoters in urban areas. Although Pennsylvania made such meetings illegal in 1810, trotting courses and horse clubs were established in the larger cities by 1825. Despite Pennsylvanians' being anything but sympathetic to commercialized sports, the trotting course became so popular that racing was legalized in 1833.

Cricket clubs appeared in Boston and New York in the 1790's, but it was Philadelphia that soon became the home of the American game, mainly through the influx of English workers into the woolen industry there. South of the Quaker city quoit clubs thrived in the larger towns. Prize fighting in the 1840's and 1850's grew in favor among more disreputable urban elements, and bull baiting, dog baiting, and cock fighting sometimes found enthusiasts in the large city.

But the transition was slow and the sports of these decades retained many rural as well as urban characteristics. Few cities in the United States had attained a metropolitan status when organized sport began to win a following around 1830. In that year less than 2 million Americans out of a population of almost 13 million lived in communities of 2500 or more people, and only New York and Philadelphia had passed the 100,000 mark. Baltimore, Boston, New Orleans, and Charleston followed in order, and no other city's population exceeded 25,000. The turf depended on urban crowds more than did any other sport, but the racing centers of the South (except for Charleston and New Orleans) were still frontier towns or small settled communities. Richmond had a population of 16,060; Louisville, 10,352; Norfolk, 9816; Lexington, 6104; and Nashville only 5566. In the rural South and West the sporting diversions of frontier folk continued until the Civil War. As Augustus Longstreet showed in *Georgia Scenes,* backwoodsmen revelled at "gander Pooling," gouging matches, cock fights, and horseshoe pitching. Even in thriving New York, where hunting and fishing were only a short walk from town, sports retained a rustic atmosphere in the early decades of the nineteenth century. By 1830, however, trap shooting establishments had opened, rowing clubs were common, prize fighting had won a foothold, and the turf was running on an organized basis. Sport was increasingly dependent for its organization on city audiences and social groups, but many of its agrarian characteristics were present up to the Civil War.

## Technological Change and the Decline of Agrarian Isolation

Various changes helped pierce the isolation and self-contained life of the farm in the years before the war. Telegraph lines went up all over the landscape, the railroad followed the steamboat from the East to the Midwest and the South, and by 1860 a network of over thirty-thousand miles of track covered the United States. An immigrant tide helped populate mid-western states, and Cincinnati, St. Louis, Chicago, Milwaukee, and Detroit gradually became western metropolises. The reaper and other new tools slowly transformed farm life; agricultural societies sprouted up; journals brought scientific information to the farmer; and the agricultural fair developed into a prominent social institution.

As early as 1838 Wade Hampton and other sportsmen were shipping race horses by rail. American turfmen were handicapped by problems of climate, food, water, and hard dirt tracks as well as by a "want of good roads, and means of communication in the interior" and "the great distance their 'strings' had to travel to the various meetings."

> On some lines there are railroads; but this is only choosing a less evil, with a tenfold risk, so badly are they managed; and, on one occasion, Col. Hampton, and two other gentlemen, having sent their horses by that conveyance, the rails broke down, the cars upset; two of the horses were killed on the spot . . . and all more or less hurt, so as to stop their running for that season.[12]

New Orleans society went to the Eclipse Course by way of a short-line road in 1837, and two years later it was reported that "the Metairie Course, drew the largest kind of a crowd, and had it not been for the breaking down of the cars on the Nashville Railroad the attendance would have been the largest ever on a race track in this vicinity." Fortunately, the shell road to the course was in good repair, and "every hack, gig, barouche, omnibus, buggy and wagon—every two and four wheeled carriage, including some carts and drays" was requisitioned. Another incident illustrating the turf's dependence on the railroad, which was seldom very dependable in this era, occurred in the race between Boston and Fashion at the Union Course in 1842. Some five thousand racing enthusiasts jammed the trains of the Long Island Rail Road, the company sold more tickets than the number of passengers it could carry, and then the trains failed to arrive at the track on time. Riots broke out among the disgusted crowd which decided to overturn the cars and smash railroad property.

By mid-century sportsmen were riding the Erie line through New York State in search of choice fishing streams while Louisville, Kentucky could announce to horsemen, "Lexington, Georgetown, Frankfort, Paris and other towns in this State, are now but a short ride from our city by railroad conveyance. Horses can come from Lexington here in five hours." Harvard and Yale rowing crews were first brought together at a New Hampshire lake in 1852 as the result of an offer by the superintendent of the Boston, Concord and Montreal line. Just prior to the war the railroad began to assume a prominent role in sporting circles. Flora Temple "hippo-dromed" from Hartford to Elmira, Detroit, Chicago, Kalamazoo, St. Louis and other centers, racing at tracks throughout the northern states from 1857 until the outbreak of war. "Flora Temple settled down to her boxcar journeys with the zest and snugness of the seasoned tourist, slept soundly amid the rattling confusion at the junction points," and ended each campaign as fresh and strong as she had been at the beginning. The Great Fair of the St. Louis Agricultural and Mechanical Association in 1859 attracted not only this renowned queen of the tracks but also horses from Virginia, Maryland, Pennsylvania, New Jersey, New York, Georgia, Arkansas, and Louisiana as well as Kentucky, Tennessee, Ohio, Indiana, Illinois, Missouri, Iowa, Michigan, and Wisconsin.

A Michigan Central Railroad Base Ball Club commenced playing in 1857. The National Association of Base Ball Players games were attended by droves of "cranks" at the Fashion Course in 1858, who rode there by way of the Fulton Ferry, a small steamer, and the Flushing Railroad. Excursion tickets were also sold in Massachusetts for the state champion-ship.[13] The Erie line carried boisterous crowds to the Morrissey-Heanan match fought near Buffalo in 1858, and at the outbreak of the Civil War hunters, fishermen, and sportsmen of all breeds were utilizing the expand-ed railroad network.

The rapid development of telegraphy in the journalistic world also helped break the shell of isolation. Following the Mexican War six leading newspapers formed the New York Associated Press (a name acquired some years later). The Western Union Telegraph Company, organized in 1855, favored the AP with low rates in exchange for a monopoly of newspaper business. James Gordon Bennett's *Herald* and Horace Greeley's *Tribune* installed telegraphic apparatus in 1846, only two years after its invention by Samuel F.B. Morse and as soon as the Magnetic Telegraph Company's line reached New York. New York achieved direct contact with New Orleans in 1848, and by 1861 San Francisco was in communication with the Atlantic seaboard. One of the first accounts of a sporting event was of the Hyer-Sullivan brawl at Rock Point, Maryland, in 1849, and the scrupu-lous editor of the *Tribune* printed dispatches of the fight. Although most reports came in by mail, sporting news was telegraphed to the *Spirit of the Times* by 1850, and during the prewar decade prize fights, horse races, trotting contests, and yachting events were occasionally reported over the wires. When two fighters met for the American championship in 1858, anxious crowds huddled around Western Union offices in many towns, and news of the victory of England's Tom Sayers over America's "Benicia Boy" Heanan was wired to various parts of the country after it was received from the steamer *Vanderbilt.*[14] Reporting of sporting events was increasing by 1860, but the real exploitation of telegraphy was to come only with the return of peace and the sporting boom after the Civil War.

## Farmers and the Agricultural Fair

Elkanah Watson's exhibition of merino sheep in 1807 and the Berkshire Cattle Show of 1810 may have been the forerunners of the annual agricultural fair, but it seems that no statewide exhibitions were held until Syracuse, New York, and New Brunswick, New Jersey, inaugurated the custom in 1841. The fairs were organized for purposes of showing sheep, hogs and other stock, as well as domestic arts, agricultural machinery, and new techniques in farming. They multiplied rapidly in the 1840's, especially in Kentucky, Tennessee, and Missouri. "Ploughing matches" were the favorite diversion until the 1850's, when trotting and thoroughbred "speed trials" became popular. The Louisville Agricultural Society held a meeting in 1830, and it was claimed that "there were persons from all parts of the United States here, and some from Europe, who spoke in praise of the racing, good order, &c."[15] But it was the ploughing match which was featured at rural fairs until the 1850's.

Although it was not the practice of most farmers, the training of trotters and thoroughbreds for racing had become rather common in the 1830's and 1840's. Around 1850 they were entering into the excitement of some local, county, and state exhibitions. Lady Suffolk's appearance at the Rochester fair in 1851 was heralded as a great attraction to the farmers of western New York: "This was decidedly the race of the season. Our State Fair had called people together from all parts of the country, and the fame of these horses attracted thousands to the course. Hundreds and hundreds wended their way to the track for the first time, to see the world-renowned Lady Suffolk."[16]

At the Clinton County fair in Keeseville, New York, the following year, however, promoters established a race course in the vicinity of the grounds and caused the state agricultural society to denounce this rising menace as a curse, both economic and moral. This statement induced many farmers to remain at home. Farm journals and society reports of the fifties seem to have given little recognition to the racing crowd, and that little was generally condemnatory. When 60,000 people attended the United States Agricultural Society's exhibition at Boston in 1855 the *Cultivator* admitted: "There is a race—we beg pardon, a 'trial of speed' to come off shortly, and the fact cannot be denied that it is this which draws such a crowd."

Many farmers remained obdurate in their hostility. A.B. Allen and R.L. Allen, editors of the new *American Agriculturist,* represented early farmer opposition to racing in 1842: "It is no part of our intentions to chronicle the trials or triumphs of the turf. There may be more or less connexion with the stouter kinds of racing bloods and the farm horse, as there generally is with the carriage horse or roadster, and with manifest advantage to the latter. But as a general rule, we are wholly opposed to this mode of testing the value of breeders; and if decidedly advantageous as a method of proving the requisite quality of serviceable horses, we should consider the *cost* in time, money and morals, far exceeding the value to be derived from it." This policy, however, did not prevent the editors from reporting the race of the day between Boston and Fashion![17] Although "trials of speed" were the great attraction of the United States Agricultural Society's fair in Philadelphia in 1856, the *Working Farmer* printed a denunciation of the racing mania:

> They do injustice to American farmers when they require them to give their endorsement to horseracing. . . . Fast horses are *not* an agricultural necessity nor even an agricultural product. No practical farmer need be told that the rearing and training of such horses is at utter variance with agricultural success; and no hard working, intelligent farmer sees his son turning his attention to the development of speed in horses, especially for competition on the track, without trembling for his success as a farmer. . . . Fast horse-flesh has no practical value since the introduction of railroads and the telegraphs. . . If we cannot have Agricultural Fairs without this accompaniment, let us wait until we can.[18]

Governor Henry Wise of Virginia, in a letter to the National Horse Exhibition, of 1858, wrote, "Improved agriculture, and the wealth it produces, will, in my opinion, do far more for the horse than ever the turf did." And the *American Farmers' Magazine* for October, 1858 stated its belief that "this yearning after the fastest horses, stimulated as it is by the hopes of a golden reward at our fairs, and wrought up to an unnatural intensity by the shouting and hat heaving of the million, and incensed over with woman's smiles, will put back, by a long period, but not forever, the day when our country will beat the world in such horses as will do our work best."

Almost all states had annual state fairs by 1858, and the prevalence of racing indicates that it was an important adjunct of the exhibition. A great part of the huge throngs which attended the larger fairs, and many of those who frequented local and county exhibitions, were townsfolk, but farmers appeared from all points of the compass, either in spite of or because of the races. The trotting and thoroughbred world of the 1850's was deeply ensconced in the annual fair, and the loss of enthusiasm in the northern states for intersectional races on the turf during these years of the antislavery struggle was more than compensated for in the popularity of races at trotting parks and fairgrounds.

## Origins of Sporting and Athletic Interest

Although the turf exemplified the most consistent trend toward organized sport in the first half of the nineteenth century, other sporting or athletic groups made some headway. Foot racing, mostly over long distances, increased in popular favor in the 1820's, and by 1835 the sport was in full swing. "Jackson," "Gildersleeve," and others gained fame in sporting circles, and races of both amateurs and professionals were held in many urban communities. Pedestrian races—both walking and running—were widely reported by the press or the sporting journal. Indian runners participated frequently, challenges and heavy betting were common, and owners of private tracks promoted races or arranged them in conjunction with agricultural fairs. A ten cent admission charge was often sought to pay the professional runner's expenses. A foot race often developed into an important local event. When "Gildersleeve" ran against a group of Indians at Buffalo in 1847, the Buffalo *Daily Courier* described the festive affair:

> The race has been a topic of conversation for a week past . . . the 'red men' runners were paraded through our streets in carriages, preceded by a band of music.
> As the hour of the afternoon drew nigh, when the race was to come off, the two streets, Main and Delaware, were literally crowded with carriages, horses, and pedestrians, wending their way to the course. When we reached it there was a larger throng than we had seen on any similar occasion.[19]

Foot racing contests continued throughout the 1850's and aroused an enthusiasm which post-bellum experimenters capitalized on in promoting track and field contests.

Competitive rowing races, often between British and American seamen, seem to have originated about the time of the War of 1812, although harbor races of an informal nature occurred even in the colonial era. Perhaps the first organized race of modern times was one in 1807 between the boats of Jean Baptiste of New York and the Chambers builders from

London. In 1811 longshoremen rowed light barges on the Hudson from
the Jersey shore to the Battery. Various boat clubs preserved the victorious
*Knickerbocker* until fire destroyed it in 1865.

A number of organizations like the Savannah Boat Club and the
Whitehall Aquatic Club formed in the 1820's, and a crowd estimated at
possibly 50,000 attended a British-American race in 1824. By 1835 boat
clubs were numerous; the Castle Garden Boat Club Association, created in
1834, held its first race at Poughkeepsie in 1837; Newburgh and the upper
Hudson had clubs; and races commenced on an organized basis on the
Schuylkill at Philadelphia. Southern clubs in New Orleans, Mobile, Savannah,
and elsewhere bought northern boats, while the Detroit Boat Club, organizing in 1839, had its first boat shipped to the West by the Erie Canal.[20]

Boston saw its first rowing regatta about 1842. In the South slave
crews rowing in galley style were pitted in competitive races, and interest
was aroused in the establishment of boat clubs. According to E. Merton
Coulter, "Boating as a sport extended from Virginia to Texas, and the
heyday of its existence was from the 1830's to the Civil War."[21] Clubs
were formed at Biloxi, Mississippi, Mobile, Alabama, and on Lake Pont-
chartrain, Louisiana, while an Aquatic Club of Georgia was formed in
1836. The coming of the Civil War, however, brought an end to these
clubs.

During the 1840's rowing races began on western waters while collegiate rowing got its start in the East. Yale students formed a boat club in
1843, Harvard followed in 1844, but it was not until 1852 that the first
contest with the boys from New Haven took place. During the 1850's
enthusiasts organized clubs in Worcester, Milwaukee, and other cities;
crews competed in Fourth of July races on the Charles River for prizes
offered by the Boston city fathers; regattas took place at Springfield,
Charlestown, and numerous other centers. In 1854 students of the University of Pennsylvania formed a University Barge Club and 1858 marked
organization of famous Schuylkill Navy. Professional rowing attained a
degree of popularity, and the champion oarsman James Lee gained a
national reputation after 1850. At the outbreak of the Civil War rowing
was firmly established as one of the leading American sports.

The history of yachting might begin with the development of the
clipper ship, but the story of organized yacht racing really commences
with the formation of the New York Yacht Club in 1844. For the remain-
der of the century that club's authority held sway with few serious challenges from outside. Massachusetts, however, was a pioneer in yacht racing,
the *Sylph* of Robert B. Forbes and the *Wave* of Commodore John C.
Stevens engaging in what may have been the first race in America. Following the ocean race of 1836, the first open yacht regatta in Massachusetts

was held in 1845 at Nahant, which remained the center of Bay State yachting until the Civil War. After the demise of a Mobile Yacht Club founded in 1847, the Southern Yacht Club was organized in 1849 at Pass Christian on the Gulf of Mexico.

Commodore John C. Stevens gave the greatest boost to the sport, however, when he won the America's Cup at Cowes in 1851. At the announcement of victory Americans overflowed with pride, clipper ship records were forgotten in this moment of glory, and the American minister to Paris, William C. Rives, congratulated the victors, stating "how much I felt our national honor and interests to be involved in the issue of any match the America might make at Cowes. . . . And what a victory! . . . to beat her in her own native seas . . . contending against a fleet of seventeen sail of her picked models of naval architecture . . . is something that may well encourage us in the race of maritime competition which is set befor us." [22] The Brooklyn and Jersey City clubs were formed in 1857 and 1858, but racing had to stand aside for commerce. The 1850's marked the exploits of the clippers and rival steamships, and the end of races for the America's Cup until after the Civil War.

Another sport in its growing pains in ante-bellum America was the prize ring. Slaves had been the first pugilists in the United States, planters frequently betting the returns for future crops on their champion black fighters. From about 1819 onwards interest grew in pugilism. But the New York *Mirror* of 1835 expressed "regret and alarm at finding reason to believe that the detestable practice of prize-fighting threatens to take root within the soil of our native land . . . . May the time never come when it shall be added to the list of our faults and vices." [23]

When a fight took place in New Jersey in 1835 an Elizabethtown public meeting asked for restrictive legislation, and the New York *Sun,* which was already covering fights, agreed: "If any law can be framed by our legislature that may aid in putting down this disgraceful practice, we hope it may be adopted." Among the noted champions of the time were James ("Yankee") Sullivan, Tom Hyer, John Morrissey, John C. Heanan, and the visiting fighters from England or Ireland who sustained most of the interest in the ring. Because of the vigilance of legal authorities and hostile journalists like Hezekiah Niles, prize fights were often held by moonlight or at dawn, usually on an isolated island where the police would seldom appear.

In the 1850's the more reputable press often ignored the fights, but sporting journals gave considerable space to ring activities. George Wilkes published accounts of fistic encounters in his *Spirit of the Times,* while the *New York Clipper,* first published in 1853 under the editorship of Frank Queen, became the prize ring's "Bible." Crowds of three to six thousand spectators were reported to the metropolitan press. In New

York, where well-known pugilists led many of the city's gangs, the prestige of recently arrived immigrant groups often hinged on their champion. When Morrissey and Heanan met near Buffalo in 1858 enthusiasm was so intense that the editor of *Harper's Weekly* railed:

> Without doubt the leading event of last week—to a large mass of the people of New York, and the other large cities—was the prize-fight which took place. . . . Other events there were . . . but all of these were overshadowed and swallowed up by the great boxing-match at Long Point. On Thursday, especially, there was nothing heard of—up town, down town and in the country—but the great prize-fight. . . . The popularity of prize-fighting as a newspaper topic is unquestionable . . . . On Thursday morning, the rush for the paper which happened to contain the only report of the fight was frantic. . . . The prize-fight was, we venture to assert, the only topic discussed that morning in bank-parlors, counting-rooms, and offices generally throughout the city—to say nothing of bar-rooms, and places of like character.[24]

The prevalence of six-shooters and a tough element at the fights caused a British observer to express his disgust with the American ring, but young Walt Whitman of the Brooklyn *Eagle,* also a critic of rowdyism, claimed: "Here, in this young, vigorous country we want no spoonies or milk-sops."

Tom Sayers and John Heanan, the English and American champions, captured the public's interest in 1860 in the most publicized fight prior to the war. Newspapers devoted pages to Heanan's preparation, departure, heroic struggle, and return to the United States. On his return from England fifty thousand admirers attended a Heanan festival at Jones Wood, New York. *Harper's Weekly* minced no words in commenting on how the opera house had virtually emptied as men clamored for sports "extras" on the fight: "We believe prize-fighting to be a degrading, brutal, and shameful practice; we consider the prize-ring a national nucleus of black-guardism, and we do not believe that pugilism is in the least degree calculated to do good when it can hardly fail to do evil." The *Weekly* continued in this vein by complaining, "Moralists must be writing and clergy-men must be preaching to very little purpose, since the bulk of the people in England and America are heart and soul engrossed in a fight compared to which a Spanish bull-bait is a mild and diverting pastime. To what purpose so many pulpits and so many sermons if the brutal prize-fighter is the hero of the day."[25]

Prize fighting made little headway in New England, and in other areas the ring's supporters were often of a volatile nature, but it seems certain that, despite the disdainful attitude of respectable journalists, a large proportion of the metropolitan population were aroused.

Just where and when baseball appeared in the United States is one of the unsolved mysteries of American history. The *Spirit of the Times,* October 24, 1857 remarked, "Base Ball . . . has, no doubt, been played in this country for at least one century." Abner Doubleday, whom historians formerly credited with originating the game at Cooperstown, New York, may never have witnessed a contest as it was played in the 1840's and 1850's. Most probably the game had grown through the acquisition of rules and techniques from other popular games of the early nineteenth century—the numerous Old Cat games, town ball, rounders, and cricket. A town ball club had organized in Philadelphia as early as 1831. Alexander J. Cartwright outlined a diamond for the Knickerbocker Club in 1845 and their first match was played at Hoboken the following year. Whatever the origin of the game, the Knickerbockers' reputation soon incited others to organize amateur teams. During the 1850's clubs centered in the New York area, and in 1858 these formed a National Association of Base Ball Players.[26] As Arthur C. Cole has claimed, the organization of this association "marked the beginning of a more regulated development under a definite code of rules; players from cities all over the Union sought admission to its ranks. Every community of any size soon had its own team." As early as 1858 the *Atlantic Monthly* referred to "our indigenous American game of base-ball, whose briskness and unceasing activity are perhaps more congenial, after all, to our national character, than the comparative deliberation of cricket."

Amherst and Williams played the first intercollegiate game of baseball in 1859, and by 1860 the baseball fever had hit the campus at Princeton and Union College in Schenectady. A crowd of ten thousand people were reported at a New York game between the Excelsior and Atlantic clubs. In New England games were held at agricultural fairs, while upper New York state was well acquainted with baseball in 1860 when the Excelsiors played in Albany, Troy, Buffalo, Newburgh, and Rochester. By this time the game had appeared in Detroit, Chicago, St. Louis, New Orleans, and San Francisco. Clubs were already playing in Nininger and St. Paul, Minnesota by 1857, a year after Chicago fielded its first team. The Civil War temporarily checked the rapid rise of baseball interest but the game was already spreading over the country.[27]

## The Spirit of Organization in the 1850's

Organization first appeared in American sport in the world of the turf in the years before 1850. By about 1830 a split-second watch costing $120 was developed; elaborate grandstands were erected; jockey clubs strove to standardize the rules; seasonal schedules (allowing horses to campaign in the South in the fall and winter and in the North in the summer) were arranged; racing times were recorded; and the spirit of organization made considerable headway. This trend was still in its formative stage, however. Meetings were held semi-annually, seldom for more than a week's duration, and schedules were often changed. Signs of loose organization were present in 1831 when the Beech Bottom Course in western Virginia followed the rules of the Union Course, Long Island; the Louisville Agricultural Society's races of 1830 were based on the rules of the Baltimore club; and the Warrenton, North Carolina, fall races of 1831 were governed by the racing code of the New Market, Virginia, track.

The length and condition of the first race tracks illustrates the irregular nature of early racing: in 1829 the Lexington Kentucky Association Course was rough and cut by two sharp hills; Richmond, Kentucky's course was 1 mile less 17 yards in length; Georgetown, Kentucky's track was 50 yards short; even the Union Course was found when surveyed in 1830 to be 30 feet over a mile. The Boydton Course was described as "considerably rolling."

Another problem of early racing was the question of weight to be carried by each horse. By 1830 "the long established usage of weights on the Southern courses" was being introduced at New York, whereas Louisville racing in 1831 followed the code used at Baltimore—except in the weight to be carried. By the fifties the spirit of organization had spread widely. Mr. P.F. Barnum, proprietor of the National Course in New York, advertised, "The races will be run with Virginia weights, the same as in Kentucky, Tennessee, Mississippi, Alabama and Louisiana." Further organization of the turf was retarded by the sectional rift preceding the Civil War.[28]

Social historians are able to record a strong array of boating, racing, cricket, and similar clubs in the years prior to mid-nineteenth century. It was only in the 1850's, however, that sport was transformed, to any significant degree, in the direction of organization. The prize ring, patronized surreptitiously, gained increasing popularity in a few metropolitan areas with the arrival of numerous English and Irish pugilists. Thoroughbred, trotting, and pacing races were introduced at the county and state fair. Baseball enthusiasts formed a National Association; yachting clubs appeared on inland waters; cricket and shooting clubs were organized for social purposes; intercollegiate athletics appeared on the sporting horizon; Turnvereins cropped up in German communities; and professional rowing acquired a wider following. In the year 1850 a New Yorker by the name of Michael Phelan, then the great promoter of billiards in America and the author of *Billiards Without A Master,* threw out a challenge for an international match, and specified the rules of play, lest there be any confusion: "The balls to be played with are to be 2 3/8 in. in diameter, and the game to be played on a true and correct cushion table." In 1859 Phelan met John Seereiter of Detroit for the first championship in America, after which Phelan reigned as champion until Dudley Kavanaugh succeeded him in 1862. Such organization was needed at a time when many styles of play were in vogue, some introduced by French cue artists, and there were few authoritative rule books available.

Promoters of racing directed their attention to the need of more general control. During the 1850's a corps of turfmen were very active. Charles S. Ellis, owner of Lady Suffolk, sponsored races at the Chicago and St. Louis courses; J.C. O'Hanlon conducted meetings at Memphis and at Columbia, South Carolina; Richard Ten Broeck and James Valentine backed turf meetings at New Orleans. Planters no longer retained the monopoly in racing of earlier decades: "The days of American aristocracy and exclusiveness are gone."[29] Local proprietors took over in numerous other communities and helped to organize the turf to the point where club rules were fairly similar and race conduct was somewhat standardized.

Lady Suffolk's racing in the South and West helped popularize the trotter, and by 1850 this filley had won $40,000. Numerous recognized trotting courses appeared around 1850, when popular interest in recreation was manifesting itself in the throngs which attended annual fairs, boat regattas, foot races, prize fights, and other sporting events. Thoroughbred racing lost some of its earlier popularity with the decline of intersectional rivalries; only 400 thoroughbreds were in training in 1847 for the fall campaigns in the South and the West (although it was thought that some 2000 foals for the year 1849 might eventually go on the running track).[30] A leading historian of the turf, William Henry Herbert ("Frank Forester") recognized this trend in racing sentiment as early as 1857: "The palmy time, then, of the Turf in America, . . . [was] between the years 1815 and 1845, the former date being a little earlier than its dawn, the latter a little later than the first symptoms of its decline." With a nod to the farmer's preoccupation with the trotting horse, he pointed out:

> Now, horse-racing and steeple-chasing can never, from their very nature, become in the true sense of the word, POPULAR. The people may love to be spectators, but can never hope to become participators in them. Since the keeping up of racing establishments . . . [requires] almost unbounded expenditure, . . . abundant leisure, constant attention, and the ownership of soil, [horse-racing] can

never extend to others than the few, the wealthy pleasure-seekers, of
any community. The masses can never pretend to those sports.

The trotting-course, on the other hand, is common to all. It is
the trial-ground and arena of the roadster, open to every one who
keeps a horse for his own driving . . . the butcher, the baker, or the
farmer, who keeps his one fast crab, trains it himself into general
condition on the road, and puts it for a month or two into the hands
of Spicer, Woodruff, Wheelan, or some other such tip-top-sawyer,
to bring it to its best time, and trot it, when the purse is to be won.

Trotting, in America, is the people's sport, the people's pastime,
and consequently, is, and will be, supported by the people.[31]

## Small Business and the Sportsman

Sportsmen in the colonial era occasionally imported fishing books and gear
from England, and by the 1730's a few merchants advertised their rods
and hooks in the *Pennsylvania Gazette.* Edward Pole offered artificial flies
to anglers in 1774. He was "the leading Philadelphia tackle-dealer in the
Hey-day of the Schuylkill River fishing clubs." Jeremiah Allen of Boston
imported bamboo, dogwood, and hazel rods prior to the Revolution. By
the 1830's anglers might visit the shops of T. W. Horsfield, Hinton's Ware-
house and Manufactory, Abr'm Brower, Charles R. Taylor, and Lewis of
3 Wall Street in New York. Fishing as sport came increasingly into vogue in
the 1820's and 1830's. Conroy's won a reputation as the leading supplier
of fishermen by the 1840's. John J. Brown, owner of an "Angler's Depot"
in New York, wrote in his *American Angler's Guide* in 1849 how "the
raft and lumbermen from the Delaware and rivers of Pennsylvania, are
seen in the fishing-tackle stores of New York, selecting with the eyes of
professors and connoisseurs the red, black, and grey hackle flies." Multiple
section split-bamboo rods were made by Samuel Philippe of Easton, Pennsylvania, who placed them on the market in 1848 through the agency of
Andrew Clerk and Company.[32]

Across the mountains in Kentucky George Snyder manufactured
reels shortly after the start of the century, and in later decades Jonathan
Meek, B.F. Meek, and Benjamin C. Milam of Frankfort, as well as J. W.
Hardman of Louisville, gained renown for their craftmanship. During the
forties merchants like P.J. Simpson and J.B. Crook of New York informed
the "sporting community" of their stocks of fish hooks and tackle. Daniel
Webster was an ardent hunter and angler, owning a trout rod called "Kill-
all" and hunting rifles such as "Mrs. Patrick," "Learned Selden," and
"Wilmot Proviso." That the manufacture of fishing equipment was already
considered indispensable to sportsmen of the time is seen in Webster's

letter of June 10, 1847, to Mr. Robert Welch of New York, who had made him three rods, silver mounted and his name engraved on each, the gift of an anonymous admirer. "The rods and reels are certainly of exquisite workmanship, and richly mounted; the flies truly beautiful, and the contents of the books ample, abundant, and well selected. Poor Isaac Walton! Little did he think, when moving along by the banks of the rivers and brooks of Staffordshire, with his cumbrous equipments, that any unworthy disciple of his would ever be so gorgeously fitted out, with all that art and taste can accomplish, for the pursuit of his favorite sport!"[33] Yet, in this same period when Webster bragged of his equipment and his intensive preparations for an angling venture, the specialized apparatus of skilled sportsmen were unknown to many a rural youth. Charles Hallock, a noted sportsman and conservationist of post-Civil War years, recalled how the rural folk of Hampshire County, Massachusetts, responded to visiting sportsmen of the 1840's who brought with them the practice of fly fishing and the enviable manufactured rods and reels.

> Ah! those were halcyon days. No railroads disturbed the quiet seclusion of that mountain nook. . . . Twice a week an old-fashioned coach dragged heavily up the hill into the hamlet and halted in front of the house which was at once post-office, tavern, and miscellaneous store—an *"omnium gatherum . . ."* One day it brought a passenger. . . . He carried a leather hand-bag and a handful of rods in a case. The village *quidnuncs* said he was a surveyor. He allowed he was from Troy and had "come to go a-fishing." From that stranger I took my first lesson in fly-fishing.[34]

Manufacture and merchandising of sporting goods was still in the pioneer stage of development during the early decades of the nineteenth century. To a great extent, fishing tackle, riding habits, saddles, and sleighs were still imported from Europe, as they had been from colonial times. After improvements were made in the percussion cap, stemming from the work of John Forsyth in 1807, hunters who appreciated the greater accuracy of the new guns no longer relied solely on the older Pennsylvania (often called Kentucky) Rifle which had proved such a trustworthy weapon and friend in clearing frontier forests, fighting Indians, and pursuing wild game. Gunsmiths began specializing in fowling pieces and various kinds of sporting rifles, James McNaughton of Virginia advertising his wares "To Sportsmen of the Field" in 1821. Trapshooting gained in popularity, as more and more gentlemen took up the rifle for sporting relaxation. By 1831 a Sportsman's Club of Cincinnati introduced traps which were soon copied by other clubs.[35]

At mid-century C.F.A. Hendricks was offering cricket bats, "Wickham's Balls, Stumps, etc.," and archery equipment; while J.W. Brunswick & Bro. of Cincinnati was already established in the manufacture and sale of billiard tables, in which trade they were soon to be challenged by the firm of Phelan and Collender. Boys' sleds were made by skilled craftsmen in the 1850's as sledding became one of the most popular sports in the Boston area. William Henry Herbert's "Frank Forester" pseudonym was used in recommending to fellow sportsmen the wares of Henry T. Cooper, importer and manufacturer of guns and "sporting apparatus." Highly prized agates for marble players, who were legion, were made by German iron mills and then exported to Holland, from whence American dealers imported both marbles and ice skates. Rods made of vine, bamboo, hazel and hickory were available at all "fishing-tackle shops," while youngsters could purchase battledores, shuttlecocks, and tops from peddlers or at any toy shop. Distributors appeared in numerous communities. The Natchez *Courier* carried an announcement in 1850: "S. Odell, would inform his friends and the sporting community, that he has just returned from New York and Boston, with an assortment of all the necessaries for the Sportsman." John Krider's "Sportsman's Depot" of Philadelphia, distributing as far west as Wisconsin, advertised: "Southern and western merchants, the city and country trade in general, can be furnished with a full assortment of every article in this line of business."[36]

Most of the equipment was naturally of the homemade variety, however, and youngsters were expected to rig up their own fishing rods, cricket bats, and varied types of balls. *The Boy's Treasury of Sports, Pastimes, and Recreations* advised youngsters to procure two small India-rubber bottles, and "having cut each of them round and round . . . into one long strip, wind them up as near as possible into the shape of a ball, using a small piece of cork as a foundation; over this, wind some worsted, until none of the India-rubber is visible, making the shape as perfectly round as possible; this should then be covered with a piece of stout wash-leather, and the ball will be complete." Only the privileged sporting class could afford the special equipment of prewar dealers. Far more important to boys of the school yard was a mother's industrious hand with needle and thread.

Advertising by hotels which featured ten pin alleys, billiard tables, and saddle horses as well as boat races, hunting and fishing became increasingly common in prewar years. Track owners were especially interested in publicizing their courses, and ladies' pavilions were frequently mentioned in advertisements and press reports of the races. The Memphis track promised to furnish female servants and a parlor for the "accomodation" of the ladies, while the men were advised: "A main of Cocks will be fought between Mississippi and Tennessee . . . preceding the races," and the "Memphis Brass Band will be in constant attendance." Lecomte's and Lexington's names were used for brands of tobacco by alert businessmen. Enterprising tavern keepers or restauranteurs occasionally made available copies of *Bell's Life in London,* the *Spirit of the Times,* and other sporting organs of interest to their patrons.[37] And steamboats and railroads were only too anxious to advertise excursions. Yet, advertising was in its infancy and one can search diligently through the journals and papers of ante-bellum years without turning up more than a brief announcement or advertisement (except for race meetings) of sporting affairs. Not for some decades would advertisers find reason to capitalize on the public's enthusiasm for sport.

Lithographic prints of yachting races, champion pugilists, and famous horses were sold by peddlers who stocked up on pictures of Nathaniel Currier (Currier & Ives after 1857), Brown and Severin, and other print-makers. Currier advised the public that "no sporting man should be without" one series of Lady Suffolk, Black Hawk, James K. Polk, and other champions. A corps of artists and craftsmen helped Currier & Ives establish its leadership in the printmaking trade. Sports of the blacks were satirized in the "Darktown Comics" of Thomas Worth; C. Severin's lithograph of Peytona and Fashion won great popularity as the first large sporting print of a thoroughbred running race produced in America; John Cameron excelled in the reproduction of horse prints; and Louis Maurer applied his artistic talents to painting the turf champions and trotting tracks of the day.

Political cartoonists gradually introduced horse racing, cock fighting, foot racing, and prize fighting themes into the party warfare of the time. Campaigns and controversies from 1824 onward featured cartoons of John Quincy Adams, Andrew Jackson, Henry Clay, Nicholas Biddle, Daniel Webster, Martin Van Buren, William Henry Harrison, and others in "A FOOT RACE," "RACE OVER UNCLE SAM'S COURSE," "SET TO BETWEEN OLD HICKORY AND BULLY NICK," "GREAT AMERICAN SWEEPSTAKES," "GREAT AMERICAN BUCK HUNT," and similar caricatures. The 1860 campaign presented the novelty of a baseball cartoon of Abraham Lincoln and his rivals with ball and bat. Frontier sports were also used for political propaganda in publicizing the homespun character and log cabin background of political candidates.[39]

Edward Troye used his inspired brush to spread the fame of "American Eclipse," "Sir Henry," "Grey Eagle," and other noted thoroughbreds. Sporting scenes gained entry into such new pictorial journals as *Graham's American Monthly, Harper's Weekly, Frank Leslie's Illustrated Newspaper,* the *Illustrated American News,* the *New York Illustrated News,* and the sporting journals. The Romantic mood in art was expressed by Thomas Birch, Thomas Doughty, George Durrie, Robert Salmon, J.G. Clonney, F.F. Gignoux, Henry Inman, Fitz Hugh Lane, and A.A. Lawrence, who captured the joys of skating or sleighing, fishing or hunting, sailing or boating. The horsemanship and games of the Indian were transcribed by George Catlin.[40]

Sporting literature was almost entirely of English origin. Accounts of English racing or cricket crept into the pages of the *Port Folio, American Farmer, American Turf Register,* and *Spirit of the Times,* while ardent sportsmen read the English sporting journals. Few works of consequence came off the American printing press from *A Little Pretty Book* in 1762 to George Washington Jeffrey's *Annals of the Turf* in 1820. Equestrian and hunting manuals, various editions of the *Boy's Own Book,* Charles Caldwell's *Thoughts on Physical Education,* and Robin Carver's *Book of Sports* all appeared in the 1830's. Outdoor sports gained a number of scribes in the 1840's with the writings of William Schreiner, William P. Hawes ("J. Cypress, Jr."), John J. Brown, John Mills, and George Ruxton. Cricket, boxing, and fishing manuals were common in the forties and fifties. William Henry Herbert ("Frank Forester"), William T. Porter, and John Krider were then telling sporting anecdotes and describing the wonders of the outdoor life and of the woods in the midst of the Romantic era.[41]

Romanticizing of nature and of rural sports also appeared in antebellum fiction, as in John P. Kennedy's *Swallow Barn* (1832). The Virginia gentleman, Frank Meriwether, in this novel symbolized his genteel clan's penchant for racing, riding, and fox and possum hunts: "He is somewhat distinguished as a breeder of blooded horses; and, ever since the celebrated race between Eclipse and Henry, has taken to this occupation with a renewed zeal, as a matter affecting the reputation of the state." And Henry Wadsworth Longfellow's epic poem won the hearts of a sentimental generation wanting to glorify the noble savage:

> Out of childhood into manhood
> Now had grown my Hiawatha,
> Skilled in all the craft of hunters,
> Learned in all the lore of old men,
> In all youthful sports and pastimes,
> In all manly arts and labors.

Prewar sporting journalism was confined to a few turf magazines and occasional reports in the press. There were long gaps in the reporting of sporting contests in most of the leading newspapers. Many papers failed to mention even the most important matches either before or after the event, and a large number of papers as a matter of policy completely ignored the sporting fraternity. The legends of the turf and the ball field were in part perpetuated in many communities only by pork-barrel sporting philosophers who met at the barbershop, blacksmith's forge, or country store. One can easily exaggerate the penetration of sport into the lives of Americans already crowding into big cities or living in rural villages, but at least there were signs already appearing which portended the great advances the world of sport would make in post-bellum decades.

One might best illustrate this growing enthusiasm for outdoor recreation and competitive sport in the few songs which took up the sporting theme. "Light May the Boat Row" (1836), "The Galloping Sleigh Ride" (1844), "Jingle Bells" (1857), and "Skating Polka" (1858) touched on rural and athletic sports. In 1847 Stephen Foster published "Away Down Souf," in which the black pines, "Ah! dat's the place for the steeple chase and de bully hoss race." His "Camptown Races" (1850) was the first song of enduring popularity composed around a sporting theme. Later generations swayed to the rhythmic nonsense of the minstrel tune:

> De Camptown ladies sing dis song,
> > Doo-dah! doo-dah!
> De Camptown track five miles long
> > Oh! doo-dah-day!
> I came down dah wid my hat caved in,
> > Doo-dah! doo-dah!
> I go back home wid a pocket full of tin,
> > Oh! doo-dah-day!
> Gwine to run all night!
> > Gwine to run all day!
> I'll bet my money on de bob-tail nag,
> > Somebody bet on de bay.

# Chapter 3

# Sporting Journalism and the Technological Revolution

# Chapter 3

# Sporting Journalism and the Technological Revolution

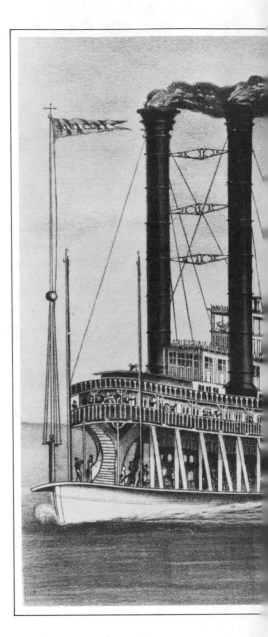

## Pioneers in Sports Reporting

James Bryce, writing at the beginning of this century, observed the American scene, noted "the passion for looking on at and reading about athletic sports," and concluded:

> It occupies the minds not only of the youth at the universities, but also of their parents and of the general public. Baseball matches and football matches excite an interest greater than any other public events except the Presidential election, and that comes only once in four years . . . (and) the interest in one of the great contests, such as those which draw forty thousand spectators to the great "Stadium" recently erected at Cambridge, Massachusetts, appears to pervade nearly all classes more than does any "sporting event" in Great Britain. The American love of excitement and love of competition has seized upon these games.[1]

What a revolution had occurred in less than a hundred years! At the dawn of the nineteenth century only the turf held any interest for the average American, and sporting enthusiasm had grown very gradually throughout the first three decades. There were many social currents, however, which were to be instrumental in creating a high degree of sports consciousness in America. Among these were the lingering outdoor heritage of a frontier society and English interest in sporting life, the colonial and early American aristocracy's support of the turf, and the more secular spirit slowly emerging on the national scene as the old theocratic-Puritanic discipline went into decline. A decided change in the urban character of the population, an extension of leisure time allied with economic prosperity and a rising standard of living, and a mounting concern for the health and physical well-being of the people contributed to the more favorable atmosphere in which sport began to appear on the national scene.

With the impact of industrialization, millions of Europeans emigrated to the United States, bringing with them their faiths, their customs, and their games. Technological improvements, ranging from the railroad and telegraph to the electric light and streetcar, gave impetus to the promotion of sport. Educational authorities slowly recognized the value of exercise, and they expressed a friendlier attitude toward the athletic interests of their students. And there were those countless pioneers in the organization of sport, men in all walks of life who founded jockey clubs, yachting associations, baseball leagues, and athletic conferences. Yet, any account of this changing outlook throughout the last century would be far from complete were it not to emphasize the indispensable role played by magazine and newspaper editors who championed the cause of sport.

In the years between the American Revolution and the age of Jacksonian democracy there arose a widespread interest in journalism of every conceivable kind. Religious, literary, economic, and, above all, political topics were discussed so widely that newspapers and magazines cropped up everywhere to exploit this popular interest. As horse racing and—by the 1830's and 1840's—field sports and athletic games gained an ever greater following, enterprising journalists set out to capture fans as subscribers. The fame of *Bell's Life in London* (1821) reached across the Atlantic to the young republic, and Americans who followed the English turf, ring, and cricket fields were forced for a time to rely on the *Weekly Dispatch* (1801) and similar publications.[2] There was enough interest emerging in horse racing throughout the Middle Atlantic states and the South to encourage experimentation with sporting journals. "Sporting Intelligence" appeared as an occasional item in *The Port Folio* of the early years of the century, but it was John Stuart Skinner who pioneered with articles in the *American Farmer* (1819) and the *American Turf Register and Sporting Magazine* (1829) and introduced the first turf column, "The Sporting Olio," in 1825. At least two other journals appeared during the twenties: *Annals of the Turf* (1826), published by George W. Jeffreys in North Carolina; and the *Farmer's, Mechanic's, Manufacturer's and Sportsman's Magazine,* published briefly in New York in the years 1826-27.

The 1830's brought forth the greatest of the ante-bellum sports editors in William Trotter Porter, a country journalist who left Vermont to work in New York. On December 10, 1831, he published the first copy of the *Spirit of the Times,* which was destined to become the leading sporting journal of the middle years of the nineteenth century. "York's Tall Son" won a nationwide reputation as "an oracle in the sporting world" through his publication of the *Spirit* and of the *American Turf Register,* which he purchased in 1839. Porter merged his *Spirit* with the *Traveller,* suffered financial reverses in the 1830's and 1840's, allied himself with George Wilkes and eventually wound up as editor for the latter's publication, generously entitled *Porter's Spirit of the Times.* Meanwhile, other experiments were being made. A short-lived *Cabinet of Natural History and American Rural Sports* was undertaken at Philadelphia in 1830; Cadwallader Colden, an authority on pedigrees, published the *New York Sporting Magazine and Annals of the American and English Turf* in the thirties; and the *Illustrated Police News,* founded in Boston in 1842, began its long career. In 1845 Porter took on the editorship of a new *American Turf Register and Trotting Calendar,* a position he held for ten years. The *Spirit* achieved a national reputation and was relied upon by newspapers everywhere. More than a hundred papers printed extracts from its account of the Boston Fashion race in 1842. By 1859, however, newsmen were awakening to the public interest and more than a hundred editors and reporters attended the Great Fair of the St. Louis Agricultural and Mechanical Association. Porter became one of the greatest promoters of horse racing; he was a devotee of angling; he opened his pages to cricket, foot racing, rowing, and yachting; and he gave a decided lift to the game of baseball in the 1850's. It has sometimes been claimed that Porter published the first box scores and "dope" sheets, and that he labeled baseball the "national game."

It was Porter who published the sporting sketches by Henry William Herbert, writing under the pseudonym of "Frank Forester" in order to conceal his identity from the literary and historical worlds in which he had high aspirations as a writer of historical romances.[3] Forester came from England as a young graduate of Cambridge, became a teacher of Latin and Greek, and founded the *American Monthly Magazine* in 1833. He was persuaded to publish a series of articles in the *American Turf Register* in 1839, and became keenly interested in writing books on hunting and fishing. His sporting reputation spread to all corners of the Union. An artist and a poet, Forester's genius in describing scenes of field and forest made him the first nationally famous sports writer.

A man of great personal vanity and pride, a recluse for long periods, quarrelsome in nature, somewhat eccentric and addicted to fancy clothes, Forester continued to write historical works but soon found that his pen, when turned to sporting literature, was much more remunerative. Among his principal works were *The Warwick Woodlands* (1845), *My Shooting Box* (1846), *Frank Forester's Field Sports* (1849), *Frank Forester's Fish and Fishing* (1850), and *Frank Forester's Sporting Scenes and Characters* (1882). His classic two-volume study entitled *Frank Forester's Horse and Horsemanship of the United States and British Provinces of North America* (1857) remains the most valuable of all contemporary studies of thoroughbred and trotting horses. As a contributor of sporting sketches to magazines and as the most noted of literary craftsmen in this field, Frank Forester became a legend to sportsmen of later generations.

George Wilkes, who had been connected with some of the sensational New York tabloids of the 1840's, founded the *National Police Gazette* in 1845. After he bought the *Spirit of the Times* in 1856, he sold the *Police Gazette* to George W. Matsell, who carried it through the Civil War era. Upon William T. Porter's death the old *Spirit* was allowed to die and Wilkes published a new journal called *Wilkes' Spirit of the Times* from 1859 to 1866, after which he dropped his own name from the masthead. Wilkes realized the publicity value in controversial issues, and carried on feuds with F.L. Dowling of *Bell's Life* and with several American sports editors. Since he was acquainted with the racing and pugilistic interests of the barroom fraternity, he proved to be a much sounder man than his predecessor in balancing his books, and the new *Spirit* enjoyed a prolonged career as a leading journal for sportsmen of every breed.

A few other periodicals appeared in the years before 1865. *The California Spirit of the Times* (1854), the *Horse Journal* (1855), the *Philadelphia Police Gazette and Sporting Chronicle* (1856), *Billiard Cue* (1856), *Sportsman* (1863), and San Francisco's *Our Mazeppa* (1864) all devoted articles to the sporting scene. The most important of the publications of the period, however, was the *New York Clipper,* founded by Frank Queen in 1853.

Queen was born to working class parents in Philadelphia in 1823, and became a printer's apprentice and ran a stationery store and newspaper stand until he ventured into the newspaper business in New York. He joined Harrison Trent in founding the *Clipper,* soon bought Trent's interest, succeeded in building up the journal's circulation, became "a man of social popularity," erected a new Clipper Building in 1869, and attained a high position in the sporting world of the 1860's and 1870's. Queen seems almost to have vanished from the journalistic scene though his office was for some years a popular site for arranging fights, and he was highly respected by sportsmen as an arbiter and authority. The *Clipper* became the prime popularizer of the diamond, employed the pioneer baseball writer and statistician Henry Chadwick, and encouraged most athletic activities. It was one of the few journals which strove to defend the prize ring, and by the 1870's it was considered one of the three leading journals of the "Sporting Press."

In the ante-bellum era, turf and athletic sports were more directly aided by magazine editors like Skinner, Porter, Wilkes, and Queen than they were by the newspaper press. American Eclipse and Sir Henry inaugurated an exciting North-South rivalry on the race course in 1823, and by the 1830's there was thoroughbred racing and trotting on numerous tracks from New York, Pennsylvania, and Ohio to Virginia, Kentucky, and Louisiana.

Foot racing and the ring, as well as rowing matches and cock fighting, were increasingly popular after 1830. A large newspaper public became deeply interested in such horses as Boston Blue, Eclipse, Boston, Fashion, Peytona, and Lady Suffolk; many came to know the notorious deeds of James (Yankee) Sullivan, Tom Hyer, John Morrissey, and John C. Heanan in the prize ring; others recalled the exploits of James Lee on the rowing course or "Deerfoot" and "Jackson" on the running track. Such New York papers as the *Transcript* and the *Sun,* as well as the Philadelphia *Public Ledger,* began reporting horse races and prize fights in the early thirties.[4] The New York *Weekly Mercury* and then James Gordon Bennett's New

York *Herald* featured trotting matches, thoroughbred racing, and prize fights during the 1840's. When Fashion met Peytona in 1845 the *Herald* commissioned eight reporters to cover the event, published four "extras," and devoted the entire first page of one issue to describing the crowd, the race, and the tumultuous proceedings. In 1847 the *Herald* employed "pony express" riders to hasten the news of the Sullivan-Caunt fight from Harper's Ferry to New York, and two years later it published reams of newsprint on the Sullivan-Hyer brawl in Maryland. This interest in the ring was not confined to such sporting centers as New York, Buffalo, Baltimore, and New Orleans. Wisconsin had been in the Union for only one year when telegraphic reports informed readers of the Milwaukee *Sentinel and Gazette* on February 10, 1849: "Sullivan was then removed from the ring by his friends, his face dreadfully mangled." The Chambersburg, Pa., *Cumberland Valley Sentinel,* February 12, 1849, noted "the wonderful excitement in the public mind" as crowds waited anxiously for the results.

Although the *Herald* regretted the necessity of reporting such escapades, Bennett's exploitation of the sporting world forced more scrupulous editors to emulate his policy. The Sullivan-Morrissey bout at Boston Four Corners, New York, in 1853, the pugilistic record of William Poole who was murdered by a rival gang in 1855, the Morrissey-Heanan match in Canada in 1858, and the celebrated Heanan-Sayers contest in 1860 were discussed and deplored by numerous newspapers.[5]

Horace Greeley was as assiduous as any editor in capitalizing on the sensational Poole murder, and he sent a reporter to cover the Morrissey-Heanan fight. He allowed six columns of coverage on October 22, 1858, all the while excoriating the prize ring: "The thing is whereby its natural gravity of baseness it sinks. It is in the grog-shops and the brothels and the low gaming hells." Nor was Henry Raymond of the New York *Times* sleeping at the switch. The *Times* never developed a real interest in sport until the turn of the century, but from its very first years it recognized the news value of the more important races and fights. Threatening the public authorities if any event like the recent prize fight should occur, Raymond wrote in the October 14, 1853 issue:

> With the benefits of a diffused education; with a press strong in upholding the moral amenities of life; with a clergy devout, sincere and energetic in the discharge of their duties, and a public sentiment opposed to animal brutality in any shape; with these and similar influences at work it is inexplicable, deplorable, humiliating, that an exhibition such as the contest between Morrissey and Sullivan *could* have occurred.

Well might religious journals like the *Independent* attack city newspapers for filling their columns "with the loathsome details of prize fights, street fights, and the personal history and adventures of bullies;" well might the *Budget* of Morrissey's home town of Troy, New York, suggest "that it cannot redound to the credit of a city like this to receive a victor of the prize ring with a demonstration like those awarded to the world's benefactors, and to which only they are entitled;" well might irate local editors and vitriolic critics attack the New York press for publicizing such outrages on public decency. But men were coming from as far away as New Orleans to the Morrissey-Heanan fight on October 20, 1858; reporters were sent by the papers; from "an early hour in the evening, according to the *Herald,* until past midnight the spirit of the prize ring was prevalent in every bar room, bowling alley and billiard saloon in the city;" mobs hung about telegraph offices in many towns; while the *Times* noted, "Southern planters and dry goods merchants bet on the result of the conflict, a mighty, populous, and refined metropolis waits with hushed anxiety to know which of the two ruffians had his pate first broken, or his chest stove in by the other." Such things were news!

A revolution in the dissemination of news occurred in the prewar decade with the extension of telegraph wires throughout the United States, and with the enlargement of the newspaper format as improvements were made on the old Napier double cylinder press and the Hoe type revolving cylinder press. Yet, the sporting calendar of the 1840's and 1850's was anything but continuous from January to December. There was little to write about in the winter months, the organization of sport was still in its formative stage, prize fights or athletic contests were held only sporadically, and the public mind was not yet ready for the intensity of exploitation which characterized the press of the decades following the Civil War. With the possible exception of Bennett, no newspaper editors could equal Skinner, Porter, Wilkes, or Queen in the encouragement and promotion of sport through their journals. Mention should also be made of the occasional articles appearing in the *Atlantic Monthly, Harper's Weekly,* and *Frank Leslie's Illustrated Newspaper* during these years, although the literary, religious, and intellectual journals either ignored or were oblivious to the growing concern for sporting matters.

## Magazines of the Late Nineteenth Century

Sporting journals reported the occasional athletic contests and numerous races which were held throughout the North during the war, thereby providing at least a base from which to operate when Americans by the thousands began to flock to the ball park or the track at the end of the war. As the center of horse racing passed from an impoverished South to the more prosperous North and Midwest, it soon took on most of the commercialized characteristics of urban life. Two of the three leading New York journals of the postwar years were primarily for followers of the turf; George Wilkes' *Spirit of the Times* and the newly founded *Turf, Field and Farm* (1865). Three sportsmen of high reputation made the latter an authority in the sporting world: Sanders D. Bruce, Hamilton Busbey, and Frederick G. Skinner. Bruce, a Kentuckian and a graduate of Transylvania University, was a colonel in the Civil War before he founded *Turf, Field and Farm.* Publisher of an American stud book, a breeder's guide, and *The Thoroughbred Horse,* Bruce was respected as highly as any man on racing matters. Busbey, an Ohioan by birth, served as a judge at tracks and horse shows and later wrote *The Trotting and Pacing Horse in America* (1904) and *History of the Horse in America* (1906). Skinner, a thoroughbred authority and son of John Stuart Skinner, was publisher of *Turf, Field and Farm* from 1886 to 1889. *Turf, Field and Farm,* appealing for the support of the more respectable elements of society, advertised: "The paper denounces pugilism, and all low, disgusting sports." Like other sporting journals it printed material on virtually every outdoor diversion which was not tainted with the evils of gambling or commercialization, as well as on military affairs, the theatre, and general news.

A host of other turf journals appeared over the next three decades. Some like *Western Horseman* (1877), *Horseman and the Spirit of the Times* (1881), *American Horse Breeder* (1882), and *Horse Review* (1889) gained fairly wide circulation. The four mentioned reached or surpassed 15,000 copies in the 1890's. The most famous editor and publisher of the last decades of the century was John H. Wallace, who drifted from Iowa to Pennsylvania and New York, published *Wallace's American Stud Book* (1867), organized the National Association of Trotting Horse Breeders in 1876, and was the chief bulwark in the defense, popularization, and improvement of trotting. His greatest contribution to racing was *Wallace's American Trotting Register,* founded in 1871, but his deepest influence on the public was through his agricultural and horse journal, *Wallace's Monthly,* established in 1875. For a generation he was the foremost statistician and commentator in the trotting world.

One of the most successful turf editors was Charles J. Foster of the *New York Sportsman* (1865), who had helped on the *Ohio Statesman,* had written for and then worked on the *Wilkes' Spirit of the Times* during the Civil War, and had edited sporting books. Another was F.E. Pond ("Will Wildwood"), whose Chicago publication of *Horse Review* made him a popular figure in sporting circles. A host of writers and editors appeared on the scene to fill the pages of more than a score of turf journals.[6] Racing, however, no longer monopolized the interest of the sporting world, and the *Spirit of the Times* declined in both importance and circulation. None of the turf periodicals exceeded 20,000 subscribers after 1880, and much of this was caused by a shift in popular interest as water sports, prize fighting, baseball, cycling, and other athletic pursuits came to the fore on the sporting scene.

That the rural diversions of agrarian America were not forgotten in the postwar years of industrial expansion and urban development is obvious from even a cursory glance at the periodicals devoted to field sports and outdoor life. First among such journals to appear in the postwar era was the *Sporting Times and Theatrical News* (1867). It was only in 1873, however, that Charles Hallock founded *Forest and Stream* and brought the publication of field sports to a new journalistic high. A scientist and pioneer in conservation, Hallock became the editor of *Nature's Realm* long after leaving *Forest and Stream*. He published directories and guides for anglers and hunters, including such works as *The Sportsman's Gazetteer and General Guide* (1877) and *Hallock's American Club List and Sportsman's Glossary* (1878). One of those sporting editors who carried columns of amateur athletics and the turf as well as field sports, Hallock consistently deplored commercialism and held high the banner of respectability. Editorial policy was declared in the opening issue of August 14, 1873:

> The Publishers of *Forest and Stream* aim to merit and secure the patronage and countenance of that portion of the community whose refined intelligence enables them to properly appreciate and enjoy all that is beautiful in Nature. It will pander to no depraved tastes, nor pervert the legitimate sports of land and water to those base uses which always tend to make them unpopular with the virtuous and good. No advertisement or business notice of an immoral character will be received on any terms; and nothing will be admitted that may not be read with propriety in the home circle.

No man did any more for hunting and fishing in the postwar era than this sporting journalist who founded the International Association for Protection of Game in 1874 and formulated the first uniform game laws in 1875.

Field sports were not a particularly lucrative phase of journalism, and many of the magazines had very hazardous careers.[7] Among the most successful were *American Field*, edited by N. Rowe ("Mohawk"); *American Angler*, published by William Charles Harris (an author of fishing guides and books and angling editor of *Outing*); *Field and Stream*, edited by William Bleasdell Cameron and still one of America's top sporting journals; and *Sports Afield,* edited by Claude King. *Sports Afield* reached an unusual circulation for field sport journals of about 23,000 in 1898. G.O. Shields ("Coquina"), editor of *Recreation,* organized the League of *American* Sportsmen in 1898 and the Camp Fire Club. He was a fish and game conservationist and an author of hunting, fishing, and camping books.

Far and away the most responsible magazine for acquainting the public with the wonders of life in the mountains, the lakes, the forests, and the streams was *Outing* (1882), which was published by Albert Pope and reached an average circulation of 88,000. During the eighties it featured camping, outdoor life, and travel, as well as aquatic and athletic sports. With the cloud which hung over professional baseball in the nineties *Outing* eliminated all mention of the game for a decade, but respectable homes, schools, and public libraries subscribed to this most popular of the journals featuring field sports. Many prominent sports writers contributed to its issues, and the youth of America found it one of the most entertaining and adventuresome of all the monthlies. It is beyond proof but a reasonable speculation to suggest that *Outing's* success was related to the pictorial journalism of *Harper's Weekly, Frank Leslie's Illustrated Newspaper,* and other publications of the day, and that *Outing* may have been responsible for the great interest taken in outdoor life by such magazines as *Saturday Evening Post, Collier's,* and *Illustrated American.* Children's journals like *St. Nicholas Magazine* and *American Boy* also turned to sporting themes at times.

Between 1865 and 1900 an athletic impulse swept over the nation, and the amateur game of baseball made powerful strides forward in winning the popular support of men and women of all classes. Athletic and aquatic sports and the cult of physical education all were subject to journalistic exploitation.[8] Henry Chadwick, who also edited guides for the House of Beadle & Adams and for A.G. Spalding, gave baseball a decided lift with his short-lived *Ball Players' Chronicle.* This was followed by Francis C. Richter's *Sporting Life,* which was published in Philadelphia and employed regional correspondents throughout the country. Athletics, wheeling, yachting, tennis, and prize fighting were all discussed, but baseball statistics and gossip were the backbone of Richter's paper. O.P. Caylor, Brand Whitlock, Harry Palmer, and countless other writers contributed to *Sporting Life.* In 1888 Richter publicized a sworn circulation of 45,000 and in 1889 he claimed the largest circulation of sporting and baseball journals. Only Al and Charlie Spink's *Sporting News* served as a rival in these years. With the fame of the St. Louis Browns in the ascendant in 1886, the *Sporting News* gained in support but had an irregular history until World War I. After helping Ban Johnson establish the American League in 1900, the *Sporting News* won a wider audience and inherited the title once held by Queen's *New York Clipper* as the "Bible of baseball."

Among the prominent sports writers of the 1890's one must not forget the impeccable Caspar Whitney, journalist of many talents and sporting editor of *Harper's Weekly,* or Walter Camp, the great proponent of baseball and collegiate football. These two men, who together originated the custom of All-American selections, were ardent propagandists for the preservation of the amateur spirit.

A brief cycling craze occurred in the United States in 1869, but it was not until the Centennial Exhibition in 1876 in Philadelphia that manufacturers began to recognize that there was a market for the bicycle as a vehicle for travel, exercise, and sport. Albert Pope's manufacturing enterprise helped sponsor a cycling fad which mounted throughout the 1880's, gained the support of the League of American Wheelmen, and then became a middle-class mania during the depression years of the 1890's. And, once again, the journalists leaped into the breach and helped promote the gospel of sport. Magazines devoted to cycling multiplied beyond all reason, and with the passing of the popular excitement at the turn of the century the vast majority either consolidated with other journals or expired.[9] One of the most important of these was Albert Pope's *Wheelman,* edited by S.S. McClure, which merged with *Outing* in 1883, while Charles Pratt's and C.W. Fourdrinier's *Bicycling World* reached 28,760 subscribers in 1892 before going into a decline. Charles Mear's *Cycling Gazette* hovered in the vicinity of 15,000 in 1896, and the League of American Wheelmen's *Bulletin* averaged almost 94,000 in 1898.

Although *Scribner's* and *Atlantic Monthly* printed an occasional article, sport was treated with caution by editors dedicated to respectable journalism. The man on the street, however, was the target of a novel tabloid, the *National Police Gazette.* It was taken over by a young immigrant editor in 1877 and soon became the widest selling sporting organ in the United States. Richard Kyle Fox, who arrived from Belfast in 1874 with $5 in his pocket, was so successful with his new venture that within six years he was able to erect a new home for the journal at a cost of one-quarter of a million dollars. For a time the *Police Gazette* was the "most lurid journal ever published in the United States," featuring buxom showgirls, scandals, hangings, red-tinted paper, and spicy stories. Pictures and photographs were exploited to the full, while crime and sex were the dominant themes of the early years.

The *Police Gazette,* however, rapidly invaded the world of sport. When an edition of the Paddy Ryan-Joe Goss fight of 1880 kept the presses running for weeks and reached the 400,000 mark, Fox was convinced and set out to make his journal the principal authority on prize fighting. The *Gazette's* subtitle was *The Leading Illustrated Sporting Journal in America.* William E. Harding, author of several biographies of pugilists, was the sporting editor during the years of growth in the 1880's when the journal fought for the legalization of prize fighting. He introduced a column of sporting news and, with the success of professional baseball under the guidance of such figures as William Hulbert, Harry Wright, Chris Von der Ahe, Charles Comiskey, and Albert Spalding, discussed diamond gossip under "Our National Game." By reducing subscription rates to saloons, barber shops, and hotels, he was able to attain a steady circulation of 150,000 copies which went into virtually every city and town of America.

Many newsstands refused to sell the tabloid, but barkeepers and barbers saved them for their male clients, young and old.[10] All the attacks of Anthony Comstock's Society for the Suppression of Vice, and all the fines or settlements on pending lawsuits failed to halt the journal's success in these years. As "the arbiter of the masses in sports and the gay life," the *Police Gazette* brought fame and a certain distinction to its owner, whose silk hat and Prince Albert coat were known everywhere in New York. Edward Van Every claimed that "it was as an arbiter of sports news that the *Gazette* came into world-wide prominence," and that "it was the Fox success that eventually made the heads of even the most conservative of daily papers appreciate . . . the circulation worth that was to be found in giving increased prominence to doings in the world of sports." Much as this estimate slights the contributions of Porter, Wilkes, Queen, the Bennetts, Dana, and Pulitzer, there is at least a grain of truth in the claim, and it was Fox alone of all the magazine publishers who edited a periodical which reached the masses on a national scale.

Postwar sporting magazines, although generally of limited circulation, anticipated the newspapers in capitalizing on the growing interest in sport.[11] In 1872 Frederic Hudson in his famous *Journalism in the United States* admitted the newspaper world's limited interest in sport and stressed the point that magazines "unquestionably give more information on the subjects they treat than the general newspaper can."

## Yellow Journalism and the Sports Page

Metropolitan newspaper editors of the postwar era soon awakened to popular interest in sport. The younger James Gordon Bennett made the *Herald* the foremost New York oracle for sporstmen in the late 1860's. Allotting considerable space to baseball, prize fighting, and horse racing, in the winter of 1866 Bennett exploited through transoceanic cable dispatches the victory of his yacht *Henrietta* over the *Fleetwing* and the *Vesta.* An athletic, outdoor man, he introduced polo into the United States and established numerous prizes for yachting and racing contestants.

Sport was well on the way toward becoming a national institution in the early 1870's, but it was to be another decade before the metropolitan newspapers made their great bid to capture the sportsminded public. Only then did the press begin to recognize the true value of continuous and imaginative sports reporting. By the early 1880's professional baseball established itself on a more secure footing; prize fighting gained a new grip on the popular mind in the meteoric rise to nationwide fame of John L. Sullivan; tennis and polo had been added to the more genteel sports of high society; competitive games caught on in the colleges and the armories of national guard units as well as in a few public schools; and even the farmer was diverted by the racing feats of Goldsmith Maid or Maud S.

Prior to this time reporting had usually been assigned to fans, local correspondents, and green young newspapermen. Although specialists had been employed on turf columns and the *Times* as well as the Brooklyn *Eagle* had taken on Henry Chadwick as their baseball and cricket expert during the 1850's, it was only in the eighties that the art and the value of sports-writing was really discovered.

There were exceptions, however, among them the New York *Evening Telegram,* the Chicago *Tribune,* the New Orleans *Daily Picayune,* and the San Francisco *Chronicle.* Perhaps the first San Francisco editor to realize its import was Thomas Flynn of the *Chronicle,* and the first sporting editor in Pittsburgh, in all probability, was John H. Gruber of the *Post,* who was official scorer of the National League for many years. Charles A. Dana of the New York *Sun* and Joseph Pulitzer of the New York *World* outdid all the previous efforts of the Bennetts and within a few years developed the first regular sports page. Dana had developed sports reporting over a period of years, making it "one of the *Sun's* strongholds." Amos Cummings, his managing editor, would allot "half a page to a race at Saratoga or Monmouth Park" and Dana "would encourage Amos to neglect his executive duties so that the paper might have a good report of a boxing match."[12] The *Sun* did much to promote the interests of the prize ring, and even the publisher was an interested spectator, despite the prevailing opinion about the depravity of pugilism. When Sullivan met Charlie Mitchell at the old Madison Square Garden on May 14, 1883, the New York *World,* parodying a scene-by-scene unveiling of an epic drama, observed the reporter's row at ringside and noticed: "Mr. Charles A. Dana looking like Homer, at one end, and Mr. Roscoe Conkling, looking like a faded caricature of himself, at the other, lent the newspaper row their antipodal dignity." One of the

first papers to offer detailed information and sporting gossip, the *Sun* of
the middle 1880's had only one rival in the fight of daily papers for the
support of the sporting public.

That rival was, of course, the New York *World,* purchased in 1883 by
Joseph Pulitzer. Pulitzer invaded the eastern publishing field and founded
what was probably the first separate sports department. He gave prominent
space to important events in the racing, yachting, pedestrian, football, and
billiard worlds. While deprecating a prize-fight crowd which, with the
exception of a few celebrities, "was made up of sporting men, athletes,
gamblers, roughs, thieves, arabs, and that great brute element that under-
lies all civilization and only comes together when there is a hanging, a mob
or a fight," the *World* devoted three columns of the first page to the contest. Nellie Bly, ace reporter for the paper, interviewed Sullivan and
William Muldoon on August 7 before the Kilrain fight in 1889. She was
not the first woman in the field of sports, however, for the New York
*Times* sent "Middie" Morgan to races and cattle shows as early as 1870.
Throughout the eighties sport expanded in many directions, and by 1895
the *World* was reporting every activity, while sending correspondents and
artists to the training quarters of Charlie Mitchell and James J. Corbett. In
the *World Almanac and Encyclopedia* for 1894 the paper claimed, "The
entire sporting world recognizes *The World* as fistiana's authority . . . .
*The World* continues to be the only paper in America whose decisions on
turf questions are final," and the following year the *Almanac* blatantly
boasted:

> In all departments of sports *The World* has taken the lead . . . .
> *The World* has continued to be the leading authority on racing . . . .
> The National Trotting Circuit and the National L.A.W. racing circuit
> were covered by special and expert correspondents . . . . The great
> public discussion opened up by *The World* as to the propriety of
> women riding bicycles was one of the features of the summer.

It would be senseless to give precedence to the Bennetts, Dana, or
Pulitzer in crediting any one person with the creation of the sports page,
so gradual was the process. But to the degree that "yellow journalism"
was responsible for the sporting impulse of the 1880's and 1890's, the
influence of the New York *World* cannot be overestimated. Also the New
York *Evening Sun* and the Pittsburgh *Press* were pioneers in the publication of "sporting extras" which helped the game of professional baseball
immensely. After the Corbett-Sullivan fight in 1892 the Louisville and
Nashville railroad carried 15,000 copies of the New Orleans *Times-
Democrat* and the Illinois Central rushed another 20,000 copies north-

ward. The battle for circulation was a torrid one. Frank Luther Mott writes in his study of *American Journalism:* "Emphasis on sports was characteristic of the yellow press, which developed for that department a slangy and facetious style. This exploitation did much to promote national interest in league baseball and in prize fighting."

Newspapers in every section of the country felt the impact of sporting journalism. The New York *Evening Post* of William Cullen Bryant was reluctant to enter the field, but Bryant's lieutenant, Carl Schurz, urged the news editor to give round-by-round accounts of the Paddy Ryan-John L. Sullivan fight in 1882. By the nineties almost all the great newspapers in the leading cities had "sporting editors" with trained staffs. Joe Vilas of the New York *Sun,* Benny Benjamin of the San Francisco *Chronicle,* and Charles Dryden, who worked in both San Francisco and New York, were leaders in organizing sports departments.

The most important developments in sporting journalism, outside of New York, were taking place on the Chicago newspapers. Charles Seymour of the *Herald,* Finley Peter Dunne of the *News,* and a reporter for the *Times* were the creators of a novel style among baseball writers, a style based on picturesque jargon, lively humor, and grotesque exaggeration.[13] Although the Chicago *Tribune* had begun the reporting of sports events, it was less a pioneer than its metropolitan rivals. While the East was producing experts the West was producing humorists, and, as Hugh Fullerton has observed, "The style of reporting baseball changed all over the country."[14] Dunne's influence may be seen in the *Times* columns of 1888, shortly after he came over from the *News.* One reporter, who relished the job of "riding" the Chicago club, wrote on September 26 of that year.

> The ninth inning of yesterday's ball game was a marvel of beauty. To describe it one needs a big stretch of canvas, a white-wash brush, a pail of green paint, and an artist's hand. Words are hardly expressive enough. . . . Mr. Schoeneck is a large secretion of fat around considerable bone and muscle, and he knocked the ball out of the diamond and puffed down to first base. . . . Immediately after which Mr. Buckley bunted the ball and went to first, his fatness moving to second. . . . The inning had not been particularly gorgeous up to this moment, but with the hitting of a fly by Mr. Hines it took on a resplendent and glorious aspect, for Mr. Van Haltren got under the fly, gauged it with his blue eye, and muffed it beautifully. . . . When the ball reached Capt. Anson it had lost much of its virulence and was bounding gently along, smiling the while. But if it had been a chunk of lava fresh from the bowels of the earth it could not have had more fun with Capt. Anson, for it rollicked out of his hands and

into them again and all over his person, blithely tapped him in the face, and danced away. Indeed, it was a beautiful error, that one of Anson's—a regular sunset error flushed and radiant with shadings of purple and a mellow border. . . . Mr. Van Haltren picked it up and looked about irresolutely. He was debating whether he should sacrifice skill to art, and being a young man of no high culture in this respect, he esteemed art as naught, but hurled the ball to the plate to catch Mr. Hines. But art was triumphant after all, for Mr. Van Haltren's irresolution had been fatal. The ball came to the plate a second after Mr. Hines crossed safe, and Mr. Raphael, Mr. M. Angelo, and Mr. Turner will have to take a seat near the door.

With the transition from Henry Chadwick's restrained prose to the fabulous narratives of the new school, sportswriting increasingly favored the national game. During the ensuing decade many of the leading names in the sports world were baseball writers like Harry Weldon, Ban Johnson, and Ren (Deacon) Mulford in Cincinnati, Al and Charlie Spink in St. Louis, John Gruber of the Pittsburgh *Post,* Timothy Murnane of the Boston *Globe,* Frank Richter in Philadelphia, Joe Campbell of the Washington *Post,* Harry C. Palmer of the Chicago *Tribune,* and John Foster, Sam Crane, O.P. Caylor, and Charles Dryden in New York.

Caylor had written for the Cincinnati *Enquirer,* contributed to Frank Richter's *Sporting Life* and to *Harper's Weekly,* and wrote for the New York *Tribune.* Along with Weldon and Dryden, who was called the "Mark Twain of baseball" by Hugh Fullerton, Caylor was one of the recognized baseball authorities of the newspaper world. Dryden, rising out of poverty and the career of a hobo, joined the Chicago *Times* in 1889, moved to Tacoma and then to the San Francisco *Call.* As a baseball writer he was induced to join the *Chronicle* and then the *Examiner,* finally going to Hearst's New York *Journal* in 1895. Bitten by wanderlust, he later went to other papers and to the Chicago *Tribune* in 1907. Fullerton, writing in the April 21, 1928 issue of the *Saturday Evening Post,* contended that "regardless of what the present generation of baseball reporters is doing to promote the welfare or add to the box-office receipts of the club owners, the sport owes its popularity and probably its continued existence to earlier generations of scribes who gave their talents and the newspaper space of their bosses to popularize the game and its players."

The professional game went into eclipse in the columns of many papers during the 1890's, after the public reacted unfavorably to the drinking and rowdyism of the players and the war among club owners. It may well have been the baseball writers who really carried the game through these dark years.

Despite the cloud which hovered over professional baseball, the nineties gave every sign of being a watershed in sporting history, and a young man from California invaded New York to inaugurate a new chapter in journalism. William Randolph Hearst, who had featured sports in his San Francisco *Examiner* and who was deeply interested in baseball stories, bought the New York *Journal* in 1895 and immediately made it the arch-exponent of all the sensationalism of the yellow press. The *Journal* assembled an unexcelled staff including specialists like Charles Dryden for baseball, Ralph Paine for rowing, Paul Armstrong for boxing, and Robert H. Davis, who did the ghost writing for numerous champion athletes. Hearst papers acquired a monopoly of "inside" information concerning the Corbett-Fitzsimmons fight in 1897, and their aggressive tactics may have led to the collapse of numerous sporting journals at the turn of the century. In an unparalleled exploitation of every phase of athletic life the *Journal* was the first to develop the modern sports section.

It was the metropolitan and then the smaller city dailies which sponsored teams, promoted contests, and brought the lingo of the diamond, the turf, the ring, the links, and the gridiron to the great American middle class. After 1894 the *New York Clipper* became a theatrical journal, eventually ending up as *Variety,* and after 1900 the circulation of the *National Police Gazette* fell off rapidly. At the turn of the century most local newspapers were just beginning to exploit it, but the pattern of twentieth-century sporting journalism had been cut, and the coming of age of such writers as Charles Van Loan, Ring Lardner, Damon Runyon, Joe Vilas, R.B. Hanna, Irvin Cobb, Hugh Fullerton, Bozeman Bulger, Grantland Rice, and John Kieran was in great part the result of the journalistic achievements of the nineteenth century.

While there had been a corresponding increase of periodicals in such fields as religion, education, agriculture, science, and the arts during the century, there was no department in the daily press which was changing and expanding as rapidly as that of sports in the 1890's. The sports section of the modern era was at hand.

## Editors on the March

With such pioneers as the *Spirit of the Times,* the *New York Clipper,* the *National Police Gazette* and other sporting journals as a precedent, new periodicals appeared in the next two decades, among them *Golfer's Magazine, Baseball Magazine,* and *Yachting. Collier's* and the *Saturday Evening Post* played a great part in drawing national attention to sport and a host of prominent journals began to capitalize on the mounting public enthusiasm. Baseball won the support of editors around the year 1910 and was often featured in the most respectable magazines. Many of the nineteenth-century sporting journals continued well into or through the first two decades. But the growth of a national interest was increasingly more dependent on the spectacular treatment by the daily press, and the earlier nineteenth-century leadership maintained by such sporting editors as Porter, Wilkes, Queen, and Fox was lost as their journals went into decline or ceased publication.

Sports reporting lagged in the Far West and the South until the end of the last century. Although the San Francisco *Chronicle, Bulletin* and *Examiner* all featured sports along the Barbary Coast, the press of the Pacific states reflected the limited enthusiasm of those who had made the long trek over the plains as settlers or 49'ers. Pioneer conditions prevailed throughout much of the West until the late years of the century and left little time for revelry. In 1900 the Los Angeles *Daily Times,* Seattle *Post-Intelligencer* and Oregon newspapers gave scant coverage, though within a decade the sports department would become an important feature of western journalism.

By 1906 the Tacoma *Daily Ledger,* Denver *Daily News,* and Salt Lake City *Deseret Evening News* all gave evidence to a rising sports-consciousness in the West. Portland, Oregon, previously unconcerned with such frivolities, represented the trend toward fuller coverage. This was accomplished, according to George Turnbull's *History of Oregon Newspapers,* through rising interest and better organization in sport, increased space made available by the linotype and smaller costs of type composition and pulp paper, the development of department-store advertising, and the appearance of the exclusive "sporting editor."

Southern sporting journalism, which had been every bit as active as that in northern metropolitan centers before the Civil War, had to weather almost a half century of social and economic recovery before the region became fully receptive to the modern athletic movement. As late as 1916 the Dallas *Morning News* offered little more than brief summaries and statistics, but the tradition which lingered on in such old sporting centers as New Orleans, Louisville, Nashville, and Memphis caught on with journals in Little Rock, Atlanta, and smaller cities of the region.

Midwestern newspapers, headed by the enthusiastic sports policies of the Chicago dailies, rivalled the East in reporting from the turn of the century through World War I. Frank Luther Mott designated the years 1892-1914 as a period in newspaper history when sporting news underwent a remarkable development, being "segregated on special pages, with special make-up pictures, and news-writing style." This was especially true of Muncie, Indiana, where sporting news expanded more rapidly than any other news category in the years 1890-1923, rising from four percent of the total news coverage of "Middletown's" leading paper in 1890 to sixteen percent in 1923.[15] Sporting news in 1920 was universally prominent in metropolitan papers, including the conservative *New York Times* of Adolph Ochs, and it was rapidly winning converts among the editors of smaller cities and towns.

## The Technological Revolution in Full Swing

Ante-bellum sport had capitalized on the development of the steamboat, the railroad, the telegraph, and the penny press, and in succeeding decades the role of technology in the rise of sport proved even more significant. Although fight crowds still chartered steamboats, they lost much of their early importance. The *Chauncey Vibbard* carried sports crowds of the 1860's, however, and the Hudson River League of the 1880's depended on riverboat transportation. The Civil War failed to halt turf meetings and outdoor recreation in the North. It was, however, only with the return of peace that the nation felt a new sporting impulse and began to give enthusiastic support to the turf, the diamond, the ring, and other outdoor activities.

The game of baseball, spreading from cities to towns and villages, became a national fad, and matches were scheduled between distant communities. A tournament at Rockford, Illinois, in 1866 was attended by teams from Detroit, Milwaukee, Dubuque, and Chicago. In 1867 the Washington Nationals toured the Midwest, and a year later the Philadelphia Athletics, Brooklyn Atlantics, and the Morrisania Club of New York visited St. Louis. In 1869 Harry Wright's Cincinnati Red Stockings were able to make a memorable transcontinental trip from Maine to California and a New Orleans club visited Memphis, St. Louis, and Cincinnati. When the Red Stockings made their tour by boat, local lines, and the Union Pacific it was reported: "The boys have received every attention from the officers of the different roads. . . . At all the stations groups stare us almost out of countenance, having heard of the successful exploits of the Club through telegrams of the Western Associated Press."[16]

Baseball clubs made use of the 1870's rapidly expanding telegraph network and the organization of the National League in 1876 was only possible with the continued development of connecting lines. The Memphis Reds sent a printed circular to the Boston team in 1877 stressing the reduced rates for any club visiting St. Louis or Louisville.[17] In the 1886 edition of *Spalding's Official Base Ball Guide* the Michigan Central advertised: "The cities that have representative clubs contesting for the championship pennant this year are—Chicago, Boston, New York, Washington, Kansas City, Detroit, St. Louis and Philadelphia. All of these cities are joined together by the MICHIGAN CENTRAL Railroad. This road has enjoyed almost a monopoly of Base Ball travel in former years." Through-out the last three decades the expanding railroad network played an indis-pensable role in the popularization of the national game.

A widespread interest in thoroughbred and trotting races also was in great part sustained by the expansion of the railroad network. *Turf, Field and Farm* pointed to the need for better transportation arrangements and predicted, "The completion of the Pacific Railroad will not be without effect upon the blood stock interests of the great West."[18] A year later the Harlem, Rensselaer and Saratoga Railroad Company arranged to con-vey race horses at cost by express train from New York to Saratoga. Jerome Park, Long Branch, and Gravesend catered to New York crowds, Baltimore attracted huge throngs of sportsmen, and in California the con-struction of lines into the interior of the state encouraged racing. In the 1870's western turfmen began sending their horses by rail to Eastern tracks, the Grand Circuit linked Hartford, Springfield, Poughkeepsie, and Utica with Rochester, Buffalo, and Cleveland, and racing associations formed in virtually every section. The Pennsylvania advertised "the Superior Facilities afforded by their lines for reaching most of the Trot-ting Parks and Race Courses in the Middle States." When Mollie McCarthy and Ten Broeck raced at Louisville in 1877, "Masses of strangers arrived by train, extra trains and steamboats." People from "all over the land" attended the Kentucky Derby in 1885, the City Council declared a holi-day, and sixteen carloads of horses were sent from Nashville to Louisville. Agricultural fairs, with the cooperation of numerous companies, drew thousands to their fairground tracks, and the railroads encouraged inter-sectional meetings by introducing "palace stock cars" in the middle eighties.

In the decades after the Civil War an apologetic but curious public acquired a "deplorable" interest in prize fighting, and railroad officials were not slow to capitalize on the crowd appeal of pugilism, despite its illegality. When Mike McCoole met Aaron Jones in 1867 at Busenbark Station, Ohio, the railroad sold excursion tickets to the bout and sporting men from the East were in attendance; another McCoole fight in 1869 encouraged the lines to run specials from Cincinnati and other nearby cities. After 1881 John L. Sullivan, the notorious "Boston Strong Boy," went on grand tours of the athletic clubs, opera houses, and theaters of the country, his fights in the New Orleans area with Paddy Ryan, Jake Kilrain, and James J. Corbett luring fans who jammed the passenger coaches. When the Great John L. met Kilrain near Richburg, Mississippi, in 1889, the Northeastern Railroad carried a tumultuous crowd from New Orleans to the site, even though Governor Robert Lowry of Mississip-pi issued a proclamation against the affair and called out armed guards to prevent any invasion of the state. After the brawl the governor proceeded to request the attorney general "to begin proceedings to forfeit the charter of the Northeastern railroad."[19] Sullivan returned to Mississippi as a popular hero when Governor Hill of New York granted extradition papers. He was jailed, given bail, and finally freed after paying over $18,000 in fines and expenses. Companies expressed only minor concern for such sporadic events, it is true, but the prize ring was greatly aided by their cooperation.

Poor connections, uncomfortable cars, and the absence of lines in rural sections remained a problem for some years. Albert G. Spalding recalled the conditions of 1880: "Thirty years ago the greatest drawback to Base Ball . . . was the lack of communication between the smaller cities. Many a time I have known a team of young ball players to take a tramp of four or five miles to play with the team in a neighboring town and walk all the way home after the game was over."

Many of the difficulties and inconveniences of travel persisted through these expansive years of railroading, but the improved transportation of the post-bellum era encouraged all sports. Shortly after the war ended a New York crew visited Pittsburgh to participate in a regatta held on the Monongahela River. When the Biglin brothers entered a boat race at Poughkeepsie in July, 1865, a large number of spectators from "Canada West" came down on the morning train from Albany.

Intercollegiate athletics depended on railroad service for carrying teams and supporters to football, baseball, and rowing, as well as track and field contests. The first intercollegiate football game between Rutgers and Princeton was attended by a group of students riding the train pulled by "the jerky little 'dummy' engine that steamed out of Princeton on that memorable morning of November 6, 1869." Two years later special trains carried an excited throng to the Cape May yacht races. Harvard's crack baseball team made the first grand tour in 1870. Playing both amateur and professional clubs, Harvard won a majority of the games played in New Haven, Troy, Utica, Syracuse, Oswego (Canada), Buffalo, Cleveland, Cincinnati, Louisville, Chicago, Milwaukee, Indianapolis, Washington, Baltimore, Philadelphia, New York, and Brooklyn. Amateur and professional cycling races also took place throughout the country, and by the nineties many lines carried cycles as free freight while professional riders could tour their National Circuit in luxury cars. The nature of the transportation revolution was demonstrated in the trip of a Denver cycling delegation to Chicago and then on to an Asbury Park (New Jersey) meeting![20]

Rod and gun enthusiasts relied on major roads and branch lines into rural preserves. Anglers of the seventies were advised: "The lines of Pennsylvani [sic] Railroad Company also reach the best localities for Gunning and Fishing in Pennsylvania and New Jersey," while the Grand Rapids and

Illinois served northern Michigan as "The Fighting Line." The Chesapeake & Ohio, "the Route of the Sportsman and Angler to the Best Hunting and Fishing Grounds of Virginia and West Virginia," advertised "Guns, fishing tackle, and one dog for each sportsman carried free."

The trans-Mississippi West, like the more remote areas of the East, had been opened to sportsmen by the 1860's, and a decade after the war the Chicago and Northwestern and the Burlington, Cedar Rapids and Northern Lines proclaimed their advantages for hunters and fishermen seeking prairie chickens, duck, geese, brant, deer, bear, brook trout, lake salmon, pike, pickerel, and bass. In the Far West sportsmen rode the Central Pacific, the Southern Pacific, and other lines; in the plains region there were the Union Pacific, Kansas Pacific, and the Atchinson, Topeka, and Santa Fe as well as smaller routes; and in the South rural railroads like the Selma, Rome and Dalton and the Western Alabama reached into isolated areas of every state. Of Montgomery it was said: "The central position of this city and its excellent railroad and river communications with all parts of the State, render it one of the best initial points for sportsmen in the whole State."

The South, however, lagged behind other sections in the development of organized athletics, and this was in great part due to the vast distances and the inferior railroad systems which prevailed from 1860 to 1920. Virtually every region of the United States was nonetheless becoming accessible to the devotees of field sports in the latter part of the century.[21] By the nineties almost every realm of sport had shared in the powerful impact of the railroad on American life, and in the years down through the First World War this influence continued unabated.

The expansion of sporting news in the years following the Civil War was directly related to the universal usage of telegraphy, which made possible instantaneous reporting of ball games, horse races, prize fights, yachting regattas, and other events. Box scores, betting odds, and all kinds of messages were relayed from one city to another, and by 1870 daily reports were published in many metropolitan newspapers. In that year the steamboat race of the *Natchez* and the *Robert E. Lee* was reported throughout the country in what may have been the most extensive telegraphic account of any nonpolitical event prior to that time. Not only did the newspapers make a practice of publishing daily messages from all corners of the sporting world, but crowds formed around Western Union offices during any important contest.

The United Press began operations in 1882 and five years later the New York office had three wires which could "drop reports simultaneously to seventy towns and cities." The Associated Press sent its representatives to the Sullivan-Kilrain fight in 1889, reporters appeared in New Orleans from "every prominent journal in the Union," and Western Union was said to have employed 50 operators to handle 208,000 words of specials following the brawl. When John L. was whipped by Jim Corbett three years later the New York *World* claimed three hundred saloons and billiard halls in the city received the news from the Crescent City. Poolrooms and saloons were often equipped with receiving sets to keep customers and bettors posted on baseball scores, prize fights, and track results.

The "bookie" soon became a permanent fixture on the sporting scene as newspapers set up bulletin boards for the crowds to linger around. The *Tribune Book of Open-Air Sports* stated in 1887 that professional baseball scores were wired at the end of each inning to every large city in the country, "and the result is awaited with equal interest by hearty farm boy and city swell." Henry L. Mencken nostalgically recalled how, since there were few sporting "extras" in the eighties in Baltimore, "the high-toned saloons of the town catered to the fans by putting in telegraph operators who wrote the scores on blackboards."[22]

The rise of sporting journalism, as we have seen, was closely related to the development of a national telegraphic network. The sports page of the eighties and nineties was not solely the result of improvements in telegraphy, however, for popular interest had encouraged the employment of specialists who were as quick as the publishers to capitalize on the news value of sporting events. Although the telegraph was no longer the one indispensable means of communication as the telephone and wireless came to the fore at the end of the century, it did retain its functional importance in recording daily box scores and racing statistics. Concentration of news distribution helped in reporting sporting news as the AP grew from 63 members in 1893 to 1300 in 1922. The World Series was reported throughout the nation for the first time on a single circuit 26,000 miles in length, operating from the Boston and Brooklyn parks to "the office of every leased wire member newspaper." The traffic agent of AP received a congratulatory message from Thomas A. Edison, who recognized this as a great advance in instantaneous telegraphic communication: "The Associated Press must be wonderfully well organized to be able to accomplish what was done in the ball game. Uncle Sam has now a real arterial system and it is never going to harden."[23]

The Atlantic Cable, successfully laid in 1866 by Cyrus Field, overcame the midcentury handicap of reporting two- or three-weeks-old English sporting news. At the end of that year, with the aid of AP's newly established office in London, James Gordon Bennett, Jr. featured cable dispatches of the great ocean race. When the Harvard crew rowed against Oxford on the Thames in 1869, "the result was flashed through the Atlantic cable as to reach New York about a quarter past one, while the news reached the Pacific Coast about nine o'clock, enabling many of the San Franciscans to discuss the subject at their breakfast tables, and swallow the defeat with their coffee!" [24] The combination of cable and telegraph aroused a deeper interest in international sport. Nor must we ignore that forerunner of the modern radio, the wireless which was demonstrated publicly in America for the first time in the yacht races of 1899. From Samuel F.B. Morse to Guglielmo Marconi the revolution in communication encouraged the rise of sport.

Public interest in sport was also intensified by a number of inventions which revolutionized the printing process. By 1830 the Napier double-cylinder press was imported from England and developed by R. Hoe and Company. This press printed the cheap and sensational papers which were the first to regularly record horse races, prize fights, and foot races—the New York *Sun*, the New York *Transcript*, and the Philadelphia *Public Ledger*. In 1846 the Hoe tupe-revolving cylinder press was introduced by the *Public Ledger*, enabling newspaper publishers, after improvements were made in the machine, to print 20,000 sheets an hour. Other inventions facilitated the mass publication of the daily paper, making possible the sensationalized editions of Bennett, Dana, Pulitzer, and Hearst. With the arrival of the new journalism of the 1880's, sporting news emerged as a featured part of metropolitan newspapers which were reaching vast audiences through enlarged editions.

Publishers also aided in the era's popularization of outdoor sport. From the 1830's onward American sporting books appeared in greater and greater numbers, and by the time of the Civil War cheap methods of publication had led to the amazingly popular dime novel. While the majority of these thrillers and shockers concerned the wild west or the city detective, athletic stories and manuals were put out by the leading publisher, Beadle & Adams.

After the establishment of A.G. Spalding & Brothers in 1876 the *Spalding Guide* developed into the leading authority on rules of play, and the *Spalding Library of Athletic Sports* included all sorts of handbooks. The *New York Clipper* published a theatrical and sporting *Clipper Almanac* from the 1870's onward, while newspapers like the New York *World*, the New York *Tribune*, the Chicago *Daily News*, the Washington *Post*, and the Brooklyn *Daily Eagle* issued almanacs listing athletic and racing records and sporting news. Richard K. Fox of the *National Police Gazette* issued *Fox's Athletic Library* and sporting annuals. By 1900 book publication had grown to astronomic proportions when compared to the Civil War era, and the Outing Publishing Company offered more than a hundred titles on angling, canoeing, yachting, mountain climbing, hunting, shooting, trapping, camping, cycling, and athletics.

At the turn of the century publishers improved techniques and expanded their output. They became more proficient at attracting attention to the world of sport. And in the years prior to 1920, as intercollegiate and interscholastic athletics as well as physical education came to the fore, the contribution of publishers became even more manifest.

Mass-production manufacturing methods were still in their infancy in post-Civil War decades, but the factory system became ever more deeply entrenched and the individual craftsmanship of ante-bellum years slowly yielded the market to large dealers. The sporting goods business never attained any great economic importance in the nineteenth century, but much of the popularity for athletic games and outdoor recreation was due to standardized manufacturing of baseball equipment, bicycles, billiard tables, sporting rifles, fishing rods, and various other items. Michael Phelan, who in 1854 developed an indiarubber cushion thereby permitting sharp edges on billiard tables, joined with Hugh W. Collender in forming Phelan and Collender, the leading manufacturer until the organization of the Brunswick-Balke-Collender Company in 1884. Gymnastic apparatus, invented by Dudley A. Sargent and other physical educators, was featured by many dealers, while the readers of *American Angler, Forest and Stream,* and other journals were kept informed of the latest models of rifles, shotguns, rods, and reels. Although most children played with restitched balls and a minimum of paraphernalia, college athletes, cycling enthusiasts, and professional ballplayers popularized the products of George B. Ellard of Cincinnati, Peck & Snyder of New York, and their competitors. The pioneer manufacturers of baseballs were John H. Mann and J. Ryan and Company, while Hillerich and Bradsby won fame as the makers of the "Louisville Slugger." Improved implements were offered by various companies, Andrew Clark & Co. putting out a lighter fishing reel with a removable spool. Some magazines like *The Youth's Companion* gave balls or fishing tackle for new subscriptions.[25] Even the personalized sport of sledding was invaded as the Flexible Flyer and other brands gained fame among the youngsters.

As a renowned pitcher for the Boston and Chicago clubs and then as promoter for the latter, Albert Spalding had turned to the merchandizing of athletic goods shortly after the formation of the National League. One of the most avid sponsors of the national game, he branched out into varied sports in the eighties, and acquired a virtual monopoly over athletic goods by absorbing A.J. Reach Co. (1867-) in 1885, Wright & Ditson (1871-) in 1892, as well as Peck & Snyder (1865-) and other firms. By 1887 the Spalding "Official League" ball had been adopted by the National League, the Western League, the New England League, the International League, and various college conferences, and balls were sold ranging in price from five cents to $1.50. It was through mass manufacture of base-balls and uniforms that Spalding gained such a leading position in the eighties and nineties, but the market was restricted and manufacturers had to resort to ingenious methods to meet the situation when difficulties arose. To make the most profit on bats Spalding bought his own lumber mill in Michigan, while Albert Pope had to overcome a lack of cooperation from the rolling mills in his first years of bicycle manufacture. To gain an even greater ascendancy over his rivals Spalding advertised his wares in his *Library of Athletic Sports,* where the products of competitors were often derided as inferior in quality.

The sewing machine was one of many inventions which made possible the more uniform equipment of the last decades of the century when local leagues and national associations took shape throughout the United States. Canoeing and camping were other diversions which gave rise to the manu-facture of sporting goods on an ever larger scale.

In the later years of the century the department store and the mail-order house began to feature sporting goods. Macy's of New York began with ice skates, velocipedes, bathing suits, and beach equipment in 1872, although all sporting goods were sold by the toy department. By 1902, with the addition of numerous other items, a separate department was established. Sears, Roebuck and Company, meanwhile, devoted more than eighty pages of its 1895 catalogue to weapons and fishing equipment, and within a decade featured not only hunting and fishing equipment but also bicycles, boxing gloves, baseball paraphernalia, and sleds.[26] In the first two decades of this century the sporting goods business increased more than seven-fold as the leading dealers strove to meet the public demand.

When Thomas A. Edison developed the incandescent bulb in 1879 he inaugurated a new era in the social life of the cities. Although the first dynamo was built within two years, gas lighting did not give way immedi-ately, and the crowds which jammed the old Madison Square Garden in New York in 1883 to see John L. Sullivan fight Herbert Slade still had to cope not only with the smoke-filled air but also with the blue gas fumes. The Garden had already installed some electric lights, however, although at a six-day professional walking match in 1882 the cloud of tobacco smoke was so thick that "even the electric lights" had "a hard sturggle to assert their superior brilliancy" over the gas jets.

On a similar occasion the New York *Sun* for August 7, 1883 reported that "the noisy yell of program, candy, fruit and peanut venders who filled the air with the vilest discord" failed to discourage the crowd. The philosophically-minded reporter wondered what Herbert Spencer would think of "the peculiar phase of idiocy in the American character" which drew thousands of men and women to midnight pedestrian contests.

Within a few years electric lighting and more comfortable accommodations helped lure players and spectators alike to YMCA's, athletic clubs, regimental armories, school and college gymnasiums, as well as sports arenas. In 1885, at the third annual Horse Show in Madison Square Garden, handsomely-dressed sportswomen revelled in the arena, "gaudy with festoons of racing flags and brilliant streamers, lighted at night by hundreds of electric lights," while visitors to the well-lighted New York Athletic Club agreed that "fine surroundings will not do an athlete any harm."[27] The indoor prize fights, walking contests, wrestling matches, and horse shows were a far cry from the crude atmosphere of early indoor sport. In 1890 carnivals were held at the Massachusetts Mechanics' Association by the Boston AA and at the new Madison Square Garden in New York by the Staten Island AC. The California AC in San Francisco featured a brilliant electric arc light; the horse show attracted fashionable New Yorkers to the Garden; and indoor baseball, already popular in Chicago, was taken up in New York's regimental armories.

A decade of electrification, paralleling improvements in transportation and communication, had elevated and purified the atmosphere of sport. The saloon brawls of pugilists in the 1850's and 1860's were gradually abandoned for the organized matches of the 1880's and 1890's. At the time of the Sullivan-Corbett fight in the New Orleans Olympic Club in 1892, an observer wrote in the Chicago *Daily Tribune,* September 8, 1892: "Now men travel to great boxing contests in vestibule limited trains; they sleep at the best hotels . . . and when the time for the contest arrives they find themselves in a grand, brilliantly lighted arena."

Basketball and volleyball, originating in the YMCA in 1892 and 1895, were both developed to meet the need for indoor sport on winter evenings. The rapid construction of college gymnasiums and the building of more luxurious clubhouses after the middle eighties stemmed in great part from the superior appointments and more brilliant lighting available for athletic games. Abortive experiments with outdoor athletic carnivals, bicycle meets, and horse races were made in the 1880's and 1890's, but lighting proved successful in indoor arenas. Much of the urban appeal of sport, as crowds turned out to six day bicycle races, basketball games, and prize fights, was directly attributable to the revolution which electric lighting made in the night life of the metropolis between 1880 and 1920.

Electrification, which transformed everything from home appliances and domestic lighting to power machinery and launches, exerted an influence on the course of sport through the development of rapid transit systems in cities from coast to coast. Horse-drawn cars had carried the burden of traffic since the 1850's, but the electric streetcar assumed an entirely new role in opening up suburban areas and countryside to the pent-up city populace. Soon after the Richmond, Virginia, experiment of 1888, the streetcar began to acquaint large numbers of city dwellers with the race track and the ball diamond. Experimental lines had been laid even earlier, and Chicago crowds going to the races at Washington Park on the Fourth of July in 1887 were jammed on "the grip." One reporter for the *Tribune* noted the "perpetual stream of track slang," the prodding and pushing, and the annoying delay when it was announced that "the cable has busted." Trolley parks, many of which included baseball diamonds, were promoted by the transit companies.

By 1896 there were said to be at least one hundred companies which maintained parks to increase the passenger traffic. While commercialized amusements were the chief attraction, sports facilities were often provided. Ball teams were encouraged by these same concerns through gifts of land or grandstands; and the crowds flocked to week-end games on the cars. One Texas official declared: "We find it profitable to keep in with the baseball people; they are well patronized in Galveston." When Edward Barrow, future molder of the New York Yankees, took over the Paterson club in the midnineties, Garret H. Hobart, president of a trolley line, built a park between Passaic and Paterson.[28] Popular interest in athletic games in thousands of towns and cities in the early years of the twentieth century was stimulated to a high degree by the extension of rapid transit systems, a development which may possibly have been as significant in the growth of local sport as the automobile was to be in the development of inter-community rivalries.

Numerous inventions and improvements applied to sport were of varying importance: the stop watch, the percussion cap, the streamlined sulky, barbed wire, the safety cycle, ball bearings, and artificial ice for skating rinks, among others. Improved implements often popularized and revolutionized the style of a sport, as in the invention of the sliding seat of the rowing shell, the introduction of the rubber-wound gutta-percha ball which necessitated the lengthening of golf courses, and the universal acceptance of the catcher's mask.

Charles Goodyear's vulcanization of rubber in the 1830's led to the development of elastic and resilient rubber balls in the following decade, and eventually influenced the development of golf and tennis balls as well as other sporting apparel and equipment. The pneumatic tire, developed by Dr. John Boyd Dunlop of Belfast in 1888, revolutionized cycling and harness racing in the nineties. Equipped with pneumatic tires, the sulky abandoned its old high-wheeler style, and the trotter and pacer found it made for smoother movement on the track. Sulky drivers reduced the mile record of 2:08.75 by Maud S. with an old high-wheeler to 1:58.50 by Lou Dillon in 1903 with a "bicycle sulky." According to W.H. Gocher in *Trotalong* the innovation of pneumatic tires and the streamlining of the sulky cut five to seven seconds from the former records, which was "more than the breeding had done in a dozen years." The pneumatic tire, introduced by racing cyclists and sulky drivers, went on to play a much more vital role in the rise of the automobile industry and the spectacular appeal of auto racing.

The camera also came to the aid of sport in the decades following the Civil War. Professional photography had developed rapidly in the middle period of the century, but nature lovers became devotees of the camera only when its bulkiness and weight were eliminated in the closing years of the century. Development of the Eastman Kodak after 1888 found a mass market as thousands of Americans put it to personal and commercial use. Pictorial and sporting magazines which had been printing woodcuts since the prewar era began to introduce many pictures taken from photographs, and in the late 1880's and early 1890's actual photographic prints of athletes and outdoor sportsmen came into common usage. *New Cabinet* photographs of pugilists, cyclists, ball players, wrestlers, oarsmen, pedestrians, and billiard experts were sold by the *National Police Gazette* to those who would part with a dime. *Harper's Weekly, Leslie's Illustrated Weekly, Illustrated American,* and the *National Police Gazette* featured photography, and by the end of the century the vast majority of their pictures were camera studies. Newspapers recognized the circulation value of half-tone prints, but because of paper and technical problems they were used sparsely until the New York *Times* published an illustrated Sunday supplement in 1896, soon to be imitated by the New York *Tribune* and the Chicago *Tribune.* The year 1897 saw the half-tone illustration become a regular feature of metropolitan newspapers, rapidly eliminating the age-old reliance on woodcuts.

At the turn of the century sport was available in visual form to millions who heretofore had little knowledge of athletics and outdoor games. Photography developed throughout the nineteenth century as an adjunct of the science of chemistry. Chemical and mechanical innovations were also responsible for the improvements of prints and all kinds of reproductions. Woodcuts were featured in the press, engravings were sold widely, and lithographs were found in the most rural home. Nathaniel Currier (later Currier & Ives) published hunting, fishing, pugilistic, baseball, rowing, yachting, sleighing, skating, trotting, and racing prints for more than half a century. Cheap prints, calendars, and varied reproductions of sporting scenes did much to popularize the famous turf champions and sporting heroes of the era.

It was in 1872 that Edward Muybridge made the first successful attempt "to secure an illusion of motion by photography." At the instigation of Leland Stanford, already a noted turfman, he set out to prove whether or not a trotting horse at any time had all four hoofs off the ground. By establishing a battery of cameras the movements of the horse were successively photographed, and Muybridge later turned the technique to "the gallop of dogs, the flight of birds, and the performances of athletes." In his monumental study entitled *Animal Locomotion* (1887) he included thousands of pictures of horses, athletes, and other living subjects, demonstrating "the work and play of men, women and children of all ages; how pitchers throw the baseball, how batters hit it, and how athletes move their bodies in record-breaking contests."[30]

Muybridge is considered only one among a number of the pioneers of the motion picture, but his pictures had presented possibly the best illusion of motion prior to the development of flexible celluloid film. A host of experimenters in the late 1880's gradually evolved principles and techniques which gave birth to the true motion picture. Woodville Latham and his two sons made a four-minute film of the prize fight between Young Griffo and Battling Barnett in 1895, and showed it on a large screen for an audience, an event which has been called "the first flickering, commercial motion picture."[31] When Bob Fitzsimmons won the heavyweight championship from James J. Corbett at Carson City, Nevada, in 1897, the fight was photographed for public distribution. With the increasing popularity in succeeding years of the newsreel, the short subject, and an occasional feature film, the motion picture came to rival the photograph in spreading the gospel of sport.

When sport began to mature into a business of some importance and thousands of organizations throughout the country joined leagues, associations, racing circuits, and national administrative bodies, it became necessary to utilize on a large scale the telephone, the typewriter, and all the other instruments so vital to the commercial world. Even the phonograph, at first considered a business device but soon devoted to popular music, came to have an indirect influence, with the recording for entertainment of such songs as "Daisy Bell," "Casey at the Bat," "Slide, Kelly, Slide," and, early in the present century, the national pastime theme, "Take Me Out to the Ball Game." All of these instruments created a great revolution in communication, and they contributed significantly to the expansion of sport on a national scale.

The bicycle, still an important means of transport in Europe but something of a machine-age casualty in the United States, also had an important role. In the brief craze of 1869, according to Albert H. Pope, in excess of a thousand inventions were patented on the bicycle. Clubs, cycling associations, and racing meets were sponsored everywhere in the years after the Philadelphia Centennial display, and the League of American Wheelmen served as a spearhead for many of the reforms in fashions, good roads, and outdoor exercise. Albert H. Pope was merely the foremost among many manufacturers of the "velocipede" which became so popular among women's clubs, temperance groups, professional men, and, at the turn of the century, in the business world and among the trades. As a branch of American industry the bicycle was reputed to have developed into a $100,000,000 business in the 1890's. Mass production techniques were introduced and Iver Johnson's Arms and Cycle Works advertised, "Every part interchangeable and exact." The Indiana Bicycle Company, home of the Waverley cycle, maintained a huge factory in Indianapolis and claimed to be the most perfect and complete plant in the world: "We employ the highest mechanical skill and the best labor-saving machinery that ample capital can provide. Our methods of construction are along the latest and most approved lines of mechanical work."[32]

Much of the publicity given to competing manufacturers centered around the mechanical improvements and the speed records of their products. Between 1878 and 1896 the mile record was lowered from 3:57 to 1:55.20. While one critic recognized the effect of better riding styles, methodical training, improved tracks, and the art of pace-making, he contended in the April 11, 1896 issue of *Harper's Weekly:* "The prime factor . . . is the improvement in the vehicle itself. The racing machine of 1898 was a heavy, crude, cumbersome affair, while the modern bicycle, less than one-sixth its weight, equipped with scientifically calculated gearing, pneumatic tires, and friction annihilators, represents much of the difference."

Roger Burlingame has contended that the bicycle "introduced certain technical principles which were carried on into the motor car, notably ball bearings, hub-breaking and the tangential spoke."[33] Little did cycling enthusiasts realize that in these same years a much more revolutionary vehicle, destined to transform our way of life, was about to make its dramatic entry.

One of the last inventions which the nineteenth century brought forth for the conquest of time and distance was the automobile. During the last decade the Haynes, Duryea, Ford, Stanley Steamer, Packard, and Locomobile came out in quick succession, and the Pierce Arrow, Cadillac, and Buick were to follow in the next several years, along with dozens of other cars like the Waverly, Hupmobile, and Peerless. Manufacturers of bicycles had already turned to the construction of the motor car in a number of instances. As early as 1895 H.H. Kohlsaat, publisher of the Chicago *Times-Herald,* sponsored the first automobile race on American soil. One of the features of this contest which was run through a snow-storm and won by Charles Duryea, was the enhanced reputation achieved for the gasoline motor, which had not yet been recognized as the proper source of motor power. A number of European races like those from Paris to Rouen, and Berlin to Potsdam inspired American drivers to take to the race course. The experimental value of endurance or speed contests was immediately recognized by pioneer manufacturers. Nor were they slow to see the publicity value of races featured by the newspapers. Car builders looked upon road and speedway races as "marketing devices" to win public interest.[34]

Henry Ford "was bewitched by Duryea's feat," and he "devoured reports on the subject which appeared in the newspapers and magazines of the day." When other leading car builders sought financial backing for their racers, Ford, after earlier failures, determined to win supremacy on the track. After defeating Alexander Winton in a race at Detroit in 1902, Ford's achievements as a speed merchant were recorded in the popular journal aptly entitled *Horseless Age.* In later years he was to contend, "I never thought anything of racing, but the public refused to consider the automobile in any light other than a fast toy. The industry was held back by this initial racing slant, for the attention of the makers was diverted to making fast rather than good cars." The titan of industry apparently had forgotten that in his younger years he said, "I believe that track racing is of inestimable value to the trade and to the development of the art of automobile building." The victory over Winton was his first race, "and it brought advertising of the only kind that people cared to read." Bowing to public taste, he was determined "to make an automobile that would be known wherever speed was known," and set to work installing four cylinders in his famous "999." Developing 80 horse power, this machine was so frightening, even to its builders, that the fearless Barney Oldfield was hired for the race. Oldfield had only a tiller with which to steer, since there were no steering wheels, and he was reported to have uttered a last-minute prediction: "This damn thing may kill me but the records will show I was going like hell when it got me." This professional cyclist, who had never driven a car (until the previous week), established a new record and helped put Ford back on his feet. The financial support of Alex Y. Malcomson, an admirer of "999," gave him a new start: "A week after the race I formed the Ford Motor Company."[35]

The next few years witnessed the establishment of Automobile Club of America races, sport clubs in the American Automobile Association, the Vanderbilt Cup, and the Glidden Tour. The St. Louis *Post-Dispatch* for August 5, 1900 headlined the "First Automobile Race in the West" although there were only thirty-five cars in the city at the time. Reporting on the third annual Glidden Tour in 1906, the August 11 issue of *Scientific American* defended American cars, heretofore considered inferior to

European models: "Above all else, the tour has demonstrated that American machines will stand fast driving on rough forest roads without serious damage to the cars or their mechanism. Engine and gear troubles have practically disappeared, and the only things that are to be feared are the breakage of springs and axles and the giving out of tires. Numerous shock absorbers were tried out and found wanting in this test; and were it not for the pneumatic tires, which have been greatly improved during the past two years, such a tour would be impossible of accomplishment."

The Newport social season featured racing, Daytona Beach soon became a center for speed trials, Savannah had its Grand Prize Race, and tracks were built in various parts of the nation, the first of which may have been at Narragansett Park as early as 1896. Not until the years just prior to World War I did auto racing attain a truly national popularity with the establishment of the Indianapolis Speedway in 1911. Some 80,000 spectators flocked to the track the following year, a crowd composed of mechanics, racing enthusiasts, and mere onlookers.

The "Good Roads" movement gained impetus with road racing in some areas. A Tampa historian claims that the Tampa to Jacksonville round-trip race in 1909 gave birth to good roads and that this eventually had a "tremendous bearing on the future of Tampa . . . and the entire state of Florida." Auto races became an annual event at Iowa state and county fairs in 1916, though reckless drivers were prohibited from raising dust storms and scaring town shoppers on every state course.[36] Henry Ford had long since lost interest, however, while the Buick racing team of experts like Red Burman and the Chevrolets was discontinued in 1915. By then mass production had turned the emphasis toward design, comfort, and economy. Although racing was not abandoned and manufacturers still featured endurance tests in later years, the heated rivalry between pioneer builders had become a thing of the past. The automobile, however, gradually transformed the transportation habits of the American people and encouraged intercommunity rivalries in the World War I era.

Meanwhile, motorboat races, motorcycle climbs, air meets, and endurance flights capitalized on the public fever for higher speed and spectacular performances. By 1900 Daimler boats had proven the desirability of gasoline motors in power launches and smaller craft. Sir Alfred Harmsworth (later Lord Northcliffe) established the Harmsworth Trophy for international competition in 1903. Even the depression of 1907-1908 failed to halt the mounting sales of motorboats. The spotlight was thrown on airplane racing in 1909 when Glen Curtiss won the James Gordon Bennett trophy at Rheims, France. Los Angeles held the "First Great Aviation Meet" in 1910, in which year racing carnivals were held by the Harvard Aeronautical Society and at Belmont Park in New York. New

York newspapers like the *Herald* and the *Times* realized the widespread interest in aviation, as well as did the Boston *Globe* and Chicago *Evening Post,* who all put up large cash prizes.

The *Independent,* November 3, 1910, referred to the "new sport of the air" and speculated that the airman "is the true superman, a veritable *deus ex machina* . . . . He is playing with the aeroplane now. By and by when he gets tired of the new toy he will set it to work. In the meantime youth will have its fling. It will spend its time in sport and perhaps do a little fighting too." Cross country racing became the vogue among airmen in the next few years, and the sport thereby revealed much about the proper construction of planes. When Galbrath Rogers made the first trans- continental flight in 1911 he needed 49 days because of all kinds of mechanical delays which deprived him of the $50,000 Hearst prize, but thirteen years later Lt. Russell Maugham flew from New York to San Francisco in less than 22 hours. Although mass production, laboratory experimentation, efficiency studies, and the inventor's imagination con- tributed more heavily to mechanical improvements, the impact of sport on the machine was a vital one in these years.

Technological developments in the latter half of the nineteenth and the first two decades of the twentieth century transformed the social habits of the Western world, and sport was but one of many institutions which felt their full impact. Fashions, foods, journalism, home appliances, commercialized entertainment, architecture, and city planning were only a few of the facets of life which underwent rapid change as transportation and communication were revolutionized and as new materials were made available. There are those who stress the thesis that sport is a direct reac- tion against the mechanization, the division of labor, and the standardiza- tion of life in a machine civilization,[37] and this may in part be true, but sport in the years between the Civil War and the First World War was as much a product of industrialization as it was an antidote to it.

While athletics and outdoor recreation were sought as a release from the confinements of city life, industrialization and the urban movement were the basic causes for the rise of organized sport. And the urban move- ment was, of course, greatly enhanced by the revolutionary transformation in communication, transportation, agriculture, and industrialization.

The first symptoms of the impact of invention on nineteenth-century sports are to be found in the steamboat of the ante-bellum era. An intensi- fication of interest in horse racing during the 1820's and 1830's was only a prelude to the sporting excitement over yachting, prize fighting, rowing, running, cricket, and baseball of the 1840's and 1850's. By this time the railroad was opening up new opportunities for hunters, anglers, and ath- letic teams, and it was the railroad, of all the inventions of the century, which gave the greatest impetus to intercommunity rivalries. The telegraph and the penny press opened the gates to a rising tide of sporting journalism; the sewing machine and the factory system revolutionized the manufacture of sporting goods; the electric light and rapid transit further demonstrated the impact of electrification; and the bicycle, the automobile, and the airplane gave additional evidence to the effect of the transportation revolution on the sporting impulse of the years before 1920.

In the twentieth century the rapidity with which one invention followed another demonstrated the increasingly close relationship between technology and social change. No one can deny the significance of sportsmen, athletes, journalists, and pioneers in many organizations, and no one can disregard the multiple forces transforming the social scene. The technological revolution is not the sole determining factor in the rise of sport, but to ignore its influence would result only in a more or less superficial understanding of the history of one of the prominent social institutions of modern America.

# Chapter 4

# The
# Athletic Impulse,
# 1860-1890

**EYTONA AND FASHION.**

IN THEIR GREAT MATCH FOR $20,000.

OVER THE UNION COURSE L. I. MAY 13TH 1845, WON BY PEYTONA.

Time 7: 39¾ 7: 45½

rned, Rider, Blue jacket, Black cap

FASHION light Chestnut, Rider, Purple jacket, Green cap.

LITH. & PUB. BY N CURRIER, 152 NASSAU ST. COR.

UNION COURSE L.I. Tuesday May 13 th 1845 Match—the **NORTH** vs the **SOUTH** $10,000 aside $5000 forfeit, 4 Mile heats.

The[n] Kirkman of Alabama entered Ins. Ch — **PEYTONA** by Imp Glencoe out of Giant

[...] by Abdallah [...] by Imp Leviathan [...] yrs [?] the "Baron" T.F.Falmer

Henry K. Toler of New Jersey entered W[m] Gibbons's Ch. m. **FASHION** by Imp Trustee out of

Bonnets o' Blue [the Dam of Mariner etc] by Sir Charles 6 yrs 124 lbs       Joseph Laird

Time of First Heat 1st Mile  1.54        Time of Second Heat 1st Mile

    2nd   "   1.53                    2nd   "

    3rd   "   1.57                    3rd   "

    4th   "   1.55¾                   4th   "

    Total=7.39¾                          Total

Chauncey Depew, noted lawyer and corporation director, was engaged in one of those perorations for which he was famous as an after-dinner speaker. The occasion was a testimonial banquet in honor of Walter Camp, who in 1892 was already recognized as one of the authorities in the world of athletics. In a serious vein, the speaker noted the tremendous change which had taken place in the years since the Civil War:

> There has always been a singular prejudice among the American people against muscular training. It is not twenty-five years since a large majority of the men and women of this country associated physical training and athletic superiority with a close-cropped, bullet head, and intellectual pre-eminence with a frail figure and a hacking cough, surmounted by a dome of thought. All of us who are in middle life can remember the minister, the lawyer, or the doctor of the village who could box, belonged to a ball club or was a member of an amateur rowing association had no hope of success. It was felt that such tendencies were incompatible with the care of estates, the curing of bodies or the saving of souls.[1]

By the middle years of the nineteenth century, however, interest in recreation had appeared throughout the United States. The popularity of picnics, excursions, summer resorts, museums, minstrel shows, and agricultural fairs, as well as the circus and the theater, demonstrated a new and mounting demand for entertainment of all kinds. It was in this more favorable environment that the common man of the Jacksonian era gradually threw off many of the shackles of his Puritan heritage. While convictions about proper conduct and respectable diversion were to change during the next hundred years, and while this enthusiasm for new forms of recreation met stern resistance in every part of the country, a mere look at the activities of the prewar generation is convincing proof that the seeds of change were at work in the American mind. It was in this atmosphere that outdoor sport began to capture the popular imagination, when suddenly a fratricidal struggle divided the nation into two hostile camps and impeded the sporting movement. Despite the interval of war the three decades from 1860 to 1890 were to witness a renewed enthusiasm for the turf, aquatics, field sports, and, especially, athletic games.

## Civil War

A war which split the nation and reached down and touched the personal life of every American diverted public interest from sport to more vital issues, but it did not completely alter the recreational pursuits of the people. Sporting activities were maintained throughout the northern states during much of the conflict although the South had little time for play. Baseball enthusiasts suffered a decided blow as the National Association's membership fell from 54 teams in 1860 to 34 in 1861—and then suspended operations. Whereas there were 62 clubs in the area of New York city in 1860, there were only 28 in 1865.

Just how common baseball playing was in the army is dubious, although there is evidence that it was a fairly frequent occurrence. Yankee soldiers apparently demonstrated the New York game to men of the West and the South. Games were held even in prison camps. A.G. Mills, a major figure in the rise of professional baseball, claimed to have played in a South Carolina prison camp before forty thousand soldiers. Soldiers off-duty often sparred or wrestled. "Next to music," writes Bell Irvin Wiley, "Johnny Reb probably found more frequent and satisfactory diversion in sports than in anything else. When leisure and weather permitted, soldiers turned out in large numbers for baseball."[2] The southern soldier occasionally played at football, cricket, quoits, boxing, wrestling, foot racing, swimming, and hunting, not to mention the widespread popularity of card games.

George Haven Putnam, reminiscing on an impromptu game in 1864, told how he played on a baseball nine in Texas which was forced to use a field outside the fortifications and beyond the line of pickets, even though this was prohibited by army regulations: "Suddenly there came a scattering of fire of which the three fielders caught the brunt; the center field was hit and was captured, the left and right field managed to get into our lines . . . . The Rebel attack, which was made with merely a skirmish line, was repelled without serious difficulty, but we had lost not only our center field but our baseball and it was the only baseball in Alexandria."[3] The commanding general delivered them a severe reprimand, but after a Union defeat at Sabine Cross Roads necessitated quick evacuation of the forces, the baseball incident was soon forgotten.

On the northern home front sport was handicapped by the flow of youths into the army. Some were able to avoid military service, especially by hiring substitutes, while many a parent strove to keep his son in school or college. The Turner movement suffered a decided setback as thousands went to war. Rowing was temporarily suspended at Harvard and Yale. Horse racing, however, continued in the North, and even in the battle-scarred city of Lexington, Kentucky. Louisville, Philadelphia, New York, Chicago, and Paterson, New Jersey, held intermittent meetings. Saratoga, a center of trotting in the 1850's, inaugurated thoroughbred racing in 1863 under the sponsorship of William R. Travers and John Morrissey. Offspring of the immortal Lexington, whose skeleton was sent to the National Museum in Washington on his death in 1875, began to win fame on northern tracks as Kentucky, Asteroid, and Norfolk dominated the racing scene. Agricultural fairs continued to sponsor races, and Dexter made his first appearance on the trotting course in 1864, driven by Hiram Woodruff at the Fashion and Union courses in New York. By this time dozens of communities were holding races throughout the entire North. Billiards proved to be a popular pastime and the "National Tournament" of 1863 was such a huge success that state tournaments were also held. One enthusiastic admirer of the new game of baseball, recognizing the handicaps caused by war, stated:

> Although the past season has been one of gloom and despondency, rather than one of joyful merriment and recreation, we are pleased to note that the young men composing our various base-ball organizations have gallantly stood by their noble pastime, and have not permitted even an adverse tide to cripple or stay the growth and prosperity of our National Game.[4]

Pugilists were particularly active, and the celebrated Mike McCoole fought Joe Coburn for the American championship in 1862. Joshua Ward rowed against James Hamill in widely heralded races. Even the anglers were active as the New York State Sportsmen's Association held its first casting contests in 1864. War on the sea forced the New York Yacht Club to abandon its annual regatta in 1861. Regular races were held in succeeding years, the New York club holding its regatta during the seige of Richmond in 1864, by which time thirty-five craft were enrolled with the Brooklyn Yacht Club. But the toll of the war on yachting had been heavy.

Four years of war impeded the advance of sport in the North, but many athletic organizations and sporting clubs survived the conflict. In the South the effects of war on civilian life were more sharply felt. Horse racing died "south of Kentucky," the Charleston season fell off, and New Orleans lost its leadership of the American turf: "The war had swept away the racing institutions of the South, the breeding studs were broken up, and the blood-horse bridled and made to do service in the army . . . the people had no heart for the pastimes of the turf; racing was abandoned, horses of royal lineage scattered; and when the war closed, the old jockey clubs were disorganized—bankrupt."[5] Devastation of plantations brought an end to fox hunting, and the customary matches between slaves as fighters or oarsmen were abandoned. In conquered territory there was a Mississippi Valley Base-Ball Club at Vicksburg, but members complained, "We are compelled to get up games among ourselves, as there are no other clubs on the River south of St. Louis."[6] At the end of the war the South, impoverished and in a state of social upheaval, was ill prepared to engage fully in the competitive world of sport.

War-weary veterans returning from the battlefield carried a knowledge of baseball into remote rural areas, and nines began to appear immediately throughout the southern and western states. Immediately following combat a revival in the turf, baseball, and yachting took place, and many new games soon won widespread recognition. Although war had hindered the advance of sport in the early 1860's, the stimulus given to manufacturing and industrial expansion helped lay the economic basis for the sporting impulse of the 1870's. It may well be that the postwar sporting fever was based on a widespread desire to relax and forget the rigors of the past, a tendency noted in the aftermath of wars in more modern time. And of even greater importance was the preservation of the Union, which made it possible in later years to develop intersectional rivalries in athletic competition.

## "I Sing the Body Electric"

Ante-bellum visitors to the United States often noted the beauty of the American girl but regretted, as did Harriet Martineau, the poor posture of women who all too commonly avoided any form of physical activity. Nor was the average American male, except for the southern sportsman, likely to practice even the rudiments of muscular exercise. Because of an absorption in business affairs, few Americans retained their athletic habits beyond adolescence. While tales of the superhuman skill or muscular power of fabled strong men were reported in the press and merged into the national folklore, during the ascendancy of New England transcendentalist thought the purely physical was held in low esteem. As a writer in *The Atlantic Monthly* for March, 1858 maintained, "There is in the community an impression that physical vigor and spiritual sanctity are incompatible." Manly strength remained an asset of the farmer and frontiersman, but urban conditions seemed to militate against any form of athleticism. Oliver Wendell Holmes, author and physician, disparagingly observed that "society would drop a man who should run round the Common in five minutes." To his disgust he admitted, "I am satisfied that such a set of black-coated, stiff-jointed, soft-muscled, paste-complexioned youth as we can boast in our Atlantic cities never before sprang from loins of Anglo-Saxon lineage."[7]

In these same years attention was given the problem of physical health by a few educators like Emma Willard, Catherine Beecher, and Dio Lewis, who publicized the need of walking, dancing, and exercise. Horace Mann considered the problem in his 1843 report on education in Massachusetts, the *Ohio Journal of Education* in 1852 pioneered in discussing the "Physical Education of Females," and in the years just before the war the Tom Brown books helped encourage teachers' conventions to direct attention to the health of students. Changing religious opinion was reflected in the Cincinnati *Star in the West* for December 6, 1856, which maintained that "while we concede to the fullest extent the sinfulness of neglecting the spiritual and intellectual faculties of our nature, we cannot see that it is any less a sin to neglect the physical. God made man to develop all his faculties to the highest possible degree—to stand erect, with broad shoulders and expanding lungs, a picture of physical and moral perfection." Thomas Wentworth Higginson, Holmes, and others called for more ardent support of the athletic movement, while Walt Whitman's *Leaves of Grass* preached the exaltation of the body as part of the soul in "I Sing the Body Electric:"

> If any thing is sacred the human body is sacred,
> And the glory and sweat of a man is the token of manhood
>     untainted,
> And in the man or woman a clean, strong, firm-fibered body,
>     is more beautiful than the most beautiful face.

At the return of peace to America the interest of the public in health was heightened by the greater attention given to sanitation and medical care. Exercise was thought by many to be the solution of health problems, and the newly-founded *Turf, Field, and Farm* argued, "It is better than doctor's physic, or all of the patent medicines in the land."[8] The *New York Clipper* in 1869 considered baseball clubs to be "missionary organizations preaching the new gospel of health in a most effective manner, and arousing an interest in physical exercise for which many an otherwise dyspeptic and jaundiced youth would have reason to be thankful in years to come." In postwar years numerous publications appeared, among them the *Herald of Health, Hall's Journal of Health, Good Health, Health and Home, Dr. Foote's Health Monthly,* and *Annals of Hygiene.* Leading magazines carried articles on health and sporting journals constantly praised the role of athletics and field sports in achieving the ideal of a sound mind in a sound body. Within a single generation a great transformation was to take place.

## Rise of the National Game

The collapse of the Confederacy and the return of men to civilian life inaugurated a new epoch in American history and a new era in American sport. More than any other sport, baseball grew in national favor in the next quarter century. In 1866 Charles A. Peverelly, an early authority on recreation, claimed, "The game of Base Ball has now become beyond question the leading feature of the out-door sports of the United States," mainly because of its low expense, its excitement, and the small amount of time required.[9] Another baseball enthusiast contended:

> Of all out-door sports, base-ball is that in which the greatest number of our people participate, either as players or as spectators . . . it is a pastime that best suits the temperament of our people. The accessories being less costly than those of the turf, the acquatic course, or the cricket-field, it is an economic game, and within the easy reach of the masses. The merchant may associate himself with a leading club of amateurs for a mere bagatelle, the schoolboy may join a junior club at a mere trifling expense, and the GAMIN can and does play ball for nothing. It has become the rage with all classes and conditions.[10]

By 1860 there were 54 clubs represented in the National Association of Base Ball Players, but the Civil War cast a blight on organized leagues until the end of hostilities. When delegates convened in 1865 there were 91 clubs represented—48 from New York, 14 from Pennsylvania, 13 from New Jersey, and others from Maine, Kansas, Missouri, and Kentucky. Arthur Pue Gorman became president of the Association in 1866, and under his leadership the membership roll expanded rapidly. Baseball enthusiasm spread throughout the Midwest, and by 1867 there were 145 member clubs in Illinois, Indiana, Ohio, and Wisconsin. A group of government employees formed the nucleus of the National Base Ball Club of Washington, D.C., which toured the West in the same year. (The Nationals had met the Philadelphia Athletics on the White House "lot" in the summer of 1865, and three years later President Johnson directed the Marine Band to play at their games.) By rail and by steamboat the Washington club visited Columbus, Cincinnati, Louisville, Indianapolis, and St. Louis, as well as Chicago and Rockford, Illinois, arousing a keen interest at every city.

In 1867 there were 237 teams represented in the National Association; nearly a score of clubs were active in San Francisco; and James Parton, the historian, was impressed with the current rage. New York held the distinctive claim of "the home of baseball," the Massachusetts Game having collapsed with the Civil War. This new diversion was being widely heralded as "The National Game." By this time New York ranked behind Illinois, Ohio, Pennsylvania, and Wisconsin in the number of enrolled amateur clubs, and in the South sportsmen quickly took up ball and bat.

Despite the hardships of Reconstruction, according to E. Merton Coulter, "Baseball made its appearance immediately after the Surrender and it was participated in by all classes of people from clerks in the stores to gentlemen of leisure." Mobile had five clubs in 1868; Thomas E. Watson served as captain of the Up and At Em Club of Thompson, Georgia; an Alabama Association of Base Ball Players was organized in Montgomery, composed of clubs from five cities; and further proof of the Southern baseball fever came with the organization of the Louisiana State Base Ball Association.[11]

In the years immediately following Appomattox tremendous crowds came out to enjoy the baseball fad. When the Mutuals of New York met the Atlantics of Brooklyn in 1865, a throng of 20,000 spectators looked on. Vehicles, grandstands, sheds, and trees failed to accommodate the teeming crowd which surpassed, according to the *Spirit of the Times,* "any gathering ever convened to honor this popular pastime." Amateur clubs appeared in cities, small towns, and villages. "Baseball tourneys were in the air" in Iowa in 1866 and a state association formed the following season. Toledo had four clubs in 1866, while teams were active in 1867 in Mobile, Louisville, Nashville, Denver, Helena, Leavenworth, Topeka (three clubs), Cedar Rapids, Cincinnati, and other cities of the South, the Midwest, and the West.

The *Leader* of Lake City, Minnesota, quipped: "The game of Base Ball has become so much the *style* that nearly every village and hamlet has its club, and to a member of the first nine is now looked upon as being nearly as honorable a position as a seat in the Legislature." In many towns the game was first adopted by socially prominent young men, the Cincinnati Baseball Club of 1866 being composed mainly of Harvard and Yale law graduates while the Cedar Rapids players were "members of the best families . . . and most of them were active in the business life of the city." Umpires often officiated wearing a silk hat, sporting a Prince Albert coat, and carrying a cane. Democracy was at work, however, and two years later the great pork metropolis was represented by thirty-four clubs as the baseball fever swept over Ohio.[12]

At the beginning of the 1870's the diamond was already one of the nation's chief forms of recreation. *Beadle's Dime Base-Ball Player* emphasized that players must have the characteristics of true manhood. One study mentioned ball playing as a pastime "in which the Americans indulge with rare gusto." In rural areas "Saturday afternoon is usually assigned to . . . [ball playing] , on which occasions the young men are as active and expert in throwing and catching, or striking the ball, as if they had been idle all the previous week instead of having had to work in the fields with the utmost energy."[13] In South Carolina during the early seventies ama-

teur clubs appeared throughout the countryside. When the Carolina Club
of Charleston played at Orangeburg, a crowd escorted them from the railroad station and feted them at a banquet. According to the *Rural Carolin-
ian,* "Public match games between nines from a distance, which lead to
dinners and picnics are frequent." Clarence Darrow recalled the lure of
baseball for young boys in Ohio towns of the 1870's:

> It seems to me that one unalloyed joy in life, whether in school
> or vacation time, was baseball. . . . I have snatched my share of joys
> from the grudging hand of Fate as I have jogged along, but never has
> life held for me anything quite so entrancing as baseball; and this, at
> least, I learned at district school. When we heard of the professional
> game in which men cared nothing whatever for patriotism but only
> for money—games in which rival towns would hire the best players
> from a natural enemy—we could scarcely believe the tale was true.
> No Kinsman [Ohio] boy would any more give aid and comfort to a
> rival town than would a loyal soldier open a gate in the wall to let an
> enemy march in.[14]

The *Spirit of the Times* for April 19, 1873, enthused over the progress of the rural diamond: "The game is truly a national one. In every
little town and hamlet throughout the country we find a ball club, generally two, bitter rivals, at it with hammer and tongs, dong-dong the entire
summer, as though all creation depended on the defeat of the other crowd,
and then away goes a challenge—to the next town, and from there to the
next, and so on."

During the middle of the decade, with the Panic of 1873 causing
mounting distress among baseball promoters, the game underwent considerable reorganization. Professionalism had entered the scene with the
Cincinnati Red Stockings tour in 1869. Although the Boston Baseball
Club reported a net profit of slightly more than $3000 in 1875, the season
ended with almost every club facing bankruptcy. Owners obstinately refused to reduce the 50¢ admission fee during 1876, despite the prolonged
depression. The season of 1877 was also a failure financially for most professional clubs. At the end of that season, when players were earning from
$800 to $3000, the secretary of the newly organized National League
wrote, "The salaries of players must come down, and players so understand
it, and are preparing themselves for it. If the fancy prices are paid in the
future that have been in the past, and the Clubs 'come out of the little end
of the horn' at the close of the season, they will have no one to blame but
themselves."[15]

Discovery of the curve ball's effectiveness by Arthur Cummings and other pitchers, the closeness of pennant races, and the higher level of playing skill helped tide organized baseball through the dark years of depression. By 1881 many clubs were out of the red, and, as is seen in the *Spalding Guide* reports, the professional game prospered throughout most of the eighties. The Chicago White Stockings sold Mike (King) Kelly to Boston in 1887 for $10,000, and when they later sold John Clarkson for a similar sum, the diamond reached a new peak of prosperity. Baseball in Dixie came to the fore with the organization of Georgia, Alabama and Tennessee in the Southern League in 1885 and the Texas League in 1888, these being years of economic recovery in the New South. To build up attendance ladies' days were instituted, and appeals were made to men of prominence to help in the promotion of the game. This was never an easy matter, as was seen in the case of Chattanooga: "That place wants ball. The money could be raised in two days, but the trouble there, as in all other cities, is to find men who will take the office of president, or some position that would start the movement."[16]

In the late eighties baseball flourished on an estimated annual $10,000,000 exchange of money and investment, winning, according to its boosters, "the support of business man and mechanic, clerk and capitalist alike." More than 350,000 Brooklyn fans turned out for the season of 1889, establishing an average of more than 5000 per contest and an attendance record for professional baseball. Throughout the land the game had made a remarkable advance in the quarter century from 1865 to 1890.

Clerks of the commercial houses in larger cities joined in the social clubs and organized baseball and athletic leagues. The *Ball Player's Chronicle* in 1867 joyously claimed that "almost every large manufacturing establishment in the country has its 'nine'." Employers were often unsympathetic to the sporting activities of their workers, but the baseball fever was widespread in some of the large concerns of New York in 1869. Factories in St. Louis began sponsoring clubs, while bank clerks and the clothing industry placed teams on the diamond. Play in commercial leagues received little publicity in the press, but commercial and neighborhood athletic clubs were fairly common by the middle eighties. "Compositors do battle with pressmen, weavers with dyers, the hands in the wholesale department with the hands in the retail store. Any morning you may read in the *Sun* or the *Star* that a certain valiant lithographer, for instance, offers to row or to wrestle with any other lithographer for the championship of the lithographers."[17]

In rural areas town rivalries on the diamond helped penetrate the social isolation. Although published in 1884 with the aim of popularizing baseball, particularly among children, Noah Brooks' *Our Base Ball Club* illustrated how small town fans reacted to the game. Many of the town-folk disapproved since numerous games had been thrown, but the town's isolation did not prevent the outbreak of a baseball epidemic:

> It was the dead of winter, and, except a few teams slowly pull-ing in from the outlying country, with a few farmers in quest of the necessaries of life from the town stores, very little life was visible about the place. Occasionally, a fierce snow storm would sweep over the town, blocking the streets, and cutting it off from all communi-cation except by railroad. The main street would be desolate. . . . Around the hot stoves in the lounging-places, down town, grown men were talking of baseball, and small boys, hanging eagerly on the outer edges of the groups, drank in with silent intelligence the words of wisdom that dropped from the lips of their elders.[18]

Colorful players already were gaining widespread fame. John Clark-son, Mike Kelly, Adrian Anson, Dan Brouthers, Harry Wright, and other stars of the diamond held high rank among the heroes of American youth. In 1890 Mike Kelly's friends in San Francisco, Chicago, New Orleans, Boston, New York, and Rochester presented their idol with a home valued at $13,500. A community's interest in the local team was variable, but the spirit of victory whetted many a city's enthusiasm for the game. The old Philadelphia Athletics of the American Association did much to spread interest throughout the country, and when they won the championship in 1883 Philadelphians exuded overweening pride in their team. On the return of the Athletics to the Quaker City, "The neighborhood of the railway-station . . . was thronged with tens of thousands of people of all ages and colors and of both sexes." Those who had watched the bulletin boards during the series welcomed their heroes with a torchlight parade, fireworks, decorated streets, an electric light display, and a banquet "attended by many of the prominent men of the city." They were present-ed with the freedom of the city theaters, with watches, medals and testi-monials, "and altogether they have been treated like heroes worthy of the proudest distinction."

On a similar occasion: "The Poughkeepsie Base Ball Club arrived home . . . previously having won the championship pennant of the Hudson River League. The club was met at the wharf by a crowd with a band of music and escorted to carriages, gayly decked with flags. . . . Main Street was ablaze with fireworks, all of which was followed by a banquet."[19] Although these may have been exceptional demonstrations of municipal spirit, local pride in the home club had developed strongly in many towns and cities during the 1880's.

## The Athletic Club

American athleticism was promoted by coteries of enthusiastic individuals who banded into clubs in every organized sport. This era from 1860 to 1890 was, in many ways, the age of the athletic club. In the years before many colleges granted permission for organized athletic teams, the college baseball, rowing, or football association was little more than a student-sponsored athletic club. Rowing clubs cropped up everywhere after Appomattox, about two hundred being formed between 1865 and 1867, while the passing years found cricket clubs flourishing in New England and in many cities like Baltimore, Buffalo, Pittsburgh, Detroit, Milwaukee, and San Francisco. Amateur baseball teams comprised the heart of the game throughout these decades, despite the greater publicity showered on the professional. Bowling, boxing, tennis, racquets, and finally golf were encouraged by numerous private clubs which were patronized by young men of high society. Even the fire companies competed in mule racing, ladder raising, running contests, and baseball. Much of this interest in sporting or athletic clubs was also encouraged by the social distinction attached to societies of yachtsmen, turfmen, and cyclists.

No single agency gave a greater impulse to sport than the formalized athletic club of the metropolis. When William B. Curtis, John C. Babcock, and Henry E. Buermeyer founded the New York Athletic Club in 1868, they inaugurated a new era in athletics. By 1871 the club had acquired a tract at Mott Haven and sponsored an annual spring track and field meet. During the 1870's other groups of athletes appeared as rivals to the NYAC, among them the Staten Island, the Manhattan, the American, and the Pastime clubs. The Chicago Athletic Club came into being in 1871, the Young Men's Gymnastic and Athletic Club of New Orleans the next year, and by 1877 the Olympic Club of San Francisco (which claims to have originated around 1860) began to sponsor track and field games. In the 1880's New Orleans had its Olympic Club, while Providence, Philadelphia, Baltimore, Pittsburgh, Cincinnati, Cleveland, Detroit, Chicago, and St. Louis were well represented by similar organizations, some of which were composed of "many young men from the very best families."

These formal clubs inspired the organization of many neighborhood and institutional athletic societies. In 1887 one writer claimed:

> Athletic clubs are now springing into existence in the United States in such profusion as to baffle the effort to enumerate them. Scarce a city can be found having a population of more than 30,000 inhabitants, in which there is not at least one club of this class. In the large cities, there are from five to twenty-five; sometimes even more.

Many societies, founded for social, literary or military objects, have added gymnasiums to their other resources for the entertainment of their members. In New York City there are twenty-one clubs founded primarily to promote an interest in gymnastics and general field exercises, besides numerous German Turner societies; and there are in addition a great number of riding, boat, bicycle, ball-playing, archery, bowling and yachting associations for fostering special forms of athletic sports. . . . It would be impracticable to enumerate the athletic clubs of the smaller cities of the United States. Nearly every Caledonian, St. George's and German society of the country is, to a certain extent, an athletic club. Nearly every college and academy has its own athletic association. The total number is several thousand.[20]

This presents a decidedly favorable picture of the facilities afforded by athletic clubs of every description, but we find that Boston's clubs centered on cycling or boating, the Pullman Athletic Club was "the only distinctively athletic organization which Chicago may be said to possess," and Philadelphia's Fencing, Athletic and Sparring Club was "the only one of its kind in the city." Many a community in the South and West as well as in the East was represented by no other athletic organization than the local nine.

During the 1880's the increase of enthusiasm for physical education and the rapid construction of gymnasiums was in part stimulated by college athletics, by the more general recognition of the value of *mens sana in corpore sano,* by the YMCA, by the Turnverein, and by the sprouting athletic clubs throughout the nation. The first athletic clubs sponsored track and field meets and produced such great athletes as Lon Myers of the Manhattan AC, the first American to consistently defeat the best English runners both at home and abroad, and John Owen of the Detroit AC. It soon became desirable, once the more wealthy clubs had their own gymnasiums, to include fencing, handball, wrestling, boxing, gymnastics, and other athletic activities. Even baseball and football teams were placed on the diamond and the gridiron, and games with the colleges became an annual event.

The formal athletic club was in great part responsible, also, for the extension of the club idea to National Guard units and United States Army posts. Little attention was paid to the athletic interests of men in military service until the end of the century, but the struggle to promote physical exercise and competitive sport goes back to the Civil War era. Regimental baseball teams that were organized during the war were the pioneers of sport in the military. The *Army and Navy Journal* in 1868 remarked: "One good, at least, from the great evil of the late war, came from its accustoming two millions of our people, most of them young, or in the prime of life, to military training. No great war, however, calling upon the nation as a whole, is likely to occur for many years. For the physical training of the people, we must rely on the popular national sports."

By the late seventies company rifle matches developed into serious rivalries, while athletic games were held in the West by the Fourth Infantry Regiment at Fort Sanders, Wyoming. The Twenty-third Regiment of the New York National Guard inaugurated its armory contests in 1879. Fort Sanders and Fort Russell matched their teams the next year, while it was reported in 1884 that in the army departments of California and Columbia "nearly all the posts have gymnasiums and many athletes among the troops." Soon thereafter athletic carnivals were sponsored by Brooklyn's Thirteenth Regiment and the Twelfth Regiment, with William B. Curtis of the *Spirit of the Times* and E. Plummer of the *New York Sportsman* officiating. The Fifth Maryland Regiment Athletic Club of Baltimore had a membership exceeding five hundred. Boxing, baseball, and football teams competed in contests throughout the decade, and some military men supported a call to post commanders for a policy of "Athletics in the Army." The contention was that physical training "would do more than any single thing to reduce the rate of desertion," and athletic associations of National Guard regiments were considered an inducement to enlist.[21]

Meanwhile, rowing had become popular in the navy after the Civil War, especially with the encouragement given young midshipmen at Annapolis by the Academy's superintendent, Admiral D.D. Porter. Races were sometimes arranged spontaneously between the crews of ships, as was narrated by Admiral Robley Evans in *A Sailor's Log*. Of equal or greater interest were the baseball games which became a diversion for seamen in foreign ports. While the records of the early clubs in the navy are scanty, we know that officers of the *Pensacola* had a team and that the game was played in Japan in 1879 by officers of the United States fleet and the Yokohama Base Ball Club. In the next few years matches were held between the crews of the *Minnesota* and the *New Hampshire,* the *Portsmouth* and the *Jamestown,* and other ships. When the *Brooklyn* went on cruise in the years 1881-1884, the officers opposed the crew in a ball game at the English Cricket Club in Montevideo. By the end of the decade seamen had taken to the diamond during leave hours as one of their most popular forms of recreation.[22]

Around the metropolitan area of New York in 1890 it was claimed, "The growth of athletics has been nowhere more clearly manifest than in our militia regiments. The building of such immense armories as those of the Seventh in New York and the Thirteenth in Brooklyn has given the regimental athletes room enough to hold games indoors, and has greatly stimulated winter exercises of all sorts. Nearly all the regiments now have athletic clubs. . . . It is easily seen that the encouragement of athletic sport among members of the National Guard is an excellent thing for that branch of the service. Young men who keep 'in condition' and who are trained to walk and run and jump and play ball, are certainly capable of better service in the field than they could render without such training." [23]

Some YMCA's such as those in New York and Providence formed athletic clubs, and in the latter city in 1887 there was a High School AC. William Penn Charter School became famous for outdoor sports, maintaining a six-acre playing field in the suburbs. Students of Central High School in the same city banded into an athletic association as early as 1876, largely concentrating on baseball until football began to challenge its popularity in the eighties. Then the students began to imitate college teams, and by 1889 football enthusiasm was so great that Central High had its school yell. Such pioneering in high school athletics portended the amazing popularity of school sports in the early years of the twentieth century.

The athletic club in all its manifold types was the cornerstone of the era of organization. Inspired by the exploits of famed metropolitan clubs as well as by college associations, clubmen from coast to coast did much to promote the athletic movement of the era 1860-1890.

## Athletes on the College Campus

One of the notable trends in American education between 1860 and 1890 was the revolution against the sedentary habits of college students. College authorities often remained indifferent or hostile to the new spirit of athleticism, but almost every campus felt an upsurge of sporting interest. Physical education gained headway and most established colleges either obtained or campaigned for adequate gymnasium facilities before the end of the 1880's. Baseball caught on widely in the colleges, the Williams-Amherst game of 1859 inaugurated an era of intercollegiate competition in eastern schools, while teams appeared at such institutions as the University of Virginia and the University of Georgia soon after the war. Rowing was revived at Harvard, Yale, Brown, and Trinity, and it soon became a major sport at Wesleyan, Dartmouth, Amherst, Columbia, Bowdoin, Massachusetts Agricultural College, Cornell, Williams, Hamilton, Union, Princeton, Pennsylvania, Rutgers, and Annapolis. By 1871 the need for a Rowing Association of American colleges was apparent. In 1876 an American Intercollegiate Football Association began to organize the gridiron game.

Track and field sports won many followers with the creation in 1875 of the ICAAAA, which laid the groundwork for the Amateur Athletic Union's control after 1888. Lacrosse was played on a few eastern campuses, the boxing ring became an adjunct of the better gymnasiums, and even polo attracted some privileged college students. The entire realm of athletics was greatly encouraged by the avidity with which games and contests were played on the campuses of American colleges.

In the years following the Civil War baseball rapidly acquired its title as the American national pastime. College baseball prospered, deriving much of its popularity from the public's interest in professional clubs. It was the only rival of rowing and football in eastern colleges, while its following in the South and West usually exceeded that of any sport. Large universities and many small colleges fielded teams which fought for the glory of "the old school." By 1874 Henry Chadwick noted that Northwestern, Kenyon, Manhattan, New York University, and Seton Hall were represented on the diamond.[24] Almost every major eastern and midwestern institution sponsored teams. The inexpensiveness of paraphernalia (gloves, masks, and equipment other than bats, balls, and uniforms, were not yet in vogue), the adaptability of men of all kinds of physique to the game, the stimulus given to college baseball through competition with teams from YMCA's, athletic clubs, and professional ranks, and the benevolent attitude of college administrators all contributed to the rise of the diamond in intercollegiate ranks.

During this same decade rowing became the most honored of sports in the East among those privileged colleges provided with the necessary facilities and resources. In 1876 (the year of the Philadelphia Convention, Custer's massacre at the Little Big Horn, and the furious Hayes-Tilden campaign) the New York *Evening Post* ignored the formation of the National League in its annual chronology of important events, listing the college rowing races as the only major sports events of the year. Regattas at Saratoga Lake in the middle 1870's were highly publicized by the press. The New York *Daily Tribune's* first page gave an unprecedented tribute of five columns to the rowing fever of the 1875 regatta, as more than twenty thousand holiday celebrants converged on the famed resort. Cornell emerged the victor, but the spirits of all the undergraduates were high as cheering students marched in battalions about the town crying "C-o-l-u-m-b-i-a" and "Yale! Yale! Yale!" Organized cheering had already appeared on the scene.

After the regattas of the 1870's rowing never again gained the preeminence in college sport it had enjoyed, but the crew remained a major element in athletics throughout the rest of the century. Rowing had introduced the hired coach to the campus and Robert Cook at Yale, Ellis Ward

at Pennsylvania, and Charles Courtney of Cornell were among the most
renowned authorities of the era. Limited to those colleges with suitable
water courses, rowing felt the rising competition of baseball, football, and
track athletics by 1890, but in the development of American intercollegiate athletics it had played an indispensable role.

Track and field athletics, popularized to some extent by the Scottish
Caledonian games of the Civil War era and by the meetings held by the
New York Athletic Club, developed into a major interest of college students in the middle 1870's. Races were held at Saratoga in 1874 in conjunction with the rowing regatta, and the *Harvard Advocate* was pleased
that "at least we have the various foot contests so well known in the
British universities." The Intercollegiate Athletic Association was formed
among a few eastern colleges, but interest lagged until the 1880's when
the rising enthusiasm for track and field sports encouraged Cornell, Union,
Syracuse, Rochester, and other upstate institutions to band together in
1885 in a regional conference called the New York State Intercollegiate
Athletic Association. Amherst, Williams, Brown, Bowdoin, Dartmouth,
Trinity, and Tufts organized a New England Intercollegiate Athletic Association. Tradition, however, obstructed this as it had other athletic movements, and many conservative leaders in American colleges remained
apathetic if not hostile to intercollegiate sport. President Buckham of the
University of Vermont stated in 1875 that "neither the character of our
community nor the traditions of the college are such as to encourage
sporting habits. A large proportion of its students, large enough to determine the prevailing tone of the institution, are sons of farmers . . . and
would regard it as beneath the dignity of a free-born Vermonter to expose
their muscle in public, like gladiators in the amphitheatre." [25]

Throughout the South and Midwest interest in track and field athletics lagged behind the East. With the rise of state universities the sport
gradually gained a foothold on the campus, and Michigan held its Ann
Arbor open games in the 1880's. Track athletics were popular in the colleges of Iowa, Indiana, and Ohio, as well as at the universities of Wisconsin and Illinois. Among the smaller colleges of the Midwest, however, there
was a conservative attitude toward physical education. Arthur Ruhl,
writing two decades after this period, stressed this lag in sporting interest:

> What was true of New England and New York was true of the
> Middle West and the Pacific Slope, although in the smaller colleges
> of the Middle West the new sport was slow in striking fire. And . . .
> many of these little colleges gave scant attention to any sort of sport
> in those days, and what tentative interest the undergraduates them-
> selves happened to take was likely to be frowned upon by the

faculty. Most of these small colleges were either coeducational or strongly sectarian, or both. In the first there was likely to be a feeling that there was something incompatible between athletics and a decorous gentlemanliness, and in the latter sport was looked at askance as flippant and of the flesh fleshy. Those who had these institutions in charge were generally men who had come from good old New England stock, or who had been brought up in the stern school of the pioneer, and it was naturally very difficult for them to look upon mere games as anything but a waste of time.[26]

Track and field athletics in American colleges were given a decided stimulus by the athletic clubs of the 1870's and 1880's, and annual amateur championships like those of the New York AC at Mott Haven were open to the best men of club and campus alike. Among the leading track and field men of the 1860-1890 period were H.H. Lee of Pennsylvania, Evart Wendell and Wendell Baker of Harvard, F.M. Bonine of Michigan, and C.H. Sherrill of Yale, the man most responsible for popularizing the crouching start for sprinters. Even in 1890, however, interest in track was limited to relatively few institutions and clubs in the major cities; the public schools were slow to organize meets; the press gave little attention; and the average citizen was only vaguely aware of its popularity in sporting circles. The great era of track and field sports on the intercollegiate level was to open with the coming of the new century.

Football is a sport of such universal interest today that it seems difficult to remember that back in the 1870's and 1880's it was the Johnny-come-lately of intercollegiate athletics. Played as a kicking game by students at numerous colleges in the first half of the century and popularized by such pioneer clubs as the Oneida of Boston, football did not attain a prominent position in intercollegiate sport until the 1880's in many eastern institutions, and it only began to emerge as a truly national pastime in the early years of the present century.

Intercollegiate football began with the Rutgers-Princeton contests of 1869; Columbia placed a team on the gridiron the next year; Yale entered the intercollegiate scene in 1872; and Harvard met McGill University on Jarvis Field in 1874 in the first intercollegiate game of Rugby football, in which running with the ball rather than kicking was featured. The Massasoit House at Springfield, Massachusetts, was the scene of a small convention in 1876 which formed the Intercollegiate Football Association, but it was not until the late 1880's that football was widely accepted outside the larger eastern colleges. In 1881 Michigan invaded the East to play Harvard, Yale, and Princeton. Lafayette, Lehigh, Dartmouth, Wesleyan, Pennsylvania, Stevens Institute, West Point, and Annapolis were all fielding teams by 1890, while the Western Intercollegiate Football Association (including Iowa, Kansas, Missouri, and Nebraska) was created in that year.

Something of the primitive nature of football in this era is seen in the numerous quarrels over rules, the faculty abolition of games, the size of crowds such as that of the Harvard-Yale game of 1884 which drew the comment that there were "at least 3000 people in attendance," the more general interest in baseball in southern and western colleges, and the small expenditures involved. Faculty sentiment toward the rough-and-tumble game of football may be seen in the twenty-five to four vote for abolition at Harvard in 1885. Financing of the team was an early problem, one which the Harvard club met by drawing $705 in gate receipts in 1875 and which Wesleyan authorities resolved by granting $600 to football in the early 1880's. Football gained a popular following on a few of the ivy-covered campuses of eastern colleges, and William L. Kingsley could write in 1879 that at Yale it was "more generally popular among the students than either boating or baseball," but it was to be accepted on a national basis in the colleges and schools only in the nineties.

Other sports were taken up by college students in the era 1860-1890. Archery proved popular at girls' schools; gymnastics were featured in physical education programs; a few polo teams were organized; an Intercollegiate Cricket Association operated in the East; and an Intercollegiate Lacrosse Association developed as a branch of the National Lacrosse Association. Even boxing and wrestling were popular, although only on an interclass or informal basis while the growth of baseball, rowing, football, and track athletics, along with these other minor sports, cannot obscure the fact that college athletics were only in their formative years prior to 1890; the college was a vital factor during postwar decades in making the American people conscious of the growth and popularity of organized sport.

## Physical Education and Athleticism

Physical training gained widespread support only after the Civil War, but its introduction as a formalized study in America began with the pioneer efforts of Charles Beck and Charles Follen in the Boston of the 1820's. The founding of Round Hill School by Follen, J.G. Cogswell and George Bancroft was a landmark in the history of physical education. German gymnastics, based on the principles of Friedrich Ludwig Jahn, who founded the Turnvereine movement in Prussia, were introduced by Beck at Round Hill School while Follen was establishing a public gymnasium for the city and the first American college gymnasium at Harvard in 1826.[27] The first Turnvereine were organized by Friedrich Hecker in 1848 in Cincinnati, but it was the Revolution of 1848 which gave impetus to the movement in the United States as thousands of exiles came to our shores. In 1851 the United Turnvereine of North America (the American Turnerbund) held its first national turnfest in Philadelphia; by 1859 there were 73 societies with over 5000 members; by 1865 the Turner societies reorganized themselves into a Nordamerikanischer Turnerbund; the German system of gymnastics was introduced into the schools of Kansas City, Chicago, Cleveland, Omaha, Canton, Holyoke, Lowell, Davenport (Ia.), St. Joseph (Mo.), Denver, and Washington, D.C., between 1885 and 1890. The Turner influence was said to have been dominant in introducing gymnastics in the schools of fifty-two cities with a total population of over sixteen millions. Largely influential in this movement was Dr. Carl Betz, one among many Turner authorities who agitated for physical education in the schools. Between 1880 and 1890 the Turners themselves multiplied rapidly, jumping from 186 to 287 societies and from 13,387 to 35,912 members.[28] During the late 1880's the Swedish system of gymnastics was also introduced widely. As agencies sponsored by recent immigrant groups, such organizations contributed greatly to the rise of popular interest in physical education.

Although German immigrants featured physical education in antebellum years, it was only during the Civil War era that American educators began to turn a friendly ear to its advocates. On the brink of war Amherst College, under the leadership of W.A. Stearns, formally began a physical education program, the first of its kind in the United States. In 1859 President Stearns had recognized this need in his report to the trustees:

> Many of our students came from farms, mechanic shops, and other active occupations, to the hard study and sedentary habits of college. Physical exercise is neglected, the laws of health are violated, the protests and exhortations of instructors and other friends are unheeded. The once active student soon becomes physically indolent, his mental powers become dulled, his physical movements and appearance indicate physical deterioration. By the time Junior year is reached many students have broken down in health, and every year some lives are sacrificed. Physical training is not the only means of preventing this result but it is among the most prominent of them.[29]

Dr. Edward Hitchcock of Amherst, Dr. Dudley A. Sargent of Harvard, and George Goldie of Princeton led in the development of gymnastics and were recognized as leading authorities. Dio Lewis opened the Normal Institute for Physical Education in 1861, the earliest American school for training teachers in that field. American colleges were soon alive with an interest in the use of gymnastic apparatus, and a surge of gymnasium construction swept over the campus. Between 1860 and 1885 gymnasiums appeared in surprising numbers but it was in the middle eighties that construction was most active. While there were at least thirty-five colleges in 1885 which had some kind of facilities, the Commissioner of Education report for 1886-1887 stated that there were seventy-seven known colleges with gymnasiums. An important step was taken in 1885 when the American Association for the Advancement of Physical Education was founded. Leading magazines printed articles on the value of physical education and Harvard fitness tests conducted through the eighties showed that there were 250 students in 1890 whose strength tests surpassed the highest score recorded in 1880! Yet, physical education was still in its infancy. In 1886 it was pessimistically reported that "no city system of schools can be considered as up to the standard of the day that has not gymnasiums and teachers of gymnastics sufficient for the pupils of all grades. It is to be regretted that no one of our American cities can be named where such provision exists."[30] And less attention was paid in southern and western colleges than in the East.

Much attention was being directed toward manual and industrial training in these years, thereby restricting the emphasis on physical education. Only 89 of 419 public secondary schools of the United States reported physical culture programs in 1887; only 50 of 172 endowed academies, seminaries and other private secondary schools for girls reported similar programs; gymnasiums were found at 13 private schools for girls, 81 for boys, and 57 for both sexes—a total of 151 in private schools.[31] Just as depressing to the ardent champion of physical education was the picture of facilities in secondary schools in 1890, when only 94 of 2526 public high schools reported gymnasiums. Well might Professor Emil Hausknecht of the Realschule in Berlin, reporting on his tour of 1892-1893, note the lack of facilities for secondary schools. He may have partially explained the lag behind German gymnasium facilities in citing the popularity in the United States of open air sports such as rowing, canoeing, camping, angling, cycling, football, lawn tennis, and lacrosse. While many colleges and most secondary schools throughout the United States had the most meager facilities for physical education programs throughout much of this period, a great transformation was taking place in the eighties.

Physical training and athletics were also promoted outside the turn-vereines and the field of education. One institution was of paramount importance—the YMCA. The Young Men's Christian Association, founded in England by George Williams, spread gradually throughout the United

States in the 1850's. Confined to those of a definitely Protestant religious inclination, its leaders pursued a conservative policy toward athletics in its early years. A "Y" convention in 1860 favored athletics and gymnastics as "a safeguard against the allurement of objectional places of resort." Having learned of the interests of young men during the Civil War and profiting from the inspiration of such directors as Robert R. McBurney of New York and Robert J. Roberts of Boston, the YMCA rapidly became a center of physical culture.[32]

Although the pioneer religious leaders of the "Y" questioned the rising emphasis on things athletic, the mounting appeal for *mens sana in corpore sano* began to take effect. McBurney opened the 23rd Street YMCA in 1869 and a gymnasium, bowling alleys, and baths were made available for the first time to all members. Associations in San Francisco and Washington, D.C., opened gyms in the same year. Soon such outstanding Christian spokesmen as Henry Ward Beecher and Washington Gladden heralded the arrival of a new age in which the "Y" was to have bowling alleys and billiard tables as well as reading and social rooms. Between 1883 and 1887 the number of YMCA's equipped with a gymnasium leaped from 68 to 168, with about 50 paid directors, while other less fortunate centers engaged informally in baseball, football, rowing, swimming, bowling, weight lifting, and calisthenics. At the end of the decade about one fourth of all associations were encouraging physical culture.

The Young Women's Christian Association, growing during the war years, had failed to meet the demand for facilities for its members, one critic observing, "There is, indeed, no adequate reason why the privileges of the gymnasium and the bowling alley should not be theirs at certain hours and under proper restrictions."[33] The YWCA at Boston held the first athletic games for women in 1882. By 1890 physical education was becoming a key part of the Young Women's Christian Association program and many buildings either maintained a gym or planned on its construction when funds would become available. But the appeal of physical exercise was strongest among young men and *Harper's Weekly* noted in 1890 that the "Y" in New York was fully committed to physical training, maintaining that "almost every well-organized Young Men's Christian Association in the city and neighborhood has now its athletic department, and many of them have gymnasiums. It is the muscular form of Christianity that seems to take best among young men." Not only did the associations, under such new leadership as that given by Luther Halsey Gulick, accomplish much in persuading Christian families of the value of physical training, thus piercing the lingering veil of Puritan austerity, but they also encouraged the extension of athletics beyond the campus to the heart of the thriving metropolis.

## Three Decades of Organization

When war came to an end clubs and associations took on new life, and throughout the remaining years of the century organization remained one of the most vital factors in the growth of American sport. In 1865 the Nordamerikanischer Turnerbund, popularly called the North American Gymnastic Union, was created to bring greater uniformity to the societies throughout the United States. The late sixties were formative years in the sporting revival of the latter part of the century: in 1868 the New York Athletic Club was founded and the Cincinnati Red Stockings toured the country in 1869 as the first professional baseball team. In the same year gymnasiums were constructed in several YMCA's and intercollegiate athletics made headway as soon as the students returned to the campus.

It was only in the 1870's, however, that countless minor groups, societies, and clubs merged their interests in regional associations and bound themselves to rules of play and conduct administered by committees with constitutional power. Organization went on apace in other fields of sport. The year 1870 saw the birth of the National Association for the Promotion of the American Trotting Turf, in 1873 the Grand Circuit officially opened, and in 1876 the National Association of Trotting Horse Breeders was founded. The thoroughbred turf benefited greatly from the opening of Long Branch, Pimlico, Belmont, New Orleans Fair Grounds, and other courses, as well as from the inauguration of the Kentucky Derby at Churchill Downs. In similar fashion a small nucleus of baseball clubs created the National Association of Professional Baseball Players in 1871; in 1876 the National League was founded to rid the diamond of its prevailing ills; and the late seventies witnessed the rise of several minor leagues which died an early death. Rowing came into prominence as an amateur sport through the regattas at Lake Saratoga, the combining of several eastern colleges in a Rowing Association of American Colleges (1871), and the appearance of a more united front by the National Association of Amateur Oarsmen (1872). Aquatic sports were also encouraged through the founding of the Seawanhaka Yacht Club and the New York Canoe Club in 1871, as well as the America's Cup Races of 1870, 1871, and 1876. Marksmen came together under the National Rifle Association in 1871, and local gun clubs multiplied rapidly in cities like Memphis, which had five in 1885.

Track and field athletics were more closely scrutinized after the Intercollegiate Association of Amateur Athletes of America (ICAAAA) came into being in 1875. Even the amateur bowler might look to the National Bowling League (1875) for guidance and information, the "noble game" had its Cricketer's Association of the United States (1878), and the

National Association of Archers (1879) served the same purpose for students of the bow and arrow. Although football was still limited to a few universities, an American Intercollegiate Football Association (1876) helped eliminate the differences in style of play. Athletics in the American college were finally put on a more stable footing with the formation of the National Association of Amateur Athletes of America (later reorganized as the National Collegiate Athletic Association or NCAA) in 1879. In short, athletics in the 1870's underwent a rapid process of organization.

During the decade of the 1880's the sporting movement manifested itself in an even more decided tendency toward closer supervision and more efficient regulation. Such personalized recreations as cycling, canoeing, skating, and croquet were given an impetus by the activities of the League of American Wheelmen (1880), the National Canoe Association (1880), the National Croquet Association (1882) and the United States Skating Association (1884). The first ski tournament was held by Norwegian-Americans of Minnesota in 1884. Although the vast majority of Americans had no direct relationship with these governing organs, the contests sponsored and the rules promulgated by them did much to popularize sporting diversions among many previously uninterested people.

This decade also found tennis enthusiasts organizing the United States Lawn Tennis Association (1881), a few golf addicts introducing the game in New York, and a number of socialites combining in the United States Polo Association (1890). Athletics and physical education were stimulated by the foundation of the International Training School of the YMCA at Springfield, Massachusetts, in 1885; by the gradual introduction of athletic games in the YWCA; by the growth of the American Association for the Advancement of Physical Education; and, particularly, by the historic formation of the Amateur Athletic Union (AAU) in 1888. From the birth of the AAU it was engaged in a continuous struggle to gain recognition and control over athletic organizations of all kinds, but it was destined to be one of the great champions of sport in the United States. Sports were further promoted by the creation of a rival to the old National League in the American Base Ball Association in 1882 and the formation of the American Trotting Association in 1887, while even fishing and shooting were showing the first real signs of organization in the National Rod and Reel Association and the National Gun Association.[34]

These governing bodies suffered through years of resistance and noncooperation; their authority was usually much less than the title of the organization indicated. Nor can it be forgotten that there were no national controlling bodies for the thoroughbred turf or the prize ring. Thousands upon thousands of Americans bought bicycles or canoes, went swimming or fishing, and played at croquet or billiards without any consideration of the policies or the playing codes of any sporting organization.

By 1890, however, it was quite obvious that the age of organized sport had arrived. It can truly be said that it was in the 1870's and 1880's that the spread of intercollegiate sports, the popularity of athletic clubs, the establishment of control bodies for even individualized recreation, the advance of physical education, and the growth of interest in baseball jointly assisted in the establishment of organizational bodies in most important athletic activities. In turn, these administrative agencies, operating within the framework of a much more closely regulated world of sport, contributed immensely to the enthusiasm for athletic and sporting diversions.

# Chapter 5

# The Triumph of Athletics, 1890-1920

If the three decades after 1860 saw an athletic impulse sweep over the country, it was in the succeeding thirty years that the athletic spirit became a permanent part of the American social scene. The nineties, the prosperous years of the new century, and the First World War comprise an important epoch in the history of sport. It was in this period that the militant young organizations and the crusading sportsmen of the late nineteenth century won many crucial battles in attaining, within one generation, general recognition of competitive athletics as an entrenched national institution.

Whereas attacks on the past excesses of sport had been confined to small pressure groups or individual spokesmen seldom able to win any unified support, athletic games were challenged on several fronts in the years after 1890. Champions of the athletic cause were almost completely successful in beating back the tirades of bitter critics and in winning the general approval of the American people. Nowhere was this manifested more forcefully than in the enthusiastic recognition of athletics by the colleges and schools of the nation. Baseball's faltering prestige eventually recovered from a decade of troubles, while football soared into prominence as a collegiate, scholastic, and sandlot game. Basketball, volleyball, and other athletic activities gained footholds for the first time. While the diamond maintained its pre-eminence as the national pastime, it was the triumph of athletics in all its forms which was the distinguishing characteristic of these three decades of sport.

## Clouds Over the Diamond

Professional baseball seemed to be coming of age and hopes were high in the 1880's; however, the following decade proved to be one of confusion and disillusionment. The minors began to prosper and the Western Association caught on beyond the Mississippi, but the year 1890 witnessed one of the most calamitous setbacks in baseball history. Friends of the diamond were shocked at the decline of prestige resulting from the Brotherhood War. The National Agreement of 1882 and its reserve clause had been anything but popular with many players. Then, in 1885, a new National Agreement established a top salary of $2000, freezing out all other leagues except the National and the American Association. The noted ballplayer and manager, John M. Ward, had forewarned of trouble. Writing in *Lippincott's* in August, 1888, he argued, "In speaking of this reserve-rule I ought to notice an abuse which has sprung up under it. Clubs sometimes retain men for whom they have no possible use simply for the purpose of selling them to some other club. In this way the player loses not only the benefits a free contract might give, but also the amount paid

for his release." Ward became a leader of the players' revolt, and on
November 4, 1889, a "Manifesto of Brotherhood of Base Ball Players"
was issued. In rebuttal the National League advertised:

> To the Public—
> To correct a misapprehension in the public mind as to the
> alleged 'enormous profits' divided among stockholders of League
> Clubs, it may be interesting to know that during the past five—and
> only prosperous—years, there have been paid in cash dividends to
> stockholders in the eight League clubs less than $150,000 and during
> the same time League players have received in salaries over $1,500,-
> 000. The balance of the profits of the few successful clubs, together
> with the original capital and subsequent assessments of stockholders
> is represented entirely in grounds and improvements for the perma-
> nent good of the game, costing about $600,000.

The term "magnate" was a gross exaggeration of the vested interests
in baseball, and Fred Lieb has questioned whether all sixteen franchises
(including real estate, stands, and reserved players) represented an investment exceeding $1,000,000. Nevertheless, in 1890 the Brotherhood—or
Players League—waged a financial war with the National League and the
American Association. Financial ruin stalked many of the professional
teams. In the American Association one club fell two months in default
on salaries and the players worked on a cooperative plan. Gloomy, indeed,
were the season's reports: "It is a patent fact that the season which is now
closing has been the most disastrous campaign financially that has ever
been known in the history of the national game." One editor deplored the
war and feared this "almost fatal decline of a great National institution."[1]
Professional baseball men responded to the crisis as the Players
League collapsed. Many owners resorted to Sunday games in 1892, and
Chicago followed suit the next year. The depression of 1893 did not hit
the diamond immediately, although crowds were smaller than in 1889
when Brooklyn set an all-time record. Eventually the national crisis made
itself felt, and a majority of minor leagues "fell by the wayside" in 1896,
*Spalding's Guide* blaming this on the financial distress of the country.
Renowned beyond all others of the diamond were such veterans as
William (Buck) Ewing, Mike Kelly, Adrian (Pop) Anson and "Wee Willie"
Keeler. When the first-named player died in 1906 the Chicago *Tribune*
recalled, "Ewing was a Cincinnati product, born and bred, and a graduate
of the most prolific of all baseball schools in this part of the country, the
'bottoms' that skirt the Ohio river," and, "as champion catcher of the
country [he] earned the fame that made the name of 'Buck' Ewing known

to every schoolboy that has handled a baseball in the last twenty years."
At the peak of his fame Kelly was possibly the most colorful player in the
game, his name destined to go down in baseball lore in the call, "Slide,
Kelly, Slide!" Anson, whose career spanned the era 1871-1898, was one
of the greatest players and managers of the time; on the field his chief
prowess was in batting, and as a manager he did much to encourage ball
teams to patronize the better hotels in each of the League cities. Keeler's
fabulous batting achievements with the Orioles are still in the record book.
Nor should we forget Ned Hanlon, that great manager of the riotous
Baltimore Orioles. Ewing received the top salary in his day of $5000 and
the pitching ace Amos Rusie earned $4500, sums thought by many critics
to be outrageously exorbitant.

In their struggle to regain a popular hold on the affection of the average American, baseball men of the nineties suffered under the handicap
of spotty reporting in the better newspapers and magazines. Despite
attempted reforms, the professional game had lost many of its friends.
Even the general introduction of gloves and the new styles of play developed were of little help.

Then came the Spanish-American War. Poor attendance in major and
minor leagues was blamed on the war as seven of the twelve National
League teams faced deficits, but a contrary charge was made that fans
were alienated by "the outrageous conduct of many managers and players" and the failure of reform plans. The waning century well might
question just what lay ahead for the professional diamond.

These years of difficulty were explained in part by the mushrooming
of golf, cycling, and football enthusiasm, by the Brotherhood War, and by
depression, but another explanation centered on the "evils" of the sport:

> The decline in the popularity of the game, which is now much
> lamented by American newspapers and by lovers of clean sport, is
> due mainly to the lawlessness that the club owners and managers
> encourage in the play. . . . No wonder attendance at the game falls
> off and women dislike to go. In the cities embraced within the
> National League complaints of rowdyism on the field are universal
> and continuous. . . . They [the franchise owners] are in the game for
> money, and if they cannot win by fair means, they do not hesitate to
> resort to foul means. The lovers of baseball can bring them to their
> senses by continuing to remain away from the games. Appeals
> through the press are useless; they can be reached only through their
> pockets.[2]

In 1889 the *Spalding Guide* had urged the inclusion of a "prohibition plank" in all baseball contracts as the only cure for the prevalence of drunkenness. In baldest terms it charged: "The two great obstacles in the way of success of the majority of professional ball players are wine and women. The saloon and the brothel are the evils of the baseball world at the present day." Throughout the decade constant "kicking" and abuse of umpires by the players turned games into a perpetual state of anarchy. The New York *Times* for September 23, 1900, carried the following:

> Rowdyism by the players on the field, syndicatism among the club owners, poor umpiring, and talk of rival organizations—these are the principal causes accountable for baseball's decline. There is still another cause. That is the growth in popularity of other sports . . . if they (the baseball 'magnates') are so anxious to see their team win and thus swell gate receipts that they will condone and even encourage unsportsmanlike behaviour by their players, then their presence as 'magnates' is a menace to the welfare of the game, and the sooner they are out of it the better for the game. . . . The players deny that they contemplate another brotherhood. It is well that they do not, for the brotherhood trouble in 1890 was a blow from which the game has not yet recovered.

As professional baseball staggered through a calamitous decade, the Brotherhood War, the depression, the rise of new sporting fads, the apathy of the respectable press, and maladministration within its own ranks all contributed. "Magnates" struggled to revive interest through consolidation of the American Association and the National League as early as 1892. And then came the new threat of Ben Johnson's American League, which acquired many stars from the teams that disbanded in 1899. Launched largely on the financial backing of its vice-president, Charles W. Somers, who had an interest in the Boston, Cleveland, Philadelphia, and Chicago clubs, the new league was immediately successful. Formation of the National Association of Minor League clubs in 1901 also strengthened the game. Finally, in 1903, a peace pact was signed between the major leagues, and the organization of modern professional baseball took on a permanent character. Garry Herrmann, president of the Cincinnati Reds, headed a National Commission for the control of organized baseball.

Although the World Series' final game of 1903 drew a meager crowd to see the Boston Americans win the first championship and although much of the press gave only passing notice, by the end of 1904 baseball scribes were heralding the complete renaissance of the diamond. "The season of 1905 was the baseball year par excellence. There was never anything like it", according to the *Illustrated Outdoor News.* Making an appeal for respectability with the recruiting of college men like Christy Mathewson of Bucknell, Mike Lynch of Brown, and Walter Clarkson of Harvard, the professional game soon acquired a grip on the public mind far stronger than at any time in its history. Stop

Despite the retarded growth of the game in professional circles, most Americans never lost their enthusiasm for the national pastime. The California League got under way in 1897 and proved a popular success.[3] Baseball remained the major sport of many colleges and the development of "inside baseball" (stressing the strategy, signals, and highly integrated team play popularized by the notorious Baltimore Orioles) made the game more exciting.[4]

Thousands of communities were represented by local teams. The *World Almanac* for 1901 noted the failure of "magnates" to see the rivalry of other sports or to rectify the evils of the professional game, but confidently prophesied, "The inherent attractions of baseball are such that no matter what blundering management may do to lessen the financial profits of the professional business, itself, it can have but little effect on the national game at large." Emporia, Kansas, at the turn of the century was a typical town of 10,000 souls, and, according to *The Autobiography of William Allen White,* "In the summer the town's baseball team played the teams from other towns in Kansas, in Soden's Grove. And of a late summer afternoon, the town gathered at these games with noisy loyalty and great excitement. . . . The ball game was the only public summer sport." Indoor baseball was catching the public's attention. Armory games were held in the larger cities, and from Chicago the game spread throughout the United States in the nineties. By 1900 there were leagues reported throughout the country and *Spalding's Illustrated Catalogue* claimed, "Every large commercial house has its team." The future of baseball and its sidekick variants seemed secure.

## The Good Old Days of the National Game

Arbitration of the conflict between the National and American leagues, commencement of the World Series of 1903, and a general attack on rowdyism by President Harry Pulliam all contributed to the promotion of public confidence in the game. When the outlaw Tri-State League finally joined the National Association, "Organized Baseball" comprised 34 leagues with 256 clubs and 4400 players. In 1906 the majors and the minors combined attracted 20,000,000 fans, and two years later the *Spalding Guide* reported: "The wonderful growth of the public's interest in Base Ball during the last half decade has attracted many hundreds of thousands of people to the game to whom its history previous to the last four or five years is unknown, or at least hazy."

Statistics proved the sustained interest, for in 1909 the National Association of Minor Leagues employed more than 7000 players and there were estimated crowds totaling more than 24,000,000 spectators throughout the nation. One observer noted that "it is doubtful that any season since baseball became a fixed institution in this country has seen so much progress made as in the year 1909." This was due to the elimination of wrangling, the rise of a flock of capable young players, and the better accommodations at ball parks. The Associated Press recognized the trend and began to expand its baseball coverage. World Series games between Pittsburgh and Detroit in 1908 illustrated this heightened enthusiasm for the baseball championship. Streetcar traffic in the Smoky City was relegated to side streets during the game "owing to the thousands who stood in front of bulletin boards," and the mayor issued a proclamation calling upon the people to decorate the city for the welcoming home of their club.[8] Baseball might well claim its traditional title when Walter Camp declared two years later in *Century Magazine,* "The national game has no rival, and is growing greater every year."

The World Series of 1912 interfered with the presidential campaigns of Wilson, Taft, and Roosevelt as thousands upon thousands hovered over tickers, congregated around bulletin boards, and waited for the details in the daily newspapers. Justices of the Supreme Court were said to have passed bulletins of the game from one to another. One commentator observed that "for the moment the whole country seemed to be in the grip of baseball. Now, however, the great struggle is over and politics can rule the land."[5]

By 1913 the diamond world included over 300 clubs in 43 minor leagues employing 8588 players, or about double the number in 1906. The year 1913 was a prosperous one, but "Organized Baseball" was hovering on the rim of the abyss. The professional game had won new fans all through the depression of 1907, but it could not withstand the onslaught of warfare with the Federal League at home and the German Empire abroad.

When Robert B. Ward, the Brooklyn baking czar, and Charles H. Weeghman, the owner of a lunch room chain in Chicago, teamed up with Phil Ball in the formation of the Federal League and waged a disastrous war with the established leagues, attendance fell off. By investing about $1,000,000 and by signing about 40 Big League players, the Federal League made a fight of it for two years. Although the clubs felt no compunctions in publishing false figures, it was known that the total 1915 attendance fell below that of 1909. Only three of the Federal clubs and none of the International League met expenses.

Open warfare led to a race for high salaries as such stars as Tris Speaker, Christy Mathewson, Walter Johnson, and Ty Cobb received the startling sums of $15,000 or more. Excessive expenses and diminishing crowds embarrassed the warring factions and almost led to the collapse of organized ball. By the end of the 1915 season the number of players in the minors declined drastically, and the Blue Ridge, Texas, and other leagues were forced to finish their seasons early in order to save their vanishing bankrolls.[6] Hopeful addicts predicted a revival with the settlement of the baseball war, but the next season was so unprofitable that the Players Fraternity threatened to strike when minor league clubs failed to pay full salaries as a result of the season's losses. Then came the real war, only eight leagues completed their schedules in 1917, and not until 1919 did the diamond take on a new spirit of confidence and activity. Stop

Progress in the prewar era was demonstrated with equal clarity in the growth of investments and property values. In 1907 Ralph Paine, a sports authority, claimed, "Baseball as a vocation is an astonishing economic study."[7] Few players in 1905 received a salary of $5000, but by 1910 Ty Cobb was paid $9000 and by 1915 he was reputedly receiving $20,000 annually. Baseball's popularity in the prewar years accounted for a general rise in salaries, and during the Federal League affair the stars were able to extort unprecedented sums from rival owners.

Prosperity was best evidenced in the capital outlay of clubs. The National Association of Minor Leagues in 1909 had investments estimated at more than $20,000,000. The phenomenal prosperity of the New York Giants organization, from its purchase by Andrew Freeman "lock, stock and barrel" for $49,000 in 1894 to its acquisition by John T. Brush in 1903 for $125,000, and from that transaction to its sale to C.A. Stoneham in 1919 for slightly less than $1,000,000, was a commentary on the trend of the times. Charles P. Taft, brother of the president, was baseball's largest investor in 1912, and other promoters included the Fleischmans of Cincinnati, Barney Dreyfuss of Pittsburgh, Charles Ebbetts of Brooklyn, Charles Somers of Cleveland, and Benjamin Shibe of Philadelphia.

Valuations on baseball property spurted upward. In 1911 and 1912 baseball parks were built or renovated in Pittsburgh (Forbes Field), Philadelphia (Shibe Park), New York (Polo Grounds), Chicago (Commiskey Park), and Washington. Brush was credited with the growth of the scouting system, used as an attempt to corner outstanding players for the Giants, and the appeal of this colorful team to the New York fan enabled him to reap annual profits of from $100,000 to $300,000. When Jacob Ruppert and T.L. Huston bought the American League franchise of the Highlanders, later to be known as the Yankees, in 1915 for $460,000, when a $60,000 investment in Sportsman's Park, St. Louis, was sold for $425,000 the same year, and when Harry Frazee joined Hugh Ward in the purchase in 1916 of the Boston Red Sox for $675,000—all three of which had been cheap franchises at the turn of the century—the value of baseball property became obvious to other interested investors.

While there was little real wealth among the owners, franchises in the second decade were sometimes estimated at close to a million dollars, a far cry from the purchase of the Detroit club in 1903 for $50,000 by W.H. Yawkey, multimillionaire son of the lumber and ore magnate W.C. Yawkey. Small as it was in comparison to the giants of the business world, baseball was already being described as a vested interest.

And how might we account for this revitalizing of the diamond? The quest for respectability was a potent factor. Reform of the conduct of players and an improvement in the attitude of the fans were evident. Robert Smith, one of the most entertaining baseball historians, maintains that rowdyism continued unabated as the populace gradually acquired a more unabashed attitude toward the rough-and-tumble nature of the game, and he contends that there was a "tacit conspiracy" on the part of sports writers to tone down the sharp controversies and language of the old-time reports.[8]

In part this may have been true; in the main it is misleading. Baseball men, as was true in most sports, aspired toward respectability. Bozeman Bulger in the *Literary Digest* told how Governor John Tener of Pennsylvania was chosen president of the National League for the "prestige and dignity" he would bring to the game. Had not President Taft opened the 1910 season by throwing out the first ball? When the fabulous Boston Braves of 1914 defeated Connie Mack's Athletics in four successive games, Cardinal William H. O'Connell helped welcome home the new champions. On the other hand, the more skeptical were not persuaded by Governor Tener's appointment and many felt, "To make one's living out of play is not the highest kind of work . . . and hireling amusers have never stood high in the esteem of thoughtful people in our age or country." That the diamond had not attracted the best of youth was constantly pointed out in the inimitable stories of Ring Lardner, whose debunking was described by Gilbert Seldes as "the pinprick report that baseball players were ignorant and childish and stupid and not a little mean spirited." The new League president, however, appealed to the public's favor in calling ball players "professional men" and in arguing, "Baseball players are not miners or hod carriers or ditchdiggers."[9]

The struggle was an unending one. In a series of baseball articles for *Collier's* in 1909 Will Irwin observed, "Little by little this strong control of a body of men with ethical responsibility toward a Puritan public has reacted on the profession, raising its standards and its personnel." Connie Mack and Hugh Fullerton, the reigning prince of sports writers, noted the role of the college man in the transformation of the conduct and manners of professionals. Comparing the game of the nineties with that of 1911, Fullerton stressed the role of commercialization and higher salaries in attracting a better class of players. Billy Sunday, the evangelist and former ball player, proclaimed that the level of conduct was "higher and broader than ever." During 1915 there was an insidious growth of baseball "pools," and President Tener waged a virulent attack upon them. A veteran baseball reporter, H.B. Hanna, surveying his twenty-five-year career of writing, maintained in 1916 that the spirit of rowdyism was dying out. Charles A. Comiskey, one of the great pioneers in modern baseball, a few years later recalled, "Formerly sport was not regarded as a proper calling for young men. It is beginning to assume to rightful place in society. . . . Year by year a higher and higher class of players come into the game."[10]

Despite the attitude of newspaper reporters and the crudeness of many players, the more rapid entry of college players into professional ranks, better policing of the ball parks, and a continued battle for the patronage of women made the quest for respectability a real one. More competent umpires were found when the $1500 maximum salary of 1901 was raised to $3000 in 1911. The more respectable tone of baseball—and there was no danger that it would ever be too dignified and high brow— did much to encourage new customers to pass through the turnstiles and become acquainted with the national game.

Baseball's rise to predominance in sport was also the result of a series of very spectacular and colorful personalities. John McGraw became the highest paid figure in the diamond world, and the press made him a mythical titan, feared and respected by all. The son of an Irish father who had been a section hand, McGraw rebelled against the drudgery of farming and railroad work, worked his way up through the minor leagues, played a key role in the development of the Baltimore Orioles, and finally emerged as the most publicized man in the professional game. The public acclaimed his aggressive tactics, and, according to Frank Graham, "In his vigorous leadership—even in his rowdy tactics—he had the support of the New York baseball writers." McGraw's genius in the building of the Giants' system and his bellicose antics before the crowd did much to arouse public interest.

The most spectacular player of the New York Giants was Christy Mathewson, an idol of baseball fans throughout the nation and the most famous pitcher in the game. "Matty" brought a certain tone of respectability into baseball, and, upon his death, a *Commonweal* editorial for October 21, 1925 paid him the tribute:

Christy Mathewson was, of course, a wonderful pitcher—no other man probably has ever brought a President of the United States half way across the continent to a seat at a crucial game; and certainly no other pitcher ever loomed so majestically in young minds, quite overshadowing George Washington and his cherry tree or even that transcendent model of boyhood, Frank Merriwell. . . . Such men have a very real value above and beyond the achievements of brawn and sporting skill. They realize and typify, in a fashion, the ideal of sport—clean power in the hands of a clean and vigorous personality, a courage that has been earned in combat, and a sense of honor which metes out justice to opponents and spurns those victories that have not been earned.

These were the brightest years of such stars of the diamond as "Rube" Marquard, Eddie Collins, Chief Bender, Hans Wagner, Napoleon Lajoie, and the fabulous "Rube" Waddell. Fans compared the $100,000 Athletics' infield with the Cubs' trio of Tinker to Evers to Chance. Detroit's Ty Cobb left a trail of permanent records behind him as he was generally acclaimed the greatest player in the history of organized baseball. His baserunning, hitting, and fielding, along with a fiery temper and ruthless determination made him the terror of the American League.

During the era from 1905 to 1920 a new star arose in Washington and became a household name. Walter Johnson with his paralyzing fast ball was to win more contests than were won by any player in the modern game. Only the great Cy Young of earlier fame excelled "The Big Train" in the record book. The spectacular appearance of a cluster of brilliant performers was instrumental in the rise, once again, of baseball to preeminence in American sport.

The sympathy of the press, the playground movement, the growing interest of women, the popular songs and humor of the day, the increasing use of the automobile, the expansion of school athletic programs, and the rise of many ambitious park programs were instrumental in establishing the supremacy of the diamond. Moving picture houses were showing World Series films by 1916, while electric scoreboards lured throngs of fans who eagerly awaited game scores.

America's entry into war, however, dealt a severe blow and brought hard times to the diamond. Secretary of War Newton D. Baker issued a "Work or Fight" order, but the 1918 season was curtailed, in all probabilities, not from any opposition by President Wilson or a government agency but because of dwindling gate receipts. An intermediary relayed a message to the editor of *Spalding's Baseball Guide* stating that the president "sees no necessity at all for curtailing the baseball schedule." That schedule was concluded on September 1, 1918, and only one minor league club was said to have finished the season. ~~Stop~~

To those during the interval between the armistice and Versailles who worried over postwar baseball General Peyton March, Chief of Staff of the U.S. Army, wrote in a letter to Ben Johnson, "Unless there are some changes in the situation which now seems impossible there is no reason known to us why the great national game should not be continued as usual next year [1919]. The wholesome effect of a clean and honest game like baseball is very marked and its discontinuance would be a great misfortune."[11] Whatever temporary alarm baseball men felt in 1918 dissipated with a national revival of enthusiasm in the next two seasons.

## Formative Years of the Gridiron

Cycling, golf, yachting, track athletics, prize fighting, basketball, bowling, and the turf all prospered in the sporting atmosphere of the nineties, but none of these diversions developed so rapidly as the American game of football. Whereas a few thousand fans attended the contests of the eighties, the next fifteen years were marked by greater public interest, more colorful gridiron spectacles, and a decided increase of support from the press. The Thanksgiving Day game between Yale and Princeton attracted widespread attention as the folk in North Carolina mountain towns were said to have kept watch on the telegraphic bulletin.

From a geographical standpoint the pigskin game had developed into a national sport by the end of the last decade. The South witnessed its greatest contest in 1894 as the University of Virginia clashed with North Carolina before 8000 enthusiasts. Michigan met Vermont, Dartmouth, Harvard, Princeton, and Cornell on an eastern jaunt. Intersectional rivalries were further stimulated after Dartmouth travelled to Chicago for a Thanksgiving Day game with the Chicago Athletic Club. Colorado took up the game, and the Denver AC played Baker University as 8000 fans looked on. By 1895 the Oakland AC was planning to invade the East to challenge the Chicago teams, Michigan and Cornell, an undertaking involving many transportation, financial, and academic difficulties at that time. According to the San Francisco *Bulletin,* "Never before has an eleven crossed the Great Divide from the Golden West." Thanksgiving Day was celebrated in 1895 before an unprecedented throng in Little Rock's history as some 3500 strong watched the greatest of Arkansas cycling meets and a football game against a Memphis team.[12]

The gridiron was becoming national in scope when 5000 games involving 120,000 players were said to have been played on Thanksgiving Day, 1896. The University of Chicago's team became the first western eleven to defeat a strong eastern university as Cornell was crushed on Marshall Field in 1899. On the Pacific coast Stanford and the University of California usually drew an overflowing crowd after the commencement of their rivalry in 1892, and great excitement prevailed when one game ended in a catastrophe. Twenty thousand horrified spectators saw a section of the stand give way and a number of fans killed by falling into vats of boiling water!

During the decade most eastern colleges were represented on the gridiron. West Point first turned to football in 1890, and in another decade the president, his cabinet members, and high-ranking officers were attending the Army-Navy games. Princeton and Yale usually played the Thanksgiving Day game before colorful crowds in New York, but by 1900 the Harvard-Yale game had become the classic of the fall schedule. Copying the New York *Sun* and the New York *World,* large newspapers throughout the country featured the autumn classics. Football was already known for its ferocity, but leaders of society like Walter Phelps Dodge and the Cornelius Vanderbilts put the seal of approval on it by making personal appearances.

The 1890's laid the groundwork for the future organization of the gridiron. It was only in this period that intercollegiate competition reached the smaller colleges, and most of the institutions of the South and West.[13] Although the University of Minnesota's first season of "scientific football" (involving coaches, schedules, and long trips) was that of 1890, colleges all over America were taking to the game. Athletic associations took hold and helped popularize the hiring of professional coaches. When Henry Q. Williams appeared at Minnesota in 1900, he became one of the pioneers of the Big Ten gridiron, sharing that distinction with Fielding Yost and Amos Alonzo Stagg.

Coaching was often done by amateurs in this period. Roscoe Pound, famous dean of Harvard Law School in later years, helped promote football in Nebraska in the nineties, and at the turn of the century Vernon Parrington did some coaching at the University of Oklahoma. Colleges from coast to coast, except for a few ivy-clad eastern institutions, went to little expense in fielding their teams, and Syracuse University's gate receipts were less than $1300 in 1892. Alonzo Stagg, the first physical education director with professorial status in the Midwest, recalled, "The West inevitably was playing inferior football. The game was so new that it had not yet caught the public's interest, the gate receipts were trivial, and there were no prep schools and few high schools playing the game to feed the colleges with trained material."[14] Within a few years, however, Chicago was a valiant foe for any college eleven and the chief rival of Michigan's "champions of the west."

The game sunk its roots more deeply into American life as the high schools eagerly took to the gridiron. Games were played from Boston to Seattle and by the beginning of the new century its growth seemed assured. Somewhat belatedly the St. Louis *Globe-Democrat* of 1901 noted the rise of football on the local scholastic scene: "For the first time since Rugby football became a feature of St. Louis school life, the games were well attended yesterday, something like 12,000 persons witnessing the four played in which local white schools took part. In addition, the game between the colored elevens at Hanlon park in the morning was well patronized. . . . The general play in all the games showed a marked improvement, and the game seems destined to at last secure the same firm hold on public affection here that it has won for itself elsewhere throughout the United States."

That organization lagged in smaller towns is obvious. Although high schools in larger cities were playing the game widely in the nineties, many boys in rural areas never saw a football. Donald Herring, in his *Forty Years of Football,* remembered that "as yet the complete and complex organization of sport that even for youngsters we now take for granted had not reached down to our age and out into the rural districts of Pennsylvania." By the beginning of the new century football was passing from its formative stage and might well make its claim to being a national game.

Educators of the earlier era had raised the cry against intercollegiate athletics because of the distraction to students, the extended trips to other colleges, and the distortion of academic ideals. The years after 1890 gave birth to sporadic campaigns against the brutality of football.[15] Many were the critics of alumni zeal, mounting gate receipts, and uncontrolled enthusiasm for gridiron spectacles. But the future of football itself, expanding from the budding rivalries of the 1880's to the nation-wide game of the new-born century, was seriously called into question.

The New York *Daily Tribune* had excoriated the dangers of football in 1889, maintaining that maimed players should be reported by the press under the "casualties" column. "Flying wedges" and "mass plays" dominated the game, and fisticuffs were a common occurrence; a contest without serious injuries was cause for congratulation. The latter years of the century found some improvement, and the New York *Evening Post* noted that much of the rough play disappeared in the major contests of 1895. A little later one critic in the *Chicago Tribune* remembered that "the contests became so bloody that the pulpit and the press attacked the game until momentum plays were largely abandoned."

Criticism centered not only on injuries but also on the threat of professional athletes. The "tramp player" carried his services from school to school, and to complicate the picture there were those who posed as

amateurs while playing for money under assumed names. Distinguished
professional players caused misunderstandings in the eastern colleges. The
University of Missouri abandoned its recruited team of 1895 and, through
an agreement between the faculties of the Missouri and Kansas state
universities, professionalism was stamped out. In the next year six men
who had sold their services to the Pittsburgh team for a game with Allegheny College were expelled from the Chicago Athletic Club. Proselytizing
was a real threat in 1905. James D. Hogan, Yale's renowned athlete, was
charged with accepting, in good faith, a suite in exclusive Vanderbilt Hall,
meals at the University Club, a ten-day trip to Cuba paid by the athletic
association, the $100 John Bennett scholarship, free tuition, a monopoly
on the sale of score cards, and a position as cigarette agent of the American Tobacco Company.

Despite the reform of playing rules, football remained a game of
rough-and-tumble power plays. Death stalked the gridiron in 1902 and
twelve fatalities aroused an appeal in the *Journal of the American Medical
Association* for abolition of the game. A survey of college presidents and
deans published by Charles Thwing in The *Independent* relieved some of
the hostile pressure through their general agreement that despite its faults
football was beneficial to college life. Walter Camp and the rules committee strove to rectify the evils, but by 1905 the public clamor was extremely raucous. Although football seemed to have more friends than enemies,
a severe crisis loomed on the academic scene. Shailer Mathews, dean of
the Divinity School of Chicago University, flared up in *The Nation:* "Football to day is a social obsession—a boy-killing, education-prostituting,
gladiatorial sport. It teaches virility and courage, but so does war. I do not
know what should take its place, but the new game should not require the
services of a physician, the maintenance of a hospital, and the celebration
of funerals." President Theodore Roosevelt attended the Army-Navy game
of 1905 and pondered the issue during the ensuing weeks. A real crisis was
reached when a Union College player was killed in a game against New
York University. Chancellor Henry MacCracken thrust the issue into the
limelight with an immediate appeal for a convention of college presidents
to outlaw the game. His telegraphic appeal to President Eliot failed to get
the expected response since the latter did not directly control Harvard's
athletic policy. The Harvard president, however, did criticize any reform
by committees, coaches, and umpires who had "ruined the game," and he
charged, "There seems to be a well nigh universal consent that the present
game is intolerable."[16]

A more antagonistic position was taken by President Nicholas Murray
Butler of Columbia University, who, despite the aroused opposition of the
student body, maintained that the pulpit, the press, and the platform, as

well as the parents of the students had called for the universities to curb misguided athletic tendencies. Columbia, Northwestern, Cumberland University, Union College, and Wisconsin were but a few of the colleges which suspended or considered dropping the sport. An adverse faculty vote at the latter institution was defeated only through the efforts of President Charles Van Hise and Professor Edward Birge, with the newly gained support of Frederick Jackson Turner.[17] Reform was essential. On this point all agreed, friend and foe alike. Walter Camp urged the introduction of a "ten yards in three downs" rule to open up the game. The Big Nine abolished football "as it is," and the conference planned for shorter schedules, lower gate fees, and the elimination of preliminary training periods. Pacific Coast schools were set on reform regardless of the action of eastern authorities.

But the friends of football were not caught sleeping. The Chicago faculty opposed abolition, while Presidents Arthur Hadley of Yale, Joseph Swain of Swarthmore, George Harris of Amherst, and Cyrus Northrop of Minnesota wrote in defense of a game too good to be abolished. In general, the cry was not against the dangers but the foulness and brutality of most contests. Foremost of the defenders of the sport, though generally silent on the subject, was the sportsminded president in the White House. A conference in New York of thirteen colleges passed a resolution against abolition and for reform, a new Intercollegiate Athletic Association was formed, the forward pass opened up the game, and the gridiron was given another lease on life.

In 1906 an historian of American education wrote that "the game has been increasing in popularity at the colleges and also in the attention which it commands from the general community. It has become the great American academic game."[18] A stimulus came in the form of intersectional contests, and when the Carlisle Indians defeated the University of Minnesota in 1906 it was the first East-West contest held in Minneapolis. By the outbreak of war in Europe southern colleges were occasionally scheduling northern opponents. Although Stanford and California, following the leadership of presidents David Starr Jordan and Benjamin Ide Wheeler, abandoned the American for the English game in 1906, they came back into the fold a decade later.

Football was again attacked in 1909 as a direct result of the heavy casualties caused by a revival of mass play and the decline of the forward pass. In the *American Review of Reviews for December,* 1909, the charge was made, "It is fast growing to be the opinion of thoughtful people outside of academic circles that the mania for sports and contests of physical prowess in our colleges and schools has gone so far that it constitutes an evil of great magnitude."[35] Fear of abolition by numerous faculties and of legal restriction by some of the states drew forth further reforms on the part of the Intercollegiate Athletic Association. The Washington, D.C., Board of Education discontinued public school contests, the Board of Superintendents recommended abolition of the game in the public schools of the state of New York, while Boston and New Haven took similar action.

Football had endeared itself to too many hearts to be abandoned so easily. The press was more friendly, and many voices were raised in defense of the game. Presidents W.H.C. Faunce of Brown, James H. Baker of Colorado, S.E. Mezes of Texas, Frank Strong of Kansas, George E. Mac-Lean of Iowa, Harry P. Judson of Chicago, W.O. Thompson of Ohio State, Woodrow Wilson of Princeton, and Jacob G. Sherman of Cornell were for reform but definitely opposed to abolition. Few gave serious attention to the Stanford president's cry that football is "a sport that destroys the best there is in American youth."

This third attack within seven years demonstrated ever more convincingly the deeply rooted nature of sports in the American college. There was little alarm over the consistent opposition of men like David Starr Jordan and Simon Newcomb, or over the skeptical attitudes of G. Stanley Hall and A. Lawrence Lowell. The new president of Harvard, in his inaugural address of 1909, warned that "college life has shown a marked tendency to disintegrate, both intellectually and socially. To that disintegration the overshadowing interest in athletic games appears to be partly due." But he recognized that this exaggerated prominence of sport was "due rather to the fact that such contests offer to students the one common interest, the only striking occasion for a display of college solidarity."[19] Perhaps the most encouraging words were voiced in *Collier's* by the president of Notre Dame, Father John Cavanaugh, who scoffed, "I would rather see our youth playing football with the danger of a broken collarbone occasionally than to see them dedicated to croquet."

In the ensuing seasons, although injury lists increased as many schools took up the game, the number of fatalities declined. More frequent use of the forward pass, particularly after the startling display by Mike Dorais and Knute Rockne in Notre Dame's victory over West Point in 1913, added the new elements of skill and unpredictability to the spectacle. Greater newspaper coverage, a wider appeal of outdoor games, and a general acceptance of the value of contact sports all contributed greatly to the rise of football during the second decade. Parke Davis, football historian and statistician, reported that in 1914 there were 450 colleges, 6000 secondary schools, and some 15,000 other teams playing football, with an overall total of 152,000 active players. An avalanche of publicity fell upon such great players of the first two decades as Walter Eckersall of Chicago, Jim Thorpe of Carlisle, Eddie Mahan of Harvard, Elmer Oliphant of the Army,

Paul Robeson of Rutgers, and George Gipp of Notre Dame, while school-boys in every town or city played their hearts out on sand-lots in imitation of their gridiron heroes.

The financial side of collegiate football and other athletic games was demonstrated in the building of new stadiums and in the rapid rise of gate receipts. Syracuse was fortunate in the philanthropy of John D. Archbold, and, on the suggestion of Chancellor James R. Day, built one of the finest stadiums in America. Edgar Palmer gave a magnificent stadium to Prince-ton, and the Yale Bowl, subscribed by graduates of the university, sup-planted Harvard's as the finest football arena in America. Within a decade the gridiron had emerged as a major factor in college life, and it was esti-mated in 1914 that 150 reported colleges spent more than $2,000,000 annually on athletics. Varsity teams at the various universities were listed as expending the following amounts, most of which went to football.[20]

| | | | |
|---|---|---|---|
| Harvard | $160,000 | Minnesota | $30,000 |
| Cornell | 75,000 | Pennsylvania | 24,000 |
| Wisconsin | 45,000 | Pittsburgh | 20,000 |
| Brown | 40,000 | Vanderbilt | 20,000 |
| Leland Stanford | 30,000 | Columbia | 15,000 |
| California | 35,000 | | |

Alumni coming out of American colleges organized as pressure groups for the purpose of recruiting strong teams. Intercollegiate football was featured in the press, and the names of such famous coaches as Amos Alonzo Stagg, Glenn (Pop) Warner, Percy Naughton, and Fielding (Hurry Up) Yost were known to all sporting people. Walter Camp's "All-America" selections attracted national attention to the great players of the day. Football suffered with the entry of America into World War I, many col-leges suspending activity for the duration. It was played widely in army camps, however, and men returned from the service interested in following up the game. General Leonard Wood, a former player on the Pacific Coast, exemplified this spirit in stating, "I thoroughly believe in the sport because the men who played it made good in the war."[21] It would not be long before the gridiron would once again emerge, with mounting intensi-ty, as the most popular sport on the intercollegiate scene, as well as in most public, private, and parochial schools.

## Origins of Basketball

Indoor sport became more popular in the late years of the century with the construction of gymnasiums for schools, colleges, YMCA's, clubs, and armories. Gymnastic exercises proved to be less appealing to physical education classes than group play in organized games. James Naismith originated a game for the young men of Springfield College and the YMCA in 1892 at the instigation of Dr. Luther Gulick, who had expressed the need of a new sport for physical education students. Developed as an indoor recreation for the winter months when sportsmen were confined to the gymnasium, its growth was less spectacular than that of golf or auto racing, in part because of limited playing facilities and an apathetic press. Within a decade, however, the new court game had won a small army of advocates.

Played with frequently altered rules and in small gymnasiums, converted basements, or on open air courts, the game struggled through an experimental stage. Until 1915, and even after that date in some areas, there were two sets of rules, those of the colleges and those of the AAU. Rebounds were permitted off the walls in the early years, and rough play was the norm. The primitive style of these years was demonstrated in a final score of 8-7 as Yale defeated the Central YMCA of Brooklyn before an unusual crowd of 1200 spectators. According to a report in the New York *Times* for January 26, 1896, "One of the rules of basketball playing says that if the spectators hoot or hiss or annoy the players by making a noise, the umpire may stop the game and declare the visitors the victors."

Although it received slight publicity, basketball caught on with those who sought wintertime exercise. Dr. Naismith claimed: "Basketball was accepted by the high schools before the colleges took it up as an organized sport. I believe that the younger boys who played in the YMCA gymnasiums took the game with them into the high schools. It was only after these boys graduated from high school and entered college that basketball really began to take hold in that institution." [22] Geneva and Iowa seem to have been the first men's colleges to play the game, while Stanford, Yale, Pennsylvania, Wesleyan, Trinity, Nebraska, and Kansas were early converts. Girls at Smith, Vassar, Wellesley, Bryn Mawr, and Newcomb soon took to the court. Miss Clara Baer of Newcomb eliminated the most strenuous characteristics, developing a nine court game, captain ball, and the three court division. Mrs. H.L. Carver introduced the game to Texas in 1893. Denver high schools formed the first known league in 1896 and by 1897 basketball was played at fifty-seven athletic clubs. Yale travelled to Chicago in 1899, eastern colleges formed an Intercollegiate League and the game was exhibited at the Buffalo Exposition in 1901; by the early 1900's it was played on campuses everywhere and caught the interest of churches, armories, settlement houses, and industrial organizations.

The YMCA, the army, and the navy carried the court game abroad. American troops introduced it in the Phillipines after the Spanish-American War; it was played among the builders of the Panama Canal; women participated in Japan by 1900; Nome, Alaska had adopted the game by 1906; and it gained a foothold in the West Indies as it became a national sport in Puerto Rico. Missionaries also carried the game to many lands, Robert Gailey taking it to China in 1898 and Drs. Charles Siler and Max Exner helping to spread it over the next decade. A missionary taught the game in Brazil, while Indians, Burmese, and Ceylonese all were playing on the court by 1920.[23] Yet, Dr. Naismith's sister never forgave him for leaving the ministry, and she never went to see a game!

James E. Sullivan, noted president of the Amateur Athletic Union, sagaciously predicted in 1901 that basketball was "apparently America's coming indoor game."[24] Convinced of this, the AAU successfully extended its control over amateur ranks even in the Midwest by disqualifying offending teams "for life." Kansas and Indiana became two of the hotbeds of basketball enthusiasm, but it was only in the era of World War I that it really began to win widespread public attention.

## Military and Naval Activities

National Guard regiments had been in the forefront of the athletic movement in the 1880's. By the early 1890's the armory was one of the most important centers of sporting activity, and in 1897 a Military Athletic League was organized. In the Navy the impulse also caught on. The cruiser *Detroit's* baseball team was crowned "Champions of Uncle Sam's Navy" in 1897, and two years later every ship in the North Atlantic Squadron had a nine.[25] The battleship *Iowa* scuttled the cruiser *Philadelphia* for the championship of the Pacific Coast Squadron in 1900. Secretary of the Navy Paul Morton informed A.G. Spalding in 1905, "The officers who have the responsibility of the administration of the enlisted personnel of the Navy recognize Base Ball as one of the very best influences in connection with the discipline of the ship." Prizes were awarded to rowing crews as well as baseball, football, and fencing teams. Championship boxing matches became traditional, and all sailors were expected to learn the art of self-defense.

The navy increasingly recognized the attraction felt for sports among the crews and the inducement it created for men to enlist. It was thought to be a means of keeping the crews content. Rear Admiral Robley D. Evans, commanding the North Atlantic Fleet and "booming athletics in the navy," in the *Illustrated Sporting News* of 1905 commended athletic interest from the point of view of morale and alertness: "That the morale of athletics is very high is beyond cavil; and I have always contended for that which will raise the morale of the service. . . . That the athlete has muscles, nerves, eyes and brain which unconsciously work in unison, is axiomatic; it is just such qualities as these the officers and men of the United States Navy must possess if we are to continue to uphold its proud traditions." Ex-president Theodore Roosevelt asserted, "It is an admirable thing to have boxing on board our warships."

Athletics began to win the sympathy of high-ranking officers in the army. Both Theodore Roosevelt and the War Department favored exercise and baseball as a part of military training, even on Sunday and despite Women's Christian Temperance Union objections. Garrisons were encouraged to hold games. Track and field athletics stirred up keen rivalries in such large posts as Leavenworth (Kansas), and Sam Houston (Texas), where infantry contingents were centered. It was claimed "the meets embrace an elaborate programme, and are attended by every one from the department commander to the sergeant-major," while the military carried sport to the Philippines, Puerto Rico, the Canal Zone, and Cuba.[26] Sports were fostered in the armed services more than in any earlier era, and in World War I they developed into an integral part of military and naval routine.

## Diverse Trends on the National Scene

Bowling became something of a winter season fad by 1892. *Harper's Weekly* noted that "matches are arranged, prizes contended for, and the sport generally conduces to a more perfect *entente cordiale* between the sexes." The American Bowling Congress had taken root in 1895, and by 1900 there were more than one hundred bowling clubs engaged in tournaments in New York City, where there were commercial leagues among bank, wholesale drug, fire insurance, and life insurance clerks.

The little world of polo expanded from eight clubs in 1890 to thirty-three in 1904. German-Americans sponsored an annual National Schuetzen Fest after 1895. Professional oarsmen were accused of chicanery, and the public increasingly turned to other commercialized sports. Amateur rowing remained popular, and the Schuylkill Navy maintained at least a dozen boat houses with an average value of $10,000.

In the early years of the new century organizations like the American Rowing Association, the National Ski Association, the Intercollegiate Soccer Football Association, and the National Collegiate Athletic Association took hold. Wrestling promoters at the old Madison Square Garden drew large crowds to see Hali Adlai ("the Sultan's lion"), Tom Jenkins the American champion, and other titans of the mat. And the Far West was already outdistancing other sections in the training of swimming champions. Handball caught on with the athletic clubs and was played widely in California. Winter sports and carnivals began to attract attention. Ice hockey was played at New York and Pittsburgh athletic clubs as well as in the eastern universities and schools. Volleyball, increasingly popular in the YMCA and the grammar schools, won a legion of fans among soldiers in the army camps of World War I. Six-day bicycle racing was promoted in the nineties in the hippodromes of many cities. All these were swirling currents in a great sporting flood.

On the intercollegiate scene where football emerged as the dominant sport some institutions experimented with handball, fencing, ice hockey, and other athletic activities. Rowing in eastern colleges retained its popularity, and as many as thirty crews trained at both Harvard and Yale for their annual race. When President William Rainey Harper of the University of Chicago made a plea for the endowment of athletics and physical education departments, the triumph of college sport seemed complete.[27]

In many ways the most colorful of all sports was that western institution, the rodeo, which became an organized activity of its own peculiar brand. An outgrowth of friendly competition on the range where rival ranchers would put up stakes on their best men, the rodeo was promoted by traveling organizers who enticed cowboys from distant ranches. Texas cowboys in Cheyenne in 1872 engaged in a steer riding exhibition, and a bronco busting demonstration was given some months later at this crossroads of the cattle drives. A "Cowboy Tournament" was held in Denver in 1890, but that city's "first well-advertised, well-organized cowboy contest" was held in 1896 and Cheyenne's in 1897.[28] The rodeo eventually became an annual feature in the life of the cowboy, a means of showing to all the world the prowess he had attained in mastering the West.

There were years when the AAU, the YMCA, the colleges, and other athletic agencies were engaged in a constant struggle for power. Caspar Whitney foresaw a dreary future for the Amateur Athletic Union because of its encroachments on other organizations. As sports editor of *Harper's Weekly* he contended, "The AAU has humbly accepted so many undignified affronts—small wonder its branches disregard their affiliations—small wonder it has grown to be considered as an organization with multitudinous rules and by-laws, and no-power, or still worse, no wish, to enforce them. . . . If the cause of amateur sport had been nearer its heart than the feverish wish to add clubs to its roll, it would today be strong and respected."

Despite such a dire commentary it was called "the strongest and most influential organization of amateur sportsmen in the world." An 1898 tabulation listed an active membership of 45,000 in the Western, Pacific Northwest, Southern, Pacific, Central, Atlantic, New England, and Metropolitan associations, and allied membership of more than a quarter of a

million in the League of American Wheelmen, the YMCA, the North
American Gymnastic Union, the ICAA, the Western Intercollegiate AA,
and the Canadian AAA. The metropolitan area of New York was the core
and the eastern states with their greater population were most strongly
represented, although the Far West had a surprisingly large contingent of
members.

The Penn Relays became the greatest of track and field carnivals
after 1893, but spectator appeal was still lacking and only with the growth
of the Olympic Games would it be possible for the stellar performers of
the cinder path to acquire international reputations. The West, however,
was successfully challenging the East by 1905. Colleges east of the
Mississippi swarmed to the Penn Relays, while track and field sports
dominated the sports activities of the athletic clubs. Alvin Kraenzlein,
Arthur Duffey, John Hayes, Jim Thorpe, and James (Ted) Meredith established world records and won international titles in these prewar years.
Western high schools were already imitating the eastern emphasis on
schoolboy athletics, city authorities featured running and jumping contests in annual grade school championships, and track and field was recognized as one of the three major sports in which a schoolboy might win his
varsity letter.

Many colleges and universities had encouraged interclass games prior
to 1910 and had instituted intramural systems, but it is generally recognized that the modern intramural program dated from about that time.
W.P. Eaton canvassed a number of prominent colleges in 1910 and discovered that general participation of students in athletics reached a level
of about 80% at Amherst and Princeton, 75% at Harvard, 67% at Yale,
49% at the University of Virginia, 40% at Vanderbilt and Washington
University, St. Louis, and between 35% and 40% at Chicago and the
University of Missouri, whereas only some 10% to 12% were active at the
University of California. Another study of this period of 80,000 male
college students and 26,000 females revealed that 32% males and 18%
females participated in some form of athletics. A more comprehensive
survey in 1913 revealed that among 150 institutions and 111,600 men,
over 18,000 (10.6%) participated in varsity games and over 45,000
(40.3%) in nonvarsity contests, totaling just about half the students. Most
revealing was the discovery that of 142 reporting colleges, 37% took no
interest in sports other than on the intercollegiate level. As yet in its formative period, the intramural movement spread out its arms in this decade,
with Cornell reporting 4000 of 4600 male students (87%) engaged in some
form of athletics in the year 1914-1915.[29]

In the years embracing World War I the intramural movement received
a decided impetus from the emphasis on physical fitness. The Secretary of

War urged, "The gospel of college athletics should be athletics for all," and the NCAA convention in Washington agreed to stress intramural sports. Supervised sports were first required of students in women's colleges largely between 1906, when Wellesley introduced the idea, and 1918.[30] Something of the trend is indicated in the increase of colleges with gymnasiums from 114 in 1909 to 209 in 1920. One may justly observe that, although confined to a select group of colleges in the years before 1910, the intramural program planted its roots and prospered in the ensuing decade, especially with the advent of war.

## World War I and the Athletic Crusade

The rising standard of living, the growth of the city, and the extension of leisure time were paramount among the social forces which promoted the athletic impulse. But historical movements need not always follow logical rules of causation, and some great detonating force may be imperative to the development of a movement which otherwise might lay dormant. Such a detonator in the history of American sport was the participation of American military and naval forces in World War I. The postwar generation came to rely almost universally on the explanation that war had done more than anything else to indoctrinate our people with the gospel of sport. If analysts of postwar sport exceeded the mark, they should not be charged with grievous error since those critical years cleared the path and set the stage for the greatest sporting epoch in modern history.

When the young men of America swarmed into army camps from New York to San Francisco they were given rigorous physical training as preparation for combat. Selected athletes were organized into regimental and divisional teams, and many of the stellar performers of the decade added to their sporting fame as participants in military and naval contests. Great masses of troops played at volleyball, football, baseball, and boxing, many of them for the first time in their lives. Each naval district had its athletic director, and Walter Camp acted as General Commissioner of Athletics for the United States Navy. Men were introduced to many indoor sports which were little known to those from rural areas. Wrestling, hockey, basketball, and swimming attracted thousands to the large auditoriums of naval stations. As Lawrence Perry's *Our Navy in the War* mentioned, "Boxing tournaments, station championships, and army-navy championship bouts were given with crowded houses everywhere." Swimming tournaments stemmed out of the great need for instruction of seamen, while baseball, football, relay races, and track athletics were also promoted.

Newspapers gave extensive publicity to post and camp competitions. Clark Griffith originated a "Bat and Ball" fund, and such newspapers as the Pittsburgh *Post* collected old footballs, bats, and odd types of athletic equipment for the army camps. Americans might well have marveled at the incongruity of sporting spectacles at naval posts and military camps while the nation was struggling to organize an expeditionary force to whip the Hun. Some may have wondered as they read of campaigns for athletic funds during the battle of Verdun and the outbreak of the Russian Revolution. Many colleges, particularly in the East, abandoned intercollegiate schedules, and the traditional golf, tennis, and yachting tourneys were dropped as the nation came to grips with the realities of war. Thousands turned out to the race track, however. Professional baseball continued in halting fashion, schools maintained their interscholastic games, many colleges played at least skeleton schedules, and men in the armed services found athletic games their greatest diversion.

The War Department responded to a popular demand in the army for athletic equipment. One allotment included 17,500 sets of boxing gloves, 7000 baseball mitts, 21,100 baseballs, 3000 footballs, 7000 soccer balls, 3500 volleyballs, and 1750 medicine balls. Later shipments exceeded these figures especially in baseball equipment. The army drew heavily on the personnel and resources of the YMCA, and 300 athletic directors took charge of the sports program operating 836 athletic fields. The YMCA sent scores of these directors overseas and spent between one and two million dollars on athletic equipment. The Knights of Columbus and the Jewish Welfare Board also contributed vigorously and generously in the promotion of recreational programs.

Commencement of the occupation program and the delay in shipping two million men home gave an unprecedented opportunity to athletic directors. Under the directorship of Elwood S. Brown, the YMCA carried the burden of athletic activities in France until General Order 241 made athletics and mass games a matter of military schedule. In June, 1919, General John J. Pershing received Pershing Stadium in Paris from the "Y" and then presented it to the French people. This stadium was meant as a token gift in the hope "that the cherished bonds of friendship between France and America forged anew on the common field of battle may be tempered and made enduring on the friendly field of sport."[31] Opening an athletic carnival between the allied armies, General Pershing declared, "Conscious of the service which athletes rendered and of the influence athletic training had in making victory possible, it seems a fitting conclusion that our labors in a common cause should be celebrated by a great tournament in which athletes of the allied nations will join in friendly contest."

Throughout the months of demobilization the athletic program continued, the American Red Cross sponsored boxing tourneys at Paris, and a young marine by the name of Gene Tunney won an AEF championship. American occupation troops engaged in games at Cologne and other cities of the Rhineland. It was a program for mass organized sport which had never been presented to any army in our history.

On the domestic scene Dr. Joseph E. Raycroft served as Chairman of the Athletic Division, War Department Commission on Training Camp Activities, perhaps the largest athletic program in the modern era prior to 1920. Through this system of training it was said that "4,000,000 men are marching back to the ranks of citizens with a new idea of the place recreational athletics has in the life of a nation." Dr. Raycroft, according to the New York *Times,* might be called "the boxing Moses of the United States Army" since he was largely responsible for winning the support of the athletic directors. They helped win over many of the soldiers who were reluctant at first to engage in boxing because of the unsavory reputation of the ring.[32]

The war caused some speculation about the proper place of sports in our national life. Propaganda against the Hun and the Bolshevik had left its mark, even on the American intellectual. Professor William Lyon Phelps made the fleeting judgment: "The average Anglo-Saxon has sporting blood. . . . If they had only developed the love of sport forty years ago, the German behaviour in the present war might possibly have been somewhat less detestable. I am sure that if the Russians were devoted to baseball, football, tennis, track athletics, some barriers of misunderstanding between Slav and Saxon might fall."[33] Many Americans were of the same conviction.

Those who worried about the postwar era speculated on what boxing in the army had done to American men and how the pugilistic underworld might be attacked, while those concerned with the advance of amateurism agreed with Dean LeBaron Briggs of Harvard, who warned in *The Nation* for August 24, 1918: "Reforming athletics is about as hard as reforming society. A convulsion has come. . . . Intercollegiate athletics are brought face to face with the problem that confronts America, and by the same tremendous force, the war for the mastery or the liberation of the world. Like America, they will stand or fall according as they choose between luxury and simplicity, trickery and integrity, the senses and the spirit."[34] Most Americans were too tense over the swaying tide of combat as Hindenburg's forces made their last drive in the spring of 1918 and then they were too elated over the armistice to do much worrying about the future.[35] Sport could take care of itself. When the boom in sports followed the war there was cause to wonder whether or not the prewar struggle for reform had fallen into silent obscurity. The gap of the war era may partially explain the uncontrolled and misdirected course of sporting enthusiasm in the 1920's.

What had the war done for sport? It had minimized the activities of most all civilian groups, to be sure, but it returned millions of men so tired of war and so recently trained in athletic games as to comprise a tremendous core from which the gospel of sport might spread. Industrial athletics were promoted as an outlet for the workers, and volleyball became extremely popular. Newspapers acquired new readers of the sports page, gymnasiums and athletic clubs found many new converts, and those foremost in the commercialization of sports acquired a reservoir of enthusiastic spectators.

On June 28, 1919, the New York *Times* ran an editorial, "The Revival of Sport," in which the spirit of the day was enunciated: "The nation, released from years of gloom and supression, is expressing the reaction by plunging into sport." On the last day of the year the paper printed Secretary Baker's speech before the NCAA deploring the rejection of thirty-five percent of all draftees as physically unfit and paying tribute to athletics: "Our soldiers played ball from Paris to the Rhine," he said, "We carried over there with us American recreational ideals and standards. Men in the ranks learned to play games they had never indulged in at home. The mountain boy saw a tennis net for the first time. It was the wholesome and attractive substitutes that kept the young men away from the immoral side of life during their service in the army."[36] All the momentum of the athletic impulse was released on a generation tired of war.

# Chapter 6

# Of Gentlemen
# and Pugs

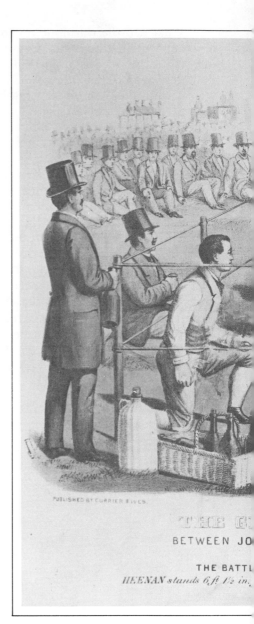

PUBLISHED BY CURRIER & IVES.

THE G[...]

BETWEEN JO[...]

THE BATTL[...]

*HEENAN stands 6 ft 1½ in.*

152 NASSAU ST NEW YORK.

T FIGHT FOR THE CHAMPIONSHIP.

EENAN "THE BENICIA BOY," & TOM SAYERS "CHAMPION OF ENGLAND",

ch took place April 17th 1860, at Farnborough, England.

O 2 HOURS 20 MINUTES 42 ROUNDS, WHEN THE MOB RUSHED IN & ENDED THE FIGHT.

eight 190 lbs. Born May 2nd 1835.    SAYERS stands 5 f. 8 in. fighting wt 150 lbs. Born 1826.

The triumph of American capitalism in the late nineteenth century was achieved through ingenuity, imagination, and courage as well as luck, chicanery, and exploitation. A new social aristocracy comprising men who amassed fortunes in railroads, coal, iron, lumbering, oil, manufacturing, and finance rose to prominence on the national scene. Millionaires of humble origin now sought to mix with longstanding devotees of the arts. They and their families attended the theater and opera, built country homes, visited the more select vacation centers, paid obeisance to the tomes on etiquette, joined social clubs, patronized symphony orchestras, and participated in all the diversions of the privileged class. Many were strongly imitative of the English, bitten by the bug of "conspicuous leisure." Thorstein Veblen at the end of the nineteenth century stressed the role of sport in an economic society where "competition is in large part a process of self-assertion on the basis of these traits of predatory human nature," and, in an era when Social Darwinists were emphasizing the survival of the fittest, competitive sport found a receptive audience in the leisure class.

Veblen noticed "the facility with which any new accessions to the leisure class take to sports, and hence the rapid growth of sports and of the sporting sentiment in any industrial community where wealth has accumulated sufficiently to exempt a considerable part of the population from work."[1] It was only natural that devotees of the turf and the hunt, yachting, cycling, golf, and tennis organized in social and sporting clubs, while thousands of others with free time took to the woods with angling rod or hunting rifle.

While middle class men and women (including farmers, small businessmen, and all kinds of employees exclusive of the sparse ranks of organized labor) were slow to adopt the recreations of high society, there were many of the so-called dangerous elements who frequented the saloon, poolroom, and gambling house or the track, arena, and ball park, where they found release from a life of frustration in the metropolis. Gamblers, saloon keepers, athletic bums, and all the parasites of the sporting world did much to perpetuate public suspicion and hostility, but they were also responsible for satisfying the betting propensities of an urban populace. There were, of course, the mounting hordes of new enthusiasts attracted by the press, but one cannot avoid the impression that it was the two polar extremities of society which were the first to rally behind sport and were responsible for the later enthusiasm of white collar employees, industrial workers, and all the other components of American middle class society.

## Commercialization of the Turf

A number of bankruptcies occurred on the turf during the Civil War, but the return of peace and prosperity instilled new blood in racing. Fortunes made during years of conflict and in the prosperous period following the war were diverted to the turf as Leonard W. Jerome, August Belmont, G.L. Lorillard, William R. Travers, E.J. Baldwin, Leland Stanford, and James R. Keene poured their fortunes into breeding and racing. John Morrissey, ex-pugilist, gambler, and politician, opened a track at Saratoga in 1864 and encouraged its patronage with the Travers Stakes. Saratoga meetings proved a success socially and financially from the start. With the return of peace interest revived around metropolitan New York. Leonard Jerome and the newly-formed American Jockey Club, seeking to rid the turf of less desirable elements, inaugurated a new era at Jerome Park in 1866. The influence of this track in the attraction of a distinguished clientele, in the promotion of interest among the fashionable set, and in the organization of new jockey clubs penetrated every level of racing and went far to persuade the public of the respectability of the turf.

Long Branch and Pimlico stirred racing circles with their inaugural programs of 1870. During the seventies the Pacific Jockey Club held spectacular races at Ocean View Park, San Francisco; the Fair Grounds at New Orleans opened in 1873; Pimlico's Preakness Stakes were inaugurated the same year and Belmont's Withers Stakes the next. In 1875 the Kentucky Derby and Kentucky Oaks were run for the first time at Churchill Downs. In addition to the backers of eastern tracks, men of high reputation in other areas assumed responsible positions in the promotion of the turf. General Phil Sheridan became the first president of the exclusive Washington Park Jockey Club, Chicago, in 1884; while Col. H.A. Montgomery, who had been instrumental in making Memphis a leading cotton market of the South, had formed the New Memphis Jockey Club two years earlier.

So violent a racing fever hit Baltimore in 1877 that the Senate adjourned, ostensibly to permit the committees to study impending business, and politicians evacuated Washington on the day of the great race of Parole, Ten Broeck, and Tom Ochiltree.[2] During the years of Reconstruction the Association Course at Lexington held meetings, as did the Woodlawn Course at Louisville, the Blood-horse Association at Nashville, the Chickasaw Jockey Club at Memphis, the Metairie Course at New Orleans, and the Magnolia Course at Mobile. Civil War raids on southern plantations by both Confederate and Union cavalry had depleted many areas of their best thoroughbreds, but "the racing tastes of Southerners were not so high but that they could be reasonably satisfied by nags that were left." New Orleans fans nostalgically recalled "the palmiest days of the old Metairie" and continued to hope for the return of prosperity to the southern turf. And in southwestern cities like San Antonio and Dallas racing was winning a following.[3]

Thoroughbreds of nationwide fame in these decades included Harry Bassett, Ten Broeck, Iroquois, Hindoo, Hanover (founder of a popular blood line), and Salvator, who was ridden to victory over Tenny by the celebrated black jockey, Isaac Murphy, in a famous match race in 1890. By the late 1880's breeding had become a business of large proportions; while Kentucky remained the center of breeding, extensive farms were founded in New Jersey and California, Leland Stanford's Palo Alto stables shipping more than a hundred horses valued at about $200,000 to New York in 1890. The Sheepshead Bay course opened on Long Island in 1880, and the Coney Island Jockey Club held its first meeting there.

In 1882 the St. Louis Derby was inaugurated, while Latonia, Kentucky, rose to challenge Louisville and Lexington in 1883. Memphis introduced the Tennessee Derby the following year, and Chicago's Washington Park opened with the renowned American Derby. Racing proved so popular in the New York area that the Brooklyn Jockey Club was organized and the first running of the famous Brooklyn Handicap was held in 1887. By the nineties New York City had emerged as the hub of thoroughbred racing, and the halcyon days of ante-bellum Charleston and New Orleans remained little more than romantic memories.

Interest in the post-bellum track was increasingly diverted to the trotter and the pacer. Josh Billings, the noted humorist, pictured the fair of the late 1860's and wrote, "thar was two yoke ov oxens on the ground, beside several yokes ov sheep and a pile ov carcort, and some worsted work, but they didn't seem to attrakt enny simpathy. The people hanker fur pure agrikultural hoss trots." Dexter succeeded Flora Temple as the national favorite, in the seventies Goldsmith Maid established an unchallenged ascendancy, and during the eighties Maud S. reigned as queen of the trotters. When the Maid appeared at St. Joseph, Missouri, in 1871 the town went wild and visitors were lured by huge posters throughout the countryside: "Everybody talked horse, eat [sic] horse, drank horse, slept horse, dreamed horse. Wherever you went in private house, hotel, saloon, or workshop, horse racing was the chief topic of discussion."[4]

Such drivers and trainers as Hiram Woodruff, Budd Doble, Ed Geers, and John Splan added much to the color of harness racing as crowds gathered to watch favorite speedsters spin over the turf. Farmers in every section of the United States turned to training promising nags, and the agricultural fair, often sponsored by the Grange, served as the backbone of harness racing. By 1868 there were 1367 state, county, and district fairs, at most of which the drivers competed for prizes, while the trend in purse money was shown in the increase at the Sacramento Fair from $935 in 1867 to $3150 in 1872.

Not until 1870 was the trotting course placed on an organized basis with the formation of the National Association for the Promotion of the

Interests of the American Trotting Turf. By that time fairs were reviving in the desolated South, trotting enthusiasm was sweeping throughout the West, annual races were a fixture at most fairs, and John H. Wallace was preparing to issue his authoritative *Trotting Register.* Organization was desperately needed "to check the growing flood of corruption which threatened to engulf the trotting turf." Giving unstinted support to the National Association in 1871, the *Spirit of the Times* agreed that "it should embrace *all* the places at which the public may expect trotting to be conducted upon fair, honest, manly principles."[5]

Opening of the Buffalo Driving Park, inspired by Cicero J. Hamlin, set the standard for trotting courses throughout the country. Fairs began to stagger their dates and the Grand Circuit, then known as the Quadrilateral, commenced operations in 1873. Prosperity was fabulous. Purses at the Cleveland and Rochester meetings in 1866 totaled $15,650, but by 1875 the Grand Circuit's purses almost reached the quarter-million-dollar mark. The Panic of 1873 then began to take effect, purses fell off, and harness racing entered a period of hard times, only to revive in the next decade. In western New York fairs regularly featured races, while few states could challenge the enthusiasm for trotting in Wisconsin. It was stated that millions of dollars were invested in the trotting horse industry, that Mr. J. Case of Racine had put almost one-half million dollars in breeding, and, by 1884, that N.W. Kittson of St. Paul had "more money invested in trotters, pacers, and thoroughbreds than any other man in the world, his total expenditures in the purchase of horses and farms . . . having been in the vicinity of $2,000,000."

So great was the widespread interest that "these millionaire horsemen with their mammoth establishments and invested thousands, represent but a small fraction of the money employed in this special industry. The average farmers are, after all, the real trotting horse breeders of Wisconsin, and their name is legion."[6] From Maine to California "speed programmes" were included in annual fairs, and in 1886 there were about eight hundred tracks on which harness racing was held. From the sale of Dexter in the late sixties for a record $33,000 to the sale of Axtell in 1889 for $105,000, the popularity and the value of the trotter increased steadily.

Foreign visitors frequently remarked on the American preoccupation with the trotter. Chicago was singled out as being "noted for its fast trotting horses, the wide, level, straight and withal softly paved streets, being eminently suitable for the rapid movements of the crowds of spidery vehicles." Captain W.E. Price exclaimed at the record times and novel gigs: "The Americans get immensely excited over these races, and all attempts of the police to restrain them are ineffectual." Another tourist observed, "Trotting is as national on the American side of the Atlantic as preaching."[7]

When Benjamin Harrison entered office in 1889, metropolitan racing had definitely come of age. Garden City track in Chicago had the greatest meeting in the history of the West, while Washington Park offered $25,000, the Kansas City Jockey Club $15,000, and the New Jersey Trotting Circuit $32,700 in prizes. In 1891 the Belmont stables brought a record two-thirds of a million dollars. By 1894, however, hard times had set in. Dwight Akers has described this era in dramatic fashion:

> Like every other American business of the time, the breeding of horses had been overextended. There were too many work horses and too many pleasure horses to find jobs in an America whose activities were so suddenly and so narrowly contracted. . . . Horses were sold for what they would bring—it was little enough. . . . In many instances, the stock was dispersed, barns were razed and training tracks plowed up and turned into fields for the growing of grain. . . . To the croakers of evil fortune it seemed that the great days of the American light-harness horse were about over. . . . In cities electric and cable cars had already eliminated the horse as a means of mass conveyance. The growth of traffic had pushed the fast roadster out to the suburbs beyond the sound of the policeman's whistle or had driven him off the highways altogether.[8]

Racing survived the depression in spite of the scarcity of money. The Grand Circuit boosted its total purse money from $230,000 in 1889 to $375,000 in 1894. On the West Coast the Undine Stable collected $14,025 from a total of nearly $150,000 offered for 235 races, and the Pacific Jockey Club advanced purses aggregating $32,000.[9] Elias (Lucky) Baldwin's great Santa Anita Ranch and the stables of Leland Stanford were leaders in the West. Prospering as it did, racing naturally attracted the interest of state governments, and Tom Platt, the political boss of New York, wired state senators to change their tune and vote for the Percy-Gray and Wilds bills which alloted the state a five percent tax on gross receipts at the track.[10]

Western sportsmen had asserted their independence in 1887 in the formation of an American Trotting Association. By 1898 nearly two thousand meetings were held annually in the United States and Canada, involving more than $3,000,000 in purse money. These were also the brilliant years of Nancy Hanks, Lou Dillon, and Dan Patch. How integral a part of life racing had become in some areas is reflected in the humorous jibe:

> The love of the sport of kings is as much a part of the nature of a Tennessean as his innate and intense admiration for his sunny

Southern clime. This is true of all classes of citizens. It has frequently
been said, but with some degree of exaggeration, of course, that a
Tennessean's affection extends to his horse, his wife, his dog and his
country, and in the order named.[11]

By 1900 Tod Sloane was earning $75,000 for a year's jockey fees,
while revolutionizing British racing with his crouching style. William C.
Whitney, who had lately established a breeding farm near Lexington and
was to bring about a remarkable revival of the meetings at Saratoga, and
Richard Croker were sending horses abroad. It was no surprise to sportsmen that between 1895 and 1905 racing taxes of the state of New York
soared from $27,220.74 to $190,256.30. European trotting reached a
peak of popularity in the 1890's and, until the Revolution of 1917,
American trainers emigrated to Russia in considerable numbers. Exports
of trotting horses abroad rose from about 100 in 1893 to 3000 in 1903.

That many races mounted in value between 1890 and 1905 is
evidenced in the great stakes of the day:[12]

| Stakes | Place | 1890 | 1905 |
|--------|-------|------|------|
| American Derby | Washington Park | $15,260 | $26,325 (1904) |
| Belmont Stakes | Belmont Park | 8,500 | 17,240 |
| St. Louis Derby | Fair Grounds, St. L. | 3,280 | 10,685 |
| Suburban Handicap | Belmont Park | 6,900 | 16,800 |
| Brooklyn Handicap | Aqueduct | 6,900 | 15,800 |
| Travers Stakes | Saratoga | 4,925 | 8,350 |

That numerous stakes remained unchanged or declined in value is also
clear. At Churchill Downs the Kentucky Derby dropped in value from
$5460 to $4850, while the Kentucky Oaks followed suit. The Withers
Stakes at Belmont fell off in value, and in Chicago racing was suspended
in 1895, 1896, and 1897. Many stakes declined during the middle nineties,
perhaps as a result of the protracted depression, reviving only after 1902.
By 1906 purse values totaled $1,500,000, while the state of New York
collected about $200,000 in taxes which were distributed to agricultural
societies.

Racing had been fortunate in producing a string of great thoroughbreds from Salvator and Domino to Hamburg and Africander. A prominent turf historian believed that "any one of the five champions of 1903
could so far eclipse the efforts of Boston, Fashion, Henry, Eclipse, Lexington, Lecompte, and all that galaxy of the olden time, that they would
seem poor horses indeed."[13]

Several major tracks were maintained in Kentucky, but thoroughbred racing increasingly centered in large metropolitan areas like New York, Chicago, and San Francisco. If not the all-embracing passion that occasionally swept over the people of the ante-bellum era, turf enthusiasm remained high throughout the years at the turn of the century. Great as was its financial prosperity, however, the track was plagued by an omnipresent rough element as well as bookmakers, gamblers, and dishonest jockeys. Michael Dwyer, George E. (Pittsburgh Phil) Smith, and Stephen L'Hommedieu gained a certain notoriety as the heaviest "plungers" of the decade, along with John W. Gates and John A. Drake.[14]

Due credit for turf prosperity must be extended to the organizers of the Jockey Club in 1894 for their formulation of standard rules of track conduct. Improved railroad facilities were provided and good times returned with the ascendancy of the Republican party under McKinley and Roosevelt, while public officials and the press softened their criticism with the increase in racing taxes. The atmosphere of the early twentieth century was turbulent, however, for reform was everywhere the topic of the day. Muckraking, women's rights, temperance, Social Christianity, and similar crusades were under way, and their advocates were extremely vocal. As sport loomed ever larger on the horizon, what could be more natural than a storm of protest over the menace presented by the racing world?

Western Union underwent a withering attack from the Police Commissioner of New York in 1904, when direct charges were made that gambling was sponsored by its wire services, while Kentucky formed a Racing Commission in 1906 for the better control and protection of the turf. Cancellation of racing meetings occurred in many states from 1906 to 1908, and Governor Charles Evans Hughes of New York undertook his famous crusade against gambling and pool selling. Employment of any device for betting and the practice of any form of pool selling were illegal according to the statutes of the state of New York.[15] The Chicago turf collapsed after 1906 when Illinois paid obeisance to the reform spirit of the time.

The yellow press allotted ample space to the racing addict and devoted charts to the statistics of the turf, but financial reverses became general after 1910. Arthur Brisbane, maestro of the Hearst syndicate, levied war on racing in the Empire State and helped weld the moral crusade which eventually abolished betting at races through the legislation fashioned by State Senator Foelker and Governor Hughes. Although purses and stakes distributed to American horsemen totalled $4,351,691 for 1908, by 1911 they had dropped to $2,331,957. James R. Keene's stables collected more than a quarter million dollars in 1908 and the immortal Colin's earnings surpassed $140,000; but such returns became impossible in the next few years and by 1918 racing was so depressed that prize horses were sold abroad by leading turfmen.

It was not until 1917 that purse and stakes winnings approached the old level of 1908. On the eve of our entry into the great war in Europe a revival in the size of crowds occurred at many tracks. Omar Khayyam captured a purse of more than $16,000 before a crowd of 40,000 in the greatest Kentucky Derby in history. A series of brilliant horses—Old Rosebud, Regret, Exterminator, and Sir Barton—won fame in the Derby between 1914 and 1920. Pari-mutuel betting had proved an instant success after Colonel Matt Winn introduced the machines at Churchill Downs in 1906. Oral betting cropped up on many tracks to evade legislation against bookmaking. Moral resentment against racing seems to have been lost in the more crucial issues at stake in the world of 1914-1918, and the statutory attack was relaxed. The Belmont and Preakness Stakes rocketed upward in value after 1916, workers flush with ready cash made a parade to the $2 window, and sportsmen noted the "returning prosperity of the turf in 1917."[16]

Falling heir to the great traditions of the nineteenth-century turf, harness racing held the good will of most communities and was spared the legislative attacks of state governments. Edward H. Harriman contributed generously to trotting at Goshen in 1909 when that track was in distress, Thomas W. Murphy led the parade of winners from 1909 to 1914, the most famous driver was the veteran Ed (Pop) Geers. Uhlan, prince of trotters, established an unbelievable world mile record of 1:58 and some 15,000 trotters competed for $6,000,000 in purses and stakes in 1912, at a time when thoroughbred winnings totalled less than $2,500,000. Harness racing remained generally prosperous throughout the first two decades in spite of the popular appeal of the automobile. Traditions established in rural nineteenth-century America, however, now had to yield to the mounting interest of cities and smaller towns in baseball, football, and other athletic games. Whether or not the appeal of harness racing was as strong as in the previous generation, old veterans and their enthusiastic offspring helped to magnify the legends of famous trotters and pacers, and trotting continued to intrigue fairground crowds with its colorful and picturesque style of racing.

## Heyday of Yachting

Peace brought new opportunities to zealous yachtsmen urgently awaiting the sport's revival. Additions to the fleets of New York harbor such as the schooners *Fleetwing, Phantom,* and *Maria* in 1865 caused a renewed enthusiasm for regattas. American prestige soared higher than ever in 1866 with the sensational victory of James Gordon Bennett, Jr.'s *Henrietta* over the *Fleetwing* and the *Vesta* in their transoceanic race from Sandy Hook to the Isle of Wight. By the late sixties revival of the America's Cup races was awaited with anticipation in all yachting circles.

In the years following the collapse of the Confederacy yachting thrived on the aristocratic backing of such men as James Gordon Bennett, Jr., Pierre Lorillard, Jr., and J. Malcolm Forbes. It also benefited from the prevailing economic prosperity.

By 1869 there were at least fifteen yacht clubs in the United States. America's Cup Races of 1870, 1871, and 1876, as well as those of 1881, 1885, 1886, and 1887, did much to arouse popular interest in water sports in many sections of the United States. New England, with its numerous harbors and coves, held regattas surpassing all but New York. In 1865 the Boston Yacht Club and in 1866 the Atlantic Yacht Club were launched; South Boston and Lynn followed in 1868, Quincy in 1874, and Hull in 1880. Local clubs not meeting the specifications of the New England Yachting Association in 1884 were to be found in many towns.[17] In the middle eighties the *American Yachting List* included seventy-five clubs and 1870 yachts, by 1888 there were a reputed one hundred twenty clubs, while the Seawanhaka-Corinthian was considered the most progressive and active of all organizations.

Concentrated mostly in cities located on a suitable body of water, clubs were already active in Savannah, St. Augustine, and Mobile. Sailing predominated over yachting in Gulf waters at Biloxi, Pass Christian, and other centers. "New Orleans is quite large enough to be getting beyond model yacht racing," according to the *Daily Picayune* of August 17, 1870, "Nothing but the war has kept us from having our Magics, Dauntlesses, Fleetwings and Sapphos. Money, however, is now flowing southward once more, and we look forward, at no very distant day, to witnessing races in the deep blue water of the Gulf." Yachting and sailing thrived on the Great Lakes at Buffalo, Cleveland, Toledo, Chicago, Milwaukee, and throughout the state of Michigan.

Progress was not so rapid on the Pacific Coast. In 1868 a number of San Francisco gentlemen formed what was later called the San Francisco Yacht Club (1873) and then the Pacific Yacht Club (1878) and the Corinthian Yacht Club (1886). The task of establishing a new government and building new cities, however, left little time for recreation. While the East had a leisure class with large steam or sailing yachts capable of going to sea, "Here in California we have no leisure class, to speak of, and our very wealthy men generally 'run to horse'. . . . Our yachts are smaller, fewer in number comparatively, and are only used on Saturday afternoons and Sundays as a general thing. Moreover, most of our yachting is confined to the bays, the Pacific Ocean in these latitudes being pacific only in name and not in reality."[18]

During the late eighties interest reached a high pitch. Victories by the *Puritan,* the *Mayflower,* and the *Volunteer* brought fame to the leading designer of American yachts, Edward Burgess. The Burgess name became a symbol of success on the water. Funds of $11,500, of $10,172 and $30,000 were granted by clubs to the designer and his family, while Harvard College in 1889 conferred on him "the unique honor of the A.M. degree for excellence in ship designing."[19]

When the *Coronet* outsailed the *Dauntless* in a transAtlantic race from New York to Queenstown in 1887 the press exploited the event to the fullest. As W.P. Stephens claimed, "The publicity given to the sport by the daily press, and the large amount of technical detail published by the special yachting journals, aided greatly in introducing the sport in many remote and isolated localities." Sailing on inland waters and lakes increased rapidly at a time when Britain was recapturing her old hold on the merchant marine, while the prestige of American sailing vessels retarded our conversion to steam. Of all factors at work between 1860 and 1890—geographic, social economic, or moral—the most vital to the rise of yachting interest was the emergence of a larger, richer leisure class in urban communities, using the yacht or sailing craft both as a vehicle of pleasure and a mark of social distinction.

Yacht races were a characteristic feature of the social season among the "elite" just prior to the turn of the century. But notwithstanding the fact that America's Cup challenges attracted considerable attention in 1899, 1901, and 1903, the sporting flood of the twentieth century proved too great a distraction for the continued prominence of yachting. Sir Thomas Lipton's *Shamrock* boats revived interest, but no Cup race was sailed between 1903 and 1920. Wilhelm of Germany helped establish the Kaiser's Cup; King Edward VII of England donated a trophy for sloops and schooners in 1905; and a new cup was substituted in 1912 by King George V. Annual competitions continued until the war, but the yachting fever of the past century, which excited all New York and was splashed over the front pages of the national press, was no more.

In 1906 ocean racing came to the fore with the California to Honolulu race and the small-boat race to Bermuda. Sailing became slightly more democratic as less expensive boats, like those of the "Bug" and "Star" classes built by William Corry and his imitators, appeared on the market. Sailing clubs were encouraged with the organization of the Star Class Association of America in 1915 and its junior division four years later. Among the prominent races for yachtsmen were those for the Canada's Cup, the Seawanhaka Cup, the Lipton Cup, and the Walker Cup.

At the same time local clubs held their own contests and cruises. Many of the "mushroom aristocracy," scorned by the older, established families, bought their own sailing or steam yachts and flaunted their wealth on the waters off Newport, presaging the "Twilight of the Social Gods."[20] The decline of yachting as an American sport was relative, not absolute. As national attention was increasingly diverted from the affairs of the elite to the problems of the machine age, thousands of sailing craft set up their riggings on coastal and inland waters, but the sporting public no longer thrilled to the legends and excitement of the glorious days of nineteenth-century racing. One more stronghold of the sporting gentleman was falling before the surge of popular interest.

## Age of Cycling

In the late 1860's a bicycling fad swept France, and arrangement of races like that from Paris to Rouen followed immediately. Other Europeans soon took to the open road and the cycling fever crossed to England. Pierre Lallement and A.D. Chandler of Brookline both helped introduce the "velocipede" in the United States and a number of races were held in 1869. But it was the Centennial Exposition's display of English wheels at Philadelphia in 1876 which inspired Colonel Albert Pope to enter the field. Pioneer bicycle and automobile manufacturer, ardent crusader for the free use of roads and parks, publisher of sporting journals, promoter of the Good Roads movement, and propagandist for establishing the Massachusetts Highway Commission and the federal government's Bureau of Road Engineering, Pope made and lost a fortune in the encouragement of cycling and outdoor sport.[21]

Although it was not destined to play the economic role of the steamboat, the locomotive, the automobile, or the airplane, the bicycle and its devotees cannot be overlooked by the social historian. Throughout the horse-and-buggy age in the middle of the nineteenth century construction of hard-surfaced roads had been neglected. English cyclists struggling over muddy, bumpy roads looked with scorn on the American countryside. Yet, the sprawling metropolis and the country town held thousands of dwellers eager to get out and explore the beauties of nature. The Boston Cycling Club of 1878, under the leadership of Frank W. Weston, was a leading light in stirring up cycling interest, and within two years there were so many addicts and so many clubs that the need for an effective organization governing the sport was apparent. Toll companies had been known to forbid travel on their turnpikes, and officials had the nasty tendency to close off city streets and parks. In January, 1886 the cry was still heard in *Outing:* "Around many of our cities the wheelman must still be ready to fight his way with the obtuse or reckless or malicious occupants of horse-drawn vehicles, and often with equally depraved roughs on foot."

The zeal of the League of American Wheelmen did not go unheralded. President Bates predicted that a veritable economic revolution would result from the cycling movement:

> With good roads, the average rapidity of travel with horses will largely increase. Much heavier loads will be hauled. Transportation will consume less of the farmer's labor and profits. The cost of living in villages and cities will diminish and be less liable to needless fluctuations. Farms will greatly increase in value; and their nearness to market will not be so essential as it now is. The average life of working and road horses, and of wagons and carriages of all kinds, will be much enhanced; and life will be better worth living. To these reforms the rapidly growing army of wheelmen are and will be the most enthusiastic and personally interested contributors.[22]

Public inertia in accepting the outwardly grotesque high-wheeler; scarcity of roads suitable for pedalling through the countryside; resistance of municipal authorities to the use of thoroughfares and park lanes; limited production and high prices of manufacturers; and handicaps of women riders before the invention of the drop-frame all retarded the formation of clubs. Racing helped win the support of the press, however, and a Cyclists' Touring Club soon claimed an army of 30,000 riders, while the LAW membership rose to 12,000 by 1889.

Appeals to the clergy were frequent in the early issues of cycling magazines, which generally adopted a somewhat snobbish tone: "Until society is sufficiently instructed as to the value of the bicycle and learns also that ministers are made of the same flesh and blood with themselves, our clerical brother will certainly be the target of criticism and the occasion of many a smile," but it was found that "the increasing number of ministerial bicyclists indicates a rapid improvement in public opinion."[23]

Women have frequently played a decisive role in the growth of American sport, and nowhere is this more evident than in the cycling mania of the Mauve Decade. Thousands of eager sporting women who hesitated to pass the turnstiles of the race track and the ball park rushed to take up pedalling their safety cycles on parkways and country roads. Central Park in Manhattan opened its paths in 1887 and women flocked to its winding trails. According to the Cincinnati *Commercial Gazette* in 1894, "The debating and literary societies have begun early this fall on their discussions, 'Shall the Ladies Ride Bicycles?' "

Manufacturers were overwhelmed with orders as prices descended to the $30-$50 bracket. From Minneapolis Mr. P.J. Kennedy bemoaned his trials on an eastern search for cycles in 1895:

> My observations all over the country wherever I went, showed me that the demand was not local at all, but the result of a vast wave of increased popularity for the wheel everywhere. . . . Dealers everywhere are complaining that they cannot get a fifth of their orders filled, and it is perfectly true, but at the same time all the factories, most of them with increased capacity over last year, are running double time with double forces. That gives you some idea of what wheeling has come to. There never was such a demand for any manufacture in the last 25 years as there is now for the bicycle.[24]

Hard times in the middle nineties failed to halt the cycling fad, although it may well have been that the lowering of bicycle prices was due to the tight money situation as well as to increased manufacture. E. Benjamin Andrews recalled: "Bicycle makers multiplied and prospered despite the panic of 1893. Sewing machine and arms companies turned to the manufacture of bicycles. . . . Clothiers complained that only cycling suits could be sold. Liquor dealers in some sections could not vend their wares in intoxicating quantities even among young men who had formerly indulged freely." It was claimed in 1896 that at least $100,000,000 had been spent in the United States on the wheeling mania, and about ten percent of all national journalistic advertising in 1897 was devoted to bicycling.[25] Among the patrons of the Humble Cycle Co. were the Royal Family of England, W.L. Biddle and A.J. Drexel, Jr., of Philadelphia, and the New York contingent of F.W. Vanderbilt, Stuyvesant Fish, James Stillman, J.P. Morgan, Charles Peabody, E.L. Godkin, and Seth Low. Even the Czar of Russia was pictured on his cycle. Men and women of high and low estate bought models from the scores of agencies maintained by such companies as Columbia, Spalding, Overman, Olympic, Pierce, Liberty, Crescent, Syracuse, and the Waltham Manufacturing Company. By 1891 the Pope Manufacturing Company had offices in Boston, New York, and Chicago and supplied six hundred agencies. The growth of century clubs, the armies of riders enlisted in the LAW, and the tremendous expansion of the cycling industry were indicative of popularity of wheeling in the nineties and the first years of the new century.

And then the bottom fell out of the cycling market for sportsmen. The automobile and country club may have had some effect. Contemporary analysis offered various explanations, among which were accessibility to the immediate countryside with the building of trolley lines, concentration of cycling factories under great monopolies (forty-five active factories were reputedly gathered under one management), and collapse of the League of American Wheelmen due to its failure to advertise. The decline in exports was due in part to the raising of tariffs abroad.

The bicycle craze had made a profound impression on the social life of the nineties. Some attention was given by men like General Nelson A. Miles to the use of bicycles for military purposes; Philadelphia maintained a "Bicycle Squad" of twelve policemen; New York's Commissioner of Street Cleaning encouraged its use; a Wheelmen's Protective Co. offered insurance on cycles; and some midwestern groups formed state bicycle detective associations to halt the sale of stolen machines in the cities. Doctors signalled their approval of cycling exercise, while Frances Willard and the temperance movement concurred, but cycling was said to have hurt the piano and barbering trades and to have altered much prejudice on observance of the Sabbath. Political activity on behalf of good roads was championed by LAW president Charles E. Luscomb's circular letter: "The League of American Wheelmen is bound to secure better roads, and you, as a wheelman are expected to assist at the polls. . . . Work up a quiet interest among your friends to attend the primaries; find out how the candidates stand, and vote for good roads candidates only."[26]

Public enthusiasm began to waver at the turn of the century, and in 1899 Chicago's park commission refused to permit any future Memorial Day races. There were about three hundred establishments with capital amounting to thirty million dollars in 1903, which fell to less than six million dollars in 1905: "the popularity of the bicycle is waning, and manufacturers are turning to automobiles as a means of keeping their workmen busy."[27] The LAW secretary-treasurer had to recognize in 1904 that cycling had been declining for several years. Almost every cycling magazine collapsed, and by 1905 wheeling was generally considered one of the erstwhile fads of the nineties. Despite the financial backing given in 1902 to the American Bicycle Company by John D. Rockefeller, the manufacturing of wheels dropped off drastically. In 1900 it was noted: "*The Washington Post* has observed a marked decline in the use of the wheel. Society seems to have given it up altogether, and now it is chiefly used as an article of utility to get clerks and workmen to and from their business. . . . Here in New York it has been evident for some time that the 'craze' was over," although shopboys, newsboys, carpenters, and tradesmen had learned to use the bicycle for business purposes.[28]

Roger Burlingame, a leading student of American invention, assessed the role of the bicycle in glowing terms:

> The bicycle, thus equipped [with pneumatic tires], had a far larger social significance than is generally credited to it. It introduced the first idea of individual speed and was the first inexpensive means of rapid individual travel. It brought a medium of exercise which was simultaneously healthful and pleasurable to millions of people. It began, in America, the new agitation for good roads which has culminated today in our great highway system. . . . [Cycling organizations acquired] a certain political power from their very size and they presently turned their attention to state agencies. When we consider the extent of the vogue—the quantity of recreation, camping, racing, 'nature' and other clubs which sprang up, the use of the bicycle for pseudo-scientific expeditions, for police, in the army, for messenger service, for mail, for newspaper delivery and as an adjunct to the telegraph; the long-distance competitions, the road races, endurance contests and an infinity of other matters—we may understand this power. And for finances there were, of course, the manufacturers, who saw the necessity of highways to the extension of their business.
>
> There began, therefore, one of the first great campaigns of mass propaganda . . . that the nation had seen. . . . The press took up the cry of the knickerbockered men and bloomered women, and several states revived their highway commissions as a result.[29]

Conservative farmers, skeptical of new ways and hostile to road taxes, were already beginning to resent the motor car as cycling tours lost their appeal to urban clubs.

## Rise of Tennis and Golf

Lawn tennis and golf were further examples of the British influence on the rise of American sport. Developed by Major Walter Wingfield from an early French and English game, tennis was inaugurated on the Staten Island Cricket and Baseball Club's grounds in 1875 through the efforts of Miss Mary Outerbridge, who had picked up a net, rackets, and balls from regimental stores on the island of Bermuda. Shortly thereafter Dr. James Dwight and Fred Sears began playing on a private court at Nahant near Boston. Within two years the game was introduced at Newport, Plainfield, New Orleans, and the Germantown cricket grounds. Establishment of the Marylebone and All-England rules and the Wimbledon tournament (1877), along with the spectacular play of the Renshaw brothers, attracted attention in collegiate and social circles. Despite the use of the Ayres ball and the organization of private clubs, uniformity in playing regulations and equipment was not achieved for some years.

Richard Sears dominated the courts of the 1880's, while Dwight, "the first player anywhere to analyse strokes and tactics and write about them for the guidance of others,"[30] fathered the United States Lawn Tennis Association (1881) through two decades. National championships were held before the fashionable set at the Newport Casino grounds as Oliver Campbell, Bob Wrenn, Fred Hovey, Holcombe Ward, Beals Wright, Malcolm Whitman, and William Larned developed tennis into a faster, more athletic game. The little world of tennis players failed to win widespread acclaim in these early years, but this was in part due to the determination in social circles to confine the game to the élite. Southern California, however, had its Pacific States association by 1890. Between 1883 and 1895 USLTA membership grew from forty clubs to 105 clubs and ten associations. Interest in the West soared after the 1896 doubles championship of the Neel brothers of Chicago and after Dwight Davis offered a prize cup for international competition in 1900. The Davis Cup victory in 1900 renewed interest at the turn of the century, and in 1905 Miss May Sutton returned from Wimbledon with our first English championship.[31]

Through the years tennis underwent a transformation from the aristocratic game of the turn of the century to the semipopular sport of the second decade. The United States failed to regain the Davis Cup in the decade from 1903 to 1913, but by the latter date there were players in every section of the country, and definite signs of West Coast proficiency were in evidence. When Maurice McLaughlin and Mary Browne, fellow Californians, carried both national titles back to the Pacific Coast in 1912, a new era had opened. Of humble origin, McLaughlin had learned the game on the public courts of San Francisco. To the amazement of the social set at Newport and Forest Hills, this red-headed "California Comet" swept over all the names of the eastern courts and, with a blistering service, revolutionized the game from one of placement and skill to one of blinding speed and stroking power. Fans needed only to read of his thundering service to be convinced of the new tone of masculinity in tennis. John Kieran has described the influence of the Californian:

> Then came a larruping Lochinvar out of the West: Maurice E. McLaughlin. . . . He brought tennis down to the common ground. It was no longer a game for the Four Hundred—not the way Red McLaughlin played it. He made it a game for the millions, for the young fellows at the small clubs about the country and the youngsters just starting out on the courts in the public parks. . . . No

longer did the man in the street or the boy in public school regard it disdainfully as a sissy sport.[32]

Exaggerated as this view may be, it gives some idea of McLaughlin's significance in the rise of the game. William T. Tilden, always a keen student of the court, maintained: "McLaughlin was the turning-point in American tennis. He made a lasting impression on the game. . . . Cyclonic, dynamic energy, embodied in a firey-headed boy, transformed tennis to a game of brawn as well as brains . . . and all the rising young players sought to emulate the game."[33]

Other developments in American life also contributed to the game's popularity. It was an era of financial prosperity as well as one of expanding interest in other athletic games. McLaughlin soon found rivals of equal ability. Although he defeated Norman Brooks and Anthony Wilding in Davis Cup play in 1914, others soon captured his laurels, among them William Johnston, R. Norris Williams, and R. Lindley Murray. Sports critics were already contending that a new mecca of tennis was rising on the Pacific Coast as a result of the favorable climate and the prevalence of courts. Among the women of this decade the four greatest names were Mary K. Browne, May Sutton Bundy, Hazel Hotchkiss Wightman, and Molla Bjurstedt, the first three of whom were Californians.

Tennis was not abandoned during the years of war, and many star performers entered "patriotic tournaments" sponsored by various clubs. Throughout this whole period, despite the new vigor injected into the game, tennis, even more than golf, remained suspect in the eyes of the masses. By the end of the decade popular opinion was definitely more favorable, yet some proponents of the game found it necessary to seriously campaign against the effeminate sound of the term "love" and the press referred to agitation in favor of "he-man tennis." Enthusiasm was fanned in the schools, players scampered over baselines in every town and city, and many middle-class families constructed their own private courts.

The new game of golf, an importation from Scotland and first organized at a Yonkers-on-Hudson dinner hosted by John Reid, fascinated a leisure class of sportsmen who nurtured it into prominence within a decade. America's first country club had opened at Brookline in 1882 as a social center for the aristocracy of polo, racing, and the hunt. St. Andrews in Westchester County was merely the first of a group of isolated clubs which experimented with golf, but the game soon spread so rapidly that the United States Golf Association was founded in 1894. In the same year Theodore A. Havemeyer, the "Sugar King," capitalized the Newport Country Club at $150,000 with a host of wealthy incorporators including

James A. Stillman, Cornelius Vanderbilt, Perry Belmont, John Jacob Astor, Robert Goelet, and other giants of the financial world.[34] Newport had its first golf course by 1890, the first women's championship was held at Meadowbrook in 1895, and within another five years the Baltusrol tournament attracted women from thirty-eight clubs between Boston and Chicago.

USGA membership soared to 103 clubs in 1898 and professional golf had already appeared. The Golf Association of Philadelphia and New York's Metropolitan Golf Association entered on the scene in 1897. The game was introduced in the Far West at Tacoma in 1894, at Portland in 1895. There were twenty courses on the Pacific Coast by 1897, leading to the creation of a Southern California Golf Association two years later. Clubs were formed in St. Louis, Denver, Colorado Springs, Salt Lake City, and other western communities. Washington society had its Chevy Chase Club where Justices Melville W. Fuller and John M. Harlan, Secretaries Elihu Root and Lyman Gage, Senators Joseph Foraker and Chauncey Depew, as well as General Nelson Miles and Thomas Nelson Page, the Beau Brummel of the greens, practiced their shots.[35]

An invasion by England's famed Harry Vardon in 1900 popularized the game as he played courses at Palm Beach and St. Augustine and then swept all before him in the North. Sponsored by A.G. Spalding & Company, Vardon toured the country as far as the Rocky Mountain region of Denver. At the beginning of 1899 there were an estimated 887 golf clubs in the United States, 154 of which were west of the Mississippi River. Public interest was attracted to this sporting hobby of the socialites, and interscholastic tourneys were held before the end of the century. Public golf opened at Van Cortlandt Park in New York in 1895, and soon spread to Boston, Rochester, Buffalo, Indianapolis, Toledo, Chicago, and elsewhere, but the game retained an aristocratic air, pursued mainly by the leisure class.

A pioneer golf promoter, surveying the status of the game in 1904, acknowledged that the best courses in America, such as Garden City, Myopia, and the Chicago Golf Club, could not be compared to "the classic golf courses in Great Britain and Ireland."[36] Introduction of the lively Haskell ball in 1902, however, and the play of Findlay Douglas and Walter Travis heightened interest in the game. A group of influential men organized the National Golf Links of America in 1908, and within two years there were more than twenty outstanding tournaments. Among its leading members were Finley Peter Dunne, Robert Bacon, Henry Clay Frick, Elbert H. Gary, J. Horace Harding, J. Borden Harriman, Robert Lincoln, W.D. Sloane, James A. Stillman, William K. Vanderbilt, Harry Payne Whitney, and Charles B. MacDonald.

Prominent men from all walks of life drew attention to the game. John D. Rockefeller, Andrew Carnegie, William Howard Taft, and other public figures played golf for diversion, for exercise, and, frequently for the correction of digestive ailments. President Taft's love for the links was intense. His example led many to risk donning golfing togs, and it was said that, with the single exception of the Philippines, no subject appealed to him more than golf and its possibilities as a popular pastime.

In the years prior to World War I Jerome D. Travers, Charles E. (Chick) Evans, and Francis Ouimet brought new life to the links with their development of a hard-driving style of play, and golf galleries steadily increased in size. Ouimet's spectacular victory in the National Open of 1913 over the world's greatest golfers was the first truly international championship won by an American and the first positive sign of a new generation which would shake the British golfing dynasty to its very foundations. When Harry Vardon visited the United States for the second time in 1913 he recognized a great improvement in American players and courses, despite the scarcity of bunkers. The general superiority of English players was still recognized in golfing circles, but by the end of the decade such names as Hagen, Barnes, Stirling, Ouimet, and Evans had dimmed the exalted reputations of some of England's greats. By 1920 Vardon observed that American courses had been tremendously improved and that Britain had found a worthy rival in the ancient game.[37]

Chicago, with Charles B. MacDonald as its first golfing missionary, became the nucleus from which the West acquired an interest after the turn of the century. Main Street and Middletown folks joined their local clubs, and by the time President Wilson felt compelled to declare war on the German Empire the head of the USGA estimated that nearly 2000 clubs were operating in the United States. Yet, the very fact that twenty years of organization had not extended the game very far beyond those in higher income brackets was proof enough, in the popular mind, that golf was a rich man's sport. Although doctors, lawyers, businessmen, and even ministers took to the fairways, the country club set was restricted to a relatively small clique. Many cities followed the lead of Chicago in the building of public courses, but golf still wore the mantle of gentility.

## The Leisure Class and the Dangerous Classes

Democratic as America may have been in the closing decades of the century, class distinctions were maintained with unabated ardor. High society became a mélange of distinguished old families and aspiring members of the commercial aristocracy. Sport could not throw off many of the bonds of tradition. Even at the turn of the century society still remained in control of leading tennis and golf associations; fox hunting prevailed among wealthier eastern and southern families; many continued to flock to Newport, Saratoga, and other resorts; horse shows remained a notable event on the social calendar; the venturesome element accepted the "horseless carriage" as a substitute for "coaches and four"; yachting remained essentially an aristocratic monopoly; racquets and squash were played only by the metropolitan élite; and polo showed no signs of being vulgarized by the masses. Such a tendency was not all bad, for the code of the sporting gentleman was sustained largely by this class and by those in collegiate circles who had grafted this ideal to their amateur athletic rules. Whatever its effects, high society strove to isolate itself from the popular games of the day, to shun contact with the rougher elements, to keep free of contamination by the denizens of the gambling world, and to retain an aura of privilege and distinction in its favorite diversions.

That sport had spread throughout all classes and won adherents among white collar workers, bankers, professional men, and laborers was obvious. That there was a mingling of social classes on college and school gridirons, on sandlots, at the "Y", or on the public links was equally evident. The turf no longer remained under the tyrannic control of a few eastern families, baseball parks attracted fans from all classes, and the athletic clubs of swank New Yorkers or Chicagoans were imitated widely by middle and laboring class organizations of school, church, or factory. But this democratic trend did not destroy the bastions erected by the social élite, nor did it immediately raise the standards of the element so deeply entrenched in commercialized metropolitan sports. Sport was welcomed by the average citizen, but it still retained traditional barriers between gentlemen and pugs.

The game of polo was particularly illustrative of this snobbish attitude. Although James Gordon Bennett, Jr., introduced Americans to the game, the leading sponsor in pre-World War I years was Harry Payne Whitney, who captained the teams which won the International Cup from England in 1909, 1911, and 1913. Metropolitan newspapers gave only fleeting attention, and it was almost confined to those few college fours or private clubs which could afford a string of ponies. The matches of 1911 were reported primarily by society columnists rather than sports writers on the premise that polo was less a sports spectacle than a social event. Something of the later popularity of the game may be attributed to the first World War. In 1919 General Peyton March encouraged the promotion of polo in the army by promising to supply mounts and equipment. Polo, however, never reached far beyond the confines of the leading socialite families who were not interested in making it a popular game.

At the other extremity of American society were those fanatical devotees of metropolitan sports who frequented the saloon, gambled at the track, loitered in the poolroom, made a haunt of smoke-filled billiard parlors, and became the camp followers of contemporary pugilists. The term "sporting man" had long carried a dubious connotation, and idealists of amateur sport berated these questionable characters as parasites, riff-raff, rowdies, toughs, and pugs. In the long quest for respectability which sportsmen had made the pug had remained anathema. For years the association was drawn in the press and impressed on the public mind that contaminating influences in professionalism were due to the gambler and the rowdy. Despite the growing popularity of billiards, pool, and bowling, they were long associated with the frequenters of the gambling house and, for those proprietors who sought the patronage of the middle class, it was a difficult struggle to throw off this association in the public mind. Little need we wonder that the gentleman champion of sport, dedicated to an amateur ideal, feared the corrupt or parasitic tendencies of the sporting underworld.

## Saloons, Poolrooms, and the Gambling Fraternity

In the years when commercialized sport first struggled for recognition the pioneer sponsors were the saloon and the poolroom. Pugilists of pre-Civil War New York often congregated at Frank Stuart's gambling house in Park Place, and it was with the backing of Stuart that Yankee Sullivan went into his ill-fated clash with Tom Hyer in 1849. The saloon of Izzy Lazarus in Buffalo was a noted sportsmen's center in the fifties. Tavern keepers learned the benefits to be derived from the sporting fraternity, as was shown in an advertisement of Wm. Clark's Saloon in New York: "Ales, wines, liquors, segars, and refreshments. All the sporting news of the day to be learned here, where files of the *Clipper,* and other sporting papers are kept. Here also may be seen numberless portraits of English and American pugilists. . . . A room and other facilities are also at all times in readiness for giving lessons in sparring under the supervision of the proprietor. Drop in, and take a peep."[38]

After the war fighters sought their customary haunts in the barrooms and poolrooms of the city, and in the seventies and eighties. Harry Hill's served as the meeting place of sporting men and pugilists. It was there that William Muldoon got his start on the road to fame as the most renowned Greco-Roman wrestler of the era and where John L. Sullivan waged his first New York fight. Although most matches were still fought in secluded glens, on barges, or over the Canadian border, many were held in barrooms. In 1889 the St. Louis populace became belligerent over the fatal

ending of a bout in the Dally Brothers' saloon before a crowd composed
mostly of "pool alley sports." The tie between saloon keepers and pugilists
was fully demonstrated in running newspaper accounts of Sullivan's
escapades in barrooms from coast to coast.

Enthusiasts of the track and the diamond also frequented the saloon
or the poolroom. Odds on the races were wired into countless parlors, and
baseball "bugs" awaited returns at the neighborhood cigar store or drinking establishment. Henry Chadwick noted in 1873 that "the past season's
experience stands forth as affording unmistakable evidence of the fact
that the greatest evil the system of professional ball playing ever encoun-
tered . . . is that arising from the pool-selling business inaugurated in
1871." When the Baltimore team was at home H.L. Mencken's father
consistently attended the games: "When it was on the road, he would
slip away from his office in the late afternoon to glim the score at Kelly's
oyster house in Eutaw Street." He also recalled how a cigar store attached
to his father's business at 7th and G streets in Washington, D.C., was
"baseball headquarters" for the city, and he there came to know most of
the great players of the era. Atlanta had its baseball exchange "in which
all the games the Atlantas play away from home are reported in detail on
a large blackboard, and with pegs numbered to represent the men, the
game can be watched as closely as if the spectators were actually on the
ground." [39] In the life of the city these establishments served a unique
purpose in the promotion of gambling and of sport.

Professional gamblers were often the promoters of sporting events.
John Morrissey sponsored the race track meetings at Saratoga, and John
Chamberlin operated the gambling emporium and track at Long Branch,
in which Jim Fisk, Pierre Lorillard, and William (Boss) Tweed were investors. John W. (Bet-a-Million) Gates was willing to wager on anything,
although Faro, Poker, and the turf were his favorites, and the Dwyer
brothers raced their horses at the major meetings. Bud Renaud, noted
southern gambler, promoted numerous prize fights, the most spectacular
of which was the Sullivan-Kilrain match in 1889.

Gambling men were among the premier sponsors of the turf, and
the bookmaking racket thrived at metropolitan tracks. In the 1870's
Anthony Comstock commenced an attack on the turf by publishing
*Gambling Outrages; Or Improving the Breed of Horses at the Expense of
Public Morals.* Bookmaking was at the core of gambling on the turf.
When the 1884 season closed in New Orleans, Captain Ira E. Bride and
his staff of pool sellers set out for Memphis before going on to take charge
of the Chicago pools, the privilege for which cost $4400 per day. During
the New York season of 1886 local officials harassed the bookmakers
incessantly, causing the treasurer of the American Jockey Club to com-

plain to a reporter "that if betting was stopped on race courses Jerome Park would have to close its gates, breeders would cease to raise thoroughbreds, and the business would go to smash." The police were persistent, however, and jailed Alfred H. Cridge, "the father of bookmakers in New York."

By 1890 the gambling world had sunk its teeth deeply into the turf. Although there were those who resented the presence of undesirable elements at the track, it is not too much to say that the saloon keeper, the poolroom operator, and the bookmaker had been greatly responsible for arousing widespread interest in the turf, the diamond, and the ring. Whether a larger segment of the public would have been won to the armies of sportsmen had this connection been broken is one of those insoluble problems the historian must leave to others more certain of the predictability of social reaction, but one cannot discount Arthur Schlesinger's contention: "Despite its wide popularity . . . racing failed of universal favor because of the evils of betting and fraud which ordinarily attended it and which neither the true friends of the sport nor the enactments of legislatures could suppress."[40] That those institutions which sponsored this betting and fraud had attracted attention to commercialized sport seems, however, beyond dispute.

## Titans of the Prize Ring

Pugilists of the late nineteenth century attained a recognition and popularity unknown before the war. A majority of the outstanding fighters continued to come from recent immigrant groups or from the ranks of touring pugilists from Ireland and England.[41] Although relatively small crowds attended bouts featuring Mike McCoole, Tom Allen, Jem Mace, Joe Goss, Paddy Ryan, Jake Kilrain, Charley Mitchell, and John L. Sullivan, millions heard the names of the great champions. By the eighties the number of matches reported in metropolitan newspapers indicated that the ranks of pugilists were rapidly gaining a host of recruits. Sparring in the athletic club added to the prestige of the ring, and the appearance of several colorful bare-knuckle champions helped capture the public imagination.

Prize fighting failed to win the social esteem its prewar devotees had expected as the churches and the law remained hostile. There was the restraining power of Puritan prejudice; a widespread and well-founded belief was held that pugilists were surrounded by gamblers, thieves, and social outcasts; the opposition of churchmen to the brutality and the dramatization of the ring was strong; the vigilance of many municipal and county officials to prevent fights in their localities had to be faced; a lack of organized control plagued the pugilistic world; and the exclusion of prize fight reports from most reputable magazines and many local papers presented a barrier of silence which the ring could penetrate only with difficulty.

Hard as the task proved to be, however, prize fighting aroused enthusiasm among the hotblooded men of the postwar generation. Whereas state and local authorities prevented many contests, the local theater or opera house in larger cities engaged noted "professors of pugilism" to give exhibitions on the stage. When this was not feasible, matches were held in out-of-the-way places, and many a fight was overlooked by the local sheriff. In the 1880's John L. Sullivan fought on a barge on the Hudson River near Yonkers, made a tour of Michigan, boxed a series of exhibitions for a Philadelphia theater, whipped Paddy Ryan in a bout in Mississippi, boxed Charlie Mitchell and others at Madison Square Garden in New York, broke his arm on Patsy Cardiff's jaw before ten thousand fans in Minneapolis, gave hundreds of exhibitions throughout the United States with a theatrical troupe, performed for the hometown folks in Boston, and talked boxing with the Prince of Wales while touring England and Ireland.

Popular interest, centering largely in the metropolis but spreading slowly into the most rustic community, grew rapidly as boxing was encouraged in the athletic clubs, YMCA, and colleges. Public authorities, however, were reluctant to ignore the stipulations of the law, except in those instances where contests were merely exhibitions of the science and the art of boxing. That Louisiana and Mississippi forbade the fights of the eighties, that many a contest was held in a secluded spot beyond the surveillance of the police, that the clergy remained almost uniformly opposed to the iniquities of the ring, that many a fighter found an outlet for his talents only in Colorado mining camps, in San Francisco, or in Mexico—all were indexes of the slowness of change in social approbation.

Although the enforcement of curbs on fighting had wide support, public enthusiasm mounted as Jack Dempsey (The Nonpareil), Jack McAuliffe, and George Dixon dominated the lesser weight classes, while Sullivan's matches with Ryan, Mitchell, and Kilrain won for him a fame unmatched by any athlete of the period. This Boston titan roamed the country as champion of the world and proceeded to bully, boast, and battle his way into public acceptance as the first of our legendary sporting heroes. As the nineties opened and the press gave increasing space to the ring, several other pugilists had established reputations, among them Bob Fitzsimmons, Peter Jackson, and James J. Corbett. From San Francisco came Gentleman Jim to do battle with the Boston Strong Boy. The scene: Olympic Club, New Orleans, September 7, 1892.

Derided by the ministry and men of culture, the gladiators nonetheless found themselves no longer social outcasts but heroes of an excited nation. Corbett outclassed the aging Sullivan, and the modern age of pugilism dawned. Professor William Lyon Phelps of Yale described in his *Autobiography* the reaction of his clergyman father:

> In 1892 I was reading aloud the news to my father. My father was a good man and is now with God. I had never heard him mention a prize fight and did not suppose he knew anything on that subject, or cared anything about it. So when I came to the headline *Corbett Defeats Sullivan* I read that aloud and turned over the page. My father leaned forward and said earnestly, 'Read it by rounds!'[42]

The friend of Theodore Roosevelt and in later years a temperance advocate, John L. long remained the athletic hero of many an American boy. John P. Marquand has written, "In the days when nice little boys wore long curls and velvet blouses and lace collars and cuffs and posed for their portraits with their hands on the heads of faithful New Foundland dogs, Sir Galahad was not the hero of the youth of America, in spite of the Victorian effort to make this come to pass. The hero of this age and the man who had the most influence on boyhood's wish fulfillment was John L. Sullivan, the Champion of the World. There has been no other pugilist in the history of the prize ring, either in England or America, not excepting the bookish Mr. Tunney or even the universally respected Joe Louis, who has ever assumed such a role . . . [and] by some amazing alchemy his memory has outlived the Goulds and the Sages and the Harrimans and the Vanderbilts."[43]

Sullivan's defeat was first-page news in Boston and every city of the land. The day after the fight the respectable New York *Times* editorialized, "For a decade or more Sullivan has been swaggering about as an unconquerable person . . . [and] the dethronement of a mean and cowardly bully as the idol of the barrooms is a public good that is a fit subject for public congratulation." Better informed writers, recognizing the advantages of the Marquis of Queensbury rules, evaluated the fight as the old generation of gladiators against the new generation of boxers. Sullivan, however, was credited with introducing gloves and eliminating much of the former bare-knuckle brutality so that contests might be held before gentlemen at athletic clubs. Corbett was acclaimed the innovator of an entirely new style of scientific boxing.

Despite appeals of ring followers that boxing was an art, members of the clergy soon heightened their crusade against all forms of pugilism.

Archbishop John Ireland, a fighter of the first order on social issues, had
headed the opposition to a prize fight at St. Paul in 1891, and Governor
William R. Merriam of Minnesota had prevented it by calling out the
militia. The International Law and Order League also forced the attack
on prize fighting. When Mitchell and Corbett sought a site for a match the
next year, Lyman Abbott and T. DeWitt Talmage came out in opposition.
Clergymen were not alone in their hostility: Christian Endeavor responded
with a protest by several hundred members in Brooklyn; five thousand
people attended a protest rally in St. Paul; Governor Claude Mathews of
Indiana prevented any match at Roby; thousands signed a petition of the
YMCA; and Governor Roswell P. Flower of New York prohibited holding
the contest at Coney Island. Although Louisiana and Mississippi remained
the weak links in the war on pugilism, the South was equally adamant in
its hostility to the ring. When Corbett and Fitzsimmons planned to meet
in a Texas match in 1895, Governor Charles A. Culberson, backed by
Governor James P. Clarke of Arkansas, called a special session despite his
wife's contention that nine out of ten men wanted the fight. Passage of
his bill was achieved after a brief but very stormy battle, the relevant
section reading as follows:

> Section 1. Be it enacted by the legislature of the State of Texas,
> that any person who shall voluntarily engage in a pugilistic encounter
> between man and man, or a fight between a man and a bull or any
> other animal, for money or other thing of value, or for any cham-
> pionship, or upon the result of which any money or anthing of value
> is bet or wagered, or to see which any admission is charged, either
> directly or indirectly, shall be deemed guilty of a felony, and upon
> conviction shall be punished by imprisonment in the Penitentiary
> not less than two nor more than five years.[44]

Under such a withering attack prize fighting remained a profitable
livelihood for only the very successful, most fighters invading the tank
towns for small purses. Fitzsimmons and Jeffries met at the fashionable
New Coney Island Sporting Club, but a hostile legislature passed the Lewis
Law in 1900 to prohibit all public boxing matches. Governor Theodore
Roosevelt was thought to be in favor of a law permitting any match under
ten rounds, but the knockout craze and the decline of the boxing art
disgusted even friends of the ring. How poorly managed and how little
esteemed the world of pugilism was in certain respectable circles is seen
in the critical account of the New York *Times,* May 12, 1900, which
discussed Corbett's failure to regain the title from Jeffries: "There was
an absence of any propensity to gamble on the result, and this was taken

by the knowing ones to indicate that there was little confidence in the genuineness of the fight. 'Fake' was the word heard oftenest wherever the sporting element congregated."

When Jeffries fell before the bludgeoning fists of Jack Johnson at Reno in 1910, the world of pugilism fell on evil days. What little prestige had been won for the ring by the dapper Corbett and clean-living Fitz-simmons was lost in the onslaught of opinion against this indiscreet black champion. Jeffries, corpulent and aging, gamely tried a comeback as the "white hope," but he was easily defeated by Johnson in a match which had so inflamed the relations of white and black people that a series of race riots broke out in towns and cities throughout the land. In Pitts-burgh, according to one account, "Riots swept a mile of the 'black belt,' along Wylie avenue and Fulton street. . . . Trolley cars were held up and the white passengers jeered." Outbursts occurred in Philadelphia, Washing-ton, Baltimore, Norfolk, Wilmington, Pueblo, St. Louis, Chattanooga, Houston, Little Rock, Cincinnati, Dayton, Kansas City, Atlanta, New Orleans, and other centers with black colonies.[45]

When the black champion and Jeffries had planned to stage the fight in San Francisco, Governor James N. Gillett prohibited the bout, appar-ently on a warning from the Chairman of the Foreign Affairs Committee of the House of Representatives who threatened to deprive the city of the impending Panama Fair. Much as Johnson had done to stimulate black pride and to stir boxing ambitions in black youth, his conduct was not always viewed as exemplary. As the New York *Times* declared in an April 6 editorial, "The elevation of Johnson has not been of benefit to his race; his fall from his pinnacle will, we fancy, be looked upon complacently by all intelligent colored folk."

Prize fighting began to flourish on a much broader basis. The Fraw-ley law in New York stirred a boom in the ring throughout the country. Professional promotion, headed by James W. Coffroth and Tex Rickard, put boxing on a more respectable plane and made it more profitable. California, supposedly the bastion of the pugilistic world, administered a shock to the game in 1914 when the law permitting bouts was repealed, but laws were eased in New Jersey, Minnesota, and other states in the war years.

American entry into World War I and the millions of men who for the first time learned that boxing can be an excellent physical conditioner enabled the ring to exploit a heretofore latent enthusiasm. Jack Dempsey, a rising young slugger from Colorado, amazed the world in 1919 with his pantherlike speed and lethal blows in a devastating conquest of Jess Willard. A new day dawned for the ring. Although a disappointing crowd of only 20,000 appeared at ringside under the broiling Toledo sun, receipts reached a total exceeding $400,000, and for several minutes of gallant but ineffectual fighting the retiring champion received $100,000. Nor did fighters in the lighter ranks suffer any decline in popular support. These years were the heyday of Stanley Ketchel, Battling Nelson, Joe Gans, Benny Leonard, and other memorable ring figures. And in the great cities numerous neighborhood boxing clubs encouraged young hopefuls to seek their fortunes inside the ropes.

Of much less interest to the general public were the wrestling contests of prewar years. The year 1905 marked the end of an illustrious career for Tom Jenkins, the one-eyed champion who did so much to introduce "catch-as-catch-can" at the expense of the methodical Greco-Roman style. Frank Gotch won the title and remained the world's outstanding wrestler until his retirement in 1913. The Gotch-Hackenschmitt match in 1909 attracted 40,000 Chicago fans, but the mat game gradually fell into disgrace and newspapers refused to print accounts. The faking of contests led to wrestling's doom in many cities and to the disorganization that prevailed down through the years after the First World War. Wrestlers became "groaners" and applied every trick of the hippodrome.

Not that members of the trade (one cannot call it sport) ignored the better tastes of the public. Foul play and histrionics, mingled with a display of strength and real ability, pleased the crowd, but there was a constant appeal made to the respectable classes. Once the war had ended, wrestling took on new life as some of the better matchmakers put on worthy contests. When Wladek Zbyszko defeated Ed (Strangler) Lewis in 1919 it was reported: "The Garden was so jammed with the greatest crowd that has been in the Garden since before the war. . . . Many men of prominence including judges, bankers and clubmen from Fifth Avenue, were in the boxes. There were hundreds of women in the jam and there has seldom, if ever, been so much enthusiasm at a sporting event in the history of the old arena."[46]

The appeal of such matches was strong but with the exception of a few metropolitan centers the public cared little for the usual hippodrome. Amateur wrestling was sponsored by the AAU and the YMCA, and constituted part of the Olympic program, but it would require some years to become a popular collegiate and scholastic sport. Too many Americans associated the ring and the mat with gamblers, parasites, riff-raff, and the pugs.

# Chapter 7

# Urbanization and Democratization

Metropolis! The American of the latter half of the nineteenth century awakened to a new force in national life as disappointed sons of the soil and desperate refugees from the Old World crowded into urban centers. Civic problems mounted rapidly in postwar years, and the doors were opened wide to political corruption and economic exploitation. It was in this turbulent era that the populace turned to commercialized amusements and sports as their chief source of recreation. Athletic exercise and life in the great outdoors were encouraged by those who saw their potential value for improving the morale and health of crowded city dwellers. Horse racing in the second half of the nineteenth century became increasingly dependent on metropolitan crowds and on betting at the tracks. Baseball as a professional and even as an amateur game flourished in towns and cities, while intercollegiate contests appealed mainly to audiences in larger towns and cities. Commercialized sports such as bicycle racing, prize fighting, wrestling, and pedestrianism were all dependent on gate receipts. Sports were promoted by numerous city organizations which were struggling to meet the growing social ills of an all-too-rapidly expanding metropolis. The YMCA, the athletic club, the public school, and various amateur and professional organizations centered themselves in cities and towns, and a sporting spirit emanated from their zealous activities.

Urban areas encouraged sport through better transportation facilities, a growing leisure class, a higher standard of living, more available funds for purchase of sporting goods, and the greater ease with which leagues and teams could be organized. Perhaps it is no coincidence that athletic games were popularized nationally in a postwar era greatly preoccupied with better sewerage, sanitation, and health problems. While it is true that many were handicapped by the overcrowding of American cities and a consequent loss of play areas as the city rapidly expanded, this was not a serious issue in most urban areas until the end of the century.

It was largely to the town or the city that the immigrant brought his games and recreational customs, and in the city that he first felt the spirit of Americanization spread by sport. Millionaires who ventured into yachting, office girls and young ladies of leisure who turned to cycling, and prize fight enthusiasts who backed their favorite challengers were largely from the town or city. Bowling and billiards prospered from the loose money spent by men lounging around the parlors at night, while race courses, baseball parks, gymnasiums, and country clubs were dependent on urban groups for their support. The small town often experienced a wave of sporting interest comparable to that of the city, but this was because of a similar spirit evolving in surrounding communities not too far distant. Vacationing at a summer resort or at the shore became the vogue. And it was from town and city that hordes of anglers and hunters escaped on vacation, responding to the call of the wild. In the seventies Frank Queen's *New York Clipper* ran a sporting column entitled "Metropolis." Metropolitan newspapers incorporated sports pages in their dailies, city authorities belatedly sponsored competitive athletics, and the sporting goods industry in great part depended on urban labor. Fairs were held and trotting meetings centered usually in the largest community of the county or state. The Grand Circuit, the great yacht races, indoor athletic games, commercial leagues, and motorized sport were all sponsored in metropolitan centers. This was because it was obvious that such sports could hardly flourish in rural areas where there were neither the transportation facilities, audience, nor wealth to support them.

## Leisure Time and the Metropolis

Urban influences on the world of sport made their appearance in the pre-Civil War era, and by 1860 the increasing concentration of city populations created a demand for more recreational outlets. A western newspaper like the Springfield *Weekly Illinois State Journal* for April 25, 1860 criticized New York journals for stressing the Heanan-Sayers fight and expressed the opinion that interest was confined to the "fast" men and boys "who make up a considerable portion of the population of the large cities, but who are fortunately almost unknown elsewhere." The physical ailments of city dwellers at that time were noted by the January 28 issue of *Harper's Weekly* which deplored the "unhealthy constitution, the pulmonary men and women, the childless wives, the dyspeptic men, the puny forms, and the bloodless cheeks which characterize the population of our great cities at the present day." Blaming the commercial spirit of preceding decades for the abandonment of exercise, the editor pleaded for "muscular education" for the young men and women of American cities.

At the end of the Civil War attempts to escape from the cramped quarters of the metropolis became more common. Excursions made an increasingly greater appeal, and the New York *Herald* for July 16, 1865 advised:

> There are a great many ways to go out of town, and one of the easiest is to go to the Fishing Banks. Being easy, it is popular. While whole circles of men and women are wondering, like Othello, where they can go, counting the expense up this river and down that railroad, and canvassing the price of board at all the half fashionable watering places, the large and sensible public, that never had a thought of Saratoga, puts a little luncheon in one pocket and a dollar in the other, hunts up the Fishing Banks boat, and, presto!

is out of town. . . . Up she steams, a neat little craft, with the merry passengers laughing everywhere, colors flying, bells ringing, and the lively musicians doing their best on the promenade deck.

This enthusiast, in urging townsmen to get away from "the heat and turmoil of the city," advised, "Try it, ye denizens of the dirty streets, and see what a world there is just outside the city."

Frank Leslie's *Illustrated Newspaper* for October 30, 1869, discussed "Playing Baseball Under Difficulties in the Streets of New York." Despite the traffic jams of Gotham's narrow streets, "Boys will be boys. . . . No cars nor trucks, no apple-women nor fire-engines, can interrupt their games. There are few places in the city proper of sufficient size to permit ball-playing; but as the young fellows will play, they choose the most convenient streets, and fire away in spite of all travel and obstruction." First glimmerings of this urban problem, destined to become one of the unsolved riddles of recreation in the twentieth century, were appearing on the national scene. Out of the demands of city life arose the need for supervised play.

In the overly rapid expansion of American cities in the 1870's and 1880's all too little consideration was given to the leisure-time recreations of the masses, and the vanguard of sporting enthusiasts had to contend with the indifference of public authorities. Whereas only a little more than 6,000,000 Americans lived in cities or towns of more than 2500 people in 1860, by 1890 the urban population had grown to more than 22,000,000, while the rural population only doubled in that same period.

In the 1880's many of the evils of city life were already well entrenched: the sweat shop, the omnipresent saloon, the tenement districts, the prevalence of juvenile delinquency, and a host of other municipal problems were in dire need of reform. Yet through the years from 1830 to 1870, hours of labor had dropped from about 12½ to 11 among the general population. Although the schools, the YMCA, private clubs, and other agencies took up the cause of providing better recreational and sporting facilities, most American cities had not yet taken effective measures to meet the pressing problem of leisure time. All too frequently the commercialization of sport thrived on the inactivity and negligence of city fathers in the promotion of outdoor recreation.

Signs of progress did appear, however, especially with the growing concern for the building of city parks. When the National Association of Base Ball Players was organized in 1857 a committee was appointed by the convention to secure grounds in Central Park. Boston, Philadelphia, and New York pioneered in city parks as civic-minded citizens like William

Cullen Bryant, Andrew Jackson Downing, and Frederick L. Olmstead crusaded for the setting aside of large areas for the use of the people.[1] Skating became the rage in the Civil War period and grew with the years, some 50,000 New Yorkers using Central Park in one week in the winter of 1870-1871. *Harper's Weekly* for August 14, 1869 noted: "For several years the children of our schools have been allowed the use of the playgrounds of the Park. Any child attending the public schools of the city may have the privilege of the playgrounds, upon application to the Commissioners of the Park, with a certification from his or her teacher." With such obstacles, however, little encouragement could be given to organized games. Although croquet was introduced on the girls' playground, "the practice of adult clubs of match games, and the objectionable features that have become the frequent attendant of these games, have been effectually prevented." It was not until the latter years of the century that city parks began to open their fields to competitive games.

Chicago pioneered in opening up its parks to sportsmen. Washington Park seems to have been opened in 1876 to teams seeking a place to play games, the ban on cycling in Lincoln Park was lifted in 1882, and tennis courts were constructed in the South Parks in 1886.[2] Prospect Park in Brooklyn was used by 416 tennis clubs representing 6000 members, if we can believe the *Brooklyn Daily Eagle Almanac* of 1887, which also recorded 12 croquet, 3 archery, and 6 bicycle clubs, as well as 456 baseball games on the Parade ground. Although Fairmount Park in Philadelphia and a number of newly acquired tracts in New York were put into use, the challenge was not met as rapidly in many other cities. The perspicacious Charles Eliot recognized the city's dilemma in 1891:

> All about our large cities and towns the building-up of neighborhoods once rural is going on with marvelous rapidity, and the city population is progressively excluded from private properties long unoccupied, but now converted into brick blocks and wooden villages, mostly offensive to the eye. Meantime the municipalities take no measures to provide either small squares or broad areas for the future use of the people. . . . A notion has been spread abroad by assessors and frugal citizens who prefer industrial or commercial values to spiritual and aesthetic or joy-giving values, that any area exempt from taxation is an incubus on the community. . . . One would infer, from democratic practice, that in democratic theory public parks and gardens were made for the rich or the idle, whereas they are most needed by the laborious and the poor. . . . The urban population in the United States have not yet grasped these principles.[3]

Although certain private clubs and institutions were sponsoring sport in the city, the athletic impulse was neutralized in part by the lethargy of urban authorities. In the quest of outdoor sport, as open land disappeared and the public failed to recognize the urgency of remedial action, the city presented many obstacles. The athletic impulse, commercialized sports, and activities of the well-to-do all marked the progress of the sporting world, but sport for the metropolitan masses could come only with the awakened interest of the period of reform.

## Urban Reform and the Populace

Industrialism and the urban movement created many social problems at the end of the nineteenth century, and, rising to the challenge, public-spirited citizens and social agencies began to ponder seriously the evils of city life. Municipal corruption, the trust, the slum, and all the festering sores of overcrowded cities were attacked by a group of reformers including Henry George, Henry Demarest Lloyd, Edward Bellamy, Frank Parsons, Richard T. Ely, Washington Gladden, Jacob Riis, and other forerunners of the "muckrakers." As the working man sought shorter hours and greater recreational opportunities, the need for more parks, playgrounds, school gymnasiums, summer camps, and other facilities became more pressing.

While the American city dweller still groped with the problems of traffic congestion, tenement districts, crime, police reform, and political graft, he had already undertaken with little publicity the task of beautifying his environs. In certain metropolitan centers new libraries, art galleries, museums, parks, and playgrounds appeared during the 1890's, and one of the Windy City's park commissioners at the beginning of the new century envisioned Chicago as the Paris of America. The people of Boston, Chicago, Philadelphia, New York, Cleveland, Washington, and San Francisco had already begun to give attention to their park and playground needs.[4]

In the struggle of municipal authorities to improve recreational facilities for the populace, the YMCA gave increasing attention to athletics. There were 205 "Y" buildings valued at $8,350,000 in 1890, and the number of associations continued to grow, until by 1919 there were more than 1000 buildings valued at $96,000,000. In the late 1880's there were 327 associations of a total of 1273 which supported physical culture programs, and the gymnasium "attracted to the buildings and rooms a larger percentage of the associate members than any other feature or agency," but in 1898 the YMCA could report 1415 associations in existence, 552 of which stated that they had a program of physical training.[5]

Athletics proved such a popular feature of "Y" work that inter-association contests were promoted through the establishment in 1895 of the Athletic League of North American Associations. Luther Halsey Gulick emphasized the essentials of a rounded personality and created the "Y" triangle of body, mind, and spirit. The new symbol was adopted in 1895.

Physical training thus became an official feature of the YMCA. Gulick recognized as well as any man of his day the role the "Y" had to take in combatting the evils of the congested city, and in the 1890's he asserted his influence over various directors in other associations.[6] In collaboration with the 14th Regiment Armory, the Brooklyn Central "Y" began an open athletic meet in 1903, and similar programs were held in other communities as the associations encouraged sports in Sunday schools and industries. Athletics games were more slowly incorporated into the program of the Young Men's Hebrew Association, but in the period before the war progress was made.

Private clubs, high schools, colleges, armories, commercial houses, and some industries also sponsored athletic teams in the late years of the century.[7] Another urban institution of the late 19th century was the "boys' club," patterned after E.H. Harriman's Tompkins Square Club of 1876, which by 1907 had nightly admissions in excess of 1000 and which sponsored numerous athletic teams. It was during the administration of Theodore Roosevelt, however, that most American cities first undertook an ambitious program of civic improvement of recreational and athletic facilities.

If the park and playground movements made less progress than their sponsors expected in the last years of the century, it was in part due to the necessity of confronting even greater problems. Public health, sanitation, hospital, rapid transit, prison facilities, and other areas had to be given priority over the aesthetic and recreational interests. The populace had to be educated to its needs. Henry Smith Williams, writing in the February 16, 1895 issue of *Harper's Weekly,* recognized the dilemma and pointed out one safety valve and positive agent of reform:

> But we are living in the age of cities. Year by year the population of the civilized world masses itself into larger and larger communities, and lives on an average a more and more sedentary life. . . . Meantime the struggle for existence, though becoming harder and harder, is less and less a physical struggle, more and more a battle of minds. . . . It has become proverbial that our cities were stocked with 'new blood' from the country, and the succeeding generations

of city-bred descendants were progressively degenerate. Plainly this
must not continue if the gregarious impulse is to be increasingly
obeyed and the average status of our race maintained or carried
forward. And gradually the idea gained acceptance that in physical
development lay the remedy. Hence the introduction of calisthenics
in our schools, the building of gymnasia for our colleges, the spring-
ing up of athletic clubs in our cities, the amazing popular interest
in athletic games, and, lastly, the marvelous conquest of the bicycle.

That city dwellers were naturally attracted to sport in the late nineteenth and early twentieth century was evident. According to Arthur M.
Schlesinger, Sr., "The athletic awakening of the 1880's and 1890's added
a new dimension to American life. . . . Sometimes it seemed as if the
mass of people could take an interest in nothing else," and by 1905
Frederick Howe saw enough signs of civic progress to prophesy: "Just as
the monumental cathedrals which everywhere dot Europe are the expression of the ideals and aspirations of mankind, so in America, democracy
is coming to demand and appreciate fitting monuments for the realization
of its life, and splendid parks and structures as the embodiment of its
ideals."[8]

Americans were an optimistic people, as Herbert Croly, James Bryce,
Josiah Strong, Abbé Klein and other observers noted. The promise of
American life, however, required the rise of a powerful social conscience,
vocal in its protest against the confiscatory and destructive characteristics
of the capitalistic system. A new school of reformers appeared, among
them Thorstein Veblen, Ray Stannard Baker, Ida Tarbell, Upton Sinclair,
John R. Commons, and Lincoln Steffens. The spirit of progressivism and
reform penetrated to the heart of American society and brought Theodore
Roosevelt, Woodrow Wilson, and Robert La Follette to the center of the
political stage.

Sport had served as one of the safety valves of the overcrowded urban
populace and may have been an important factor in the retention of much
of nineteenth-century optimism after the disappearance of the frontier.
Other elements in this maintenance of faith in the future were the compensations derived from education, cultural progress, science, religion,
business prosperity, a rising living standard, expanding economic frontiers,
and greater opportunities at other forms of recreation. But Americans,
facing a new century of industrialization, mass production, total war, and
unpredictable business cycles, would be increasingly in need of safety
valves for the mounting tensions of urban life. In all the recreational pursuits of the years from the late nineteenth century to the end of World
War I sport was a principal and at times the dominant factor.

## Recreation for the Masses in the Roosevelt-Taft-Wilson Era

Richard T. Ely, one of the early champions of playgrounds, public gardens, and parks, believed that "half of the wrong-doings of young rascals in the cities is due to the fact that they have no innocent outlet for their animal spirits." The playground movement originated in the sand box innovation in Boston in the early 1880's and soon attracted some attention in New York and other cities. Brooklyn organized a playground movement in 1888, and New York followed the next year. Abram S. Hewitt served as the first president of the New York Society for Parks and Playgrounds in 1891, and when park officials were reluctant to build grounds, he issued a report for the Small Parks Committee in 1897 stating that "the law should be amended as to *require* playgrounds to be made part of a park."[9]

Although the Outdoor Recreation League formed in 1898 and the playground movement antedated the year 1905, its greatest impetus came in the following years. Michigan cities reputedly had no playgrounds in 1906, but the passing decade witnessed the building of playgrounds and the training of leaders in seventeen municipalities. South Park, Chicago, opened in 1905 as a pioneer experiment in the provision made for athletic fields, gyms, and other facilities. Los Angeles and Pittsburgh were competitors with Chicago in the erection of recreational centers. In 1906 the formation of the Playground Association of America was a notable step in the athletic movement, especially in the guidance of that organization by Luther Gulick and Joseph Lee. By 1912 Seattle was claiming a higher proportionate expenditure than any other city, having spent $1,000,000 on playgrounds and $4,000,000 on parks and parkways. Although Seattle had no playgrounds in 1900, it had 22 in 1912 and plans for a vast extension of the program. City planning commissions at this time were seriously considering the problem.

Tom L. Johnson of Cleveland was one mayor who encouraged the playground movement, and he was reputed to have said, "When I die I hope the people will make a playground over my body. I would rather have the children romping over my grave than a hundred monuments." Whereas there were only 41 cities with a total annual playground budget of $15,000 in 1906, ten years later there were 480 cities reporting a municipal playground movement. Park acreage expanded rapidly: a comparison of land in four types of recreation areas in municipalities in the Chicago region showed 174.83 acres in the 1901-1910 period but 1001.09 acres in the 1910-1920 period.[10] Women's clubs were especially active in sponsoring playgrounds, and, with Illinois as the pioneer, they were in great part responsible for legislation on physical education in 25 states between 1915 and 1921.

One of the great problems of reform was the existence of boys' gangs which settlement workers struggled to divert to athletic games. Through the athletic club composed of gang members it was felt that not only muscular development but intellectual and moral benefits could be achieved. Although the difficulty in meeting the needs of a rapidly grow-ing population became almost insuperable, the city and the state never-theless had made considerable progress in the playground movement by 1920.

When the New York Public Schools Athletic League was founded in 1903 by General George W. Wingate, cities throughout America promptly imitated the idea. Competitive games, and especially volleyball, were introduced on the grade school level. New Orleans, Baltimore, Seattle, Newark, Troy, Buffalo, Cleveland, Birmingham, Tacoma, San Francisco, and Kansas City were sponsoring public school athletic leagues in 1909 and countless other cities followed their lead. A survey of the 75 largest Nebraska high schools in 1909 revealed that 95 percent of these schools were then engaged in interscholastic athletics. Another study made in 1904-1905 covering 555 American cities in various population categories showed that 345 had high school athletic associations, and the popularity of the major sports was shown in that 432 had football, 360 had baseball, 213 had basketball, and 161 had track teams. The consolidated school movement, already under way, enabled rural children to enjoy the games and athletics of the town and city schools.[11]

All these movements were related to the noticeable enthusiasm on the sandlots of every American community. One baseball fan in *Collier's* for August 12, 1911, maintained, "The real baseball, where grit is learned, wits sharpened, and the battling spirit of Yankee ambition first takes fire, is the baseball of the back lots." First lessons in American democracy were often learned on the corner lot by many an Irish, German, or Swed-sih lad, not to mention the Jewish, Italian, and Polish boys who avidly took to organized games. Much available space was disappearing, especially in large urban centers, but ingenious youngsters in every American town and city found some abandoned lot overgrown with weeds and tall grass, full of rocks and holes, where they could meet their rivals in glorious combat.

The institutional church of the eighties and nineties had approached the Social Gospel through the introduction of libraries, meeting rooms, auditoriums, and gymnasiums. By 1904 a Sunday School Athletic League was organized in Brooklyn and a Catholic league in New York. In less than a decade there was a "tremendous growth in church athletics." Even the rural church began to recognize, ever so slowly, the value of recreation and sports. Catholic men in the Knights of Columbus sponsored numerous boxing and athletic exhibitions at their smokers. Military authorities co-operated with the public schools, allowing schoolboys to hold practice sessions and games in their armories. The universality of sport has been described by Owen E. Pence: "Every institution centered in the life of youth, either by compulsion or choice, assumed some degree of leadership in athletics."[12]

Public reaction to organized games was reflected in the interest of social workers and educators. It was also demonstrated in the growing support of sport in business and industry. For example, the Pabst Brewing Company offering trophies for athletic contests, auto races, aero clubs and horse shows at the start of the century. As early as 1905 some of the leaders in the American Federation of Labor tried to form an international union of professional baseball players. Some fifty baseball leagues were said to be in operation in Chicago in 1909, including such teams as "the Banker's League, the Stockyards and the Commercial Houses." The YMCA held classes in many factories in these early years of industrial sport. As Germany declared war on Russia in 1914, the Bethlehem Steel Company was engaged in another kind of war at the time. Charles Schwab, its renowned head, was spending lavishly to recruit the best soccer aggre-gation in the country, and many stars were persuaded to sign by Schwab's piratical but enticing offers.[13]

By the middle of the second decade numerous industries promoted athletics among their employees. Among the business organizations and industries sponsoring athletic clubs were R.H. Macy's and John Wana maker's of New York, Johnson and Johnson of New Brunswick, General Electric of Schenectady, Michelin of Milltown, New Jersey, and Borden's Milk and Metropolitan Life of New York. Wanamaker employees, banded together in an athletic association which founded one of the annual winter athletic classics, the Millrose Games. Basketball was rising in popularity, and Philadelphia had its Industrial League of Basketball Clubs. Few indus-tries went as far as the Goodyear Company and employees who sponsored baseball, football, track, hockey, skating, basketball, volleyball, tennis, and even cricket. Akron's other factories formed a City Industrial League and engaged in athletic contests. Nor were sports neglected by the United States Steel Corporation, which apparently found that recreational and athletic facilities made for better workers.

General prosperity, a more truly national appreciation of sport, and the increase of leisure time were all contributory to the growth of indus-trial athletics. Whereas in 1909 the number of those who worked less than 54 hours per week was only 15.2 percent of the industrial class, by 1923 this group had increased to 68 percent. Hours of work were still long in the years prior to 1920, but industrial sponsorship of organized sports was making rapid headway.

Urban conditions had eliminated much of the physical exertion required of women in early America. Although basketball had been quickly accepted in the 1890's and field hockey had been put on an organized basis at Bryn Mawr, Radcliffe, Smith, Wellesley, and Vassar as early as 1901, it was only in the years 1906 to 1918 that supervised sports were first required in American women's colleges. Sportswomen trailed Alexa Stirling and Molla Mallory to the golf links and tennis courts, but there was still a very strong reaction in educated circles against overly athletic sports for women. James E. Sullivan, Secretary of the AAU, opposed the hiring of male teachers for girls' athletics, discouraged training periods or interschool competition, and felt that women were discredited by competition. The Amateur Athletic Union refused to register any female competitors, a definite indication of public opinion on the proper place of women in sport.

Public school athletic leagues and playgrounds aroused some interest among girls, but in any comparison with the strides made in the athletic interests of boys, little was done for girls. In the limited confines of academic walls this lag was not so evident. The records of Vassar College revealed that, among 7077 students at the college from 1884 to 1920, the average height increase was 1.3 inches, while the average weight increase was 6.5 pounds (though this may have been due as much to improved diet as to physical exercise). The rise of interest among collegiate women is shown in the decline over the first two decades of the present century of those who participated in no sports whatever from 26.5 percent to 6 percent.[14] One must not forget that this was far from characteristic of the average woman. Golfing, swimming, and cavorting at games like tennis, softball, volleyball, and basketball, more American girls were introduced to sport than ever before, but the general belief that competitive rivalry and strenuous athletics impeded the social and physical development of young women did much to hinder more active feminine participation.

Part of the crusade for social reform was directed into a war on juvenile delinquency. Athletic games were encouraged in boys' clubs and settlement houses as a bulwark against the evils of the slum and such "demoralizing amusements" of the city as vaudeville, the theater, saloons, and gang clubs. Thomas Evans observed in the *Annals of the American Academy of Political and Social Science* for November, 1907: "The settlement should manage the athletic sports of the young people . . . for it has been proven that the athletic sphere when taken hold of properly may be one of the largest fields of usefulness in neighborhood work, since all classes of people will rally more enthusiastically about athletics than anything else."

Rev. Josiah Strong wrote in the same year that the saloon was "the clearing house of athletic and sporting news" as well as a "poor man's club," a social center, and a meeting place of labor union groups. He recognized that it was generally felt that the playground diminished delinquency and he concluded: "Play . . . is an essential part of a normal childhood. A child, therefore, who is robbed of a playground is robbed of a large part of his childhood. . . . If God gives the instinct, man ought to provide the playground."[15]

In *Twenty Years at Hull-House* Jane Addams attested to the popularity of athletic contests among boys which diverted them from "the sensual and exhausting pleasures to be found so easily outside the club." Hiram House in Cleveland and South End House in Boston, among other settlements, recognized the value of sports programs and playgrounds in combatting juvenile delinquency. Jane Addams later wrote of the interest of men and boys in the diamond in Chicago: "The theater even now by no means competes with the baseball league games which are attended by thousands of men and boys who, during the entire summer, discuss the respective standing of each nine and the relative merits of every player. During the noon hour all the employees of a city factory gather in the nearest vacant lot to cheer their own home team in its practice for the next game with the nine of a neighboring manufacturing establishment and on a Saturday afternoon the entire male population of the city betakes itself to the baseball field."[16]

Theodore Roosevelt recognized the city's responsibility to youth. In a letter of congratulation to General Wingate on the founding of the Public Schools Athletic League in 1903, he wrote:

> The great congestion in population which, of course, means the crowded streets as well as the crowded houses, has resulted in depriving the children of New York of opportunity of exercise, especially in the tenement house districts, so that their physical development tends to drop below the normal. The energies they should work off in wholesome exercise, in vigorous play, find vent in the worst feats of the gangs which represent so much that is vicious in our city life. It is a great disadvantage to a boy to be unable to play games; and every boy who knows how to play base ball or football, to box or wrestle, has by just so much fitted himself to be a better citizen.[17]

In his tireless efforts to improve the lives of the underprivileged, Jacob Riis noted a decline in gang warfare and juvenile delinquency with the establishment of parks and playgrounds, and he contended that the youth who engaged in outdoor sports had neither the time, the desire, nor the energy for dissipation: "It is the idle fellow who falls into that trap."

Sport's contribution in the war on juvenile delinquency was accepted on all sides, perhaps too enthusiastically at times. It received the confirmation of Lillian D. Wald, another noted social worker, who wrote *The House on Henry Street* in 1915 and maintained that clean sport and competition decreased gang warfare and hostility between national groups. The police cooperated by roping off streets for the playing of games, and social workers enthusiastically promoted team play.

Racial and national differences were accentuated in the latter half of the nineteenth century as the immigrant wave turned from the north and west to the south and east of Europe. Irishmen and Germans, who had come to America in post-Civil War decades and had become storekeepers, railroad men, or saloon operators, were by the end of the century beginning to penetrate the professions, business, and the world of politics. But a new force was operating on the immigrant class at the end of the nineteenth century. As more and more ships debarked hopeful peoples from Italy, Greece, Poland, Russia, and other southern and eastern European areas, new barriers confronted their "Americanization." Industrialism had transformed the face of America and altered the opportunities of the immigrant. He became "associated with the laboring class and inherited its psychology and status in an industrial economy. . . . For the immigrants were now frequently thought of as comprising a distinct class, in America but not of it."[18] Difficult as it was for the children of these immigrants to escape the life of manual labor, many determined to become identified with everything American. Countless boys and girls of all nationalities seeking outlets for these pent-up desires entered into competitive sports.

Immigrants were attracted to sport or reacted against it almost as soon as they settled down to a normal existence. Michael Pupin, destined to win lasting fame in American science, was persuaded to attend Columbia University in great part by the fame of its Henley crew of 1878. Oscar Handlin has noted how this sporting interest mounted after 1880 among the adults who recognized the lack of social distinctions and among gang members who emulated athletic heroes. "Increasingly the thoughts of the children were preoccupied with the events of the world of sport within which were played out the vivid dramas of American success and failure," and, though there was parental perplexity at "the infantile antics of grown men playing at ball," the status concept of these transplanted Europeans weakened: "Even the older folk indeed derived a kind of satisfaction from the fame of men who bore names like their own, as if John L. Sullivan or Honus Wagner or Benny Leonard, somehow, testified to their own acceptance by American society." But the old order changeth slowly, and Mary

Antin, admitting in 1914 that "the baseball diamond may supplement the schoolroom and the pulpit in the training of American citizens," nonetheless warned, "We shall not look in the sporting columns . . . for the names of contemporary Americans who are likely to secure us a place of honor on the scrolls of history."[19]

Philadelphians held their first annual Field Day at Franklin Field in 1908 and New York City opened recreational opportunities to its children as Mayor Gaynor inaugurated the "Safe and Sane Fourth of July" in 1910. From the beginning we find a general mingling at these games of all nationalities and religions, among them such typical names as Cohen, Goldberg, Rosenberg, Goldstein, Schwartz, Crowley, Dugan, McLaughlin, O'Donnell, Reilly, Sullivan, Paterno, Balzarini, Solari and Anderson, to mention only a few. This interethnic movement became general on the playgrounds of the larger cities. Interinstitutional athletics were promoted, and in Baltimore one league was composed of clubs representing such organizations as the Light Street Mission, St. Paul's Guild House, Epworth Hall, Messiah Church, Govans YMCA, and Public School No. 49.

Not all sporting activities were conducive to the amalgamation of national groups. The Scotch, Irish, and German athletic clubs which multiplied in the 1880's sometimes accentuated the exclusiveness of the ethnic identity of their respective immigrant populations. They did add to the fervor for athletics among young clubmen, however, and as these hyphenated organizations began to compete with one another they enhanced the fusion of national groups.

German names became prominent on the football teams of midwestern colleges before 1909 and were found in all sports from bicycle racing to baseball. The Poe brothers of Princeton, the most noted of football families, Honus Wagner of the Pittsburgh Pirates, Archie Hahn of Michigan, and Alvin Kraenzlein of Pennsylvania indicated the entry of those of German descent on the sporting scene. Basketball attracted young enthusiasts of many nationalities, particularly in the largest cities where the YMCA, YMHA, churches, and boys' clubs made their limited facilities available. As Jewish boys were thrown against Italians and German youths competed with the Irish, contests frequently became unruly, but the give-and-take of combat created a mutual respect on the part of all participants. The concept of sportsmanship entered the games of the school, the settlement, the YMCA, the YMHA, and the church, as well as supervised contests of institutions for the deaf and the blind. Even the prisons began to encourage athletic competition. Sportsmanship broke the bonds of its aristocratic origins and was taken over by peoples of all creeds and color, emerging as a new force in the American mind and a subject for the pulpit, the platform, and the soap box.

## Fair Play and the Democratic Spirit

Americans of every walk of life increasingly recognized the potential value of sport as a promoter of the democratic spirit. Perennial vigilance in the clash between amateur and professional codes drew forth a continuous eulogy of sport for sport's sake. The threat to the spirit of sportsmanship manifested in commercialization and overemphasis during the first two decades was constantly asserted. The sportsman's code was inculcated into a generation of sandlot players and country club members alike. Professor Hugo Munsterberg, who claimed that only American humor excelled sport in breaking down social distinctions, speculated on social aspirations toward true equality and remarked:

> If the members of the community feel themselves really equal, they will lay special importance, in their social intercourse, on all such factors as likewise do not accentuate external differences, but bind man to man without regard to position, wealth, or culture. This is the reason of the remarkable hold which sport has on American life. . . . And yet even the fervour with which the spectators on the grand-stand manifest their partisanship is only another expression of the fact that the average American is intensely moved by sport; and this interest is so great as to overcome all social distinctions and create, for the time being, an absolutely equal fellow-feeling. . . . Around the grounds sit labouring men, clergymen, shop-boys, professors, muckers and millionaires, all participating with a community of interest and feeling of equality as if they were worlds removed from the petty business where social differences are considered.[20]

Fair play and good sportsmanship were often identified with the democratic ideal. One of the finest descriptions of the sporting code came from the pen of an eminent sports writer, Mr. Grantland Rice:

> For when the One Great Scorer comes
>     To write against your name
> He writes—not that you won or lost—
>     But how you played the game.

Fair play demands that all who participate in the contest must abide by the rules, and in sport the competitor is most sharply confronted with this necessity. Lessons of defeat went far to strengthen the moral fiber of youth. All too frequently schoolboys were supervised by coaches ill equipped to reinforce their moral character, but the general movement of this era toward state regulation of athletic programs aided mightily in the rise of a qualified coaching profession.

The identification of the concept of fair play in sport and in democratic life was gaining wider acceptance. Otto Mallery, writing in 1910 on
"The Social Significance of Play," contended:

> It seems a far cry from the ideal of fair play in boys' games to
> the ideal of fair play in the political life of our democracy, yet it can
> be demonstrated that the ideals of fair play and team play are im-
> portant in forming the character of a community.
> In the games of the street every boy is for himself. Victory
> belongs to the shrewd, the crafty, the strong. Team games of the
> playground require the submission of the individual will to the
> welfare of the team. Rigid rules inculcate fair play. A boy has the
> option of obeying the rules or not playing at all. New standards are
> set up; standards of self-control, of helping the other fellow, of
> fighting shoulder to shoulder for the honor of the team, of defeat
> preferable to unfair victory. These standards when translated into the
> language of political life we call Selfgovernment, Respect for the
> Law, Social Service and Good Citizenship.[21]

Luther Gulick, one of the truly great promoters of the athletic ideal,
also demonstrated the affinity between the sporting code and the democratic concept of the law. Firmly believing in play as a preparation for
democracy, he illustrated the effect of competitive games on youth: "The
morality developed during the years of competition is legal, individual,
combative. The greatest indignation is felt by the small boy in that period
at any one who violates his rights, who will not play by the rules of the
game, who fails to observe the law of justice. . . . There is, however, a
more comprehensive morality that comes in with the team games. Here
enters the element of devotion to the whole, of loyalty to a group. . . .
The team games develop respect for law, in a rudimentary form, to be
sure, but in a form capable of growth. The boy that is caught cheating or
lying to his own crowd is ostracized."[22]
In an era when large numbers of foreign-born citizens and their
children were adjusting to the American way of life, the code of fair play
and good sportsmanship was widely praised as promoting good citizenship
and deeper understanding of our democratic institutions. Although the
repetition of such ideas was most frequently found on the sports page, an
ever increasing realization of sport's significance worked its way into the
inner fabric of the American mind.
G. Stanley Hall, writing in his pioneer study *Adolescence* in 1907,
recognized the social value of sport for the teenage child. At this stage of
physical development, he wrote, "a new spirit of organization arises which
makes teams possible or more permanent. Football, baseball, cricket, etc.,

and even boating can become schools of mental and moral training. . . . Group loyalty in Anglo-Saxon games, which shows such a marked increment in coordination and self-subordination at the dawn of puberty as to constitute a distinct change in the character of sports at this age, can be so utilized as to develop a spirit of service and devotion not only to town, country, and race, but to God and the Church." Although most educational reformers adhered to the principles of personalized, individual play, many of them seemed to incline toward a more spirited promotion of athletic rivalries. The ethics and philosophy of sport were seen to coincide with the ethics and philosophy of Americanism.

All groups in the population were affected. Immigrant and native, man and boy, woman and girl, capitalist and laborer, Jew and Christian— all responded to this growing national consciousness of the great possibilities in organized games. More and more they realized that the great issue of the day in sport was not simply amateurism as opposed to professionalism (strong as the prejudice remained) but the moral and educational value to be derived. The American spirit was being modified, at least, by our athletic interests. Frederick L. Paxson, distinguished historian of the frontier, writing on "The Rise of Sport," noted the change of national character, personal conduct, and public opinion from the indifference to corruption of the post-Civil War years to the more respectable ethics of the twentieth century. Sport had played its role: "And who shall say that when our women took up tennis and the bicycle they did not as well make the great stride towards real emancipation; or that the quickened pulse, the healthy glow, the honest self-respect of honest sport have not served in part to steady and inspire a new Americanism for a new century."[23]

## Sectionalism, Nationalism, and Internationalism

> "The most important thing in the Olympic Games is not winning, but taking part; the essential thing in life is not conquering, but fighting well."
>
> —Baron Pierre de Coubertin

One of the foremost contributions to this more national enthusiasm for athletics was the spread of games from a local to a sectional and, at times, a nationwide level of competition. Sport was well on the way to being national in spirit by 1900. Organizers of professional baseball, collegiate football, and track athletics, and certain performers on the links, tennis courts, and other fields of play were holding national championships and spreading the spirit of sport from the Atlantic to the Pacific.

But the broad base of sport was only lightly affected. Sectional prejudices against the dominance of eastern sport appeared at least as early as the late sixties and developed through the years. Baseball remained primarily a local game of small towns or cities and of closely-knit leagues; football teams still hesitated to schedule games more than a few miles away; and the only real source of comparison in deciding championships was in the newspaper. Walter Camp, Caspar Whitney, and the principal sports publishing houses strove to nationalize the rules of various sports, but many organizations remained in a state of hostile rivalry. For years the YMCA, the AAU, the intercollegiate rules associations, and other bodies ignored each others' regulations. To an unprecedented extent it was the first decades of the twentieth century that experienced a statewide, regional, and, at times, national organization of sports.

Athletics made rapid headway in the Far West. In 1905 James E. Sullivan noted, "The city [Portland, Oregon] is the same as Frisco, St. Louis and other western cities. That is, they lack the organized schoolboy leagues, military leagues, church leagues and leagues of athletic clubs. I am convinced that in many western cities the very foundation of our athletic structure is being neglected, and that is, the formation of clubs and leagues and the giving of open games." But such attractions as the Penn Relays, national tennis and golf tourneys, AAU championships, and similar events interested young athletes on a wider scale in the succeeding fifteen years.

Among the tennis stars of this period one must list such westerners as Maurice McLoughlin, William L. Johnston, Mary K. Browne, May Sutton Bundy, and Alice Wightman. And they were but the most publicized of a growing group of California enthusiasts. Harry Hooper and Frank Chance were the vanguard of a horde of western players to invade the Big Leagues, while baseball flourished on the West Coast throughout the Federal League war. Nor was that solid base of sport, the playground movement, ignored. In the public schools of the West a branching out of interest was demonstrated in the growth of the traditional state championship. Oklahoma's first track championship was held in 1905 and by 1916 we find 500 athletes attending the games at Norman.[24]

As athletics caught on in the West, football prospered. Eastern colleges retained only a slight edge on western rivals, and none at all on midwestern teams. When "All-America" selections in 1918 failed to name a Harvard, Yale, or Princeton player, one critic in *Collier's* stated, "It is the story of football's prarie fire sweep after the forward pass opened up the game and the old dynasties fell from power with a crash."

South of the Mason and Dixon line it was the same story in slower tempo. In the 1890's Glenn ("Pop") Warner had gone to Georgia to develop football interest. A series of famous coaches such as John Heisman (Clemson), Dan McGugin (Vanderbilt), and Mike Donahue (Auburn) helped raise the reputation of southern football. The high school game lagged in southern climes, but during the years of World War I strong southern teams gave a decided impetus to gridiron interest in that region.[25]

Baseball was more firmly established in the South when the Southern Association was organized in 1910 and joined the National Association the next year. The limited sizes of cities and the long jumps by rail, however, were definite obstacles. Golf became increasingly popular, as did tennis and other outdoor sports, although various games of northern cities, including handball, squash, and lacrosse were not widely known.

Sport in general lagged in the South during this period. The playground movement, so needed in an area where child labor laws were now turning children out of the factories, was not zealously promoted. With short school terms and long summer vacations, southern children might easily have been attracted to organized athletics. The race problem and the substandard revenues of southern cities may partially explain the lag, as might the nature of the climate. As the poverty of southern cities diminished, however, and the New South really made economic progress, sport in the schools became increasingly popular. According to Francis Simkins, "Important changes became evident at the time of World War I. Colleges and schools popularized gymnastics. Northern tourists demonstrated the advantages of golf and other outdoor sports, Southerners appreciated the claims of certain northern magazines concerning the benefits of physical culture. Fear of the sun succumbed to an appreciation of its health-giving qualities. Young women cultivated the bronzed skin in preference to the fair one."[26]

The groundwork for intersectional sport had been laid. Within the states themselves many communities were drawn more closely together by the formation of district and state athletic associations in the public schools. By 1926 there were forty-five states with organizations for promoting interschool contests, most of which had been based on the constructive work of the 1905-1920 era.

Many critics might complain that the philosophy of physical superiority and the will to win, sometimes at any price, were detrimental to the best form of citizenship. The tide was swinging, however, to a widely held confidence on the part of the public of the merit of sporting ideals and vigorous play. Sport was emerging as an important institution in American life. John A. Krout, aware of many of the excesses and evils of commercialized sport, nonetheless later wrote in his *Annals of American Sport*: "Probably the most socially significant contribution of modern team play has been its powerful influence for national solidarity. Whether on municipal athletic field, on school playground, or on college campus, American youth learned much more than successful cooperation and good sportsmanship. As representatives of many nations, drawn from families of widely varying cultural backgrounds, they found a common denominator in competitive sports. Athletic prowess in group competition proved a truly democratic force, often countering tendencies toward class and caste distinction."

By 1920 sport had become associated, in the minds of millions of Americans, with local and national prestige and with democratic society. Sport had, through development from a local to a regional and national basis, done much to unify the social interests of men and women from Bangor, Maine, to Spokane, Washington. It carried with it an *esprit de corps* which gave the auto worker in Detroit a common interest with the farmer from Missouri or the ranch owner from Texas. The lingo of the playing fields was spoken in barber shop, hotel lobby, barroom, and club as well as at church, school, or public meeting. Contributions of sport to democracy have entered the American mind in subtle ways, but these contributions have been significant. Far-seeing observers acknowledged the potential value of sport, but warned that its merits lie in the leadership it received. Where ideals of fair play, equal opportunity, and good sportsmanship were encouraged, the majority seemed to have been converted to the wholesome benefit of rugged, vigorous competition. Much of social democracy lies in men of every class rubbing shoulders, and in sport this tendency is more marked than in most other spheres of everyday life.

> If, as many think, England is now at the zenith of her power and greatness, where will the traces of her paramount influence upon the nineteenth century be sought by the Buckles of two centuries hence? Not so much in the imitation by other nations of our representative institutions of trial by jury, of freedom of the press, or even in the wide diffusion of English books, as in the reproduction all over the world of some of our lighter social peculiarities . . . most of all, in the contagious passion for our national pastimes.

Anthony Trollope may have been slyly jesting in this prophecy of 1868, but it is true that American interest in athletics grew out of that British sporting renaissance of the Victorian Age. The turf, cricket, and fox hunting gradually were forced to share the limelight with rowing, association football, and track events. Waning interest in cock fighting and the decline of respectability in the boxing world opened the way to popular enthusiasm for athletics in the British Isles.

As English youth flocked to the playing fields of their famous schools, Rugby and other games swept throughout the upper classes of English society. Even the masses attended annual spectacles such as rowing on the Thames or the famous Derby. Although the coal miners of Wales and the children in knitting mills had no time for the athletic diversions of the élite, British enthusiasm for sport became legendary in the nineteenth century. In 1868 Trollope might caution "That English Sports may remain as long as England remains, and that they may remain among the descendants of Englishmen to days in which perhaps England herself may exist no longer, is our wish as sportsmen; but . . . should it ever become unreasonable in its expenditures, arrogant in its demands, immoral and selfish in its tendencies, or worse of all, unclean and dishonest in its traffic, there will arise against it a public opinion against which it will be unable to hold its own."[27]

By 1876 President James McCosh of Princeton was alarmed at the growth of "wickedness" in the Oxford-Cambridge races, charging that the authorities at both universities found the gambling element so deeply entrenched that "it was difficult for the college authorities to interfere."[28] As the century progressed the wail of protest against overathleticism mounted in England, and sport was charged with all the vices of the commercial world. The English athlete reigned supreme over his only challenger, the aspiring American, as the Continent failed to respond to competitive athletics. The record books listed countless British champions in rowing and swimming, running and cycling, tennis and golf. The nineteenth was an Anglo-American century in sport and, until the last decade, it was an epoch of English pre-eminence.

This athletic supremacy had its effect on Anglo-American relations. Emulation of things British did not die with the Federalists. As the nation grew in industrial power, as frontier civilization steadily passed from the American scene in the late years of the century, and as the nature of world power, military and naval, revealed itself to Americans, there rose a mounting inclination toward Anglo-American amity. This course is also illustrated in the story of Anglo-American sport.

Only the élite of American women entered the field of organized sport. From croquet they turned to cycling and were greatly responsible for the wheeling mania of the nineties. Few went to the gymnasium, except in the colleges. Masculine games like baseball, football, and track and field demanded too great exertion for their long dresses and cumbersome apparel, too strenuous action for the feminine mores of the period. Most women found their household duties more than enough to fill the daylight hours. In addition to the church, which remained their principal interest, they sought their recreation as spectators at the track, the ball park, or the theater.

American women did turn in limited numbers to more genteel games, however. As they did so they imitated their English sisters to a startling degree. When Queen Victoria's daughter took to the bicycle, there occurred "a national glow of emulation;" when English women began to compete on the tennis court and golf links, women of society hesitatingly did the same.

American women golfers remained inferior to the English, who were admired for the length of their drives and their more manly style of play. In 1891 the Shinnecock Hills Golf Club became the first organized women's club, and in the nineties men's courses were opened to feminine enthusiasts. Golfers abroad were not to be bothered by the "weaker sex," but American sportsmen gladly shared their links. Miss Beatrix Hoyt attained the reputation of being the first great American woman golfer. The turn of the century found one hundred and thirteen women, from thirty-eight clubs between Boston and Chicago, competing at the Baltusrol tournament in New Jersey, the largest entry in any women's tourney in early golfing history. Even then, however, the same admiration was held for Anglican supremacy on the links. An American critic in 1901 observed:

> We must admit that, as a race, they [the British] are stronger and more athletic than we are, and more accustomed from childhood to outdoor sports of all kinds. They have a greater natural love for such things and will probably always excel us in them; so that while in time we may be able to furnish a few players who will rank with England's best, still I doubt if the day will ever come when we shall feel able to challenge 'all England' with an 'all American' team.[29]

British supremacy was valiantly maintained in the world of feminine sport.

Britain's impact on the sporting world contributed much to the growth of an Anglo-Saxon theory of supremacy. As the nineteenth century broadened and deepened the grip of democratic institutions in the English-speaking world, pride in England's history led historians to view her past as a continuous struggle for human freedom. Meanwhile, the United States emerged from the tiny republic of 1789 to extend protective arms over the continent and the great Pacific Ocean as far as the Philippines. This was a century of expansion for the British and American empires, while Germany, the Saxon home of this new race, attained paramount power on the continent and great heights in music, scholarship, and science. Little need we marvel at the rise of a theory of Anglo-Saxon destiny. The *Spirit of the Times* for July 17, 1875 urged American youth to emulate British athleticism, decrying the effeminacy of the modern Italians and southern Europeans but firmly alleging: "There can be little doubt that the English owe much of their national independence of character to their love of manly sports."

International competition, after its brief appearance in the victory of the *America* in 1851, was sustained during the Civil War period only through visiting cricket teams and the prize fights held here and abroad.

The postwar years saw sporadic attempts to arouse interest in the boating rivalries of American and English universities. *Frank Leslie's Illustrated Newspaper* followed the Harvard-Oxford race in 1869 and observed: "The rivalry not unnaturally excited considerable national feeling in the people of both countries; for there were few on either side . . . who did not heartily wish success to the representatives of their native land in this novel aquatic rivalry." Noting the role of sport in the British military, Lloyd S. Bryce made "A Plea For Sport" in the May, 1879 issue of the *North American Review:* "As a means of bringing the family of nations into more friendly relations, international athletic contests have within a few years proved to be very effectual." Wheelmen, track athletes, horsemen, cricketers, rifle experts, and other sportsmen traveled between the United States and England. Even the baseball world sent its emissaries of good will to foreign lands, Harry Wright taking a team to England in 1874 and A.G. Spalding leading an expedition around the world in 1889. It was only in the nineties, however, that any popular interest in international competition developed in the athletic world.

Scholars, as well as the world of journalism, made use of sport. As both historian and sports enthusiast, Professor William Milligan Sloane excoriated the saboteurs of sport and maintained, "It is a serious truth that other nations wonder at the proud position of the Anglo-Saxon race, and that they attribute the fine ripe qualities of maturer life to the beginnings born on playing fields and developed in the seriousness of conflict."[30] President Eliot, in a different spirit, was later to question any effect of athletic interest on patriotism by exposing the records of Harvard men in the Spanish-American War. The case for Wellington's tribute to the playing fields of Eton had been overworked by the sporting scribes of the age, but the idea of the gridiron and the diamond as mimic battlefields training future guardians of the republic has passed down through the annals of American sport.

A skeptical academic world berated this growing threat of athletics to the old university ideal. Increasingly, men of scholarship took up the cudgel FOR or AGAINST intercollegiate games. The world of journalism engaged at times in the controversy. E.L. Godkin bewailed in the *Nation* for December 7, 1893: "There was the greenback craze, and the cholera craze, and the granger craze, and now there is the athletic craze." On the other hand, a rising young politician in New York named Theodore Roosevelt wrote that "the true sports for a manly race are sports like running, rowing, playing football and baseball, boxing and wrestling, shooting, riding and mountain climbing." That athletically-minded individual maintained:

In a perfectly peaceful and commercial civilization such as ours there is always a danger of laying too little stress upon the more virile virtues—upon the virtues which go to make up a race of statesmen and soldiers, of pioneers and explorers by land and sea, of bridge-builders and road-makers, of commonwealth-builders—in short, upon those virtues for the lack of which, whether in an individual or in a nation, no amount of refinement and learning, of gentleness and culture, can possibly attone. These are the very qualities which are fostered by vigorous manly out-of-door sports.[31]

The American debt to Britain was not forgotten. Albert Bushnell Hart of Harvard acknowledged that debt by writing in the *Atlantic Monthly* in July, 1890: "While German youths still exercized with a sword and American youths with a trotting-sulky, young Englishmen ran, rowed, played cricket, and revived football and tennis." Professor Hart attributed this unique development to ancient customs, climate, and the English schools. As war with Spain neared, Henry Cabot Lodge spoke briefly to a Harvard alumni gathering:

I happen to be one of those, Mr. President, who believe profoundly in athletic contests. The time given to athletic contests and the injuries incurred on the playing-field are part of the price which the English-speaking race has paid for being world-conquerors. . . . Individualism carried to its last extreme has made Poland a geographical expression. Social efficiency has made the English-speaking people the conquering race of modern times. . . . A nation must have that spirit [of victory] to succeed in the world, and a college must have that spirit to succeed in the nation.[32]

Whether or not American sport was really so instrumental in securing the bonds of friendship between the two peoples, whether or not it was a potent factor in the welding of a healthy and united nation, many enthusiasts thought so. How deeply this penetration of athleticism went into the future alignment of warring powers is questionable, but as one of many factors it is not to be ignored.

Misunderstandings often arose as a result of the excited passions of sportsmen, but international rivalry descended to a new low in 1895 with Lord Dunraven's denunciation of American yachting officials and his refusal to race his *Valkyrie VII* against the *Defender*. The *St. James Gazette* confessed, "Once again the great Anglo-American sporting contest has ended muddily in a fiasco and quarrel, not an unusual experience."[33]

American feeling ran high over the accusations of the British challenger:

> Lord Dunraven's attitude was a dissapointment to American yachtsmen. He knew crowding was a condition to be met in yacht races here, as elsewhere. He made trouble through a vague charge of fraud, then shifted ground and refused to sail because he was not assured a clear course. . . . When he returned to England he was easily the most unpopular Englishman who ever left this country. It is hard to justify, in American eyes, what is popularly called 'quiting,' no matter what motives govern the act. There is a feeling in this country that a sportsman should 'take his medicine' when once embarked in a sporting venture, come what will. This Lord Dunraven did not do.[34]

A committee composed of Edward J. Phelps, J. Pierpont Morgan, William C. Whitney, Alfred Thayer Mahan, and George L. Rives absolved the crew of the *Defender,* convincing many Americans of Dunraven's poor sportsmanship. There were those, however, who felt that too much sharp practice had entered into the defense of the America's Cup. The *fin de siecle* yachting world might well feel grateful for the generous sportsmanship of Sir Thomas Lipton on the defeat of his *Shamrock* in 1899. Sir Thomas engaged in yachting to help cement Anglo-American friendship, but he was also keenly concerned with the publicity value of the America's Cup in the extension of his great commercial enterprises in beef and tea.

The rival claim of athletics on the American public restricted the popularity of yacht racing, but it remained one of the great spectacles of the sporting world. On race day all sorts of paraphernalia was worn, the city took on a holiday mood, and the big race was the talk of sporting world for weeks on end. In 1891 *Manning's Register* recorded 116 yacht clubs and 3268 yachts, but by 1895 there were more than 200 clubs and about 4000 yachts in the United States. Most of these were small pleasure models which were popularized at the end of the century. America's leading designers were Edward Burgess, A. Cary Smith, J. Beaver Webb, and Nat Herreshoff, builder of the *Vigilant, Defender, Columbia* and *Reliance.*

Despite all its sustained popularity, public interest in yachting was relatively weaker after 1902 than it had been at any time since the late 1860's. Racing yachts increasingly became the toys of the millionaire who sacrificed utility and safety for speed, while most vessels were now built for cruising. Many of these were of the steam yacht class, but steam yachting held little of the glamor of the sailing ships of old. Although sailing as a recreation of the upper middle class at vacation time was rising in popularity, the age of the great yachting spectacle was rapidly passing.

With the opening of the Penn Relays in 1893 and a startling victory of American athletes over the London Athletic Club at New York two years later, American track and field men at last felt equal to their British competitors. British sportsmen stood amazed. In noting the widespread excitement of the English press the *New York Athletic Club Journal* quoted the satirical London *Weekly Sun:* " 'Rule Britannia' is but the last despairing wail of a played out race. We are no longer athletically or nautically supreme; indeed we are very small beer." Modern track athletics really stem from the excitement aroused in the closing years of the century. The London AC's visit was headlined by the New York *Times* as the "Most Sensational Athletic Meeting Ever Held." Meanwhile the University of California, which had sent a team to the intercollegiate championships as early as 1890, won the meet held by the Western Intercollegiate Amateur Athletic Association, forewarning such conquered foes as Michigan, Iowa, and Illinois that the Far West was catching the spirit of modern athletics.

From the zealous work of Pierre de Coubertin the modern Olympic Games were instituted in 1896. When an unheralded group of college athletes tramped off to Athens and stunned all European sportsmen with their victory, the value of international athletics was acclaimed by the journalistic world. *Harper's Weekly* for April 18, 1896, praised the Olympic Games with their "aim which will commend itself to all who have the advancement of humanity and civilization at heart, namely, the advancement of international comity, of good fellowship among nations, in their common delight and interest in the culture of man's physical life, health, and vigor." The hopes of sportsmen often exceeded their grasp. David St. Clair had sagaciously observed in the *Illustrated American* for October 5, 1895, "It is believed by some that these great festivals of sport and athletics will do more to remove national prejudice and make the world acquainted with itself than any other agency of civilization. International sport certainly does one of two things. It helps nations to better understand one another or else the contests tend to widen the chasm."

International yachting races created one of the great sporting traditions of the nineteenth century, but the new century experienced a sporting tide which centered popular interest on athletics. English and American golf tourneys, particularly the "amateur" and "open" championships, contributed mightily to the spread of the golfing fever, and Davis Cup matches drew thousands of new converts to the tennis court. Intercollegiate rowing and the stimulus given to soccer by colleges and industries helped foster international rivalries. Foreign racing drivers tried out their German, French, Italian, and English models against the best of American cars. American colleges and professional teams visited Japan hoping to spread the lure of the diamond, and American track and field athletes gained unprecedented renown in the Olympic Games. W.T. Stead's *Ameri-*

*canization of the World* recognized this rapid surge to sporting supremacy and in 1901 noted the value of cricket to the Australians as a nationalizing force and "the political importance of athletics and of sport generally as a means of promoting a sense of unity among the English-speaking peoples of the world."

When the Americans returned from Athens in 1906 as Olympic victors, President Roosevelt cabled, "Uncle Sam is All Right." Only the slightest coverage of previous contests had appeared in the American press, but by 1908 the games held in London were attracting widespread attention. This spectacle, attended by the British royal family, proved to be one of the most unpleasant events in the history of international sport. The marathon race (in which British officials almost awarded victory to a Greek runner who collapsed and was assisted to the tape as the American Johnny Hayes finished) touched off an avalanche of criticism. James M. Sullivan, Walter Camp, and others admitted that the games had contributed little but discord, jealousy, and distrust; nevertheless, they appealed for fairer reporting by the press and contended that the Olympic festival might yet prove one of the prime instruments in attaining international peace.

During the years before 1912, imperialistic rivalries, which had drawn nations into crises at Fashoda and Algeciras, in China, Indonesia, Africa, and the Near East, were driving European powers into the Triple Alliance or Triple Entente. Although military and naval races, secret treaties, imperialism, and jingoism formed a malignant undercurrent threatening to disrupt the peace, most Americans, Englishmen, Germans, Russians, Frenchmen, and Italians were not primarily concerned with the imminent threat of war. Only in such a light can we comprehend how sincerely Europeans and Americans of that era believed in the value of sport as a possible harbinger of lasting peace.

Disillusionment over the London games of 1908 failed to discourage those who looked forward to 1912. Stockholm proved the answer to those who demanded abandonment of the Olympic Games. Some four hundred journalists from twenty-seven nations flocked to the Swedish capital, while athletes from many nations announced by their very numbers to the world at large that they were at last converted to the athletic spirit of the age.

Arnold Bennett was inspired to write in *Harper's Monthly* that "Your United States" was not a sporting country, since the European fanaticism was missing in the land of baseball and football! This, however, was not the normal reaction, and the *Vossische Zeitung* of Berlin editorialized:

> America's triumph at Stockholm is not the triumph of spasmodic training or of organization, as that term is commonly under-

stood, but the national fruit of the long and systematic inculcation of the athletic spirit in American youth. And by the athletic spirit America means not only the rational, uniform development of the body to the highest state of perfection from boyhood up, but the development of all those qualities of mind which are indispensable to preeminence in sports. . . . Americans race with their heads as well as with their legs, and their Olympic victories are won on the playgrounds of their school days. This is the only reason that we can give for the monotonous reappearance of the Stars and Stripes at the Stadium mast-head of Stockholm.[35]

*Blackwood's Magazine* typified British hostility to overspecialized athletics by contending that the United States contingent was "run on business lines" and that America's victory was attained neither through American athletic superiority nor British decadence, but through professionalism alone. On this side of the water, however, the *Nation* claimed that it was the United States and the Olympic Games which were instrumental in stirring athletic consciousness among Europeans.

This seemed like a tempest in a teapot when the storm broke over Jim Thorpe's amateur status after he had won the decathlon and pentathlon. American authorities admitted that he was "an Indian of limited experience and education in the ways of other than his own people," but he was "deserving of the severest condemnation for concealing the fact that he had professionalized himself" by playing for money in an obscure southern baseball league. In a classic remark which defies one's sense of logic, they contended: "That he played under his own name would give no direct notice to any one concerned, as there are many of his name." While the International Olympic Committee recalled the prizes of the man called by the King of Sweden the greatest athlete in the world, the Swedish official report included Thorpe's records and the fact that his Swedish opponent who was belatedly awarded an Olympic title refused to accept the American's medals.[36] The tempest has not yet blown over.

Following the Stockholm Games of 1912 extensive plans were laid for a Berlin meeting in 1916, but Sarajevo and the German invasion of Belgium altered the course of sporting history. Not until 1920 were the Olympics to be held again. International sport virtually disappeared in the holocaust of war. The Davis Cup series which had remained unbroken from 1900 to 1914 was discontinued in 1915, to be revived only four years later, while the America's Cup race was suspended for the duration.

The influence of the United States became paramount in this period for the first time in sporting history. Our sports, long obscured by English pre-eminence, began to react on the British. American Rhodes Scholars

distinguished themselves in athletics at Oxford by winning all the first
places in 1913 and by showing that all Americans were not "professionals."
In 1914 Harvard became the first American crew to win the Grand Chal-
lenge Cup on the Henley. Oxford and Cambridge established a traditional
series of track meets with Harvard, Yale, Princeton, and Cornell. And the
British came to recognize such champions as the cycling "phenom" A.A.
Zimmerman, the court tennis star Jay Gould, and the golfing wizard
Walter Hagen.

Whatever animosities may have been aroused in the Olympic Games
and other international contests, the two nations had become more closely
allied in prewar years, and Anglo-American sport had stimulated a bond
of friendship as well as a recognition of mutual respect. A minor factor in
the alignment of allied feelings prior to the war, sport was now proclaimed
one of the means of future understanding. To those who little realized
how deeply the spirit of nationalism was ingrained in the peoples of the
western world the potential of sport as a harbinger of peace and good will
seemed unlimited.

# Chapter 8

# Social and Cultural Implications, 1860-1920

# Chapter 8

# Social
and Cultural
Implications,
1860-1920

In the years before the Civil War interest in sport was so casual that only the slightest imprint was made on the social and cultural life of the American people. By the 1850's, however, signs of general concern were seen in the sporting press and literature, in the sale of sporting goods, in art prints, and in popular songs. Throughout the next six decades this impact was felt ever more strongly as sport grew into a national institution in both city and country. Business capitalized on the manufacture of sporting goods and on the crowds attending outdoor contests; advertising slowly utilized sporting themes; and investments in racing, yachting, and commercialized promotion rose rapidly. Court decisions helped to clarify the legal status of professional ball players; educators and critics engaged in a running debate on the evils and values to be found in athletics; and the growing interest of women, the improved environs of sports arenas, the relaxing of the blue laws and of the Puritan Sabbath, and the greater respectability acquired by various games now attracted all but the most skeptical. For the first time Americans could begin to claim a sporting literature, and enthusiasts were to influence our language, art, music, humor, dime novels, light drama, and motion pictures.

### Private Enterprise Lends a Hand

When Boston lured thousands of farmers and city dwellers to the Mystic Park races in 1869 the relationship of sport to the local business scene was evident:

> [There was] a perfect hub-bub of Jubilee and Turf sports, of crowding hungry strangers, busy hotel keepers and effervescent life generally—a perfect harvest for small tradesmen, cigar dealers, billiard rooms—and must the "Modern Athens" blush to own it—rumsellers. Lodgings are scarce and exhorbitant in prices—daily on the increase at that,—a good chance now for some Gothamite to buy up all the available rooms and relet them at an tremendous advance. Even the bootblacks are busy at fifteen cents a shine, and impudent at that, cooly requesting you to stand in line and take your turn.[1]

Rural sports brought thousands of city dwellers to the country while seashore resorts and inland watering places were crowded with vacationists, and farm houses, taverns, and hotels took in wandering sportsmen.

Peck & Snyder and Horsman's Base Ball and Croquet Emporium of New York, George B. Ellard & Co. of Cincinnati, and Bassler of Boston were among the main sporting goods houses of postwar years. As early as 1867 the *Ball Players' Chronicle* boasted:

The business of supplying material for the several games of ball now in vogue, such as Base Ball, Cricket and Croquet, has increased to such a degree of late years as to amount to a very extensive and important branch of our trades and manufactures. Especially is this the case in reference to base ball materials. Five or six years ago clubs procured the balls they played with from two or three makers, and one bat maker could supply almost the whole demand. Now there is a regular bat and ball manufactory in each city, and in the metropolis we have half a dozen regular base ball emporiums where bats, balls, bases, uniforms, shoes, etc., can be supplied in quantities, manufacturers turning out bats by the thousand, and balls by the hundred, where they previously sold by the dozen and singly.[2]

By 1872 billiards had evoked "a manufacturing and commercial enterprise hardly second to that which the *piano-forte* creates," and, "In almost every village of two thousand inhabitants, and, indeed, in many with less population, a billiard table (with usually an accompanying one) is to be found in some public house, the favorite hotel, or the most elegant 'saloon' of the village . . . while throughout the larger towns and cities of the Union, from the capital of Maine to the remotest southern and western boundaries of the republic, billiard tables are found in large numbers."[3] From the days when Martin Van Buren's table became a political issue until Benjamin Harrison's and Mark Twain's addiction to the cue, billiards had developed as a favorite game of many people who dared to disregard mid-Victorian prejudices.

Most prominent of the pioneer sporting goods companies was A.G. Spalding & Brothers. Appearing on the scene at a time when mass production of goods was feasible for the first time, branching out from Chicago to New York, Spalding was the monarch of the business in the late years of the century. By the end of the eighties the company advertised its wares to schools, colleges, teachers, clubs, and individuals at reasonable prices. Hundreds of individual craftsmen and small enterprisers built canoes and hunting boats or put out new models of sporting rifles and fishing rods. Barton & Company, Thomson & Son, Abbey & Imbrie, Fowler & Fulton, Hawks & Ogilvy, Schuyler, Hartley, & Graham—among others—supplied the sportsmen of New York. As trapshooting clubs quickly took to the range after the invention of clay birds by George Ligowsky in 1880, concerns like Woeber & Varwig of Cincinnati, G.P. Kolb of Philadelphia, Globe Shot Co. of St. Louis, Henry Sears & Co. of Chicago, and Joseph C. Grub & Co. of Philadelphia established their brand names. Remington breechloaders for hunters were featured mainly by Schuyler, Hartley & Graham, who merged with E. Remington and Sons in 1888 and cultivated the sporting market until World War I.

As sleds, skates, bicycles, balls, bats, gloves, croquet sets, golf clubs, tennis racquets and a host of other items were produced on a mass production basis at the turn of the century and as manufacturing and distribution were concentrated in the hands of Spalding, Sears-Roebuck, and the larger department stores, the economic aspects of sport took on new proportions. With the rising popularity of basketball, volleyball, bowling, and winter games, city and state scholastic associations, the activities of private agencies, and the demand for paraphernalia for the armed forces in World War I, sporting goods (exclusive of athletic apparel and guns) reached a manufacturing value of almost $40,000,000 at the end of the war.

Professional ball clubs operated on a budget of $70,000 for the season in the eighties, gate receipts to commercialized events or college games were very modest until the late nineties, few prominent citizens entered the promotional field because of the small financial inducements, municipal support of recreation came slowly in prewar years, and the gambling fraternity was only beginning to capitalize on sport. Investments in gymnasiums, playgrounds, and parks, in ball fields, arenas, and stadiums, in country clubs, yacht clubs, race tracks, and other facilities did rise rapidly, however, in the three decades before American entry into the European conflict. The development of fishing and hunting reserves, watering spots, seaside resorts, and summer hotels was also significant, and even in the 1880's, when croquet, baseball, canoeing, and archery were featured at vacation centers, it was said that no country-seat or summer resort was complete without tennis courts. Further evidence of the economic nature of sport was to be found in Western Union's wire services and in newspaper employment of reporters and purchase of AP and UP press services. Concessionaires in local areas slowly yielded the field to large-scale operators at the end of the century. Harry Stevens built a scorecard franchise into a gigantic chain of concessions serving hot dogs, peanuts, and soda pop at ball parks and race tracks. With the passing years sport took on greater significance in the family budget and the national economy.

If any activities surpassed hunting and fishing in the amount of capital involved, they were horse racing and yachting. Churchill Downs, Pimlico, Saratoga, Jerome Park, Belmont, Arlington Park, and scores of other racing establishments comprised a total investment of many millions of dollars, while the trotting tracks of America may well have surpassed the value of thoroughbred courses. Among leading owners of thoroughbreds in 1890 were Leonard Jerome, D.D. Withers, August Belmont, William L. Scott, Alexander Cassatt, Michael Dwyer, and J.B. Haggin, the Anaconda copper king. Lucky Baldwin, Leland Stanford, Pierre Lorillard, and hundreds of other breeders invested heavily in their farms, and the Rancocas stables in New Jersey won fame on the track with the great Iroquois as its leading light. Stanford created a fabulous racing empire as he "proceeded to ride his new hobby as it had never been ridden elsewhere." "Supremacy on the racetracks of the world became his goal, and boards of strategy met regularly . . . to plan and perfect the campaign."[4]

Bristol, Rhode Island, home of the Herreshoff Manufacturing Company during the war, had put out 1500 small craft of varied designs by 1870. The Eastern Yacht Agency was established by Edward and Sidney Burgess in 1884, and after the success of their boats in the America's Cup races of the eighties the company was swamped with orders. Other designers of sailing craft enjoyed the new wave of business prosperity. J.B. Van Deusen, A. Cary Smith, Albertson Brothers, and Poillou Brothers all established thriving businesses and high reputations in the yachting world. The American Yacht Club sponsored annual regattas in order to improve the speed, comfort and safety of steam yachts, and by the late 1880's a fleet of rivals to William K. Vanderbilt's $750,000 *Alva* were sailing the seas.

Advertising was also utilized to capitalize on sporting interest. Street car companies encouraged local ball teams, the Metropolitan Company offering a playing ground to the Atlanta club of the Southern League in 1889. Cigarette and tobacco brands like the Peerless, the Plug Chewing, and the Lorillard Yacht Club Smoking Tobacco as well as Croquet, Iroquois, and Our Club Rooms cigars appealed to the sporting trade. Pugilists, ball players, and race horses were pictured on cards collected by eager youngsters, indicating "their interests and their naughty habits." The Lipton Beef Company's poster entitled "Champion Pugilists of the World" carried John L. Sullivan's endorsement: "After a fair test of your extract of beef, both as a beverage and as a muscle and health producing food, I am well convinced it is the best thing of the kind in the market. Yours sincerely, John L. Sullivan." One celebrated New Orleans restauranteur in 1892 actually claimed: "What caused the knock-out was the good meal that Corbett ate last night at Antoine's Restaurant, prepared by the renowned Jules Caesar Alciatore." Dr. Greene's Nerve Tonic claimed to have cured Harry Brooks, "America's Greatest Walker and Athlete," of nervous prostration and exhaustion. Hotels offered purses at the great races, while railroads advertised their services to prize fight, baseball, cycling, and racing fans as well as hunters and anglers. In 1900 the Santa Fé Route featured "Golf in California under summer skies in midwinter." In succeeding years Ty Cobb and other famous sportsmen endorsed all kinds of products in the sporting journals, and preparatory schools like Peddie, Tome, Culver, Staunton, Kemper, Colby, Augusta, and Western stressed their athletic facilities and programs.[5]

Commercial artists and advertisers came into their own in the first two decades. *Collier's, The Saturday Evening Post, The Ladies Home Journal, The Woman's Home Companion,* and similar journals featured athletic and outdoor cover girls as well as articles or columns on health. *Dress, The Delineator,* and *Vogue* slowly opened their pages to designers of sports clothes. In 1910 *The Delineator* noted that the Vanderbilt Cup race had "started the moth ball rolling earlier than usual . . . while the shops are full of the most sporty-looking motor wraps and polo coats imaginable." Wanamaker Sports Togs were advertised in 1917, when Murad cigarettes and clothiers like Hart, Schaffner and Marx were appealing to sophisticated members of the country club and racing set.[6]

Shredded Wheat capitalized on the sporting proclivities of the American youngster, forewarning the public of the later household curse caused by "The Breakfast of Champions" and other cereal slogans. Underwear and corset concerns stressed the advantages of their styles to the athletic man and woman. In spite of this trend, however, advertising was only beginning to recognize the value of sports appeal, especially since respectable magazines were overwhelmingly dedicated to the interests of the American woman. Postwar years would see a steady increase in this phase of advertising.

## The Law and the Courts

Judicial tradition has been little affected by legal problems stemming from sport, which has always been accorded the most casual consideration by the Bar and the Bench. But the course of sport has been directed to a considerable degree by the exigencies of the law. Fish and game legislation was championed by sportsmen conservationists of the 1870's and 1880's, later influencing the programs of Cleveland, Roosevelt, and their successors. A general attack on Sunday games and a perpetual prosecution of the gambling menace were also reflected in numerous decisions between the Civil War and World War I.

Most court cases revolved around player contracts and Sunday sports. Judicial decisions gradually tempered the attack on baseball, allowing cases to be decided by local option and popular consent. Defenders of the national pastime contended professional baseball was not a monopoly but a government, and one of such private power without which the game would have been disrupted and destroyed in a state of chaos. August Herrmann of the National Baseball Commission, in commenting on a 1914 resolution in the House of Representatives, welcomed an investigation of organized baseball and fearlessly maintained the "established privileges of national agreement clubs."[7]

Players' rights were protected by the courts in numerous instances. One may pass back through the years to 1882 and find there the refusal to uphold the "reserve clause" in Allegheny Base Ball Club *v.* Bennett. In 1890 the decision in Philadelphia Ball Club, Ltd. *v.* Hallmann *et al.* stated most forcefully that if the defendant ball player "sold himself for life to the plaintiffs for $1400 per annum" and yet could be set adrift arbitrarily, on ten days' notice, "then it is perfectly apparent that such a contract is so wanting in mutuality that no court of equity would lend its aid to compel compliance with it."[8]

There were differences in the construed meaning of "mutuality" of contract. In general, players were legally defended from suit, but to whom could they turn? Banishment to the "bush leagues" hung as a constant threat over their heads. Baseball authorities avoided the courts whenever possible, fearful of their weak legal position and of the tarnish which would mar the reputation of the game.

Cases continued to arise in succeeding years: Metropolitan Exhibition Co. *v.* Ward (1890), Philadelphia Ball Club, Ltd. *v.* Tojoil (1902), and others. Owners were also protected at times. When James E. Dolen sued the Metropolitan Exhibition Company for $25,000 in 1887 for loss of an eye from a foul ball at the Polo Grounds, he claimed negligence because no screen was provided behind the catcher. The New York *Sun,* for March 22, summarized the case: "Judge Donohue dismissed the complaint. . . . He said that the company appeared to have taken all necessary precautions to prevent accidents, and when a ticket to the grandstand was sold it was a mutual contract between the company and the purchaser that a seat would be provided and a game of ball played. That ended the contract, and the spectator must take all risks of accident."

Throughout the first and second decades of this century, baseball men strove to maintain public confidence, but critics continued attacking the "baseball trust." Will Irwin, in a *Collier's* article of June 12, 1909, remarked that the player was caught "in a system of slavery mitigated by public acclaim and managerial generosity." Starting his career with a Class D team at $10 a Sunday, rising through the minors to the big leagues, then drifting back to the bush leagues as a veteran, the player must abide by dictates of the National Commission and his own manager. Without an opportunity to play outside of the organized leagues, the player must bend his knee to the owner's decree: "It is take our terms or get out of baseball." Irving Sanborn referred to the "White Slaves of the Diamond" and vilified some magnates who were "masters with whom Simon Legree would hesitate to shake hands."[9] Cartoonists of the period delighted in picturing leering magnates hovering over a player shackled with ball and chain.

But the public took this lightly, for how could men engaged in play be slaves? Napoleon Lajoie, prince of second basemen, could not appear in Pennsylvania because of a broken contract, but fans everywhere applauded him as a sports hero. The "established privileges" of organized baseball were generally recognized by the sporting public. Discussing litigation over the Baltimore Federal League club's claim for damages from the baseball war of 1914-1915, the New York *Times* for April 15, 1919 editorialized:

It may be that the present organization does violate the Sherman law; for it operates quite successfully against outside competition, and it puts the players very much at the mercy of the men who own the clubs. But experience has shown that both of these arrangements are in the public interest, so long as the public wants professional baseball. . . . In the end unrestricted bidding for the players would almost certainly lead to the concentration of the men who could command high prices in New York and Chicago, where the clubs earn the highest profits; and if New York and Chicago always won the pennants interest would die out.

Sunday sport, although less the center of controversy than the Sunday theater, remained a thorn in the side of conservative religious groups and sporting circles alike. By 1885 the Memphis *Appeal* pointed out the problem of Sunday baseball, and many papers seemed to recognize both the need for proper observance and the value of relaxation to the overworked. Changing sentiment was seen in a New York *World* editorial of May 11, 1886 which criticized New Jersey laws prohibiting boys' sports on Sunday. The *National Police Gazette* campaigned for an open day, admitting all the while that there was "a general prejudice against playing baseball on Sunday."[10]

Religious opposition remained strong and in 1886 the Chicago Reform Alliance ended Sabbath racing in the Windy City. Even in 1914 Big League baseball was permitted on Sunday only in Chicago, Cincinnati, and St. Louis. Schedules of other clubs were completed by playing games away from home. In the Empire State as early as 1913 sentiment favoring Sabbath games was demonstrated in the approval of twenty-seven of thirty-two mayors, and Supreme Court Justice Gilbert Hasbrouck made the issue simply one of disturbing the peace. A study in 1917 showed that lax enforcement prevailed under the many special provisions of state laws, that fines generally were limited to those over fourteen years of age and, particularly, to professional teams, the common prohibition of boisterous sports being confined to those "breaking the peace."[11] By the end of

World War I interest in weekend sports caused numerous communities to relax their Sabbath laws. Tennessee's Supreme Court rendered a decision that the aged blue laws of 1803 did not apply to Sunday baseball, thus encouraging the game in Nashville, Memphis, Chattanooga, and other cities. The old Puritan Sabbath of an agrarian era was fading before urban demands and the continental habits of those who came from abroad into the industrial environment of twentieth-century America.

## Critics and Educators on the Firing Line

The mushroom growth of intercollegiate contests caught fire and then blazed into one of the most virulent educational controversies of the years before World War I. As early as March, 1880 *Popular Science Monthly* charged, "a positive and serious evil of athleticism is, that it tends to become a power in the schools, rivaling the constituted authorities." Betting, hiring of "pseudo-students," professional coaching, and commercialization of college athletics gave fuel to bitter critics. College teams often found their most popular opponents among professional clubs, and the threat of a professional invasion of intercollegiate sport alarmed thoughtful people of the 1880's. Dudley A. Sargent deplored the trend toward professionalism and warned that "betting will ever be the bane of competitive contests."[12] Three years after the college had originally banned football for its brutality, the *Harvard Report on Athletics* declared in 1888 that "during recent years a strong, and in every respect objectionable tendency had developed to break down the line between athletics practiced for sport, social recreation and health, and athletics practiced in a competitive spirit in emulation of professional athletes and players."

Vilification of the cult of athleticism in colleges increased in the nineties, and hired coaches were made the target. Robert Cook's fame with the Yale crew had done much to make the sporting world realize that winning teams demanded expert instruction, but as Yale and Princeton men scattered to coaching positions throughout the United States critics howled in derision. At the time *The Nation* and similar publications were wailing against the athletic craze, Amos Alonzo Stagg was hired by the University of Chicago to bring distinction on the gridiron and the diamond. Long trips and loss of study time stirred President Frederick Barnard of Columbia to complain in 1888: "This is an evil inevitable while the present system is maintained, and is of sufficient magnitude to justify . . . an absolute prohibition of intercollegiate games altogether."[13]

Equally virulent in his hostility to this competitive mania, Charles Eliot lacked the tact and imagination needed for reforming collegiate sports. Great as were his achievements in the establishment of outstanding graduate schools and the elective system at Harvard, Eliot seemed to pursue a confused policy toward athletics. According to Henry James, Eliot's imperfect knowledge of competitive sport was exposed when on one occasion he thought a college pitcher not only deceptive but also ungentlemanly for looking at one base and throwing to another! In his animosity toward foolish and pernicious sporting expenses, Eliot deplored the "constant economy and inadequacy in expenditure for intellectual and spiritual objects." Later he would bow to the generosity of Harvard graduates in the building of a great athletic plant on Soldier's Field, but in 1894 he remained unstintingly critical of contemporary overemphasis on athletics:

> When thus exaggerated, they interfere with, instead of clarifying and maintaining mental activity; they convert the student into a powerful animal, and dull for a time his intellectual parts; they present the colleges to the public, educated and uneducated, as places of mere physical sport, and not of intellectual training; . . . they induce in masses of spectators at interesting games an hysterical excitement which too many Americans enjoy, but which is evidence not of physical strength and depth of passion, but of feebleness and shallowness; and they tend to dwarf mental and moral preeminence by unduly magnifying physical prowess. . . . In short, football cultivates strength and skill kept in play by all the combative instincts, whereas the strength most servicable to civilized society is the strength which is associated with gentleness and courtesy.[14]

Academicians, and thoughtful observers, then as now, varied in the intensity of their interests. William Milligan Sloane was an ardent proponent of football for its similarities to war. Francis A. Walker, famed economist and president of the Massachusetts Institute of Technology, encouraged physical exercise, rabidly followed athletic contests, and contended, "This nation has long shown the painful need of more popular amusement, of more that shall call men, in great throngs, out into the open air, of more that shall arouse an interest in something besides money-getting or professional preferment." Immediately after the Spanish-American war Franklin H. Giddings remarked in *Democracy and Empire*: "It is doubtful if the transition from chronic warfare to a busy industrial civilization materially diminishes the demand for primitive virtues. . . . Consequently it is not among primitive men only that physical prowess is valued above all other gifts. . . . The prize fighter, the athlete, the military hero, the imperturbable leader who can withstand the assaults of malignity, these are the popular idol." And the philosopher of loyalty, Josiah Royce, within a few years stressed the values of strength and skill in a lecture on "Some Relations of Physical Training to the Present Problems of Moral Education in America." Less interested than any of these was William Graham Sumner, famed sociologist living in the midst of an athletically-minded generation of Yale students, who noted in 1905, "The last game I attended was on Thanksgiving Day, 1876." James McCosh was proud of the gymnastic program he introduced but deplored the excess of concern with things athletic: "Meanwhile, let Princeton proclaim that her reputation does not depend on her skill in throwing or kicking a ball, but on the scholarship and the virtue of her sons."[15]

Friends of organized athletics were valiant in defense, stressing the improvement in student health, the decline of illness and absences, the remarkable increase of strong men in college classes of the eighties, and the diminishing problem of tobacco and alcohol. Some noted the decided moral uplift derived from athletic interest, the disappearance of riots and rowdiness, the increasing respect for college property, and the danger of turning students to temptations of the theater and saloon if sports were barred by the authorities. Already sport was said to provide a "safety-valve for the superabundant physical effervescence of the young men" in our colleges. As the possibilities of applying athletics in education became manifest, appeals were made to the teacher to appreciate and to direct games, since an effective teacher must keep in touch with his students' interests. By 1889 Professor Nathaniel Shaler of Harvard had been converted heart and soul: "We must bear in mind the fact that the revival of athletic sports in this country has been of decided advantage to our people ... [and] whatever steps may be taken to guide this impulse in our youth, we must take pains not to stop the spring whence it flows."

The National Education Association began to recognize that it must pay close attention to such agencies in the popularization of physical education as the YMCA, the Turner societies, the American Association for the Advancement of Physical Education, The WCTU, Chautauqua, and the teachers colleges, which were following the leadership of Francis Wayland Parker's Cook County Normal School. In 1891 a report on physical education appeared in the *Journal* of the NEA, and from that time the society was greatly concerned with the topic. The educative, moral, co-operative, and individual values of games and sports were widely accepted, and by 1892 State Superintendent A.B. Poland of New Jersey claimed that "so far from being an evanescent fad or fashion," physical culture was "an absolute necessity for the well-being not only of the present generation, but of generations to come."[16]

Asserting that few among university teachers were as intolerant toward athletics as the more irate critics were, Professor Frederick Taus-

sig, the tariff expert, came to the defense of sport in the middle nineties
when professionalism had reached new heights. Alarmed at the public's
excessive interest and the exaggerated tenor of the press, however, and
aware that some schools were gaining fame from athletic teams alone,
Taussig recognized that lasting reputation depends on the intellectual contributions of a university. Although disturbed by the sensational aspects
of commercialization, Taussig was profoundly optimistic on the future of
democracy and compared sporting enthusiasm to a keen party spirit in the
political realm. He showed considerable wisdom in maintaining, "We have
not too much of pleasure and romance in our everyday American life and
can welcome everything that gives it a brighter and happier aspect."[17]

Friend and foe thrashed out the effects of athleticism on the American university long after the nineteenth century, and with the rise of intercollegiate football at the turn of the century it became an even more
strenuous battle of the educators.

Once the crisis in intercollegiate football waned after 1905, there
was much less unqualified condemnation of competitive games. A split
among educational authorities on the value of organized sport remained,
but the assault had generally lost its intensity. Faculties and educational
critics now turned their attention to the dangers of overemphasis and
improper leadership.

More and more the issue became one of guidance, of direction of
sport into proper channels. As sport became an institution deeply embed-
ded in the national character, it became imperative that intellectual leaders
should try to educate the public to a more enlightened perspective on its
place in American life. Led by Dean Briggs of Harvard, educators began
to meet this challenge. G. Stanley Hall, in the tradition of those nineteenth-
century scholars who found much merit in the character-building attributes
of sport but who warned against abuses, wrote in 1904 that "athletics
afford a wealth of new and profitable topics for discussion and enthusiasm
which helps against the triviality and mental vacuity into which the inter-
course of students is prone to lapse. . . . It gives a new standard of honor
. . . . It supplies a splendid motive against all errors and vices that weaken
or corrupt the body. It is a wholesome vent for the reckless courage that
would otherwise go to disorder or riotous excess."[18] An education survey
made in Cleveland in 1916 illustrated the increase in respect for athletics
held by the authorities:

> There is no incentive to make a supreme effort or to acquire a
> surplus of ability. The spiritual value of competition in which boys
> of this period are absolutely engrossed is the maximum effort which
> it calls forth. In the majority of cases the chief difference between

men in the presence of a crisis lies in the relative capacity for extreme effort. This capacity is part of one's character. Competition is an essential in the moral training of children. . . . The pre-pubescent years from 10 to 12 are, for the majority of boys, especially favorable for the beginning of athletic interest and skill. If participation is delayed beyond the elementary school period, sufficient interest and skill for personal participation in later years are far less likely to be developed.[19]

In 1916 Gamaliel Bradford recorded an experience which illustrates not only the changing attitude toward school games but also the author's sensitive and perceptive mind:

> For fifteen years now I have followed the school-boys not only in their games, but two or three times a week in their daily practice, and it has been one of my most agreeable and interesting diversions. First, I love to watch and study the character of boys. Nothing brings this out more than sports, or, rather, I suppose school pursuits perhaps bring the character out equally; but, at any rate, on the athletic field character is revealed in the most subtle and fascinating way. . . . To see the stolid boy, who has no fear because he has no imagination; to see the nervous boy who conquers his nerves, or in the immense stimulus of excitement forgets them altogether, or better still uses them to gain his victories; to see the hard-working boy, who has no natural gifts for muscular glory, but by sheer persistence attains decided skill in the end, and even surpasses those naturally more gifted—all these and many more varieties are to be seen, in all their varied limitations and combinations.[20]

If the vast majority of educators became resigned to the permanent hold of sport on the American school and college, critics did not yield the day. The violence with which the enemies of football assaulted the game in 1905 and 1909 and the widening recognition of the alumni menace to collegiate athletics demonstrated continuing interest in reform. Flagrant violations of "summer baseball" regulations, the long-standing feud of the NCAA and the AAU, the issue of intercollegiate athletics in war time —these and many other incidents aroused the ire of caustic cynics and critics throughout the second decade.

Scholastic life, in the eyes of the critic, was undermined by athletics which fostered an excess of distraction to the student, a nonacademic self-advertisement for schools, a false conception of the athlete's prominence in university life, an unwanted pressure in collegiate circles, a demand for expert coaches rather than inspiring leaders, a neglect of nonathletes, an inordinate expense for the institution (particularly smaller colleges), a gambling menace, and an undue influence on the lower schools. So firm a hold had athletes on the academic world in 1904 that President William Faunce of Brown told the National Education Association that the era was one of systematic prevarication: "We are living in a time when college athletics are honeycombed with falsehood, and when the professions of amateurism are usually hypocrisy. No college team ever meets another today with actual faith in the other's eligibility." President William Rainey Harper of the University of Chicago deplored the pressure put on high school lads to choose a college on the basis of athletics and bemoaned a virtually universal impression that colleges had one standard for athletes and another for students. Such fears were somewhat exaggerated, despite the widespread belief that athletic prowess had become the chief drawing power of the university. A study of eight Western Conference and eight Ohio institutions for the years 1905-1924 seemed "to indicate that the average high school graduate chooses his college for reasons other than football success."[21]

Woodrow Wilson, who had been in charge of the sports policy for a time at Princeton, expounded his philosophy of the role of athletics in an ideal university, advising the athletic-minded generation of 1910 that sports were wholesome and necessary to every normal youth, inculcating the spirit of sportsmanship and of moral living: "But athletics and mere amusement ought never to become serious and absorbing occupations, even with youngsters." Wilson's interest in athletics *per se* was academic. He resented the fact that in the colleges the "sideshows" had swallowed the "circus," and he felt that men could not be prepared for the problems of the modern world where sport played a major role in the curriculum.[22]

Outside as well as inside academic walls two themes proved to be of general concern: the protection of amateur ideals and the social danger implicit in spectator sports. As commercialization crept into all forms of recreation after the Civil War the threat to sporting ideals was recognized. *Forest and Stream & Rod and Gun* maintained in 1880: "The mighty dollar is the controlling agency in every branch of social and public life. Possibly this generalization may sufficiently account for the mercenary element of so many forms of alleged sport. Generous emulation in physical strength or skill gives place to sordid clutching after purses, gate money, entrance fee or prize—provided this last be convertible into cash."

By this time 'ringers' were beginning to invade college games and scandals in prize fight circles and professional baseball stirred up widespread protest. Caspar Whitney, Walter Camp, and others glorified the

amateur and warned against the professional in the nineties. Amateurism
was strengthened by vigilant agencies like the YMCA, the U.S. Lawn
Tennis Association, the U.S. Golf Association, and the Olympic authorities. The ICAAAA and the AAU campaigned against the longstanding evil
of professionals masquerading as amateurs, cashing in on prize awards.
General Palmer E. Pierce, first president of the NCAA, fought zealously
for faculty control in the colleges.

Although the New York *Times* maintained in 1900 that "sports are
held in public esteem in precise ratio to their freedom from all professional practice," signs of change were in the air. As the professional diamond
became more respectable and popular interest in the World Series mounted,
the journalistic world paid increasing respect to the national pastime. By
1914-1915 *The Outlook* and similar magazines withdrew much of their
attack on professionalism and shifted it to those areas where the facade of
amateurism was maintained by those who were really professionals. Controversy now tended to rage over the right of college athletes to play
summer baseball for money as an employee of a business firm or pleasure
resort.

Observers of the social scene, however, still worried over the decline
of the amateur code and over the effect of commercialized sport on urban
audiences. Much less is heard of *mens sana in corpore sano* and much more
of the alarming parallel between the pageantry of Roman gladiatorial
contests and the mass appeal of spectator sports: "The disease of *spectatoritis* is abroad in the land. . . . We are still a long way from the Roman
amphitheater and the Spanish bullfight, but *spectatoritis* leads that way."[23]
Professionalism and spectatoritis continued to bother thoughtful critics
and moralists concerned with the role sport should play in American life.

The old veil of outright hostility was lifted, however. As conservative
an educator as the unenthusiastic Abbot Lawrence Lowell professed a
belief, in his Thomas Lectures at Yale, that athletics do not seriously
affect study (for athletes would find other means of dissipation) or
attendance at class. An old veteran of the baseball field and the golf links,
William Howard Taft was quoted on the improvement in collegiate life of
the second decade:

> We have made great improvements in intercollegiate athletics,
> due to rigid limitations by agreement. We confine intercollegiate
> athletics now to undergraduates. It is not possible for a man to grow
> old in college athletics by studying first for one degree and then
> another until he becomes a man of thirty or thirty-five. This was a
> great abuse in my day. A man could go through the academic depart-

ment, and then through the scientific department, and then through the medical school, and continue to win victories on the diamond or the football field until he had nearly passed the military age.[24]

It was this realization that athletics had created a more wholesome atmosphere in the American university which won new adherents to the cause. Throughout the first two decades, on playgrounds or in physical education classes, there developed a general acceptance of the merits of organized games under proper leadership. Stalwart defenders of athletics fought valiantly for confidence and good will among the colleges, and it may well be that the athletic impulse helped promote the community-of-interest ideal among these institutions.

Sport, in its most intricate manifestations, had eaten into the framework of higher education and then into the vast, rambling body of the public and parochial schools. It was through the parents' concern for their children's health as well as scholastic and social interests that the general public responded to the athletic movement. Seventy-five of the largest and best high schools were surveyed in Nebraska in 1909 and, of the 95 percent engaged in interscholastic contests, 91 percent reported an easing of discipline, 97 percent better school spirit, and 92 percent higher scholastic standards.[25] Better sportsmanship, interinstitutional trust, opposition to recruiting, and the perennial quest to maintain a true scholastic perspective became common topics of discussion. One cannot sense, despite public criticism and the coming of a great war, any semblance of a real crisis when the future of athletics was in doubt. Sport had arrived as a national institution by 1920 and had become the bandwagon around which rallied students and alumni, business and transportation interests, advertising and amusement industries, cartoonists and artists, juvenile authors and sports columnists.

## Feminine Approval and Public Recognition

It has hitherto been the greatest drawback to the popularity of sports and pastimes in this country that ladies have been prohibited, by the ridiculous customs of American society in this respect, from being spectators at any trial of skill in those manly games and exercises which in England are countenanced by the fairest of Britain's nobility. Of late years a great change has been introduced here . . . [and] experience has shown that nothing tends so much to elevate the game, to rid it of evil influences, to lead to proper decorum and to gentlemanly contests than the countenance and patronage of the ladies. . . .

But if you wish to realize the great advantage the presence of ladies at matches is to the game, just mark the behavior of a large assemblage at an exciting contest where no ladies, or but half a dozen or so at most, are to be seen, and that of a crowd where a hundred bright-eyed fair ones occupy seats as interested spectators. At the one, profanity and ill-feeling, partisan prejudice and open gambling, are prominent features; while at the other, the pride which curbs men's evil passions in the presence of ladies frowns upon all such exhibitions, and order and decorum, and the absence of profanity, mark the presence of the civilizing influence of the fair sex.[26]

Brought to America as a Victorian pastime at "country homes and garden parties," croquet won many addicts in the immediate post-bellum years: "It began the process, later accelerated by archery, tennis, and bicycling, of bringing women out of stuffy living rooms and parlors to participate in out-of-door exercise with men. . . . In both the country and the city, wire wickets on lawns became a sign of conformity with the latest dictates of fashion." The roller skating rage also contributed greatly to this emancipation process, as did the ice rink. Young ladies sported fur-trimmed tunics, ermine hats, knit lamb's wool leggings, and high boots in 1871, and the *New York Clipper* observed, "The new fashions for skating dresses are very elegant and attractive."[27]

Recreation for the American woman, however, was more likely to be found in her interest in continental novels and poetry, in sewing circles and church suppers, in camp meetings and visits to the seashore. Many girls rolled hoops, played marbles, skated, or took long walks in the woods, yet they hardly enjoyed the freedom of sun-tanned lads diving in the old swimming hole or playing baseball. Never risking the social sin of being seen at prize fights, they were almost always a notable minority at the races, and, handicapped by their hoop skirts or offended by the rough language of the players, they were seldom found in the grandstands. English girls of the late nineteenth century were referred to as the open-air type in contrast to their American "cousins" who clung tenaciously to the old ideal of pallid cheeks, narrow waists, and frail wrists.

The American woman's sporting diversions remained an object of controversy down to the First World War. Should she ride the wheel in 1895? She was riding by the thousands in 1896. Was it ladylike to golf in 1892? She was golfing from Key West to the Pacific by the end of the decade. Should she take to athletic sports in 1890? She was engaging in basketball, baseball, rowing, winter sports, and aquatic carnivals in the college of 1900. Limited as sports may have been to those of money and leisure, a change in sentiment inevitably accompanied the rise of feminine interest: "Not play golf? Why, of course you play. Everybody plays, or talks of playing, for not to be well up in the sports of the day is a mistake few *fin de siecle* women are guilty of."

A feminine enthusiast might look back on the Victorian Age and philosophize, "With the single exception of the improvement in the legal status of women, their entrance into the realm of sports is the most cheering thing that has happened to them in the century just past." Women, however, pursued the athletic craze of 1900 mildly; golfers were still forced to wear skirts which touched the tops of their high shoes; newspapers ridiculed the bloomer costume and there was "a storm of sermons on immodesty." When Stanford and University of California coeds met in a basketball game in San Francisco no men were allowed to look on; doorkeepers, janitors, and ushers were all women; and reports to the press were made by feminine writers. Even so, the faculties forbade a return match.[28]

Sport for women in schools, factories, and small towns was to be largely a twentieth-century phenomenon. Seeds were taking root, nevertheless, as we have noted in the playground movement, girls' athletic leagues, college athletics for young women, and varied physical education programs in the Roosevelt-Taft-Wilson era. Newspapers and magazines gradually opened their pages to feminine games. Even a few daring souls, like the two wives of sporting men from Louisville who attended the boxing carnival in New Orleans in 1892, began to ignore social taboos—although as late as 1908 only "a score of women" appeared among ten thousand spectators at the Battling Nelson-Joe Gans lightweight title fight on the San Mateo hills in California.[29]

As spectators of pedestrian matches, cycle races, baseball games, and horse races, women continued the process of breaking down Victorian prejudices against the sporting life. Emily Post, asking "What Makes A Young Girl Popular?" in 1910, noted the athletic craze and observed: "Grace includes not alone aymmetry of movement, but all accomplishments in activity, such as dancing, skating, swimming, riding, and also any especial gifts, such as a talent for music or acting." By 1919 a reporter noted: "More women are attending the world's series than any previous baseball spectacle. . . . The shyness of the women fans is a thing of the past, and they now shout and yell at the players with just as much frankness as the men."[30]

Throughout the Victorian era the quest for respectability became pronounced in every field of sport. Many early amateur baseball clubs were composed of young lawyers, students, and scions of the "best families," but youths from the city streets and ruffians from the worst elements of the populace soon caused alarm to spread among the early advocates of the game. The Excelsior Club had become the model for the ball teams of 1860, and at the end of the Civil War it was acclaimed for standing "at the head of the list, socially speaking." But the appearance of clubs in every section of the teeming metropolis and in every stratum of society led to fear for the future of the game. One critic in 1867 warned that "the friends of baseball will soon understand that unless we can swing clear of 'sports', blacklegs, and rowdies, the whole thing will degenerate into a mere gambling institution." When a "gang of more than a score of New York ragamuffins" were jailed for cursing and swearing while playing on the Sabbath, the *Ball Players' Chronicle* editorialized: "We hope every one who thus offends the moral tastes of the community, will be equally as promptly punished. Blasphemy and obscenity follow close upon the heels of such crowds." An old-time ball fan described the conduct of San Francisco crowds: "I well remember a habit the gamblers among the spectators used to have, that surely savored of the wild and wooly west. Just as a fly ball was dropping into the fielder's hands, every gambler who had a bet on the nine at bat would discharge a fusillade from his six-shooter, in an endeavor to confuse the fielder and make him miss the ball."[31]

Gambling became a parasite on baseball in the seventies as pools operated in flagrant defiance of the law and of public sentiment. Guiding spirits of the diamond became alarmed, especially after the Louisville club's scandal of 1877. Corruption threatened the existence of the infant National League. The Boston *Post* for November 5, 1877 reported: "An investigation into the doings of the Louisville club during the past season reveals the fact that A.H. Nichols, J.A. Devlin, Geo. W. Hall, and William Craver have received bribes and sold games. Nichols and Devlin confessed. All have been expelled and they are now ineligible for positions in the league clubs. McCloud, a New York pool seller, has been acting in conjunction with them." Respectable journalism lamented the gambling menace:

> It would be difficult to name any recreation which can be conducted in public, from horse-racing to base-ball, that has not been debased by the infusion of the gambling element. Base-ball, indeed, has steadily declined in popular interest during five years past. It is a great pity that the game should have fallen into disrepute, for it is a wholesome and healthful pastime, not a costly diversion. . . . If the promoters of these games cannot cure the evil, nobody can. And if dishonest managers persist in their schemes, they will soon find nobody simple enough to attend their humbug shows.[32]

The National League was unable to eradicate much of this corruption for some years, and the return of prosperity to the nation and to baseball at the end of the seventies brought only limited improvement in the conduct of games. The baseball world was accused of blasphemy, hard drinking, and low moral standards during these years of economic exploitation when political and business ethics reached new depths. Drunkenness was considered "the most conspicuous evil that was connected with professional ball playing during 1884," and it was stressed that "whatever may be said about prohibition in political circles, most assuredly it is the only law which should prevail on the subject in the ranks of the professional fraternity, from April to November each base ball year."[33]

These were the years of the rise of the American Association (and the sale of liquor on its grounds). The umpire was slowly given greater authority, and while the fans were screaming, "Kill the Umpire!" it was said, "Some defensive armor for protecting the umpire against bad language and beer-glasses is imperatively called for." As defenders of the game pointed to the growing respectability of ball players in morals, intelligence, and "keen regard for the amenities of social life", athletics were enjoyed at the vacation school held at Dwight L. Moody's Northfield Seminary. The *Northwestern Christian Advocate* noted that, "the forehead of a certain celebrated baseball celebrity slopes backward rather more decidedly than does that of Walter Scott, Cavour, Castelar, and Gladstone. Home-rule bills need a bit more of brainroom than does a home run."[34]

The prize ring struggled to make itself more reputable, despite a strong contingent of rowdies who were close to the sport. When two pugilists sought to settle their differences near St. Louis in 1873, the Chicago *Times* reported, "Arrangements for the mill between Hogan and Allen are being perfected very quietly, for fear of magisterial interference. The fight will undoubtedly come off within the next 24 hours, but the exact time and place will not be known to any but a select and trusty few." Such secrecy surrounding ring encounters was slowly abandoned, and, no matter how illegal such contests might be, by 1890 fight news was widely reported in the press. The ministry in general seemed to be opposed to such sport. T. De Witt Talmage recalled the national interest in the Sullivan-Ryan fight in 1882: "I had no great objection to find with it. . . . I saw no reasonable cause why the law should interfere between two men who desired to pound one another in public." It was to be noted, however, "I stood alone almost among my brethren in this conclusion." One local paper editorialized "Blue-blooded Boston is disgusted with the notoriety the Hub has gained through the brutal victory of its hard-hitting son, Sullivan." Legal prosecution of prize fighting and public condemnation of the carousing habits of John L. Sullivan and his associates testify to the failure of pugilism to attain the respectability its sponsors sought.[35]

The American turf appealed to the "better elements" for popular support throughout the latter decades of the century, and references to the presence of ladies, public figures, pillars of society, and even clergymen at the track were common. When *Wallace's Monthly* made its appearance in 1875 it made a declaration "in favor of banishing the pool-seller from every race and trotting course in all this broad land." Yet, the conservative restraints of Puritanism had not withered away and the gambling which raged at the track aroused the ire of layman and preacher alike. In 1887 the ministers of Brooklyn were aroused "to do a good deal of work outside of our pulpits, outside of our churches, on the street and in the crowds. . . . Brooklyn was disgraced before the world by our race tracks at Coney Island, which were a public shame!"[36] Charles Parmer has pointed out the dependence of the track on bookmaking:

> This opportunity to bet freely was offered when a new element took stance on the American racecourse after the Civil War: the *bookmaker,* the professional gambler who made a book of wagers, betting *against* every horse in a race. The bookmaker . . . was necessary to the commercial turf. . . . Race meetings had been opened with professional gambling forbidden; and had been closed with great loss. So the racing associations not only tolerated the bookmaker; they urged him to come and make himself at home.[37]

By 1891 W. B. Curtis estimated that total annual betting on races in the United States reached almost $200,000,000 and that expenses in maintaining telegraph and betting services exceeded $5,000,000, while bookmakers and poolsellers paid more than $2,500,000 annually for track stalls. As the undesirables were eliminated from better tracks, a host of outlaw courses cropped up, like the notorious Guttenberg in New Jersey as well as those in Virginia and Maryland. Cooperation of the police at the tracks and other sporting events increased in the latter decades, and rowdyism was steadily brought under control.[38]

By inducing prominent citizens to assume responsible positions in local racing associations, by catering to feminine enthusiasts, and by establishing more rigid rules for membership in the jockey clubs, the better tracks aspired to maintain their traditional links with the social aristocracy and to constantly reassure the public of their honesty and respectability.[39]

Some sports were relatively free of the gambling menace. Intercollegiate contests before World War I were attended largely by students and followers of the "old school" and by those who could afford the costly tickets of a big game. Yacht, tennis, golf, polo, and cycling organizations prided themselves in the belief that they were limited to men and women of distinction and good breeding, while athletic clubs and YMCA's made much of the high caliber of their members. Archery, cricket, rowing, croquet, fishing, and canoeing were accepted by the public as rational forms of recreation needing no justification or defense. Even in these sports, however, the authorities often seemed as anxious to maintain prestige as to acquire new participants.

In the years prior to the European holocaust baseball pools were investigated continually by the district attorney's office, and in 1915 President Tener inaugurated a systematic attack on the "insidious" mushrooming of gambling dens. Even so, baseball rapidly won the public's approval and hearty support. Popular confidence in the honesty of the professional game rapidly became the rule of the day. Reform of the conduct of players, more respectable treatment of games in the press by sports experts, and spread of participation on the sandlot or playground helped the national pastime acquire a unique position in the hearts of the people.

Horse racing was another matter, for the turf was engulfed in a whirlpool of gambling and reform. Western Union's Racing Department went under attack in the press in 1904 as pool rooms (not always identical with billiard parlors) were found in most cities. Racing staggered through more than a decade of virulent criticism. Organization of the thoroughbred turf undertaken by the New York Jockey Club had only partially eliminated bribes, throwing of races, or widespread gambling. Kentucky was forced in 1906 to create a State Racing Commission, probably the first public controlling agency in the United States, and reform crusades took hold in many states in 1907 and 1908. *The World's Work* contended, "There is a grain of truth in the ancient fiction that racing improves the breed of horses; but the greater truth, the more important truth, is that racing lowers the breed of men." Poolselling in any form was declared unlawful in several cases in New York in 1908 on the grounds that it was illegal to employ devices for betting.[40]

Most spectacular of all the reform movements was the vigorous campaign of Governor Charles Evans Hughes of New York. Hughes tackled the issue of betting, stating to the legislature that it was promoted by "those who would sacrifice the morals of our youth by extending the area of unnecessary temptation; who would inflict needless suffering upon helpless women and children . . . and who would imperil the welfare of thousands of our people simply because of their selfish desire to make money out of gambling privileges." Exposing the flagrance with which poolselling and bookmaking flourished "unrestricted under what amounts to legal protection," Governor Hughes went to the people: "This is a scandal of the first order and a disgrace to the state. The bills are not aimed at racing or at race tracks or at property. They are aimed at public gambling, prohibited by the constitution, condemned by the moral sense of the people, irrespective of creed, and conceded to be the prolific source of poverty and crime." How deeply racing entered into the politics of the Empire State was demonstrated in a speech to his fellow Republicans, wherein he stated that "we have always been a party of moral purpose. If the party does not practice that it will go steadily into a decline. Here is one of these questions where you are not trying to execute some impossible moral reform by visionary legislation. The abolition of this evil will be the saving of thousands of men who are now going to their ruin. The Republican party cannot afford to dodge this issue."[41]

The law as finally passed in 1910 was the death knell of racing in the state for some years. When oral betting was substituted for bookmaking in succeeding racing campaigns, Justice Townsend Scudder was attacked by the Society for the Prevention of Crime for his decision in a "test case" in 1917. Racing recovered during the war years, but the moral crusade of the preceding decade did much to tarnish its reputation in the public mind.

Next to horse racing, in the eyes of social reformers, came the menace of the ring. Gambling had appeared in bowling, cycling, and yachting circles, but this received little attention compared to the combination of forces which retarded public approval of both wrestling and boxing. Prior to the war of 1914-1918 religious elements and respectable society united in discouraging attendance at professional fights. When Olsen the Dane defeated champion Gus Roeber in 1900, betting was high among his Scandinavian friends despite rumors that, like most other wrestling matches of the time, the contest was "fixed." Pugilism still wore its old tainted garments and only gradually attracted a loyal clientele. After aging Jim Jeffries fought Jack Johnson at Reno in 1910 a public storm broke loose. A campaign for the prohibition of fight films was launched, headed by the United Society of Christian Endeavor. Governor Fred Warner of Michigan made the blast: "The brutal contest at Reno between the black stevedore and the white boiler-maker has sealed the doom of the ring contest between humans. . . . Such a fight brings into the limelight the riffraff of society, the element that drove horse racing from the list of clean sports." *The Independent* charged: "Decency and good order require that the public exhibition of these pictures should be prohibited. It is bad enough to pervert the morals and ideals of a community with such shows. But it would be much worse to allow them to incite race riots throughout the country."[42]

Popular feeling was reflected in a congressional bill to prohibit interstate transportation of fight films:

Be it enacted by the Senate and House of Representatives of the United States of America in Congress assembled, that it shall be unlawful to send or receive, by mail, railway, express, water service, or in any other manner, from any state, territory or the District of Columbia, or to bring into this country from any foreign country, any film or other pictorial representation of any prize-fight or encounter of pugilists, under whatever name, or any record or account of betting on the same. Any person violating the provisions of this act shall be punished by imprisonment not exceeding one year or a fine of not exceeding $1000, at the discretion of the court.[43]

There was no national boxing association to regulate conditions of the game, state laws prohibited professional bouts, addicts of the ring still were compelled to seek contests held in "tank towns," and Johnson and Jess Willard had to go all the way to Havana for their championship bout in 1915.

State laws were gradually altered or disregarded, but it was World War I which provided the impulse necessary to the revival of the ring. The *Northwestern Christian Advocate* recognized an upsurge of interest: "When the war is over and a return to the daily life of peace is had, we may be assured the prize-fight will be so thoroughly ensconced in American sports as to necessitate another long and wearisome campaign of education and legislation to push it back a second time into obscurity. . . . The swing in favor of cigaret-smoking and 'boxing' is too strong to be hurled back now, or during the war. But churchmen must sit tight, or rather stand firm in their opposition to these things. . . . The Church must maintain unyielding opposition thereto." How difficult their cause would be was observed by alarmed religious groups. When the Dempsey-Willard fight was held in Toledo in 1919, the churches of Ohio strenuously opposed it, though they were unable to persuade the Ohio legislature. New York passed the Walker Law in 1920 and the floodgates were thrown open.

At the end of the Civil War bowling was popular not only among the old Dutch burghers and German settlers in New York but was played widely in beer gardens in many states. From outdoor greens to clay courts to slate slabs, the game steadily underwent transformation. Until the eighties bowling alleys, like skating rinks or ice cream parlors, were called "saloons," after which time bowling was played in private clubs, Y's, a few churches, and on private estates. Commercial alleys, along with ice skating and dancing, were often featured by the Amusement Palace in the nineties. Clubs in New York and Brooklyn organized a National Bowling Association in 1875, followed by an American Amateur Bowling Union in 1890. Finally, in 1895, the American Bowling Congress was launched to standardize rules of play and lift the reputation of the game.

Slowly but surely the game began to win new fans in YMCA's and athletic clubs as well as among a few daring young women. By 1899 Chicago had some 20,000 keglers, nearly 100 clubs, and ten bowling leagues. Then said to be one of the most popular diversions for members of the Chicago Athletic Club, bowling was slowly gaining in social prestige. "It is within the memory of every one in Chicago when bowling alleys could be found only in saloons, and a woman who played the game would have been looked upon as something of a prodigy. . . . There was a common superstition that the game was fit only for roughs and had no place among the sports recognized as legal. A club initiating it would have been ostracized from society and its members prosecuted." Even at the end of the century this condition still prevailed, much as the enthusiast might claim for the game. The Brunswick-Balke-Collender Company's 1914 catalogue still emphasized the propriety of women bowlers, but by 1916 sufficient interest had developed for the organization of a Woman's National Bowling Association, later renamed the Women's International Bowling Congress.

Billiards, of course, remained a diversion of clubs and private homes or the sport of taverns, saloons, and hotels. Even in recent years promoters have failed to win the approval of most women. Whether the freer movement of women in large cities and the adoption of many industrial recreation programs will eventually overcome a centuries-old prejudice remains to be seen. Brunswick promotional literature, noting the prestige accruing to bowling as it freed itself from the "questionable following" of the "pool hall" and as leagues of players from clubs, industries, churches, and the professions lent "tone," has recognized a still existent problem: "The game of billiards can enjoy the same honor, can bask in the same public favor. It's simply a matter of attitude, of setting up for, and catering to, the same high class trade and of supervising the management of the billiard center so that it is a clean, attractive, and popular gathering place for young and old of both sexes."[44]

A generation of mounting interest in physical education and an immediate concern with the bodily health of the American soldier aroused considerable discussion during the war years. Studies like *Educational Hygiene from the Pre-School Period to the University* (1915) by Louis W. Rapeer, *Healthful Schools* (1918) by May Ayres, Jesse Williams, and Thomas Wood, and *Health Education in Rural Schools* (1919) by J. Mace Andress expressed public interest in the health of the child and the healthy benefits of sport. James H. McCurdy, editor of the *American Physical Education Review,* opened his magazine to medical discussions of the effect of athletics on the heart. Dr. William Middleton, for example, found cardiac hypertrophy, accentuated dilatation, and lessened resistance, whereas Dr. Roger Lee discovered little conclusive proof of damage to the "athletic heart." The concern of America in the twenties with the health of its citizens was in great part activated by the focussing of public attention on the high number of rejected draftees. And, of course, while the tobacco-consuming public was to grow through the years, appeals were made to athletically-minded youth to forego cigarettes as an impediment to success on the playing field or the running track.

Americans were concerned throughout the years between the Civil War and World War I with the moral and legal problem of Sabbath observance. This new threat to Puritan tradition and practice seemed to grow in proportion to the tide of Europeans reaching our shores and to the commercialization of society. As ministers and their congregations became increasingly concerned, local laws were passed to prohibit ball games and other sports as well as to close the theater and the saloon. In Dubuque, Iowa, businessmen and the clergy opposed Sunday ball: "The influence of the pulpit in favor of the game will be a great advantage that would be turned against them should it be turned into a Sunday game." Hundreds of New Yorkers rode the ferries to Weehawken to play baseball in the middle eighties, causing a reporter to observe, "Whatever the law of New Jersey may be in regard to Sunday base ball playing, it is inoperative in the neighborhood of Weehawken."[45]

Edward Hitchcock and Dio Lewis were among the physical culturists who had supported the temperance cause. Inasmuch as the athlete in training could not indulge in tobacco and alcoholic beverages, temperance advocates looked with favor on wholesome outdoor sports. Appealing to "All Knights of Labor, Trades Unions and Other Labor Organizations," Frances Willard noted that "famous athletes, pedestrians, rowers and shots are men who do not cobweb their brains, or palsy their nerves with alcoholic drink." She scored an even stronger point with her promise that the WCTU would aid the Knights of Labor in their "efforts to secure the [Saturday] half-holiday, which, we believe, will do so much to change the Sabbath from a day of recreation to one of rest at home and for the worship of God."[46]

Laws remained on the statute books of almost all states, continuing to prohibit hunting, fishing, shooting, racing, cock fights, and prize fighting. In urban areas, however, the Sabbath was losing its hold as California rescinded its law in 1883 and "all through the summer of 1884 Sunday base-ball games, in defiance of law, were reported from Chicago, St. Louis, Cincinnati, Indianapolis, Louisville, Milwaukee, Dubuque, and Kansas City." James Bryce observed several years later that metropolitan centers like Chicago, Cincinnati, New Orleans, and San Francisco had liberalized the rules of observance and that "the strictness of Puritan practice" had disappeared, but "the American part of the rural population, especially in the South, refrain from amusement as well as from work."[47]

Widely scattered communities, with different religious and national groups, reacted differently. A Bostonian in 1895 might not enter a beer garden whereas thousands visited such "dens of evil" in Milwaukee; New York might close its theaters on Sunday while the playhouses of Cincinnati, Chicago, St. Louis, and New Orleans remained open; Philadelphians might not play baseball but Iowa cities conducted championship series. Those of Puritanic background who were alarmed at the advance of the Parisian Sabbath were already being warned that "practical conformity of one's outward life to the spirit of the Christian religion does not involve treating Sunday as a day on which recreation is a moral offence," since Christ had proclaimed, "The Sabbath was made for man, and not man for the Sabbath."[48]

The Puritan tradition refused to yield, however, and quarrels over Sunday observance were to rage well into the twentieth century. At the Olympic Games in Paris in 1900 French mismanagement of the scheduled events compelled the American team to compete on Sunday. Although most college delegations grudgingly consented, eight of thirteen University of Pennsylvania men refrained from entering the games on the Sabbath, an indication that many athletes were not anxious to discard their religious convictions in order to win an Olympic medal.

Meanwhile, the Women's Sabbath Alliance had taken up a crusade against Sunday golf, urging women to abandon the practice and set an example for the men. Mrs. Darwin R. James, leader of the movement, charged, "All criminals start on the downward path by working on Sunday. If golfers only considered that they were starting their caddies in a life of sin by making them work on Sunday, they would give up their Sunday games." In Cleveland contemporary fears were well illustrated in a *Plain Dealer* warning: "Sunday baseball is the entering wedge of an 'open Sunday.' Its legalization is planned to be followed or accompanied by the legalization of Sunday poolrooms, and then barrier after barrier would be swept away and, instead of the orderly Cleveland Sunday with its restful peace, there would soon be the 'wide-open' Sunday of Chicago and St. Louis."[49] While convictions were hard to obtain, a New York statute warned:

> All shooting, hunting, fishing, playing, horseracing, gaming, or other public sport, exercises or shows, upon the first day of the week, and all noise disturbing the peace of the day, are prohibited.[50]

And so dawned a new century. Rev. Charles H. Eaton of New York was representative of the liberal clergy when he proclaimed, "I do not hesitate for a moment to affirm that every law and regulation in regard to Sunday observance, resting on religious reasons, should be abrogated."[51]

"Blue laws" against sport remained on the statute books of all states
except California as late as 1915, however, and public officials often enforced them so stringently as to make them ridiculous. When the Chicago
White Sox conquered the Cubs in the 1906 World Series on a Sunday, Rev.
John Roach Straton, an admirer of the diamond, deplored such desecration: "It is a shame and a disgrace to any community as enlightened and
civilized as Chicago that Sunday baseball should be tolerated and indulged
in, not only by professionals but by boys and young men in general, many
of the better classes. It has been shown times without number in history
that society always suffers from the desecration of the Sabbath."[52] Many
thinking people changed their attitude toward recreation on the Sabbath
and favored the opening of art galleries, museums, and parks, but they still
hedged on the issue of Sunday sports and opposed any commercialization
of the Lord's Day.

Foreign observers mentioned the confusing diversity of state laws and
the "draconian rigor" of enforcement in many states, but the ingenious
evasive spirit of the average American was also noted. In Illinois, as in
earlier times, they had changed to bowling with ten pins rather than with
the traditional nine because "nine pins" had been prohibited by state law!
Riding, yachting, automobiling, and aviation were generally left untouched
by the law in 1910. James Bryce observed in 1911, "The habit of playing
outdoor games and that of resorting to places of public amusement on
Sunday have much increased of late years."[53]

Boston permitted individualized recreation like swimming, skating,
and tobogganing, "but anything in which a ball is used is still anathema."
Among the more prominent sympathizers with amateur sport on Sunday
were G. Stanley Hall, Joseph Lee, Lillian Wald, and William Howard Taft.
Lee, in a pamphlet entitled *Sunday Play*, heartily recommended that "it is
in the interest of Sunday, of its fuller realization, that we shall remove the
fetters we have placed upon it." By 1913 *The Outlook* recognized the
existence of a violent fight over Sabbath observance in the press of the
country and the tendency of a large percentage of mayors to favor local
option. Taft was quoted as saying at that time, "There should be no objections to playing it [golf] on the Sabbath day if one attends to his religious
duties first. Church in the morning and golf in the afternoon on Sundays
is an excellent compromise."[54]

This spirit was by no means representative of the convictions of a
large segment of the American public. Much of the holdover from Victorian conformity restrained millions from abandoning strict observance of
the Sabbath in the custom of their forefathers. A general leavening of
opinion was taking place, however, and in larger urban centers the trend
was especially noticeable. Lillian Wald recalled how in the 1890's richly
attired golfers crowded on trains or ferries bound for the suburbs and a

Sunday's sport, while underprivileged lads were chased by the police as
street Arabs when they engaged in games. By 1914, however, the police
had been converted to the spirit of the sporting crusade and they obliged
by closing off streets from city traffic: "Happily some of the early prejudice against ballplaying on Sunday has vanished."[55]

Churches were regularly confronted with the issue of Sabbath sport,
but the clergy in general seem to have been less belligerently vocal in
public controversy. The liquor traffic, public crime, and other social issues
were of more immediate concern, and the value of sport in the prevention
of juvenile delinquency helped win over some who had been hostile. There
was agitation in 1913 on Sunday sport, reflected in the comments of the
Indianapolis *News,* Buffalo *Express,* and such New York newspapers as the
*Sun, Globe, World,* and *Tribune.* The New York *Tribune* stated that "certain sports on Sunday, conducted so as not to disturb the day's peace,
contribute to the health of and make for good morals in the community."
The American Sunday-School Union in 1915 acknowledged that a solution
of the "attack" of organized Sunday sport and the retention of a Sabbath
of refining and Christianizing influence was "a large part of the problem
of the modern Church."[56]

World War I did much to bring to fruition social movements of long
standing in America, among them prohibition, the women's vote, and the
more liberal Sabbath. At the height of the war in Europe, when our troops
were helping the French and British launch the great counteroffensive of
1918, an influx of government workers in Washington, D.C. impelled the
opening of professional baseball on Sunday. Ex-president Theodore Roosevelt, who on entering office in 1902 had been cautious not to leave the
impression that he was a sporting president, was now reported favoring
Sunday baseball. But the 131st General Assembly of the Presbyterian
Church in the United States of America, meeting in St. Louis in 1919,
decried the desecration of the Lord's day and condemned state legislatures
for easing laws. It was resolved: "That the general assembly reiterates its
strong and emphatic disapproval of all secular uses of the Sabbath day, all
games and sports, all unnecessary traveling and excursions, and urges upon
all employers of labor and captains of industry to recognize the need of
the laboring man for his weekly rest day, and secure him in this right and
thereby insure his larger efficiency and happiness and the greater prosperity
of both capital and labor."[57] The Sabbath had to remain a day of rest.
Tradition remained strong within the churches, particularly in small towns
and rural sections; the country was undergoing a resurgence of fundamen-
talism; and liberal laws appearing on statute books were rigorously criticized. Concern for more crucial issues and return of men from the armed
forces, however, were major factors leading to the more open Sabbath
attained in the years after the armistice.

## American Culture and the Sporting Life

So strong was the grasp of Puritanism on the mid-nineteenth century mind and so conservative was the public attitude in succeeding decades that the penetration of sport into even the peripheral areas of culture could only be slight. Strong conviction prevailed that athletic exercise and aesthetic appreciation were antipodal in nature. American literature, thriving on the rich heritage of the New England past and colored with a strong streak of transcendentalism, was hardly a fertile field for interest in mundane sport. William Dean Howells might write in *Silas Lapham* of the thrill of a trotting match on the open road, Mark Twain might picture "fishin'" along the Mississippi, and thousands might read the blasts at athletics by the English author, Wilkie Collins. But the theme had little appeal to most authors of the time. Nor did any prominent historian, from Jared Sparks, George Bancroft and James Ford Rhodes to John Bach McMaster, Frederick Jackson Turner and Charles Beard, delve into the sporting interests of the American people.[58]

Juvenile literature offered somewhat larger opportunities. William Taylor Adams, renowned as "Oliver Optic," published the *Boat Club Series* in the 1850's and the *Yacht Club Series* between 1872 and 1900. *Oliver Optic's Magazine for Boys and Girls*, which he edited from 1867 to 1875, served as a source of juvenile literature, while the publishing house of Beadle & Adams brought out numerous stories and rule books. In the postwar era C.A. Fosdick came out with a *Sportsman's Club Series;* Mark Severance wrote of rowing, boxing, and cricket in *Hammersmith: His Harvard Days* (1878); and Noah Brooks pioneered in baseball fiction with *The Fairfield Nine* (1880) and *Our Base Ball Club* (1884). None of these rivalled Thomas Hughes' classics, *Tom Brown's School Days* and *Tom Brown at Oxford,* but they were harbingers of the flood of juvenile stories of the turn of the century. The House of Beadle & Adams published Bracebridge Hemyng's *The Captain of the Club,* Frederick Whittaker's *Pluck Wins,* and Joseph Badger's *The Bay Jockey or, Honesty versus Crookedness,* all in 1879. Among its later handbooks were *Dime Base Ball Player, Dime Guide to Swimming, Dime Book of Cricket, Dime Hand-Book of Croquet, Dime Hand-Book of Yachting and Rowing,* and books on winter sports, skating, curling, football, and track and field. Even though the juvenile field was largely preempted by dime-novel tales of the Wild West or the Big City, *Frank Leslie's Boys' and Girls' Weekly* occasionally printed outdoor and athletic stories.

Sporting literature worthy of the name made a modest but increasingly impressive appearance in postwar years. Incipient Isaac Waltons in earlier decades depended in great part on the angling lore and sporting publications of the British, but from the 1840's onward, as we have seen, field sports and the beauty of the American landscape were romanticized by a number of writers. A land which produced such ardent devotees of rod and reel as De Witt Clinton, Daniel Webster, Horace Greeley, Thurlow Weed, Chester A. Arthur, Henry Ward Beecher, Joseph Jefferson, Jay Cooke, and Grover Cleveland could not fail to develop a literature of its own.

Thaddeus Norris pioneered in the latter half of the century with *The American Angler's Book* (1864), rivalled by Robert Barnwell Roosevelt's *Game Fish of the Northern States of America and British Provinces* (1862), *Superior Fishing* (1865), and *The Game Birds of the Coasts and Lakes of the Northern States of America* (1866). William Cowper Prime's *I go a-fishing* (1873) and George Dawson's *Pleasures of Angling* (1876), along with "Frank Forester's" ever-popular works sentimentalized rural sport, while detailed information was to be found in John H. Walsh's *Encyclopedia of Rural Sports* (1874), Charles Hallock's *The Sportsman's Gazetteer* and *General Guide* (1877), and numerous guidebooks.

By the eighties works on the great outdoors appeared frequently. Public interest was aroused by numerous articles in *Harper's Monthly,* and the love of the outdoors of Robert Roosevelt's nephew Teddy was recorded by the latter's facile pen in *Hunting Trips of a Ranch Man* (1885), *Ranch Life and the Hunting-Trail* (1888), and *The Wilderness Hunter* (1893). Numerous books on buffalo hunting and western sport were published. With the conquest of space by the postwar railroad, fishermen could travel afar and readers might vicariously enjoy the techniques and woodland adventures of Charles Orvis and A. Nelson Cheney (eds.), *Fishing with the Fly* (1883); Professor Alfred M. Mayer (comp.), *Sport with Gun and Rod in American Woods and Waters* (1883); Judge Lewis B. France, *With Rod and Line in Colorado Waters* (1884); Henry P. Wells, *The American Salmon Fisherman* (1886); G.O. Shields ("Coquina"), *Cruising in the Cascades* (1889); Edward A. Samuels, *With Fly-Rod and Camera* (1890); and Henry van Dyke, *Little Rivers* (1895) and *Fisherman's Luck* (1899). Approximately one hundred works related to American fishing were published between 1870 and 1901, and over the past half century this landslide of books on outdoor life has become an avalanche.[59]

Turf history was described in Hiram Woodruff's *The Trotting Horse of America* (1869); the memoirs of John Splan and Ed Geer; the works of John H. Wallace, Hamilton Busbey, and their colleagues; Charles Trevathan's *The American Thoroughbred* (1905); and Henry Coates' *A Short History of the American Trotting and Pacing Horse* (1906). Men of leisure were attracted to yachting accounts like J.D. Jerrold Kelley, *American Yachts, Their Clubs and Races* (1884), Ed Burgess, *American and English Yachts* (1887), Fred Cozzens et al., *Yachts and Yachting* (1887), R.T. Pritchett et al., *Yachting* (1894), Winfield Thompson and Thomas Lawson,

*The Lawson History of the America's Cup* (1902), and W.P. Stephens, *American Yachting* (1904). Diamond lore and the merits of the game received treatment in C.A. Peverelly, *The National Game* (1866), John M. Ward, *Base-Ball* (1888), Mike Kelly, *Play Ball* (1888), George Tuohey (comp.), *A History of the Boston Base Ball Club* (1897), Adrian Anson, *A Ball Player's Career* (1900), and Seymour Church, *Baseball* (1902).

The ring was represented only in the hack writing of William Harding of the *National Police Gazette,* Robert De Witt's *The American Fistiana* (1873), the "autobiography" of John L. Sullivan, specialized manuals of Billy Edwards, J.B. O'Reilly, and others, and similar publications. Athletics and outdoor sport were championed in Charles Pratt's *The American Bicycler* (1880), *Cassell's Book of Sports and Pastimes* (1881), *The Tribune Book of Open-Air Sports* (1887), Edward Hartwell's studies of physical training, William Patten's *The Book of Sport* (1901), the diversified works of Henry Chadwick, Caspar Whitney, Walter Camp, and Harry Palmer, the tennis books of J. Parmly Paret, and the scores of titles in *The Outing Library of Sports* and *The American Sportsman's Library*. In the years immediately preceding World War I A.G. Spalding, Al Spink, Parke Davis, and James Anderson directed attention to the historical side of sport, unprofessional as their efforts may have been.

Hardly had the troops returned to their homes before baseball enthusiasm appeared everywhere. By October 24, 1867 the *Ball Players' Chronicle* noted: "Some individuals have since become monomaniacs over it; have employed its technical expressions during their prayers, at the table, and in business transactions. 'Red hot,' 'a grass cutter,' a 'skyscraper,' a 'corker,' a 'tip,' and other similar terms, are common phrases." With due allowance for the expansive nature of the foregoing claim, baseball fans acquired a growing knowledge of terms and phrases. In 1888 the bat was already an "ash," a "willow," or a "stick," and the unforgivable sin of striking out was variously identified as "caressing the mist," "compressing the atmosphere," "cutting holes in space," "fanning the air," and "pushing air." Thousands of enthusiasts learned the terminology of the racecourse, while yachtsmen had a technical language of their own. The American language, however, had absorbed few sporting phrases into general usage at the end of the century, and the lingo of the playing field was to be found in sporting journals rather than in established magazines and newspapers.

The arts tell much the same story. It is true that two of America's greatest painters often turned to sporting themes. Winslow Homer's *Skating in Central Park* (1858), *Croquet Players* (1865), *Long Branch* (1869), *Snap The Whip* (1872), *A Fair Wind* (1876), *Huntsman and Dogs* (1891), *Shooting the Rapids* (1905), and *Harper's Weekly* sketches were seminal experiments in sporting art. Oliver Larkin acclaimed his woodland watercolors such as *A Good Shot* (1892), *Deer Drinking* (1892), *Two Men in a Canoe* (1895), and *Eagle's Nest* (1902) as a milestone in painting and observed: "Among these pine-shaded lakes and dense autumn woods Homer's contemporaries could relive their own experiences as hunters and fishermen."

It was Thomas Eakins, however, who became most intimately acquainted with the sporting world and developed into the most versatile of American nineteenth-century sporting artists. Even he was to paint with restraint, perhaps from a reluctance to offend the public sense of propriety after his experience at the Pennsylvania Academy. Eakins rowed on the Schuylkill and "many of his early pictures were of rowers." *Max Schmitt in a Single Scull* (1871), *Pair-Oared Shell* (1872), *The Biglen Brothers Turning the Stake* (1873), countless sailing scenes and *Swimming Hole* (1883) expressed his love of outdoor exercise.[60]

Arthur Frost's baseball and golf sketches, Philip Hale's love of the prize ring *(Between Rounds),* and Currier & Ives' prints reflected the mounting enthusiasm of the latter part of the century, isolated as they may have been from the dominant stream of late Victorian artistic taste. Little if anything was achieved in sculpture until John McNamee finished *The First Base* while in Rome in 1873, a work praised by one critic as the first of an American athlete and for a "boldness and originality of conception."[61] Art and sculpture were little impressed with the athletic impulse of post-Civil War years, but popular illustrators in *Harper's Weekly, Frank Leslie's Illustrated Newspaper,* and other pictorial journals utilized sporting themes. In the 1870's Thomas Nast used athletic settings only in occasional instances, but by the early 1880's public interest was recognized by Joseph Keppler and other caricaturists like Thomas Worth, James A. Wales, Victor Gillam, Frederick Opper, and Eugene (Zim) Zimmerman.

Applying sharp wit and brutal drawing, these artists exposed political corruption and pomposity and were prone to argue such controversial issues as the race question, anti-Catholicism, civil service, and imperialism. Following in the footsteps of the *New York Graphic,* magazines like *Judge, Puck,* and *Life* added new dimensions to political warfare as well as popular humor. Victor Gillam's 1889 cartoon in *Judge* caught the lighter mood as John L. Sullivan addressed a dazed and blood-spattered football hero: "If that kind of work is eddication, young feller, I orter be a perfesher at Yale, m'self." Later years found illustrators using baseball, tennis, golf, prize-fight, and other sporting situations in the more genteel and sophisticated jokes, satire, and humor.[62]

Something of the contemporary enthusiasm was recorded in popular music. J.K. Kalbfleisch's "Live Oak Polka" (1860) and John Zebley's

"Home Run Quick Step" (1861) set the pattern. During the diamond
mania of 1867 "The Baseball Fever", "Base Ball Polka", and "The Base-
ball Quadrille" made an appearance, followed the next year by "Hurrah
for Our National Game." "Home Run Polka" and "The Red Stockings
Schottisch" greeted Cincinnati's pioneer professional club in 1869. An
Erie City club's polka was published in 1868, the Lowell club's "Silver
Ball March" appeared in 1870 and "Tally One for Me" in 1877. The
Waverly Boat club had its "Waverley Galop" (1868) while skating songs
like "Skating Galop" (1864), "The Central Park Polka" (1865), "Our
Skating Park" (1868), "The Enchanted Tide" (1869), and "Flirting on
the Ice" (1877) had their brief hour, followed by "Gliding in the Rink"
(1884) and "The Skaters" (1885). "Croquet" came in 1866 and the
pedestrian tunes "Weston's March to Chicago" (1867) and "Go-As-You-
Please Grand Galop" celebrated one of the popular contests of the era.
Hunting, riding, and fox hunting songs also were sung. "Casey At The Bat"
was set to music after 1888, rivalled by "Slide, Kelly, Slide" (1890),
"Finnegan the Umpire" (1890), and "O'Grady at the Game" (1891). And
cycling tunes were published in such collections as S.C. Foster's *Wheel
Songs* (1884) and T.S. Muller's *Club Songs for Wheelmen* (1888). Many of
these were of purely local popularity, but the interest of the postwar
generation was clearly evidenced by the sheet music of the period.[63]

Although signs of change in the public attitude toward sport were
also to be seen to a limited degree in the arts at the end of the century,
those who led the movement toward a higher culture seldom gave much
attention to the outdoor life. As sport grew into a national institution in
the period from 1890 to 1920, however, its cultural implications were
somewhat more discernible. Most talented authors continued to ignore
the world of sport, but writers of boxing yarns invaded the field of the
short story. Richard Harding Davis spun the tale of *Gallegher* in 1891,
while Jack London had a "tense interest in game and sport" and an "un-
quenchable joy in the leopard-like beauty of an athlete." As a frequenter
of the Oakland Athletic Club he acquired a great love of ringside, reporting leading fights for the San Francisco *Examiner* and the New York
*Herald,* writing of the ruthlessness of *The Game,* and telling many stories
of the wild. And O'Henry portrayed the pugilist in "The Higher Prag-
matism."

Rupert Hughes, Brand Whitlock, Ring Lardner, Charles Van Loan,
Franklin P. Adams, Heywood Broun, Damon Runyon, Irvin S. Cobb, and
Will Irwin turned their talents to sports writing or fiction. George Fitch's
"Siwash" stories pictured college life in pre-World War I years. If any book
in the lighter vein of sporting humor and satire deserved the accolade of

"classic" it was Lardner's *You Know Me Al* (1916), the epic of a "bush leaguer" whose ignorance and vanity were held up to public scorn:

> Indeed, it is probable that Ring Lardner's place as an American classic will be as a reporter of new phases of the American character, best seen through the satiric realist's eyes. In sports, particularly, there had come to be a new cohesion of American society, powerful over the imagination of millions. It had its own code, its own language, its own comedies and tragedies, its own heroes and buffoons . . . . Yet a corrupting commercialism, as inevitable as elsewhere in American life, gave an opportunity to the realist that such a romantic of a previous generation as Richard Harding Davis would have been unable to take.[64]

Juvenile literature contributed significantly to arousing interest among youngsters of the first two decades. Father Francis J. Finn, S.J., had written *Tom Playfair or Making a Start* (1891) and *That Football Game* (1897) for Catholic youth. Of *Tom Playfair* the author wrote, "I started this story with nothing else in mind than to present, once and for all, my ideal of the typical American Catholic boy." In 1896 Gilbert Patten (Burt L. Standish) began pouring out a story every week for the publishing house of Street and Smith on the greatest of schoolboy heroes, Frank Merriwell. This furious output was maintained from 1896 to 1913, comprising 208 titles and an unknown total publication estimated at more than 25,000,000 copies. By the early 1900's the Merriwell sales reached about 135,000 copies weekly. With the waning of boyish interest, Frank's heroic performances were followed by those of his younger brother Dick. After 1910 Patten began to look for other athletic themes and mass-produced the *Cliff Sterling* (1910-1916), *College Life* (1913-1928), and *Oakdale* (1916-1925) series. To Gilbert Patten go the laurels for bringing to youth the drama of the diamond, the gridiron, the cinder path, and the rowing course.[65]

Juvenile athletic stories began to stream from the pens of Ralph Henry Barbour *(Behind the Line, Double Play, On Your Mark!)*, Lester Chadwick *(Baseball Joe* series), Zane Grey *(The Shortstop, Red Headed Outfield)*, Leslie W. Quirk *(The Freshman Eight, The Fourth Down)*, Ralph D. Paine *(The Stroke Oar)*, Edward Stratemeyer *(The Rover Boys, Dave Porter* and *Lakeport* series), and Charles Emmet Van Loan *(Big League, Inside the Ropes, Fore!)*, to mention but a few of the authors of boys' books. Nor were the authors of girls' stories untouched by the spirit of the times, as novels by Gertrude Morrison, Jessie Flower, Janet Aldridge,

and other authors utilized the importance of athletic rivalries in girls'
schools as an integral part of the plot.

Merriwell, Baseball Joe, Stover of Yale, and the Rover Boys were
athletic idols worshipped by millions of young Americans. As heroes of
youth they inspired the fair play on the fields of sport and good conduct
in the game of life. Triumph ultimately and inevitably came to those who
played the game, and incalculable numbers of readers were inspired with
a love of competition which had important undertones for our national life.

Americans have always inclined to the extravagant and picturesque
in their language. Partly from the imaginative mind of the frontier, partly
from a subconscious revolt against English cultural domination, and partly
from a jovial and democratic spirit, they have created slang in almost every
walk of life. America's folklore and speech were molded by a myriad of
interests, all distinct segments of our national life: the love of the sea; the
adventure of mining; the vastness of her rivers, mountains and plains; the
stimulating imagery of railroading; the devotion to business enterprise and
to politics; the inventive nature of men in a machine civilization; and the
prolonged western movement have all added to the richness of our speech.

As B.A. Botkin has observed, the origins of "tall talk" were among
pre-Civil War hunters and trappers and sportsmen of turf and field, in tales
of Davy Crockett and Mike Fink and in "such as produced the hunting
and sporting yarns that filled William T. Porter's virile journal of oral and
anecdotal humor, *The Spirit of the Times.*"[66] We have incorporated
words into our language from our recreational interests as well—from
music and dancing, automobiling and flying, theater and motion pictures.
But there is a strong conviction that, since the maturation of industrialism
in the late nineteenth century, no institution in American life, excluding
the broad field of the sciences, has contributed more colorfully or more
voluminously to our language than that of sport. Humor and slang have
drawn extensively on the lingo of field and stream as well as of the playing
fields, the racing courses, and the athletic arenas.

There is comparatively little evidence prior to the nineties that sport
had a profound effect on the literature or the everyday speech of the
American people. Gradually, however, sporting journals and the sports
page of the press noted the drama and, at times, the ridiculous pomposity
of baseball patter; terms of the trotting course and the yachting world
were widely understood during the latter decades of the century; a baseball "phenom" or a cycling "scorcher" were known to the initiated in
post-Civil War years. But when we turn to political speeches, scholarly
studies, religious tracts, and fiction there was virtually a complete absence
of sporting terminology.

From the late 1880's onward, however, there was a parallel growth of sporting slang and popular enthusiasm for sports. *The Bookman* noted in 1901—less than two decades after the new style of journalism developed by Chicago baseball writers—the "absurdity and atrocious taste of it all" when a baseball was never called a ball but a "sphere," "pellet," "pea," or "leather."[67] An English observer noted in 1908:

> Never before in the world's history has slang flourished as it has flourished in America. And its triumph is not surprising. It is more than any artifice of speech the mark of a various and changing people. America has a natural love of metaphor and imagery; its pride delights in the mysteries of a technical vocabulary. . . . And not many tongues but many employments have enhanced the picture-esqueness of American slang. America has not lost touch with her beginnings. The spirit of adventure is still strong within her. There is no country within whose borders so many lives are led. The pioneer still jostles the millionaire, the backwoods are not far distant from Wall Street. The farmers of Ohio, the cowboys of Texas, the miners of Nevada, owe allegiance to the same government, and shape the same speech to their own purpose. Every state is a separate country and cultivates a separate dialect. Then came baseball, poker, and the racecourse, each with its own metaphors to swell the hoard. And the result is a language of the street and camp, brilliant in color, multiform in character, which has not a rival in the history of speech.[68]

As collegiate and professional sport became subjects for popular music, vaudeville, journalism, theater, advertising, humor, short story, and juvenile literature, the proper place of sporting terminology was debated. When a professor of the University of Chicago railed at the "patois" of the diamond, the Washington *Post* came to its defense. The Charleston *News and Courier* boldly proclaimed, "Long may the lingo live," whereas the Atlanta *Constitution* questioned such florid expressions as "clattered across the pan," "dented the platter," "got pinked in the pants," and similar descriptive phrases.[69]

Whatever the attitude of pure linguists may have been, Americans were reading the sports pages, revolutionized by Leonard Washburne, Charles Dryden and their confreres, or they were laughing at the cartoons of *Life* and *Puck*. The value of sport was more readily recognized even in the most distinguished publications of the new century. *The Bookman* pointed out in 1910: "A few years ago the conventions were such that no general magazine would even have considered an article on sport. But what a change! During the last four and twenty months it has been almost impossible to pick up a magazine that did not contain some kind of an article on baseball." [70]

Humorists explored a new-found gold mine. Finley Peter Dunne's "Mr. Dooley" reflected on the state of the nation and on the diversions of the people: "I've told ye that in me time I was a gran' futball player . . . . T'was fr'm watchin' me kick that th' navy got their idee in long distance shootin'. Besides it don't seem that there ar-re anny old men nowadays. It used to be that a man iv fifty was thought to be too seenile f'r anny useful warruk. But nowadays ye'll see dashin' young la-ads iv sixty-five full iv Boolgarian buttermilk wallopin' a goluf ball aroun' th' lot." Satirizing the growth of international sport, he observed, "I don't know what's goin' to happen to this Anglo-Saxon supreemacy iv ours if these here despised subjick races gets started in our spoorts. A few years ago ye'd as soon expict to see an archbishop on a thrapeze as an Eyetalyan or a Frinchman or a Bahaymyan winnin' a race." [71]

In the transitional years at the turn of the century, when Winslow Homer was painting many of his woodland water colors, Thomas Eakins continued to demonstrate his devotion to portrayal of Philadelphia life and typically American scenes, in great part influenced by his close friend, Walt Whitman. His interest in sculling was neglected as he became a frequenter of boxing and athletic clubs. New heights in sporting art were attained in *Taking the Count* (1898) and *Between Rounds* (1899), while Eakins' *Salutat* (1898) was to be considered possibly the best male nude ever painted by an American. "Nothing absorbed him more than a surgical operation," according to F.O. Matthiessen, "unless it was a boxing match." Something of his love of the drama of sport, which Eakins felt so strongly as to invite prize fighter friends into his home, was handed on to such pupils as George Luks, John Sloan, William Glackens, and Everett Shinn. [72]

Eakins had pioneered in portrayal of horses and humans in a state of motion in *Fairman Rogers Four-in-hand* and *Swimming Hole,* introducing "a new dynamics" in painting. [73] A provocative painter with sporting instinct was now to capture the excitement of the ring as well as the spirit of other sports in *Stag at Sharkey's* (1909), *Polo Game* (1910), *Golf Course, California* (1917), and *Tennis at Newport* (1920). A former athlete at Ohio State University and a constant attendant at private athletic clubs, his interest in boxing developed to the point where he eventually became America's most celebrated artist of the ring. To Bellows there was no more dramatic clash in nature than the fury and the ruthlessness of combat within the ropes. His growing devotion to sport was to flower in an avalanche of lithographs and paintings in postwar years. It was in great part his spirit which, in the tradition of Thomas Eakins, motivated a num-

ber of aspiring young artists of a later era to abandon the traditional
aversion for sporting scenes.

With the exception of R. Tait McKenzie, few sculptors consistently
turned to sporting themes. Herman MacNeil, Cyrus Dallin, and James
Fraser memorialized the American Indian's outdoor life while Solon
Borglum's "sculpture of Western genre" caught the drama of bronco
busting in *Rough Rider* and Frederick Remington sculpted bronze statu-
ettes of the cowboy. As the nude was more readily accepted at the end of
the century, the athletic body was featured in the works of John Dono-
ghue *(Young Sophocles)*, Gutzon Borglum *(The Flyer)*, Bessie Vonnoh
*(Allegresse)*, Janet Scudder *(Victory)*, and Alexander Calder *(Depew
Memorial Fountain)*. Although the nude invaded American art with the
decline of Victorian propriety and with the impact of French realism, it
seems reasonable to assume that the athletic movement was in part responsible for the changing concept of decency in art.[74]

Charles Dana Gibson, who had been an illustrator of amateur athletics in *Harper's Weekly,* acquired a towering reputation as creator of the
Gibson Girl, giving an impetus at the turn of the century to the portrayal
of the outdoor girl and of organized games, particularly in a note of irony
and of humor. Among the more interesting of his illustrations were "The
Champion," "Is A Caddy Always Necessary?" "Two Strikes and the Bases
Full," "The Coming Game," "A Little Incident," "Her First Appearance
in the Costume," and "The Art Museum of the Future," all of which
satirized the sporting diversions of the new century. Edward Penfield,
master of poster designs, illustrated the pleasures of seashore, horse show,
and steamship travel as well as racing, swimming, and coaching, and in
1899 he published a Golf Calendar. And a host of illustrators now employed camping, sailing, riding, golfing, swimming, and varied athletic
scenes for stories in as well as covers on the popular magazines.

From the age of the clipper ships to the yachts and sailing craft of
Herreshoff, Burgess, and their successors, draftsmanship and knowledge of
the sea were combined to produce ever more graceful and speedy models.
Craftsmen applied their artistry to guns, rods, canoes, golf clubs, and other
sporting equipment. Athletic, fishing, yacht, and country clubs challenged
more than a few architects of the era. McKim, Mead and White designed
the new Madison Square Garden in the 1880's and the Shinnecock Hills
Golf Club in the 1890's, by which time the functional demands of
YMCA's, college gymnasiums, sports arenas, and clubs attracted at least
passing attention from the architectural profession. With the introduction
of reinforced concrete the modern stadium made its appearance at Harvard in 1903, and these colosseums of the twentieth century proved to be
"a new and vital note in American architecture."[75] But the greatest degree

of originality was demonstrated in the twentieth-century country club. Talbot Hamlin pointed this out almost three decades ago:

> The American country club is purely a native institution, in which American architecture has found a peculiarly congenial opportunity. Long, low, rambling lines lend themselves readily to picturesque groupings; style becomes important, for it is character that counts—a character of intimacy, comfort, welcome, widespreading quiet informality. Whether Georgian or English or purely styleless and picturesque, the success of the best American country clubs is the charm that inevitably comes from the frank expression of these qualities.[76]

The humor and the pathos of outdoor life and games attracted a growing corps of cartoonists. Thomas (Tad) Dorgan, H.C. (Bud) Fisher, and Fontaine Fox were in the front ranks of a parade of cartoonists who helped build the comic page. John T. McCutcheon's cartoons of Chicago life portrayed the sports of college youth, the golf set, Derby Day, and the simple games of "A Boy in Springtime." Rube Goldberg in the New York *Mail* introduced the comic strip to the sports page.

It was on November 15, 1907 that the San Francisco *Chronicle* published the first issue of "A. Mutt," joined in 1909 by "Little Jeff," developed into the celebrated "Mutt and Jeff" strip which was syndicated by the Hearst press and became the first comic strip concerned with race-track affairs. Mutt and Jeff, inveterate racing addicts and tipsters, became the forebears of such later strips as "Barney Google," "Minute Movies," "Joe and Asbeztos," "Joe Palooka," and "Ozark Ike." A new audience of suburban commuters in the 1907-1910 period were seeking on the comic pages "a good chuckle about characters concerned with matters in their own world of club life, poker games, golf, fishing, and the hazards of marriage."[77] And the caricaturists carried on in the tradition of Joseph Keppler; free coinage of silver, the Spanish-American war, and reform were subjected to the incisive attacks of political cartoonists. Teddy the Rough Rider was the first of our athletic presidents, playing tennis, wrestling, sparring, riding horseback, and sailing. Interludes in his heavy appointment schedule might even find him "chopping down a few trees, swimming across Long Island Sound or taking ten-mile marathons. No President ever worked so hard turning out material for cartoonists."[78]

Acrobats had long been featured in circuses and variety shows, and during the eighties new acts featured outstanding athletes of the era. Lester and Allen's Minstrels presented William Muldoon and John L. Sullivan, and Muldoon organized his own Athletic and Specialty Company. In 1889 the Eden Musée in New York presented Sullivan and Kilrain in wax, Adam Forepaugh's circus starred a boxing elephant called "John L. Sullivan," and a popular song making the rounds was entitled "Let Me Shake the Hand that Shook the Hand of Sullivan."

During the last decade, when life was hardly as gay as tradition has pictured it, the entertainment world continued to capitalize on the popular appeal of the athlete in spite of depression, agrarian and industrial strife, and the war with Spain. Mike Kelly, James J. Corbett, Bob Fitzsimmons, Mike Donlin, and other heroes of the diamond and the ring paraded the boards from time to time. Sullivan appeared in *Honest Hands and Willing Hearts, A True American, The Man From Boston,* and *Uncle Tom's Cabin,* while the great black champion Peter Jackson played Uncle Tom in another version. Never an important factor in show business, athletic thespians continued to infest the world of vaudeville through the passing years.

Theatergoers were occasionally offered melodramas like *In Old Kentucky, The Sporting Duchess, Sporting Life, The County Fair,* and *A Base Hit,* while Weber and Fields developed a poolroom skit. In the new century sporting scenes were introduced in *David Harum, The College Widow, Strongheart, Brown of Harvard* (starring Hernry Woodruff), *Cashel Byron's Profession, The Vanderbilt Cup* (with Elsie Janice in her first Broadway role), *Wildfire* (featuring Lillian Russell), *A Gentleman of Leisure* (with Douglas Fairbanks), *The Amazons, The Girl and the Pennant, The Indestructible Wife,* and *Forever After.* Following the opening of the Hippodrome in 1905 thousands of sightseeing tourists and native fans viewed water ballets like *Neptune's Daughter,* the daring costumes of swimming star Annette Kellerman, and spectacles like *The Auto Race, Sporting Days,* and *The International Cup.*

Motion picture pioneers also introduced news reels and experimental films in rapid sequence. William K.L. Dickson produced *Corbett And Courtney Before The Kinetograph* in 1894. His *History of the Kinetograph* appeared the next year featuring scenes from most of the major sports. In 1897 Tilden and Rector photographed the Corbett-Fitzsimmons match for their Veriscope Company, accidentally catching a pickpocket in action and thereby leading to his arrest, the first legal use of the motion picture. George Sadoul, historian of cinema, called this the first film of considerable length projected in public which recorded an important event.[79] Thomas A. Edison made such shorts as *Hurdle Race* (1896), *Cock Fight* (1896), *The Ball Game* (1898), *America's Cup Races* (1899), *Bicycle Paced Race* (1901), and *Africander Winning the Suburban Handicap* (1903), while Edwin S. Porter's *America's Cup Race* was filmed in 1899. American Mutoscope, Vitagraph, Edison, and independent producers printed reels on trout and bass fishing, sculling, track and field, football, baseball, ice boating, yachting, skating, horse racing, motorboating, and ocean bathing between 1896 and 1914.

Essanay produced *The Baseball Fan* and began recording the annual World Series in 1908. *The Girl and the Halfback* appeared in 1911 and *Love and Vengeance* in 1914, while Mack Sennett featured Charlie Chaplin in *The Knockout* (1914) and *The Champion* (1915). By 1915 there were one-reelers like the "Athletic and Physical Culture Series" and "World's Greatest Athletes." Comedy with a sports theme was exploited in *Little Sunset, Rafferty Stops A Marathon Runner,* and *The Silent Co-Ed. Casey at the Bat* and *Sporting Blood* hit the silver screens in 1916. With the end of the war news reels and short specials were steadily supplemented by feature films.[80]

"Slide, Kelly, Slide" yielded to Ernest Thayer's ballad of "Casey at the Bat," rendered to clamoring audiences by De Wolf Hopper for a generation:

> Oh! somewhere in this favored land the sun is shining bright;
> The band is playing somewhere, and somewhere hearts are light.
> And somewhere men are laughing, and somewhere children shout;
> But there is no joy in Mudville—mighty Casey has Struck Out.

Harry Dacre's "Daisey Bell" ("A Bicycle Built for Two") won lasting popularity after 1892, and cycling songs did not go out of fashion until the new century. "Since Katie Rides a Wheel" (1893), "Sweetheart I Love None But You" (1895), "Angel Grace and the Crimson Rim Syracuse" (1895), "Ma Ca'line" (1897), "The Pretty Little Scorcher" (1898), "An Easy Mark" (1899) and "American Wheelmen's March" (1899) proved cycling's popularity in the nineties.

A vaudeville song in *The Wizard of Oz* satirized rough play on the gridiron:

> Just bring along the ambulance,
> And call the Red Cross nurse,
> Then ring the undertaker up,
> And make him bring a hearse;
> Have all the surgeons ready there,
> For they'll have work today,
> Oh, can't you see the football teams,
> Are lining up to play.

Blacks sang "Brother Noah Gave Out Checks For Rain" in 1907.

Albert Von Tilzer and Jack Norworth composed the most unforgettable of all baseball songs in 1908, "Take Me Out to the Ball Game:"

> Take me out to the ball game, take me out with the crowd,
> Buy me some peanuts and Cracker Jack,
> I don't care if I never get back.
> Let me root, root, root for the home team
>     if they don't win it's a shame,
> For it's one, two, three strikes,
>     you're out at the old ball game.

Barber shop quartets and the phonograph soon made this a national tune. George M. Cohan helped publicize "Take Your Girl to the Ball Game" in the same year, while the vaudeville team of Hite and Donlin featured "Stars of the National Game:"

> If I'm somewhat hank-y-panky
> O'er a game that's strict-ly Yan-kee,
> When I have explained my-self,
> You'll blame me not at all;
> We as barefoot kids have played it,
> And the fact should be pa-rad-ed,
> There is nothing in it with our own base-ball.
> I'm as dip-py and as daf-fy,
> As a daf-fo-dil in May,
> When the heroes of the Diamond
> Come up-on the field to play.
>
> Chorus:
>
> Then it's hats off to Old Mike Donlin . . .
> To Wagner, La-joie and Cobb . . .
> Don't forget Hal Chase and fox-y Mister Chance
> Who are always on the job, . . .
> Good old Cy Young we root for, . . .
> And fielder Jones the same, . . .
> And we hold first place in our Yan-kee hearts
>     for the Stars of the Na-tion-al Game.

"Let's Get the Umpire's Goat" and "I Can't Miss that Ball Game" followed during the baseball fever of 1909-1910. With the waning of vaudeville, however, sports tunes seem to have gone out of fashion except for a few of the old classics.

Metropolitan entertainment and recreation appealed to all classes, whether it be opera, legitimate stage, symphonic concert, and art exhibition, or vaudeville, nickelodeon, dime museum, and amusement park. While the legitimate theater, literature, art, and serious music remained virtually impervious to the appeal of sporting themes, there was impact in the lingo of the sports page as well as the comic strip, juvenile leterature, popular music, vaudeville, and the nickelodeon during the era from Lincoln to Wilson. Sport as an art in itself was ignored by both champions and foes. They failed to appreciate the perfection of performance, the physical skill, the instinctive expression, and the rhythmic grace of the athlete. The potentialities of sport in the arts were only slightly recognized despite the work of Homer, Eakins, Bellows, London, Lardner, and their associates.

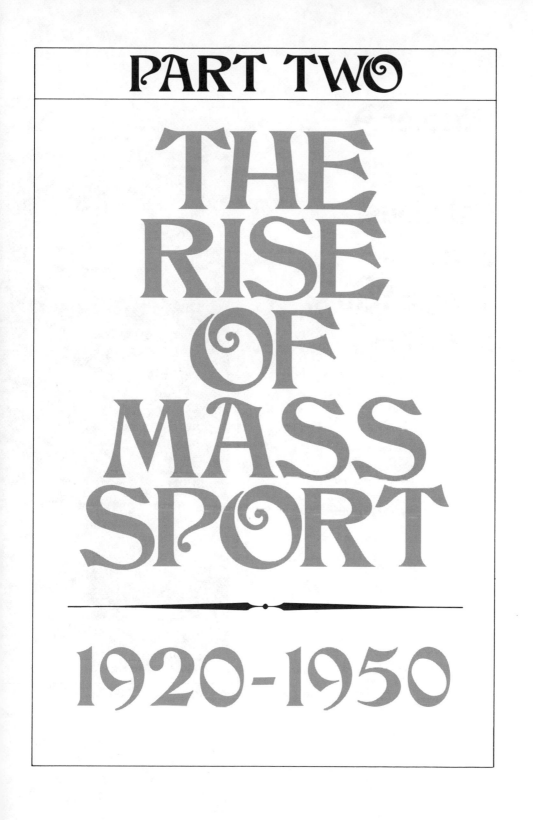

# PART TWO

# THE RISE OF MASS SPORT

## 1920–1950

# Chapter 9

# Fabulous and Tragic Years, 1920-1935

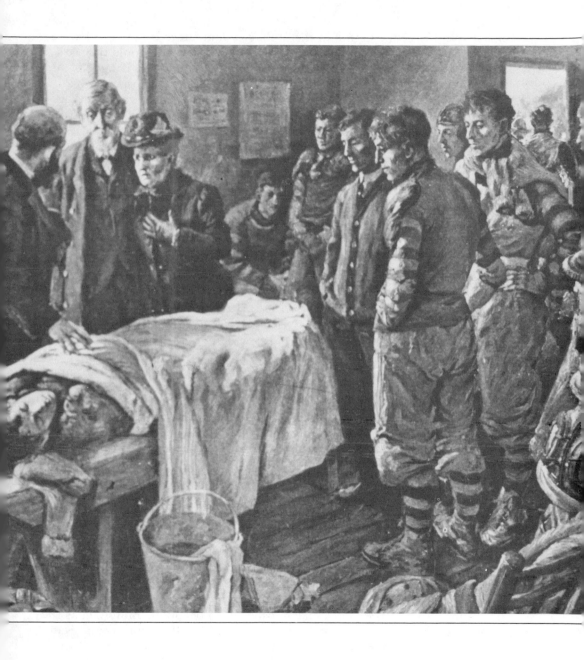

Sport swept over the nation in the 1920's and, at times, seemed to be the most engrossing of all contemporary interests. Although people from every walk of life pondered the issue of prohibition, discussed the League of Nations, and speculated on the endless spiral of business prosperity, millions spent much of their time tinkering with the family car, flocking to the movies, loafing at the club, fiddling with a balky radio receiver, or going to ball games. It was an era of intellectual ferment as the theories and ideas of Max Planck, Albert Einstein, Alfred North Whitehead, Havelock Ellis, Sigmund Freud, H.G. Wells, George Bernard Shaw, and Eugene O'Neill dominated the arts and sciences. For most of the public, however, the most popular figures of the day were Mary Pickford, Douglas Fairbanks, Lon Chaney, Tom Mix, Rudolph Valentino, Charlie Chaplin, and the Barrymores who attained a fame rivalled only by Enrico Caruso, Paul Whiteman, Harry Houdini, Will Rogers, or Charles Lindbergh. And there was also Babe Ruth, Knute Rockne, Red Grange, Bill Tilden, Bobby Jones, Helen Wills, and Jack Dempsey.

There were, of course, such giant national figures as Henry Ford, Thomas A. Edison, Herbert Hoover, and Alfred E. Smith; there were the Clarence Darrows, the Sinclair Lewises, the H.L. Menkens, and countless others; and there was the notorious Legs Diamond and Al Capone. But more than in any previous era entertainers, actors, musicians, aviators, and athletes were in the limelight. In a decade dedicated largely to escapism, adventure, and general levity, sport gained the publicity which made it one of America's foremost social institutions.

## Landis, Ruth, and the National Game

Immediately after the war a sporting fever broke out throughout the United States. So successful was the financial year of 1919 that wartime gloom over baseball's future dissipated overnight. Bleacher seats which formerly sold for 25¢ went into the discard as a new price range of 50¢, 75¢, and $1 tickets was instituted. The New York Yankees were soon called "the greatest drawing card in history" as they established attendance records in five of eight American League cities.

The diamond received a shot in the arm with the Supreme Court decision in 1922 which denied that baseball transactions were commerce. The minor leagues enjoyed similar prosperity under Judge Bramham as the American Association attracted more than 1,500,000 spectators and Kansas City alone lured more than 300,000 fans to its park. At the dedication of Yankee Stadium in the spring of 1923, Governor Alfred E. Smith threw out the first ball, and an all-time record crowd of 74,200 Yankee fans watched the Babe smash a home run to baptize the $2,500,000 "House That Ruth Built."

By 1930 the major leagues attracted more than 10,000,000 spectators, and observers of the national scene offered several explanations for
the baseball boom. Dyed-in-the-wool baseball fans pointed to the game's
traditional role as the national pastime.[1] The economist or social historian
might have stressed the wave of prosperity which prevailed through the
postwar decade. Sports writers generally lined up in two camps: those who
proclaimed the mighty popularity of Babe Ruth and those who lauded
the crusading spirit of Commissioner James Kenesaw Mountain Landis.

Commissioner Landis was drawn from the federal bench to the position of baseball czar in a desperate move by the magnates to restore public
confidence. The notorious "Black Sox" scandal of 1919-1920, wherein a
number of prominent members of the Chicago White Sox were banished
from baseball for life because of their reputed complicity in throwing the
Series of 1919, frightened promoters of the game. Hugh Fullerton scath-
ingly rebuked the club owners for pursuing a policy of secrecy and white-
washing "for the good of the game."[2] Drastic action was also needed at
the time to overcome Ban Johnson's autocratic control of the American
League. Judge Landis, who had once fined the Standard Oil Company a
record $21,500,000 and was noted for his vigor, integrity and courage,
appeared to be an ideal man for the job. With an excellent sense of
propriety Landis eulogized the game: "We might stand to have the business
smirched, and perhaps we men might look upon it cynically; but we must
keep baseball clean for the sake of the kids and not permit anything to
destroy their faith in its squareness and honesty. Baseball is something
more than a game to an American boy; it is his training field for life work.
Destroy his faith in its squareness and honesty and you have destroyed
something more; you have planted suspicion of all things in his heart."[3]
Much as this may have represented an emotional appeal of vested interests
for the confidence of the public in the integrity of baseball, it also expressed the commissioner's personal outlook on the game.

The Chicago jurist did much to restore and maintain public confidence in the diamond. Even John McGraw confessed that "the greatest
constructive baseball move of recent years" was the creation of a commissioner, and especially in the choice of Landis."[4] Others like President
John A. Heydler of the National League came to the assistance of the
reform movement. He helped reorganize the old National Commission.
But all the reformers played secondary roles to the fierce and ruthless
justice with which Landis cleaned up the game and the vigilance with
which he stood guard against corruption.

In 1920 a new star rose out of Boston into the baseball firmament.
George Herman (Babe) Ruth, sold to the Yankees for $125,000, entered
upon the most highly publicized career in the history of American sport.
Boisterous and unpredictable, he endeared himself to fans who revelled in

his lofty home runs and to boys who crowded around the exit gates at every park he visited. Colorful, humorous, boylike in his ways, Ruth proved his ability both at bat and in the field, and his name reached the most isolated homesteads in the land.

Heywood Broun, always a keen critic of the sports world, discovered the magical power of this new titan of the diamond: "The joy of watching Ruth lies in the fact that he is so palpably intent upon victory. There is never a moment when he is not trying. One feels that no crusader has ever been more firmly convinced of the righteousness of his cause. . . . Babe Ruth has been a considerable factor in breaking down party lines. Even in hostile towns the rooters like to see Ruth make home runs."[5]

The Sultan of Swat was not without rivals. Tris Speaker, Ty Cobb, Rogers Hornsby, Walter Johnson, and Grover Cleveland Alexander were rounding out memorable careers in the 1920's, and a host of new stars appeared, among them Paul Waner, Lou Gehrig, Frank Frisch, Tony Lazzeri, and Lefty Grove. But the "kingpin" of baseball was the Babe.

Fans in Dallas and other distant cities read in 1920 how Cleveland had gone "baseball mad," and first-page priority was alloted the World Series between the Cleveland and Brooklyn clubs. One reporter informed the nation, "Ohio had two contenders for the presidency of the United States and one contender for the baseball championship of the world. Ask anyone in the State today who's going to win and they'll answer 'Cleveland!' It would never occur to anyone to think that the questioner might be referring to Ohioan Cox or Ohioan Harding and the trifling matter of the country's presidency."[6]

In one of the most dramatic episodes of American sport the nation's capital took on the air of a madhouse in the autumn of 1924. President Coolidge addressed a tremendous throng who greeted the Washington Senators when they won the league crown, and baseball electrified the atmosphere in Washington during the next ten days. In late September the pennant fever had eliminated the presidental race and the League of Nations controversy from public attention. When the beloved veteran Walter Johnson dramatically strode to the mound in the ninth inning of the last game of the Series and then pitched the Senators to victory in the fourteenth, Washington let the lid blow off: "Thousands are tramping the streets in the wildest celebration ever seen in baseball. From the White House to the Capitol the clamor rises. The streets are full of jostling, joy-crazed citizens, blowing horns, manipulating rattlers, firing pistols and making a din that can be heard for miles. On the banks of the Potomac there is bedlam and madness tonight."[7] Although foreign legations would soon realize that this was not violent revolution but mere baseball hysteria, the thrilling grip of baseball on the public was amply demonstrated. Every

autumn baseball fever would spread like wildfire until the World Series
was history.

Despite the popularity of the professional game, social forces were
at work undermining public preoccupation with the diamond sport.
Mighty as the figure of Babe Ruth loomed in sporting lore, popular as the
World Series were, the baseball boom was a deceptive one. Sandlot ball
was widely played in the early 1920's, but in 1925 the National Amateur
Athletic Federation estimated that participation among boys fell off 50%
between 1923 and 1924. Delegates to the National Baseball Federation's
convention in 1926 agreed that the game exhibited signs of dying in small
communities and was in jeopardy in the younger organized clubs of the
cities. College baseball suffered heavily, and the rabid interest of high
schools in interscholastic football did not encourage the diamond game.
As sports of all kinds won new converts, baseball discovered more powerful rivals than ever before.

Alarm over baseball as the sport of the average boy was best expressed
by Byron "Ban" Johnson, founder of the American League. Embittered as
he may have been at his defeat in the struggle against Landis, Johnson
spoke earnestly in warning:

> At a time when every large city boasts a great stadium, vaster
> than any Roman amphitheater, it may seem absurd to declare that
> baseball is deteriorating rather than progressing, but this is my firm
> opinion. The strength of the game does not lie in costly parks and
> huge investments, but in the heart of the American boy, and this
> once-solid foundation is steadily weakening. It used to be that base-
> ball was the one outlet for athletic aspirations, and every youngster's
> dream was to be a major leaguer, but today we have football, golf,
> basketball and tennis, each one making its direct appeal to the grow-
> ing boy. Baseball is doing nothing to meet the competition, and the
> corner-lot game has been permitted to dwindle away to a vanishing
> point. . . . Unless remedial action is taken vigorously and quickly,
> nothing is more likely than that baseball will drop down to a third or
> even fourth rate American sport.[8]

The American boy was not in immediate danger of losing his baseball
heritage, however. Publicity from the press, the newsreel, and the radio
reminded him constantly of the close race in the major leagues, while baseball lore continued to grow with the passing years. A constant quest for
respectability surmounted the "Black Sox" scandal of 1919, and high
salaries in the Big Leagues attracted the eye of every aspiring player in
high school, college, or semipro ball. Baseball was, however, in a precarious

state in the early 1930's and there was urgent need to encourage the sand-lot game. This was accentuated by the onset of the Depression and the crisis in the major and minor leagues.

By 1932 one minor league after another was folding up and the framework of the professional baseball world was giving signs of complete decay. The Eastern League quit because of insufficient funds, the Three-I, Cotton States, and Interstate circuits folded, and other leagues from coast to coast faced the same demise.

In the midst of the crisis Commissioner Landis maintained there was nothing wrong with baseball but the Depression itself. Players' salaries were everywhere reduced. Jimmy Foxx of the Philadelphia Athletics, at the height of his career and popularity after winning the batting crown, was compelled to accept a salary cut because of financial losses of the club. Even the baseball commissioner's contract was reduced in 1933 and 1934 from $65,000 to $50,000, while the aging Babe Ruth's salary dropped from $80,000 in 1931 to $35,000 in 1934. The Pacific Coast League voted a return to 25¢ and 40¢ minimum admission fees of an optional nature. Sincerely alarmed at the distress of the diamond, President Heydler of the National League issued a statement to the players urging them to do all within their power to improve the game: "This personal appeal is made to you on the eve of the start of a season which probably will put to the acid test the popularity of our national game and directly affect your livelihood as a player. Never before have we faced more stringent money conditions or keener competition from other sports, motoring, and amusements." In an appeal obviously directed toward the public as well as the player, he quoted a recent statement of President Roosevelt: "Major league baseball had done as much as any one thing in this country to keep up the spirit of the people."[9]

## King Football

Football rode the crest of a vigorous educational crusade in the twenties as hundreds of thousands of American youth entered colleges across the land. With the falling of leaves on gray autumn days footballs were tossed about by boys in every community. From sandlot to stadium, from grammar school to university, youngsters played the game with unequaled enthusiasm. The avidity with which high schools supported teams, expanded their athletic plants, constructed stadiums, and arranged extensive schedules with neighboring or distant communities was amazing. But it was the collegiate world which formed the spearhead in forcing national attention on the gridiron, for it aroused violent attacks against and loyal defense of the autumn sport. Discussions of "football hysteria" and "King

Football" flared into disputes over countless phases of the game. Scholarship, safety, overemphasis, professionalism, advertising, and all the evils of commercialism were flung into the cauldron of heated controversy, and the same issues soon assumed large proportions on the scholastic scene.

Intersectional sport set off on the right foot in 1920 when Dartmouth traveled to Seattle to play the University of Washington before the largest throng in the football annals of the Northwest. Michigan and Ohio State forewarned the Midwest of this postwar hysteria when in 1922 they inaugurated the new stadium at Columbus before an assemblage of 75,000 cheering fans. Arch Ward of the Chicago *Tribune* recalled, "When the 1920 season unfolded, giant stadia were rearing their steel and concrete contours high into the sky in the prairie cities and towns which were seats of the great universities."[10] The Western Conference found its total receipts exceeded $2,000,000 from the games of 1923 which lured more than 1,000,000 men and women through the turnstiles; the Army-Navy game rose to the status of a national classic, the Rose Bowl emerged as a great annual athletic carnival; the Stanford-California rivalry achieved national prominence; and the South was definitely established as a power in gridiron circles.

During the early 1920's the popularity and prestige of Notre Dame's teams, coached by a dynamic Norwegian named Knute Rockne, became prodigious. Men and boys everywhere heard of the exploits of the Four Horsemen and the Seven Mules from South Bend. But the greatest publicity ever showered on any player in the history of the game came to the "Galloping Ghost" from the University of Illinois, Harold ("Red") Grange. Nationally recognized as the finest back in years, Grange flashed his number "77" on the gridirons of the Midwest, and once skeptical eastern writers were soon spreading his name to the remotest corners of the land after his remarkable exhibition at Franklin Field.

Intercollegiate football attained such flamboyant publicity and wide popularity that it was enveloped in the social milieu. College youths were frequently portrayed as law-breaking carriers of racoon-coat pocket flasks; gambling on college games was charged as a major scandal; the recruiting and publicizing of gridiron stars attracted the vigilant attention of university authorities; and the spectacle of thousands of rooters gathered in mammoth coloseums led many analysts of contemporary life to warn of the decadence of Rome in a similar epoch. Universities and smaller colleges alike were accused of seeking nationwide publicity through their powerful football squads, and all the old evils of commercialism, professionalism, and distraction from the true purpose of a university were hashed over in the press as football's role in collegiate life became the core of an educational controversy.[11]

For the first time in American sporting history the fame of college football players rivalled that of heroes of the professional diamond. When Walter Camp died in 1925 his traditional selection of All-American teams passed into the able hands of Grantland Rice. As the old method of selection by individual writers became obsolete, newspaper chains announced All American teams which for the first time showed how football power was shifting westward to Michigan, Illinois, Northwestern, Chicago, Notre Dame, Southern California, Stanford, and the University of California. Amos Alonzo Stagg, Glenn S. (Pop) Warner, Andrew (Andy) Kerr, Gilmour (Gil) Dobie, Howard Jones, Robert C. (Bob) Zuppke, Fielding (Hurry Up) Yost, Dr. John B. (Jock) Sutherland, William (Bill) Roper, and Knute Rockne were coaches whose names were known to millions of Americans.

Considerable fame came to a group of southern experts including Ray Morrison, Dana X. Bible, Dan McGuigan, Madison (Matty) Bell and Wallace Wade. Fritz Crisler and Bernie Bierman stood out as the most successful coaches of the early depression years as Princeton, Minnesota, Alabama, and Stanford, challenged the supremacy of Notre Dame, Michigan, Pittsburgh, and Southern California.

The most abbreviated list of gridiron heroes must mention Ernie Nevers of Stanford, Chris Cagle of the Army, Benny Friedman and Benny Oosterbaan of Michigan, Herb Joesting and Bronko Nagurski of Minnesota, Wesley Fesler of Ohio State, George Cripp and Frank Carideo of Notre Dame, Ken Strong of New York University, Paul Scull of Pennsylvania, Barry Wood and Ben Tichnor of Harvard, and Wally Koppisch of Columbia.

Notable in the early twenties, before major universities collected most of the outstanding stars by scouring the backwoods for every good prospect, were those representatives of smaller colleges whose brilliance compelled football authorities to give them due recognition. Among them were William (Fats) Henry of Washington and Jefferson, J.R. Weaver, J.B. Roberts and A.N. (Bo) McMillin of Centre, Frank Schwab and Charles Berry of Lafayette, and Homer Hazel of Rutgers. Despite the gloom of the Depression a procession of stars including Jerry Dalrymple of Tulane, Bill Corbus of Stanford, Harry Newman of Michigan, Don Hutson of Alabama, Cotton Warburton of California, Gaynell Tinsley of Louisiana State, Pug Lund of Minnesota, and Jay Berwanger of Chicago added to the lustre of gridiron history.

Every college treasures memories of the legendary exploits of its gridiron heroes of the Golden Age. No previous generation had idolized so many heroes of the football field, and only the game of baseball produced as many players of great reputation. Other sports had a Bill Tilden, a Walter Hagen, a Bobby Jones, a Jack Dempsey, a Gene Tunney, an Earl

Sande, a Johnny Weismuller, a Gertrude Ederle, a Charles Paddock, a Tommy Hitchcock, or a Helen Wills, but football fans in every community could talk of the deeds of local gridiron stars. And the most famous of all was the immigrant boy who lived to make the name of Knute Rockne one of the most beloved in the America of the twentieth century.

Although thousands of schools had played football since the turn of the century, interscholastic and intramural football made startling progress in this decade. In such areas as eastern Ohio, the Lehigh Valley and the hard coal towns of Pennsylvania, the city of Chicago, along with the high schools of every larger city, the interscholastic game won a host of fanatical supporters. In general, southern communities lagged behind other sections up to the Depression as facilities remained primitive, crowds small, and most southern interest centered on the intercollegiate game. State championships and state athletic bodies were organized throughout the nation, and educational requirements gradually drove out the informal method of coaching by the town "sport" or some local athlete. During the years of boom and depression the game most highly publicized in the newspapers of all but the largest communities was interscholastic football. Many collegiate customs and traditions were initiated, and high schools surpassed the universities in the enthusiasm with which they organized pep rallies, athletic clubs, cheerleading, and victory celebrations. Buttons, pennants, streamers, gay outfits, and feathered hats were standard paraphernalia for important games on a sunny Saturday afternoon, and a "what the hell do we care," "rip 'em up, tear 'em up, rip 'em up right" spirit infected local sportsmen. Despite metropolitan newspaper publicity on collegiate and professional sport, local interscholastic games were the foremost sporting interest of the average town or small city. And in Chicago a city championship of the early thirties amazed the authorities by drawing more than 120,000 fans.[12]

Sandlot football developed into an institution of its own, and touch football proved a popular variation admirably suited to smaller lots. Compared to the open spaces of small towns, metropolitan areas were ill-equipped for playing fields larger than the playground, but games of touch football on hard-surfaced streets or school playgrounds entertained the neighborhood.

When the Carnegie Report of 1929 and the economic collapse of that year synchronized to stir up a wave of criticism of intercollegiate sport, the college athletic world entered upon a period of crisis. Presumptuous analysts lauded the student's greater interest in academic life, welcomed the decline of intercollegiate spectacles, and prepared obituary notices for "big time" collegiate sport. A noticeable rise in intramural games, increasing popular interest in professional football, and the caprice of a fickle public were offered as explanations for the hard years which fell on college football. Others realized that declining gate receipts at gridiron spectacles meant a curtailment of all college athletics.

As early as 1930 the state universities of Iowa and Nebraska began to deemphasize the athletic program, and many minor sports were eliminated throughout the South and Southwest when gate receipts dropped from 5 percent to 25 percent in those areas. A Carnegie report for 1931 maintained that the fall of gridiron receipts was widespread. Athletic funds were cut in half at the University of Oklahoma and at Oklahoma A&M, Governor William H. (Alfalfa Bill) Murray threatened to veto any appropriations of the state legislature which were not radically reduced.

Many institutions were not affected immediately and football often prospered even in those areas most deeply discouraged over financial losses. Colleges began to cut their admission fees in 1930 and 1931 to counteract the decline of crowds. A 1931 survey of the Associated Press revealed that "four out of every five institutions have been forced either to economize sharply on athletic expenses or curtail activities," but it also admitted, "Depressed business conditions have not hit all of the major colleges by any means, notably in such sections as the Pacific Northwest, Rocky Mountain and Southwest areas where football 'booms' were enjoyed last fall." [13] Noted gridiron powers like Yale, Notre Dame, and Southern California still took in more than $1,000,000 annually, but the overall situation was bleak as receipts of the Big Ten fell below $2,000,000 for the first time in years. Appeals for attendance were made by auctioning off footballs and by publicizing the needs of charitable organizations.

During the Hoover-Roosevelt campaign of 1932 conditions became even more stringent. Such tradition-ladened institutions as Yale and the University of Pennsylvania joined the toboggan in lowering ticket prices. The University of Illinois was forced to withdraw financial support from varsity teams in swimming, tennis, gymnastics, water polo, and golf when football receipts fell to the lowest level since the exciting era of Red Grange and the opening of Memorial Stadium in 1923. Dartmouth and Cornell, as well as many other schools, were forced to retrench. General reduction of gate receipts was recognized at the NCAA convention of 1932. At a time when Franklin D. Roosevelt was struggling to introduce his New Deal program, the annual Poughkeepsie Regatta was cancelled. Syracuse, the Catholic University of America, UCLA and other colleges curtailed or suspended spring programs.

## Golf and Tennis Attract National Attention

In the 1920's Americans of all classes and ages read sports-page accounts of the fabulous feats of Walter Hagen, Gene Sarazen, Bobby Jones, and

Glenna Collett. They witnessed the construction of links and country clubs, found golfing articles in the most respectable magazines, and learned new lingo such as "on the green," "down the fairway," "off the tee," "in the trap," and, of course, the perennial call of "Fore!" Others laid out private tennis courts, promoted public and school tournaments, and rallied to the game of tennis as one of the great sports of the decade. Whereas golf and tennis, originally games for the social aristocracy, had made considerable headway prior to the World War, the postwar generation was to raise them to games of national prominence.

In 1922 there were 533 active or allied clubs of the United States Golf Association, but in 1930 the number of member clubs had grown to 1195,[14] while public and daily fee courses appeared everywhere. Just what the cause for this tremendous expansion of golfing interest was is difficult to discern. Certainly the prosperity of the great middle class during the economic boom was a major factor. The United States Golf Association's annual report for the year 1923 estimated that more than 3000 golf and country clubs had expended over $88,000,000 on land, equipment and other items, and that over $200,000,000 was expended by their members. National interest in all sports and in outdoor life was also contributory. Spectacular performances by brilliant golfers like Hagen and Jones added to the public enthusiasm. A more enthusiastic press, thousands of local promoters, and the concern of municipal governments for better recreational facilities were all vital to its popularity. Golf architects such as Arthur W. Tillinghast, W.C. Fownes, Seth Raynor, and Maurice McCarthy created some of the world's most beautiful courses, and these were rapidly imitated.

When Jock Hutchinson of Chicago became the first American to win the British Open in 1921 the old feeling of inferiority began to wane. Another golfer of great brilliance who won the National Open in the following year was a young Italian boy named Gene Sarazen. National tourneys and the Walker Cup matches stirred widespread interest. Golf acquired followers in the clubs organized in such colleges as Georgia Tech, California, Drake, Stanford, and those of the Big Ten. Eastern teams soon felt the competition of midwestern and western institutions, but as late as 1933 either Harvard, Yale, or Princeton had won all but one of the intercollegiate championships since 1897. The intercollegiate individual championship was shared after World War I by students from colleges all over the United States as Yale and Princeton found capable and successful challengers in Columbia, Dartmouth, Tulane, Georgia Tech, Georgetown, and the universities of Oklahoma, Michigan, and Texas. Although never a prominent scholastic sport because of the expense involved, golf slowly won adherents in many high schools as thousands of boys took to caddying.

Golf was commonly associated with those of the social clique who were popularly called "the country club set." The sport failed to attain the stature of a national pastime but it did attract a multitude of players to public courses where the fee was nominal. It also aroused the interests of millions who had never owned a club or sliced a drive but who had heard of Tommy Armour, Gene Sarazen, Jim Barnes, Johnny Farrell, George Von Elm, Walter Hagen, Chick Evans, Francis Ouimet, Leo Diegel, or Bobby Jones. With the onset of the Depression public links sprouted up like mushrooms. New York's metropolitan area maintained seventeen municipal golf courses while Chicago had ten in addition to some fifty daily fee courses in its environs. Los Angeles and San Francisco followed in close order, the courses of each city constantly crowded with hordes of golfing addicts who played throughout the year in the favorable California climate. The first municipal links championships were held at Toledo in 1922, and President Harding presented a cup for inter-city competitions which began in the following year.[15]

One country club after another lavished funds on the construction of new links which might attract the wealthier members of the community as well as the famous players of the day. Nearly $5,000,000 was invested in 1922 in the Westchester-Biltmore Country Club at Rye, New York. The Olympic Fields Club of Chicago turned down a New York syndicate's offer of $2,500,000 for its four-course layout which was claimed to be the largest private links in the world. Clubs, often organized for social purposes, featured dancing, dining, card playing and drinking. Many members belonged for the purpose of meeting the proper people, selling insurance, and doing business, while young socialite girls often lounged about the club in hopes of catching an eligible bachelor.

Much as common talk of the community might satirize "the country club set," golf won the affections of millions of sportsmen. That it was a game for gentlemen was evidenced on every hand. Golfing ethics demanded silence on every tee and green, required trust in one's partner keeping proper score, and made courtesy on the fairways an ironclad law. Damon Runyon, acquainted with the ethics of the prize ring and the race track, recognized the sterling nature of the game: "Show us a golf-playing town and the writer will show you a town in which refinement is above the average."[16]

Women had always been a major factor in golf's rise to prominence in sport, and among the great names in feminine golf were such pioneers as Mrs. Dorothy Campbell Hurd and Mrs. Caleb Fox. Alexa Stirling gradually relinquished her dominant position to Glenna Collett, probably the most outstanding woman golfer the United States had produced. Greatest of women golfers was Miss Joyce Wethered of England, and English women were still respected as being generally superior to their American rivals, but at long last the gap was narrowing. Maureen Orcutt and Edith Cummings came to the fore in the late twenties, and the early thirties found Helen Hicks and Virginia Van Wie at the top. Enjoying the rustic atmosphere of woodland and rolling fairways as well as the male companionship, feeling less physical limitations in a game requiring rhythm, touch and skill, using special tees to shorten the course, and taking great pleasure in the social atmosphere of a club—women did much to bring golf into prominence.

Walter Hagen's career went far toward the establishment of the professional game on a permanent basis. Although he was theatrical and petulant on the links, "Sir Walter" ruled as an almost unchallenged monarch in professional circles. But, this was the "Golden Age" of sport, little gold fell into the pockets of the "pros," for purses were small. They found lucrative jobs, however, at the leading clubs, the Pasadena, Florida club paying Hagen a reputed $30,000. Winner of eleven major national and international titles, Hagen's confidence was legendary, his style was colorful, and his skill was acclaimed by all who followed the game. On many occasions he appeared late on the scene, and once, after accepting an invitation to play with Warren G. Harding, he kept the President waiting at the first tee!

While Hagen ruled the professional links, no player attained the popularity and reputation of Robert Tyre Jones. Winner of a long string of championships in the British Open, the British Amateur, the United States Open, and the United States Amateur tourneys, the young star from Atlanta rose as a titan of the links. Graceful in his swing, phenomenally accurate with his putter, modest and poised, Bobby Jones was respected as a gentleman, admired as a sportsman, and envied as a competitor. His fame lured thousands to the big matches, and huge galleries followed him over the course. The crowds which composed these golfing galleries provided a living for the professionals by reason of the admission fees. Bobby Jones maintained the best standards of amateurism as his fame carried over the radio and through the press into the family circle. Every incipient golfer wondered how "The Emperor Jones" would chip out of the trap or approach the green.

When Jones won all four major amateur and open championships in 1930, the sporting world stood agog. America's ace golfing analyst and sports columnist, Grantland Rice, prophesied with amazing foresight that Bobby Jones "had piled up a record this generation will never see equalled." New York welcomed him back from England in the midst of this historic campaign with a tremendous ticker-tape ovation. Later he was given the greatest reception in the history of Atlanta, and young black caddies proudly sang, "Mr. Bob brought home de bacon." In September he completed his famous Grand Slam at Ardmore, and "the Georgian came to the pinnacle of all golfing fame on the green far down the valley where the trail ended."[17] Even today veterans everywhere refer nostalgically to "The Era of Bobby Jones."

Luxurious golf and country clubs, like urban athletic clubs, were hit a disastrous blow after the collapse of Wall Street. Membership fell rapidly and dues or fees dropped by more than half between 1929 and 1933. There were 1134 clubs affiliated with the United States Golf Association in 1930, but only 763 in 1936. A survey by Herb Graffis for *Golf* and *Golfdom* claimed 5727 courses in operation at the time. Between 1929 and the middle thirties sale of golf balls, "woods," and "irons" dropped to less than half. While private clubs were gripped with hard times, or went into bankruptcy from the overcapitalization of the 1920's, the number of municipal golf courses increased from 300 to 700 during the depression decade.[18] By 1935 the country club atmosphere of the twenties was little more than a nostalgic memory.

After World War I tennis discarded much of its aristocratic trappings, and rapidly emerged as a popular sport. Among the factors in this heightened interest were the popularity of the game in the colleges, the Davis Cup matches, an array of colorful players, the country club, and the more general construction of school and public courts. The New York *Times* of September 3, 1921, ventured to state, "Waterloo may or may not have been won on the Eton playing fields, but far greater victories, victories for which diplomacy is striving, of international understanding, cooperation and friendliness, are and will be won in friendly contests like those at Forest Hills." French, English, and Australian players competing at Forest Hills or the Germantown Cricket Club brought greater international significance to the game. By 1923 there were about 2000 tennis courts in 75 leading cities of the United States as well as an incalculable number in smaller towns, at vacation resorts, and at private schools and colleges in rural areas. Chicago, Los Angeles, St. Louis, Philadelphia, and Washington were already outstanding centers of municipal tennis.[19]

Industries experimented with the game, while private courts were built adjoining the homes of countless families of upper or middle-income groups. National attention was directed to the courts even more by the spectacular stars of the twenties: William (Little Bill) Johnson, Vincent Richards, R. Norris Williams, Henri Cochet, Suzanne Lenglen, Réné Lacoste, Helen Wills, and William (Big Bill) Tilden, all of whom brought color to the game by their brilliant play.

The newspaper and the radio played up Davis Cup and national championship matches, and it was said when Helen Wills lost to Suzanne

Lenglen that it was "a game which made continents stand still, and was the most important event of modern times exclusively in the hands of the fair sex." [20] When "Queen Helen" finally reached the heights of her game at the end of the decade, her supremacy was unchallenged, even with the arrival of Helen Jacobs on the tennis scene. A similar mastery over the field was displayed by William T. Tilden, whose spectacular escapes from defeat, theatrical exhibitionism, and overwhelming strokes captured the imagination of tennis fans from coast to coast. John Kieran has portrayed his great role in tennis:

> England, Australia, the Continent, the United States—with raquet in hand, Big Bill was monarch of all he surveyed. No one could stand before him.
>
> Big Bill was more than a monarch. He was a great artist and a great actor. He combed his dark hair with an air. He strode the court like a confident conqueror. He rebuked crowds at tournaments and sent critical officials scurrying to cover. He carved up his opponents as a royal chef would carve meat to the king's taste. He had a fine flair for the dramatic; and, with his vast height and reach and boundless zest and energy over a span of years, he was the most striking and commanding figure the game of tennis ever had put in court. [21]

## The Passing Scene

Millions of Americans flocked to rivers and lakes to enjoy the relaxing and exhilarating sport of swimming. The annual visit to the shore gained in popularity, while the YMCA and the Boy Scouts continued to stress water sports in the pool or at summer camps. Competitive aquatics were stimulated through national championships, the Olympic Games, and attempts to conquer the English Channel. Johnny Weismuller and Gertrude Ederle reigned as idols of swimming enthusiasts. Rifle matches remained popular, a new American Trapshooting Association was formed, and colleges competed annually in the National Intercollegiate Rifle Match. More money was collected through hunting licenses and fines than ever before as the great outdoors beckoned to increasing hordes of sportsmen.

Rowing retained its popularity at the traditional schools. Navy's victory in the 1920 Olympic Games, Yale's in 1924, and California's in 1928 were featured events of the era, while the Harvard-Yale classic was losing out to the more general interest in the Poughkeepsie Regatta. The heyday of American polo was reached during the twenties as Argentine, Irish, and English teams made visits to these shores. The United States Army won the world's military championship, and Meadow Brook matches attracted the Prince of Wales, Lord and Lady Mountbatten, and the top members of society. The United States Polo Association organized nine circuits, and intercity tournaments were held in 1925, but the inordinate expense, the distraction of other sports, and the coming of the Depression seemed to prove that it was still the private preserve of the social aristocracy.

With the introduction of basketball to junior high schools and the more rapid consolidation of rural schools, this game caught on with a new intensity. A national invitation interscholastic basketball tournament was held in 1923 at the University of Chicago and Indiana became the hotbed of the court game. In "Middletown" it was found: "Hundreds of people unable to secure tickets stand in the street cheering a score board, classes are virtually suspended in the high school, and the children who are unable to go to the state capital to see the game meet in a chapel service of cheers and songs and sometimes prayers for victory."[22]

The *Outlook and Independent* showed that in 1929 basketball's triumph was spectacular: "In many schools, especially in the Middle West, it has driven baseball out of existence. Publicity followed promptly. A further aid in the Middle West was the building of play halls in towns and small cities."[23] Some interest was aroused by professional teams such as the New York Celtics, on which Nat Holman, Joe Lapchick, and other famous stars played, but its promotion by school authorities was infinitely more important on the national scene. In Utah the Mutual Improvement Association organized 800 teams throughout the state, and gymnasiums were found in towns of 1500 people. When teams met for the national interscholastic championship in 1927 many clubs from the East and Midwest had to share the spotlight as Idaho, Oregon, Texas, New Mexico, Colorado and South Dakota sent representatives from the West while the South sent teams from Georgia, Florida, South Carolina, Mississippi, Kentucky, Virginia and Arkansas. The East and Midwest naturally had their usual numerous representatives. By 1930 the University of Kansas contests attracted 46,300 spectators, and the game was more popular than ever in neighboring colleges. Slower in attaining major-sport recognition in the schools of the East and the South, basketball was nonetheless becoming one of our greatest participant and spectator sports by the early thirties.

Winter sports were introduced on a wider scale at the Olympic festival of 1924, and the traditional American interest in skating, sledding, skiing, and hockey was maintained. Hockey developed as rapidly in the 1920's as any other winter sport through the adjustment of the game to children's conditions on ponds or flooded lots. Skates alone were needed in the way of equipment; a curved branch and a mashed tin can might easily serve as hockey stick and puck. In 1920 an Intercollegiate Hockey League was formed. Although the old Western Hockey League of Frank and Lester

Patrick disbanded, professional hockey in the mid-twenties gained a following in large metropolitan centers with the entry of the Boston Bruins, New York Americans, New York Rangers, Chicago Black Hawks, and Detroit Red Wings into the National Hockey League to battle for the Stanley Cup. Ice skating, building on the missionary work of Irving Brokaw in the previous decade, had its heroines in the spectacular Maribel Vinson and the graceful young Norwegian, Sonja Henie.

Since the informal kicking of footballs about the campus in pre-Civil War years there has always been some intramural sport. The accent on intercollegiate and interscholastic games in the late nineteenth and early twentieth centuries left a gap in student life which was not adequately met until the 1920's. Mass interest in sport at the time of World War I stimulated a boom in intramural activities, although it was "not until about 1925 . . . that intramurals began to infiltrate the high school programs; and it was not until 1930 that the movement in high schools was well under way."[24]

The college was somewhat quicker to promote organized intramural programs. In 1921 the University of Michigan required outdoor athletics for everyone on the basis of a claim that the war had demonstrated that American men were physically deficient. President David Kinely of the University of Illinois, where 7500 men and women engaged in sports, recommended athletic credit toward degrees. At the same time more than 10,000 students were reported participating in eighteen sports at Ohio State. In the mid-twenties Williams, Princeton, Wisconsin, and other colleges had a vast majority of students in intramural sport at one period of the year or another. The 1926 report of Dean Edmund H. Day of Michigan instituted an even more general program with the building of a stadium, intramural building, women's athletic hall, and women's playing field.[25] Many colleges had nine out of ten students participating in some branch of intramural sport in 1930.

By the first years of the Depression even the educational centers of the great metropolis maintained extensive programs, most of which were hit less by hard times than were varsity programs. In 1938 a survey of men's colleges showed that in colleges of more than 1000 students those in intramurals averaged 65 percent while 50 percent of the undergraduates in smaller institutions took part, and faculty control proved to be the predominant system.[26] Within two decades the colleges had induced more boys and girls than ever before to join their classmates in touch football, softball, archery, basketball, field hockey, badminton, tennis, swimming, and other activities in the general sports program.

Grammar schools of both town and city sponsored volleyball teams organized into community-wide leagues, and both the public and parochial schools maintained athletic leagues. A health-conscious postwar generation rallied to the support of physical education and backed the intramural movement. Whereas only an estimated 5.7 percent of high school students of the United States were enrolled in such courses in 1922, within six years there were 15 percent, and by 1934 participation in intramurals had rocketed upward as 50.7 percent of high school students were taking physical education courses. Surveys of the twenties showed that athletics were almost always the first choice of junior and senior high school students.[27]

## Commercialization of the Turf, the Ring, and Motorized Sport

Postwar American sportsmen gave rapt attention to the racing world, which resulted largely through the appearance, within a short period of time, of several truly great thoroughbreds, the most prominent of which were Exterminator, Man O'War, and Zev, popular victor in the 1923 Kentucky Derby. Many experts have judged Exterminator (popularly called "Old Bones") the greatest thoroughbred in racing history. This horse won fifty of one hundred starts in all conditions of weather and at all distances. But the public's imagination was caught by Man O'War, whose record-breaking performances found millions cheering "Big Red" home. Although campaigned only as a two- and three-year-old in 1919 and 1920, Man O'War won all but one of his races, his sole defeat coming from a poor ride. After three decades Man O'War is still the one thoroughbred symbolizing the wonder horse of the turf, and he was chosen by Associated Press writers as the greatest horse of the half century.

Other horses were to sustain that popular interest, among them Black Gold, Crusader, Gallant Fox, and Twenty Grand. Earle Sande, the most renowned jockey of the era, rode Gallant Fox to one of the most spectacular campaigns in racing history in the year 1930. But the horses themselves were only partly responsible for widespread interest in the track. A national sporting fever, postwar prosperity, and an increase in value of stakes won by such leading stables as those of Harry Payne Whitney and John R. Madden, along with the cooperation of press and radio, all contributed to the popularity of the turf. Track fans also found sympathetic supporters in numerous state legislatures as Illinois legalized racing in 1927, Florida in 1931, and California, Michigan, New Hampshire, New Mexico, North Carolina, Ohio, Oregon, Texas, Washington, and West Virginia soon thereafter.

The Florida land boom and the opening of Hialeah added much to the racing scene. Between 1920 and 1930 the total number of racing days in the United States rose from 1022 to 1653 and the number of races held from 6897 to 11,477. In 1920 only 4032 horses campaigned annually compared to 8791 ten years later, and, while American horsemen had won stakes and purse money totalling $7,773,407 in 1920, they were collecting $13,674,160 in 1930. When Man O'War captured the Belmont Stakes in 1920 he won less than $8000, but Gallant Fox collected $66,040 for the same race a decade later.

The desperate economic situation of the early 1930's gave a frightening scare to the turf, and by 1933 stakes and purses had dropped to $8,516,325. It was 1937 before earnings passed the level of 1930, although from 1934 to 1939 they rose steadily from $10,443,495 to $15,911,167. Despite this increase the average earnings remained stationary in the depression decade as some 13,257 horses ran in 16,041 races in 1940 compared to only 8791 horses in 11,477 races in 1930.[28] Something of the threat to the turf in the early years of the Depression can be seen in the decline of earnings in the three classic races:[29]

| Belmont Stakes: | 1930 | Gallant Fox | $66,040 |
| | 1935 | Omaha | $35,480 |
| Kentucky Derby: | 1930 | Gallant Fox | $50,725 |
| | 1935 | Omaha | $39,525 |
| Preakness Stakes: | 1930 | Gallant Fox | $51,925 |
| | 1935 | Omaha | $25,325 |

In 1930 there were 371 stakes worth $3,082,489, averaging $8,308.59, but by 1933 there were only 286 stakes worth $1,355,819, averaging $4,740.62, while yearling sales declined in average value from $1,966 in 1930 to $569 in 1932. Hard times had come to the turf in full force in the early thirties.

Under a broiling sun at Toledo in 1919 Jack Dempsey beat Jess Willard decisively and won the heavyweight championship of the world. From that day the "Manassa Mauler" became the central figure of the prize ring. Under the guiding hand of promoter George (Tex) Rickard, boxing emerged as one of the three or four most important commercialized sports in America. The Dempsey-Willard "gate" of $452,000 in 1919 was eclipsed by that of $1,600,000 in the Dempsey-Carpentier fight of 1921. The New York *Times* devoted a total space of about 47 columns in the issue reporting the struggle at Boyle's Acres, and Harding's signing of the peace treaty with Germany was squeezed into one column on the first page. More than 75,000 fans congregated in Jersey City despite public criticism against holding the fight:

Cavil as the seriously minded may, rage as do reformers of contemporary morals, the few minutes of boxing in Jersey City today— all may be over before a spectator has time to sneeze—stand preeminent in the interest of millions from the Hudson round the globe to the Seine. Affairs of state are forgotten, the great in other walks and spheres vanish into the wings, even the destiny of a nation loses attention, the absorbing question is, who wins? The answer will be shouted through a million telephones, flashed across the sea by cable, transmitted from ship to ship by wireless. Singapore and Manila will want to know it as well as London and Paris, the camp in the wilds as well as the metropolitan club. Mr. Harding, David Lloyd George and Aristide Briand will doubtless be interested, also judges, professors and bishops—and even reformers. The answer must be left to the principals, Mr. Dempsey and Mr. Carpentier. The sooth- sayers of sport are not to be depended upon, not even George Bernard Shaw. All are biased or the prey of prejudice.[30]

The building of the new Madison Square Garden and a succession of great fighers did much to popularize the ring. Tex Rickard, John Ringling, and the Sports Alliance were charged by the National Boxing Association with a monopoly of boxing in New York, but Rickard had been greatly re- sponsible for bringing boxing out of the dirty, smoke-filled arena into the sports palace. When Luis Firpo of the Argentine knocked Dempsey from the ring in 1923 and then was soundly beaten by the ferocious champion, distinguished figures from all walks of life were at ringside: Elihu Root, W. E. Vanderbilt, Foxhall Keene, and Florenz Ziegfeld, to mention only a few. Franklin D. Roosevelt, Mrs. Theodore Roosevelt, Mrs. Nicholas Longworth, and Don Juan Riano, ambassador from Spain, had attended the Dempsey-Carpentier fight two years earlier, and critics and reformers could no longer claim that only rowdies attended the prize ring.

National attention centered on the Philadelphia contest in 1926 between Dempsey and Gene Tunney. Held as a feature of the Sesqui- Centennial celebration in the Quaker City, more than $2 million was spent in admission fees and members of the Chamber of Commerce estimated that between $3 million and $5 million were dropped into the laps of Philadelphia businessmen.

College boxing won new fans, the American Legion sponsored bouts, and finally the Golden Gloves tourney was established by the New York *Daily News* in 1927 and the Chicago *Tribune* in 1928. Charity gave its approval to fights for such causes as the Catholic Big Sisters, The Italian Hospital Fund, and Mrs. William Randolph Hearst's Milk Fund. Radio broadcasts of all major bouts excited a large segment of the public, and newsreels entertained the movie audience.

Jack Dempsey attained a popularity comparable to that of John L. Sullivan, but there were other outstanding fighters in this great era of the prize ring. Paul Berlenbach, Tommy Loughran, Harry Greb, Mickey Walker, Jack Sharkey, Joe Dundee, Tony Canzoneri, and Benny Leonard comprised a group of colorful fighters unsurpassed in pugilistic history. One of the significant trends in boxing was the decline of Irish dominance of the ring with the rise of Italian and Jewish boys. In the depths of the Depression Dempsey, Tunney, and Rickard had passed from the scene, however, and the prize ring had begun to fall once again into the shadows in popular interest as Jack Sharkey, Max Schmeling, Primo Carnera, Max Baer, and Jimmy Braddock proved to be fly-by-night champions.

Motorized racing seemed to hold its appeal, at least outwardly. In 1920 Gaston Chevrolet was killed in a tragic accident which reminded the public of the risks in racing, but the eighth annual national road race was won by Ralph De Palma before 60,000 spectators.[31] Indianapolis Speedway lured ever larger throngs each year until 160,000 fans watched Ray Keech win the title and $40,000 in 1929. Motorboat competitions were publicized through the victories of Gar Wood's *Miss America* boats in the Harmsworth Trophy races. The Gold Cup and President's Cup races at Detroit and Washington, D.C. drew more publicity to motorboat racing.

Air meets had tended to center on the annual agricultural fair until World War I, and when the public began to show interest after the war meets were held at fairs and exhibitions. By 1920 racing was featured in aviation circles. At a convention in Atlantic City opened by Woodrow Wilson's radio message in 1920 it was planned that twenty "great international and national aerial contests, which will start a new epoch in aerial sport and stimulate progress in aeronautic art" would be discussed. At that time a Los Angeles Aeroplane Rally, an Alaska Air Derby for seaplanes, and an International Aerial Derby Across the United States were being planned, while the Aerial League of America was encouraging college men to fly by the establishment of intercollegiate trophies.

James Doolittle popularized air races in the twenties and thirties as did Al Williams, Frank Hawks, Roscoe Turner, Alexander Seversky, and Howard Hughes. From Ruth Law and Phoebe Fairgrave to Amelia Earhart and Jacqueline Cochran, the aviatrix engaged in racing and a Woman's Air Derby was organized. Newspapers, private corporations, and the military sponsored air meets, altitude and endurance tests, and speed races, and the meets helped advertise new models.[32]

Schneider Cup, Pulitzer Trophy, and Marine Trophy races drew the eyes of the public to the air. Balloon and air races; endurance experiments such as Lindbergh's crossing of the Atlantic and the Navy's flight around the world; altitude contests—all added to public interest in aviation. The building of the aircraft carriers *Lexington* and *Saratoga,* military and naval experiments, General William Mitchell's campaign for air power, dirigible flights of the *Shenandoah, Los Angeles,* and *Graf Zeppelin,* and the increased importance of airmail service and commercial aviation also contributed to public interest in the air world in the twenties and early thirties.

Automobile racing maintained something of its grip on the public, but the novel and sensational aspects began to wear thin and popular interest began to wane as racing became increasingly commercialized. The public was infinitely more concerned with new annual automobile models than with spectacular speed records of the racing dromes. Few industries in America experienced as rapid a development as that of automobile manufacturing, and the new car became the obsession of the masses rather than the classes. In 1900 annual production of passenger cars was just above 4000, and in 1910 it reached 181,000, but in the next two decades the industry mushroomed into national importance, with annual production figures approaching 2,000,000 in 1920 and surpassing 4,500,000 in 1929. The earlier influence of racing on the sale of cars rapidly disappeared.

Much had been learned from air racing. The great St. Louis Air Meet, the National Air Races, and augmented military sponsorship of racing had focused the public eye on air power. In 1931 the British "declared that racing types consumed more money than could be spared from amounts available for the regular needs of aviation," but both the United States and Great Britain "had learned more than they openly admitted, for the British winner in 1931 was the prototype of the famous Spitfires of 1941, and the Curtiss racer had a profound effect upon all later United States naval and military designs."[33]

Major automobile producers were less interested in special high-power models than in such selling points as sleek lines, mileage per gallon, wearing quality, and comfort. Model-T Fords, utilitarian in design, were a far cry from the speedsters of the racing track. The public might be occasionally stirred by the air records of Jimmy Doolittle, the motorboat races of Gar Wood, or the Daytona Beach speed tests of Major H.O.D. Seagrave, Ray Keech, and Captain (later Sir) Malcolm Campbell, but racing in the machine age lost much of its color and popularity.

The twenties were years of rapid commercialization of sport. Professionalism won new converts among followers of the diamond, the ring, and the turf, as well as in the commercialized world of hockey, bicycle racing, golf, bowling, and professional football. The entry of Red Grange into the National Football League in 1925 gave that organization, which originated in 1920, a lift that carried it through years of adversity until the lush days of the Depression. All sorts of contests were held, including dog sled races in Utah. Commercialization and the popularity of professional sport gave publicity to sports which were heretofore relatively unknown. Amateur ideals may have suffered, it is true, but the generation of the twenties and early thirties had become much more intimately aware of the role of competitive athletics in our national life.

## Radio and a National Audience

Radio came of age in the hectic 1920's, and sport was soon seized upon as an entertainment feature. Although the sports craze of those years was given its greatest encouragement by the metropolitan and local press, broadcasting for the first time brought the drama of ringside, diamond, gridiron, and racetrack into homes from coast to coast. Western Electric and Manufacturing Company's establishment of Station KDKA (Pittsburgh) in 1920 placed radio on a commercialized basis, and thousands of amateur enthusiasts from all areas of the country soon encouraged the formation of organized broadcasting systems.

Music and news broadcasts were the standard programs in the early years of radio, but sports events were rapidly absorbed into the entertainment schedule. On April 11, 1921 Johnny Ray and Johnny Dundee fought in the Smoky City's Motor Square Garden. KDKA then made the first broadcast of a boxing event and then proceeded to broadcast the Davis Cup matches of that year. David Sarnoff of the Radio Corporation of America and Major Andrew White, editor of *Wireless Age,* brought the Jersey City match of Dempsey and Carpentier to thousands of listeners in "halls, theaters, sporting clubs, Elks, Masonic and K of C clubhouses, and other meeting places." [34] This was achieved only through the use of an American Telephone and Telegraph wire to station WJY in Hoboken and through the cooperation of the National Amateur Wireless Association. In October WJZ (Newark) went on the air with bulletins of the World Series, and naval vessels in New York harbor picked up the news.

General Electric, Westinghouse, and American Telephone and Telegraph entered this virginal communication field in 1922, when the radio public of some 60,000 receiving sets was large enough for stations to resort to planned programs and advertising. Sports programs were featured regularly in the autumn, Grantland Rice announcing a play-by-play account of the Yankee-Giants World Series over WJZ. With the aid of Western Union and the New York *Tribune,* Charles Popenoe used the Series to publicize his station. [35] College football games were put on the air in October and November; WJZ covered the contests played at the Polo Grounds; and a special broadcast of the Chicago-Princeton game at Stagg Field was announced over WEAF by loudspeakers in Park Row. [36]

As the radio fever caught on throughout the country, the sports reporting of Graham McNamee, Bill McGeehan, and other announcers was featured by WEAF, WJZ, and WBAY (New York); WJAR (Providence);

WBZ (Springfield, Mass.); WEAC (Boston); WGY (Schenectady); WJAX (Cleveland); WIP (Philadelphia); WWJ (Detroit); WGN (Chicago); WEAO (Columbus); and, of course, KDKA (Pittsburgh).

When the Washington Senators met the New York Giants in the national capital for the World Series of 1924, Western Union sent out a record 2,200,000 words, while the details were relayed from the wires of the American Telephone and Telegraph Company to more than 100,000 scattered sets. News of the game was relayed by WEAF to other stations, and reached at least a half million radios from coast to coast. By the fall of 1924 college football games were broadcast weekly, and, as a tremendous expansion of the radio industry took place in the next three years, sport came to play a larger role in the broadcasting schedule. By 1927 there were 6,500,000 receiving sets, a Federal Radio Commission was established, and the National Broadcasting Company had to meet the challenge of the Columbia Broadcasting System.

On the rainy night of September 22, 1927, Jack Dempsey fought Gene Tunney in Chicago for the heavyweight championship. Graham McNamee and Phillips Carlin described the long count and Tunney's valiant recovery while millions listened on an NBC hook-up of more than sixty stations. The morning headline of the New York *Times* read "Millions Listen On Radio." So great was the pre-fight enthusiasm that one department store sold $90,000 worth of radio equipment in two weeks, "most of which was attributed to the big fight" that proved to be "a great stimulus to the radio business."[37]

With the ring capitalizing on the airwaves just as the diamond, the gridiron, and the turf had done, sport owed much of its rapidly expanding support to the phenomenal popularity of radio, which by 1928 had passed the 10,000,000 sets mark. In 1927 NBC commenced its annual World Series broadcasts; Clem McCarthy and Ted Husing came along to announce the great horse races; while Graham McNamee's name became a household word among those who followed Knute Rockne's Notre Dame, Jock Sutherland's Pittsburgh, or Glenn Warner's Stanford. The arrival of Charlie Gelbert, Terry Moore, Frankie Frisch, Dizzy Dean and that "Wild Horse of the Osage," Pepper Martin on the St. Louis scene made the Gashouse Gang the most colorful club in baseball, while the great Yankee, Athletics, and Detroit clubs of the early thirties won a vastly wider audience as millions listened in to hear the exploits of Lefty Grove, Carl Hubbell, Lou Gehrig, Charlie Gehringer, and other stars of the day. In the depths of the Great Depression for the first time a nation could listen to on-the-spot reporting of the great sporting events of the day.

# Chapter 10

# Recovery, War, and Peace

# Chapter 10

# Recovery,
War,
and Peace

A photograph

Bobby putts in the course of th[e]

THE "JONE[S]

THE CALM BEFORE THE SHOT

tch with Perkins. English champion, at Brae Burn, while a big gallery holds its breath.

# COMPLEX" ON THE GOLF LINKS

Americans could hardly believe the headlines when the stock market crashed on October 29, 1929. A decade of overspeculation, watered stocks, mounting personal debts, foreign investment, and high tariffs now reaped the whirlwind, and the nation's morale slowly weakened. Out of confusion and panic a plethora of panaceas appeared. The Townsend Plan, Huey Long's "Share Our Wealth" campaigns, Father Coughlin's radio forays, and the diatribes of the *Daily Worker* added a touch of pathos, anger, and disillusionment to the dreary thoughts of millions. The Hoover Administration tackled the Depression by instituting the Reconstruction Finance Corporation and other forms of government aid, but by late 1932 banking had reached a new crisis. Franklin Delano Roosevelt's election demonstrated a desperate resolve on the part of the American people to meet national paralysis with new leadership.

New Dealers created a host of alphabetical agencies to solve problems of unemployment, relief, farm credit, banking, and other critical issues. The Works Progress Administration transformed the physical face of the nation and the morale of the jobless worker. The WPA stimulated recreation through thousands of parks, swimming pools, dance pavilions, picnic grounds, athletic fields, and playgrounds. National parks recorded in one year more than 16,000,000 tourists bent on fishing, hunting, camping, or sight-seeing. Adventurers everywhere took to the open road, and in New England hostels cropped up for cyclists.

Young men in Civilian Conservation Corps camps constructed ski runs, picnic areas, camping grounds, and boating facilities for park tourists. Special ski trains carried "tens of thousands out of Boston, New York, Pittsburgh, Chicago, Salt Lake City, Portland, San Francisco and Los Angeles."[1] State parks also lured millions of fishermen, hunters and casual automobilists. Municipalities entered into the spirit of recreational promotion. Jones Beach, created by Robert Moses and Mayor La Guardia, was but one of many metropolitan projects. Thousands of small communities, largely supported by federal aid, built public parks with swimming pools, athletic fields, stadiums, and other recreational facilities, and government assistance to recreation reached a level unmatched in any era of American history.

In the "angry decade" of the strike-ridden thirties labor organizations swelled their ranks and the CIO soon rivalled the AFL in membership. The American people were aware that a new epoch in economic life had opened and that free private enterprise had many adjustments to make, and they did not abandon their democratic heritage. As freedom and the value of the common man took on new meaning, this consistent loyalty of the people was in great part preserved by their sense of humor and love of play.

## The Road Back

Much of professional baseball's recovery from the depths of the Depression lay in the gradual improvement of economic conditions, but the baseball world itself was in great part responsible. Branch Rickey's development of the St. Louis Cardinals' farm system was imitated by other clubs, even under the disapproving eyes of Judge Landis. Men like Tom Yawkey in Boston and Walter Briggs in Detroit poured money into their clubs and farm systems, Yawkey reputedly spending $3,500,000 on the Red Sox. The rise of the St. Louis Cardinals, Detroit Tigers, and Boston Red Sox as leading baseball powers went far to prove the value of capital resources and of extensive training systems.

Night baseball proved to be another pillar firmly supporting the tottering structure of the diamond. Experimentation with the night game occurred as early as 1880, but none of the succeeding trials, including that of the old Federal League, proved successful. The first promising nighttime ventures took place in Des Moines and Wichita in 1930. The Texas and Pacific Coast leagues quickly followed the lead, and members of the American Association and the Eastern, Piedmont, Southern, International, and Western leagues installed arc lights despite skepticism of what was then considered a novelty. "Social historians may record 1930 as the year of the emergence of night baseball," reported *The Outlook* in 1930: "Starring in the starlight is now common from coast to coast, confined by no means to bush-league clubs." No boost to the game of baseball comparable to the innovation of night contests had taken place in years. Although major league owners were reluctant to follow the minors or the "bush-leagues," vigilant and businesslike men such as Branch Rickey, Larry McPhail, and William V. Wrigley became enthusiastic over the potentialities of after-dark play.

Not until 1935, however, was the night game introduced in Cincinnati for the first time in the majors. As an antidote to the Depression, the innovation saved many clubs. Little Rock's *Arkansas Gazette* reported, "As a result of night baseball, better baseball and a general improvement in conditions in the South [in 1936] the Southern Association, 'old faithful' of the minors, will return this season to the 'million a season attendance' for the first time since 1931." [2] President William Harridge of the American League still favored limitations of night baseball to seven games in 1940, and only in the forties did it gain universal acceptance, but its role was a vital one in hastening the recovery of professional teams throughout the land. Twilight ball also was a factor in the popularity of industrial and semipro teams. Daylight saving time and the shorter working day occasioned by slack production schedules aided in the popularizing of twilight games.

Babe Ruth's fading brilliance left baseball without its most popular hero, but Jimmy Foxx, Al Simmons, Mickey Cochrane, Lou Gehrig, Bill Dickey, Bill Terry, Lefty Gomez, Charlie Ruffing, Charlie Gehringer, Joe Cronin, Babby Hartnett, Carl Hubbell, Chuck Klein, Hank Greenberg, Pepper Martin, and countless other stars kept interest alive. New York's Yankees remained the terror of professional baseball as they won the World Series six times in the thirties. Jerome (Dizzy) Dean, eccentric but matchless pitcher of the Cardinals, became the diamond's most colorful player. A new generation of youngsters often dreamed of pitching for the Cardinals along with "Me and Paul" and the "Gas House Gang" instead of smashing out home runs for the Yankees. Before the decade was over a young outfielder from San Francisco was the talk of the American League, but Joe Di Maggio had to share the limelight with "Rapid Robert" Feller of the Cleveland Indians.

Among the many factors contributing to the restoration of baseball as paramount in American sport were the support of teams by industries, by the American Legion, and by the newly-founded National Baseball Congress of semiprofessional teams. Some 3,000,000 youngsters with their eyes on a Big League contract competed in the early years of the American Legion Junior Baseball tourneys. In 1931 Ray Dumont conceived the idea of a congress of semipro teams, a tourney was held at Wichita in 1935, and the organization continued to grow through the years with the aid of the major leagues. By 1950, in the "First Official Interhemisphere Playoff," the Fort Wayne Capeharts won over the Osaka All-Kanebos at Tokyo in a series attended by 317,000 Japanese fans.

Resurgence of diamond interest was also evident in the spectacular rise of softball. Mushball, indoor ball, playground ball, softball, and whatever other disguises the game may have taken in the passing years were never abandoned in the gymnasium or on the playground. It was in the late twenties, however, when Ban Johnson and other critics bewailed the decline of baseball as our national pastime, that softball began to win widespread support. Tournaments were encouraged in Chicago after 1930 by Leo H. Fischer of the Chicago *American* and by H.H. Pauley. Its virtues were espoused by the National Recreation Association, and the idea of a nationwide tournament was sold to the Century of Progress Exposition of 1933. An Amateur Softball Association, with George Sisler as president, was formed in 1934, and within a year an estimated 2,000,000 Americans were playing on more than 60,000 organized teams. By that time there were about a thousand lighted parks for night softball, mostly in the Midwest. One "wildcat professional" named Matt Rupert earned $50,000 in one season! The game rapidly won favor in the automobile factories of Detroit, and it soon became a favorite in the schools and colleges. Enthusiasm was nationwide: Little Rock sponsored its first annual tourney in 1935, Salt Lake City had two parks reserved on a rotation schedule of four games per night, and Utah held its first state championship in 1936.[3]

Softball, more adaptable to both sexes and to all ages, less expensive to maintain and lacking little of the dash and drama of baseball, rapidly attained the position of one of America's favorite recreations. By 1940 there were some 300,000 organized clubs and the Amateur Softball Association claimed at least 3,000,000 affiliated players. Veterans of Foreign Wars posts promoted junior softball, and a "Cripple A League" of oldsters who played a simplified version reputedly had 2500 teams in Chicago. A new support of the diamond world had been found, and at the end of the Depression interest in baseball seemed as keen as ever.

The road back from the Depression was ever more in evidence in the years 1933-1935. Only a few months after Roosevelt's election the collegiate athletic scene showed signs of improving health. Long a weak link in intercollegiate athletics, the South was not yet represented among the first twenty colleges in attendance, but the famous football teams fielded by Alabama and Tulane and the fantastic fervor with which Huey Long supported Louisiana State University were signs of better times for sport in Dixie.[4] From 1933 to 1935 the Far West experienced a football "boom," while even the great drought failed to halt the upward swing of attendance at Big Six games. Also, the recession of 1937-1938 had little effect. High school football developed in many areas into a fall pageant of gay crowds, extensive schedules, and high pressure publicity. Few observers seemed aware that the gridiron sport was losing out in one area, that of the small college which could no longer compete with the larger private and state universities. "When we are frank about it, we have to admit that at the present time most small colleges—maybe a few fortunate ones don't have to—but most are taking money to finance their athletic programs from the general funds of the college." [5]

No era in gridiron annals produced more brilliant names, from Ben Ticknor, Barry Wood, Gerry Dalrymple, Frank Carideo, Wesley Fesler, Harry Newman, Jack Buckler, Bill Corbus, Don Hutson, Bobby Grayson, Pug Lund, Bobby Wilson, and Jay Berwanger to Clint Frank, Larry Kelley, Sammy Baugh, Davey O'Brien, Whizzer White, Gaynell Tinsley, Marshall Goldberg, Nile Kennick, Sid Luckman, and Tom Harmon. Although the East still was represented by occasional strong clubs at Columbia, Princeton, Fordham, and Pittsburgh, most of the powerful teams were found in other sections. Alabama, Tulane, Tennessee, Texas Christian, Michigan, and Southern California rose up to challenge the supremacy of Notre Dame and the new national champions from Minnesota, who scaled the heights under the tutelage of Bernie Beirman. And the pageantry of the college game was utilized by public officials, chambers of commerce, and local businessmen to popularize the Orange Bowl (1933), Sugar Bowl (1936), Sun Bowl (1936), and Cotton Bowl (1937) as rivals of the traditional Rose Bowl (1920).

Collegiate sports of every variety prospered in the years of the New Deal. Ed Krause, Al Bonniwell, John Wooden, and other stars won national fame on the basketball court, though none rivalled Stanford's brilliant Hank Luisetti. Ned Irish introduced doubleheader contests at Madison Square Garden in 1935 and inaugurated the National Invitation Championship three years later. James Naismith, originator of the game who had lived to see it develop into a national sport, paid this tribute: "I think that Ned Irish has done a wonderful thing for the game. He has made it national instead of sectional."[6] The NCAA then established its annual tourney in 1939, Madison Square Garden became the mecca of basketball, and teams composed of former settlement house, "Y", and boys' club players helped spread the athletic fame of St. John's University, Long Island University, and New York University.

By 1936 there were reputed to be more than 50,000 organized teams and 80,000,000 spectators at contests conducted by every conceivable agency. Industries and commercial houses, playground and recreation directors, sports writers, and school authorities paid heed to the winter-long appeal of the court game. At the end of the decade all except six states conducted championship tourneys and about 95 percent of American high schools maintained teams.[7]

Sports lovers will not soon forget the exploits of such cinder path stars as Bill Carr, Ben Eastman, Bill Bonthron, Gene Venzke, Archie Sam Romani, Don Lash and tireless Glenn Cunningham, whose mile and 1500-meter duels with Bonthron and Britain's unforgettable Jack Lovelock made track history. Among the sprinters Frank Wykoff, Eddie Tolan, Ralph Metcalfe, and the immortal Jesse Owens were outstanding. The onslaught on track and field records continued, but even the Olympic Games could not conceal the decline of interest in track athletics in the United States.

Although the early thirties witnessed a drop in athletic funds, by 1935, most collegiate associations were carrying on normal functions. Colleges discovered that handball, fencing, badminton, lacrosse, and soccer had a special appeal to many students. Michigan and Yale dominated inter-collegiate swimming circles, while Ohio State produced a string of champion divers. Boxing and wrestling tourneys were held for the national championship under AAU auspices. Wisconsin, Penn State, Virginia, and Louisiana State sponsored boxing on a large scale, while wrestling was emphasized at Lehigh, Oklahoma A&M, and scores of other institutions.

Baseball never regained its former popularity as a campus sport, but golf, tennis, and rowing survived the critical years. Harvard, Navy, Wisconsin, and Cornell sponsored strong crews, although leadership had already passed to the Pacific Coast as the universities of California and Washington set the pace. The names of Hiram Connibear, Al Ulbrickson, and Russell (Rusty) Callow were destined to take an honored place in the annals of rowing.

Eastern students occasionally played at racquets, rugby, and squash, but in most colleges interest centered in the traditional sports. High schools generally supported the four major sports, although tennis, swimming, wrestling, and even golf won many recruits. Sport in school and college was more alive than ever at the end of the Depression.

As the Depression had deepened unemployment mounted, millions of families found it impossible to spend freely on commercialized amusements, and juvenile delinquency (illustrated by the Dead End Kids) developed into an ever greater national problem. Consequently social life in the schools took on more significance. Dancing, drama, clubs, and the school band shared with athletics in meeting student needs of the time. This was especially true among the children of the underprivileged, and while Jewish and Protestant groups strove to meet the needs of their youngsters in the YMHA, YMCA, and church and school programs, the plight of Catholic boys and girls was resolved in great part through the spectacular development of the Catholic Youth Organization.

Bishop Bernard Sheil, who had pitched a no-hit game for St. Viator's College in a 1906 contest against a Western Conference champion Illinois team and who had received offers from the major leagues, approached his superior, George Cardinal Mundelein: "Your Eminence, I want to run the biggest boxing tournament this city has ever seen." As Arch Ward of the Chicago *Tribune* has remarked, "That was the first time that the Cardinal had been approached with a proposal that souls could be saved by a punch in the nose."[8] The CYO, founded in 1930, promoted boxing and basketball tourneys. Catholic Scouting and CYO Vacation Centers were introduced, and programs soon blossomed into every area of the social life of the young. Through the passing years this organization, on a diocesan basis, has attracted millions of youngsters throughout the nation. Although a parochial institution of predominantly Catholic membership, it has been operated on a nondenominational, interracial basis. Each year in Chicago the CYO and B'nai B'rith champions meet on the basketball court. With coaches like Tony Zale in boxing and Bernie Masterson in football, with a host of Catholic sportswriters in the religious and secular press, with the aid of the Knights of Columbus, and with a nationwide recognition of the moral and physical values developed in the CYO, this great movement and its founder have been honored by the commendations of dignitaries in every area of American life. If some feared parochial education and training as a divisive factor on the contemporary scene, few have doubted the achievements and the value of the Catholic Youth Organization.

In 1931 the Boston and Maine Railroad sent out its first ski trains, in 1932 the Winter Olympics at Lake Placid drew the attention of many winter sportsmen, and by 1935 the trek to northern ski trails had become an annual winter custom. Railroads, sports clothes designers, and fashionable stores all encouraged the enjoyment of winter sport. According to Frederick Lewis Allen, "department stores were importing Norwegian specialists and building ski-slides; the Grand Central Station in New York was posting prominently in its concourse the daily temperature and snow data for a dozen skiing centers in New England and New York, and rural hotelkeepers in icy latitudes were advertising their unequalled skiing facilities and praying nightly throughout the winter for the snowfall upon which their fortunes depended."[9]

Aided by the work of the WPA in state and national parks, ski sales totalled $3 million in 1938, and about $6 million was spent on ski clothing.[10] Symbolic of the new enthusiasm was the founding of Sun Valley through the efforts of W. Averell Harriman and the Union Pacific Railroad. An International Ski Meet and Winter Sports Show held in 1936 in New York was attended by 80,000 interested visitors. Vermont and Michigan became great winter playgrounds and popularized community snow carnivals. In 1930 there were about 75 ski clubs with some 3500 members, but by 1940 there were thought to be 2,000,000 skiers in the United States.

Horse owners found little solace in these years of distress, but public interest was sustained and the decade had its share of colorful thoroughbreds. Equipoise, Twenty Grand, Cavalcade, Omaha, Bold Venture, War Admiral, and Sea Biscuit headed a long list of great horses. Alfred Gwynne Vanderbilt became a leading figure in turf circles, and Hirsch Jacobs gained fame as a trainer. The rebuilding of Hialeah in 1931, opening of Santa Anita in 1935, and technical advances of the era (the totalisator, automatic gates, electric timers, photo finish, saliva and urine tests, and better methods of horse identification) were also of prime importance.[11] Pictorial magazines acquainted many with the track, and a flood of turf journals encouraged betting on the races. At the end of the decade parimutuel betting was legal in more than twenty states as legislatures responded to the gambling fever. Azucar won the inaugural Santa Anita Handicap in 1935, earning a record sum of $108,400. When William du Pont, Jr.'s Rosemont captured the 1937 Handicap, 50,000 spectators attended and wagered over $1,500,000. Sportsminded Californians, enthusiasts from the movie colony, and energetic promoters with extravagant purses contributed to the rise of the western turf. Symptomatic of this national trend was the interest aroused in 1938 when Sea Biscuit defeated War Admiral in the most celebrated match race of modern times. As the nation emerged from the Depression the turf rapidly regained its former appeal.

The Hambletonian, which had originated at Goshen, developed into the annual classic for trotters. Hanover Shoe Farm's noted line of harness racers was led by the majestic Greyhound, who set world records at one, one and one-half, and two miles and won 32 of 36 starts between 1934 and 1940. But hard times had so affected earnings that in 1933 the top pacers won less than $5000, and in 1935 when Greyhound won all of eight starts he earned a mere $26,712. Billy Direct broke Dan Patch's mile record and became the first pacer ever to run the mile in 1:55. Both trotters and pacers depended on the Grand Circuit and annual county or state fairs before World War II, but harness racing was no longer the center of popular interest that it had been in the days of Lady Suffolk, Flora Temple, Dexter, Goldsmith Maid, Maud S, Nancy Hanks, Lou Dillon, and Dan Patch. Only with night racing and pari-mutuel betting was racing to revive in the post-World War II decade.

The withering hand of the Depression struck for a time in bowling circles. Between 1925 and 1930 organized teams registered with the American Bowling Congress had risen from 12,000 to 43,000, but only 41,000 teams were still registered in 1935. With the gradual national recovery of the next five years, bowling won thousands of new adherents, and in 1940 there were 132,000 member teams. Old masters like Joe Falcaro and Andy Varipapa competed with a mounting army of keglers, including such experts as Joe Norris, Ned Day, and Hank Marino. Women increasingly appeared at the alleys in the thirties, and throwing strikes and spares became one of the favorite diversions of industrial workers. Luxurious, well-lighted, neatly-kept alleys were built to appeal to a wider public as bowling came out of the basement. By 1939 some 4600 bowling alleys reported receipts of $48,819,000, about twice the amount for all professional baseball clubs and more than the total for auto, dog, and horse tracks in the United States.

Chicago, Detroit, Milwaukee, and Cleveland waxed enthusiastic over the game. Pekin, Illinois in 1937 had 120 men's and 50 women's teams in a population of 16,000.[12] Competitive bowling made no fetish of amateurism as $170,000 in prizes were distributed at the ABC tourney at Cleveland in 1939. There were reputed to be 70,000 alleys and 12,000,000 occasional or regular bowlers in the United States, Canada, and Hawaii.

By 1940 bowling had truly become a sport for the masses, being available night and day, rain or shine, and remaining relatively inexpensive compared to golf, skiing, fishing, or hunting. The National Duck Pin

Bowling Congress, organized in 1927, made rapid headway, and by 1938 there were about 200,000 league bowlers and a grand total of 600,000 duck pin addicts in the United States. Duck pins appealed to women because of the lightness of the balls and the skill involved. Small towns and rural communities were attracted to the game by the minor investment required.

In the midst of the Depression New York remained the center of billiard parlors and bowling alleys in the East. Among the great masters of the cue were Welker Cockran, Charles Peterson, Willie Mosconi, Ralph Greenleaf, and inimitable Willie Hoppe, most durable of all sports champions. Games were played at college fraternities, social clubs, and YMCA's, while the popularity of billiard parlors and pool rooms is evident in the receipts of $38,631,000 in 1939. Participants in other contests of skill formed the National Horseshoe Pitchers of the United States, the National Archery Association, and the National Shuffleboard Association. St. Petersburg, Florida, mecca of retired couples, became the center from which shuffleboard was carried by tourists to the rest of the nation. Shuffleboard provided a popular diversion in hospitals, on shipboard, in playgrounds, at recreation centers, in parks and at the seashore. Interest in firearms was sustained by the National Rifle Association and the American Trapshooting Association's annual Grand American Handicap at Vandalia, Illinois.

Gene Tunney's retirement in 1928, the Wall Street crash, the ensuing financial distress, and a scarcity of great heavyweights led to a decline of popular interest in the prize ring. Max Schmeling, the German champion, won the heavyweight title in 1930 in a fight with Jack Sharkey, only to lose it two years later to the same foe. Primo Carnera, an Italian giant with little fighting ability, won the title in 1933 in what seems to have been a publicity stunt on the part of boxing promoters, only to lose to California playboy, Max Baer, and he in turn to Jimmy Braddock. The one bright light in heavyweight ranks was Joseph Louis Barrow, former sharecropper and automobile worker. The "Brown Bomber" from Detroit won the title in 1937 and proceeded to overwhelm every opponent until his entry into military service. His fights with Schmeling attracted an international audience intrigued with the rivalry of an American black and a German "Aryan." Except for Louis, no figure did more to keep boxing alive in the depths of the Depression than did Mike Jacobs through his Twentieth Century Sporting Club.

As the Depression brought unemployment and poverty, some 8000 young men fought in the professional ring, while thousands learned the fundamentals in Golden Gloves tourneys. During the Depression decade Maxie Rosenbloom, Barney Ross, Jimmy McLarnin, Tony Canzoneri, and a host of black boxers including John Henry Lewis, Kid Chocolate, and the unforgettable Henry Armstrong plied their trade in the ring. But the rich purses of the 1920's were no longer in the offing, and the prize ring lost public esteem due to the mediocrity of many fighters. Although Joe Louis aroused new hope among boxing enthusiasts and private sponsors bought radio time to broadcast matches, the professional ring failed to regain the glamor of the era of Dempsey, Tunney, and Rickard.

Competitive sport was exploited in the promotion of sporting spectacles characteristic of the hippodrome. Professionalization and commercialization of sport flourished, and sportsmen set out to win "the big money." Wrestling promoters found that the matches of veteran Ed (Strangler) Lewis, Jim Londos, Everett Marshall, Joe Savoldi, Daniel O'Mahoney, Man Mountain Dean and Bronko Nagurski had great drawing power in large and small cities from coast to coast. Fans came to accept the buffoonery of matmen as part of an evening's hilarious entertainment. Carnival spirit also invaded sport through other channels. Ice shows became ever more popular as Sonja Henie and Maribel Vinson toured the country. Theaters produced ice extravaganzas; prominent hotels and vacation resorts hired expert skaters; and aquacades were featured in the exhibitions at Chicago (1933), Cleveland (1937), New York (1939-1940), and San Francisco (1939-1940). Roller rinks sprouted up in amusement parks and crowded business areas as well as along the open highways of America. Speed skating, dancing, figure skating, and skating in pairs appealed to the younger generation, and the sport was well on its way to national popularity at the end of the Depression. Soapbox coaster derbies, originating in Dayton, Ohio, became the rage in hundreds of towns after the national championship became an annual spectacle at Akron.

Automobile, motorboat, airplane, and motorcycle racing continued throughout the decade. Billy Arnold, Louis Meyer, and Wilbur Shaw gained national fame on the Indianapolis Speedway, but the English retained a stranglehold on speed records as Sir Malcolm Campbell, Captain G. E. T. Eyston, and John Cobb easily surpassed the 1929 record of 231 mph. Midget auto racing was extremely hazardous and of little value of a technological nature, but it attracted thrill seekers who revelled in the jockeying cars as they skidded crazily and occasionally jumped the guard rail. Gar Wood drove *Miss America X* at a speed of almost 125 mph in 1932, and Sir Malcolm Campbell established a world speedboat record of 141 mph in 1939, only to have these records eclipsed. Although the Harmsworth Trophy was discontinued as the Depression assumed worldwide proportions, enthusiasts helped popularize the Gold Cup and Albany-New York races. Amateurs attached motors to all kinds of craft, and by 1938 some 1,600,000 powered boats plied the water courses of the United States.

Air racing continued to thrill crowds as the nation became air-minded. The Cleveland Air Races were inaugurated in 1931 and Jimmy Doolittle (later an Air Force general and war hero) won the Bendix Trophy for the California to Cleveland flight. Transcontinental races, altitude contests, glider exhibitions, parachute jumps, and trial bombings were all featured in air carnivals which attracted the best pilots of the age. Threat of war loomed ever larger at the end of the decade and attention was diverted to the problem of mass production for military purposes, but a national consciousness of air power had been in great part aroused by the air meets held at rural as well as metropolitan airports.

Easterners had for some time known of bronco riding and steer roping from the Wild West shows of many American circuses, the Hundred and One Ranch, and the Buffalo Bill exhibitions. The Rodeo Association of America was organized in 1928, and Pendleton, Oregon, Cheyenne, Wyoming, and Madison Square Garden, New York City attracted leading competitors. Prizes to winning contestants lured many cowboys off the range to join the rodeo circuit, where outstanding performers like Clay Carr and Everett Bowman won the title of world's champion cowboy. Rodeos became an annual fixture in score of western communities, luring tourists to Denver and all points west. Western influence on the carnival of sport also appeared in the dude ranch.

The first years of the New Deal saw a decided impetus to the building of recreational facilities. Whereas 1036 cities reported organized public recreation programs in 1934, by 1935 some 2190 cities were active in the field, while the number of employed leaders jumped from 28,368 to 43,419 and expenditures rose from $27,065,254 to $41,864,630, much of it through federal aid.[13] At the end of the decade expenditures surpassed $57,000,000. Community boards, committees and recreation associations, social centers, memorial building associations, Parent Teachers Associations, "Y's," civic improvement bodies, welfare federation settlements, charitable organizations, Kiwanis, Lions, Rotary, women's clubs, industrial plants, chambers of commerce, men's clubs, lodges, the American Legion, churches, colleges, schools, boys' clubs, park and playground trustees, government agencies—all helped sponsor recreation for purposes of health and morale in the depths of the Great Depression.

Something of the magnitude of American sport and recreation can be found in the numerous federal agencies which came to the aid of the public recreation movement through the years. In 1941 the Division of Recreation was created within the Federal Security Agency. The Corps of Engineers, National Park Service, Fish and Wildlife Service, Forest Service, Public Housing Administration, Tennessee Valley Authority, Federal Works Agency, Bureau of Reclamation, Children's Bureau, Extension

Much of professional baseball's recovery from the depths of the Depression lay in the gradual improvement of economic conditions, but the baseball world itself was in great part responsible. Branch Rickey's development of the St. Louis Cardinals' farm system was imitated by other clubs, even under the disapproving eyes of Judge Landis. Men like Tom Yawkey in Boston and Walter Briggs in Detroit poured money into their clubs and farm systems, Yawkey reputedly spending $3,500,000 on the Red Sox. The rise of the St. Louis Cardinals, Detroit Tigers, and Boston Red Sox as leading baseball powers went far to prove the value of capital resources and of extensive training systems.

Night baseball proved to be another pillar firmly supporting the tottering structure of the diamond. Experimentation with the night game occurred as early as 1880, but none of the succeeding trials, including the ventures took place in Des Moines and Wichita in 1930. The first promising of the old Federal League, proved successful. The Texas and Pacific Coast leagues quickly followed the lead, and members of the American Association and the Eastern, Piedmont, Southern, International and Western leagues installed arc lights despite skepticism of what was then considered a novelty. "Starring in the starlight," reported The Outlook 1930 as the year of the emergence of night baseball. "Social historians may record 1930: able to the innovation of night contests had taken place in years. Although "Starring in the starlight is now common from coast to coast, confined by no means to bush-league clubs." No boost to the game of baseball compar- major league owners were reluctant to follow the minors or the "bush- leagues," vigilant and businesslike men such as Branch Rickey, Larry McPhail, and William V. Wrigley became enthusiastic over the potentialities of after-dark play.

Not until 1935, however, was the night game introduced in Cincin- nati for the first time in the majors. As an antidote to the Depression, the innovation saved many clubs. Little Rock's Arkansas Gazette reported, "As a result of night baseball, better baseball and a general improvement in conditions in the South [in 1936] the Southern Association, 'old faith- ful' of the minors, will return this season to the 'million a season atten- dance' for the first time since 1931."2 President William Harridge of the American League still favored limitations of night baseball to seven games in 1940, and only in the forties did it gain universal acceptance, but its role was a vital one in hastening the recovery of professional teams throughout the land. Twilight ball also was a factor in the popularity of day occasioned by slack production schedules aided in the popularizing industrial and semipro teams. Daylight saving time and the shorter working of twilight games.

all to be involved at mid-century.
over $100,000,000 annually on
the great problem of sport

there are some
on the pavements
to make a
them
training of
ool of

rks Projects Admini-
alf of the recreational
ged many communities
dollar-matching basis.
prosperous ones. Govern-
untry, and promote recreation
letic fields and playgrounds and
wimming pools were constructed
ere erected and 5625 repaired. Between
A expended $941 million on recreational
ed $1,170,000,000, or 10.3 percent of all
cter estimated that the New Deal spent more
on recreational facilities, and sport absorbed

ic crisis had passed, spectator sports prospered
1941 consumer expenditures on spectator sports
1929 by more than 60 percent. Bowling, tennis, winter
, hockey, softball, football, and baseball flourished during
ven golf weathered the Depression, although many clubs
doors because of falling memberships and rising taxes. Con-
of public links and conversion of clubs to daily fee courses did
to make golf more available to the general public. Golf, however,
the brunt of the Depression more than other participant sports as
aying, instructional, and caddy fees declined between 1929 and 1941
from about $91,000,000 to $64,000,000. Fees to athletic and social clubs
also dropped off from $148,000,000 to $73,500,000 during these years
of stress.[17] Participant sports in general, however, proved increasingly
attractive during the Depression.

## Playing Field, Battlefield, and World War II

When the Continent fell under the iron heel of the Axis powers in 1940, world affairs pushed sporting news into the background. Conversion of industry to the manufacture of war weapons drew millions of unemployed back to work. High wages and steady employment created a favorable economic environment, and industrial sport grew by leaps and bounds. In 1941 it was predicted that some 40,000 semipro baseball games would be played on opening day. And then came Pearl Harbor! As the nation went to war professional baseball, intercollegiate football, prize fighting, golf, and all forms of motorized racing were critically affected. Baseball underwent a transformation even more complete than that of the era of the Great Depression. Major League owners cheered a "green light" letter from President Roosevelt which made possible the staging of Big League games over "the four difficult war seasons which followed:"[18]

THE WHITE HOUSE
Washington

Jan. 15, 1942

My dear Judge:-

Thank you for yours of January fourteenth. As you will, of course, realize the final decision about the baseball season must rest with you and the Baseball Club owners—so what I am going to say is solely a personal and not an official point of view.

I honestly feel that it would be best for the country to keep baseball going. There will be fewer people unemployed and everybody will work longer hours and harder than ever before.

And that means that they ought to have a chance for recreation and for taking their minds off their work even more than before.

Baseball provides a recreation which does not last over two hours or two hours and a half, and which can be got for very little cost. And, incidentally, I hope that night baseball can be extended because it gives an opportunity to the day shift to see a game occasionally.

As to the players themselves, I know you agree with me that individual players who are of active military or naval age should go, without question, into the services. Even if the actual quality of the teams is lowered by the greater use of older players, this will not dampen the popularity of the sport. Of course, if any individual has some particular aptitude in a trade or profession, he ought to serve

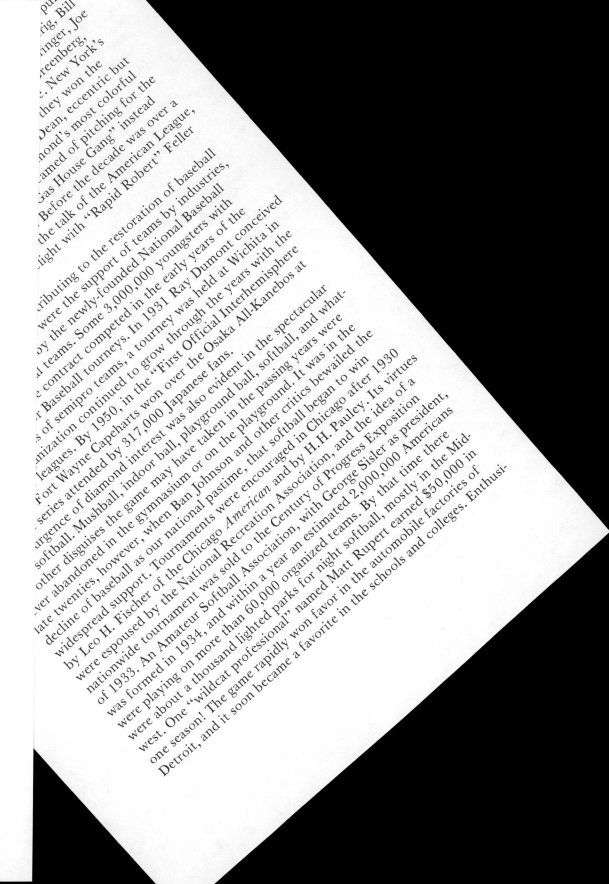

the Government. That, however, is a matter which I know you can handle with complete justice.

Here is another way of looking at it—if 300 teams use 5,000 or 6,000 players, these players are a definite recreational asset to at least 20,000,000 of their fellow citizens—and that in my judgement is thoroughly worthwhile.

> With every best wish,
> Very sincerely yours,
> (Signed) Franklin D. Roosevelt

Hon. Kenesaw M. Landis
333 North Michigan Avenue
Chicago, Illinois

Conscription rapidly depleted professional ranks in 1942, and ten minor leagues failed to open the season. While the armies of the Third Reich and the USSR were locked in mortal combat at Stalingrad, soldiers in every American training camp hovered tensely over their radios—listening to the dramatic World Series victory of the St. Louis Cardinals over the New York Yankees! Baseball reports were brought to troops throughout the war. Short-wave radio transmission of World Series games was made to men from the Arctic Circle to the Tropics, while the *Stars and Stripes* and the *Sporting News* carried diamond gossip to USO clubs, camp libraries, ships at sea, and combat units.

On the home front industrial sport gained new recruits by the thousands as workers flocked into aircraft and armament production. Night games became a regular feature, while contests were held at all times of the day to accommodate the "swing shifts" and "night shifts." More than 90 percent of the armed forces and about 60 percent of the civilian population favored continuation of professional baseball, according to public opinion polls;[19] but scarcity of gasoline, governmental restrictions on travel, and conscription were enough to cause a decided drop in attendance. Spring training, for example, was confined to areas north of the Potomac and Ohio rivers by an agreement between Commissioner Landis and Joseph B. Eastman, director of the Office of Defense Transportation.

By the summer of 1944 professional baseball found an opening in the dark clouds as attendance soared in the National, American, Pacific Coast, and International Leagues, as well as in the American and Southern Associations. The Fifth War Loan drive received considerable stimulus from organized baseball, and at one New York game the sale of war bonds reached a total of $56,500,000. The absence of star players and Judge

Landis' death were overshadowed, naturally, by the titanic struggle which raged from D-Day on the Normandy beaches through the Battle of the Bulge into the spring of 1945.

Similar difficulties confronted every area of sport. High schools continued to play extensive schedules, touch football proved particularly popular at air bases and induction centers, and even weary infantry trainees batted a volleyball in their company street. In many of the smaller colleges, however, football was suspended and most schedules reduced. Service teams filled the gap as army, navy, marine, coast guard, and air corps elevens took the field, but war took its toll and the rationing of gas and tires, along with the prohibition of railroad specials to sporting spectacles, created difficulties for leagues and conferences, amateur and professional alike. Army training units refused their men permission to engage in intercollegiate athletics, ignoring the participation of naval V-5 and V-12 units. High school football was less directly affected because of the age requirement, and interscholastic games in many areas surpassed those of the colleges in popular interest. McKinley High School in Canton, Ohio, played before 115,000 to 130,000 fans a year in this period; neighboring Massillon refused to be outdone and fielded some of the strongest schoolboy teams in the country.

West Point became the goal of most athletically-inclined officer trainees as Glenn Davis, Felix (Doc) Blanchard, Arnold Tucker, and a brigade of brilliant players ran through and over their opposition. Even more public interest was aroused by the growing popularity of various T-formations developed by Clark Shaughnessy, George Halas, Don Faurot, and other coaches. And the professional game continued to grow as Sammy Baugh, Sid Luckman, Don Hutson, Mel Hein, and an array of stellar players won an ever stronger following for the Washington Redskins, Chicago Bears, Green Bay Packers, New York Giants, and rival clubs.

The "Whiz Kids" of the University of Illinois; outstanding fives of the University of Utah, DePaul, and Oklahoma A&M; growing interest in interscholastic basketball; and rising enthusiasm throughout the South were all indicative of the steady progress made by the court game. Bowling claimed about 15,000,000 keglers who played on 180,000 alleys in 1942. Telegraphic match play attempted to counteract CDT restrictions on transportation in 1943, while women engaged in war work crowded the alleys and teams representing business concerns or industries were active in every community. By 1945 over 13,000 billiard tables and 3000 bowling alleys were in use at American military and naval bases.

Golfers felt the impact of war as the War Production Board restricted the use of rubber in balls and of steel in club shafts. Many country clubs were transformed into recreation centers, and the USGA called off all national tourneys for the duration. While many leading players had entered the armed forces, Byron Nelson and Harold (Jug) McSpaden shared in winning most of the PGA tourneys in 1944. A year later Nelson dominated the scene with earnings exceeding $60,000 in war bonds and with a winning streak of eleven successive tournaments. Voted the nation's top athlete in both years, "Lord Byron" took his place in the history of American golf alongside such greats as Francis Ouimet, Walter Hagen, and Bobby Jones.

Tennis, track and field athletics, swimming, rowing, yachting, and sailing remained in the background during the war; athletic goods and hunting supplies were scarce, and the prize ring had to struggle along without many of its champions. Winter sport retained its popularity, but national interest centered on the battlefields of the world and on the heroic deeds of soldiers, sailors, and airmen. American heroes, at least for the duration, were the warriors in combat.

Free circulation of wartime earnings made an unprecedented volume of money available for betting at the track. Whirlaway caught the imagination of the nation at the start of the decade and millions applauded the erratic but spectacular performances of "Mr. Bigtail." Warren Wright's Calumet Farm rapidly rose to dominate the racing scene in great part through the work of its trainer, Ben Jones. Although the War Mobilization Board temporarily prohibited the transportation of race horses and closed all tracks in 1945 until the allied armies swept to victory in Europe, racing had another banner year in which 17,000,000 fans flocked to see the bangtails run. Mrs. Elizabeth Graham, of "Elizabeth Arden" cosmetics fame, saw her Maine Chance Farm earnings surpass even those of Calumet. Rising yearling prices, a tremendous betting fever, and the fantastic earnings of leading stables were all indicative of the wartime prosperity of the turf. At the conclusion of World War II an estimated 881 breeding farms operated in 40 states, the total acreage of which was said to be three times the area of Rhode Island.

Most noted of the breeders formed a Kentucky group including Colonel E.K. Bradley, Samuel D. Biddle, Warren Wright, and the Widener family, as well as such prominent Californians as W.E. Boeing, Louis B. Mayer, and prominent members of the movie colony. Walter P. Chrysler, Jr., Mrs. Dodge Sloane, William Du Pont, Alfred G. Vanderbilt, William Helis, and Fred B. Koonts also poured their fortunes into breeding farms.

World War II hampered most activities, but General Walter L. Weible, director of military training for the Army Service Forces, recognized that competitive sport was vital in the training of future soldiers. Admiral Chester Nimitz credited athletics at a South Pacific recreation center with a tremendous contribution to the building of morale, and General Brehon

Somervell, chief of the Service of Supply, claimed that the sandlots and
Big League parks were doing their share in winning the war. Henry L.
Stimson recorded a discussion of the Cabinet at the White House about
the Army-Navy game. The secretaries debated "with such seriousness and
diversity of opinion that the president suggested that he would appoint a
committee to determine it." John G. Winant, ambassador to Great Britain,
recognized the grip of sport on the American people:

> Today your fathers and brothers fight bravely on the far-flung
> battlefronts of the world. I like to think, as I know many of them
> do, of the playgrounds, athletic fields, swimming pools and beautiful
> parks in communities all over America. In their mind's eye they see
> your smiling faces and know your carefree life. They remember it
> was good to live in that kind of country. They are determined that
> you and all of America's children shall continue to have that kind of
> life.[20]

## Peace and the Postwar Boom

By the summer of 1946 the United States was "in the midst of its greatest
sports revival."[21] Clashes between Commissioner Albert Chandler and Leo
Durocher, the return of former diamond luminaries, the entry of black
players into the majors, a series of exciting pennant races, the virtually
universal attention drawn to baseball by television after the 1947 Series,
the prevalence of night contests, and the high-pressure publicity of the
metropolitan newspaper were all factors in the return of baseball to the
center of the sporting scene. Fantastic salaries, general travel of teams by
air, and an improved efficiency of play over that of wartime were indicative of changes for the better in the national game. College baseball was
given a lift when the NCAA championship was established in 1948, the
University of Texas winning two successive titles in 1949-1950. By the
latter forties softball reputedly attracted as many as 125,000,000 spectators annually. Today there are over 8000 leagues and nearly 1,000,000
players in the Amateur Softball Association. As industries and municipal
recreation programs sponsored softball everywhere, it has become one of
our most popular pastimes.

The gridiron was equally affected by the sports boom. Midwestern
football retained its reputation as the center of the collegiate gridiron
world when Notre Dame, Ohio State, Michigan, and Illinois returned to
their former glory and Michigan State gained renown. The sharpest rise in
gridiron fanaticism took place in the South and Southwest, where the
universities of Texas and Oklahoma had the outstanding teams. Although

bowl games contributed heavily to this sectional trend, general commercialization of southern football was the major factor. A "black market" in star players was "exposed," the most notable instance being the resignation of Tom (Shorty) McWilliams from West Point to play for Mississippi State. Exaggerated commercialization was general in every section, however, as athletic scholarships and football dormitories were established on many campuses.

Professional football, soaring to new heights in public interest during and immediately after the war, underwent an eclipse for several years in a struggle between the All-America Conference and the National Football League. Consolidation saved the game, and by 1953 it drew more spectators than at any time in its history. Interscholastic games absorbed such commercialized characteristics of the collegiate gridiron as recruiting, costly equipment, highly paid coaches, post-season games, and large stadiums. Junior high school sports, increasing since the Depression, came under close surveillance as educators were markedly concerned with contact sports and exploitation of children.[22]

Few athletic games recorded a more sensational rise in popular interest than basketball. The years after World War II saw an almost constant growth of the court game. Establishment of state, regional, and national championships, ever growing recognition by the press, and devotion of radio and television time were all instrumental in basketball's rise to prominence despite strong criticism levelled at the emphasis placed on tall players. In Oklahoma, it was said: "Every kid plays basketball as soon as he can throw ten feet," while the game remained the major scholastic sport in Indiana, Kentucky, and other states. A coach of the Allentown, Pennsylvania, state championship high school team was given a new automobile and was said to be the "most esteemed" citizen of the city. The *Athletic Journal* stated in 1949 that about 18,000 high schools in the United States were preparing for state tournament eliminations.[23] Attention was drawn to the game by the spectacular play of teams from the University of Kentucky, Oklahoma A&M, St. Louis University, Holy Cross, Bradley, City College (of N.Y.), the University of Kansas, La Salle, and other institutions. The expert coaching of Phog Allen of Kansas, Adolph Rupp of Kentucky, Henry (Hank) Iba of Oklahoma A&M, Clair Bee of Long Island University, and Nat Holman of City College made basketball a complex and exciting game for the spectator who thrilled to the exploits of George Mikan, Bob Davies, Bob Cousy, Paul Arizin, and other hoopsters who went on to star in professional ranks. Much interest was also aroused by the antics and skills of the world-famous Harlem Globe Trotters, headed by the amazing Goose Tatum.

Wartime restrictions on the manufacture of golf balls and clubs were soon lifted, and many country clubs reopened. Professional tourneys featuring Sammy Snead, Bobby Locke of South Africa, Cary Middlecoff, and Lloyd Mangrum attracted huge galleries. Ben Hogan's spectacular recovery from an automobile accident and Babe Didrickson's return to championship form following a serious operation gave to devotees of the links a hero and heroine unrivalled by champions in other games of the postwar world. Texans might well hold their heads high with pride.

The Tam O'Shanter Country Club in Chicago set the pace in prize money, and more than 50,000 onlookers were in the gallery on the last day of its 1946 tourney. Whereas in the middle of the Depression annual prizes totalled only about $100,000, by 1947 over $600,000 were distributed, and by 1954 Tam O'Shanter's "world championship tourney" alone offered purses exceeding $200,000. But the most prized championships were still the United States Open, the PGA, the Masters, and the British Open. New York, Pennsylvania, California, Illinois, and Massachusetts maintained the most courses affiliated with the United States Golf Association, in rough correlation to their populations.[24] Players returned to the greens and fairways in droves. A sport for professional and business men and their wives as well as for an increasing number of laborers, golf regained its former hold on the public.

Amateur tennis languished with the growing popularity of so many other sports, but professional ranks lured Don Budge, Bobby Riggs, Jack Kramer, Pancho Segura, and other champions, thereby adding to the long-standing woes of the United States Lawn Tennis Association. Continuous domination of the Davis Cup matches until 1951 and the rise of such talented players as Pancho Gonzales, Ted Schroeder, Vic Seixas, and Tony Trabert softened the loss in general tennis interest. Supremacy in the amateur game shifted, however, to Australia with the appearance of Frank Sedgman and Lewis Hoad. The courts have had no dynamic group of players comparable to those of the 1920's and 1930's when Ellsworth Vines, Fred Perry, Jack Crawford, Don Budge, Helen Jacobs, and Alice Marble carried on in the tradition of Bill Tilden, Bill Johnston, R. Norris Williams, Rene Lacoste, Henri Cochet, Suzanne Lenglen, and Helen Wills. Pauline Betz and Jack Kramer alone ranked with the champions of the past until Maureen (Mighty Mo) Connolly started to wreak havoc on the courts of the world at mid-century. In order to restore interest in the amateur game the Lawn Tennis Association was finally forced to relax its overly strict amateur code.

The Hambletonian annual classic at Goshen and night races at Roosevelt Raceway, Long Island proved a boon to harness racing enthusiasts who by 1948 were betting close to $200 million at pari-mutuel tracks. Among the noted thoroughbreds of the decade Whirlaway and Citation were outstanding, with Alsab, Count Fleet, Assault, Armed, Stymie, Coaltown, Capot, and Ponder in close pursuit. American pride was somewhat lowered by the remarkable victories of a foreign invader named Noor, whose successive wins over the great Citation in 1950 will be long remembered. Tom Fool and Native Dancer added their laurels to the annals of the turf. By 1953 racing employed close to 50,000 men, had a payroll of a quarter billion dollars, and maintained 20,000 horses in training and 22,000 on breeding farms. Real property (including 83 tracks) reached beyond $700,000,000. Racing purses passed the $60,000,000 mark, mutuel bets approached $2,000,000,000, attendance exceeded 26,000,000, and state revenues were just under $120,000,000.[25] The American turf seemed to profit from general prosperity and inflation to a degree unmatched by other spectator sports, and it was looming as an issue of considerable consequence on the political scene.

War had demonstrated the value of skiing when the army formed its Tenth Mountain Ski Division. Winter sports continued to lure several million weekend sportsmen annually. Claudette Colbert, Norma Shearer, and other movie stars set the fashion vogue. Businesswise, skiing was a profitable enterprise: "Every inn and farm house near Vermont's famed runs . . . was heavily booked, at from $2 to $20 a day."[26] A National Bowling Writers Association helped focus the sports page reader's attention on league competitions, while individual or team standings were extensively tabulated in statistical columns. Between sixteen and eighteen million bowlers of all types, from novice to expert, spent over $200,000,-000 on fees and equipment in 1947, and the American Bowling Congress had nearly 2,000,000 members in 1953.[27] Roller skating owed its rising popularity mainly to the young in heart. Rinks were built in all sections of the country as the Roller Skating Rink Operators Association and the United States Association sponsored national championships in speed racing, fancy skating, and team relays. As many as 17,000,000 skaters were reputed to be roller enthusiasts in the sports boom following World War II.

Participant sports of an aquatic nature also revived after 1945. Larchmont's yachting regattas were the largest in the nation, Seawanhaka-Corinthian and Manhasset Bay sponsored popular competitions, and in 1947 175 yacht clubs were active on the waters of Long Island Sound, 33 of which were banded into a Yacht Racing Association. *Lloyd's Register of American Yachts* for 1948 noted at least 6000 owners of sailing or power yachts, 7192 yachts, and over 775 yacht clubs for the younger set and the availability of "Snipes," "Lightnings," and "Stars" costing from $650 to $2200 had done much to democratize the former yachting and sailing monopoly of the privileged classes.[28]

A new corps of baseball stars appeared in the years after 1945, among them Hal Newhouser, Tommy Henrich, Lou Boudreau, Ralph Kiner, Yogi Berra, Jackie Robinson, Roy Campanella, and Robin Roberts, who shared the baseball spotlight with veterans like Joe Di Maggio, Ted Williams, and Stanley Musial. Fans of the late forties and early fifties identified with such gridiron stars as Frank Albert and Norm Standlee, Bill Dudley, Glenn Dobbs, Frank Sinkwich, Charley Trippi, Johnny Lujack, Doak Walker, Charlie Justice, and Dick Kazmaier. Among the professionals Robert Waterfield, Steve Van Buren, Spec Sanders, and Otto Graham came on to rival such "old-timers" as Johnny Blood, Don Hutson, Ace Parker, and Ward Cuff. George Mikan, Gus Broberg, Ralph Beard, Alex Groza, Robert Kurland, George Glamack, Ray Evans, Ed McCauley, Bob Cousy, and Clyde Lovellette were but a few of the stars of the basketball court. Willie Pep, Tony Zale, Sugar Ray Robinson, Joe Walcott, Kid Gavilan, and Rocky Marciano secured their niches in the annals of boxing. In seeking to rival Canada's Barbara Ann Scott, Andrea Mead Lawrence, Tenley Albright, Gretchen Fraser and the brilliant Richard (Dick) Button won Olympic or world titles in winter sports. Women attained ever greater distinction, the most prominent of whom were Pauline Betz, Louise Brough, Sarah Palfrey Cooke, Margaret DuPont Osborn, Doris Hart, and Maureen Connolly in tennis; Ann Curtis and Florence Chadwick in swimming; Vicki Draves and Sammy Lee in diving; and Patty Berg, Louise Suggs, and the greatest of all women athletes, Mildred (Babe) Didrickson, in golf. Joan Pflueger won the Grand American Trapshoot in 1950, the first of her sex in history to defeat all male competitors.

Radio and television played great roles in the postwar world. When the Mutual Network carried the World Series of 1947 it estimated that 72.2 percent "of all radio homes were tuned into one or more of the contests, as compared with a figure of 60.6 a year ago." WOR (New York) broadcasted the Sunday game which, according to the Hooper survey, was listened to by 91.5 percent of "those listeners interviewed on the telephone," a record for a New York station.[29] Television capitalized on sport. By 1950 approximately 7,500,000 sets received the World Series telecasts which were viewed by some 40,000,000 fans.

Inspired by Carl Statz of Williamsport, Pennsylvania in 1939, Little League baseball for youngsters, although criticized for its emphasis on competition and intersectional play as well as on health grounds, received the approval of a national health forum, the Catholic Youth Organization, YMCA's, police, firemen, churches, and other sponsoring agencies. J. Edgar

Hoover of the FBI testified, "By diverting the physical energy of youth into constructive channels, Little League baseball helps curb juvenile delinquency," and the 150,000 boys in 2800 registered leagues in 1953 demonstrated the same enthusiasm. While educators were disturbed at overemphasis in juvenile sport, Biddy Basketball and Midget Football also made a tremendous appeal in hundreds of communities. It was maintained that more spectators watched Little League games in 1953 than there were in all major league parks. Arthur Daly of the New York *Times* said of Little League, "The kids love it, and so do the parents. That's a combination impossible to beat." [30]

Social workers found, "Athletic games and sports serve more individuals as participants and spectators than does any other feature of the community recreation program, and an amazing growth of these activities has been noted since the war." Industrial teams cooperating in public sports programs accounted for much of the excited interest in local baseball, softball, football, bowling, and other activities. So great was interest in all forms of recreation that bills authorizing the development of a federal recreation service were introduced in the 80th Congress, although they were not considered. [31]

War had cut into the heart of the 1940's, and even the postwar boom could not obscure its impact. Sport still faced the threat of competing amusements and recreational diversions—radio, television, movies, and motor travel. The Liberty Broadcasting System organized by Gordon McClendon inaugurated a daily narration of Big League baseball games throughout the country. Within two years it claimed to be the third largest system in the United States, thereby inspiring the Mutual Network to introduce its Game of the Day in 1950. George Trautman, head of the minor leagues, gave publicity to radio broadcasting and television as the causes of the collapse of minor league attendance in 1950. [32] As the nation passed mid-century, however, interest in sport seemed to have reached a level unmatched in our history.

## International Sport in Recent Decades

Sport was occasionally acclaimed as an agent of international understanding in the optimistic years following Versailles. Revival of international yachting with the America's Cup races of 1920, the fights of Carpentier, Firpo, Stribling, and Schmeling, the commencement of the Oxford-Cambridge track meets with Princeton-Cornell and Harvard-Yale teams, the racing of Epinard, Sun Beau, and other foreign horses, and international matches in many sports encouraged those who cherished the Olympian oath. Sir Thomas Lipton's sportsmanlike attitude aided Anglo-American friendship in a decade when the British war debt was hotly debated. Lord Dewar said of the 1920 yacht races: "Sporting events such as this form between Great Britain and the United States a golden chain which will never lose a link." President Harding, commenting on an Oxford-Cambridge versus Princeton-Cornell track meet, observed, "I know that in the past years such friendly competitions have done much for the promotion of those splendid relations between our country and the Government and people of the United Kingdom." Senator George Wharton Pepper of Pennsylvania, at the laying of the cornerstone of a new $5,000,000 Pen Athletic Club building in Philadelphia, encouraged sports among nations as well as games for industrial workers and added, "I am of the opinion that there is a great peacemaking power in common standards of fair play and that the noble army of sportsmen throughout the world is destined to be a peace army of no mean strength."

The Outlook in 1924 maintained, "The real significance of the greatest of Olympiads is its powerful influence in furthering the cause of amateur sport, friendly international rivalries and therefore good will among men." [33] And there were the persistent advocates of the American Olympic Committee who refused to recognize the relationship between sport and politics in the rise of totalitarianism. But this constitutes about the strongest case that could be made. Chancelleries of the various powers gave no serious consideration to the Olympiads or other rivalries, state documents on international problems ignored them, students of power politics were equally silent, the press emphasized victories rather than the spirit of friendly rivalry, and a series of unpleasant episodes at Antwerp in 1920, Paris in 1924, and Amsterdam in 1928 gave no sign of improving relations between nations. The Davis Cup, Walker Cup, and temperamental stars like Bill Tilden or Walter Hagen often aroused as much resentment as good will.

English sporting interest revived in 1920, and it was asserted that the "great national journals which are read by the general public tend more and more to subordinate the larger interests of the country to sport and sporting gossip." [34] With the passing years national lotteries in racing and association football sustained the common man's interest, while Bunny Austin, Fred Perry, Jack Lovelock, Henry Wooderson, and Henry Cotton, along with Commonwealth athletes like Percy Williams, Jack Crawford, Bobby Locke, Jack Bromwich, Frank Sedgman, and John Landy kept England's sporting heritage alive on the international scene. The morale of the English people was to get a great lift from the remarkable exploits leading to the conquest of Mount Everest and the achievement by Roger Bannister of the first four-minute mile in history. Following World War I, however, Britain's nineteenth-century athletic supremacy was eclipsed by rivalry of athletes from every major country of the world.

Sporting enthusiasm manifested itself in the French Republic, in part from the conviction that the war had demonstrated the need for physical training and in part as a tendency to forget the tragedy of the war years. Réné Lacoste, Jacques Brugnon, Jean Borotra, and Henri Cochet rose up to dominate the tennis courts of the world in the late twenties, while the most famous woman in France was Suzanne Lenglen, "known to millions who had never heard of Colette or of Madame Curie." On the industrial scene, however, the Left often rivalled the Right in the subsidization of clubs, although the former was prejudiced in the belief that "sport might be brutal, its teaching might inculcate those false ideas of physical prowess and unintelligent achievement which it was the business of education to destroy."[35] Except for the Tour de France and the careers of tennis stars and prize fighters, the French seldom demonstrated an intense enthusiasm over international contests.

Throughout the twentieth century a steady development has taken place in the sporting habits of the western world, at times in a natural response to the love of sport and at times as an instrument for the spread of nationalism. A Scandinavian bloc encouraged track athletics and winter games, and the sporting world will long remember the exploits of Hans Kolehmainen, Paavo Nurmi, Sonja Henie, Gundar Haegg, and Torger Tokle, who helped introduce the world to the love of the great out-of-doors.

The Japanese took to the cinder path, tennis court, swimming pool, and baseball diamond. Visits of American college and professional teams helped in the organization of a league of six universities in 1925. Even China showed some awareness of the athletic cult as Chiang-Kai-Shek ordered all pupils and teachers above the secondary level to train regularly in one athletic sport: "Athletics, as a means of developing the physique of the people, should be regarded as an important part of the program for strengthening of the race and the salvation of the nation." Indian and other oriental participants in the Asiad (Asian Games) proved an opening wedge for the development of athleticism in the Far East.

Latin America also took to the playing fields. In addition to horse racing, polo, tennis, and jai-alai, Mexicans and Central Americans began to encourage basketball on school playgrounds, while indoor arenas were built in Brazil. Baseball was widely played in Venezuela, Peru, the Caribbean area, and even Yucatan. Josephus Daniels noted that by 1940 "it was so universal [in Mexico] that I often stopped at open fields to see boys playing and rarely missed an intercollegiate game."[36] Babe Ruth's death rated enormous headlines in the Mexican press. The game's popularity in rural Mexico, where federal schools were the center of impromptu and organized games, was obvious to the most casual tourist. Athletic games were said to have been "the greatest aid in the emancipation of Latin

American women from the cloistered life imposed upon them for generations." Although music, dancing, the promenade, and bull fighting remained the favorite diversions of men and women south of the border, the impact of American sports was clearly evident.

Lenin's Russia, struggling to modernize industry and agriculture and to overcome the limitations of a dominantly rural economy, had little time for play and sport. As millions of children entered schools of the USSR, as working schedules were eventually shortened, as Moscow, Kharkov, Kiev, and new industrial cities like Magnitogorsk grew into vast metropolitan centers, and as the Stalinist Soviet regime paid increasing attention to music, ballet, folk customs, art, and the theater, interest in sport began to develop. Walter Duranty reported in 1928 that "the whole youth of Russia is sport crazy and is beginning loudly to demand press attention." By the middle thirties he was to find a decided rise in sports consciousness and active participation in the Red Army, the Soviet Air League, and the Communist Youth and Young Pioneer movements, noting "it is no exaggeration to say that youth of both sexes in urban centers are as devoted to sports as Americans."[37] Sidney and Beatrice Webb stressed the "universalism" of interest,[38] and a Supreme Council for Physical Culture was appointed by the Central Executive Committee.

World War II exacted a terrible toll on Russian youth, but enthusiasm continued to mount in the Soviet Union where sport remained directly subservient to the state and had been made a compulsory part of the industrial worker's daily routine. Despite the tendency of Russia to participate only in international working men's track and field carnivals of the twenties and thirties, in immediate postwar years, Soviet weight lifters began competing throughout the world while football and basketball players and skaters won European or world championships,[39] and teams were sent throughout the satellite states. Wrestlers and gymnasts excelled at the Olympic Games held at Helsinki in 1952, where the world was given fair notice of Russian intentions to surpass other nations on the field of sport. In the Iron Curtain countries sport caught on with a vengeance. The Czech Emil Zatopek startled the world with his disregard for world records in distance running, while the Hungarians, long active on the Olympic scene, proved their versatility at Helsinki.

Italians formed their Alpine Club in 1863 and Rowing Club in 1894, and in cycling, fencing, football, gymnastics, rifle marksmanship, and automobile and airplane racing they have won international championships. While their country was seething with industrial strife, Italian athletes engaged in virtually every contest at the 1920 Olympic Games. When Mussolini's Black Shirts made their "march" on Rome in 1922, the stage was already set for a sporting revival. Fascistification of social and cultural life took place through the national organization of leisure-time activities in the Dopolavoro. In 1926 the National Italian Olympic Committee was designated as a subordinate organ of the Fascist party to supervise all physical education and sports activities.[40] Signor Marairglia announced in 1929:

> Sport is not an end in itself. . . . Fascism avails itself of the various forms of sports, especially those requiring large groups of participants, as a means of military preparation and spiritual development, that is, as a school for the national training of Italian youth. By popularizing and militarizing sports requiring large groups, Fascism accomplishes perhaps its greatest governmental work. All Italian youths placed under the same discipline will begin to feel themselves soldiers. In this way there is built up in spirit a formidable militant organism which is already a potential army.[41]

Subsidizing of athletes, publicizing their achievements, and rewarding champions became standard policy with the Fascist government. When Luigi Beccali won the 1500-meter race at Los Angeles in 1932, it was proposed that a lifetime pension or job be given the popular hero. Arenas like the Mussolini Stadium at Rome and Il Littoriale at Bologna were erected to glorify fascist sport, and as late as 1939 Italians were still making extensive preparations for the Olympic Games scheduled for the Eternal City in 1940. Under a vigorous and athletic Duce, sportsmen played a prominent role in the pageantry of Fascist Italy.

Except for the deer hunting and outdoor life of the landed gentry, German sport was fairly well confined to the walking habits and simple games of youth until the development of the Turnverein in the nineteenth century. Gymnastics were stressed under the supervision of Turner societies, inspired by Friedrich Jahn and his followers. By the end of the century fencing was popular among university students, hiking and camping were favorite forms of recreation, while playgrounds and parks appeared in Breslau, Berlin, Konigsberg, and other large cities in the pre-World War I era. The Wandervogel organized walking clubs, the German army sponsored a "Young Germany" movement, and the government established an Imperial Commission for the scientific investigation of sport and bodily exercise. A football league and numerous athletic clubs also appeared, but organization lagged and the poor showing at the Stockholm Olympics in 1912 aroused a widespread demand for reorganization of the sports program. An imperial committee was appointed to prepare for the intended Berlin Games in 1916, specialists studied the athletic situation in the United States, and hundreds of meets had been held or

were being planned in the army and the schools of the Fatherland when
war was declared in 1914.[42]

Four years of war drained the blood of the best of German youth,
but active interest in sport developed in the Weimar Republic. It was only
with entry into the League of Nations in 1926 and readmission to the
Olympics in 1928 that Germany once again could play its role on the
international sporting scene. The revival was noted by Emil Ludwig and
Miriam Beard. Sports extras began to appear in the press, and athletic
successes at Amsterdam in 1928 gave proof of the enthusiasm developed
under the Republic. A large contingent came to Los Angeles in 1932, but
with the elevation of Adolf Hitler to the chancellorship in 1933 sport
was integrated with the National Socialist movement under a policy of
*Gleichschaltung.*[43]

The Fuhrer had expressed his views on sport in *Mein Kampf:* "In the
folkish State physical training . . . is not the concern of the individual . . .
but a requirement of the self-preservation of the nationality, represented
and protected by the State." Encouraging the schools to allot more time
to boxing, Hitler commended it for promoting aggressiveness, decision,
and physical versatility: "Thus the meaning of sports is not only to make
the individual strong, versatile and bold, but it has also to harden him and
to teach him how to bear inclemencies." In a remarkable statement he
argued, "If our entire intellectual upper class had not been educated so
exclusively in teaching refined manners and if instead of this it had learned
boxing thoroughly, then a German revolution by pimps, deserters and
similar rabble would never have been possible."[44]

Hitlerjugend (Hitler Youth), under the direction of Baldur von
Schirach, eliminated Catholic Youth as well as Protestant organizations.
Jewish athletes were virtually ignored. *Commonweal* and *Catholic World,*
American Catholic journals, charging that competition was limited to
members of Hitlerjugend and the Arbeitsfront and that both paganism
and discrimination were characteristic of German sport, urged a boycott
of the 1936 Berlin Games. More than a hundred Protestant clergymen and
educators advocated withdrawal. A petition in protest against the German
disregard for fair play was signed by the Reverends S. Parkes Cadman,
Henry Sloane Coffin, Harry Emerson Fosdick, John Haynes Holmes, Rein-
hold Niebuhr, and Albert W. Palmer, among others. Luther Weigle, Tyler
Dennett, Mary E. Wooley, and Frank P. Graham protested for the academic
world, as did William Green and the AFL, Mayor Fiorello La Guardia, the
National Council of Methodist Youth, *Time, Nation, Christian Century,*
black newspapers, the Jewish War Veterans, and a number of leading
senators and governors. A prominent member of the Olympic Committee
merely responded to all this with petulance: "To those alien agitators and

their brethren stooges who would deny our athletes their birthright as American citizens to represent the United States in the Olympic games . . . our athletes reply in the modern vernacular, 'Oh yeah!' "[45]

There were strong arguments, however, for disassociating sport from politics, and the western press did not generally sumpathize with the furor in the East. When the AAU and NCAA finally gave their approval, the die was cast. Berlin was now to have its hour of pageantry and glory. A Reich Sport Bureau was created in the Ministry of Interior and Hans Von Tschammer und Osten, Reichs Sport Leader, was charged with preparation for the festival. In the midst of beautiful sports arenas, Olympic banners and Nazi swastikas flying from the windows, with military bands, search-lights, and 100,000 SA and SS troops serving as policemen or goose-stepping in an Olympic parade, little wonder the Associated Press reported the "most dazzling military spectacle that Berlin has ever seen."

Despite the crowns won by Jesse Owens, John Woodruff, Archie Williams, Cornelius Johnson, Glenn Morris, Forest Towns, Glenn Hardin, Earle Meadows, Ken Carpenter, Jack Medica, Adolf Kiefer, Dick Degener, Marshall Wayne, Marjorie Gestring, Dorothy Poynton Hill, and American champions in basketball, rifle marksmanship, weight lifting, wrestling, and women's gymnastics, the Germans were thrilled in achieving, even if in-formally, their first Olympic victory. Athletes of 51 nations participated in the spirit of good fellowship, and the universality of interest was demon-strated by the London *Times*, which remarked that "the whole world has taken to sport with a zest and precision which Great Britain, the originator and teacher, finds it hard to rival."[46]

Germany was not yet ready to quit the international sporting scene. Gottfried von Cramm continued his tennis exploits abroad, and German boxing teams fought in England, while youth were being trained in "motor sports" by the National-Socialist Motor Corps. Autobahnen and motor-ways were built to test "new racing cars as pace-setters of technical ad-vancement." Proud German propagandists boasted, "In the great German and international sporting events Germany is becoming more and more predominant. In 61 races in the years 1934 to 1937 German cars won 55 victories."[47] But the end was drawing near. Well might the western powers have wondered when the Reich's tennis stars were refused passports to participate at Forest Hills in 1939! That love of sport survived World War II was strongly manifested even in the midst of a society miraculously raising itself out of the ruins. Memories of the fascist era remained strong as Dr. Gerhard Schroeder, Federal Interior Minister, warned "that enthusiastic free sport in the Federal Republic must not be confused with future train-ing measures necessary for military service."

American athletes and American-trained instructors helped carry the gospel of sport throughout the world. Delegations of athletes to the Olympic Games proved the increasing sports consciousness of the peoples of capitalistic, socialistic, and communistic ideologies in every area of the world. Bob Mathias, Mal Whitfield, Wes Santee, Rev. Robert Richards, Harrison Dillard, and others proved ambassadors of good will in postwar track meets abroad. The Harlem Globe Trotters were in demand in many lands, American college teams visited Latin America, and even Leo Durocher followed in the footsteps of A. G. Spalding, John McGraw, Connie Mack, and Babe Ruth as an emissary of the national pastime in the Far East. Although preservation of peace and promotion of good will in an age of clashing ideologies and constant nuclear threat depend mainly on political, economic, military, and cultural relationships, the leavening force of international sport, facilitated by the revolution in air transport, became an element of real significance to the peoples of the world.

# Chapter 11

# Business, Industry, and the Economic Scene

# Chapter 11

# Business, Industry, and the Economic Scene

P. & A. photograph

SOLDIERS' FIELD, WI

This picture of Chicago's great stadiun
seats w

THE TUNNEY

170,000 PEOPLE ARE EXPECTED TO PAY $3,000,000 TO SEE THE FIGHT

made at the time of its dedication. Mr. Rickard's carpenters have been adding acres of ring
the arena, and vast bleachers beyond the permanent tiers of seats.

EMPSEY FIGHT: A WORLD SPECTACLE

The penetration of sport into every level of our educational system, into the programs of social agencies and private clubs, and into leisure-time pursuits has been so progressively successful as to mark it as one of the important social trends of the past two generations. This is most obviously seen in the vastly greater interdependence of business and sport and in the heightened concern of both management and labor in recent decades.

## Business and Sport in Modern America

It has been mainly in the period since World War I that sport has become an integral part of the business world, affecting such varied areas of our economic system as finance, fashion, journalism, trade, transportation, communication, insurance, advertising, sporting goods manufacture, and those marginal enterprises which profit from expenditures incidental to sport. Facilities ranging from golf courses and athletic stadiums to swimming pools and playgrounds have been constructed by private and public organizations alike. In 1931 *Golfdom* reported 543 municipal courses in 46 states and 700 daily fee or pay-as-you-play courses in addition to the private golf clubs from Maine to California. By 1934 there were more than 5000 courses covering between 400,000 and 500,000 acres with an estimated valuation of $850,000,000. In 1946 alone almost 1500 cities reported expenditures exceeding $51,000,000 in recreational projects, while 46 cities and a single county issued bonds totaling over $22,000,000.[1] The construction of facilities and maintenance of programs became a factor of consequence in financial circles.

Limited but growing attention was given by women's magazines to the playtime clothes of boarding school or college girls and society matrons of the second decade of the century, and fashion experts of the twenties noted the increasing determination of women to share in the outdoor recreations of men. Designers seized on the popularization of sports styles for devotees of riding, golf, tennis, swimming, and boating: "When women of high social standing indicate their approval of a type of sports attire, it becomes safe for us to turn our creative and productive resources toward that merchandise." Madame Frances was credited with the major role in the creation of this new fad, while Don Diego, Nicholas Haz, and other designers gained recognition through styles for bathing, ski, and skating outfits. Pleated golf skirts, short-sleeved "jumpers," tennis frocks, and riding costumes were popular, and in 1923 a fashion editor could claim "sports clothes are today the usual thing."[2]

Abbreviated pants were prohibited by New York's Metropolitan Golf Association, but "shorts" were accepted on Chicago's links by 1934 and steadily won universal approval after "Bunny" Austin and Dorothy Round dared to wear them at Wimbledon and Helen Jacobs abandoned pretty billowy skirts for more practical attire. This is but a later chapter in the feminine revolt against nineteenth-century dress which goes back to the bloomer fad, cycling dresses, and Annette Kellerman's prewar one-piece swimming suits as well as to the reforms achieved through Parisian and Hollywood styles. Sweaters, sports jackets, sports clothes, hunting and fishing attire, and all the novel forms of sporting fashion have stemmed in great part from the sporting habits of the last several decades.

Newspapers increasingly recognized the appeal of sport in building up local circulation, while the nationwide syndication of AP or UP releases and the words of prominent columnists gave a new dimension in sports reporting. Stanley Woodward credited the sporting pages of the average metropolitan newspaper with attracting approximately one-quarter of all its subscribers and purchasers.

Virtually all popular magazines and a number of the professional journals, both historical and literary, featured sport, at least occasionally, whether in the form of news, fiction, reminiscences, or pictures. During the past decade such journals as *Sports Digest* (1944), *Sport* (1946), *Sports Graphic* (1946), *Sports Album* (1948), *Sports Leaders* (1948), *Sport Life* (1948), *Sports World* (1949) and *Sports Illustrated* (1954) have made their appearance. *The Sporting News, Baseball Magazine, Football Annual, Ring, Yachting, Motor Sport,* and other publications comb all the gossip of the sporting world; horse racing addicts and the gambling fraternity have been the source of revenue for dozens of form sheets which have capitalized on the success of the old New York *Morning Telegram* and the *Daily Racing Form.* Book publishers have increasingly recognized the commercial value of sport, A.S. Barnes and G.P. Putnam leading the field in recent years. The sports sections of public libraries is largely a development of the past decade.

Since 1920 the pageantry of sport has strengthened its grip on the American people and great spectacles (like the Kentucky Derby, the Indianapolis Speedway championship, the Gold Cup, the Akron soapbox derby, the Cleveland Air Races, or the Rose, Sugar, Cotton, and Orange Bowls) attract thousands of visitors whose bulging purses bring joy to local merchants, hotel owners, chambers of commerce, managers of nightclubs and theaters, restauranteurs, and concessionaires with their hot dogs, peanuts, and pennants. The Harry Stevens food chain, developing out of a score card concession in Columbus around 1890, has made a fortune from sports crowds. It has often been only through concessions that professional clubs have been able to show a profit. For example, the Chicago Cubs sold 1,368,876 hot dogs during the 1946 season and made a total profit of $279,000 from 24 concession items. Fourteen clubs in the majors alone reported net income from concessions in 1929 at $582,800, in 1939 at $850,300, and in 1950 at $2,936,300.[3]

Thousands of full-time and part-time jobs have been created in such varied fields as education, professional promotion, industry, retail sale, public recreation, journalism, radio, and television. Among those who derive a living at least in part from sport are physical education teachers, athletic directors, playground leaders, camp counselors, managers, coaches, trainers, officials, professional athletes, promoters, ticket agents, club owners, horse breeders, columnists, authors, script writers, radio and television commentators, manufacturers, and employees, salesmen, maintenance personnel, vendors, and, of course, professional gamblers. Western Union, American Telephone and Telegraph, the radio networks, and motion picture theater chains, construction engineers, and real estate agencies have constantly profited from the public enthusiasm, as has virtually every important chamber of commerce in the United States. Bus companies and railroads have increasingly capitalized on sports crowds since World War I, running special excursions to Big League games, offering combination tickets to collegiate football spectacles, or transporting ball clubs and barnstorming groups from city to city. Special ski trains operating out of northern cities have been largely responsible for the upsurge in winter sports enthusiasm since the Depression, much to the delight of sporting goods dealers and managers of winter resorts.

The technological revolution which so altered the social patterns of American life in the nineteenth and early twentieth centuries continued to exert a tremendous influence on sport. Mass ownership of automobiles eased the problems of hunters and anglers and made possible the weekend migrations of ribbon-bedecked caravans to high school and college games. When Epinard raced Sarazen at Latonia, Kentucky, in 1924, the bulging hotels and private homes of Cincinnati let loose a flood of visitors who jammed the trolleys, taxis, and private cars in "one long and unending stream" while others arrived by special trains from all over the Midwest. Garage men in the Windy City estimated that the Dempsey-Tunney fight of 1927 drew "$250,000,000 worth of cars . . . to Chicago bearing passengers for the fight," while special trains pulled in from Los Angeles, New Orleans, Tulsa, Akron, Pittsburgh, New York, St. Louis, Nashville, and points in Texas and Florida, and a few even came by air.

Since the twenties this trend has steadily developed. Air travel has been taken up by most of the major colleges and professional clubs since World War II, thereby opening up new opportunities in intersectional and international sport. While revolutionizing the sporting scene, despite the continuing of sectional conferences, transportation has thus brought sport further into the realm of business as crowds jam gas stations, restaurants, bars, motels, tourist homes, hotels, theaters, and department stores.

The business side of sport is also reflected in the great increase in gate receipts, small as that factor may be in relation to revenue from admission receipts in the motion picture industry. By 1930 Harvard, Yale, and Pennsylvania all had gate receipts in excess of one million dollars, and the past two decades have seen an astronomic rise in the revenue of such universities as Notre Dame, Ohio State, Tennessee, Kentucky, Southern California, and the University of Texas. While expenditures have often surpassed receipts in many colleges, this was often due to expansion of facilities, high salaries, generous scholarships, and other factors which cannot obscure the significance of the large-scale business operations of most of the major athletic powers. That Yale's athletic plant of 1931 (consisting of a $4,300,000 Payne Whitney Memorial Gymnasium and facilities and fields covering 830 acres) or Michigan's extensive system have been of benefit to their respective institutions can hardly be argued.

In 1924 there were less than 20 stadiums in America, exclusive of race tracks and speedways, seating more than 20,000 spectators, but in 1952 the figure had risen to at least 130.[4] The WPA program helped in the construction of many stadiums and recreation areas during the years of depression, but wartime shortages and postwar priorities limited the building of new and expansion of old facilities until recently, and war memorials have often taken the shape of a gymnasium or stadium rather than to repeat the uninspired statues so common after 1918.

Salaries of players and coaches rose remarkably during the twenties. Upton Sinclair railed against the $10,000 salary of the Stanford coach in 1922 because it exceeded that of any professor in the history of the university.[5] Knute Rockne, Dana X. Bible, Glenn Warner, Clark Shaughnessy, Jock Sutherland, Wallace Wade, Bernie Bierman, Fritz Crisler, Robert Neyland, and Frank Leahy earned salaries far in excess of the highest of the twenties, while their staff assistants frequently were more highly paid than most professors. The income issue embarrassed many university administrations and, in the case of state institutions, some governors. Little did the critics of sport in the 1920's (considering Babe Ruth or Jack Dempsey exceptions who did not disturb the public's economy-mindedness) foresee the day when outstanding performers in every professional sport would earn more annually than many business executives. That an outstanding sports reporter, often syndicated from coast to coast, might receive more than $50,000 per annum, was also beyond their ken.

While it is all but impossible to estimate the total annual outlay of the American people on sport or expenditures incidental to sport, figures presented by Robert R. Doane indicate the trend in recreation between 1860 and 1920:[6]

| | National expenditures | Education | Recreation |
|---|---|---|---|
| 1860 | $  4,548,000,000 | $     42,000,000 | $     11,000,000 |
| 1890 | 10,987,000,000 | 289,000,000 | 130,000,000 |
| 1920 | 70,508,000,000 | 1,347,000,000 | 2,000,000,000 |

By 1916 recreation costs had surpassed those of education, at the end of the 1920's about 5.5 percent of all expenditures were of this kind, and had more than doubled the outlay for education, and in 1937 it was estimated that the public spent 8.12 percent of the national income on leisure-time pursuits, more than the Treasury Department collected from all tax sources.[7] Sporting goods comprised a small proportion of these expenditures, however, and from 1909 to the Depression they annually consisted of only about 5 percent of the total. Census reports (which excluded firearms, ammunition, and such unclassified items as playground equipment, motors, boats, yachts, bicycles, etc.) reveal the value of manufactures, which serve only as a rough index of expenditures:[8]

| Year | Establish- ments | Capital | Average no. of workers over the year | Value of manufactures |
|---|---|---|---|---|
| 1880 | 86 | $1,444,750 | 1,401 | $  1,556,258 |
| 1890 | 136 | 1,693,776 | 2,008 | 2,709,449 |
| 1900 | 143 | 2,015,437 | 2,225 | 3,628,496 |
| 1909 | 180 | 6,617,000 | 5,321 | 11,052,000 |
| 1919 | 188 | . . . . . . . . | . . . . | 22,839,991 |
| 1929 | 242 | . . . . . . . . | 10,793 | 58,289,000 |
| 1939 | 350 | . . . . . . . . | 13,816 | 64,754,000 |

The Depression decade saw the value of products fall off from $58,289,000 in 1929 to $25,267,000 in 1933 and then rise to $44,461,000 in 1937 and $64,754,000 in 1939. According to J. Frederic Dewhurst's *America's Needs and Resources,* consumer purchases of sports equipment dropped more than $200,000,000 between 1929 and 1933, recovering steadily thereafter.[9] By 1936 *Business Week* noted a boom in sporting goods due to a popular reaction against years of depression, to the exten- sion of leisure time, and to the availability of more money. Prosperity returned to many of the haunts of the sporting fraternity as bowling alleys and billiard parlors reported receipts in 1939 of more than $87,000,000, horse and dog tracks took in over $43,000,000, and 276 professional baseball parks sold tickets to the sum of nearly $25,000,000.

Numerous competitors appeared to rival A.G. Spalding, among the foremost being Wilson and MacGregor-Goldsmith, followed by the Pennsylvania Rubber Company, Brook Shoes, and Riddell. Name brands appeared — King Sportswear, Hodgman Athletic Clothing, and Catalina and Jansen in swimming suits, as well as numerous sweater and T-shirt concerns. One of the significant developments has been a greater volume of over-the-counter trade, with the "middle masses" in the medium- and low-priced field adding a new dimension to the former dependence on team outfitting and on the leisured classes. When one remembers that the value of sporting and athletic equipment rose from $23,839,991 in 1920 to $163,039,000 in 1947, it is possible to get at least an idea of the development of this specialized branch of manufacture.

Frank Menke liberally estimated an annual sports bill of $4,000,000,-000 for the years 1938 to 1941, including travel costs and all kinds of incidental expenses for such costly recreations as fishing, hunting, motor boating, golf, bowling, and skiing. Recent estimates indicate the rapid increase in expenditures since World War II. Receipts of bowling alleys, pool and billiard parlors, race tracks, sports promoters and commercial operators exceeded half a billion dollars in 1948, and this did not include school or college contests. Some three million skiers spend about $200,-000,000, yachting and sailing enthusiasts $600,000,000, and hunters an estimated $4,000,000,000 on equipment, transportation, lodging and other aspects of their favorite sports. Claims of more than $1,000,000,000 annually for sports clothes have been made by the clothing industry. Whatever the amount that the public spends on sport, directly and indirectly, it has become a factor of considerable importance in the national economy.[10]

Since World War I business has recognized the advertising value of sport in countless ways. Department stores, oil companies, cigarette concerns, radio and television manufacturers, automobile companies, and soft drink distributors like Coca Cola and Canada Dry have featured exciting moments, but the real promoters of sports advertising have been the Gillette Razor Company and the brewers of Budweiser, Schlitz, Falstaff, Miller, Pabst, and other beers. Radio and television have garnered much of this trade. Vacation centers in Florida, California, and the land of winter sports lured tourists with their sports attractions. During the hectic boom days of the 1920's the Miami Chamber of Commerce boasted:

The Climate Supreme, The Tourist's Delight, The Motorist's Mecca, The Fisherman's Paradise, The Golfer's Wonderland, The Polo

Player's Pride, The Surf Bather's Joy, The Aviator's Dreamland, The Yachtsman's Rendezvous, The Tennis Player's Happiness, The Horse Racing Utopia, The Hi-Li Player's Haven. . . . Truly the Outdoor City.

Housing developments and apartment projects in the twenties featured sporting facilities as well as accessibility to churches, schools, and theaters. New York real estate men stressed the availability of facilities in residential areas and the golf courses, swimming pools, tennis courts and playgrounds at the Towers in Jackson Heights and the Shellball Apartments in Kew Gardens, as well as Soundview, Oliver Cromwell, Kingston Gardens, Fleetwood Hills, Wingrey, and other projects. Later federal, municipal, and private housing developments considered the problem of recreation areas, one of the most interesting of all plans being the model community designed by Frank Lloyd Wright and displayed at the exhibition of his work in 1951 at Florence, Italy.[11]

Nor was business alone in capitalizing on this mode of advertising. The armed services stressed the athletic side of military life and the Marine Corps discovered: "Other advantages than that of the attraction of wearing a uniform and serving the flag had to be found in order to interest new men sufficiently to join the organization. Sports, educational advantages, and demonstrations to arouse public interest were hit upon as the necessary inducements."[12] Moving picture magazines found it desirable to photograph film stars at sport and play, schools and colleges publicized their athletic programs, and the appeal of competitive games was recognized by institutions of every kind.

## Industrial Recreation and Organized Labor

Industrial recreation has surged forward in recent decades, despite the suspicion which continues between labor unions and management. Some observers believe that industrial recreation is in its infancy even now, and that it will flourish only with the attainment of mutual confidence between labor and management. Teams representing steel companies and shipyards competed for the national soccer football championships in the 1920's, while Carnegie Steel, Goodyear Tire and Rubber, Hershey Chocolate, mining companies, and other industries offered club houses, playgrounds, and athletic fields to their employees. Oakland, California, Jackson, Michigan, and Akron, Ohio, were leaders in setting the pace in industrial recreation programs in 1920; Oakland's Industrial Athletic Association attracted teams from automobile, electric, lumber, paint, gas, and box companies to its volleyball games, and motors, electric, cotton, and lamp factories entered teams in the basketball tourneys.[13]

In 1925 a survey by the Metropolitan Life Insurance Company listed recreational programs under the sponsorship of the Paterson Industrial AA, including the National Cash Register Co., Endicott-Johnson Corp., American Rolling Mill Co., Sears Roebuck, Goodyear Tire and Rubber Co., General Motors, General Electric, Westinghouse Electric and Manufacturing Co., and United States Steel.[14] The United States Bureau of Labor found in a 1927 survey of 319 companies that athletic clubs were maintained by 59 industries, baseball diamonds or athletic fields by 157, baseball teams by 223, tennis courts by 50, golf courses by 13, soccer teams by 41.[15]

Mathew Woll of the AFL and other observers contended that participation in sport by workers was on the decline: industries reputedly dropped sports programs; movies, parks, and motoring distracted workers; and municipally sponsored recreation filled the gap as plants abandoned their programs.[16] While workers may have lost some of their former enthusiasm for weekend ball games and picnics, industrial recreation prospered in most areas just as it did in New York where the Metropolitan Industrial League included Standard Oil, New York Edison, the Mack Motor Company, Interborough Rapid Transit, the leading insurance companies, and other concerns.

Industrial sport was highlighted by the interest of American railroads. The YMCA had encouraged athletics on the railroad since the late nineteenth century, but after World War I the Illinois Central, the Pennsylvania, the Louisville & Nashville, and the Missouri Pacific lines, among other systems, all showed a growing awareness of sport in the field of recreation. The *Illinois Central Magazine* featured "Sports Over the System," the *Louisville & Nashville Employes' Magazine* ran "The Way We Play," and the *Missouri Pacific Lines Magazine* carried a "Sports Along the Line" department. A "Railroad Baseball Championship of the World" was projected by the Pennsylvania and the Missouri Pacific lines, the New York Central had its many athletic associations, an American Railway Bowling Association was organized, railroad YMCA teams were promoted, and individual systems had their golf, basketball, tennis and gun clubs as well as ball teams and bowling associations, which were very popular among women employees.[17]

Some attention was given to recreational programs in industry by leading authorities on industrial management. Companies were advised to avoid any interference with employee organizations, even when the concern paid for club houses and facilities. Richard H. Lansburgh pointed out many of the problems to be faced: the need for a satisfactory wage scale so that workers would not demand that the money poured into recreation be diverted to their pay envelopes; the good will of employees; the internal politics which would inevitably arise; maintenance of bonafide amateur teams; and the distractions from routine work. "In small towns, where the company team is in reality the town team, these objections are frequently outweighed by the good-will which the team will build up in the community." Lansburgh recognized, however, the potential value of improved spirit, health, and team play, "that most valuable asset to any industrial concern," as well as the tendency to develop plant leaders. The real worth of plant recreation, except where keyed to a community program, was also questioned. William B. Cornell, however, contended that pleasant, healthful recreation saved the worker from agitators and "corner orators painting for him fancied wrongs," and he championed the improved morale and teamwork, which is "the backbone of business just as it is in football or baseball."[18]

Industrial recreation has grown rapidly since the onset of the Great Depression. Chicago Industrial Recreation Surveys of the late 1930's revealed that almost half of the plants studied maintained recreational programs, most of a limited nature, that 85 percent of all recreation was in the form of athletics, that approximately one-third of the companies had at least a softball or bowling team, and that industrial recreation was still growing. A nationwide poll of 639 companies revealed in 1940 that 245 had recreation programs. Of these 87 percent supported bowling, 74 percent softball, 54 percent basketball, 40 percent golf, and 34 percent baseball. Typical of the better company program was that of General Electric in Schenectady during the war, where employees had lighted playing fields, a gym, and bowling alleys; the Lynn plant had 50 softball teams; and other G.E. plants sponsored golf leagues.[19]

Postwar surveys reveal a decided tendency toward the promotion of industrial recreation programs, particularly by trade unions. The United Automobile Workers established its Recreation Department in 1937. President Walter Reuther of the UAW and William Green of the AFL encouraged community as well as union programs. Sports fans of the fifties recall the spectacular Phillips Oilers of the National Industrial Basketball League, which included teams sponsored by General Motors, Goodyear Tire and Rubber, and other concerns. Championships sponsored by the National Baseball Congress, the Athletic Institute, the American Bowling Congress, and the Amateur Softball Association attracted hundreds of participating company teams. According to the *Industrial Sports Journal* there were more than 20,000,000 employees participating in industrial sports in 1951. At mid-century it was claimed that "between six and seven thousand companies, labor unions, and employee associations are known to be active in promoting sports," while industrial recreation in some form was sponsored by "as many as twenty thousand organizations."[20]

The pioneer work of the International Ladies Garment Workers Union in the second decade, encouraged by David Dubinsky from the 1920's onward, was imitated by recreational groups throughout organized labor. By mid-century the ILGWU had seventy locals, joint boards, and councils with sports programs. When a furor arose over American participation in the 1936 Olympic Games, a number of unions organized the World Labor Athletic Carnival in protest, attracting nearly 25,000 spectators to its games held simultaneously with those in Berlin.[21] As part of a left-wing protest against American entry in the Games, *Sport Call* (the official organ of the Workers Sports League of America) editorialized: "International brotherhood, closer friendly relations and better understanding between peoples of the world's nations is the objective of all Olympics. Capitalism and capitalistic sports organizations have failed in this respect and have only themselves to blame for this failure. All capitalistic governments are teachers of nationalism and some countries reach fanatical ends in teaching it. . . . The only truly brotherly relations between nations and peoples of the world are brought about by organized labor and labor sports organizations."[22] Labor was in an aggressive, combative mood in the middle thirties, and unions made special appeals to unity in their ranks:

> We believe firmly and unshakably that a labor sports movement can be built only on a pure and unadulterated labor basis and in complete independence and freedom from any shackles whatsoever. We believe that just as genuine trade unionism can flourish only if it is built by and for organized labor, so a labor sports movement can plant its roots and grow healthily in labor soil only and without looking for guidance from outsiders. . . . Any decision that commits the trade unions and their sports movement to the AAU and other groups outside of Labor's ranks will greatly retard the growth of a genuine labor sports movement in our country.[23]

Few among the mass of American labor suspected the motives of either organized sport or management with anything resembling this left-wing standpoint. Employee participation since the Depression was, to a great extent, in competitive games. While a small segment might stress "the fallacy of capitalistic sport which teaches rivalry in competition between clubs and countries," thereby breeding egotism and nationalism, the ranks of American labor continued to engage in competition on the ball field, the basketball court, and the bowling alley.

Union objectives in industrial sport were stressed in a 1940 statement issued by the Committee on Recreation and Athletics of the Amalgamated Clothing Workers of America, which endorsed "sport and recreation offered through union channels:"

The Department of Cultural Activities during the past two years has encouraged the various locals and joint boards to sponsor sports, athletics, and other group games for the benefit of the members. . . . Group recreation and sports of all kinds are of the utmost physical and social benefit to workers in modern industry; at the same time they are too frequently beyond the means of our members as individuals. The union is in a position to bridge the gap by offering facilities and direction on a cooperative basis. . . . Inter-union matches and competitions should be arranged whenever feasible, so that union members in various centers can meet each other in the friendly, constructive atmosphere which sport competition provides.[24]

New problems arose after World War II, especially in the migratory movement of many workers into suburban areas far from the plant, but the unions continued to sponsor recreational and sport programs.

Industries undertook recreation programs with three main ideas in mind: fostering of better feeling between employer and employee, the increase of productive power among contented workers, and the advertising value of athletic teams. Widespread reluctance of management to undertake recreational programs developed lest labor be alienated. Competitive bidding for charters in local leagues by both management and union caused friction at times. A company might seek a charter in order that it may blazon the firm's name on the team's sports jackets or so that its name will appear in the press, whereas the union local might have the same purpose in view: to bring it publicity and an increase in membership.

The crucial issue still perplexing those who are concerned with the penetration of sport into industry is whether or not it has benefited labor-management relations. In 1919 A.H. Wayman's report on Carnegie Steel Company employees concluded that industrial athletics had led to an improvement in their physical alertness and their spirit of true sportsmanship as well as to a "closer welding of the heterogeneous groups of employees, together with a closer and more friendly relationship between workers, foremen and superintendents."[25] The Metropolitan Life Insurance Company survey of 1925 recognized that competitive sports were easy to organize among employees, that they stimulated interest rapidly, that they contributed to company morale, and that they provided amusement for a large part of the population in small towns. However, the report found that, for the most part, competitive sports appealed mostly to younger workers and American-born employees. The Labor Bureau reported in 1928 a need for sports programs, maintaining that the specialization and monotony of work in industry made it "imperative" to provide an incentive to workers, "and nothing, it seems, can better meet this need for self-expression than the friendly rivalry and interest furnished by competitive sports and games."[26] A 1940 study, finding that indoor recreation appealed more to weary workers than outdoor sports, noted that track meets, baseball games, and other contests on both an interdepartmental and an interplant basis had developed "desirable morale among the workers."[27]

The chief deterrent to the spread of industrial sport has been the recurrent charge of paternalism. *Personnel Journal* recognized that, above all else, no matter what the system of industrial recreation, "It must not be paternalistic."[28] Organized unions were frequently wary of management's motives in sponsoring programs: "Employers have been reluctant to assume direction of the leisure-time activities of their employees because this step, even more than other phases of personnel and welfare work, is open to the charge of paternalism."[29] One survey maintained that "progressive union leaders have always fostered intralabor recreation as a powerful socializing force, both in arousing the interest of nonunion workers and in keeping a union group intact."[30] The void has at times been filled with joint promotion by unions and by management, but the burden has been increasingly absorbed by union locals or the national union itself.

## Capitalism and Sport in Perspective

There are those critics who maintain that sport has found capitalism a most fertile soil for the growth of the athletic movement, that our industrial civilization has warped sport to suit its own purposes, and that organized games have been driven relentlessly into commercialized channels with the profit motive supreme. Some have maintained that athletic games have been scourged with a trend toward uniformity, and that they have been stimulated by a general reaction of frustrated workers against the machine. Capitalism has also been accused of encouraging sport in order to maintain the *status quo,* to quell youthful radicalism, and to mold "bourgeois" forms of recreation. This attack increased in the two decades following the Wall Street collapse of 1929. John R. Tunis, a noted sports authority and crusader against commercialization, maintained: "The American attitude toward athletics is simply a part of the general attitude toward life in this country, the belief that civilization consists chiefly in bigger and better Buicks." Ferdinand Lundberg emphasized the extent to which "America's 60 Families" lavished fortunes on private swimming pools and thoroughbred horses, while the Du Pont family owned thirty yachts, the Forbes family thirteen, and the Vanderbilt family ten. Aristocracy of sport no longer rules the headlines, but the conspicuous consumption described a half century ago by Thorstein Veblen is far from dead.[31]

Others argue with great conviction that the rise of sport in modern times was originally motivated by a general desire to react against the mechanization of life. Lewis Mumford tells us that sport alone provides the "glorification of chance and the unexpected" which was extruded by the "mechanical routine in industry," and Arnold Toynbee observes that organized games and sports are "a conscious attempt to counterbalance the soul-destroying specialization which the division of labour under Industrialism entails." These analysts of contemporary society complain, on the other hand, that sport has merged into the pattern of our industrial civilization. Professionalism, the profit motive, commercialization, or whatever other charges may be levelled at sport in capitalistic society reflect the final culmination of industrialization.

"Thus sport," says Mumford, "which began originally, perhaps, as a spontaneous reaction against the machine, has become one of the mass-duties of the machine age. It is a part of that universal regimentation of life—for the sake of private profits or nationalistic exploit—from which its excitement provides a temporary and only a superficial release. Sport has turned out, in short, to be one of the least effective reactions against the machine. There is only one other reaction less effective in its final result: the most ambitious as well as the most disastrous. I mean war." Professor Toynbee agrees in part with Mumford's view in his contention that "this attempt to adjust life to Industrialism through sport has been partially defeated because the spirit and rhythm of Industrialism have invaded and infected sport itself." [32]

Our capitalistic-industrial society, it is claimed, has molded sport in its own image, and the source of much of this trouble is laid at the door of the college and the university. Upton Sinclair, during the boom years of the twenties, attacked an educational system wherein "college athletics, under the spur of commercialism, has become a monstrous cancer, which is rapidly eating out the moral and intellectual life of our educational institutions." [33] Critics of the depression decade contended that the capitalist had struggled to bring sport into his own hands, but they seem to have flaunted the history of American philanthropy. Gifts to colleges and universities have been, in general, in fields far from sport—in the founding of buildings or of professorial chairs and scholarships in engineering, the social studies, law, medicine, chemistry, and the physical sciences. President Angell noted that Yale's greatest expansion came in a period of infrequent football victories and that Harvard's most rapid growth occurred during a long series of defeats by Yale. According to President Hutchins, the University of Chicago along with Harvard and Yale led the list of gifts and bequests to colleges and universities between 1920 and 1937 despite the unpleasant fact that the "records of these universities on the gridiron were highly irregular, to say the least." Among the colleges Williams, Wesleyan, and Bowdoin were foremost, each with more than $5,000,000 in gifts. Deriving his information from a survey by the John Price Jones Corporation, Hutchins concluded, "Men of wealth were undeterred by the inconsequential athletic status of these colleges; it does not appear that philanthropists were attracted to their rivals by the glorious victories they scored over them."[34]

Commercialization of intercollegiate sport has mounted into a movement of social importance, however, and here the American system appears more vulnerable. Alumni groups have been notorious in the raising of funds for athletic scholarships or in recruiting athletes for their alma mater. The controversy in academic circles, aroused by the Carnegie Report of 1929, stirred educators, sociologists, and social planners to a deeper interest in our nationwide recreational problems. One of the strongest indictments of capitalistic society was that of Jerome Davis, who was convinced that "mal-creation" surpassed "re-creation" in American society: "Recreation in a capitalist culture tends to take on the color of the cultural base. This base is profit seeking. The central drive is not to provide wholesome re-creation of the lives and happiness of the people, but rather to secure the maximum amount of profit for the few."[35]

From 1850 to the present the history of sport has been one of organization, along with which has come a high degree of regimentation. Each sport creates its governing bodies, its rules committees, and its codes of regulation. As a result games have been standardized to a large degree in this relentless trend toward organization, but discipline and order have emerged out of this process. Without organization sport might well have remained the cult of our social aristocracy, enjoyed by the masses with only a vicarious or passive interest. Nor have Americans been regimented to the extent that variety and originality have been eliminated, for they have developed variations such as "bounce-out," softball, six-man football and "touch football," and the infinite variations of play patterns on the playing field as well as in the city street have continued to fascinate the sports fans, both young and old. Competitive games thrive on strategy and the element of surprise, and the American sportsman has shown an ingenuity which belies the legend that our games stifle all sense of originality.

Athletic equipment and sporting facilities have often been achieved through a public spirit seeking remedies for the evils of industrial society. Furthermore, both the nature of the business community and a frankly mercenary spirit is responsible for the confiscation of limited play areas and sandlots by real estate promoters, apartment house owners, and merchants. Nevertheless, no other society in history has attained such a plenitude of material goods directed to the sporting inclinations of the people.

Critics have contended that totalitarian governments have accomplished "more than we in making leisure a public responsibility and in furnishing recreation to their masses,"[36] but no statistical study of any country has ever shown anything to rival the stadiums, gymnasiums, resorts, pools, playgrounds, and other facilities which in several decades have appeared on the American scene. Much of this achievement lies, of course, in the reform spirit which reappears throughout our history on both the local and the national level, where public concern over education, conservation, health, unemployment, and juvenile delinquency has led to the development of our recreational resources. Nor is the capitalism of the 1950's the ruthless and anarchistic struggle of the post-Civil War generation.

Sport and the capitalistic spirit do seem to have much in common. The spirit of initiative, the need to struggle with one's own physical and mental powers, the premium set on team play and cooperation, the encouragement of competitive spirit are characteristic of both institutions. Undoubtedly there have been interacting influences between business and sport as far as competition is concerned, but the desire to rival and surpass has origins far more remote than are to be found in modern capitalism and it has had effects every bit as profound on other forms of culture throughout history.

# Chapter 12

# Social Democracy and the Playing Fields

# Chapter 12

# Social Democracy and the Playing Fields

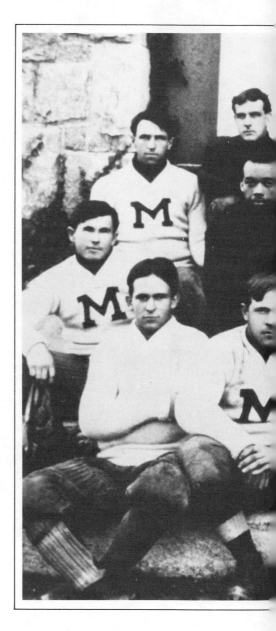

The contributions of sport to social democracy have been significant. With admirable facilities, variable terrain, and climates for every breed of sportsman, the United States offers unexcelled opportunities to devotees from country, town, or city. Except for the physical education programs of school and college, where health is of prime consideration, Americans have a freedom of choice to play or not to play at their own discretion. The private club and the social clique still cling to policies of exclusiveness, but they are of far less importance to the national sporting scene than they were at the beginning of the century. An angler is free to seek out the solitude of a mountain stream and a hunter may track down his prey without the companionship of others, but most lovers of sport are gregarious in nature and tend to join clubs, travel in groups, or participate in competitive team games.

Many forces have long been at work in molding the mixed peoples of the Old into a unified nation in the New World. Our democratic heritage, the law, the school, the newspaper, and technological innovations in transportation and communication have all contributed. And it is through the universal appeal of sport that much of this feeling of kinship and fellowship has prospered in the twentieth century. Just as intramural, interscholastic, and intercollegiate athletics encouraged *esprit de corps,* just as church leagues crossed denominational lines, and just as industrial recreation has usually contributed to the making of happier and more cooperative workers, minority groups have found in sport a process of Americanization and an instrument of social equality. And there have been other values added to our way of life despite the more sordid aspects of gambling —values which, though hard to measure, have added greatly to the development of the individual and of the democratic community.

## The State and the Law

In the development of sport both as a business and a form of recreation it was inevitable that the government and the courts should become involved. Except in the suppression of gambling or illegal amusements and in the maintenance of the Puritan sabbath, Americans traditionally looked upon sport as private in nature, to be regulated by private governing bodies. The public school movement and municipal recreation undermined this point of view to a limited extent, but the same prejudice lingered on in clubs and social agencies, colleges and industries. Boxing and racing laws had been enacted in many areas prior to World War I, but it was only from the twenties onward that the interest of the state and federal governments became significant.[1]

Following the Federal League case of 1915 and the furor caused by the Chicago "Black Sox" scandal of 1919-1920, the public waited anxiously for the decision in Federal Baseball Club of Baltimore v. National League of Baseball Clubs, rendered for a unanimous court by Justice Oliver Wendell Holmes in 1922:

> The business is giving exhibitions of baseball, which are purely state affairs. It is true that, in order to attain for these exhibitions the great popularity that they have achieved, competitions must be arranged between clubs from different cities and states. But the fact that, in order to give the exhibitions, the Leagues must induce free persons to cross state lines, and must arrange and pay for their doing so, is not enough to change the character of the business. . . . That which, in its consummation, is not commerce, does not become commerce among the states because the transportation that we have mentioned takes place . . . the restrictions by contract that prevented the plaintiff from getting players to break their bargains, and the other conduct charged against the defendants, were not an interference with commerce among the states.[2]

This decision, stating that baseball did not constitute commerce, reversed the District Supreme Court's judgement of $264,000.

Occasional tirades were made against the baseball monopoly through the passing years. Representative Sol Bloom toyed with the idea of entering a bill in the House to regulate baseball under the Interstate Commerce Act despite the Supreme Court decision of 1922. Fiorello La Guardia introduced a bill in the House advocating a 90 percent federal tax on sales of professional baseball players. When Raymond J. Cannon of Wisconsin, in the era of the New Deal, requested Attorney General Homer Cummings to start antitrust proceedings against the owners, Cummings refused to act because of the 1922 decision rendered by Justice Holmes. Although television rights, interstate farm systems of clubs, and other issues presented many new problems to the federal government in the years following World War II, the courts have continued to act cautiously in the regulation of professional sports.

Nor was the baseball world negligent in trying to prevent future action against its centralized control. Players had their own committee to consult with the owners, and were guaranteed that anyone in Major League baseball must receive a salary not less than $6000, which did much to squelch the old charges of "slavery" and "bondage." Scaled wages were arranged for every rank of minor league. Baseball men seemed to be generally content with their status, for they consistently repudiated efforts in the postwar years to unionize players. Robert Murphy tried to organize the American Baseball Guild in 1946, but the Big Leagues in that year appeased ball players by voting a minimum of $6000 salary with a maximum cut in one year of 25 percent. A pension fund, spending money on training trips, and other concessions were made, much of the credit for which goes to Larry MacPhail. Organized baseball was dragged into court despite its wariness of litigation, however. Cases of every kind from damage suits to antitrust violation were taken to court consistently in post-war years. The Mexican baseball raids of Jorge Pasquel led to legal action on the part of disillusioned players seeking to return to organized baseball in the Big Leagues.[3]

The long controversy over the social desirability of the ring also involved many a governor and many a state legislature. The Walker Law of 1920 gave the green light to prize fighting in New York. Governor A.J. Groesbeck rigorously enforced an antiboxing law in Michigan, but Governor Gifford Pinchot of Pennsylvania approved of a 1923 law creating a State Athletic Commission whose principle concern was to be the control for boxing and wrestling. With the successful return of professional fights to New York, Philadelphia, and Chicago, the fight game had acquired the legal recognition vital to its popularity. During depression years criticism eased off, and, due in part to public interest in the career of Joe Louis and in part to the growing national enthusiasm for sport, the United States Senate passed unanimously a bill to permit shipment in interstate commerce of prize fight films. Once again the state had come to the aid of sport.

Gambling made a penetration of the sporting world at every level from school to college and professional ranks. Scandals rocked the National Football League, National Hockey League, boxing circles, and inter-collegiate basketball. Even the United States Golf Association declared war on pool sellers and bookmakers in 1920 and issued occasional warnings through the years. Following World War II many states enacted laws making the "fixing" of games a criminal offense, but the professional gambler continued to reap a golden harvest.

When Grover Cleveland Alexander stifled a Yankee uprising and won the seventh game of the 1926 World Series for the Cardinals, betting commissioners along Broadway and in Wall Street claimed that there occurred the greatest turnover of bets in the history of sport. Some estimates reached as high as $20,000,000 on this one event. It was little wonder that state governments during the Depression decided to fill their empty treasuries by legalizing and taxing pari-mutuel betting at race tracks. Zechariah Chafee commented in 1937 on the new role of the state in the regulation of racing: "The State of Rhode Island and Providence Plantations acquired less than four years ago a large financial interest in betting at horse races. . . . Rhode Island now draws nearly an eighth of its total tax revenues from a business which before 1934 was an offense against public policy punishable by a prison sentence." In a conflict between the governor and the operator of Narragansett Park martial law was declared and the track shut down. Recognizing the need for a general housecleaning, Chafee compared this case to the Dreyfuss affair which exposed corruption in the French army.[4]

Betting presented its problems but the vested interests of state governments could not permit them to ignore the revenue which leaped upward through the prosperity of the turf during World War II. By 1946 about $1,760,000,000 was handled by the totalisators at pari-mutuel tracks and an additional $4,500,000,000 by the bookmakers. The Senate Crime Investigating Committee estimated that more than $20,000,000,000 was gambled annually at mid-century, and, although Las Vegas, Reno, Miami, and other centers account for much of this, sport is perhaps the major element. The postwar years have witnessed an increased interest on the part of state and federal governments in the regulation of and in revenue from sports events, either as amusement taxes or percentage taxes on betting operations.

Attacks on the location of racing tracks and pari-mutuel betting have been a constant irritant to promoters of the turf, but the legalization of racing in most states since the Depression and the elimination of the bookmaking menace in many cities finds the sport of kings in a relatively secure position at the present time. Cleanup campaigns, forced on turf authorities from Franklin Roosevelt's intervention at Saratoga Springs in 1930 to Thomas E. Dewey's concern with Yonkers Raceway in 1953, have helped preserve rather than undermine the turf world. Even the religious press found it hard to unite in opposition to the gambling problem. In 1933 the *Christian Observer* proclaimed, "To debauch the morals of the people and destroy many of the youth of the land for the sake of raising a million or so each year in taxes would seem to be reenacting the old story of Esau selling his birthright for a mess of pottage," while the *Christian Century* admitted three years later, "The only way to save racing as a clean sport is to dissociate it from gambling. The problem seems difficult."

And so it has proved to be. Tracks like Santa Anita, Hialeah, and Belmont Park have had friends in state legislatures who carried considerable political influence. The wire services paid American Telephone and Telegraph more than a quarter of a million dollars over a period of four years in the early thirties. A former newspaper circulation manager named M. L. Annenberg organized the Nationwide News Service in the twenties, and in succeeding decades the Continental Press Service gained a monopoly in the field. The Special Senate Committee to Investigate Organized Crime, headed by Senator Estes Kefauver, reported in 1951: "Everywhere this committee looked among the subdistributors of Continental it found other dummies which are captained and manned by former long-time affiliates of the wire service chiefs and the Capone mob." Wire services were leased for betting on baseball, basketball, and football as well. Western Union was accused in the Committee report of being the "backbone of the wire service which provides gambling information to bookmakers," while some telephone companies have cooperated in granting facilities to gamblers. Over the years since World War I gambling on sport grew to vast proportions, largely through the stealing of information from race tracks by the wire services: "Bookmaking provides the richest source of revenue from gambling operations and the wire service . . . is essential to big-time bookmakers." [5] Today one of the most urgent problems facing state governments is the elimination and prevention of corruption which gambling has brought into the sporting world.

## The Melting Pot of the Playing Fields

After the early 1920's the flow of the foreign-born to this country declined as a result of the new immigration acts, and the problem of the immigrant in our national life soon centered on children who comprised the second or third generation. Although the percentage of foreign-born declined, the immigrant still faced problems of assimilation and amalgamation in American society. Although large national groups continued to live in special sections of the city, men and women of European origin found that Old World customs and traditions often had to be abandoned as their children grew up in the public schools and sought to copy the ways of their friends.

Nowhere was the process of Americanization more in evidence than in sport. Walter Camp, whose enthusiasm was naturally very great, felt that "Americanization is more possible for those who come to our shores through the medium of American sport than in almost any other way." [6] Families whose chief recreation had been folk dancing or the beer garden found the children enthusiastic over athletic games. Many parents failed to understand these games and called them "foolish, wasteful, ridiculous and immoral," while the child rebelled against European forms of play and resented the parent's antagonism toward American games. The boy of the city streets who bumped up against Italian, Polish, Greek, Spanish, Jewish, Swedish and German playmates attended a school in democracy. Old prejudices against the Irish, German, or Swedish youth had been transferred through the years to the Italian, the Slav, or the Jew. In a case study of one Italian boy named "Nick," whose love of baseball aroused his family's anger, it was shown that "the adult members of the family considered baseball a foolish waste of time which should be devoted to hard work. To Nick it was not merely something enjoyable—a pleasurable activity; it was the one thing above all else that could make him an American and give him status. Because of his ability to play baseball the boys quit calling him 'dago.' "[7]

Social democracy of the sandlots became increasingly characteristic of school and college life. The playground movement and the more general availability of sporting facilities in the high school gave youths of all nationalities a greater opportunity to engage in competitive athletics. In 1925 a New York *Times* editor stressed the power of Americanization which lay in sport: "After the public schools, it is in the field of sports that we must look for the principal molding force of a sense of kind, as the sociologists call it. The baseball diamond, which is the nation's great playground, has long reflected this assimilative process." Wondering what the Ku Klux Klan must think of how "this mingling of strains and stocks and creeds should have made much progress on the playing field," he concluded, "A people that plays so well together will not spend much time in hate."

In the great metropolis and the large town the gang has remained a serious problem despite the efforts of private and public agencies, the church and the school, the policeman and the settlement worker. One of the evils of the gang in the big city, where so many organize as athletic clubs, has been the influence exerted by minor politicians. In Chicago it was claimed, "The tendency of the gangs to become athletic clubs has been greatly stimulated by the politicians of the city." The Boys' Clubs of America, the YMCA, the YMHA, police athletic leagues (like that organized in New York in 1931), the Catholic Youth Organization, the Boy Scouts of America, the Campfire Girls, and other organizations have done much to eliminate gang warfare and to bring play opportunities to boys of every race and creed. Although the foreign-born were often bewildered by the importance given to scholastic, collegiate, and professional games, the second generation usually drifted away from the recreational interests of their parents and were swept up in the athletic tide. Many of the older stocks had long since abandoned their hostility to competitive sport. The English and Scotch, both immigrant and visitor, had been most responsible for introducing track athletics, tennis, and golf. Bowling and gymnastics were popularized by the Germans, while skiing was introduced and fostered by the Norwegians. But prior to World War I the Italian, the Greek, the Slav, and the Jew played a minor role in team games.[8]

Physical education programs in the schools and the playground movement of the second decade served as leavening forces in counteracting Old World attitudes. Offspring of southern and eastern European parents gradually took interest. A generation of access to the playgrounds, of growing enthusiasm for school games, of gradually improving economic status, and of careful observation of American customs furnished the children of immigrant groups the opportunities and the desire to take part in every field of athletics.

In the decades since 1920 Italians have flocked to the playing fields, and the sporting world has been swamped with Italian names. Tony Lazzeri, Frank Crosetti, Ernie Lombardi, Phil Rizzuto, Joe Savoldi, Angelo Bertelli, Angelo (Hank) Luisetti, Tony Canzoneri, Rocky Marciano, Archie San Romani, Gene Sarazen, Tony Manero, Vic Ghezzi, Johnny Revolta, Joe Falcaro, Eddie Arcaro, and Andy Varipapa, all of Italian descent, have had outstanding careers in sport, not to mention the remarkable exploits of the DiMaggio, Garibaldi, and Turnesa families. "The third generation of Italians, facing a new environment of language and living conditions, gradually adapted itself to the sports situation in this country. They soon enough began to participate in baseball, football, basketball, tennis, and golf." An important factor in the increase of both Italian and Slavic names in sport may have been "their exclusion from upper class pursuits" while "their participation in athletics is an important agency promoting assimilation."[9]

Greeks, Lithuanians, Czechs, Yugoslavs, Poles, Syrians, Armenians, and other national groups, as well as Mexicans and other Latin Americans, participated increasingly in sandlot, school, club, industrial, and professional sports. Especially was this true in mining towns, steel centers, and in urban areas where colonies had grown since the early years of the century. The older generation of Czecko-Slovaks found that dancing, moving pictures, picnics, card games, and amateur theatricals—all of which had been important recreations to the foreign-born element in the United States—were losing ground. The Sokol retained something of its former interest to the young, but it was recognized, "With the young people, raised in this country, sports of all kinds take precedence over the forms of amusement preferred by their parents."[10] Slavic youth was represented on the field of sport by Andy Seminick, Eddie Waitkus, Johnny Pesky, and such truly greats as Al Simmons and Stanley Musial, as well as by wrestling champion Lou Thesz. Many boys of Spanish descent have entered the ring, made their way into the Big Leagues, or climbed to the top of the tennis world, among them Lefty Gomez, Mike Guerra, Mike Garcia, Pancho Segura, and Pancho Gonzales.

The American Jew has also played an important role in sport. In the early years of the nineteenth century Maccabi sports clubs had been organized throughout Europe, while David Mendoza's exploits in the English ring of the late eighteenth century have been called "a potent

psychological influence in the liberation of the Jews of England some
years later." [11] As the Jew was freed of confinement in European ghettos,
he began to participate in sport. At the Fifth Zionist Congress in 1901
Max Nordau urged the support of "muscular Judaism." Jewish names
gradually appeared on baseball rosters (some thirty in Big League ball
from 1900 to 1939), following in the footsteps of the famous catcher,
Johnny Kling. Andrew Friedman, Barney Dreyfuss, and Judge Emil Fuchs
did much to sponsor the professional diamond. Among the leading figures
in the ring were Joe Choynski, Abe Attell, Lou Tendler, Harry Greb,
Benny Leonard, Max Baer, Barney Ross, and Joe Jacobs, the impressario,
while Jewish boys have been particularly prominent in the Golden Gloves
tourneys. Since the early years of the century Jewish athletes have made
remarkable progress in intercollegiate basketball, through the training
acquired at the YMHA, the public school, and the settlement house.
Middle-class Jews took to the fairways with avidity, and by 1931 there
were more than one hundred golf clubs in the United States with a membership predominantly or exclusively Jewish. The City College of New
York's basketball team of 1949-1950, aided by two black players, became
the first in history to win both the National Invitation and NCAA tournaments. Hank Greenberg, Benny Friedman, Nat Holman, Harry Newman,
Marchmont Schwarz, Marshall Goldberg, Dave Smukler, Sid Luckman,
and Irving Jaffe are among the greats of the diamond, gridiron, basketball
court, and skating rink. It has been said that "the array of 20th cent. stars
in the United States . . . did more than any other single factor in convincing Americans that Jewish young men and women were not different from
other youths." [12]

   Discrimination against certain groups and between the nationalities
themselves, however, is all too prevalent, friction often results, and animosities are aroused. [13] But men of all creeds and nationalities have been
brought closer together, united in a common purpose and devoted to a
common loyalty. School spirit and team play have been a part of the melting pot. How much American democracy owes to the playing fields may
be open to question, but sport has done much to acquaint minority groups
with their fellow men and to break through the shell of nationalistic
animosity. While Italians have banded into Italian-American clubs (an
action characteristic of the Germans, the Irish, the Norwegians, the Greeks,
the Poles and other minority stocks), this is usually for social purposes;
other nationalities participate on their teams, and most of the athletes of
these groups also play on school, sandlot, or semipro teams where national
lines are scarcely noticed. The greatest fighter of recent decades (Joe Louis)
was a black American, the most spectacular ball player (Babe Ruth) a
German, the most publicized wrestlers (James Londos and Lou Thesz)

were Greek and Czech, the most respected football coach (Knute Rockne) was a Norwegian, and one of the most successful baseball managers (Joe McCarthy) was Irish.

Franklin D. Roosevelt wrote in 1939, "Baseball has become through the years, not only a great national sport but also the symbol of America as a melting pot. The players embrace all nations and national origins and the fans, equally cosmopolitan, make only one demand of them: Can they play the game?" Dixon Wecter, observing the extension of sport to the masses in the Great Depression, was convinced, "In sport and amusement, as in other aspects of life in America, the hallmark of caste and the stamp of prerogative had grown perceptibly dimmer." In the thirties Shane Leslie observed this process when he wrote that English class sports could not thrive in the United States: "The division into Gentlemen and Players would be a hateful and odious distinction, alone condemming the game in free-born eyes."[14] At mid-century, with the triumph of school athletics and the popularity of industrial sport, the playing fields and ball courts of America are more of a melting pot than they have ever been in the past.

## The Afro-American's Share

"No matter what the Negro may have done in religion or education, in science or art, or how well he may have achieved by serious effort, it is in the field of sport that he has made the strongest appeal to the great American public." These words of Benjamin Brawley, strong as they may seem, point to the cardinal role sport has played in the achievement of status by the "colored" race. No minority group has suffered so deeply or reaped such benefit from sport as has the American black. The black's relation to organized sport is best seen from two viewpoints: the discrimination which he has constantly faced, and the progress he has made with the opportunities he has had. His struggle for fame and fortune, his victories and his heartbreaks, are a chapter in our democratic history. Beset with poverty, long isolated in rural areas, deprived of the countless recreational opportunities of his white brothers, the black athlete is now receiving the honors and reputation he has so richly deserved.

Blacks were introduced to the white man's sports as slaves on the plantation. First among the list of famous American pugilists were Bill Richmond and Tom Molyneux, a freed slave who went abroad to fight England's great Tom Cribb. In the early years of the nineteenth century planters promoted bouts among their slaves whose winnings often far exceeded what they might earn in the fields. Crews of blacks engaged in boating regattas in the deep South, while their masters made wagers on the winners, securing their bets with future crops. Men, women, and children fished both for fun and from necessity, and many a lad found excitement at cock fights or moonlight hunts, but life was often an endless round of work. A day in the fields under a broiling sun left little opportunity or desire to engage in organized games.

With the reconstruction period, however, we hear of new interests which mounted rapidly in the hearts of black men. As many moved away from the plantation to the city and found little work, they soon took up the games of "white folks" with enthusiasm. The inexpensiveness of baseball appealed to black Americans who organized teams immediately after the war, sometimes traveling more than a hundred miles to challenge a foe in another city. Although we know very little about Negro baseball before 1900 there are some indications that blacks were actively involved in the diamond game. For example, a few black organizations contested for "the championship of the United States." Williamsburgh on Long Island was invaded by the Excelsior Club of Philadelphia in 1867, accompanied by a motley crew of fans and a band. When the Davidson County and Middle Tennessee Colored Agricultural and Mechanical Association held its first fair in 1871, ball games were played. Before the relations between the races hardened in the late years of the century, following the civil rights cases of 1883, colored teams like those in Jacksonville and Savannah often had a white following. James Waldon Johnson recalled the feverish contests of this period and the heroes of the diamond he used to read about in *Sporting Life*. It is believed that in the 1880's, when Negro teams like the Cuban Giants from Long Island and the Eclipse Club of St. Louis began playing extensive schedules, there were about twenty blacks in the organized leagues. Stars like Bud Fowler, Moses Walker, and George Stovey, however, had their careers cut short by Jim Crow laws. Black athletes were soon considered undesirable and rapidly disappeared from the ranks.[15]

Early racing was attended by many black spectators, and jockeys were frequently taken from among the slaves. Andrew Jackson's black jockey, "Dick," was hired from a Virginia owner. "Most professional riders were negroes, usually slaves, drenched with the superstitions of their race. They were privileged and sometimes pampered characters." Many young riders fresh from the cotton or rice fields and out to have a good time could hardly be relied upon and, in high spirits, they often gave a bad ride—if we are to believe the unfriendly account of "Wildrake" in the English journal, *The Sporting Review*.[16]

Black jockeys who attained prominence on the track during the later years of the century were legion. Greatest of these was Isaac Murphy, whose fame spread throughout the land. Three times winner of the Kentucky Derby, Isaac Murphy became a household name, while others like

"Soup" Perkins and "Monk" Overton were very familiar to the turf public. But the black jockey disappeared from larger and more respectable race tracks at the turn of the century. Some had made too much money and lived too high, some were accused of pooling interests or of trickery, while the public was led to believe that black jockeys had lost their former skill and were eliminated in the struggle for survival of the fittest. White jockeys formed "anticolored unions," and newspapers attacked the Black Racing Trust until the "color question" drove many a famous jockey to obscure tracks, to training, or to retirement, so that only about a dozen black jockeys were listed among some 950 licensed riders in 1930.[17]

Black Americans first began to participate in college sports about 1890. William H. Lewis, later an Assistant Attorney General of the United States during the Taft Administration, was an All-American football star at Harvard in 1892 and 1893. Howard, Lincoln, Tuskegee, and Atlanta universities began to play football in 1894.[18] But black athletes received little recognition, and few were permitted to play on those university teams most highly publicized by the press. Discrimination, always prevalent in the world of sport, was the chief core of contention in the black's rise to athletic prominence. By the nineties this "color question" was already rampant in sporting circles as blacks gained distinction as pedestrians and pugilists. Jockeys were being driven from the better race tracks, players were forced from major and minor league baseball into their own leagues, white prize fighters drew the color line, and even the cycling world found itself embroiled. N.N. Raymond, chairman of the racing board of the League of American Wheelmen, wrote to "Chief Consul" Grivot of Louisiana in 1892:

> While I am a thorough Northerner I can still appreciate the feelings of the southern wheelmen on the negro question. . . . It seems to me that the decision of President Burdett, that each division should pass a rule prohibiting the acceptance of negro applications in their several states, that such a course would make all things pleasant for all concerned. . . . There is no question of our accepting the negro in preference to the white wheelman of the south. If it should be narrowed down to a question such as that, we should undoubtedly decide that we want our southern brothers in the league in preference to the negroes of the country . . . all of us, both north and south, have a feeling of antipathy toward the colored brother, but he is not so prominent or so likely to apply for membership in L.A.W. in the north as he is in the south.[19]

One of the most famous professionals of the nineties was Marshall (Major) Taylor, a black cyclist who claimed three world records and, while racing on tracks throughout the country, fought a continuous battle against discrimination.[20]

The black American as a class was not financially capable of playing a significant role in cycling or those branches of sport confined to the aristocracy. If, however, the black was not acceptable in the sports of society, he had gained at least a foothold on the lower rungs of the social ladder. Even the New Orleans Olympic Club held mixed matches in 1892, causing a warning from a local editor who feared the danger of racial equality.

One of the pugilistic giants of Sullivan's era was a magnificently formed and brilliant fighter by the name of Peter Jackson. Although he fought many white men in both hemispheres, even the magnanimous John L. refused to cross the color line. In his famous challenge of 1892 the Boston Strong Boy charged that "in this challenge, I include all fighters—first come, first served—who are white. I will not fight a negro. I never have, and never shall."[21] And he never did.

Many colored fighters were featured in the illustrated sections of the *National Police Gazette* during the nineties. Corbett fought Peter Jackson in a sixty-round draw in 1891, but discrimination was still strong and Gentleman Jim also drew the line when he defeated Sullivan in 1892. His manager announced, "Corbett will never meet Jackson again. We are against fighting negroes any more."[22] Jeffries' retirement in 1905 left the boxing world without an acknowledged champion until Jack Johnson whipped Tommy Burns in Australia and then clinched his claim to the title in 1910. He won an easy victory over an aging Jeffries, who made a comeback only for the purpose of restoring the crown to the white race. Johnson's reign was not a popular one. When Willard won from the black champion in Havana in 1915 the crowd showed its animosity toward Johnson, and the new champion held to his previously announced decision that once he became the titleholder he would not fight another black. Inasmuch as a succession of champions had made the same decision, Jack Dempsey followed their precedent when he defeated Willard by refusing to meet Harry Wills or any other black fighter.

The career of Joe Louis was most instrumental in changing the public's attitude toward the black boxer. When Max Schmeling, the Nordic white hope of Nazi Germany, fell before the attack of the "Brown Bomber," millions of Americans recognized the courage and the stature of Joe Louis. That an impoverished black youth from the Deep South might become one of the notable names of Detroit—and of the nation—was a favorable commentary on the times.[23] Henry Armstrong, Sugar Ray Robinson, and other fighters also helped inspire respect for the black man in the ring.

The black made considerable progress in sport after 1890. In the less publicized battles of the original Joe Walcott, Joe Gans, and Sam Langford, the sporting world recognized the sterling abilities of the Negro athlete. Occasional black stars flashed over the collegiate horizon, among them Matthew Bullock of Dartmouth, Robert Marshall of Minnesota, Fritz Pollard of Brown, Duke Slater of Iowa, and Paul Robeson of Rutgers. The New York Athletic Club games and the Penn Relays opened the door to stars like John B. Taylor, the greatest quarter-miler of his day and the first American of his race to participate in the Olympic Games. By 1914 there were three black athletic clubs in New York, and the metropolitan press was taking notice of the rise of black competitors whose future was then thought to be bright.

Athletic facilities for blacks in American towns and cities, however, were inferior to those of white people. Without access to most golf courses, tennis courts, swimming pools, and playgrounds, black youth found it difficult to distinguish themselves in organized sports. Black Americans had little share in the park and playground movement of the early twentieth century, "violence and bloodshed sometimes resulting from their attempts to use available facilities." This condition prevailed longer and more effectively in the South than in other areas, where whatever tax funds were available usually went into education or housing rather than recreational facilities. By 1920 the problem was recognized as acute: "The keen desire on the part of colored people for proper recreational facilities in towns and cities is in evidence in every locality, but as yet comparatively small provision has been made for his need in this respect."[24]

Only 3 percent of all playgrounds in the United States were open to black people in 1920, and in 1927 the Chicago Health Survey exposed the disproportionately small park area for blacks. While discrimination still proved strong in Cleveland, Denver, Knoxville, and Waco, Texas, cities like Lynchburg, Virginia, and Dayton, Ohio, were opening up excellent facilities.[25]

Mayor James J. Walker and Chairman James A. Farley of the New York Boxing Commission continuously sought to force Jack Dempsey to defend his title against Harry Wills, only to finally see the championship match held in Philadelphia between the Manasseh Mauler and Gene Tunney. In 1924 Pennsylvania's boxing commission had adopted a rule prohibiting bouts between white and black fighters, but the attorney general warned that the commission's action was contrary to the Fourteenth Amendment of the Constitution. With the onset of the Depression many a black boy started the upward trail by entering the Golden Gloves as a step to professional ranks. In the late thirties Nat Fleischer, a ring authority, reported a survey which showed that in a country where the colored man was only one in ten, there were 1800 blacks among the less than 8000 professional boxers in the United States.[26]

Intercollegiate sport was another battleground. Harvard University's athletic policy did much to impress other institutions in the years since World War I. As early as 1921 Harvard cancelled a track meet with the Naval Academy and the University of Virginia rather than exclude two of her black athletes, and two decades later the Harvard Corporation advised all opponents that the university would countenance no racial discrimination in sports contests. Teams representing colleges in highly urban areas of the North and West found more and more blacks on their rosters. Homer Harris of the University of Iowa in 1936 was elected the first Negro football captain in Big Ten history. William Watson of Michigan, Delbert Russell of Wayne, and Levi Jackson of Yale are among those who have been honored with positions of leadership in intercollegiate sport. The gridiron has produced such outstanding black athletes as Kenny Washington, Buddy Young, Ollie Matson, Joe Perry, and Marion Motley, all of whom have starred in the professional game. A stream of champions has flowed forth from college cinder paths: Duke Slater, Howard Drew, De Mart Hubbard, Ralph Metcalfe, Eddie Tolan, Jesse Owens, Ben Johnson, Eulace Peacock, Ralph Sorican, Archie Williams, John Woodruff, Barney Ewell, Harrison Dillard, and many others. In 1947, alone, Charles Fonville of the University of Michigan became world shot-put champion, the Missouri Valley Conference dropped its racial ban, and more than two dozen blacks were reported on racially mixed collegiate teams.[27] The barriers began falling everywhere, even in the South, where tradition and a different social pattern served as levees to hold back the tide. In 1947 the first black to play against white collegians in the history of southern football represented Harvard at a game with the University of Virginia, and a few years later southern squads visiting the North competed with mixed teams.

Their achievements on the athletic field have meant much to the blacks of America. Of eighteen men selected by one writer as "Great American Negroes," five had attained distinction as athletes.[28] Mordecai W. Johnson, President of Howard University, was an outstanding athlete at Morehouse College in Atlanta; Charles Drew, later to originate "Banked Blood," starred in four major sports at Amherst and in the Olympics; Paul Robeson was both an All-American and Phi Beta Kappa student at Rutgers; Jesse Owens was noted for his remarkable exploits at the Berlin Olympic Games of 1936; and Joe Louis became the greatest athletic hero of Black America. Americans of every race and class have heard of the fabulous "Satchel" Paige and of Jackie Robinson, the first of his race to play in modern Big League baseball.

Educational circles noted the value of sport. One black writer presented the view that "those people who have taken part in athletics and played games are those who have inherited the earth. If they have been good for other races, I believe they are good for ours. If they develop a greater spirit of unity, a stronger race of men, if they are a bulwark against degeneracy and loss of power, and help to prepare for a fuller and more efficient life, we need them in Negro colleges today as never before in history." Those who believed in the value of sport might agree with the editor who, noting the rise of his people in intercollegiate sport, speculated on the possibility that "college athletics in America provide a laboratory for the study of racial attitudes that would be of invaluable aid in chartering a future course in methods of race adjustment." [29]

Less scholarly circles have shown even greater enthusiasm over black exploits on the playing fields. The black press, including such leading newspapers as the Pittsburgh *Courier* and the Chicago *Defender,* has responded to the race interest by devoting many columns to athletic events. When a contingent of American blacks shocked the athletic world with their amazing triumphs at the 1936 Olympic Games the Associated Negro Press boasted: "Negro America wrote her name indelibly on the records as having the best athletes in the world when her ten sons jumped and ran their way to six additional championships last week before Negro-hating Hitler." [30]

Participation by blacks in organized sport reached a critical point in the Depression. New York University and other colleges were harshly criticized in the northern press for benching black athletes in games with southern institutions. The white press had usually followed rather than assumed the leadership of public opinion, though signs of a more enlightened policy were appearing. When 30,000 fans attended the Negro All-Star baseball game in Chicago in 1940 the Chicago *Daily Tribune* allowed merely one-third of a column for coverage of the game,[31] and southern newspapers continued to grant only the most important events any space. Notwithstanding such obstacles, the tide of black athletes kept rising. Lawson Robertson, famed track and field coach of many University of Pennsylvania and Olympic teams, predicted in the 1930's "Their leap to fame in track and field will doubtless be followed by similar distinction in other sports. Certainly their glory has fired the ambition of many colored youths of possibly similar ability, who are all eager to follow the pace set."[32] Achievements in black sport were highlighted in the fifties by the acceptance of Althea Gibson in the national women's tennis championship at Forest Hills, the spectacular rise of Roy Campanella, Don Newcombe, Larry Doby, Minnie Minoso, and other black players in Big League Baseball; the weight-lifting feats of world champion John Davis; the record-shattering performances of Mal Whitfield on the cinder paths; and, of course, the fame accruing to the Harlem Globe Trotters as basketball missionaries and ambassadors of good will to Latin America, Europe, and Asia.

The path would prove to be long and difficult. In Alabama in 1941 black schools were only beginning to develop baseball, football, and track, but facilities were improving in centers like New Orleans, where NORD, a citywide recreational program, was setting the pace in the Deep South. The *Annual Report, City of New Orleans, 1950* asserted: "Provision of sufficient, well supervised recreation centers for the entire city is now an established goal of city government," and so proud were the city authorities of their program that they used it to political advantage in the 1954 mayoralty campaign.[33] Statewide athletic conferences for schools were organized in numerous southern states, though segregation was still maintained. Some of the more exclusive branches of sport held the line. The National Association for the Advancement of Colored People as early as 1929 protested the exclusion of black tennis players from the United States Lawn Tennis Association, but to no avail. Authorities of the American Bowling Congress, under pressure for a decade, only lifted the ban in 1950. In that year there were more than 150 blacks in the minor leagues and by 1952 the Texas League was cracking the southern ban with three colored players. Discrimination persisted, but with the success of Jackie Robinson's courageous venture into professional baseball, under the unwavering guidance of Branch Rickey of the Brooklyn Dodgers, the public appeared ready to accept the black as an equal on the field of sport.

Sport has given black Americans an opportunity to gain national fame they found impossible of attainment in most other fields. Success on the athletic field did much to persuade the American people that the black was no longer a listless field hand of the plantation. More permanent achievements were made daily by blacks in medicine, law, education, research, and other branches of national life, but the role of athletics, in bringing popular attention to the talents of the Negro race, has been of great significance.

A disproportionately large movement of blacks from southern rural areas to industrial centers in the North increased their familiarity with organized games, and the urban movement brought blacks into closer contact with organized sport in public schools, playgrounds, and parks. With a higher percentage of black children attending school, with facilities in athletic clubs, YMCA's, and churches being gradually opened to blacks, and with the aid given to black recreation by the WPA during the Depression, countless athletes and physical instructors were given to the colored race. The depression decade not only witnessed a great upswing in participation but also a strong movement to eliminate barriers, the black being championed by sports authorities like Jimmy Powers, and Dan Parker as well as by left-wing and communist propagandists.[34]

World War II "brought a larger consciousness of the need for organized recreation for black youth," improved opportunities in various communities, eliminated much segregation, and "developed more community leadership, responsibility, and cooperation on the part of Negroes for their youth."[35] The Olympic wreath of a Jesse Owens, the fistic crown of a Joe Louis, and the baseball prowess of a Jackie Robinson or Roy Campanella are tributes not only to these remarkable athletes but also to the sporting aspirations of their race.

# Chapter 13

# Education, Religion, and the Arts

# Chapter 13

# Education,
# Religion,
# and the Arts

From the Philadelphia Evening Public Ledger Photo Se

"WORLDLY EMPLO

The photograph shows the Athletics in
State Supreme Court rules in a majorit
the opinion. "No one, we

PENNSYLVANI

T" WHICH PENNSYLVANIA'S "BLUE" LAW OUTLAWS FOR SUNDAY

On six days professional baseball may be played in the Keystone State, but on the sevent
n, professional baseball may not be played. "Sunday is the holy day among Christians,"
ould contend that professional baseball partakes in any way of the nature of holiness.

# BANS SUNDAY BASEBALL AS UNHOLY

In the prevailing mood of escapism following the Armistice, people everywhere turned to clubs, movies, radio, jazz, dancing, travel, and sport for recreation. Public discussion of college athletics and of gambling was merely symptomatic of a general dissatisfaction with the conventionality and shallowness of national life. Among those who waged a strong campaign against the prevailing creed of success were Sinclair Lewis, H. L. Mencken, Upton Sinclair, and William Allen White, all of whom strove to shock Americans out of their complacency. Corruption and lawlessness in modern society were exposed in the Teapot Dome scandal, the Ku Klux Klan, and the gangster underworld. Undergoing further commercialization and, in spite of educational and religious opposition, the spectacle became the norm rather than the exception in everyday life. Sport's role in education, religion, and the arts is an interesting chapter in the development of the American mind.

## The Academic Scene

A. Lawrence Lowell, viewing the football hysteria of 1922, observed, "It has tended to give excessive importance to college athletic contests." The Harvard president later lamented, "Students and graduates of this generation are far more proud of their achievements on the athletic field and on the campus than in the classroom." Colleges debated employing of professional coaches, and the Eastern Intercollegiate Debating Association held a series of debates on the issue: "Resolved, That this house deplores the present condition of intercollegiate athletics."[1] Upton Sinclair presented the view that football was a tool of capitalistic alumni: "The masters of ancient Rome provided gladiatorial combats for the purpose of diverting the minds of the populace from the loss of their ancient liberties; and in the same way the masters of Modern America provide gigantic struggles on the football field."[2] Albert J. Beveridge complained that research funds were small compared to expenditures on athletics, and Abbe Ernest Dimnet bewailed the national sports mania as a corrupting force in American culture:

> The predominance of sports in schools, in the national life, in the press, not only crowds out what is or should be more important, but it creates an atmosphere in which these important things are made to appear superfluous, or even described in extremely disrespectful slang. . . . What is called culture is in danger of being regarded, in such an environment, as a specialty and not as an indispensable requisite. . . . This accounts for the fact that the American public at

large, which cannot bear the idea of foreign superiority in anything else, does not care a fig if it is beaten in the field of thought or of the arts.[3]

Prominent men in varied fields took up the cudgel. Ex-president William Howard Taft announced to fellow Yale alumni that great collegiate games were not helping the educational purposes of the university. Scholastic athletics received less attention in the press, but there were many who questioned the value of sports hysteria in the schools. William Allen White, famed editor of the Emporia *Gazette,* became alarmed with the basketball fever sweeping over Kansas in 1925 and was quoted as saying, "We are now really spending millions in America to make a lot of blind, roughnecked, yowling rooters for cheap causes." Presidents Ernest M. Hopkins of Dartmouth, Nicholas Murray Butler of Columbia, and Ernest H. Wilkins of Oberlin were among those who pondered the threat of intercollegiate spectacles. President Wilkins was forthright in his convictions and maintained, "Intercollegiate football is at the present time an enormously powerful force in the life of the nation," interfering "to an intolerable degree with the attainment of the purpose of the American college."[4]

In 1926 the American Association of University Professors published a bulletin condemning football for its hysteria, drinking, betting, overpaid coaches, and professional temptations. Sir Ernest Bain of Leeds University noted the high salaries of athletic directors and coaches in American colleges, the power of the alumni and the anxiety of administrators, as well as the monotonous way in which the stadium was always pointed out. No one attacked the hypocritical timidity of college authorities more sharply than Abraham Flexner: "They are all mad on the subject of competitive and intercollegiate athletics—too timid to tell their respective alumni that excessive interest in intercollegiate athletics is proof of the cultural mediocrity of the college graduate." Flexner charged that athletics received proportionately more money than any legitimate college activity, that the football coach was more widely known than the college president, and that professors received less than the coach: "There is no college or university in America which has the courage to place athletics where everyone perfectly well knows they belong." Bertrand Russell, amazed at the degree to which the competitive spirit had monopolized games in modern society, felt that the spirit of cooperation, which had been eliminated, could only return with a change in school games. Complaining that the athletic cult underestimated man's intelligence, he philosophized that "the belief that a young man's athletic record is a test of his worth is a symptom of our general failure to grasp the need of knowledge and thought in mastering the complex modern world."[5]

Sport was attacked as a tool of capitalistic society through which prosperous alumni distracted college youths from the radical thought of the day. Many specific abuses added fuel to the fire. The Western Conference took measures to tighten its control over players following Red Grange's bolt to professional ranks in 1925; Harvard and Princeton broke off football relations because of the unpleasant spirit of their games; West Point and Annapolis, quarreling over the eligibility of former college players, abandoned the annual Army-Navy game in 1929; the University of Iowa was expelled from the Western Conference for maintaining an athletic "slush fund;" and the Big Six expelled the University of Kansas for evading the conference rule on recruiting and subsidizing.

Various remedies were proposed. President Hopkins of Dartmouth advocated a plan based on reciprocal games, student coaches, and a simplified schedule in which only sophomores and juniors would participate. Professors at Wesleyan, Ohio State, and Wisconsin suggested plans for de-emphasizing sport, as did President Clarence C. Little of the University of Michigan. An "Athletic League of Nations" was suggested by Nicholas Murray Butler, but the abolition of gate receipts as a method to take sport out of the hands of the public and put it back in the hands of the college met with mingled response from college authorities.[6] The Gates Plan to give all varsity coaches an academic standing was introduced at the University of Pennsylvania. In the late thirties President Robert M. Hutchins of the University of Chicago recommended that all coaches be instructors and that there be an admission charge of 10¢, an extension of intramural games, and an encouragement of sports useful in later life. The overall effect of such proposals was slight, however, and the role of sport in the colleges remained as perplexing as ever.

Opponents of intercollegiate athletics were supported in many of their observations by the Carnegie Report of 1929. Subsidizing of athletes, overemphasis, and commercialization of all forms of scholastic and collegiate sport were charged against the majority of universities. Bulletin No. 23 of the Carnegie Foundation for the Advancement of Teaching was a general indictment and plea to return to the true meaning of a university. When gate receipts and crowds declined in the early years of the Depression it was widely thought that the battle was going to the critics. Even before this trend set in the New York *Times* for January 8, 1930, editorialized, "The seed is working in the ground of academe, and it is to be hoped that in time the present overgrown oak of athletics will be uprooted by a saner and more graceful growth." Hopes were high by the early thirties that amateur sport would regain its former ascendancy and that the dire threat to higher education had been conquered.

During the postwar era this attack on athletics in the university and on sport in American society was not to go unchallenged. While students and alumni enthusiastically aroused businessmen and the general public to the urgent need of a new stadium or gymnasium, friends were both articulate and adamant in their defense of intercollegiate games. Sports writers continued to glorify their athletic heroes, and educators recognized the value of intercollegiate competition. President Max Mason of the University of Chicago remained unafraid of college athletic enthusiasm as long as the building of school loyalty and of personal character prevailed. From Ann Arbor President Clarence C. Little raised his voice in defense. "In general and in particular I am in favor of intercollegiate athletics," he declared. "They bring us into contact with our neighbors—they build loyalties and character. They are in my opinion quite as valuable for women as for men. They contain too many deep personal memories of friendship otherwise missed and of examples of courage otherwise unrecognized for me to turn traitor to them now."[7]

When a bulletin of the American Association of University Professors condemned football as played in 1926, numerous educators defended the game as played at their schools. Presidents Sidney E. Mezes of the City College of New York, Walter A. Jessup of the University of Iowa, Nicholas Murray Butler of Columbia, W.H.P. Faunce of Brown, Paul Moody of Middlebury, Clifton D. Gray of Bates, and Deans Christian Gauss of Princeton and Herbert E. Hawkes of Columbia were among those who approved of football at their respective institutions. President Paxton Hibben of Princeton called athletics a "moral safeguard." The value of athletics was ably championed by President Faunce of Brown, who scored the attack on football and charged, "Much of the current criticism of football seems to amount simply to the statement that the game is altogether too interesting to be tolerated. But America will never condemn any kind of work or play because it is of absorbing interest. To find out what are the elements of supreme interest to American youth and utilize these elements in the various 'projects' of the curriculum would be the part of wisdom."[8]

Although most educators were in firm agreement as to the evils of exploitation, recruiting, and subsidization, many agreed with Albert Bushnell Hart that the Carnegie Report of 1929 took no account of the high rank of many athletes as students and disregarded the fact that "Phi Beta Kappa has an honorable record in competitive intercollegiate athletics."[9] The Carnegie Report met a mixed reception in academic circles and was violently attacked by one of the great campus athletic enthusiasts, Ralph W. Aigler of the University of Michigan Law School. In 1931, as depression clouds darkened the intercollegiate scene, President Walker D. Scott of Northwestern pointed to the history of Big Ten football in which no fatalities had occurred and stressed the fact that many of the faculty were former football players.

The temper of college alumni was tested in a 1934 report on graduates of the State University of Iowa. Overwhelmingly the graduates claimed that college athletics helped in, or at least did not hinder, their securing a college education. Charges that athletes found practice sessions drudgery were denied by 95 percent of the athletes, whereas more than 90 percent of the nonathletes claimed they would take as much or more participation in sports if they were to go through college again. All groups felt that athletics inspired courage, confidence, and a sense of team play for later life activities. This study also claimed that there was no evidence of athletes being handicapped in their intellectual, educational, psychological, and vocational preparation and that the average incomes by profession for the years 1925-1929 showed athletes or active participants leading in every field over those who had been nonactive in their college days.[10]

Conditions found in collegiate sport were duplicated in the schools, but even the severest critics of commercialism and overemphasis acknowledged that athletics were now universally recognized as a fundamental factor in education. Although grammar and high school principals were disturbed by the inevitable controversies, riots, strained relations, falsification of records, and other problems which arose out of their games, there was a growing feeling that competitive sport played an irreplaceable part in the life of our youth. Will Durant wrote that in the sex education of the young "we shall let Nature take her course, without sermons and without lies; but we shall provide the child with all the sporting goods in the catalogue, and lure it out into the sun. When a boy plays baseball with gusto his morals are good enough for me." One educational authority remarked in 1933: "The transformation that has taken place, in recent years, in the games of youth through the influence of the school playground is wonderful. The corner-lot baseball game of fifteen years ago, with its constant quarreling, profanity, and gang groupings, has given way on the playground to a game of law and order." Students of junior high school age, confronted with a world of turmoil and of challenging ideas, might look to athletics to furnish "the natural and proper correctives for the unfavorable influences of modern civilization."[11]

By the middle 1930's the attack on intercollegiate sport had been channeled into a discussion of specific evils. One figure stands out as an implacable foe of overemphasis. Robert Maynard Hutchins continued his assault on the sporting mania within university walls and did much to persuade the great institutions that athletic pre-eminence was not vital to a true university. Dedicated to the ideals of education, Hutchins preached a doctrine of deemphasis, claiming that the "emphasis on athletics and social life that infects all colleges and universities has done more than most things to confuse these institutions and to debase the higher learning in America."[12] Despite student opposition, the University of Chicago eventually dropped intercollegiate football after the 1939 season and intercollegiate sport in general in 1946. Only a few institutions have followed the precedent, though more than a number of private colleges abandoned football after World War II, largely because of its expense.

President Ernest H. Wilkins of Oberlin College surveyed 22 typical small colleges in 1938 and discovered that only two had football receipts equal to expenses. Proximity to larger universities and the greater facility with which throngs flocked to the big games in the metropolis may have been major factors in the struggle of the small college for sports patronage. Others told of the threat of commercialized sport. "Sport has a way of getting out of perspective," according to commentator Raymond Swing, who feared that "public interest in competitive games invites commercialism and commercialism entails showmanship, which is the antithesis of sport." John R. Tunis, Ernest Linderman, and others have constantly forewarned the public of the evils involved in overcommercialization. Following the war, college authorities permitted a tremendous expansion of intercollegiate games, partly in fear of the press, the radio, and the public enthusiasm for competitive sport. As Edgar W. Knight observed, "The way out of the bad conditions and the evil days on which intercollegiate sports had fallen was not clear at mid-century," but the revolt of the William and Mary faculty against overemphasis and the scandals on the basketball court and in the classroom in 1950 and 1951 apparently gave the presidents renewed courage.[13]

Sport has acquired a tradition, a loyal group of alumni, a public interest of wide dimensions, and a host of vested interests vigilant in their watch lest the crusading spirit take hold. Tunis presented a dire picture of the academic threat of football as played in the thirties: "It affects millions of students everywhere. It reaches down to the high schools and has an influence on our educational system from top to bottom. Football determines the conduct of college presidents, deans, and administrative officers. It has become an unsavory racket, and as such has no justifiable place on a college campus." As a keen observer of American ways, Stephen Leacock smiled at the inclusion of "Dry Skiing" and "Fundamentals of Golf for Beginners" in the curriculum of leading American universities. S. R. Slavson went so far as to conclude that "competitive sports are among the most unsocial of our national institutions," much along the same line of thought held by some of the writers on adolescence who stressed the anxieties which arise over physical defects or inadequacies.[14]

However, during the forties and early fifties the attack against sporting evils waned because the nation's attention had more intensely focused on national and international problems. The Great Depression, the New Deal, the rise of fascism, the Second World War, and the threat of communism during the Cold War years made people more conscious of the major issues facing America at mid-century. The end of isolation in foreign policy, the rising tide of labor unionism and social reform, and the political crises of the atomic age were of such momentous significance that the danger of commercialized sport receded to a position of secondary importance in American lives. At mid-century the public's concern with sporting interests was centered on a further democratization of recreation and on the banishing of Jim Crow restrictions, while the age-old fascination for the athletic spectacle had not lost its hold.

## The Sunday Issue

The World War of 1914-1918 brought to a focus the issue of recreation on the Sabbath. After industry was harnessed to the war effort and two million soldiers were sent overseas, religious leaders began to recognize that "blue law" traditions were fast losing their hold on the American people. Longstanding demands for Sunday sport were increasingly heard in postwar years, and with the New Deal's struggle against the Depression major gains for legalization were achieved. In 1920 Governor Calvin Coolidge of Massachusetts signed the local option bill passed by the state House and Senate. The Lord's Day Alliance and the New York Civic League campaigned against such moral evils as professional boxing, 2.75 beer, Sunday movies, and baseball, but changing opinion was illustrated in Christy Mathewson's reversal of his former hostility to Sunday baseball.

Sunday golf and baseball received the most concentrated attention during the twenties. Although "blue laws" remained in the statutes of most states, public officials became lax in enforcement. When the Lord's Day Alliance met in convention in 1923 Rev. W.W. Davis of Baltimore claimed that Sunday baseball was perhaps the most difficult problem the organization had to combat. Rashly accusing the Jewish people of controlling the entertainment field, he made the prediction that Sunday amusements and sports would suffer the fate of the liquor traffic.

It became evident that the higher the percentage of foreign-born residing in the state the weaker the "blue laws" were enforced. A survey

made by the highly controversial Dearborn *Independent* showed that the
South remained strong in its Sunday observance, as did North Dakota,
South Dakota, and Kansas. Minnesota, Michigan, Nebraska, Iowa, Indiana,
Illinois, Missouri, and Kentucky were "practically open-Sunday States
with limited districts in each State where Sunday is still observed." It also
claimed that in the 18 states with the strictest Sunday laws there were only
8 percent of foreign origin, in the 18 states with strong laws 14 percent
were foreign-born, in the 8 states with the weakest laws 14 percent were
of foreign birth, and in the 4 states with no Sunday laws 23.5 percent were
foreign-born. The Midwest was largely under a system of city control,
while the Rocky Mountain, the Pacific, and the Southwest states along
with Louisiana, were open-Sunday areas. The survey claimed that in 28
states with a population of 64,450,371 the environment was one of open-
Sunday or local option, whereas in 20 states with a population of
41,258,394 the Sabbath was comparatively well observed.[15]

The issue of Sabbath sport was argued by Bishop William T. Manning,
Rev. John Roach Stratton, Dr. C.E. Macartney, Dr. David G. Wylie, and
other leading ministers of the era. Bishop Manning condoned Sunday golf
or tennis but warned against commercialized sport. He made the statement that sports occupy "just as important a place in our lives as prayers."
Rev. Dr. John A. Ryan agreed, "Neither in morals nor in Scripture is there
any warrant for the view that participation in games is necessarily a
desecration of Sunday. The enforcement of this false notion has impelled
thousands of young persons to give up religion." Father Ryan, however,
observed, "Bishop Manning goes too far when he asserts that Sunday
sports are as important as prayers, or as powerful means of spiritual
development as religion. . . . The beneficial effects of recreational games
upon health, morality and contentment can be sufficiently emphasized
without putting them on a level with the practice of religion." The funda-
mentalist "Texas Cyclone," Rev. J. Frank Norris, blasted Sunday recreation: "It is impossible to believe that Jesus would endorse sports on the
holy day of His resurrection. Packed theaters, crowded golf courses,
Sunday automobiling have robbed the Lord's Day of its sanctity and given
us a Continental Sabbath. . . . Instead of the ministry yielding to the
flood tides of worldliness, we need a twentieth-century John the Baptist
who will call the people to repentance."[16]

Commercialized sport on Sunday was roundly attacked by Dr. Daniel
A. Poling, president of Christian Endeavor and renowned Philadelphia
minister. From New York Rev. John Haynes Holmes decried commercialized sport as "one of the great dangers to the country to-day, not to be
encouraged on Sunday or any other day." Notwithstanding the strong
prejudice against commercialism, Bishop Manning planned a new window

in the Cathedral of St. John the Divine: "The cathedral Sport Bay will stand as a visible symbol of the relationship between sport and life, sport and religion. Not only does religion not frown on sport, but encourages and sympathizes with it and gives an important place in the temple of God."[17] When the Lynds made their famous study of Muncie, Indiana, in 1825, they found that in "Middletown" the clergy still claimed the Sabbath as the Lord's Day to be observed with decorum and that Sunday baseball was still condemned by churches and a considerable part of the population. However, Sunday motoring was encouraged by newspaper advertisements, games were played in the city parks, more golfers frequented the Country Club on Sunday morning than any other half day of the week, and the Gun Club had recently shifted its weekly competitions to Sunday without serious objection.[18]

Pennsylvania remained one of the strongest bastions in defense of the "blue laws." Highly populated, a melting pot of immigrants who worked in steel mills and mines, and a state in which athletic interest had been keen since the middle of the nineteenth century, it seemed a paradox that the State Supreme Court should declare Sunday professional baseball illegal because of the "blue laws" of 1794 regarding "worldly employment." In Commonwealth v. American Baseball Club of Philadelphia the judge decreed, "We can not imagine in this sense anything more worldly or unreligious in the way of employment than the playing of professional baseball as it is played to-day. Christianity is part of the common law of Pennsylvania, and its people are Christian people. Sunday is the holy day among Christians. No one, we think, would contend that professional baseball partakes in any way of the nature of holiness."[19] Kansas was another center of opposition to the Continental Sabbath. When William Allen White's Emporia Gazette recorded a 1926 World Series game on a scoreboard for the public to watch after church, ministers attacked the newspaper. In Kentucky, on the other hand, the legislature overrode Governor Field's veto and passed the Strange-Hamilton law permitting semipro and professional baseball on Sunday. The shifting tide of Sabbath observance found golf under ban in Massachusetts and baseball illegal in Nebraska, while local option or state legislation permitted baseball on Sunday in a number of states.

During the early 1930's the more conservative centers began to loosen their restrictions. A Trenton, New Jersey, conference of Seventh Day Adventists passed a resolution in 1930 urging the legislature to repeal the state's ancient "blue laws." In 1932 Governor Miller of Alabama vetoed a local option bill, but the legislature overrode his veto; Birmingham, Montgomery, and Mobile were opened to Sunday movies, baseball, golf, and tennis. For two decades H. L. Mencken headed a drive to strike the "blue laws" from the books in Baltimore, and in 1932, by overwhelming vote, the city approved Sunday sport after 2 pm (wrestling, boxing, dog racing, and horse racing excluded).

Governor Gifford Pinchot of Pennsylvania signed the Schwartz bill legalizing Sunday baseball and football under local option, although all contests were limited to the hours 2 pm to 6 pm. One of the great citadels of Sabbath observance had been cracked at last. By the middle of the Depression the trend had definitely turned; yet South Carolina's laws still prohibited everything except some forms of golf, tennis, and swimming. Local option for football and baseball won out in Delaware in 1935, and sporting circles had gained their point in one of the strongest religious areas of the nation. Less rigid observance prevailed in the years after repeal of the Eighteenth Amendment in 1933, and after the Depression caused millions of part-time employed or unemployed people to tour the country and to engage in varied forms of popular recreation. Since the disruption of the working schedule in World War II heated discussion of Sabbath observance has waned, much as a great part of the American public still cling to their religious practices of old.

## Public Morals and Commercialized Sport

Americans of all faiths and denominations continued to oppose the more corrupt and undesirable side of commercialized sport. They continued to attack gambling, dishonesty, and cruelty. In those sports where gambling was most prominent the churchgoer supported religious movements organized for purposes of cleaning house. Horse racing returned with new vigor in metropolitan areas like New York and Chicago during this decade, and it certainly boomed in the wide-open state of Florida. But thousands of congregations continued to heed the warnings of the clergy and of public officials that race track gambling was a social menace dangerous to public morality.

It was the ring which was most vigorously attacked, however, for the pugilistic world was an ideal center of criticism. Few could deny that professional fights were brutal, that the ethics of sportsmanship were seldom recognized, that corrupt elements had worked their way into the inner circles of the boxing world, or that gambling flourished on the thousands of ring contests held every year. When Jack Dempsey met Georges Carpentier in 1921 the Board of Temperance and Public Morals of the Methodist-Episcopal Church condemned the fight, charged that women who attended such contests were degraded thereby, and maintained that this fight should be the last on American soil. The General Assembly of the Presbyterian Church in the United States also condemned the match, and a prominent clergyman charged that it was an exaltation of paganism and the flesh: "The presence of churchwomen at the ringside is the culmination of that spirit of worldliness which started in card playing, dancing, theatregoing and other selfish indulgences, which things have sapped the spirituality of many followers of the Nazarene." A board of the Methodist-Episcopal Church called on the people of Philadelphia to prevent the Dempsey-Tunney fight at the Sesqui-Centennial Exhibition, charging that such fights were not representative of American civilization and that it would be a disgrace to the city. When the two heavyweight heroes met again in Chicago the following year ministers from various sections of the country were vehement in their criticism, despite Tex Rickard's appeal to respectable people that governors, mayors, bankers, lawyers, millionaires and women would attend: "I am proud . . . to say that a huge majority of the throng will be 'nice people'." [20]

Public interest in boxing grew rapidly in the twenties in spite of such opposition. When the General Director of Moral Welfare in the Presbyterian Church of the United States opposed the Philadelphia contest, Governor Pinchot published an open letter in defense of boxing, claiming its value in war and maintaining that Pennsylvania's new law had created a more wholesome atmosphere. Since the twenties there has been frequent criticism of the ring for its fatalities, its gambling devotees, and its camp followers. The old charges of brutality and blood lust lost their sting, however, and one seldom heard the clergy complaining that women are debased by their attendance. Perhaps religious thinkers felt that their efforts were futile and that the public was not so easily aroused on such issues. Hysteria over the symptoms which led to the fall of Rome fell on deaf ears. Millions of Americans still feel that pugilism is morally wrong and that it is a public menace, but the spotlight is no longer centered on the ring.

## The Churches Sponsor Sport

Religious thought about sport underwent a change in the years after 1920 as the athletic cult became an integral part of secondary and higher education, as communities began to recognize the value of recreational programs, and as the churches began to build gymnasiums and to organize teams in church or community leagues. Outdoor sport and camping were sponsored by the Protestant Committee on Scouting (1922), the Knights of Columbus (1923), and the Jewish Committee on Scouting (1925). [21] Baseball, softball, basketball, bowling, and quoit leagues brought more and more ·churchgoers into contact with competitive games. The Catholic Youth Organization, inspired by Bishop Bernard Shiel, rivalled or surpassed Protestant groups in the sponsorship of team games, and national Catholic interscholastic championships were held. Even dancing made headway in the churches. Churches still lagged behind other institutions in sponsoring athletics, but the increasing attention directed toward such forms of entertainment indicated a gradual recognition of the moral value of sport in daily life.

Whether the changing church position was a grudging acceptance of the need to appeal to the public on more secularized terms or whether it was indicative of a genuine belief in the value of sport, the religious attitude at mid-century was no longer as discouraging to sportsmen as it was in earlier years. Ex-president Herbert Hoover expressed the moral side of properly-conducted sport for city youth in terms which many a priest or minister approved:

> Ours is a problem of creating a place where these pavement boys can stretch their imaginations, where their bent to play and where their unlimited desire for exercise can be channeled into the realms of sportsmanship. We can divert their loyalties to the gang from fighting it out with fists to the winning of points in a game. We let off their explosive violence without letting them get into the police court. And sportsmanship, next to the Church, is the greatest teacher of morals.[22]

## Modern Artists

Since World War I artists have become increasingly interested in American themes. While it is true that there have been numerous other schools and movements in recent decades (for the spirit of revolt has turned many an artist to psychological studies, to fleeting impressions interpreted in geometrical forms, and to an accent on the grotesque or the mysterious), the average artist in a Vermont village or California town has found in native scenes and the vernacular the source of his inspiration. Farmers toiling in the field, laborers working at the machine, the beauty of a New England winter, or the golden leaves of autumn woods are typical themes for a Thomas Hart Benton, a Grant Wood, a John Steuart Curry, and many another artist. And this return to interest in native scenes was signalized by a revolt against European domination. Grant Wood described this trend in *Revolt Against The City:*

> But painting has declared its independence from Europe, and is retreating from the cities to the more American village and country life. Paris is no longer the Mecca of the American artist. The American public, which used to be interested solely in foreign and imitative

work, has readily acquired a strong interest in the distinctly indigenous art of its own land; and our buyers of paintings and patrons of
art have naturally and honestly fallen in with the movement away
from Paris and the American pseudo-Parisians. It all constitutes not
so much a revolt against French technique as against the adoption of
the French mental attitude and the use of French subject matter.
For these elements of the new artists would substitute an American
way of looking at things, and a utilization of the materials of our
own American scene.[23]

With this inclination in art circles one might expect a greater interest
in sporting themes, and numerous artists have dabbled in the field. This is
particularly true of fishing and of hunting with hounds, and our public
galleries frequently feature wild life scenes.[24]

When we look at organized sport we find that George Bellows continued to express his fascination with the drama of the ringside. In lithograph and on canvas he poured out a stream of boxing studies: *The White
Hope* (1921), *Counted Out* (1921), *Introducing Georges Carpentier*
(1921) and *Between Rounds* (1923). He also completed a striking study
of the most famous of pugilists which he called *Introducing John L.
Sullivan.* After attending the famous fight in 1923 Bellows painted his
classic *Dempsey-Firpo,* while *Ringside Seats* was finished in 1924. Bellows
died the following year, having firmly established his reputation as the
foremost American artist of the ring.[25]

James Chapin fell victim to the drama of ringside in such pictures as
*A Prize Fighter and His Manager* and *Negro Boxer.* Some of the most
effective lithographs of recent years have been those of Robert Riggs,
among them *Club Fighter, Neighborhood Champ, Little Brown Brother,*
and *Baer-Carnera.* James Montogomery Flagg painted the Dempsey-Tunney
fight, and Howard Chandler Christy did an excellent canvas on the ring.
John Steuart Curry finished a water color in 1925 entitled *Counted Out,*
and the popular water colorist Joseph W. Golinkin painted numerous fight
scenes of the thirties. The gentle art of boxing has also been memorialized
in the sculpture of Paul Landowski, Mahonri Young, and R. Tait Mackenzie. Few sculptors have so ably captured the beauty of an athletic body
or the poise and grace of the athlete.[26]

Baseball has attracted a number of artists, among them James Chapin
*(Batter Up),* Paul L. Clemens *(In The Dugout),* Mrs. Marjorie Phillips
*(Baseball)* and Douglass Crockwell *(Babe Ruth's Greatest Moment).* Count-
less illustrators for the national magazines have done exceptionally fine
scenes from the diamond game. Carl Hallsthammer modeled *The Swat
King* and *Safe* in sculpture. Among those who have worked on football

themes are Benton Spruance *(Touchdown Play, Backfield in Motion)* and John Steuart Curry *(Goal Line Play).* R. Tait Mackenzie sculpted *The Onslaught,* a powerful representation of clash and struggle on the gridiron, and the works of Beatrice Fenton and Carl Hallsthammer were exhibited at the Xth Olympiad art exhibition at Los Angeles in 1932.[27] Winter sports have a natural appeal to lovers of the great outdoors. Marianne Appel's *Ski Town,* Benjamin C. Brown's *The Ski Jumper,* and Levon West's *Stem Christiana* have caught the thrill of winter sport and the awesome grandeur of the snow-covered landscape. Devotees of the turf have seen an outpouring of portraits of Man O'War, Gallant Fox, Whirlaway, and other noted horses. Randall Davey, Guy Pene du Bois, Joseph W. Golinkin, Paul Brown, and others have recorded with their brushes the glamor and excitement of a horse race.

A host of artists have entered the field. Isabelle Bishop protrayed the links in *Golf Match,* William Palmer did a golfing scene called *Indian Summer,* Robert Faucet painted Bobby Jones in the 1929 U.S. Open, and Sears Gallagher has done *Home In Two, Foursome,* and *All Even.* Some of America's athletic heroes have been memorialized in bronze or stone—Walter Johnson, Lou Gehrig, Knute Rockne, and Babe Ruth, among others. *Polo Group* by Henry Moeller captured the intense action of match play. Pierre Nuyttens did portraits of Helen Wills Moody and Sir Thomas Lipton; Kathleen Leighton painted *The Cherokee Athlete;* Percy Crosby, creator of the "Skippy" comic strip, excelled in polo drawings. Peter Hurd has given us the drama of the rodeo as well as *Landscape With Polo Players;* Carl Springchorn and Walter Speck have dramatized the six-day bicycle race; Peter Helck has painted the Indianapolis Speedway races; Reginald Marsh and others have been fascinated with the art of wrestling; Reynolds Beal has shown the New England scene in *Marblehead Yachts;* and, while the profession is not particularly interested, virtually every sport has had at least several artists who have experimented with one or another theme.

Although the Metropolitan Museum of Art in New York, the Boston Museum of Fine Arts, and the Baltimore Museum of Art gave exhibitions of sporting art some years ago, the galleries seem less interested than private collectors. There has never been a comprehensive study of American sporting art, which in itself is indicative of the attitude of the artist and the critic. Sporting art, however, has been encouraged by magazines like *Yachting, Motor Boating, Sport, Esquire,* and various turf publications. Artists have also frequently turned their talents to magazine covers and illustrations for fiction stories; national publications such as *Collier's, Saturday Evening Post,* and *Time* have used numerous themes or personalities for their covers. Another repository of sporting art is the college or private gymnasium. Madison Square Garden has an extensive boxing collection, the Payne Whitney gymnasium at Yale has scores of prints and paintings of an athletic nature, the New York AC and other private clubs have their trophy rooms, and numerous works of art are to be found in the gyms or field houses of many universities and colleges.

Architecture has turned its talents to sport in the construction of stadiums, swimming pools, ski lodges, athletic arenas, and gymnasiums. The golf architect has had a field day with hundreds of luxurious country clubs and sprawling courses. Since Willie Dunne's Shinnecock Hills course was laid out in 1891 there has developed a specialized branch of the profession, among the more successful practitioners being Thomas Bendelow, Donald Ross, Deverreux Emmett, John Dunn, Arthur Tillinghast, George Stumpp, Seth Raynor, and Bobby Jones. Designs for modern schools involve the latest improvements in construction materials, while the building of a pool or a hunting lodge must fit naturally into its surroundings.[28]

Another art form which utilized sporting themes is the motion picture, either in the hands of the amateur cameraman or the studio professional. On the screen the struggle of landing deep sea fish, the gliding motion of the sailboat, the grace of the high diver, or the power of a muscular athlete are reproduced in a way beyond the limitations of the painter or the sculptor. Films of sporting action gained a wide movie audience following the thirties, as did the sale of "sporting" reels for home use. The thrill of sport, from archery to yachting, was a weekly ritual in the newsreels of the fifties produced by Paramount News, Movietone News, or Pathé.

Still photography is yet another of the arts which have successfully exploited sport. In postwar years, the action snapshot has become an integral part of the newspaper and such pictorial magazines as *Life, Look, Sports Illustrated,* and their numerous competitors. The University of Missouri School of Journalism and the Encyclopedia Britannica joined forces in 1947 in establishing an annual competition for the best candid camera shots in news, feature, and sports. Newspaper and professional photographers have found sport—with its action, its pathos, its extremes of emotion, its beauty and its humor—a virgin field of countless opportunities.

## The Literary Mind

No great American novel has used organized sport as its central theme. Although the novelist deals with ideas, situations, and characters representative of every side of life, sport is concerned with techniques known to the fan but a mystery to the bystander. Great sports fiction demands the talents of an artist, the enthusiasm of a sportsman, and the insight of a philosopher—qualities rarely found. Among the better novels of recent decades are H.C. Witwer's *The Leather Pushers,* Phil Stong's *State Fair,* Jim Tully's *The Bruiser,* Francis Wallace's *Kid Galahad,* Bud Schulberg's *The Harder They Fall,* and Mark Harris' *The Southpaw.*

Some writers of reputation have digressed in their works to scenes or characters from the sporting world. James T. Farrell portrayed the athletic interests and sporting vanity of wayward city youth, and boxing and football scenes were treated as dramatic episodes in *The Young Manhood of Studs Lonigan.* Thomas Wolfe maintained an interest in athletics until his premature death. Sinclair Lewis, who smiled at the alarm over Sunday baseball or golf and realized the role of sport as a road to social recognition, directed his caustic pen toward the Zenith Athletic Club of Elmer Gantry and George Babbitt. It was known that "Wellspring Church, including the pastor of Wellspring, bloomed with pride that Elmer had been so elevated socially as to be allowed to play golf with bankers."[29] Popular writers and historic novelists sometimes allude to sport for local color, but this is not a general practice.

If we turn to lighter forms of literature, we find that men of high literary talent turned to sports fiction and short stories in the popular magazines. Ring Lardner, Paul Gallico, Heywood Broun, Westbrook Pegler, Quentin Reynolds, and Damon Runyon are among the many newspaper men who wrote fascinating stories in postwar years. Runyon's *Guys and Dolls, Money From Home,* and *Blue Plate Special* described the city "sport" whose life is bound up with boxing, horse racing, and the gambling underworld. Ernest Hemingway, F. Scott Fitzgerald, Lion Feuchtwanger, and Robert L. Marquand dabbled in sports stories. Numerous anthologies have been published or edited by Herb Graffis, Grantland Rice, Robert Kelley, Thomas Stix, Stanley Frank, Red Smith, Bill Stern, Stan Lomax and other enthusiasts, including Irving Marsh and Edward Ehre, editors of the annual *Best Sports Stories.* The *New Yorker* has contributed profile studies and sparkling humor. Short stories have proved excellent vehicles for projecting sporting themes.

Some sports writers of literary merit have left columns dedicated to the traditions, the humor, the tragedy, and the moral value of sport. John Kieran, Arthur Daley, Grantland Rice, and John Lardner published countless legends and humorous tales of the playing fields, the courts, the gridiron, the links, the cinder path, the track, and the diamond. Rice and Kieran made a habit of versifying, but their works have been exceptions in our sporting literature. The great mass of sportswriting might well be forgotten, sadly lacking in imagination or literary talent.[30] However, a considerable literature of an anecdotal and historical nature has come from the facile pens of Fred Lieb, Paul Gallico, Robert Smith, Lee Allen, Tom Meany, Frank Graham, Jimmy Powers, John Lardner, Red Smith, Arthur Mann, Warren Brown, and Arch Ward, among others.

An occasional rhyme by Edgar Guest or Ogden Nash, the poetical vagaries of a sports writer, or an anonymous verse in the daily press constitute about all that one can attribute to sport in contemporary poetry, except for Vachel Lindsay's "John L. Sullivan, The Strong Boy of Boston." Lindsay recalled the great Sullivan-Kilrain fight of 1889, a few lines of which describe a boyhood reaction to that famous event:

> I heard a battle trumpet sound.
> Nigh New Orleans
> Upon an emerald plain
> The strong boy
> Of Boston
> Fought seventy-five red rounds with Jake Kilrain.[31]

In American humor the penetration of sport has been somewhat more visible. Tall stories, fantastic exploits, and hoary legends have long surrounded the world of sport. Jokes about Rube Waddell and Shoeless Joe Jackson were multiplied in the era of Babe Herman, Lefty Gomez, and Dizzy Dean. Fantastic tales were told of John L. Sullivan's drinking, John McGraw's rowdyism, Babe Ruth's poor memory, and the bonehead plays of the old Brooklyn Dodgers. Contemporary humorists like Bennett Cerf in *Try and Stop Me* devoted large sections of their anthologies to sport, while Herman Hickman gained fame as a raconteur. American folklore may yet be enriched by the legends and humor which are being passed from one sporting generation to the next.

The comic strip may be called a vulgar art, but it certainly is an element in American culture. In the years since 1920 there have been numerous strips devoted to or occasionally touching on sporting topics. Barney Google, Dick Dare, Harold Teen, and Smitty entertained the American public with their occasional sporting adventures in the 1920's. Billy De Beck's Barney Google introduced Spark Plug in 1922: "At first this horse angle was introduced to amuse the racing people . . . but much to everyone's surprise, the ordinary public, that didn't know a horse blanket from a dope sheet, took Spark Plug to the private paddocks of their hearts."[32] In the years since the Depression Joe and Asbestos, Freckles, and Donald Duck have been a few of the comic strip characters interested at one time or another in sport. While Popeye and Li'l Abner have taken a whack at athletic games, the most popular of sports heroes have been Ham Fisher's Joe Palooka and Ray Gotto's Ozark Ike.

Willard Mullin has set the pace on the sports page, and H.T. Webster, Fontaine Fox, Jefferson Machamer, and other cartoonists have contributed to the humor of the comic page or the vignettes found in *Collier's, The New Yorker,* and other magazines. Political cartoons increasingly utilized sporting situations from the diamond, the ring, the cinder path, the turf, and the gridiron in order to put over a conflict of parties or a dispute between nations. In the realm of American humor the influence of sport has been felt more fully than in any part of our literature.

Whatever we may find in novels, verse, or humor, we must recognize that the impact has been slight throughout the long growth of sporting interest. In literature, as in art, the main difficulty may be the feeling that sport has no message of social significance or that sport is not a truly reputable subject for concentrated study. Rivalry, sportsmanship, struggle, sacrifice, courage are themes which sports fiction might well develop. Emotional tenseness, from elation over victory to dejection in defeat, is subject to varied interpretations. The age-old idea of personal struggle over the conflict of conscience and will is particularly characteristic of competitive sport. But such potentialities have rarely attracted talented writers. One of the most perspicacious writers on baseball history has summarized this problem:

> Despite the pervasiveness of baseball in the spoken tongue, there is little of the game in our literature. . . . There are histories of various teams and biographies of certain great players, but these are jobs of journalism. . . . It may be that our national game appears so seldom in our literature simply because American writers have wandered so far from the highroad of American life. . . . Of course, to many men and women in the book world baseball remains a bourgeois excrescence, like crowded bathing beaches and houses that look alike. To them it is past imagining to take the game seriously.[33]

## Lingo, Lexicon, and Language

Sporting lingo has grown with the American language. Nineteenth-century horse racing and baseball contributed many a colorful phrase to the speech of the common man. Academic circles held out against the crudeness of the market place, but the leavening influence of a Walt Whitman or a Mark Twain made inroads on our speech in the twentieth century. The frontier gave us the lore of the miner, the boatman, the lumberman, and the cowboy, and then came a national interest in the railroad and the steel mill. More recently Americans have been intrigued with the machine, and we have moved from an automotive era to the age of the jet plane and space

travel. Every branch of national life, from the refined speech of the
theater to the babble of the immigrant, has added to the vocabulary of
the American.

With the rise of a national press and the popularization of sporting
journalism, with millions playing organized games on the playground or
the athletic field, and with the development of a national sports-consciousness, enrichment of the American language was inevitable. Scholars still
dispute the value of slang in modern speech, but few deny the impact it
has made. Our language has escaped the narrow confines of the respectable
literature of the nineteenth century. As one scholar has written:

> An earlier solemnity in literary manner, the result of studied
> imitation of the speech of our elders in culture, has been in consider-
> able part succeeded by a national youthful gayety. Formal rule as a
> guide has been superceeded by a national use. . . . A democratic
> unwillingness to recognize a superior, which interferes with subjec-
> tion to military discipline, appears in an unwillingness to submit to
> discipline in language. There is a revolt from the conventional, a
> striving after the odd rather than the usual. In speech as in music the
> graceful and the beautiful yield to the grotesque. For the expression
> of this American spirit the frontier life of the woodsman provided
> much unrefined word material. From industrial occupations, from
> the less reputable amusements of the gaming table, the race track,
> and the prize ring, and from life on the stage came more word
> material which expressed a revolt from decorum and propriety.[34]

Whereas the turf, the diamond, and the ring contributed most to the
sporting language of the last century, other sports have made inroads on
American speech in more recent decades. Newspaper scribes had an unrivalled opportunity to experiment with the art of sportswriting. The
extremely dramatic, the grossly bombastic, and the spectacularly original
became the order of the day. It is the colorful sportswriter who has
flooded our language with a terminology for everything sensational,
exciting, humorous, or tragic in sport.

In what ways has sport penetrated our language? Presidential
speeches, editorials, articles of foreign correspondents, the speech of the
barber shop, the general conversation at clubs and fraternal societies, the
arguments of youth clustered around the corner drugstore—every phase of
American life attests to the power of what John Kieran called the "Sportsman's Lexicon." Robert Smith has pointed out the impact of baseball on
our language with such common expressions as "born with two strikes on

him," "he has something on the ball," "you're off your base," "to make a hit," "right off the bat," "to go to bat for," "to play ball with," "keep swinging," "getting to first base," and "to throw curves at." "He's a foul ball," "the third strike," "he didn't get to first base," and "to pinch hit for" are also phrases from the diamond. Phrases such as "change of pace," "hot stove league," "money player," and "What's the score?" were transferred to varied situations in many areas of modern life.[35]

When the American uses the expression "in the swim," "down my alley," "on the homestretch," "to hold the line," "to bowl over," "to shoot straight with," or "behind the 8-ball," he seldom thinks of the sport from which these phrases have been derived. Boxing has added such phrases as "hanging on the ropes," "hit below the belt," "a knockout," "to hit the canvas," "to take a dive," and "saved by the bell." The turf has been the source of such expressions as "a photo finish," "a dead heat," "jockeying for position," "in the stretch," "a dark horse," "at the post," and "as jittery as a thoroughbred." Football has not penetrated our language as profoundly, although Americans from coast to coast understand "on the five yard line," "to hit the line hard," "to run interference for," "until the last line is crossed," "in the shadow of the goal posts," and "to carry the ball." Our language has accepted "wrestling with a problem," "a stranglehold on," "to take to the mat," or "to pin his shoulders," among expressions of the wrestling game. From the golf links of forty-eight states have come "straight down the fairway," "in the rough," and "duffer." Other phrases applicable to the most diverse situations which the average person uses subconsciously in his speech might be mentioned. The very idea of fair treatment in our social life is most widely known as "fair play," "sportsmanship," or (from the playing fields of Britain) "cricket," and the American spirit of cooperation is to "play the game" or "play ball." "Home run," "southpaw," "touchdown," "K.O.," "uppercut," "haymaker" and "athletic bum" are but a few of the hundreds of terms familiar to all sportsmen.

The American Thesarus of Slang devoted more than one hundred pages to thousands of terms applying to sports and games.[36] Baseball fans recognize that professional players are often called "ivory," "slaves," or "hired hands," while a novice at the game may be a "busher," a "rookie," or a "farm hand." The boxing devotee refers to his chosen sport as "the ring," "fistiana," "cauliflower alley," or "fistic lane." Their long traditions, their popularity with the masses, their exploitation by the journalistic world, and their special appeal to the field of sports fiction—these and doubtless other explanations may be offered to account for the penetration of diamond, ring, and turf lingo into our vocabulary. The speech of the common man has been altered more visibly than that of the scholar, but the American language, for better or for worse, is becoming the language of the people.

Americans have absorbed new names of mechanical devices, new terms of warfare, and new words in the fields of industry, business and government, while psychoanalysis and sociology have added their novel terminology. Throughout the past one hundred years sport has developed a distinctive lexicon. When the language of the playgrounds, the ball fields, and the racing courses is spoken from the pulpit, the lecture platform, and the movie screen, when it is read in sporting journals and the daily press, when it is blared forth over radio or television and enters into conversation at the dinner table, one easily recognizes the major role it plays in the daily life of the people. Serious students, though few in number, are turning their attention to this unplowed field of study: "The sports writers, of course, are all assiduous makers of slang, and many of their inventions are taken into the general vocabulary."[37]

Deep as it has penetrated our language, there are reasons to question whether the encroachment of sporting terminology has been anything but quantitative. Words with meanings confined to the playing fields often fail to attain a universal meaning. Transmission of American ideas to the rest of the world will be confined to those few sports of international appeal. Nor does the extensiveness of specialized terminology lead to complete understanding even within our national boundaries. Some may know the meaning of "cousin," "windsucker," or "long shot artist," but most Americans, even with the aid of radio and television, will not understand the mysterious lingo of a horse trainer, a boxing manager, or a golf enthusiast. Yet, the impact of sporting lingo has added color to our language to a degree previously unknown in any earlier era.

## Hollywood and the Entertainment World

Appealing to a vast audience in country hamlets and in large cities, the movie industry has exploited every subject which is of interest to the general public, including almost all fields of sport. Football hysteria of the twenties was pictured in such films as *The Freshman* (Harold Lloyd), *The Quarterback* (Richard Dix), *One Minute To Play* (Red Grange), and *Casey At The Bat* (Wallace Beery). Babe Ruth, Jack Dempsey, and Gene Tunney made pictures in Hollywood. Other films included *Kentucky Derby, Racing Heart, Racing Luck, Racing Blood, Racing Fool, The Sport of Kings, They're Off, Thundering Speed, Warming Up, Slide Kelly Slide, Battling Orioles, Big Game, Brown of Harvard, Touchdown,* and *Battling Butler,* as well as *Red Hot Tires, Red Hot Leather,* and *Red Hot Hoofs.*

In the years of the Great Depression sporting enthusiasm was increasingly exploited in the movies. Charlie Chaplin had a prize fight scene in *City Lights* which reminded old-timers of his picture, *The Champion*. *The Champ* (Wallace Beery, Jackie Coogan), *David Harum* (Will Rogers), *The Prizefighter and the Lady*, *Pigskin Parade*, *Elmer the Great*, *The Crowd Roars*, *A Yank At Oxford*, and *Golden Boy*, along with *This Sporting Age*, *Kentucky*, *Stand Up and Fight*, *Indianapolis Speedway*, *Pride of the Blue Grass*, *Fighting Thoroughbreds*, *$1,000 A Touchdown*, and other films were features in which the athletic or sporting interest was highly exploited. Short sequences were often used as atmosphere in the life of the city.[38] And animated cartoons began to develop the numerous potentialities of sport in such series as *Aesop Fable* and *Paul Terry Toons*, as well as in the revolutionary art of Walt Disney.

During and following World War II the movie audience witnessed an unending stream of sporting films. Frequently the picture used sport merely as background for a love story, a musical comedy, or a serious drama, but its allure was fully exploited. Since 1940 there have been such baseball films as *Pride of the Yankees, The Babe Ruth Story, Take Me Out To The Ball Game, The Stratton Story, It Happens Every Spring, Angels in the Outfield, Rhubarb, The Kid From Left Field,* and *The Jackie Robinson Story*. Prize fighting, with its smoky arenas and physical conflict, lends itself well to the screen, and we have had *Gentleman Jim, The Great John L., Killer McCoy, Body and Soul, The Set-Up, Iron Man,* and the remarkably realistic *Champion*. Horse racing and trotting films have also been popular, among them *Home in Indiana, The Return of October, The Great Dan Patch, The Story of Seabiscuit,* and *Top o' the Mornin'*. Football stories have seldom attained the artistic distinction which one finds in films such as *Gentleman Jim, Pride of the Yankees,* or *Champion*. Pat O'Brien's portrayal of Knute Rockne in *The Spirit of Notre Dame* and of Father Cavanaugh in *The Iron Major* were among the better gridiron films of some years ago. *Harmon of Michigan, Smith of Minnesota, The Spirit of Stanford, The Spirit of West Point, Jim Thorpe—All American,* and *Crazylegs* glamorized the careers of outstanding athletic heroes. *Father Was A Fullback* satirized the trials of a college coach, and *Saturday's Hero* stressed the dangers of collegiate overemphasis.

Ice skating has been popularized to a great extent by Sonja Henie's pictures, while automobile and motorcycle racing, the roller derby, the rodeo, and golf have been portrayed on the screen in *To Please a Lady, Drive a Crooked Road, Rodeo, Fireball, Adam's Wife,* and *The Ben Hogan Story*. Another form of sporting entertainment that had audience appeal, especially among the small fry, was the swimming of Johnny Weismuller as Tarzan. Esther Williams has done more than any one in recent years to popularize water sports through such pictures as *Bathing Beauty, Neptune's Daughter,* and *Million Dollar Mermaid.*

Basketball, bowling, skiing, sailing, track and field, billiards, and similar activities are well adapted to the movie short for the teaching of techniques to athletic clinics and school audiences.

Many short films devoted to fresh and salt water fishing, to yachting cruises, and to duck or deer hunting have proved popular. *Grantland Rice Sportlight* has remained popular since the early twenties, while Warner Brothers has had its *Sports Parade,* R.K.O. Pathé its *Sportscope,* Columbia Pictures its *World of Sports,* Paramount its *Sports-Eye View,* Fox's its *Adventures of the Newsreel Cameraman,* and Metro-Goldwyn-Mayer its *Pete Smith Specialty* and *Sports Parade.* Every diversion from water skiing and polo to archery and bronc riding are filmed for local color scenes or specialty films. The cinema, to a degree greater than that of any of the other arts, has exploited sporting themes both for pecuniary and for artistic interest.

Television continues to make use of the humorous side of baseball; comedians know the value of a joke about the blockheaded fullback or the crazy southpaw; dancers sometimes incorporate sporting sequences in tap routines; and Radio City Music Hall has included sporting scenes in its musical extravaganzas. The Icecapades and other similar carnivals have been commercialized to the point of being important events on the entertainment calendar. And the television play based on sporting themes has become increasingly popular in the past several years.

Popular music has paid only passing attention to sport in such songs as "Collegiate" and "Jolting Joe Di Maggio." RCA Victor recorded the "Brooklyn Baseball Cantata" and Joe E. Brown's "How to Play Baseball." College songs such as "On Wisconsin," "The Notre Dame Victory March," and "Rambling Wreck from Georgia Tech" have been popularized through the radio and the movies as well as at football games. The Broadway stage has avoided the theme more completely than any of the arts, although even here *Golden Boy* and *Body and Soul* were successes, and other plays like *As Thousands Cheer, Early To Bed, Two on the Aisle,* and *Wish You Were Here* featured sport.

Throughout the entertainment world, as in art and literature, sport has been of only marginal interest to actors, dancers, comedians, writers, and musicians. In most of the arts, from painting and sculpture to fiction and poetry, or from musical comedies and popular tunes to the theater and the dance, the influence of sport has been of secondary significance. At the other extreme the short story, the humorous anecdote, the comic strip, the American language, and the motion picture have more fully utilized sporting themes. Although sport has not made a deep impact on the aesthetes and intellectuals in the arts, American culture has felt its impact.

# References
# and
# Bibliography

## References

### Chapter 1

1  Hiram Woodruff, *The Trotting Horse of America* (New York, 1869), 250-51.

2  William Bradford, *Bradford's History "Of Plimoth Plantation"* (Boston, 1898), 135.

3  Carl Bridenbaugh, *Cities in the Wilderness: The First Century of Urban Life in America, 1625-1742* (New York, 1938), 111-21, 274-80.

4  John Allen Krout, *Annals of American Sport* (New Haven, 1929), *The Pageant of America*, Vol. XV, 10.

5  *William and Mary College Quarterly*, III (August, 1894).

6  *Archives of Maryland*, XLIV, "Proceedings and Acts of the General Assembly of Maryland, 1745-1747," ed. by Bernard Christian Steiner (Baltimore, 1925), 647.

7  Hugh Jones, *The Present State of Virginia* (London, 1724); "The Equine FFVs," *Virginia Magazine of History and Biography*, XXXV (October, 1927), 334; *Virginia Gazette*, November 30, 1739.

8  *William and Mary College Quarterly*, II (July, 1893), 55.

9  John Hervey, *Racing in America*, 1665-1865, 2 vols. (New York, 1944), I, 99.

10  *Moreau de St. Mery's American Journey* (1793-1798), translated and edited by Kenneth Roberts and Anna M. Roberts (Garden City, 1947), 173.

11  F.A. Michaux, *Travels to the Westward of the Allegheny Mountains in the States of the Ohio, Kentucky, and Tennessee . . . undertaken in the year X, 1802*, translated by B. Lambert (London, 1805), 230-31; Louisville *Courier Journal*, May 4, 1852.

12  Barry's Gray Medley is said to have laid "the foundation for the improvement of the blood-horse in Tennessee, having been taken from Virginia to the Nashville area in 1800 by Redman D. Barry's black boy, Altamont. John Tayloe advertised in the Lexington *Reporter*, April 18, 1817, the standing at stud of Hamlintonian, got by Diomed, at the stable of William Hancock. Hamlintonian had raced against such a champion as Post Boy at Richmond and Washington during Jefferson's administration.

13  Henry W. Herbert, *Frank Forester's Horse and Horsemanship of the United States and British Provinces of North America*, 2 vols. (New York, 1857), II, 509; Charles William Janson, *The Stranger in America, 1793-1806* (New York, 1935), 217, first published in London in 1807; Charles F. Adams (ed.), *Memoirs of John Quincy Adams Comprising Portions of His Diary from 1795 to 1848*, 12 vols. (Philadelphia, 1875), VII, 159.

14  *Niles' Weekly Register*, May 31, 1823.

15  Hervey, *Racing in America*, II, 98, 177, 189. Hervey here mentions 43 tracks in 1830, 89 in 1840, but the *American Turf Register* listed 47 known tracks in 1830 —and it assumed there were many others of lesser importance. Of the 47, Virginia was in the vanguard (15), followed by Kentucky (8), North Carolina and Maryland

(4), Alabama and South Carolina (3), Pennsylvania, New York and Tennessee (2), Ohio, Mississippi, New Jersey and Washington, D.C. (1). *American Turf Register,* II (October, 1830), 93. The New Orleans Jockey Club appeared in 1828, the Eclipse Course opened in 1837, the Metairie in 1838, and the Louisiana in 1838.

16   Francis Brinley, *Life of William T. Porter* (New York, 1860), 43.

17   *American Turf Register,* III (July, 1832), 571.

18   Claude G. Bowers, *The Party Battles of the Jackson Period* (Boston, 1928), 18.

19   See "Index" in the *American Turf Register,* XIII (1842), 51-55. There were apparently many more blooded horses on the turf than these figures for 1842 would indicate. Shortly thereafter one authority on farming, deriving his information from the *Spirit of the Times,* estimated that about 2000 thoroughbred foals for the next season were expected to "come upon the turf." Cuthbert W. Johnson, *The Farmer's Encyclopaedia and Dictionary of Rural Affairs,* adapted to the United States by Gouveneur Emerson (Philadelphia, 1844), 642.

20   New York *Herald,* May 15, 1845; New York *Weekly Herald,* May 17, 1845.

21   See, for example, the work of James Brown at Philadelphia and Trenton tracks, and the leasing of the Central Course at Memphis to Mr. Linn Coch and that of the Selma and Montgomery, Alabama courses to Mr. John Clark in 1844. Among the sponsors of racing in America were Cadwallader Colden, Alexander Botts, and David H. Branch. *American Turf Register,* XII (May, 1842), 289; *ibid.,* XV (September, 1844), 570-71; Hervey, *Racing in America,* II, 103, 139, 193. Names of planters prominent in early racing can also be found in Trevathan, *Making the American Thoroughbred,* and William Ransom Hogan and Edwin Adams Davis (eds.), *William Johnson's Natchez: The Ante-Bellum Diary of a Free Negro* (Baton Rouge, 1951).

22   *American Turf Register,* XII (March, 1841), 162; XIV (March, 1841), 162; XIII (May, 1842), 289; XIV (November, 1843), 683.

23   Richmond *Enquirer,* September 20, 1842.

24   *Spirit of the Times,* XX (March 2, 1950), 30.

25   New Orleans *Daily Delta,* April 14, 1855.

26   While the 1854 race attracted some twenty thousand spectators, estimates of the crowds at the 1855 contests ranged between five and ten thousand, a poor contrast to the enormous throngs at intersectional races like the Fashion-Peytona match ten years before. New Orleans *Daily Picayune,* April 9, 1854; April 15, 1855; New Orleans *Daily Delta,* April 15, 1855.

27   *Porter's Spirit of the Times,* I (October 25, 1856), 128; Nashville *Daily News,* May 27, 29, 1860. This decline was also noted by the sporting editor, Frank Queen, in the *New York Clipper,* V (January 23, 1858), 316; by Henry William Herbert in his authoritative study, *Frank Forester's Horse and Horsemanship of the United States and British Provinces of North America,* 2 vols. (New York, 1857), I, 161; and by Ralph H. Gabriel, *The Evolution of Long Island* (New Haven, 1921), 170.

28   Hugh Murray, *Historical Account of Discoveries and Travels in North America,* 2 vols. (London, 1829), II, 412.

29  *American Turf Register*, II (January, 1831), 250; XV (November, 1844), 744.

30  Quoted in the *Spirit of the Times*, XVII (April 3, 1847), 66; J. S. Buckingham, *The Slave States of America*, 2 vols. (London, 1842), I, 353.

31  *American Farmer*, VI (November 12, 1824), 270; *American Turf Register*, XV (November, 1844), 757.

32  Andrew Jackson to Andrew Jackson, Jr., Washington, May 19, 1832; May 24, 1832; Francis P. Blair to Andrew Jackson, Washington, May 20, 1839. John Spencer Bassett (ed.), *Correspondence of Andrew Jackson*, 7 vols. (Washington, 1926-1935), IV, 441-42; *ibid.*, VI, 16. Also see George Wilkes, *Europe in a Hurry*, (New York, 1852), 67; Nashville *Daily News*, May 29, June 1, 1860.

33  Brinley, *Life of William T. Porter*, 104-105, 145; *Spirit of the Times*, XXI (April 5, 1851), 78.

34  Quoted in Robert M. DeWitt, *The American Fistiana, Showing the Progress of Pugilism in the United States from 1816 to 1873* (n.p., n.d.), 80.

35  *Illustrated American*, XVIII (October 12, 1895), 455.

36  Holliman, *American Sports*, 3-10.

37  G. M. Young (ed.), *Early Victorian England, 1830-1865*, 2 vols. (London, 1934), I, 271-280.

38  *Spirit of the Times*, XXI (June 28, 1851), 217.

39  *North American Review*, LV (October, 1842), 345.

## Chapter 2

1  Dallas T. Herndon (ed.), *Centennial History of Arkansas*, 3 vols. (Little Rock and Chicago, 1922), I, 210; J. M. Keating, *History of the City of Memphis and Shelby County, Tennessee* (Syracuse, 1888), 152-53; *Spirit of the Times*, IX (September 4, 1839), 330.

2  William R. Hogan, "Amusements in the Republic of Texas," *Journal of Southern History*, III (November, 1937), 416.

3  Ferdinand Roemer, *Texas, with Particular Reference to German Immigration and the Physical Appearance of the Country* (San Antonio, 1935), 81.

4  William R. Hogan, *The Texas Republic: A Social and Economic History* (Norman, 1946), 133.

5  New York *Daily Times*, December 13, 1855; *Spirit of the Times*, XX (October 12, 1850), 407; XXI (May 17, 1851), 150; XXI (September 27, 1851); XXI (June 28, 1851), 6.

6  George B. Merrick, *Old Times on the Upper Mississippi* (Cleveland, 1909), 144-48; William Petersen, *Steamboating—on the Upper Mississippi* (Iowa City, 1937), 431-37. David Lear Buckman, *Old Steamboat Days on the Hudson River* (New York, 1907), 79-80; Jerry MacMullen, *Paddle-Wheel Days in California* (Stanford University, 1945), 27.

7  Merrick, *Old Times on the Upper Mississippi*, 144; also see Louis C. Hunter, *Steamboats on the Western Rivers: An Economic and Technological History* (Cambridge, 1949), 405.

8   New Orleans *Daily Picayune,* December 1, 1855. For a contemporary source on the transport of horses and crowds see Hogan and Davis (eds.), *William Johnson's Natchez,* 117, 155, 225.

9   Krout, *Annals of American Sport,* 24.

10  *Southern Planter,* X (January, 1850), 4; H. Milnor Klapp (ed.), *Krider's Sporting Anecdotes* (Philadelphia, 1853), 66.

11  *American Farmer,* VIII (May 5, 1826), 54; Mills' Point *Hunter of Kentucky and South-Western Weekly Democrat,* August 17, 1842.

12  *Sporting Review,* III (February, 1840), 114-115.

13  *Spirit of the Times,* XXI (July 12, 1851), 246; Akers, *Drivers Up,* 140; *Wilkes' Spirit of the Times,* I (September 10, 1859), 4; *ibid.,* I (October 15, 1859), 84.

14  Boston *Daily Journal,* February 7-9, 1849; New York *Daily Tribune,* February 8, 9, 1849; Milwaukee *Sentinel and Gazette,* February 10, 1849; Boston *Daily Courier,* October 21, 1858; New York *Times,* October 21, 1858; New Orleans *Daily Picayune,* May 6, 7, June 29, 1860; Nashville *Daily News,* April 29, 1860. Apparently the telegraph was used in communications between clubs, a Brooklyn cricket team of the late 1840's having "received a very strong invitation by Telegraph from a few spirited old cricketers to stop at Utica and give them one day's play." *Spirit of the Times,* XXI (August 23, 1851), 319.

15  *American Turf Register,* II (January, 1831), 248-49.

16  *Spirit of the Times,* XXI (September 27, 1851), 378.

17  *American Agriculturist,* I (June, 1842), 79. Also see Henry Colman (ed.), *Fourth Report of the Agriculture of Massachusetts. Counties of Franklin and Middlesex.* (Boston, 1841), 125; *Monthly Journal of Agriculture,* I (August, 1845), 65, 71, 74; New York *Herald,* May 16, 1849.

18  Quoted in the *Plough, the Loom, and the Anvil,* IX (December, 1856), 352.

19  Quoted in *Spirit of the Times,* XVII (October 30, 1847), 422.

20  Samuel Crowther, *Rowing* (New York, 1905), 9-11.

21  E. Merton Coulter, *Boating as a Sport in the Old South* (Savannah, 1943), 5.

22  *Spirit of the Times,* XXI (September 27, 1851), 376. Edward Burgess, who knew as much about American yachting as anyone, recognized the contribution of the *America* to yachting design and to cruising and sailing. Edward Burgess, *American and English Yachts* (New York, 1887), 410.

23  Quoted in Frank Luther Mott, *A History of American Magazines, 1741-1850* (New York, 1930), 482.

24  *Harper's Weekly,* II (October 30, 1858), 690. In a fight at Boston Four Corners, New York, in 1853 the claim was made that "nearly all the farmers and citizens of that region were present to witness the disgraceful exhibition." New York *Weekly Tribune,* October 15, 1853.

25  *Ibid.,* IV (May 5, 1860), 274.

26  The origins of baseball are best discussed in Robert W. Henderson, *Ball, Bat and Bishop* (New York, 1947); Frederick G. Lieb, *The Baseball Story* (New York, 1950); Frank G. Menke, *The New Encyclopedia of Sports* (New York, 1947).

R.W. Henderson has been the leading debunker of the old Doubleday legend. The latest editions of the leading encyclopedias have accepted the Henderson version, and references to baseball prior to 1839 make it all the more convincing.

27  *Spirit of the Times* (July 7, 1860), 283; (July 28, 1860), 331; Thomas Jefferson Wertenbaker, *Princeton, 1746-1896* (Princeton, 1946), 279; *Spirit of the Times* for 1860, *passim.*; Albert Demaree, *The American Agricultural Press, 1819-1860* (New York, 1941), 132; Cecil O. Monroe: "The Rise of Baseball in Minnesota," *Minnesota History, A Quarterly Magazine* (June, 1938); Arthur Charles Cole, *The Era of the Civil War* (Springfield, Ill., 1919), 447.

28  *American Turf Register,* I (November, 1829), 162; *ibid.* (February, 1830), 273; *ibid.* (March, 1830), 361; *ibid.,* II (January, 1831), 247-50; New Orleans *Daily Picayune,* April 22, 1855.

29  *Porter's Spirit of the Times,* I (December 20, 1856), 259.

30  Herbert, *Frank Forester's Horse and Horsemanship,* 200, 247-57. Also see *Spirit of the Times,* XVIII (September 18, 1847), 350; Cuthbert W. Johnson (adapted to the United States by Gouverneur Emerson), *The Farmer's Encyclopaedia and Dictionary of Rural Affairs* (Philadelphia, 1848), 642. Among the leading trotters were such names as Black Hawk, Daniel Webster, Ethan Allen, Henry Clay, James Buchanan, Kit Carson, Tecumseh, Tom Hyer, William Booth, Yankee Sullivan, Zachary Taylor, Frank Pierce, Know-Nothing and Native American.

31  Herbert, *Frank Forester's Horse and Horsemanship,* I, 161; II, 126-27.

32  Charles Eliot Goodspeed, *Angling in America* (Boston, 1939), 285-91. This is perhaps the best account of the origins of fishing tackle in America.

33  Daniel Webster to Mr. Welch, June 10, 1847, in Fletcher Webster (ed.), *The Private Correspondence of Daniel Webster,* 2 vols. (Boston, 1857), II, 255.

34  Charles Hallock, *The Fishing Tourist: Angler's Guide and Reference Book* (New York, 1873), 18. Considerable change took place within the next decade and an accomplished sportsman soon might utilize the combined services of the railroad, telegraph, and sporting goods businesses, as was demonstrated in Frank Forester's essay, "Trouting Along the Catasauqua." See David W. Judd (ed.), *Life and Writings of Frank Forester* (London, n.d.), 270-300.

35  Holliman, *American Sports,* 7; Richmond *Enquirer,* November 16, 1821.

36  *Spirit of the Times,* XVII (March 27, 1847), 58; XX (May 4, 1850), 130; XX (October 5, 1850); *The Boy's Treasury of Sports, Pastimes, and Recreations* (4th ed.: New York, n.d.), 23, 35, 169; Natchez *Courier,* November 26, 1850; Madison *Daily State Journal,* March 26, April 13, 1855; Klapp (ed.), *Krider's Sporting Anecdotes,* 287.

37  New Orleans *Daily Picayune,* August 5, 1848; July 25, 1851; *Spirit of the Times,* XX (April 20, 1850), 106; XXI (May 31, 1851), 180; XXI (August 23, 1851), 323.

38  *Spirit of the Times,* XX (October 5, 1850), 395; Harry T. Peters, *Currier & Ives: Printmakers to the American People* (Garden City, 1942), *passim.*; Oliver Larkin, *Art and Life in America* (New York, 1949), 215.

39   William Murrell, *A History of American Graphic Humor,* 2 vols. (New York, 1933),
     I, 108, 122, 129; II, 90, 122, 129; Arthur Bartlett Maurice and Frederic Taber
     Cooper, *The History of the Nineteenth Century in Caricature* (New York, 1904),
     147, 153; Albert Shaw, *Abraham Lincoln: A Cartoon History,* 2 vols. (New York,
     1929), *passim.*

40   *M. and M. Karolik Collection of American Paintings 1815 to 1865* (Boston, 1949),
     *passim.*

41   See Robert W. Henderson (comp.), *Early American Sport: A Chronological Check-
     list of Books Published Prior to 1860 Based on an Exhibition Held at the Grolier
     Club* (New York, 1937), *passim.*

Chapter 3

1    James Bryce, "America Revisited: The Changes of a Quarter-Century," *Outlook,*
     LXXIX (March 25, 1905), 738-39.

2    British books, magazines, and newspapers antedated their American counterparts
     because of the older and general interest in outdoor sport and athletics. *Bell's Life,*
     often cited as the "Bible," was the authority for devotees of the turf, the ring, the
     hunt, and angling. Frederic Hudson, *Journalism in the United States from 1690
     to 1872* (New York, 1873), 341. Pierce Egan's *Boxiana* and other works were
     popular reading for ring enthusiasts. The *London Sporting Magazine* and the
     *English Sporting Magazine* were drawn upon for material or served as a model for
     American publishers. In the 1860's and 1870's the English published not only
     *Sporting Life* (formerly *Bell's Life*) but such journals as *Sporting Gazette* (1862),
     *Sportsman* (1865), *Sporting Times* (1865), *Land and Water* (1866), *Sporting
     Clipper* (1872), and *Fishing Gazette* (1877). H. R. Fox Bourne, *English News-
     papers: Chapters in the History of Journalism,* 2 vols. (London, 1877), II, 223,
     319-20.

3    David W. Judd (ed.), *Life and Writings of Frank Forester* (London, n.d.), 64. One
     can see some aspects of Forester's personality in the Herbert Collection at the
     New York Historical Society and in the Miscellaneous Papers and the Duyckinck
     Collection at the New York Public Library.

4    Frank M. O'Brien, *The Story of the Sun—New York, 1833-1918* (New York,
     1918), 58-59; Alfred M. Lee, *The Daily Newspaper in America* (New York, 1937),
     609; New York *Sun,* March 21, April 2, May 4, 1835; New York *Transcript* for
     the middle 1830's. This was one of the many sensationalized features of the new
     penny press, which is discussed in Willard Grosvenor Bleyer, *Main Currents in the
     History of American Journalism* (Boston, 1927), 154-84, and in Frank Luther
     Mott, *American Journalism* (New York, 1947), 228-52. Also see Isaac Clark Pray,
     *Memoirs of James Gordon Bennett and His Times* (New York, 1855), 178-85.

5    Albany *Evening Transcript,* October 13, 1853; New York *Daily Tribune,* March
     10, 20, 1855, October 22, 1858; New York *Daily Times,* October 13, 14, 1853,
     December 11, 1855, October 21, 22, 1858; New York *Herald,* October 21-23,
     1858; Boston *Evening Transcript,* October 23, 1858; Wooster, Ohio, *Wayne*

*County Democrat,* October 28, 1858; Springfield *Weekly Illinois State Journal,* April 25, 1860; Nashville *Daily News,* May 2, 1860.

6  In chronological order, and excluding those publications already mentioned, the leading journals were: *Kentucky Live Stock Record* (1875, later called *Thoroughbred Record*); *Dunton's Spirit of the Turf* (1876); *Turf, Farm and Home, and the Maine Animal* (1878); *Maine Horse Breeder's Monthly* (1879); *Breeder and Sportsman* (1882); *American Horse Owner* (1884); *Horse World* (1889); *Northwestern Horseman and Stockman* (1890); *Horse Gazette* (1890); *Rider and Driver* (1890); *California Turf* (1892); *Trotter and Pacer* (1894); *Whip and Spur* (1894); *Breeder and Horseman* (1894); *Horse Show Monthly* (1895).

7  A list of publications includes *Fur, Fin and Feather* (1868); *American Sportsman* (1871, later called *Rod and Gun and American Sportsman*); *American Field* (1874, later called *Chicago Field*); *New York Sportsman* (1875); *Afield and Afloat* (1876); *Pacific Life* (1876); *Young New Yorker* (1878); *Sporting and Theatrical Journal* (1878); *Out of Door Sports* (1879); *American Angler and Nature's Realm* (1881); *Outing* (1882); *Shooting and Fishing* (1882); *Field Sports* (1883); *Sports Afield* (1887); *Spirit of the Hub* (1888); *Club* (1889); *Sport, Music and Drama* (1889); *Sportsman's Review* (1890); *Spirit of the West* (1890); *Sports and Amusements* (1891); *Maine Sportsman* (1893); *Recreation* (1894); *Field, Forest, Shore and Hotel Register* (1895); *Young Sports* (1896); *Sportsman's Magazine* (1896); *Field and Stream* (1896); *Outdoor Life* (1897); *Outdoorsman* (1900).

8  Chronologically, these were: *Ball Players' Chronicle* (1867); Brentano's *Aquatic Monthly and Sporting Gazetteer* (1872); *Afield and Afloat* (1876); *American Cricketer* (1877); *Archery and Tennis News* (1881); *American Canoeist* (1882); *Sail and Paddle* (1882); *Sporting Life* (1883); *Amateur Athlete and Archery and Tennis News* (1883); *Sporting News* (1886); *American Yachtsman* (1887); *Sporting Goods Gazette* (1888); *Ace of Clubs* (1889); *Rudder* (1890); *New York Athletic Club Journal* (1892, called *Winged Foot* after 1911); *Bowlers' Journal* (1893); *Western Athletics* (1893); *Illustrated Sporting Review and Boxing Record* (1893); *Golfer* (1894); *Official Lawn Tennis Bulletin* (1894); *Yachting* (1894, not to be confused with the modern *Yachting* founded in 1907); *Golfing* (1894, but called *Golf* after 1897); *Bowler and Sportsman* (1894); *Mind and Body* (1894); *Triangle* (1896); *Amateur Athlete* (1896); *American Physical Education Review* (1896); *Land and Water American Lawn Tennis* (1898); *Athletics* (1898); and one might stretch a point to include the *St. Louis Sportsman and Amateur Athlete* (1901); and *Golfer's Magazine* (1902). One might also include the Bohemian athletic journal, *Sokol Americky* (1879) and the Norwegian-Danish publication, *Sportog Frilufsliv* (1897). By the end of the century college journals were publicizing athletics, while there were a number of athletic club journals.

9  Some cycling journals of short duration may have escaped the author's detection, but a partial list, at least, includes: *Velocipedist* (1869); *American Bicycling Journal* (1877); *Bicycling World* (1879); *Wheel* (1880); *Wheelman* (1882); *Western Cyclist* (1883); *American Cyclist* (1883); *Wheelman's Gazette* (1886); *Cycle Age and Trade Review* (1888); *Wheel and Cycling Trade Review* (1888); *American*

*Cyclist* (1890); *American Wheelman and Cycle Trade Gazette* (1890); *L.A.W. Bulletin and Good Roads* (1890); *Pneumatic* (1891); *Cycling West* (1892); *Cycling Life* (1893); *Cycling Gazette* (1895); *Cycler Ensign* (1896); *Cycle Trade Journal* (1896); *Southern Wheelman* (1896); *Bicycle Press* (1897); and *Sidepaths* (1898).

10   The *Police Gazette* was known as the "barber's Bible," and the magazine appealed to "tonsorial" patrons. Edward Van Every, *Sins of New York as Exposed by the Police Gazette* (New York, 1930), 145, 160; *National Police Gazette*, LVII (November 29, 1890), 14; LVII (January 10, 1891), 7; LVIII (August 15, 1891), 6; LIX (October 17, 1891), 3; LXXIX (October 26, 1901), *passim*. See Walter Davenport, "The Nickel Shocker," *Collier's*, LXXXI (March 10, 1928), 40 and "The Dirt Disher," *ibid.* (March 24, 1928), 30.

11   Of the magazines cited in this study, 1 appeared in the 1810's, 3 in the 1820's, 3 in the 1830's, 3 in the 1840's, 4 in the 1850's, 9 in the 1860's, 18 in the 1870's, 30 in the 1880's, and 48 in the 1890's. This demonstrates the great rise in the mass interest in the postwar decades, even when the growth of population is taken into consideration.

12   O'Brien, *Story of the Sun*, 394. Cummings, brilliant but rough and profane, was a decided contrast to the "fastidious and elegant Dana." Charles J. Rosebault, *When Dana Was The Sun, A Story of Personal Journalism* (New York, 1931), 167. Mark Maguire of the *Sun* was credited with inventing a chart for blow-by-blow accounts of prize fights. One historian claims that walking matches "increased the *Sun's* edition from 20,000 to 40,000 copies" when held in Madison Square Garden or other arenas. (Candace Stone, *Dana and the Sun* [New York, 1938], p. 383.) In 1888 Arthur Brisbane was sent to France to cover the Sullivan-Mitchell championship fight. (Stephen Bonsal, *Heyday in a Vanished World* [New York, 1937], pp. 33-58; New York *Sun*, March 11, 1888.)

13   Relatively little has been written on the origins of modern sportswriting, three of the best treatments being Hugh Fullerton, "The Fellows Who Made the Game," *Saturday Evening Post*, CC (April 21, 1928), 18ff.; William H. Nugent, "The Sports Section," *American Mercury*, XVI (March, 1929), 329-38; and Elmer Ellis, *Mr. Dooley's America: A Life of Finley Peter Dunne* (New York, 1941), pp. 24-30. Chicago writers were discussed in Peter D. Vroom, "Chicago's Baseball Writers," *Baseball Magazine*, I (September 1, 1908).

14   *Saturday Evening Post*, CC (April 21, 1928), 18. Eugene Field was a guiding light in the new baseball journalism. Eastern writers, however, developed a new style of prize-fight reporting in these years. Respectable journals accused the Boston *Herald* and those other papers which printed fight news, claiming: "It is the notoriety given by the newspapers to the pugilists and their doings which produces each succesive crop of them, and keeps alive the depraved interest in their contests. The silence of the press about them would do more in one year to suppress these contests than the sheriff and police can do in ten." *Nation*, LVI (March 28, 1893), 210.

15   Mott, *American Journalism*, 579; Robert S. Lynd and Helen M. Lynd, *Middletown: A Study in American Culture* (New York, 1929), 284. A great gain in coverage took place between 1900 and 1910 on the San Francisco papers, the *Examiner*

allowing 31.3 percent of its total news space, but such extravagant policies were unusual and a decline set in before 1920. Winter, *History of Journalism in San Francisco,* 6 vols. (San Francisco, 1940), IV, 31. In the winter season, of course, sport was much less prominent. Also see Meyer Berger, *The Story of the New York Times 1851-1951* (New York, 1951), 190.

16   New York *World,* August 21, 1869; Cincinnati *Commercial,* September 22, 1869; San Francisco *Evening Bulletin,* October 5, 1869. Their use of pullman cars set a precedent in sports circles. Advertising by local lines for an approaching game appeared in the Cincinnati *Commercial,* August 24, 1869.

17   Harry Wright Correspondence, 7 vols. (1865-1877), I, 40, Spalding Baseball Collection (New York Public Library).

18   *Turf, Field and Farm* (New York), I (September 2, 1865), 69; VIII (May 28, 1869), 344.

19   Dunbar Rowland (ed.), *Encyclopedia of Mississippi History,* 2 vols. (Madison, 1907), II, 142.

20   Spalding, *America's National Game,* 504; Parke Davis, *Football, The American Intercollegiate Game* (New York, 1912), 45. For other illustrations of the difficulties of railroad travel see the New Orleans *Daily Picayune,* August 13, 1869; the Walter Camp Correspondence, Box 64 (Yale University Library, New Haven); *National Police Gazette,* LIV (July 20, 1889), 10.

21   See the *Spirit of the Times,* XCII (August 19, 1876), 53; *Forest and Stream & Rod and Gun,* XII (July 10, 1879), 461; for the scores of branch lines see Charles Hallock (ed.), *The Sportsman's Gazetteer and General Guide* (New York, 1877), Pt. II, 1-182.

22   James D. Reid, *The Telegraph in America and Morse Memorial* (New York, 1887), 800-802; Oliver Gramling, *AP; The Story of News* (New York, 1940), 232; Henry L. Mencken, *Happy Days, 1880-1892* (New York, 1940), 225. For the increasing use of the telegraph in the business side of sport see the Harry Wright Correspondence (New York Public Library) and the Southern and Texas League negotiations in the New Orleans *Daily Picayune* throughout 1888.

23   New Orleans *Daily Picayune,* October 11, 1916.

24   *Frank Leslie's Illustrated Newspaper* (New York), XXIX (September 28, 1869), 2.

25   *American Artisan,* XVIII (April, 1874), 87-88; *Youth's Companion,* LIX (April 1, 1886), 125. George B. Ellard, who sponsored the Red Stockings, advertised his store as "Base Ball Headquarters" and "Base Ball Depot," with the "Best Stock in the West." *Cincinnati Commercial,* August 24, 1869.

26   Arthur Barlett, *Baseball and Mr. Spalding* (New York, 1951), *passim.*; Ralph M. Hower, *History of Macy's of New York, 1858-1919* (Cambridge, 1946), 103, 162, 234-35, 239; Boris Emmet and John C. Jeuck, *Catalogues and Counters: A History of Sears, Roebuck and Company* (Chicago, 1950), 38; David L. Cohn, *The Good Old Days* (New York, 1940), 443-60.

27   *Harper's Weekly,* XXIX (February 14, November 14, 1885), 109, 743.

28   *Street Railway Journal,* XII (May, 1896), 319; Ed Barrow, "My Baseball Story," *Collier's,* CXXV (May, 1950), 85.

29    See Robert Taft, *Photography and the American Scene: A Social History, 1839-1889* (New York, 1938), 441; Harry T. Peters, *Currier & Ives: Printmakers to the American People* (Garden City, 1942).

30    Kaempffert, *Popular History of American Inventions*, I, 425.

31    Lloyd Morris, *Not So Long Ago* (New York, 1949), 24.

32    *Harper's Weekly*, XL (April 11, 1896), 365. It is interesting that the "father of scientific management," Frederick W. Taylor, a tennis champion and golf devotee, was said to have learned through sport "the value of the minute analysis of motions, the importance of methodical selection and training, the worth of time study and of standards based on rigorously exact observation." Charles De Freminville, "How Taylor Introduced the Scientific Method Into Management of the Shop," *Critical Essays on Scientific Management*, Taylor Society *Bulletin* (New York), X (February, 1925), Pt. II, 32. Mass-production techniques, however, were only partially responsible for the outpouring of athletic goods which began to win wider markets at the turn of the century. The manufacture of baseball bats remained a highly specialized trade, while Scottish artisans who came to the United States maintained the personalized nature of their craft as makers of golf clubs. Despite the great improvements in gun manufacture, Elisha J. Lewis asserted in 1871 that there were thousands of miserable guns on the market: "The reason of this is that our mechanics have so many tastes and fancies to please, owing principally to the ignorance of those who order fowling-pieces, that they have adopted no generally-acknowledged standard of style to guide them in the getting up of guns suitable for certain kinds of sport." Elisha J. Lewis, *The American Sportsman* (Philadelphia, 1871), 435. Although numerous industries had taken up the principle of interchangeable parts, mass-production techniques were to come to the fore only with the assembly lines of Henry Ford and the automobile industry in the years before World War I. For the influence of bicycle manufacture on the automobile industry see Allan Nevins, *Ford: The Times, the Man, the Company* (New York, 1954), 186-189.

33    Burlingame, *Engines of Democracy: Inventions and Society in Mature America*, 3.

34    Lawrence H. Seltzer, *A Financial History of the American Automobile Industry* (Boston, 1928), 91; Pierre Sauvestre, *Histoire de L'Automobile* (Paris, 1907), *passim.*; Ralph C. Epstein, *The Automobile Industry, Its Economic and Commercial Development* (Chicago, 1928), 154; Reginald M. Cleveland and S.T. Williamson, *The Road Is Yours* (New York, 1951), 175-76, 194-97.

35    New York *Daily Tribune*, October 7, 1907; M.M. Musselman, *Get A Horse! The Story of the Automobile in America* (Philadelphia, 1950), 49; Henry Ford and Samuel Crowther, *My Life and Work* (Garden City, 1927), 36-37, 50-51; Nevins, *Ford*, 192-219 is the most comprehensive study of Ford's passionate interest in early racing.

36    Karl H. Grismer, *Tampa* (St. Petersburg, 1950), 228; John A. Thompson, "Early Horseless Carriage Days in Iowa," *Annals of Iowa*, XXIII (October, 1940), 455-58.

37    Lewis Mumford, *Technics and Civilization* (New York, 1934), 303-305; Arnold J. Toynbee, *A Study of History*, 6 vols. (London, 1934-1939), IV, 242-43.

## Chapter 4

1   *Yale Alumni Weekly*, March 1, 1892, p. 2.

2   Bell Irvin Wiley, *The Life of Johnny Reb; The Common Soldier of the Confederacy* (Indianapolis, 1943), 159-61.

3   George H. Putnam, *Memories of My Youth, 1844-1865* (New York, 1914), 304-306.

4   *Wilkes' Spirit of the Times*, XI (May 6, 1865), 147.

5   Charles E. Trevathan, *The American Thoroughbred* (New York, 1905), 327.

6   *Wilkes' Spirit of the Times*, XI (February 11, 1865), 372.

7   *Atlantic Monthly* (May, 1858), 881.

8   *Turf, Field, and Farm*, I (August 5, 1865), 10.

9   Charles A. Peverelly, *The National Game* (New York, 1866), 337.

10  *Spirit of the Times*, XVI (May 4, 1867), 150.

11  E. Merton Coulter, *The South During Reconstruction, 1865-1877* (Baton Rouge, 1947), 301-302. William T. Porter referred to "the National Ball play of our country" as early as 1857. *Porter's Spirit of the Times*, III (September 12, 1857), 24.

12  Writers Program of the Iowa W.P.A., "Baseball! The Story of Iowa's Early Innings," *Annals of Iowa* (April, 1941), 653; Lake City *Leader*, August 23, 1867, quoted in Cecil O. Monroe, "The Rise of Baseball in Minnesota," *Minnesota History* (June, 1938), 181; Harry Ellard, *Baseball in Cincinnati* (Cincinnati, 1907), 25, 40, 107; E.M. Eriksson, "Baseball Beginnings," *Palimpsest*, October, 1927, 335.

13  Arinori Mori (ed.), *Life and Resources in America* (Washington, D.C., 1871), 87.

14  Clarence Darrow, *The Story of My Life* (New York, 1934), 17-18.

15  Nick Young to Harry Wright, December 22, 1877. Wright Correspondence, New York Public Library, I, 1865-77, p. 62. Also see Adrian C. Anson, *A Ball Player's Career* (Chicago, 1900).

16  New Orleans *Daily Picayune*, April 15, June 28, 1888; February 25, 1889. In the *New York Clipper*, XIX (July 8, 1871), 107, it was reported of Arthur Cummings that his strong point was "his power to send the ball in a curved line to the right or the left, thus puzzling the best batsmen."

17  *Outing*, XII (July, 1888), 350-51; *Ball Player's Chronicle*, October 24, 1867; H.C. Bunner, "City Athletics," *Harper's New Monthly Magazine*, LXVIII (January, 1884), 298.

18  Noah Brooks, *Our Base Ball Club and How It Won the Championship* (New York, 1884), 52-53.

19  *Frank Leslie's Boys' and Girls' Weekly*, XXXV (October 6, 1883), 174; *Harper's Weekly*, XXVII (October 13, 1883), 654; New York *Sun*, September 7, 1886.

20  Hall (ed.), *Tribune Book of Open-Air Sports*, 332-36. At this time Brooklyn had fourteen boat clubs, as well as cycling, riding, rod and gun, tennis, canoe, and baseball clubs. *The Brooklyn Daily Eagle Almanac* (New York, 1887), 85.

21  *Army and Navy Journal,* V (July 18, 1868), 757; XIV (August 24, 1878), 37; XVII (July 31, 1880), 1059-60; XIX (May 27, 1882), 999; XXI (April 5, 1884), 727; *ibid.,* (April 12, 1884), 758; *ibid.* (May 3, 1884), 824; *ibid.* (May 10, 1884), 845. Also see the New York *World,* November 26, 1883; Chicago *Times,* September 18, 1888; New York *Daily Tribune,* November 11, 1890. That "the athletic clubs of the militia regiments may be taken as a matter of course" was stated by H.C. Bunner in *Harper's New Monthly Magazine,* LXVIII (January, 1884), 298.

22  *Army and Navy Journal,* XVIII (August 23, 1879), 43; *ibid.* (December 6, 1879), 342; XIX (June 17, 1882), 1072; XX (March 10, 1883), 726; *ibid.* (July 21, 1883), 1147; W.H. Beehler, *The Cruise of the Brooklyn* (Philadelphia, 1885), 41-43.

23  W. Kershaw, "Athletics In and Around New York," *Harper's Weekly,* XXXIV (June 21, 1890), Supplement, 473.

24  Henry Chadwick's *Diary,* A.G. Spalding Collection, New York Public Library.

25  Arthur Ruhl, *Track Athletics* (New York, 1905), 268-69, 283-84.

26  *Ibid.,* 282-83.

27  Emmet A. Rice, *A Brief History of Physical Education* (New York, 1939), 152-55; For the Round Hill School see Russel B. Nye, *George Bancroft, Brahmin Rebel* (New York, 1945), 69-70; M.A. De Wolfe Howe, *The Life and Letters of George Bancroft,* 2 vols. (New York, 1908), 172-73. The Moravian Secondary School at Nazareth Hall, Pennsylvania seems to have introduced a program in 1755, but Beck and Follen were apparently the most effective teachers.

28  Augustus J Prahl, "The Turner," in Chap. IV of A.E. Zucker (ed.), *The Forty-Eighters: Political Refugees of the German Revolution of 1848* (New York, 1950), 92; *American-German Review,* XIV (June, 1948); Rice, *Brief History of Physical Education,* 169-170, 228; Henry Metzner, *A Brief History of the American Turnerbund* (Pittsburgh, 1924), 36.

29  See Edward H. Hartwell, *Physical Training in American Colleges and Universities* (Washington, D.C., 1886).

30  *Report of the Commissioner of Education for the Year 1884-85* (Washington, 1886), cx.

31  These statistics, which have all the faults of figures based on questionnaires, are derived from the *Report of the Commissioner of Education for the Year 1886-87,* 534-43, 560-67.

32  For athletics and physical culture in the "Y" see C. Howard Hopkins, *History of the YMCA in North America* (New York, 1951), *passim.*

33  *Harper's Weekly,* XIII (December 11, 1869), 786.

34  See the *Manhattan Athletic Club Chronicle* for 1888, pp. 2-3, 20, for early charges against the AAU. The foregoing dates of organization were gleaned from numerous books on sport, from the newspapers, and from magazines. Among the authors consulted were Krout, Martin, Bent, Potter, Davis, Spalding, and Menke. The first national trapshooting tournament was held at New Orleans under the sponsorship of the National Gun Association in 1885. Even ice yachting had its devotees of organization. Sportsmen in Maine, Vermont, New York, Ohio, Michigan, and Illinois as well as in the ocean harbors and in Canada turned to sailing on the ice

in winter. Since a good ice yacht cost between $400 and $1000, the sport was confined to the well-to-do. James Roosevelt of Hyde Park headed a Hudson River Yacht Club and Poughkeepsie became the center of racing in the valley. Hall (ed.), *Tribune Book of Open-Air Sports*, 462-72. During the 1870's and 1880's even roller skating became something of a craze, rink investments in 1885 reputedly exceeding $20,000,000. Arthur Meier Schlesinger, *The Rise of the City, 1878-1898* (New York, 1933), 314.

## Chapter 5

1   Philadelphia *Press*, September 21, 1890; New York *Times*, September 8, 21, 1890; New York *Daily Tribune*, November 20, 1890.

2   *Current Literature*, XXVIII (April, 1900), 57, quoting from the Rochester *Post Express*.

3   See Fred W. Lange, *History of Baseball in California and Pacific Coast Leagues, 1847-1938* (Oakland, 1938). The national popularity of baseball, which was played by children at the age of six or seven, was noted by a French visitor who remarked that "l'habilete des jeunes Americains dans ce genre de sport, et la nation entiere temoigne de l'enorme interet qu'elle y prend." Paul De Rousiers, *La Vie Americaine* (Paris, 1892), 510-11.

4   The role of the Orioles, sponsored by the brewer Harry Vanderhorst to advertise his beer, and of Baltimore in baseball history is discussed in John H. Lancaster, "Baltimore, A Pioneer In Organized Baseball," *Maryland Historical Magazine*, XXXV (March, 1940).

5   Editorial, New York *Daily Tribune*, October 17, 1912; *Outlook*, CIV (May 17, 1913), 104.

6   Asheville *Gazette-News*, July 9, 1915.

7   Ralph D. Paine, "The Reign of Baseball," *Munsey's Magazine*, XXXVII (June, 1907), 325.

8   Robert Smith, *Baseball, A historical narrative of the game* (New York, 1947), 206-208.

9   New York *Times*, July 24, 1914.

10  G.W. Axelson and C.A. Comiskey, *"Commy," The Life Story of Charles A. Comiskey* (Chicago, 1919), 318.

11  New York *Times*, December 5, 1918.

12  Denver *Times-Sun*, November 30, 1894; San Francisco *Bulletin*, August 24, 1895; Little Rock *Arkansas Gazette*, November 29, 1895.

13  Following is a list of first intercollegiate games: (1869) Rutgers, Princeton; (1870) Columbia; (1872) Yale; (1874) Harvard; (1876) Pennsylvania; (1877) Purdue; (1878) Brown; (1879) Michigan; (1881) Dartmouth; (1882) Minnesota; (1883) Navy; (1887) Notre Dame, Cornell, Penn State; (1888) Duke, North Carolina; (1889) Southern California, Fordham, Syracuse, Iowa; (1890) Pittsburgh, Colgate, Army, Vanderbilt, Illinois, Northwestern, Ohio State, Kansas, Missouri, Washington; (1891) Indiana; (1892) Georgia, Auburn, Georgia Tech, Alabama, Tennessee,

Stanford, California, Chicago, Wisconsin, Nebraska; (1893) Tulane, Louisiana State, Oregon State, Iowa State, Texas, Mississippi; (1894) Oklahoma, Washington State, Texas A&M, Oregon, Arkansas; (1895) Mississippi State; (1896) Clemson; (1897) Kansas State, Texas Christian; (1899) Baylor. The greatest years of organization were those from 1887 to 1894. The foregoing is derived from a study of L.H. Baker, *Football: Facts and Figures* (New York, 1945), 187-533. Many small colleges took up the game earlier than some of the major universities.

14   A.A. Stagg and W.W. Stout, *Touchdown!* (New York, 1927), 159.

15   One of the early forceful defenses of American football, however, was that of Professor Nathaniel S. Shaler of Harvard who wrote in 1889: "The sport necessarily involves a system of training by which rude strength is combined with address in a very beautiful manner. . . . To the ordinary well-conditioned young man the game has some eminent advantages. It teaches him to keep a cool head in moments of great activity. In it he learns to take considerable risks of bodily pain without hesitation, and to combine his action with that of his mates. It cultivates swift judgment, endurance, and self-confidence, without which even the naturally brave can never learn to meet danger. In no other form of activity can we, during times of peace, hope to give as valuable training to youth as is afforded by this sport." N.S. Shaler, "The Athletic Problem in Education," *Atlantic Monthly*, LXIII (January, 1889), 81.

16   Boston *Daily Globe*, December 27, 1905.

17   J.F.A. Pyre, *Wisconsin* (New York, 1920), 328. The story of athletics at Wisconsin and its place in university life is most fully told in Merle Curti and Vernon Carstensen, *The University of Wisconsin: A History, 1848-1925*, 2 vols. (Madison, 1949). There is considerable material on athletics in the Turner papers at the Wisconsin State Historical Society in Madison.

18   Charles F. Thwing, *A History of Higher Education in America* (New York, 1906), 386.

19   Samuel E. Morison, *The Development of Harvard University . . . 1869-1929* (Cambridge, 1930), XXIX-XXX.

20   New York *Times*, March 22, 1914.

21   W.W. Roper, "Football—A National Institution," *Collier's*, LXIV (November 29, 1919), 14.

22   James Naismith, *Basketball, Its Origins and Development* (New York, 1941), 105.

23   *Ibid.*, 146-56, 164-65; *Proceedings of the Third Annual Convention of the Intercollegiate Athletic Association of the United States*, New York, January 2, 1909, pp. 47-52.

24   *Cosmopolitan*, XXXI (September, 1901), 506.

25   *National Police Gazette*, LXX (July 10, 1897), 13; *Army and Navy Journal*, XXXVII (April 7, 1900), 758.

26   D.A. Willey, "The Spirit of Sport in the Army," *Harper's Weekly*, L, Part II (August 4, 1906), 1100.

27   William Rainey Harper, *The Trend in Higher Education* (Chicago, 1905), 276-84.

28  Denver *Daily News*, September 7, 1890. For the first exhibitions at Cheyenne see Ernest Staples Osgood, *The Days of the Cattleman* (Minneapolis, 1929), 50.

29  For the foregoing statistics see *Collier's*, XLVII (August 12, 1911), 29; Paul Monroe (ed.), *A Cyclopedia of Education* (New York, 1911), I, 276; New York *Times*, January 31, 1915.

30  Dorothy S. Ainsworth, *The History of Physical Education in Colleges for Women* (New York, 1930), 31.

31  William H. Taft *et al.*, *Service With Fighting Men*, 2 vols. (New York, 1922), II, 51.

32  New York *Times*, May 11, 1919, Sect. II, p. 4; May 26, 1919.

33  *Atlantic Monthly*, CXII (September, 1918), 304-309.

34  *Nation*, XCV (August 24, 1918), 198.

35  Even so, crowds around the sport placards in Times Square were often five times as large as those at the news placards. Lecture of Professor James T. Shotwell, Columbia University, March 1, 1939.

36  New York *Times*, June 28, December 31, 1919.

**Chapter 6**

1  Thorstein Veblen, *The Theory of the Leisure Class* (New York, 1931 edition), 246 ff., 262, 264.

2  *Congressional Record*, 45th Cong., 1 Sess., 1877, VI, 135-36; New Orleans *Daily Picayune*, October 25, 1877.

3  Coulter, *South During Reconstruction, 1865-1877*, 297; New Orleans *Daily Picayune*, December 14, 1873, January 4, 1880; Chicago *Times*, October 14, 1888.

4  Neely, *Agricultural Fair*, 193; *New York Clipper*, XIX (October 14, 1871), 221.

5  Henry T. Coates, *A Short History of the American Trotting and Racing Horse* (Philadelphia, 1901), 553; *Spirit of the Times*, XXIV (August 5, 1871), 397.

6  New York *Herald*, April 29, 1884; Boston *Herald*, June 19, 1875; Blake McKelvey, *Rochester, the Flower City, 1855-1890* (Cambridge, 1949), 232; *Wisconsin State Agricultural Society Transactions*, XXVI (Madison, 1888), 116, 118.

7  William Robertson and W. F. Robertson, *Our American Tour* (Edinburgh, 1871), 59; M. Philips Price (ed.), *America After Sixty Years; The Travel Diaries of Two Generations of Englishmen*, 2 vols. (London, 1881), I, 94; Joseph Hatten, *To-day in America*, 2 vols. (London, 1881), I, 94. Also see James F. Muirhead, *The Land of Contrasts* (Boston, 1898), 121.

8  Dwight Akers, *Drivers Up; the Story of American Harness Racing* (New York, 1938), 238-41.

9  San Francisco *Bulletin*, August 8, 1895.

10  Philadelphia *Press*, May 3, 1895.

11  *Spirit of the Times*, May 5, 1894, 560.

12  The above and immediately following information is derived from the *American Racing Manual* for 1936, pp. 193-301.

13  Trevathan, *American Thoroughbred*, 467.

14  A good account of the relationship of gamblers to racing is Alexander Gardiner, *Canfield: The True Story of a Gambler* (Garden City, 1930), *passim*.

15  *Laws of the State of New York, II* (1908), 1873-74.

16  New York *Times*, December 16, 1917.

17  Stephens, *American Yachting*, 87; J.D. Jerrold Kelley, *American Yachts, Their Clubs and Races* (New York, 1884), 181, 358.

18  *Overland Monthly*, XVI (June, 1891), 562. Challenges for "scrub racing" were popular, but there was no yacht club in southern California in 1890. *Ibid.*, 580-81.

19  Winfield M. Thompson and Thomas W. Lawson, *The Lawson History of the America's Cup* (Boston, 1902), 138.

20  See Alfred E. Loomis, *Ocean Racing: The Great Blue Water Yacht Races* (New York, 1946), 43, 107; Frank Menke, *The New Encyclopedia of Sports* (New York, 1947), 1000; Wecter, *Saga of American Society*, 457.

21  Pope circularized thousands of chambers of commerce, boards of trade, newspaper editors, and writers in behalf of good roads. *New York Sporting Times Devoted to Bicycling and Athletics*, X (July 29, 1893), 14. Also see S.S. McClure, *My Autobiography* (New York, 1914), 148-54; Charles E. Pratt, *The American Bicycler* (Boston, 1880), 230-40, 245-47; and Harold U. Faulkner's account in the *Dictionary of American Biography*.

22  *Wheelman*, I (October, 1882), 44.

23  John L. Scudder, "The Pulpit and the Wheel," *Wheelman*, I (October, 1882), 48.

24  Minneapolis *Journal*, May 3, 1895.

25  Benjamin Andrews, *History of the Last Quarter-Century in the United States, 1870-1895* (New York, 1896), 289-90; Mott, *American Journalism*, 594.

26  Cincinnati *Commercial Gazette*, October 21, 1894. See Dulles, *America Learns to Play*, 266.

27  Gilson Willets *et al.*, *Workers of the Nation*, 2 vols. (New York, 1903), I, 143; United States Bureau of the Census, *Manufactures, 1905* (Washington, 1905), Part I, 4.

28  Editorial, New York *Times*, September 13, 1900.

29  Burlingame, *Engines of Democracy*, 369-74.

30  E.C. Potter, Jr., *Kings of the Court: The Story of Lawn Tennis* (New York, 1936), 62-63.

31  *Fifty Years of Lawn Tennis in the United States* (New York, 1931), 235-43.

32  John Kieran, *The American Sporting Scene* (New York, 1941), 87.

33  William T. Tilden, *The Art of Lawn Tennis* (Garden City, N.Y., 1922), 116-117.

34  Harry B. Martin, *Fifty Years of American Golf* (New York, 1936), 69-71.

35  T.H. Arnold, "Golfing in the Far West," *Outing*, XXXV (March, 1900), 559; St. Louis *Post-Dispatch*, October 21, 1900.

36  Charles Blair Macdonald, *Scotland's Gift, Golf. Reminiscences 1872-1927* (New York, 1928), 175.

37    Harry Vardon, *My Golfing Life* (London, 1933), 238.

38    *New York Clipper*, VIII (May 5, 1860), 22.

39    Spalding, *America's National Game*, 191; Henry L. Mencken, *Happy Days, 1880-1892* (New York, 1940), 225; New Orleans *Daily Picayune*, July 6, 1885.

40    New York *Sun*, May 28, 29, 1886. The Boston *Sunday Herald*, July 24, 1887, listed a dozen leading bookmakers; Schlesinger, *Rise of the City, 1878-1898*, 309.

41    Nat Fleischer, *The Heavyweight Championship* (New York, 1949), XIII, 55; William E. Harding, *The Champions of the American Prize Ring* (New York, 1881), *passim*.

42    William Lyon Phelps, *Autobiography With Letters* (New York, 1939), 356.

43    Donald Barr Chidsey, *John The Great: The Times and Life of a Remarkable American: John L. Sullivan* (Garden City, N.Y., 1942), XII-XIII.

44    Little Rock *Arkansas Gazette*, October 3, 1895.

45    New York *Daily Tribune*, July 5, 1910; New Orleans *Times-Democrat*, July 6, 1910.

46    New York *Times*, March 22, 1919.

## Chapter 7

1    A.J. Bixby to Henry Chadwick, October 5, 1865, Harry Wright Correspondence, I; Frederick Law Olmstead, Jr., and Theodora Kimball, *Frederick Law Olmstead, Landscape Architect, 1822-1903*, 2 vols. (New York, 1922-1928), 22-23.

2    Elizabeth Halsey, *The Development of Public Recreation in Metropolitan Chicago* (Chicago, 1940), 114.

3    Charles William Eliot, *American Contributions to Civilization and Other Essays and Addresses* (New York, 1898), 192-93.

4    Frederick C. Howe, *The City, The Hope for Democracy* (New York, 1908), 227-32, 239-48.

5    *Year Book of the Young Men's Christian Associations, 1889* (New York, 1889), 116; Richard C. Morse, *History of the North American Young Men's Christian Associations* (New York, 1913), 166; *Year Book of the Young Men's Christian Associations of North America, 1898* (New York, 1898), 6-7.

6    See Gulick's letters and data sheets in *Athletic League Letters, 1896-1911*, Archives of the National Council of Young Men's Christian Associations, 291 Broadway, New York City.

7    In 1897 one student of the United States claimed that there were 49 colleges equipped with gyms and apparatus, as well as 29 universities, 60 academies, 27 seminaries, 26 asylums, 261 "Y's", 54 athletic clubs, 12 armories, 20 private gyms, and others. He gave figures stating that of those gyms equipped with Sargent apparatus, New York had 100, Massachusetts 75, Pennsylvania 72, Maryland 27, Ohio 27, and Connecticut 22. In all the South there were 75 reported gyms of this type—about the number in Massachusetts alone. Nathaniel S. Shaler, *The United States of America*, 2 vols. (New York, 1897), II, 467.

8    Howe, *The City, The Hope of Democracy* (New York, 1908), 241.

9   Richard T. Ely, *Problems of To-Day* (New York, 1888), 242; *Playground*, No. 17 (August, 1908), 4-5; *American City*, VI (March, 1912), 577.

10  Elizabeth Halsey, *The Development of Public Recreation in Metropolitan Chicago*, 253.

11  For early mention of athletics and the consolidated school see John H. Cook, "The Consolidated School as a Community Center," *Publications of the American Sociological Society*, XI (1917), 97-105.

12  For the early interest of institutional churches see Aaron Ignatius Abell, *The Urban Impact on American Protestantism, 1865-1900* (Cambridge, 1943), 45, 155, 157, and Charles Howard Hopkins, *The Rise of the Social Gospel in American Protestantism, 1865-1915* (New Haven, 1940), 115, 155. Also see Owen E. Pence, "Young Men's Christian Association," *The Encyclopedia Americana* (New York, 1948), XXIX, 658; *Cyclopedia of Education*, I, 266; *Athletic League of Young Men's Christian Associations of North America, 1911; Reports and Minutes*, 77, Archives of the National Council of Young Men's Christian Associations; Henry S. Curtis, *Play and Recreation for the Open Country* (Boston, 1914), *passim.*

13  Thomas C. Cochran, *The Pabst Brewing Company: The History of an American Business* (New York, 1948), 265; W. Patten and J.W. McSpadden (eds.), *The Book of Baseball* (New York, 1911), 118; *American Physical Education Review*, XIV (April, 1909), 192; Morse, *History of the North American Young Men's Christian Associations*, 171; New York *Times*, August 2, 1914.

14  See Mabel Newcomer, "Physical Development of Vassar College Students, 1884-1920," *Quarterly Publication of the American Statistical Association*, December 1, 1921.

15  Josiah Strong, *The Challenge of the City* (New York, 1907), 116-17, 137.

16  Jane Addams, *The Spirit of Youth and the City Streets* (New York, 1912), 91, 95-96.

17  Quoted in James R. Sullivan, *Athletics in the West and Far West* (New York, 1905), 46.

18  David F. Bowers (ed.), *Foreign Influences In American Life* (Princeton, 1944), 50-51.

19  Michael Pupin, *From Immigrant to Inventor* (New York, 1925), 99; Oscar Handlin, *The Uprooted* (Boston, 1951), 251-53; Mary Antin, *They Who Knock at Our Gates* (Boston, 1914), 51-53.

20  Hugo Munsterberg, *The Americans* (New York, 1905), 542-43.

21  *Annals of the American Academy of Political and Social Science*, XXXV (March, 1910), 156.

22  Luther H. Gulick, *A Philosophy of Play* (New York, 1920), 189-94.

23  Frederick L. Paxson, "The Rise of Sport," *Mississippi Valley Historical Review*, IV (September, 1917), 167-68. Paxson was an early theorist on the relation of sport to the growth of the city and its needs as well as to the safety-valve hypothesis and the frontier tradition. See also H. Addington Bruce, "Baseball and the National Life," *Outlook*, CIV (May 17, 1913), 104-107 for sport and the American way of

life: "Baseball . . . is to be regarded as a means of catharsis, or, perhaps better, as a safety-valve. . . . For exactly the same reason it has a democratizing value no less important to the welfare of society than is its value as a developmental and tension-relieving agent. The spectator at a ball game is no longer a statesman, lawyer, broker, doctor, merchant, or artisan, but just a plain everyday man, with a heart full of fraternity and good will to all his fellow men—except perhaps the umpire."

24   Sullivan, *Athletics in the West and Far West,* 10.

25   See Fuzzy Woodruff, *A History of Southern Football, 1890-1928,* 3 vols. (Atlanta, 1928), I, *passim.*

26   Francis Butler Simkins, *The South, Old and New: A History, 1820-1947* (New York, 1947), 308-309.

27   New York *Times,* July 6, 1877.

28   *Outing,* VI (June, 1885).

29   William Patten (ed.), *The Book of Sport* (New York, 1901), 8.

30   William M. Sloane, "Princeton," in *Four American Universities* (New York, 1895), 139. On this point also see the comment in *Youth's Companion,* quoted in the *Northwestern Christian Advocate,* XXXV (June 15, 1887), 7.

31   Theodore Roosevelt, *Value of an Athletic Training,* 3-4, 10-11.

32   *Harvard Graduate Magazine,* V (September, 1896), 67.

33   Quoted in the San Francisco *Bulletin,* September 13, 1895.

34   Thompson and Lawson, *Lawson History of the America's Cup,* 177.

35   *Literary Digest,* XLV (August 10, 1912), 213 (extract and translation).

36   Erik Bergvoll (ed.), *The Fifth Olympiad: The Official Report of the Olympic Games of Stockholm* (Stockholm, 1913), 411.

## Chapter 8

1   *Turf, Field and Farm,* VIII (June 18, 1869), 388.

2   *Ball Players' Chronicle,* June 27, 1867, 5.

3   Horace Greeley *et al., The Great Industries of the United States* (Hartford, 1872), 392,399.

4   Oscar Lewis, *The Big Four: The Story of Huntington, Stanford, Hopkins, and Crocker, and the Building of the Central Pacific* (New York, 1938), 173-74.

5   F.L. Paxson, "The Rise of Sport," *Mississippi Valley Historical Review,* IV (September, 1917), 153; *American Angler,* I (October 15, 1881), 13; Boston *Sunday Herald,* September 4, 1887; San Francisco *Chronicle,* February 17, 1890; New Orleans *Daily Picayune,* September 8, 1892; *Smart Set,* II (November, 1900), 1; *Saturday Evening Post,* CLXXXVII, Part I (August 1, 1914), 44-46.

6   *Delineator,* LXXVI (October, 1910), 261; *Vogue,* IL (May 15, 1917), 9.

7   Charles D. Stewart, "The United States of Base-Ball," *Century,* LXXIV (June, 1907), 307-319; New York *Times,* January 6, 1914.

8   For Allegheny Base-Ball Club *v.* Bennett see *Federal Reporter,* XIV, 257-61, where the court decreed, "The contract is unreasonable and void on grounds of

public policy." Philadelphia Ball Club, Limited *v*. Hallman *et al.*, *Pennsylvania County Court Reports*, VIII, 63. A Chicago club contract of the time stipulated that the contract could be voided by the club on several grounds or "for any other good and sufficient reason." Harry Wright Correspondence, I, Spalding Baseball Collection (New York Public Library).

9  *Everybody's Magazine*, XXIX (October, 1913), 525.

10  *National Police Gazette*, XLIV (May 10, 1884), 11.

11  James Hodgson, *Digest of Laws Prohibiting Sports Or Baseball On Sunday* (pamphlet in New York Public Library).

12  *Journal of Social Science* (June, 1885), 88.

13  Edgar W. Knight, *What College Presidents Say* (Chapel Hill, 1940), 164.

14  *Harvard Graduates Magazine*, II (March, 1894), 367.

15  Francis A. Walker, "College Athletics," *Harvard Graduates Magazine* (1893-1894), 12-13; Franklin Henry Giddings, *Democracy and Empire with Studies of Their Psychological, Economic, and Moral Foundations* (New York, 1900), 317; Josiah Royce, *Race Questions, Provincialism, and Other American Problems* (New York, 1908), 255; Harris E. Starr, *William Graham Sumner* (New York, 1925), 518; William Milligan Sloane (ed.), *The Life of James McCosh, A Record Chiefly Autobiographical* (New York, 1896), 223-24.

16  *Popular Science Monthly*, XXIV (March, 1884), 588; *Forum*, II (October, 1886), 142; *Atlantic Monthly*, LXIII (January, 1889), 87; *National Education Association Journal of Proceedings and Addresses* (New York, 1891), 348-54; *ibid*. (New York, 1893), 367 68, 619; *ibid*. (Chicago, 1896), 897-98, 917-18.

17  *Harvard Graduates Magazine*, III (March, 1895), 306-11.

18  Hall, *Adolescence*, I, 229.

19  George E. Johnson, *Education Through Recreation* (Cleveland, 1916), 31-35.

20  Gamaliel Bradford, *The Journal of Gamaliel Bradford*, edited by Van Wyck Brooks (Boston, 1933), 110.

21  C. F. Birdseye, *Individual Training in Our Colleges* (New York, 1907), 158-61; *School and Society*, December 20, 1930, 841-42; *Michigan Alumnus*, February, 1905, 219.

22  Woodrow Wilson, *The Public Papers of Woodrow Wilson: College and State*, 2 vols. (New York, 1925), II, 153-54, 175.

23  Richard H. Edwards, *Christianity and Amusements* (New York, 1915), 14-15.

24  New York *Times*, December 29, 1915.

25  See Earl Cline, *Inter-High School Athletics* (New York, 1909).

26  *American Chronicle of Sports and Pastimes*, May 28, 1868, 172.

27  Krout, *Annals of American Sport*, 149; *New York Clipper*, XVIII (January 7, 1871), 314.

28  San Francisco *Bulletin*, August 6, 1895; Inez Haynes Irwin, *Angels and Amazons* (Garden City, 1933), 268-70; Anne O'Hagag, "The Athletic Girl," *Munsey's Magazine*, XXV (August, 1901), 730-37.

29  Pittsburg *Post*, July 5, 1908.

30  *Delineator,* LXXVI (July, 1910), 254; New York *Times,* October 5, 1919.

31  New York *Herald,* July 17, 1865; New York *Daily Tribune,* August 23, 1867;
Peverelly, *The National Game,* 338; Bayrd Still, *Milwaukee, The History of a City*
(Madison, 1948), 227; *Ball Players' Chronicle,* June 6, 1867, 4; Seymour R.
Church, *Base Ball* (San Francisco, 1902), 38-39.

32  New York *Times,* July 6, 1877.

33  *Spalding's Base Ball Guide for 1885* (New York, 1885), 96-97.

34  *Lippincott's Monthly Magazine,* XXXVIII (October, 1886), 448; *Northwestern
Christian Advocate,* XXXIV (May 5, 1886), 1. The effect of the skating rink craze
on divorce, sobriety, church collections and attendance was also noted. *Ibid.,*
XXXIV (January 6, 1886), 1. Also see *Outing,* XII (July, 1888), 356; *Independent,*
XL (July 19, 1888), 14.

35  Chicago *Times,* October 30, 1873; T. DeWitt Talmage, *T. DeWitt Talmage As I
Knew Him* (New York, 1912), 117-18; Easton, Pa., *Free Press,* February 8, 1882.

36  *Wallace's Monthly,* I (October, 1875), 56; Talmage, *T. DeWitt Talmage As I Knew
Him,* 174.

37  Parmer, *For Gold and Glory* (New York, 1939), 136.

38  New York *Herald,* June 14, 1864, July 19, 1865; *Wilkes' Spirit of the Times,* XI
(January 28, 1865), 340; New York *Daily Tribune,* June 14, 1869; Cincinnati
*Commercial,* August 27, 1869; Chicago *Tribune,* September 20, 1886.

39  Examples of the appeal to decency and respectability can be found throughout
sporting journals and daily newspapers. See the Nashville *Daily News,* May 29,
June 1, 1860; *Turf, Field and Farm,* VIII (January 8, 1869), 24; *ibid.,* XXVII
(July 18, 1873), 40.

40  *World's Work,* XII (August, 1906), 78-79; *Laws of the State of New York,* II (1908),
1873-74.

41  New York *Daily Tribune,* March 4, 8, 1908.

42  New York *Daily Tribune,* July 6, 1910; *Independent,* LXIX (July 14, 1910), 99.

43  San Francisco *Chronicle,* August 6, 1912.

44  See the Chicago Athletic Club's *Cherry Circle,* V (February 15, 1899), 11-12;
Brunswick's pamphlet on *The Business of Billiards* (Chicago, 1945), 10-11.

45  *Annals of Iowa,* April, 1941, 649. The New York *Sun,* May 16, 1886, commented
on thirty-one games running concurrently on Sunday in Weehawken.

46  Frances E. Willard, *Glimpses of Fifty Years* (Chicago, 1889), 413. Also see
Benjamin Ward Richardson, *The Temperance Lesson Book* (New York, 1880),
188.

47  James Bryce, *The American Commonwealth,* 2 vols. (New York, 1889), II, 52;
Wilbur F. Crafts, *The Sabbath For Man* (New York, 1885), 121; A.H. Lewis, *A
Critical History of Sunday Legislation From 321 to 1888 A.D.* (New York, 1888),
258.

48  Editorial, New York *Evening Post,* November 9, 1895.

49  New York *Times,* June 9, 1901; Archer R. Shaw, *The Plain Dealer: One Hundred
Years in Cleveland* (New York, 1942), 219.

50  Editorial, New York *Times*, June 9, 1901.

51  *Ibid.*, June 17, 1901.

52  Chicago *Daily Tribune*, October 15, 1906.

53  James Bryce, *The American Commonwealth*, 2 vols. (New York, 1911), II, 783.

54  *Outlook*, CIV (July 19, 1913), 605-607; Martin, *Fifty Years of American Golf*, 263.

55  Wald, *House on Henry Street*, 95.

56  Young, *Character Through Recreation*, 240; *Outlook*, CIV (July 19, 1913), 605-607.

57  New York *Times*, May 18, 1919.

58  The Frederick Jackson Turner Papers in the Library of the Wisconsin State Historical Society, however, contain a number of letters dealing with the problem of intercollegiate sport in the early years of the century.

59  Goodspeed, *Angling in America*, 269-80.

60  Lloyd Goodrich, *Winslow Homer* (New York, 1945), 7, 9, 10, 11, 33, 34, 35, 42, 43, 58; Oliver Larkin, *Art and Life in America* (New York, 1949), 275; Lloyd Goodrich, *Thomas Eakins: His Life and Work* (New York, 1933), 19.

61  *Independent*, XXV (January 16, 1873), 7.

62  See the files of *Judge, Puck*, and *Life* as well as Murrell, *History of American Graphic Humor;* Nevins and Weitenkampf, *Century of Political Cartoons.*

63  See Sigmund Spaeth, *A History of Popular Music in America* (New York, 1948), 165, 598; *Handbook of American Sheet Music, 1947* (Philadelphia, 1947), *passim.*, published by dealer Harry Dichter.

64  Robert E. Spiller *et al., Literary History of the United States*, 3 vols. (New York, 1948), II, 1234.

65  Father Finn, S.J., *The Story of His Life Told by Himself* (New York, 1929); John Levi Cutler, *Gilbert Patten and His Frank Merriwell Saga*, University of Maine Studies, Ser. II, No. 31 (Orono, 1934); Stanley J. Kunitz and Howard Haycraft, *Twentieth Century Authors* (New York, 1942), 1083.

66  B.A. Botkin, *A Treasury of American Folklore* (New York, 1944), 273.

67  *The Bookman*, XIV (October, 1901), 123.

68  Charles Whibley, *American Sketches* (Edinburgh and London, 1908), 216-219.

69  *Literary Digest*, XLVII (September 6, 1913), 379-80.

70  *Bookman*, XXXII (December, 1910), 335. In the years from 1910 to 1914 baseball was increasingly featured in the popular magazines like *Literary Digest, American, Saturday Evening Post, Collier's, Harper's Weekly*, and *Cosmopolitan.*

71  Little Rock Arkansas *Gazette*, July 28, 1912.

72  Frank Jewett Mather, Jr., Charles Rufus Morey and William James Henderson, *The American Spirit in Art* (New York, 1927), 58; F.O. Matthiessen, *American Renaissance* (New York, 1949), 605; Homer Saint-Gaudens, *The American Artist and His Times* (New York, 1941), 178.

73  Larkin, *Art and Life in America*, 277.

74  Mather *et al.*, *American Spirit in Art*, 198, 209-14, 217, 299.

75  *American Architect and Building News*, XIX (April 10, 1886), Plate No. 537; XXIX (July 5, 12, 1890); Thomas E. Tallmadge, *The Story of Architecture in America* (New York, 1927), 275.

76  Talbot Faulkner Hamlin, *The American Spirit in Architecture* (New York, 1926), 282.

77  John T. McCutcheon, *Cartoons by McCutcheon* (Chicago, 1909), *passim.;* Thomas Craven (ed.), *Cartoon Cavalcade* (Chicago, 1945), 12-13; Coulton Waugh, *The Comics* (New York, 1947), 49, 63.

78  Albert Shaw, *A Cartoon History of Roosevelt's Career* (New York, 1910), *passim.;* John T. McCutcheon, *Drawn From Memory* (New York, 1950), 244-45.

79  Georges Sadoul, *Historie Générale Du Cinéma; L'Invention Du Cinéma* (Paris, 1948), I, 245, 333-35.

80  See *Motion Picture World*, XXIV (1915); *Motion Pictures: 1894-1912* (Washington, 1953); *Motion Pictures: 1912-1939* (Washington, 1951); *The Film Index, A Bibliography: The Film as Art* (New York, 1941), Vol. I; also see various histories of the movies.

## Chapter 9

1   Clark Griffith, owner of the Washington Senators, believed no one man was responsible since baseball is a national game based on the broadest foundations. Interview held in July, 1947, at Griffith Stadium, Washington, D.C.

2   *New Republic*, XXIV (October 20, 1920), 183-84.

3   *American Review of Reviews*, LXIII (April, 1921), 420.

4   John J. McGraw, *My Thirty Years in Baseball* (New York, 1923), 265.

5   *Collier's*, LXIX (April 29, 1922), 12.

6   Dallas *Morning News*, October 9, 1920.

7   Editorial, New York *Times*, October 11, 1924, 1.

8   *Saturday Evening Post*, CCII (April 12, 1930), 102.

9   New York *Times*, April 11, 1933, 24.

10  Arch Ward, "Football in the Middle West," in Allison Danzig and Peter Brandwein (eds.), *Sport's Golden Age; A Close-Up of the Fabulous Twenties* (New York, 1948), 131.

11  See Howard J. Savage, *et al.*, *American College Athletics. Bulletin Number Twenty Three* (New York, 1929). This bulletin was compiled after an exhaustive investigation of college sports and is one of the best surveys of the history of campus athletics. Deeply concerned with the preservation of the amateur spirit, the survey considered such elements in sport as administrative control, health, coaching, recruiting, the press, and the value of athletics. An excellent bibliography is to be found in W. Carson Ryan, Jr., *The Literature of American School and College Athletics. Bulletin Number Twenty-Four* (New York, 1929).

As mentioned in the Foreword, the page containing references 12 through 25 for Chapter 9 was missing from the author's manuscript and could not be reconstructed.

26  Harold C. Hand, *Campus Activities* (New York, 1938), 288, 294.

27  Newton Edwards and Herman G. Rickey, *The School in the American Social Order* (Boston, 1947), 743; Walter S. Monroe and Oscar F. Weber, *High School* (Garden City, N.Y., 1928), 412-13. This trend did not diminish student interest in intercollegiate athletics. A survey of 23 colleges and universities of the 1920's showed that the percentage of space in college papers devoted to sport varied from 32 percent on intercollegiate and 4 percent on intramural at Wisconsin to 23 percent and 8 percent at Princeton, 25 percent and 6 percent at Yale, and 22 percent and 10 percent at Chicago. At Smith only 3 percent was devoted to intramural sport and there was no intercollegiate program. R.H. Edwards *et al.*, *Undergraduates* (Garden City, N.Y., 1928), 91.

28  In 1938 there were more races run in the United States than in England, France, and Australia combined—the three leading countries next to the U.S. New York *Times,* December 25, 1938, Sect. V, 6.

29  *American Racing Manual* for 1936, 204, 251, 274.

30  Editorial, New York *Times,* July 2, 1921, 8.

31  Los Angeles *Times,* November 26, 1920; New York *Times,* August 2, 1920, 17.

32  For racing in the 1920's see *Aerial Age Weekly,* XI (May 10, 1920), 283; Harry Bruno, *Wings Over America: The Inside Story of American Aviation* (New York, 1942), *passim.;* Ernst W. Dichman, *This Aviation Business* (New York, 1929), 52 ff.; *A Chronicle of the Aviation Industry in America, 1903-1947* (Cleveland, 1948); files of various aviation magazines.

33  Archibald D. Turnbull and Clifford L. Lord, *History of United States Naval Aviation* (New Haven, 1949), 212.

34  Gleason L. Archer, *History of Radio to 1926* (New York, 1938), 212-15.

35  Gleason L. Archer, *Big Business and Radio* (New York, 1939), 57. See also *Wireless Age,* X (November, 1922), 31.

36  Archer, *Big Business and Radio,* 63, 71; *The American Radio; A Report on the Broadcasting Industry in the United States from the Commission on Freedom of the Press* (Chicago, 1947), 13; *Wireless Age,* X (December, 1922), 44.

37  New York *Times,* September 24, 1927, 14.

## Chapter 10

1  Dixon Wecter, *The Age of the Great Depression, 1929-1941* (New York, 1948), 223.

2  *Outlook and Independent,* CLV (August 20, 1930), 614; Little Rock *Arkansas Gazette,* August 4, 1936.

3  *Time,* XXVI, Part I (September 16, 1935), 48; Salt Lake City *Deseret News,* July 16, 1936.

4  A new golf course, swimming pool, Hucy Long Field House (costing about $1,000,000), paid trips for students, huge band, and baseball stadium were all undertaken by the Louisiana governor. A critical account is found in Harnett T. Kane, *Louisiana Hayride: The American Rehearsal for Dictatorship, 1928-1940* (New York, 1941), 217 ff.

5  *Round Table Conference*, NCAA, December 29, 1938.

6  New York *Times*, January 31, 1939, 25.

7  *Literary Digest*, CXXII (December 12, 1936), 37; *Scholastic*, February 18, 1939, 33.

8  Arch Ward, "Everybody's Champ," in *Chicago's Tribute to His Excellency Most Rev. Bernard J. Sheil D. D. on the Twenty-Fifth Anniversary of His Consecration* (Chicago, 1953).

9  Allen, *Since Yesterday*, 149-150.

10 *Recreation*, XXV (December, 1940), 541.

11 Tom R. Underwood (ed.), *Thoroughbred Racing & Breeding; The Story of the Sport and Background of the Horse Industry* (New York, 1945), 147.

12 See J. Frederick Dewhurst & Associates, *America's Needs and Resources* (New York, 1947), 276; T.W. Kearney, "Ten Million Keglers Can't Be Wrong," in Herbert Graffis (ed.), *Esquire's First Sports Reader* (New York, 1945), 229.

13 *American City*, L (August, 1935), 65. Quotes NRA Year Book statistics.

14 *Recreation*, XLIII (November, 1949), 381. For the best discussion of governmental concern with recreation see Frederick W. Cozens and Florence Scovil Stumpf, *Sports in American Life* (Chicago, 1953), 170 ff., 186, 210-11.

15 Herbert Hoover, "Building Boys for America," in *Addresses Upon the American Road, 1933-1938* (New York, 1938), 357.

16 Donald S. Howard, *The WPA and Federal Relief Policy* (New York, 1943), 127, 130; Basil Rauch, *History of the New Deal, 1933-1938* (New York, 1944), 64; Wecter, *Age of the Great Depression*, 224.

17 Dewhurst & Associates, *America's Needs and Resources*, 284; Office of Business Economics, *National Income and Product of the United States, 1929-1951* (Washington, 1951), 196-97.

18 Spink, *Judge Landis*, 278.

19 Cozens and Stumpf, *Sports in American Life*, 210-14.

20 *Recreation*, XXXVII (January, 1944), 618; *ibid.*,(August, 1944), 225, 274; *Think*, May, 1944, 39; Henry L. Stimson and Mc. George Bundy, *On Active Service* (New York, 1947), 505.

21 *Life*, XXI (July 1, 1946), 19.

22 *Life*, XIX (December 17, 1945), 8; *Time*, XLIX (February 10, 1947), 49.

23 *Athletic Journal*, February, 1949, 20.

24 John Kieran (ed.), *Information Please Almanac, 1947* (New York, 1947), 864; Wind, *Story of American Golf*, 378; *United States Golf Association Yearbook* for 1948.

25 Frank G. Menke, *The Encyclopedia of Sports* (New York, 1953), 522-24.

26 *Time*, XLIX (January 13, 1947), 69.

27 *World Almanac and Book of Facts for 1948*, 837, 839; *Fortune*, XXXIII (February, 1946), 135; *Life*, XXII, Part II (May 5, 1947), 46; Menke, *Encyclopedia of Sports*, 210.

28  *Lloyd's Register of American Yachts, 1948* (Baltimore, 1948), 509 and *passim.*; *Life*, XXIII, Part I (July 21, 1947), 71-73.

29  New York *Times*, October 10, 1947, 50.

30  New York *Sunday News*, August 9, 1953, 78; *American*, CLI (April, 1951), 136.

31  Margaret B. Hodges (ed.), *Social Work Year Book* (New York, 1949), 429, 434; New York *Sunday News*, August 9, 1953, 78.

32  See *Fortune*, XXXVII (May, 1948), 79; *Quick*, III (August 7, 1950), 60.

33  New York *Times*, July 28, 1920, 1-2; July 26, 1921, 11; October 8, 1925, 24; *Outlook*, CXXXVII (August 13, 1924), 563.

34  *Nineteenth Century*, XC (August, 1921), 250.

35  D.W. Brogan, *France Under the Republic* (New York, 1939), 608-609.

36  Josephus Daniels, *Shirt-Sleeve Diplomat* (Chapel Hill, 1947), 439.

37  New York *Times*, February 19, 1928, Sect. III, 3; August 14, 1934, 19.

38  Sidney Webb and Beatrice Webb, *Soviet Communism: A New Civilization?* 2 vols. (New York, 1938), II, 909-10.

39  *Department of State Bulletin*, XXV (December 14, 1951), 1007-1010; *U.S. News and World Report*, XXXIII (July 25, 1952), 42, 44.

40  New York *Times*, December 7, 1926, 5; Herbert W. Schneider and Shepard B. Clough, *Making Fascists* (Chicago, 1929), 184-85.

41  G. Salvemini, *Under the Axe of Fascism* (New York, 1936), 330-37.

42  See Ernest F. Henderson, *A Short History of Germany*, 2 vols. (New York, 1919), II, 550-57.

43  New York *Times*, December 18, 1927, Sect. V, 4-5; *ibid.*, November 6, 1927, Sect. V, 8; *Report of the American Olympic Committee . . . 1928*, 1; Norma Schwendener, *A History of Physical Education in the United States* (New York, 1942), 219-32.

44  Adolf Hitler, *Mein Kampf* (New York, 1939), 614-17.

45  New York *Times*, August 5, 1935, 7; August 23, 1935, 1; October 18, 1935, 1; December 4, 1935, 26.

46  London *Times*, August 17, 1936, 11.

47  Friedrich Hiess, *Germany* (Berlin, 1936). This was a standard illustrated propaganda book issued to foreign tourists.

## Chapter 11

1  *Recent Social Trends in the United States: Report of the President's Research Committee on Social Trends* (New York, 1934), 926-27; *Recreation, Yearbook Issue*, XXXI (June, 1947), 116, 117.

2  New York *Times*, October 7, 1923, Sect. IX, 8; June 26, 1927, Sect. II, 11; December 23, 1928, Sect. VI, 7; *Collier's*, LXXX (June 25, 1927), 40.

3  *Collier's*, CXXI (March 6, 1948), 14; Edward Grant Barrow, *My Fifty Years in Baseball* (New York, 1951), 23; New York *Times*, November 10, 1953, 40.

4   See *World Almanac* for years 1925, 1953. Between 1924 and 1930 the number tripled from 16 to 47, the depression decade had a rise of from 47 to 79, and since 1940 the total has increased from 79 to 130.

5   Upton Sinclair, *The Goose-Step: A Study of American Education* (Pasadena, 1923), 372.

6   Robert R. Doane, *The Measurement of American Wealth* (New York, 1933), 67. Figures in the table are only rough approximations. The difficulty and the guess-work involved in determining the outlay for recreation and amusement, despite the census reports, is mentioned in Harold Barger, *Outlay and Income in the United States, 1921-1938* (New York, 1942), 230-31.

7   J. Weinberger, "Economic Aspects of Recreation," *Harvard Business Review* (Summer Number, 1937), 448.

8   Derived from the *Statistical Abstract of the United States*, 1909, 188; 1919, 211; 1922, 217; 1932, 756; 1948, 850.

9   J. Frederic Dewhurst and Associates, *America's Needs and Resources* (New York, 1947), 282.

10  Figures for the even years were taken from the *Statistical Abstract* for 1909, 1919, 1929, and 1939 since others were not available. Also see the Bureau of the Census, *Census of Manufactures: 1947*, Volume II, *Statistics by Industry* (Washington, D.C., 1949), 805; *Census Of Business*, VI, *Service Trade—General Statistics* (Washington, D.C., 1952), 9.03; *Business Week*, June 7, 1952, 86; *Newsweek*, XXXVIII (July 30, 1951), 42; *ibid.*, XXXIX (January 28, 1952), 56; *Life*, XXXIII (November 19, 1951), 33.

11  See the *Annual of Advertising Art in the United States* (New York, 1921), *passim.*, for post-World War I sporting themes used by such diversified businesses as U.S. Rubber, Pierce Arrow, Eastman Kodak, Colgate, Lever Brothers, Liggett & Myers, and Hart, Schaffner, and Marx.

12  Clyde H. Metcalf, *A History of the United States Marine Corps* (New York, 1939), 525.

13  *Playground*, March 1920, 584. Oakland's industrial recreation program grew from 874 to over 5000 participants between 1926 and 1930. *Industrial Recreation in Oakland* (Oakland, 1931), 14.

14  *Outdoor Recreation for Employees* (New York, n.d.), 2, 12. In the same year in St. Paul, Minnesota, there were 10 Commercial League and 10 Mercantile League teams in operation. Many industries were helping to sponsor baseball teams throughout the Midwest. *Literary Digest*, LXXXV (April 18, 1925), 69.

15  *Monthly Labor Review* (U.S. Bureau of Labor Statistics), May, 1927, 2, 3.

16  For the pessimistic viewpoint see E. E. Cummins, *The Labor Problem in the United States* (New York, 1933), 508; Carroll R. Daugherty, *Labor Problems in American Industry* (Boston, 1938), 613; and Department of Labor Bureau Statistics findings, New York *Times*, January 8, 1928, Section IX, 4.

17  *Illinois Central Magazine*, XI (April, 1923), 5; the *Louisville & Nashville Employes' Magazine*, V (April, 1929), 61-62; *ibid.* (July, 1929), 6; *ibid.* (September, 1929), 61; *ibid.* (October, 1929), 63; *Missouri Pacific Lines Magazine*, VI (March, 1929),

36; *ibid.* (April, 1929), 35-38; *ibid.* (May, 1929), 30. For the activities of Bell Telephone employees in horseback riding, golf, basketball, baseball and all kinds of sport see the *Bell Laboratories Record* section on "Club Notes" for the middle twenties.

18  Richard H. Lansburgh, *Industrial Management* (New York, 1923), 340-42; Dexter S. Kimball, *Principles of Industrial Organization* (New York, 1925), 392-93; William B. Cornell, *Industrial Organization and Management* (New York, 1928), 356-57.

19  H. L. Vierow, *Findings of Chicago Industrial Recreation Survey* (Chicago, 1939), 21; Arthur J. Todd, William F. Byron, and Howard Vierow, *The Chicago Recreation Survey, 1937,* Vol. III, *Private Recreation* (Chicago, 1938), 149 ff.; *American Federationist,* XLV (January, 1938), 21; Leonard Diehl and Floyd R. Eastwood, *Industrial Recreation* (Lafayette, Ind., 1940), 2-3; *Factory Management and Maintenance: How To Get More Production, 50 Case Studies* (New York, 1941), 141.

20  *Industrial Sports Journal,* XII (May 15, 1951), 6, cited in Frederick W. Cozens and Florence Scovil Stumpf, *Sports in American Life* (Chicago, 1953), 52. Quotes are from Cozens and Stumpf, 62. Another estimate of more than 18,000 industrial and business firms in recreation was given in George Weinstein, "Athletes in Overalls," *Coronet,* XXIX (April, 1951), 56-58. Among those concerns which sponsored major programs were North American Aircraft, Eastman Kodak, the Ford Motor Co., International Business Machines, the Peerless Woolen Mills of Rossville, Georgia, and the West Point Manufacturing Co. in Alabama.

21  Louis Levine, *The Women's Garment Workers* (New York, 1924), 297, 492-93; Cozens and Stumpf, *Sports in American Life,* 58; Harry Haskel, *A Leader of the Garment Workers; The Biography of Isidore Nagler* (New York, 1950); 266-68.

22  *Sport Call,* February, 1936, 1.

23  *Ibid.,* January, 1937, 1.

24  *Report of the General Executive Board and Proceedings of the Thirteenth Biennial Convention of the Amalgamated Clothing Workers of America,* May 13-24, 1940. *Documentary History,* ACWA: 1938-1940 (New York, 1940), 535.

25

26  New York *Times,* January 8, 1928, Sect. IX, 4.

27  Gordon S. Watkins and Paul A. Dodd, *Labor Problems* (New York, 1940), 742-43; *Personnel Journal,* December, 1939, 228.

28  *Personnel Journal,* December, 1939, 228.

29  Watkins and Dodd, *Labor Problems,* 742.

30  Daugherty, *Labor Problems in American Industry,* 506.

31  John R. Tunis, "American Sports and American Life," *Nation,* CXXX (June 25, 1930), 729; Ferdinand Lundberg, *America's 60 Families* (New York, 1938), 408-46.

32  Mumford, *Technics and Civilization,* 303-305, 307; Toynbee, *Study of History,* 305-306.

33  Sinclair, *The Goose-Step,* 370.

34  Robert M. Hutchins, "Gate Receipts and Glory," *Saturday Evening Post*, CCXI, Part 2 (December 3, 1938), 74.

35  Jerome Davis, *Capitalism and Its Culture* (New York, 1935), 272.

36  See Edward C. Lindeman, "Recreation and Morale," *American Journal of Sociology*, XLVII (November, 1941), 399.

### Chapter 12

1  One decision which may have helped clear the air for promoters was that of Justice William Hitz of the District of Columbia's Supreme Court. He dismissed a damage suit for $10,000, declaring that the spectator assumes the risk whether he sits in the grandstand with or without protection. New York *Times*, December 7, 1920, 14.

2  *American Law Reports*, XXVI, 359; (259 U.S. 200, 66 L. ed. 896, 42 Sup. Cit. Rep. for three-fold damages under Sherman Anti-Trust Act).

3  *Notre Dame Lawyer*, XIX (March, 1944), 262-72; Jay B. Topkis, "Monopoly in Professional Sports," *Yale Law Journal*, LVIII (April, 1949), 691-712; *Virginia Law Review*, XXXII (November, 1946), 1173; New York *Times*, November 10, 1953, 40.

4  Zechariah Chafee, Jr., *State House versus Pent House* (Providence, 1937), 1, 60.

5  *The Kefauver Committee Report on Organized Crime* (New York, 1951), 131 ff., 138-39, 176.

6  *Outlook*, CXXII (June 11, 1919), 252.

7  William C. Smith, *Americans in the Making* (New York, 1939), 316.

8  Frederick M. Thrasher, *The Gang: A Study of 1,313 Gangs in Chicago* (Chicago, 1927), 458 and *passim*. Henry Pratt Fairchild, *Greek Immigration to the United States* (New Haven, 1911), 124, 125, 152, 209. Among the principal recreations of Italians in 1919 were the saloon, the theater, marionettes, and moving pictures, but sport was ignored by the study of Robert F. Foerster, *The Italian Emigration of Our Times* (Cambridge, 1919), 396-97.

9  Federal Writers Project, *The Italians of New York: A Survey* (New York, 1938), 211; R. A. Schermerhorn, *These Our People: Minorities in American Culture* (Boston, 1949), 455.

10  Kenneth D. Miller, *The Czecho-Slovaks in America* (New York, 1922), 69.

11  *The Universal Jewish Encyclopedia*, I, 584. For Jewish contributions to sport also see Stanley B. Frank, *The Jew in Sports* (New York, 1936) and Harold V. Ribalow, *The Jew in American Sports* (New York, 1948).

12  *Universal Jewish Encyclopedia*, I, 584.

13  An outstanding example of discrimination was that against Japanese-Americans in California. See Edward K. Strong, Jr., *The Second-Generation Japanese Problem* (Stanford University, California, 1934), 24-25.

14  New York *Times*, May 25, 1939, 34; Wecter, *Age of the Great Depression, 1929-1941*, 243; Shane Leslie, *American Wonderland* (London, 1936), 118.

15  New York *Tribune*, October 2, 4, 1867; A.S. Young, *Great Negro Baseball Stars* (New York, 1953); Alrutheus Ambush Taylor, *The Negro in Tennessee*, 1865-1888 (Washington, 1941), 240-41; Robert Smith, *Baseball*, 317-21; James Weldon Johnson, *Along This Way* (New York, 1935), 36-39.

16  Ulrich B. Phillips, *American Negro Slavery* (New York, 1927), 314; Marquis James, *The Life of Andrew Jackson*, 2 vols. (New York, 1940), I, 268; *Sporting Review*, III (February, 1840), 115.

17  W.P. Dabney, *Cincinnati's Colored Citizens*, 179; New York *Tribune*, July 29, 1900; Parmer, *For Gold and Glory*, 150.

18  Edwin B. Henderson, *The Negro in Sport* (Washington, D.C., 1939), 5, 8, 88. New Orleans *Daily Picayune*, May 14, 1884, and August 3, 1890. By 1884 New Orleans had a boxing and wrestling tournament with numerous entries, and in 1890 an Orleans Athletic Club for colored men put on fights for mixed audiences.

19  New Orleans *Daily Picayune*, August 16, 1892.

20  Marshall W. "Major" Taylor, *The Fastest Bicycle Rider in the World* (Worcester, 1928), *passim.*

21  James J. Corbett, *The Roar of the Crowd* (New York, 1925), 165.

22  Salt Lake City *Tribune*, September 9, 1892.

23  See D.W. Brogan, *The American Character* (New York, 1944), 142-43.

24  John Hope Franklin, *From Slavery to Freedom; A History of American Negroes* (New York, 1947), 430; *Playground*, April, 1921, 85, reprinted from *Park International* for November, 1920.

25  Charles S. Johnson, *The Negro in American Civilization* (New York, 1930), 302, 306.

26  Nat Fleischer, *Black Dynamite: The Story of the Negro in the Prize Ring From 1792 to 1938*, 3 vols. (New York, 1938), I, 4.

27  Florence Murray (ed.), *The Negro Handbook*, 1947 (New York, 1949), 293 ff.

28  Ben Richardson, *Great American Negroes* (New York, 1945), *passim.*

29  *Quarterly Review of Higher Education Among Negroes*, I (April, 1933), 22; *Opportunity—Journal of Negro Life*, XXII (June, 1935), 167.

30  *Louisiana Weekly*, August 15, 1936, 8.

31  Chicago *Daily Tribune*, August 19, 1940, 21.

32  *Annals of the American Academy of Political and Social Science*, CXCIV (November, 1937), 78.

33  Federal Writers' Project, *Alabama: A Guide to the Deep South* (New York, 1941), 120. For the early history of NORD see *Proceedings of the 31st National Recreation Congress* (New Orleans, 1949), 11-16.

34  Richard Sterner, *The Negro's Share* (New York, 1943), 252; *The Black Worker*, II (August, 1936), 25.

35  *Annals of the American Academy of Political and Social Science*, CCXXXVI (November, 1944), 147.

## Chapter 13

1  New York *Times*, January 19, 1922, 1; November 3, 1925, 24; January 17, 1926, Sect. II, 1.

2  *Forum*, LXXVI (December, 1926), 838.

3  Ernest Dimnet, *The Art of Thinking* (New York, 1926), 61, 62.

4  Editorial, New York *Times*, February 19, 1925, 18; E. H. Wilkins, *The Changing College* (Chicago, 1927), 114, 115, 119.

5  Abraham Flexner, *Universities—American, English, German* (New York, 1930), 64, 65; Bertrand Russell, *Education and the Good Life* (New York, 1926), 135.

6  New York *Times*, December 22, 1930, 1, 15; *Columbia University Annual Reports*, 1931; *President's Annual Report*, 1931, 37-39.

7  *School and Society*, XXII (November 7, 1925), 581.

8  New York *Times*, January 20, 1927, 9.

9  *Current History*, XXXI (December, 1929), 560.

10 *Research Quarterly of the American Physical Education Association*, V (May, 1934), 79, 81, 82; *ibid.*, IV (October, 1933), 13, 29.

11 Will Durant, *The Mansions of Philosophy* (New York, 1929), 247; Ellwood P. Cubberley, *An Introduction to the Study of Education*, revised by W. C. Kells (New York, 1933), 338; Ralph W. Pringle, *The Junior High School: A Psychological Approach* (New York, 1937), 345.

12 Robert M. Hutchins, *The Higher Learning in America* (New Haven, 1936), 11.

13 Ernest H. Wilkins, "College Football Costs," *School and Society*, XLVII (March 19, 1938), 383; John R. Tunis, *Democracy and Sport* (New York, 1941), VII; Edgar W. Knight, *Fifty Years of American Education* (New York, 1952), 446-47. Also see Charles H. Judd, *Education and Social Progress* (New York, 1934), 195; *School and Society*, LXXIV (November 24, 1951), 333; LXXV (May 24, 1952), 333; John Lardner, "My Case Against Sport," *American*, CLII (October, 1951), 24 ff.

14 *American Mercury*, XLVIII (October, 1939), 131; Stephen Leacock, *Too Much College* (New York, 1939), 139-40; S. R. Slavson, *Recreation and the Total Personality* (New York, 1946), 96. See also C. D. Zachry and M. Lighty, *Emotion and Conduct in Adolescence* (New York, 1940), 221.

15 Dearborn *Independent* cited in the *Literary Digest*, LXXXVI (September 12, 1925), 32-33.

16 *Ibid.*, LXXXVIII (January 30, 1926), 28, 57.

17 New York *Times*, January 7, 1926, 27.

18 Lynd and Lynd, *Middletown*, 341.

19 *Literary Digest*, XCIV (July 30, 1927), 28.

20 New York *Times*, July 11, 1921, 11; September 22, 1927, 20.

21 Cozens and Stumpf, *Sports in American Life*, 100.

22 Herbert Hoover, *Addresses Upon the American Road, 1946-1950* (Stanford, 1951), 192.

23  Grant Wood, *Revolt Against the City* (Iowa City, 1935), 21, 22.

24  This trend was noticed during the Depression exhibition of Frederick Keppel & Company. *Literary Digest*, CXX (December 28, 1935), 23.

25  *George W. Bellows—His Lithographs* (New York, 1927); *The Paintings of George Bellows* (New York, 1929); Boswell, *George Bellows; International Studio*, LVI (October, 1915), 242; *ibid.*, LXXXI (May, 1925), 82.

26  Kieran, *American Sporting Scene, passim.*; Richard Elmore, "Sport in American Sculpture," *International Studio*, LXXXI (November, 1925), 98-101, gave a broad treatment of sporting sculpture of the 1920's. Among the sculptors were Laura Fraser, Charles Lopez, Douglas Tilden, John Frew, Paul Landowski, and others. Oliver Larkin claims that Mahonri Young "could draw ditchdiggers and prize fighters with a swift vitality like that of Daumier." Larkin, *Art in American Life*, 393.

27  See *Xth Olympiad . . . Los Angeles . . . 1932, Olympic Competition and Exhibition of Art, Catalogue.* Los Angeles Museum of History, Science and Art, 1932.

28  Thomas E. Tallmadge, *The Story of Architecture in America* (New York, 1927), 275-79; Martin, *Fifty Years of American Golf*, 332 ff.; *American Architect—The Architectural Review* (for 1924); *American Architect and Architecture*, February, 1938, 57-58; *Progressive Architecture*, March, 1954, *passim.*

29  Sinclair Lewis, *Elmer Gantry* (New York, 1927), 361.

30  For one highly critical approach see the *Saturday Review of Literature*, December 15, 1951, 6-7. Also see *ibid.*, April 11, 1953, 47-48, 58; *New Yorker*, XXII (September 28, 1946), 46-54.

31  Vachel Lindsay, *Collected Poems* (New York, 1939), 93.

32  Waugh, *The Comics*, 51.

33  Smith, *Baseball*, 360-61.

34  George H. McKnight, *Modern English in the Making* (New York, 1928), 552.

35  John Kieran, "The Sportsman's Lexicon," *Saturday Review of Literature*, X (July 22, 1933), 1-3; Smith, *Baseball*, 358-60; Edward J. Nichols, "An Historical Dictionary of Baseball Terminology," excerpt (State College, Pa., 1939), 4.

36  See L.V. Berrey and M. Van Den Bark, *The American Thesaurus of Slang* (New York, 1942).

37  H. L. Mencken, *The American Language* (New York, 1948), 561-62.

38  See, for example, Lewis Jacobs, *The Rise of the American Film, A Critical History* (New York, 1939), 514, for this practice in *Angels With Dirty Faces.*

# Bibliography

## SELECTED REFERENCES IN THE HISTORY OF AMERICAN SPORT

Ainsworth, Dorothy S., *The History of Physical Education in Colleges for Women.* New York, 1930.

Akers, Dwight, *Drivers Up: The Story of American Harness Racing.* New York, 1938.

Allen, Lee, *The Cincinnati Reds.* New York, 1948.

Anderson, James D., *Making the American Thoroughbred.* Norwood, Mass., 1916.

Anson, Adrian C., *A Ball Player's Career.* Chicago, 1900.

Axelson, G.W., and Charles A. Comiskey, *"Commy": The Life Story of Charles A. Comiskey.* Chicago, 1919.

Baker, H.L., *Football: Facts and Figures.* New York, 1945.

Bartlett, Arthur C., *Baseball and Mr. Spalding: The History and Panorama of Baseball.* New York, 1951.

Bealle, Morris A., *The Washington Senators.* Washington, 1947.

———*The History of Football at Harvard, 1874-1948.* Washington, 1948.

Bent, Newell, *American Polo.* New York, 1929.

Berry, Elmer, *The Philosophy of Athletics.* New York, 1927.

Blanchard, John A. (ed.), *The H Book of Harvard Athletics, 1852-1922.* Cambridge, 1923.

*Boy's and Girl's Book of Sports.* Providence, 1835.

*Boy's Book of Sports, or Exercises and Pastimes of Youth.* New Haven, 1838.

Bradley, Hugh, *Such Was Saratoga.* New York, 1940.

Braethen, Sverre O., *Ty Cobb, The Idol of Fandom.* New York, 1928.

Brinley, Francis, *Life of William T. Porter.* New York, 1860.

Brown, Warren, *Win, Lose, or Draw.* New York, 1947.

Budge, J. Donald, *Budge on Tennis.* New York, 1939.

Burgess, Edward, *American and English Yachts.* New York, 1887.

Burnes, Robert L., *50 Golden Years of Sports.* St. Louis, 1948.

Camp, Walter, *Walter Camp's Book of College Sports.* New York, 1893.

Campbell, Gordon, *Famous American Athletes of Today.*

Carver, Robin, *The Book of Sports.* Boston, 1834.

*Century of Baseball.* Cooperstown, 1940.

Chadwick, Henry, *The Sports and Pastimes of American Boys.* New York, 1884.

Chidsey, Donald Barr, *John the Great: The Times and Life of a Remarkable American, John L. Sullivan.* Garden City, 1942.

Church, Seymour R., *Baseball: The History, Statistics and Romance of the American National Game from its Inception to the Present Time.* San Francisco, 1902.

Cleveland, Charles B., *The Great Baseball Managers.* New York, 1950.

Coates, Henry T., *A Short History of the American Trotting and Pacing Horse.* Philadelphia, 1906.

Cochrane, Gordon S., *Baseball: The Fan's Game.* New York, 1939.

Coffin, Roland F., *The America's Cup.* New York, 1885.

Collett, Glenna, *Ladies in the Rough.* New York, 1929.

Connett, Eugene V., *Yachting in North America.* New York, 1948.

Cooper, John Andrew, "The Effect of Participation in Athletics Upon Scholarship Measured by Achievement Tests." Unpublished Ph.D. dissertation, The Pennsylvania State College. *Penn State Studies In Education*, No. 7, 1933.

Corbett, James J., *The Roar of the Crowd.* New York, 1925.

Cozzens, Fred S., *et al.*, *Yachts and Yachting.* New York, 1888.

Crowther, Samuel, *Rowing.* New York, 1905.

Curtiss, Frederic H., and John Heard, *The Country Club, 1882-1932.* Brookline, 1932.

Daley, Arthur, *Inside Baseball: A Half Century of the National Pastime.* New York, 1950.

Davis, John H., *The American Turf.* New York, 1907.

Davis, Parke H., *Football, The American Intercollegiate Game.* New York, 1911.

Davis, Robert H., *"Ruby Robert" Alias Bob Fitzsimmons.* New York, 1926.

Dempsey, Jack, and Myron Stearns (coll.), *Round By Round.* New York, 1940.

De Witt, Robert M., *The American Fistiana, Showing the Progress of Pugilism in the United States, From 1816 to 1873.* New York, 1873.

Dibble, R.P., *John L. Sullivan: An Intimate Narrative.* Boston, 1925.

Doggett, L.L., *Life of Robert R. McBurney.* New York, 1925.

Donovan, Mike, *The Roosevelt That I Know: Ten Years of Boxing With The President —And Other Memories of Fighting Men.* New York, 1909.

Dudley, G., and F. Keller, *Athletic Games in the Education of Women.* New York, 1909.

Dulles, *America Learns To Play: A History of Popular Recreation, 1607-1940.* New York, 1940.

Durant, John, and Otto Bettmann, *Pictorial History of American Sports From Colonial Times to the Present.* New York, 1952.

Eagan, Eddie, *Fighting for Fun: The Scrap Book of Eddie Eagan.* New York, 1932.

Eddy, Sherwood, *A Century With Youth. A History of the Y.M.C.A. from 1844 to 1944.* New York, 1944.

Edwards, William H., *Football Days.* New York, 1916.

Ellard, Harry, *Baseball in Cincinnati: A History.* Cincinnati, 1907.

Evans, Arthur L., *Fifty Years of Football at Syracuse University, 1889-1939.* Syracuse, 1939.

Evans, Charles (Chick), Jr., *Chick Evans' Golf Book.*

Federal Writers Project W.P.A. (Illinois), *Baseball in Old Chicago.* Chicago, 1939.

*Fifty Years of Lawn Tennis in the United States.* New York, 1931.

Fleischer, Nathaniel S., *Black Dynamite: The Story of the Negro in the Prize Ring from 1782 to 1938.* 3 vols. New York, 1938.

———— *The Heavyweight Championship: An Informal History of Heavyweight Boxing from 1719 to the Present Day.* New York, 1949.

Frank, Stanley B., *The Jew in Sports.* New York, 1936.

Frymir, Alice, *Basket Ball for Women.* New York, 1930.

Gallico, Paul, *Farewell to Sport.* New York, 1938.

Geer, Ed, *Ed Geer's Experience with the Trotters and Pacers.* Buffalo, 1901.

Gocher, W.H., *Pacealong.* Hartford, 1928.

———*Trotalong.* Hartford, 1928.

———*Racealong,* Hartford, 1930.

Goodman, Murray, and Leonard Lewin (eds.), *My Greatest Day in Football.* New York, 1949.

Goodspeed, Charles Eliot, *Angling in America: Its Early History and Literature.* Boston, 1939.

Graham, Frank, *Lou Gehrig: A Quiet Hero.* New York, 1942.

———*The New York Yankees.* New York, 1943.

———*McGraw of the Giants—An Informal Biography.* New York, 1944.

———*The Brooklyn Dodgers.* New York, 1945.

Griffith, Corinne, *My Life With The Redskins.* New York, 1947.

Grombach, John V., *The Saga of Sock: A Complete Story of Boxing.* New York, 1949.

Hall, Henry (ed.), *The Tribune Book of Open-Air Sports.* New York, 1887.

Hall, Valentine G., *Lawn Tennis in America and England.* New York, 1888.

Hallock, Charles, *The Sportsman's Gazetteer and General Guide.* New York, 1877.

Halsey, Elizabeth, *The Development of Public Recreation in Metropolitan Chicago.* Chicago, 1940.

Harding, William Edgar, *The Champions of the American Prize Ring.* New York, 1881.

Harris, Reed, *King Football.* New York, 1932.

Harris, Stanley, *Playing the Game from Mine Boy to Manager.* New York, 1925.

Harron, Robert, *Rockne, Idol of American Football.* New York, 1931.

Hartwell, Edward M., *Physical Training in American Colleges and Universities.* Washington, 1886.

Henderson, Edwin Bancroft, *The Negro in Sport.* Washington, 1939.

Henderson, Robert W., *Ball, Bat and Bishop: The Origin of Ball Games.* New York, 1947.

Henie, Sonja, *Wings On My Feet.* New York, 1940.

Henry, William M., *An Approved History of the Olympic Games.* New York, 1948.

Herbert, Henry William, *Frank Forester's Horse and Horsemanship of the United States and British Provinces of North America.* 2 vols. New York, 1857.

Herring, Donald Grant, *Forty Years of Football.* New York, 1940.

Hervey, John, *Racing in America, 1665-1865.* 2 vols. New York, 1944.

———*The American Trotter.* New York, 1947.

Hildreth, Samuel C., and James R. Crowell, *The Spell of the Turf: The Story of American Racing.* Philadelphia, 1926.

Hoffman, Bob, *Weight Lifting.* York, Pa., 1939.

Holliman, Jennie, *American Sports (1785-1835)*. Durham, 1931.

Hopkins, C. Howard, *History of the Y.M.C.A. in North America*. New York, 1951.

Hurd, Richard M., *A History of Yale Athletics, 1840-1888*. New Haven, 1888.

Inglis, William, *Champions Off Guard*. New York, 1932.

Jacobs, Helen Hull, *Beyond the Game: An Autobiography*. Philadelphia, 1936.

*Janssen's American Amateur Athletic and Aquatic History, 1829-88*. New York, 1888.

Johnston, Alexander, *Ten—And Out! The Complete Story of the Prize Ring in America*.
    New York, 1947.

Keeler, O.B., *The Autobiography of an Average Golfer*. New York, 1925.

Kelley, J.D. Jerrold, *American Yachts, Their Clubs and Races*. New York, 1884.

Kelly, Mike, *Play Ball*. Boston, 1888.

Kemp, P.K., *Racing for the America's Cup*. London, 1937.

Kendall, Walter G., *Four Score Years of Sport*. Boston, 1933.

Kieran, John, *The Story of the Olympic Games, 776 B.C.—1936 A.D.* Philadelphia,
    1936.

_____*The American Sporting Scene*. New York, 1941.

Kiracofe, Edgar S., *Athletics and Physical Education in the Colleges of Virginia*.
    Charlottesville, 1932.

Krout, John Allen, *Annals of American Sport*. New Haven, 1929.

Krueger, Joseph J., *Baseball's Greatest Drama*. Milwaukee, 1945.

Lacoste, Jean René, *Lacoste on Tennis*. New York, 1928.

Lange, Fred W., *History of Baseball in California and Pacific Coast Leagues, 1847-
    1938*. Oakland, 1938.

Lanigan, Ernest J. (ed.), *Baseball Cyclopedia*. New York, 1922.

Laveaga, Robert E., *Volley Ball—A Man's Game*. New York, 1933.

Leach, George B. (Brownie), *The Kentucky Derby Diamond Jubilee*. New York, 1949.

Lee, James P., *Golf in America: A Practical Manual*. New York, 1895.

Leonard, Fred E., *Pioneers of Modern Physical Training*. New York, 1919.

_____*A Guide to the History of Physical Education*. Philadelphia, 1923.

_____(Same title, third edition, revised and enlarged by George B. Affleck). Toronto,
    1947.

Lieb, Frederick G., *The St. Louis Cardinals: The Story of a Great Baseball Club*. New
    York, 1944.

_____*Connie Mack; Grand Old Man of Baseball*. New York, 1945.

_____*The Detroit Tigers*. New York, 1946.

_____*The Boston Red Sox*. New York, 1947.

_____*The Baseball Story*. New York, 1950.

Lipton, Sir Thomas, *Lipton's Autobiography*. New York, 1932.

Loomis, Alfred F., *Ocean Racing: The Great Blue Water Yacht Races*. New York, 1946.

Louis, Joe, *My Life Story*. New York, 1947.

Lucas, Charles J.P., *The Olympic Games: 1904.* St. Louis, 1905.

Macdonald, Charles Blair, *Scotland's Gift: Golf, Reminiscences 1872-1927.* New York, 1928.

Manchester, Herbert, *Four Centuries of Sport in America 1490-1890.* New York, 1931.

Marble, Alice, *The Road to Wimbledon.* New York, 1946.

March, Francis A. Jr., *Athletics at Lafayette College.* Easton, Pa., 1926.

March, Harry A., *Pro Football—Its "Ups" and "Downs".* Albany, 1934.

Martin, Harry B., *Fifty Years of American Golf,* New York, 1936.

Mathewson, Christy, *Pitching in a Pinch.* New York, 1912.

McGraw, John J., *My Thirty Years in Baseball.* New York, 1923.

Menke, Frank G., *Down the Stretch: The Story of Matt J. Winn as Told to Frank G. Menke.* New York, 1945.

——*The New Encyclopedia of Sports.* New York, 1947.

——*The Encyclopedia of Sports.* New York, 1953.

Merrihew, Stephen Wallis, *The Quest of the Davis Cup.* New York, 1928.

Metzner, Henry, *A Brief History of the American Turnerbund.* Pittsburgh, 1924.

Miller, Richard I., *The Truth About Big-Time Football.* New York, 1953.

Mitchell, Elmer D., *Intramural Sports.* New York, 1939.

Moreland, George L., *Balldom: The Britannica of Baseball.* New York, 1914.

Morse, Richard C., *History of the North American Young Men's Christian Associations.* New York, 1913.

Morton, Ira., *The Red Grange Story.*

Myers, A. Wallis, *The Story of the Davis Cup.* London, 1913.

Naismith, James, *Basketball: Its Origin and Development.* New York, 1941.

National Association of Professional Baseball Leagues. *The Story of Minor League Baseball.* Columbus, 1953.

Nichols, Edward J., "An Historical Dictionary of Baseball Terminology." Unpublished Ph.D. dissertation, The Pennsylvania State College, 1939.

Nicolson, Frank W. (ed.), *Athletics at Wesleyan.* Middletown, 1938.

O'Hara, Barratt, *From Figg to Johnson: A Complete History of the Heavyweight Championship.* Chicago, 1909.

Ouimet, Francis, *A Game of Golf, a Book of Reminiscence.* Boston, 1932.

Paddock, Charles W., *The Fastest Human: Charles W. Paddock.* New York, 1932.

Palmer, H. C., *Base Ball: The National Game of the Americans.* New York, 1888.

——*Athletic Sports in America, England, and Australia.* Philadelphia, 1889.

Parmer, Charles B., *For Gold and Glory: The Story of Thoroughbred Racing in America.* New York, 1939.

Patten, William (ed.), *The Book of Sport,* New York, 1901.

Patten, W. and J.W. McSpadden (eds.), *The Book of Baseball.* New York, 1911.

Pence, Owen E., *The Y.M.C.A. and Social Need.* New York, 1939.

Peverelly, Charles A., *The Book of American Pastimes*. New York, 1886.

Potter, E.C., Jr., *Kings of the Court: The Story of Lawn Tennis*. New York, 1936.

Powell, Harford, Jr., *Walter Camp, the Father of American Football*. Boston, 1926.

Pratt, Charles E., *The American Bicycler*. Boston, 1880.

Pritchett, R.T., *et al.*, *Yachting*. 2 vols. Boston, 1894.

Rainwater, Clarence E., *The Play Movement in the United States—A Study of Community Recreation*. Chicago, 1922.

Ribalow, Harold U., *The Jew in American Sports*. New York, 1948.

Rice, Emmett A., *A Brief History of Physical Education*. New York, 1939.

Rice, Grantland. *The Tumult and the Shouting*. New York, 1954.

Richter, Francis C., *Richter's History and Records of Baseball*. Philadelphia, 1914.

Roberts, Howard, *The Story of Football in the Western Conference*. New York, 1948.

——*The Story of Pro Football*. New York, 1953.

Rockne, Knute K., *The Autobiography of Knute K. Rockne*. New York, 1931.

Ruhl, Arthur, *Track Athletics*. New York, 1905.

Sargent, Ledyard W. (ed.), *Dudley Allen Sargent: An Autobiography*. Philadelphia, 1927.

Savage, Howard J., *et al.*, *American College Athletics*. Carnegie Foundation for the Advancement of Teaching, Bulletin No. 23. New York, 1929.

Schwendener, Norma, *A History of Physical Education in the United States*. New York, 1942.

Sharpe, Philip B., *The Rifle in America*. New York, 1947.

Sharts, Elizabeth, *Cradle of the Trotter: Goshen in the History of the American Turf*. Goshen, 1946.

Smith, Robert, *Baseball—A historical narrative of the game, the men who have played it, and its place in American life*. New York, 1947.

Spalding, A.G., *America's National Game*. New York, 1911.

Spink, A.H., *The National Game*. St. Louis, 1910.

——*One Thousand Sport Stories*. 3 vols., 1921.

Spink, J.G. Taylor, *Judge Landis and Twenty-Five Years of Baseball*. NewYork, 1947.

Stagg, A.A., and W.W. Stout, *Touchdown!* New York, 1927.

Steiner, Jesse Frederick, *Americans at Play: Recent Trends in Recreation and Leisure-Time Activities*. New York, 1933.

Stephens, W.P., *American Yachting*. New York, 1904.

Suffolk, Earl of (ed.), *Encyclopedia of Sport*. 2 vols. New York, 1905 ed

Sullivan, James E., *Athletics in the West and Far West*. New York,

Sullivan, John L., *Life and Reminiscences of a 19th Century Gladiator*. Boston, 1892.

Taylor, Marshall W. (Major), *The Fastest Bicycle Rider in the World*. Worcester, 1928.

Thompson, Winfield M. and Thomas W. Lawson, *The Lawson History of the America's Cup*. Boston, 1902.

Tilden, William T., *My Story: A Champion's Memoirs.* New York, 1948.

Trevathan, Charles E., *The American Thoroughbred.* New York, 1905.

Tunis, John R., *$port$, Heroics and Hysterics.* New York, 1928.

———*Sport for the Fun of It.* New York, 1940.

———*Democracy and Sport.* New York, 1941.

Tunney, Gene, *A Man Must Fight.* Boston, 1932.

Underwood, Tom R. (ed.), *Thoroughbred Racing and Breeding: The Story of the Sport and Background of the Horse Industry.* New York, 1945.

Van Every, Edward, *Muldoon, The Solid Man of Sport.* New York, 1929.

Vardon, Harry, *My Golfing Life.* London, 1933.

Voltmer, Carl D., *A Brief History of the Intercollegiate Conference of Faculty Representatives, With Special Consideration of Athletic Problems.* New York, 1935.

Vosburgh, W.S., *Racing in America, 1866-1921.* New York, 1922.

Walsh, Christy and Glen Whittle (eds.), *Intercollegiate Football—A Complete Pictorial and Statistical Review from 1869 to 1934.* New York, 1934.

Walsh, John H. (Stonehenge), *Encyclopedia of Rural Sports.* Philadelphia, 1874.

Ward, Arch, *The Green Bay Packers: the Story of Professional Football.* New York, 1946.

Ward, John Montgomery, *Base-Ball.* Philadelphia, 1888.

Waugh, Alec, *The Lipton Story: A Centennial Biography.* Garden City, 1950.

Weaver, Robert B., *Amusements and Sports in American Life.* Chicago, 1939.

Webster, F. A.M., *The Evolution of the Olympic Games, 1829 B.C.—1944 A.D.* London, 1914.

Wecter, Dixon, *The Saga of American Society: A Record of Social Aspiration, 1607-1937.* New York, 1937.

Weyand, Alexander M., *American Football, Its History and Development.* New York, 1926.

———*The Olympic Pageant.* New York, 1952.

White, Luke, Jr., *Henry William Herbert & The American Publishing Scene 1831-1858.* Newark, 1943.

Wignall, Trevor C., *The Story of Boxing.* New York, 1924.

Williams, Jesse Feiring, and William Leonard Hughes, *Athletics in Education.* Philadelphia, 1937.

Wind, Herbert Warren, *The Story of American Golf.* New York, 1948.

Wood, Barry, *What Price Football?: A Player's Defense of the Game.* New York, 1932.

Woodruff, Fuzzy, *A History of Southern Football, 1890-1928.* 3 vols. Atlanta, 1928.

Woodruff, Hiram, *The Trotting Horse of America.* New York, 1869.

Woodward, Stanley, *Sports Page.* New York, 1949.

Wright, George, *Sketch of National Game of Baseball.* Washington, 1920.

Wythe, George (ed.), *The Inter-Allied Games.* Paris, 22nd June to 6th July, 1919.

## MANUSCRIPT COLLECTIONS AND ARCHIVAL SOURCES

Albert G. Spalding Baseball Collection, New York Public Library.
Duychinck Collection, New York Public Library.
E.H. Hall Football Collection, New York Public Library.
Fearing Collection, Widener Library, Harvard University.
Henry William Herbert Papers, New York Historical Society.
Luther Halsey Gulick Papers, National Councils of the Young Men's Christian
    Associations, 291 Broadway, New York City.
Frederick Jackson Turner Papers, State Historical Society of Wisconsin.
Miscellaneous Papers of Henry William Herbert, New York Public Library.
Walter Camp Correspondence, Yale University Library.

## BIBLIOGRAPHICAL REFERENCES

Gee, Ernest R., *Early American Sporting Books, 1734-1844.* New York, 1928.

Henderson, Robert W. (comp.), *Early American Sport: A Chronological Check-list of
    Books Published Prior to 1860 Based on an Exhibition Held at the Grolier Club.*
    New York, 1937.

Higginson, Henry A., *British and American Sporting Authors.* Berryville, Virginia. 1949.

Phillips, John C., *A Bibliography of American Sporting Books.* Boston, 1971.

Ryan, W. Carson, Jr., *The Literature of American School and College Athletics.* New
    York, 1929.

Sporting bibliography is also to be found in a number of the leading histories and
    monographs listed in the footnotes.

# Index